FORSAKEN FREEDOM

FORSAKEN FREEDOM

Fiction

By

T. RANDALL

FORSAKEN FREEDOM, although a work of fiction about the United States defense system, is based on real probabilities. The story could take place at any time, without a moment's notice to the public. The threat of Electromagnetic Pulsing (EMP) is real whether generated through Solar Maximum, Cosmic Rays, Lightning Strikes, or Nuclear Device set off by a terrorist group. Aside from critical military and government facilities, military command and control systems, data centers, space-based defense assets such as satellites and weapons, the rest of the nation, civilian assets are unprotected and highly vulnerable to an EMP strike. Where the nation's defense system for the past fifty years has been dealt with primarily from a strategically initiated superpower threat, the defense dynamics in recent years have shifted to tactical attacks initiated mostly by Islamic extremists. It is this threat that has a high probability form bringing the U.S. nation to its knees, causing an all-out economic Armageddon.

During the span of the strategic, tactical, and cyberspace defense deployments, an army of dedicated workforce is necessary to design, develop, and implement the complexity of the defense systems. It is this army of experts from government, military, and industry sectors including scientists, engineers, technicians, operations, management, and support personnel that makes the United States a safer place to live. The story was created to acknowledge and thank every one of these experts for their commitment, dedication, and allegiance to the cause of preserving the protection and freedom of a nation. Even though the characters within this book are fictional, every one of us could have played out the role of Alex Bauer and his crew.

Special consideration in this novel is extended to the woman. Where man throughout the ages used to have the sole prerogative in fighting battles, commanding armed forces, managing the nation, there were many women supporting men's efforts in the background as unsung heroes. That, as it had been dictated by cultural heritage, at times, may not be good enough, especially in this age of technology and progress. It is for this reason that Tracy Bauer was created and given the role as primary character fighting the enemy. It should serve as reminder to the ambitious, but at times oppressed woman, whether private or career oriented, to recognize opportunities as provided through given circumstances. To inspire a nation and its citizens, the need for a heroine is just as great as for the hero.

FORSAKEN FREEDOM is a comprehensive fiction novel based on the vulnerability of the United States defense system. Extended in volume size over the average novel and, because of the complexity of the plot, many chapters are necessary in the development and subsequently segmented into a number of sub-plots merged into the main story. Making up the chapters are dozens of characters and organizations necessary that are dependent on each other in case of an all-out attack on the nation. In addition, a number of sections, traumatizing the lives of American citizens affected by an all-out attack on the nation, are illustrated.

The story, second book in the trilogy is a continuation from Book I (12 DAYS TO ARMAGEDDON) and played out over a period of several years. It is during these years the American citizen will experience tragedy and trauma imposed on each and every one from the ravages of aftermath from the EMP strike followed by the hardship of war. Many will perish in the process from starvation, sickness, and disease, especially the city dwellers. Individuals prepared for national disasters on the scale illustrated in FORSAKEN FREEDOM are mostly the Preppers and Survivalists with the vision and foresight for such a possibility. Where these factions have taken decades of intimidation, coercion, and social pressure from skeptics and debunkers, it is those people that will survive at the end. Who are the smart ones now?

The adversary, the SERPENT, principal jihad antagonist to the Unites States and the free world, flanked by his team of highly trained and educated terrorists is at his best once more. It did not take him long to realize the vulnerability the former United States was subjected. With the nation's borders down, the country in chaos, not being able to fend off foreign intrusions, he is taking the turmoil to his immediate advantage. Again, numerous nations are getting involved in his plotting for penetrating the once powerful nation, whether as ally or rival in his quest for taking over America.

The nation, due to the collapse of its political powers and military might and loss of infrastructure of the major industries with power, communication, transportation, commerce, banking and currency, is broken up into regional sectors controlled and manipulated by survivalists and overlords all out for their own interests. The common citizen not prone to join one or the other sectors will be overrun and eventually perish as a result. It only takes one harsh winter to eradicate the unprepared.

In contrast to national upheaval, the protagonist Alex Bauer and his daughters, protected by the fortitude of their Castle, will become a mighty force the Serpent has to deal with once again. Through Alex's ingenuity and inherited technology savvy aided by Tracy, Liz, and supporters, as a team in defending the nation, they become a sizable force for the Serpent over a period of several years he has to fend off during which time the struggle will take the players to various foreign ground, openness of the oceans, as well as the vast expanse of space.

Targeted for destruction by the adversary is not only the former United States nation, but its inherited forces as well including its political powers, military, industrial strengths, weapons, and every other facet within the fabric of the American life. Where the premise of the first book was that of EMP, the premise for this novel is based on the nation's secret super weapon HAARP. It is this weapon the Serpent strives for getting his hands on. As always, the adversary, based on his ingenuity and savvy achieves his means to an end, but not without getting severe resistance from Alex and his crew of righteous defenders.

LIST OF CHARACTERS

PRINCIPLE CHARACTERS

Alex Bauer – Code name "Specter." Defense analyst, home base Castle Rock, CO
Brian Harris – Former NSA Analyst, longtime friend of Alex, romantic interlude to Tracy
Hasan Hammad (aka The Serpent) – Supreme Commander, Jihad/Al Qaeda, Adversary
Lisa (Liz) Bauer – Astronaut, American Crew, Soyuz & International Space Station
Scott Brooks – Group Leader, War Dogs, Sector One, Eastern Plains, Badlands, Mississippi
Tracy Bauer – Code name "Stinger." NSA defense strategist turned Independent Warrior

ISS CREW – CURRENT MISSION

Andrei Kubalev – Cosmonaut, Commander, ISS, Soyuz Team, Moscow, Russia
Dieter Fuchs – Astronaut, Crew, ISS, European Union, Munich, Germany
Hiroshi Nagata – Astronaut, Crew, ISS, Asian Team, Nakashima, Japan
Kendrick (Kenny) Walsh – Astronaut, Commander, ISS, Houston, TX, America
Lisa (Liz) Bauer – Astronaut, Crew, ISS, American Team, Napa, CA, New United Front
Mikhail Toporov – Cosmonaut, Crew, ISS, Soyuz Team, Jihad operative, Kazakhstan, Russia
Sergei Budenko – Cosmonaut, Crew, ISS, Soyuz Team, Jihad operative, Kazakhstan, Russia
Yuri Chenkov – Cosmonaut, Crew, ISS, Soyuz Team, Kazakhstan, Russia

SUPPORT CAST – WESTERN SECTOR

Donald (Donny) Allen – Crew Chief, 477th Fighter Group, Elmendorf AFB, AK
Eagle One – AWACS, Command Post, Vandenberg, Airborne Warning System
Falcon One – Surveillance, MILSAT, Orbital Satellite Surveillance System
Gary Walters – General, U.S. AF, Mohave Desert, Edwards AFB, CA
George Wilmot – U.S. President, the White House, Washington, DC
Hector (Heck) Rivera – C-130 Squad Leader, 477th Fighter Group, Elmendorf AFB, AK
Henry "Hank" Foster – Code name "Crimson", Commanding General, Four Star, New Republic
Jack Owens – Captain, U.S. AF, Officer in Charge, HAARP System, Gakona, AK
Lee Blackwell – Colonel, Full-Bird, U.S. AF, Pacific Missile Launch Facility, Vandenberg AFB, CA
Rhonda Hicks – Chief of Operations, Pacific Missile Launch Facility, Vandenberg, AFB, CA
Raymond (Ray) Campbell – Chief of Operations, HAARP Facility, Gakona, AK
Ronald (Ronny) Cook – Commander, Base Command, Elmendorf AFB, AK
Scott Brooks – Code name "Black Night." Delta Force operative, New Republic
Thomas (Tommy) Johnson – Commander, 3rd Wing Command, Elmendorf AFB, AK
William (Wild Bill) Williams – Commander, Eleventh Air Force, Elmendorf AFB, AK

SUPPORT CAST – CENTRAL SECTOR

Allen Spencer (aka The Psychic) – Group Leader, Condors, Sector Two, Northern Plains
Big Red – Commanding officer, Col, 2nd Brigadier, Red Army, Washington, DC
Buck – Honeymooner, stranded at St. Louis en route to Niagara Falls, NY

Benjamin "Ben" Jackson – Commanding General, CINCNORAD, Colorado Springs, CO
Brodie Elliott – Command Sergeant Major, 1st Armored Division, Badlands, FT. KNOX, KY
Derek Wallace – Group Leader, Anarchists, Sector Three, Southern Region of Route 66
Doug Olsen – Plant Supervisor, Nuclear Power Station, Three Mile Island, PA
Duke Wheeler – Bad Man, Enforcer, Patriots, Badlands, Central Plains
Emma – Honeymooner stranded at St. Louis en route to Niagara Falls, NY
Hannah Thompson – Interpreter to the U.N. Secretary General, New York, NY
Jim Ross – Shift Supervisor, Nuclear Power Station, Three Mile Island, PA
Johnny Buck – Helicopter Pilot, Fort Carson, Colorado Springs, CO
Kelly – Lieutenant, 1st Battalion, Northern Command, Red Army, DC
Kimberly (Kim) – Lieutenant, 3rd Battalion, Southern Command, Red Army, DC
Mackenzie (Mac) – Lieutenant, 2nd Battalion, Central Command, Red Army, DC
Russell Wilcox – Unit Leader, Federal Penitentiary, Fort Leavenworth, KS
Rusty Norton – Group Leader, Patriots, Sector One, Badlands, Central Plains, New Republic
Scott Brooks – Group Leader, War Dogs, Sector One, Eastern Plains, Badlands, Mississippi
Wendell Nelson – Commander, Garrison U.S. Army, Fort Knox, KY

SUPPORT CAST – FOREIGN SECTOR

Dimitry Garin – Foreign Agent, Undercover contact, Volgograd border crossing, Kazakhstan
Elena – Tracy's Russian travel friend, residing at Volgograd, Southern Russia
Nikolai Chernoff – Chairman, Prime Minister, Russian Federation, Moscow, Russia
Hui Wong – Party Secretary, People's Republic of China, Beijing, China
Kazim Rashid – Secretary General, U.N., former Tribal Elder, Al Qaeda/Jihad, Pakistan

SUPPORT CAST – AL QAEDA/JIHAD SECTORS

Amin Madani – Action Officer, Jihad Mission Command, Islamabad, Pakistan
Antarah Radi – Mission Commander, Al Qaeda/Jihad, Central Sector, Chicago, IL
Bandar Malik – First Lieutenant, Al Qaeda/Jihad, U.S. Cell Alpha, New York, NY
Hakim Massoud – Terrorist, First Lieutenant, U.S. Cell Central, Chicago, IL
Jamuh Faisal – First Lieutenant, Al Qaeda/Jihad, South Cell, Miami, FL
Joseph (Yusuf) Hashim – Commander, Al Qaeda/Jihad, U.S. Cell Alpha, New York, NY
Muhab Sadek – Terrorist, First Lieutenant, U.S. Cell West, HAARP Facility, Alaska, AK
Rashid Abu – Base Commander, Al Qaeda/Jihad, Desert Base Alpha, Sudan
Sahib Mahmud – Agent, Khartoum Cell, Al Qaeda/Jihad, Sudanese Desert
Shakir Murad – First Lieutenant, Al Qaeda/Jihad, Base Camp Three, Sudan
Tariq Amman – Terrorist, First Lieutenant, U.S. Cell East, Washington, DC

THREE MILE ISLAND

Doug Olson, superintendent for the power station Three Mile Island, PA, and crew, was desperate. Most of the crew had walked off weeks ago, right after the station burnt up. Wires, electronics, sensors, computers, everything that connected to the outside power lines through insulators, transformers and long-haul wires had been fried with the blast. He still had nightmares about the traumatic event. When the station disintegrated before his eyes, first thing on his mind was to run. Run as fast as he could, from sheer fear. Most of the crew did. But after considering the implications of such an act, especially to the people in the region that had depended on his skills and expertise for decades, he quickly came to his senses. He had to uphold his promise to "never place the public in danger." It stated so in the company's Policies and Procedure Manual.

He remembered the chaotic conditions and his following actions quite vividly. After slamming down hard on the SCRAM[1] button with his fist, he had stayed on. Doug, in an initial state of panic, after assessing the immediate danger, panic gave way to his usual common sense. "Not the first time," he had calmly reminded himself, "that the system's gone into meltdown condition."

Once the jitters in the pit of his stomach had vanished and his trembling hands quieted down, his darting eyes sought out the "Emergency Shutdown" procedures. The manual, usually stored within the central console bin, wasn't there. Someone in their haste must have misplaced it. With hurried strides, he checked the tables and desks in the control room. When unable to locate the document, he increased his search parameters. He eventually located it in someone's vacated office. A sigh of relief escaped his lips. "Thank God," he exclaimed and went to work. "At least," he muttered into the quiet turned control room. "It's a starting point." It is one thing to be station manager of a nuclear power plant with responsibilities not many would want. It's another to uphold the God-like position in the wake of extreme emergency. It's where one earns his keep.

With those thoughts in mind, his confidence gradually returning, he rushed back to the control room. Where the room used to be filled with a resonating hum from energized

---

[1] SCRAM (Safety Control Rod Axe Man) was achieved by a large insertion of negative reactivity. In light water reactors, for example, this was achieved by inserting neutron-absorbing control rods into the core. Within seconds, by absorbing liberated neutrons, the rods rapidly halted the nuclear reaction.

In a pressurized water reactor (PWR), as was the case here, during normal operation, the control rods were held above a reactor's core by electric motors against both their own weight and powerful spring tensions. Any cutting of the electric current released the rods. There were other designs to assure for controlled shutdown that do not apply here.

In a boiling water reactor (BWR), the control rods were inserted up from underneath the reactor vessel. In this case a hydraulic control unit with a pressurized storage tank provided the force to rapidly insert the control rods upon any interruption of the electric current, again within seconds.

A typical large BWR would have 185 of these control rods. In both the PWR and the BWR were secondary systems (and often tertiary) that would insert control rods in the event that primary rapid insertion did not promptly and fully actuate. In addition, there were other neutralizing methods available, such as liquid neutron absorbers which may, however, cause contamination to the system, causing extensive repair or permanent shutdown.

power equipment, now, it was dead silence. "First things first," he muttered. His crew, or what remained, lingered expectantly nearby, letting him do the work. But he needed assistance. His eyes spotted the day supervisor. "Jim." Doug threw him the manual. "Give me a hand, will you?" It was easier for one to read the procedures and for someone else to execute the commands. "You read," he ordered Jim. Unfortunately, in contrast with popular belief, to hit the SCRAM button did not completely eliminate the emergency conditions, especially not with an emergency shutdown. There was more to it. Much more. But the one thing it did was save the rods from meltdown, providing everything else was functioning.

First on his immediate agenda was saving the reactor. Being the core of the system, it had to be neutralized. Instructions to do so were lengthy but the process itself was quite simple. SCRAM initiated the automated sequence for a controlled shutdown.

Doug had taken up position at the master control console, ready to take instructions. "Jim," he anxiously called out for the third time. Jim remained quiet. Where, in the past world of nuclear reactor technology, the operator would have had complete manual control over switches, knobs, and pushbuttons, in today's computerized reactor world it was the keyboard and monitor screen that did the work. But with power out, controls and control panels shut down, the plant was dead in the water. "Damned backup system," he wondered. "Why didn't it kick in?" He knew from prior emergency conditions that, although with periodic test simulations the backup diesel generators were generally reliable, providing the connecting circuitry had power. But today, not even the most critical equipment, the water pumps to keep coolant water circulating were working. There was no response from Jim or any of the controls he tried to activate. The procedures list did not provide him with a quick answer. There was none. In desperation, his eyes darted to Jim, then across the console where he finally spotted the object he was looking for, "Checklist."

With the plant gone into critical state, there was no time to read lengthy procedures. Doug tossed the manual aside with a grunt and rushed to get the list. He grabbed the list himself. His eyes rapidly scanned down entry after entry but could not find a quick solution. His face was already breaking into profuse sweat. The boiler tanks were heating up to critical state. "Dammit," he shouted wiping his eyes clear of perspiration. He could feel the heat penetrating through his skin but there was nothing he could do at the moment about his soaking body. He feverishly read on, then the last line caught his eyes. It read, "Refer to Procedures Manual."

Realizing the catch-22 entrapment, he was about to give up hope for saving the plant when it suddenly hit him, "Manual." It was the key to the solution.

"Suits!" Doug was already headed for the utility room. In spite of time consuming training and periodic exercises, both required the aid of coworkers to get their bodies squeezed into radioactive protection suits. Once secured, Jim with list in hand and Doug, grabbing a dosimeter on the way out, left for the secondary (non-nuclear) reactor room housing the turbines. Before any of these units could be manipulated, they had to find a means to stop the reactor fission. But that was in the primary sector. To gain access to this facility would mean instant death unless protected by a suit, helmet, gloves, and boots. Regardless of conditions, complete trust must be given to the manufacturing specs, if one wanted to come out unscathed from the reactor building.

The uneasy feeling plaguing both operators was clearly painted on their faces through the facial shields. The first obstacle they encountered was the isolation chamber, the entrance to the primary. The first door was no challenge. It was the second that would tell the tale. Both could already feel the excessive heat emanating though the containment lock, but the heat was still manageable. Once inside, after both doors were secured, the sweating really began, both figuratively and psychologically.

"What's first?" Step by step, with Jim reading and Doug checking, they went to work in this kitchen of hell. To begin with, there were hissing sounds coming from all sections. It was already an indication of danger. What Doug was looking for were liquid leaks, runaway motors, and failing pumps. He did not have to look very far. Where the EMP had taken out all panel controls in the main control room, the containment system deep within the walls, supported by its own battery backup system, kept on running. The heavy construction had filtered out the brunt of the strike.

Looking at the diagram was one thing, but equating the dimensions to reality was yet another. Things on paper always appeared neat compared to real, live operational objects. Here, the aging process was very much alive. Rust, cracks, and leaks were clearly visible. Water, the pulse of the system, as life-giving it was to the rods, was as destructive to the metal elements. After the initial activation of a power plant, nothing ever looked as clinically new as it had before operation. It was the degree of deterioration and assessment thereof that mattered. And that was their focus at the moment.

Doug, scanning the dosimeter in different directions, was homing in on the leaks. Nuclear fission seemed everywhere from worn valves, seals, and connections. But that, at the moment, wasn't the problem. The real problem was isolating the manual procedures for a safe shutdown.

"Core status?" Jim read from the document.

Since all indicators on the remote-control panels were inoperative, the status could only be checked via visual. And that's what Doug was staring at. "Safe."

"Lucked out on that one," Jim huffed from inside the helmet. The one thing the design specification under all conditions for a nuclear power plant insisted on was reactor core safety. To achieve that, dual and triple safety mechanisms were installed. That's were SCRAM came into the picture. Even in the absence of power and backup generators it had worked this time. The sheer weight of the suspended control rods, after released from above, dropped into the tank. Sweat was profusely running down Jim's face, blurring his vision. He could not wipe his eyes. "Deal with it," he muttered to himself.

"Next," Doug said, muffled.

"Right," Jim agreed. There were much greater concerns the inspection would very quickly reveal. "Relief tank?"

"Okay." The tank had a pressurized steam escape valve. For now, it seemed shut. That was a good thing. But once the steam pressure reached the maximum limit, it would be another matter completely. It would automatically open and allow nuclear contamination to escape into the atmosphere. That was a bad thing. It was the emission Doug was trying to prevent. It would mean an immediate evacuation, not only of Three Mile Island, but the entire Eastern Seaboard as well.

"Reactor coolant pumps?" Jim read on.

"Shut down." With the pump inoperative, the reactor cores would not receive the cooling necessary from the cold-water exchange tanks. It would only be a matter of time for the core to gradually heat up. Then, under ever-increasing pressure, the steam containment tanks would explode. It was not the first time this had happened. Chernobyl, Fukushima, were living examples.

"Not good," Jim exclaimed. "Gotta get a handle on this."

"Procedure?"

"Turn 'On' Pump," the list read. But that, with power out, was not an option. "We're screwed!" Jim exclaimed, sweating fumes. Clearly visible through the visor his breathing had elevated to hyperventilating.

"Not so fast," Doug objected. Doug had a logically oriented mind. He knew from years of problem analysis and rational applications that there was always an alternative. That's what they came in here for, to find the alternative, a manual bypass. Since he could not get the pumps turned on, cooling water had to be fed to the rods by other means. But that was not the only problem he was facing. There was the turbine generator, the condenser pump, main feedwater pump, circulating water pump—all the cooling elements—in addition to water flow. At the moment, everything seemed to be functioning as designed. But without power, not one damned thing could be activated.

"We're screwed," Jim again voiced in distress.

Disregarding his comments, Doug said, "Okay, let's get to work."

"Work?" Jim seemed already exhausted from just stepping around the room, checking for leaks.

"Condenser pump…main feedwater pump…circulating water pump," Doug ordered, "manual override." He could see clearly what had to be done. One by one, they went to work, locating, testing, and manipulating the valves. Designed for backup, the pumps contained override valves that could be operated manually. It was these valves that had to be opened to allow water circulation through bypass piping using water flow pressure from the Susquehanna River, where the island was situated. Although the river had not carried as much water in recent decades, drained for an ever-growing population, it would be enough to generate a reasonable amount of water pressure through the cooling pipes and keep the rods from overheating. With a staff on duty, although limited to monitor the water flow, it would do for the time being.

And that is how Doug saved the plant. He applied a hands-on solution. He came through. If the news wire services were still in operation, he would be heralded as hero. For now, it was only Doug, Jim, and a small crew who knew the critical state the plant was in. But, as long as the river carried water, the region was saved, and so were the people.

"God forbid," Jim wavered inside the helmet, dripping wet from sweat, "a drought."

"Got that right." In spite of the potential danger both felt relatively safe for now. What they did not know about at this time was the danger lurking outside the confinement of the island. It was a much greater danger. That danger came in the form of forces in motion. They were forces neither could comprehend at this time. With the unseen threat still lurking in the future, another panicky thought jolted Doug into the present, "Jesus Christ."

"What?" Jim turned to read Doug's face.

"The other plant!" Busy for the past hours with saving the primary power plant, he completely forgot about the secondary complex located next door. Although there were four nuclear power plants in all situated on the island, only two had been in operation for the past two decades. Number Three and Four had been shot down permanently with the last "Three Mile Island" incidence. But number Two was in the same critical state of failure. "Follow me," he yelled. Although reluctantly from sheer exhaustion, Jim and the skeleton crew fell in line headed for the next shutdown action 250 yards away.

CASTLE ROCK

"Going out Dad," Tracy called at Alex on her way out. She tried to hurry past his den without raising his attention. But as usual, his sensitive ears were tuned into the environment. "Whished you wouldn't," he shot back at her then, "Hold up." He caught up with her by the exit door. "Where you headed?" His face reflected the deep concerns he felt whenever his daughter headed out. Her being a grownup person, he had no hold on her other than that of a concerned father. But, with the nation in turmoil as it had been since the EMP attack, his concerns were not without warrant.

"Town," she answered in her self-assured way. "Don't worry. I'll be safe."

"When you coming back?"

"Don't wait up," she said, before making a hurried exit leaving a worried Alex behind. Slightly shaking his head, he returned muttering, "Gonna get in serious trouble one of these days." His worries were not so much about her being a reckless person, it was more about her getting pulled into another confrontation with the locals. And they had been more frequent in recent weeks. As good looking as his daughter was, she seemed to attract trouble, male trouble to be specific. It usually came in the form of a challenge, turned into fight. Although she never provoked an incident, so she claimed, the results were always injuries. Not so much to her as much as to the challenger. Alex was still puzzled about his once responsibly behaved daughter turned brawling barroom rebel. He had to make monetary restitutions to several local bars not only on one occasion. Bar owners did not seem to care much about the resultant damages as long as he paid up. They seem to welcome her presence since she attracted well-paying locals to their establishments ready to witness another one of her frequent challenging fights.

In the aftermath of the nation's turmoil, Tracy had gradually transformed not only her personal appearance, but also her attitude and characteristics. Once the sweet appearance of innocence, unassuming and modest, she was now committed to a cause and rather aggressive in nature. According to her, it all boiled down to rage, wrath, and vengeance. There were reasons for it. There was rage she'd felt being taken hostage several times. There was the wrath she felt having to deal with present conditions. And there was the need for vengeance she felt at the very thought of an adversary expanding his misguided principles and forces in the free world.

At first, after being confined to the Castle for months, free spirit as she was, it'd been hell even considering such a position. But, at the moment, she felt there was no alternative. Choices had been made because of present circumstances. With the condition of the nation, slaughter, massacre, and killing, living outside of the Castle was not an option unless you belonged to a gang, a mob, or a faction. Not a pleasant proposition for anyone, but those were the options.

No one could live alone anymore, not in the present society. You were either absorbed by a faction or eliminated from the land, looked upon as just another burden, another mouth to feed, and, with everyone carving out an existence, not a viable solution. For better or for worse, an individual had to cope as best as he or she could under these conditions. But, based on individual strengths and geographical advantages, there were exceptions. And one such was Alex Bauer, former government troubleshooter, intelligence analyst, and liaison contractor to the Pentagon. The government, in its once flourishing entity, might not exist anymore, but its spirit was very much kept alive. It was alive in the form of the stronghold, his daughter Tracy, and the builder of the Castle himself, Alex Bauer.

Dawn was already breaking when Tracy returned to the Castle that night. Alex, as usually was waiting for her safe return. "Glad you're back," he welcomed her. "You, all right?"

Although slightly slurred, "Just fine," was her reply. Alex suspected she was drinking more than was healthy but did not say anything or lecture her. She was an adult and seemed to take care of herself pretty well. He did not see any damaging marks on her face or body and felt relieved until next time she would venture into town again. "Your sister called," he said on her passing. "Wants you to call her."

"In the morning," Tracy promised, making her way to her private room.

Unfortunately, Lisa, his eldest daughter, to the dismay of the family, was still at large. When the nation collapsed, she had been trapped on the Pacific coast at the emergency shelters, still treating survivors from the nuclear holocaust. But Alex was assured, for the time being, her kids living with their grandma in the Napa Valley region seemed safe. The valley, due to its location to the north of the jet stream and prevalent Pacific air currents some distance from the contaminated city, to the relief of its inhabitants, so far, had been spared nuclear contamination. It was this region, remnants of a once proud nation, the former government of the United States of America had made its new headquarters: the "Western Sector."

For now, the only occupants at the Castle were Tracy and Alex. To occupy time, when they were not sparring or otherwise absorbed in intellectual and worldly discussions—and there was no shortage on rumors, originating mostly from a region called the Badlands—Alex went to work fortifying the home even more. In the wake of recent events, not only in the nation, but in the Castle as well, he saw a number of shortcomings in the infrastructure. Given a few weeks rest to let his body recover from the all-out attack in the nation the year before, he went to work. There was much to do. With the government and military unable to protect the nation and its people, not even nearby Cheyenne Mountain, Alex had no choice but to look out for himself and his family living with him.

With marauding gangs infringing from every possible direction, and no government support in sight, Alex had turned the Castle into a fortress, an island in itself. First on the agenda had been reinforcing the foundation and the framework of the fortification extending even further into the hilly slopes. Fortunately, due to being a true earth shelter, only one side of the structure was vulnerable, the front facing the valley. That included decks and the carport. Another vulnerable area was the escape hatch and heliport pad. Exposed not only to the elements, but potential attacks from air and ground above, he had decided to submerge the port into the ground. Although it required a major digging effort, the result was added safety and protection. In spite of her general remarks such as, "You sure all this is necessary?" Tracy kept supporting him, nevertheless. "Keeps me in shape," would be his standard response.

In the end, almost a year later with most defensive assets moved below ground, he was completely satisfied. And so was Tracy. To an outsider, nothing seemed to have changed to the internal structure and immediate environment. But, on the inside, the place looked like a miniature fortification any command and control center would have been proud to possess. Aside from the electronically-controlled superstructure, with manual backups to boost, the most impressive piece was the hidden helicopter port. He had decided on building that feature after acquiring the helicopter through sheer fortune.

Alex had taken possession of the craft. Although it had needed extensive repair work after two emergency crashes and aerial dogfight encounters with the Serpent, Alex had the Cobra transported on a Confederate B-17 cargo craft to Colorado Springs and, in collaboration with the shop steward and his crew at Pete Field, had the AH-1 Cobra painstakingly restored to its maximum flight worthiness. Alex did not cut corners with the restoration. Since the dollar currency had collapsed, the nation had taken to barter. With the foresight Alex had on the unstable political conditions of the past, securing some of his investments with precious metals in gold and silver, his intuitive efforts, had paid off multiple times over. People where only too willing to barter off presently rendered useless items for coins. He knew that, at some time in the future, the effort exerted on repairs would pay off as well. But that remained to be seen. For now, the craft, loaded down with its maximum weapons configuration and infrared seeking instruments, was sitting idle, secured below ground but ready at a minute's notice to deploy, give chase, and attack.

SAN LUIS OBISPO

"Unidentified objects…three incoming…approach speed Mach 2…intentions unknown." The voice belonged to Rhonda Hicks, chief of operations, Vandenberg, AFB, CA. She had been monitoring the defense shield into the pacific, as she did diligently each day. Consisting of several strategically placed arrays of short and long-range radar dishes and microwave hops between Guam, Wake and Hawaiian Islands, current and somewhat outdated defense shield, it provided General Foster and his ground team some sort of advanced warning, since he had no effective satellite system at his disposal. For all practical purposes, the satellite grid, at its whole had largely been destroyed and rendered ineffective with the terrorist attack on the nation.

Tuned in on the call were several ground control centers, including Vandenberg airbase and launch control facilities. With microphone tightly gripped into his hand, "Mission crew," Lee Blackwell, Colonel, Full-Bird, U.S. AF, Vandenberg, CA, jumped into action to relay the warning, "Wing Alpha…dispatch immediately…investigate bogey…twelve miles out." Since other ground stations had not reported the flight, he assumed the wing had been launched from an aircraft carrier close by. With missile launch capabilities still at zero capacity, left to dispatch was an F-15 fighter squadron, stationed at the local airbase and at a minute's notice to take to the air. "And get the AWACS atop." Not knowing what to expect, in case a dogfight developed, as it had repeatedly in recent times, the Boeing E-3 Sentry, airborne command post would conduct mission command and control.

Minutes later, the AWACS pilot's urgent voice broke the air, "Eagle One in position—three targets. Chinese make, Chengdu J-20.[2] Proceed mission at will." From here on out it was up to the F-15 fighter wing to make contact and assess the intruder's intentions. The sound came seconds later from the wing commander, "Attack…attack." An incoming air-to-air missile had just missed his craft but had taken out his left wingman. A steep turn upward and quick glance below assured him the pilot was able to eject. Reacquiring the hostile flight, he flipped his missile switches to Hot and ordered his right wingman, "fire at will." There were three targets to attend. "One down," the wing commander reported after his missile destroyed the first target. "Two down," his wingman reported seconds later as they watched the third target taking flight into the pacific. "One bogey left. Headed home. Awaiting instructions." The action was over in minutes. It came on so quick, not even AWACS command was in a position to act.

"Return to base," Blackwell instructed. The immediate threat had been taken care. Intrusions such as today on the Pacific coast were nothing unusual. With the EMP strike taking out the former U.S. defense shield, the Chinese military, with the support from their first aircraft carrier in operation, was demonstrating frequent intrusion on American airspace. They were testing the Pacific airspace more frequently with each passing week. The response to the kills would be up to the Chinese. For now, it seemed they were only testing the Western Sector for effectiveness. One or two losses of their craft could be

---

[2] Chengdu J-20 – Fifth generation Chinese made stealth fighter with characteristics much like the American Lockheed F-22 Rapture.

tolerated, it appeared, without being escalated into a major conflict that might end in war. For now, the threat seemed over until the next intrusion into American airspace.

Following the all-out assault on the nation, the previous year, due to the lack of effective communication with national defenses breached and the military rendered mostly ineffective due to the loss of infrastructure and support channels, the United States, as had the USSR several decades before, was broken up into several geographic regions. When the White House and the Pentagon realized the danger of a potential takeover from within and outside its borders, it was already too late. In the wake of it all, many of the military service groups attached themselves to an emerging faction, the New Republic. Without effective leadership by the government, it was only a natural process for such a faction to emerge. What was left of the nation's defense infrastructure, former command and control systems mostly positioned in and around the eastern perimeters near the Pentagon, had become too vulnerable due to the constant onslaught not only from Jihad factions, but hostile nations from across the Atlantic, as well.

San Luis Obispo, California coastal region seemed to be the most logical place to relocate the Air Force Space Command, formerly headquartered at Peterson Air Force Base in Colorado. With the base rendered ineffective, Air Force command, and what remained, consolidated many of its abandoned bases and moved its assets to this Pacific coastal town. Much construction had been completed in recent times to house the 40,000 plus personnel supporting the new initiatives, Space and Cyberspace. For the present, it was mostly a sanctuary for what used to be the pride of America's air defenses: The Pentagon, Schriever, Buckley, Belvoir, Andrews, and other Air Force commands in and around the eastern part of the nation.

According to its senior officers, it was only a temporary measure until the military regained control over the situation, but that had not materialized. It had become a permanent solution. The Armed Forces had established themselves at the western test site originally identified as Vandenberg, the new military headquarters located near San Luis Obispo. There were other branches established up and down the California coast representing support services at locations such as Beale, Edwards, March, and Travis for the Air Force; Hunter, Irwin, Presidio, and Sierra for the Army; Pendleton, Miramar, Barstow, San Diego, and Twentynine Palms for the Marines; China Lake, Coronado, El Centro, Point Mugu, Seal Beach, San Diego and other naval stations along the pacific coast for the Navy.

It was these bases and posts that would become the nation's new unified military forces, situated and fortified within the newly defined parameters of the Western Sector, governed from the seat of the relocated White House, now at the former State capital of Sacramento. And with it moved whatever was left in technology and assets in and around the once thriving Beltway. National laboratories such as Brookhaven, Argonne, Fermi, Los Alamos, Sandia, Oak Ridge, and Savannah River were abandoned and with them, their research projects. It was these facilities that became the grounds for extreme battles to gain control of their technologies.

But there was one exception. The Lawrence Livermore Laboratories located in California's Tri-Valley would remain in the hands of the Western Sector government. With the brunt of services moved west, Silicon Valley, East Bay, Richmond, and the other industrial and business parks located up and down the coast had the potential to revive engineering, manufacturing, and trade once more. But, according to statistical accounts, that would take many years to achieve. For now, because of nuclear fallout remnants at nearby San Francisco, with radiation contamination still elevated, many of the coastal regions directly inland were considered unsafe for the population.

What proved to be a valuable asset to the Western Sector was Vandenberg, specifically the missile sites with their many missile launching towers. Since Cape Canaveral was lost to the Southern Sector, predominantly controlled by the Anarchists, the site at Vandenberg was heavily fortified to protect against any intrusion and threats from terrorist attack and foreign takeover.

Fortunately for the western regions, hostile nations in and around the Pacific Rim, due to the distance across the oceans had not been effective taking hold. But, the political policymakers suspected, it would not stay this way for long. The Chinese were on the brink of expanding their military might into the Pacific oceans. Concerns were real with reminders from a not too distant past, that of the Japanese invasion to the many islands during WWII.

"What's the status?" It was Foster's voice. Since he was the most senior general at the Pentagon after the collapse of the nation, after realizing the severity of the situation, he immediately took command over the remaining resources, near and far.

"Averted." Rhonda reported. "This time." Both knew it would not take long for the next intrusion. When a country, especially a superpower, has been crippled, foreign nations were quick to take advantage over its exposed borders.

SACRAMENTO

Sacramento had become the seat of the White House for the newly created Western Sector. In addition, with the loss of the Constitution, the secession of former states, loss of centralized government, and general disorder caused by unruly citizens, the once proud United States of America had been unceremoniously dissolved into several recognized sectors: Eastern, Central, and Southern. There were no definitive borders at this time. That would come later, with the possible formation of regional regimes.

At this point, almost one year had gone by since the EMP attack. "People," George Wilmot, President at Large and Commander in Chief, was demanding attention, "order, please." This morning was another one of the weekly scheduled sessions. First on the agenda open for discussion was the compiled report from the previous week. In order of priority of offenses were the security of the state now turned Western Sector; status report on defenses, confined to its new borders; infringements on liberty and civil rights; responsibilities of the new government; citizen crimes and offences; responsibilities of local law enforcement; and new agendas.

This week, as most others issued in the recent past, was no different. People were always pushing the limits. It seemed last year's traumatic events did little to reform people on economic, personal, and political issues. There was bitching already to organize for better working conditions, better pay, and more. There were the usual complaints people had for better living conditions, food shortages, and such. *What short memories people have,* Wilmot was thinking while he waited for the board members to settle.

George Wilmot, by popular vote had been reelected into office once more. The Constitution "needs extensive rewriting to fit the new convention and borders," he told the people.

With that order on the forefront, today's session, like prior weeks, was focused on exactly that. "The new document is," as simplified as it would become, he promised, after removing many of the superfluous amendments added over the years, "still being hammered out."

Not to repeat what the nation had just experienced with the secession, the next constitution would have to address specific issues, some for the people, but, more importantly, for the protection of the government. Wilmot considered himself lucky this time. The tide could have swayed the other way, with him winding up on the chopping block, if the Patriots had gotten their hands on him. The Patriots, a faction created and supported mostly by preppers, survivalists, and ex-military loyalists emerging from the chaotic conditions after the collapse of the nation, were out for revenge. They wanted his blood, regardless of all the good things he did for the nation. "Sure," he admitted, "I could have done better. So, could have every other president. But decisions aren't always up for the president to make. There are other forces at work." For now, considering the state the nation, he was mostly satisfied with the way things were going, but that was bound to change.

Reports relayed by international wire services indicated more and more nations were making overtures toward getting their hands on what remained from the once powerful nation. With defenses limited to the Western Sector, it would be a breeze for the aggressors to take possession of infrastructure and technology, especially the experimental weaponry under development at various laboratories. Rumors had it that the closely held top-secret super weapon, the HAARP,[3] located on the fringes of the northern continent, was about to unleash its purported powers. It was this power that everybody in the world was fighting to get their hands on. That held especially true for the Adversary, the leader of Al Qaeda and Jihad, the Serpent.

For Wilmot and his localized government, it was this weapon that had become the most critical defense item in the western zone. He had to protect it at all cost. To achieve that, he planned to deploy his best tactical forces at his disposal to that region. It would not be an easy task, convincing the majority of his military echelon to relocate to northern Alaska, one of the coldest places on earth, especially not with the Russians across the Bering Strait only miles away. But it had to be done. Today was the day, although, with an extremely limited budget on hand, he had to convince the assembly to initiate the move up north. Budget wasn't the right word. There was none. For every expense he had, a few more national treasured items had to be sacrificed and bartered off. And, to his dismay, the treasure was rapidly dwindling.

---

[3] HAARP – By design, the heart of the High-frequency Active Auroral Research Program system was its transmitter array fed by a cluster of large power generators creating millions of watts of power used to heat up the upper layer of the atmosphere (ionosphere).

BRIAN HARRIS

Brian Harris was at a loss. When the spy satellites were destroyed by the blast, with them went uplinks, downlinks, relay hops, life feeds, and most of the communication infrastructure over the North American continent. Where the rest of the world was still functioning, global communication, for most part, had been severely impacted. Like many others within the National Security Agency, Brian's live had been severely disrupted. The disruption was also felt by a myriad of members from other organizations and agencies, such as the Central Intelligence Agency, the Defense Communications Agency, the Defense Intelligence Agency, combined Armed Services intelligence, the Federal Bureau of Investigation, and all the law-enforcing organizations depending on the grid for global positioning systems, weather satellites, meteorology radar, and Doppler radar.

Instant communication, for all practical purposes, for Americans had been rendered ineffective. Whereas the data and information, stored in national and developmental laboratory databanks, still existed, it would take many years to rebuild and deploy, providing there was a need and desire to do so. With the nation fragmented, each unit and citizen fighting for its own cause and existence, the outlook for that to happen soon did not look promising. The most logical entity to establish any kind of technological footing would be the Western Sector. For now, however, the Western Sector, as with the rest of the nation, was busy fending for its existence. With defense resources scaled to a minimum, it was highly unlikely anything from that sector would materialize anytime soon.

It was these conditions Brian Harris faced since his return after the final battle with the Serpent out west. Unfortunately, although the outcome was in his favor, the world's most dangerous adversary had escaped his pursuit. Replaced by a number of rogue nations, initiated mostly from the Middle East and former USSR satellite nations, the eastern seaboard had become vulnerable by their frequent attacks.

Still residing at his residence and longtime sanctuary, Baltimore, for Brian had turned unsafe. This once beautiful harbor city had turned into a battle zone with him and everybody else struggling for survival. Everywhere on the eastern front, the city dwellers were taking the biggest onslaught. New York City, Philadelphia, Chicago, Boston, and outlying areas were facing similar unsafe conditions. Where the metropolitan areas were once crowded places, today many had turned desolate. In the struggle for survival, most dwellers were seeking sanctuary upstate. Whoever dared to stay on was subjected to being terrorized. It did not take much for organized militant groups and terrorists to stake out territorial borders for controlled zones.

Although Brian hoped the population, in time, would rebuild, for now it was one against one, group against group, and, to a larger extent, organized forces against other territorial factions.

Having just awoken from a fitful sleep, Brian momentarily sat by the edge of his bed. From longtime habit, he reached for the laptop computer tossed carelessly on the edge the evening before. It had taken Brian the longest time to accept that the communication grid was gone. Still hoping to somehow make a connection, he had to keep on trying.

Today, as had been many days, there was no feedback from Carnivore or Echelon, once the most sophisticated Intel software. "No luck today," he determined, "gonna be another shitty day." Without a structured society, it would be another day to just carve out an existence. He was quickly running out of ideas on how to accomplish that. To survive, he knew he'd have to make a decision soon or otherwise get trapped in a situation he'd later regret. The visible choices were clearly limited. It was either getting recruited into the services of a regional gang, or having to fight for the Patriots. Those were the choices. He did not like either one. Until now, he had always worked alone. He preferred it that way. He could not imagine being trapped in a militant-like environment subjected to the brute, primitive, and animal type behavior found in most factions. Besides, he felt that the time had long passed for him to become a soldier. Fighter, if pushed against the wall, yes. But recruit peon or soldier, not a chance.

His personal struggle, until now, had been a fruitless proposition. While satellites still existed in orbit, they were out of reach for his computer software from home and from his former workplace. He had made a number of attempts to push his way to the office, what once was the prominent NSA complex at Fort Mead, MD, but found it had been vandalized over and over in recent months. Much of the comm and computer equipment had been damaged or removed by the vandals. "For what purpose," he questioned the insanity of it all. People, when given the chance, seemed to take things just for the sake of taking. With power and communication infrastructure gone, they'd be useless.

Presently, the inability to access a functional satellite was not his only problem. Brian had to make a decision, and make it fast. The once effective intelligence center was about to be taken over by an advancing force. A force moving in from the Atlantic, it was rapidly gaining control over the entire Eastern Seaboard. With it, government, military, manufacturing, and technology would be in the hands of foreigners before long.

While technology at this time was rendered useless, the infrastructure was a sought-out commodity very much in demand by third-world nations. Technology found in the former U.S. was second only to the gold value contained in Fort Knox, at this time held hostage by the Patriots. As it stood now, these were the two commodities used for conducting trade. Commerce was non-existent. Foreign trade, due to the loss of the dollar standard, was limited to gold and silver coins or non-existing. The banking system and Wall Street had been shut down for the same reason. The only means to acquire items were though barter. And that was marginal at best. Without effective government management, inflation had rapidly taken hold by opportunistic brokers and traders demanding ever higher cuts.

Brian made one final attempt to reach the Castle by shortwave. Unfortunately, with HAM gear the most sought-out commodity for survivable communication, he had not been able to get his hands on the equipment. Not being a prepper, he was, like most citizens, caught off guard.

He had made up his mind. "Today's the day." He would have to find transportation that would take him to the Rockies. Aside from being safe, he would be with Tracy.

Brian, like everybody else in the nation, was penniless. The few bills he'd had in his wallet that day had been rendered useless. With the dollar collapsed, nobody would take paper money. Without power, the food left in the fridge had spoiled. The few canned goods in the cupboard were gone. There was no crumb left in his lofty abode. Without food, water, and money, survival had taken over his daily life. After one last check around the apartment, he muttered one final resolution, about to lock up the place. "I'm outta here."

He was about to step outside when a sudden thought struck him. "The Coins!" Dropping the duffel, he rushed to the bedroom and began pulling out drawers. He had forgotten about the little treasure chest he used to collect souvenir coins from the many countries he had visited during his travels. He spotted the treasure chest. Pulling the metal lid open, his heart jumped with joy. His fingers gingerly sifted through the contents. Inspecting the various currencies gave him renewed assurance for the journey ahead. But the joy quickly faded at the thought for safety. "Where," he mulled, "am I gonna hide it?"

The first thing a mugger would look in would be the duffel. Then, if there was no silver or gold, would do a body search. The clothes he wore would be ransacked. He had an idea but it would take additional time. He had no option. He would have to sew the coins into the hem of the flight jacket he wore. And that is what he did. By the time he was finished, darkness had set in over Chesapeake Bay. Although his stomach was gnawing painfully, he muttered into the quiet of the night, "One more day won't matter." He sat out by the balcony for hours, enjoying one last view in the gentle breeze drifting in from the Bay.

The following day, Brian rose at daybreak. Dressed in jeans, casuals, hiking boots, a few sets of underwear tossed into the duffel, knife tucked inside one boot, handgun under the belt, he thought, "That's it." He slammed the door shut and headed for the harbor. "Best bet," he thought, "is to hitch a ride on a ship, a freighter, or anything that floats." Either way, the route would take him out in the open Bay. From there, he planned to ferry south along the Carolinas, circle the Florida coast into the Gulf, destined for Texas. From there, he would plan to somehow make it through the Lonestar State into New Mexico to hitch a ride north on I-25. With rumors about crime and hostility running rampant, not knowing what to expect on the immediate journey, he thought, if luck was on his side, "Somehow, I'll make it to Castle Rock." How long it would take or what he would face would be anybody's guess.

SCOTT BROOKS

After fighting the Jihad and chasing the elusive Serpent, Scott Brooks decided to return to the Arizona desert, the only place he felt comfortable. It's been his home and base of operations for many years. With Alex and Tracy returned to the Castle, Harris back east, the Serpent on the loose—God only knew where—his teammates deployed on missions only they knew the whereabouts of, with communication disrupted and his employer shrouded in silence, he needed time to think the situation through. Relying for most of his adult life on decisions being made by the agency, from here on he may have to decide his future on his own. Presently holed up at the CIA interrogation outpost, he was waiting for his team to show, whenever that might be. It didn't matter to him one way or another. He had enough money stashed away at Central American banks to last him a lifetime, if he lived relatively conservative. If nobody showed, he could always make his way south to his private sanctuary, a beach house in El Salvador he had acquired several years ago. But for now, he waited.

A thought had just struck him. Shaking his head in disbelief, he slapped his forehead, leaving a red imprint. "Fuck!" He had just realized that, with ATM and banks closed, he could not get his hands-on cash. "Shit," he cussed again. He finally conceded to the inevitable. "What a shitty mess." The thought alone made him decide to head south to his personal paradise by the Pacific shores. "Guess anything's better," he thought with dismay, "than carving out an existence here in this fucking wasteland." Brooks, like many trapped in loneliness, had acquired the habit of talking to himself.

He still hoped to get word in from Headquarters. An update, a debriefing, a call, any word would do. Since the generator fuel had run out he could only rely on daylight to get things done. The same was true for vehicle fuel. Somehow, his team had managed to run the Hummer dry during his absence. He hadn't pulled himself together yet to trek the distance across the desert to the nearest towns, Tombstone or Bisbee. "Towns are probably out of fuel anyway," he muttered into the quiet of the desert.

Need to make preparation for today's meal crossed his mind as nighttime crept in one more time. He did not have to worry about going hungry. He was trained to survive in deserts. Although meager, there were enough crawlers and furry things emerging from the sand during the cool of night to provide him with something to eat. He knew where to look. For water, if things became critical, he could always filter his own piss through a piece of cloth. Re-circulated, it would provide him with liquids for days, perhaps weeks. To replenish, he could always chop down a cactus branch to squeeze out the juice.

Later that evening, chewing on the last bite from a desert rat roasted over an open fire pit, a thought popped into his mind. "Yeah," he determined, "why not?" What he'd just thought of was the possibility teaming up with Bauer. "Or," he contemplated further, "pay him a visit." It would give him a reason to cross a couple of states and assess the conditions in the nation. In this place, the only sound he ever received was the howling coyotes. High spirited at the very thought of taking to the road he muttered, "Couple day's travel." With his survival skills, he could almost guarantee it wouldn't take much longer for the trip.

First day he'd make it up R-90 to I-40, then spend another day hitching over to Albuquerque to meet up with I-25. From there he'd bum a ride up north, the final leg to the Springs. Sure, he'd encounter resistance, but that wouldn't be much of a challenge in the company of the "Enforcer," his faithful companion, the .45 Smith & Wesson that was his favorite semi-automatic weapon.

Where he used to be content, holed up at any location with one or a few buddies, he suddenly found himself alone. He did not like it. After spending the last few weeks in the presence of Alex, an equally respected and capable fighter, although from different backgrounds, he'd come to appreciate the guy, even to like him. He had notions of having him on his team or being part of his, whichever way it would work out. "Tracy," he reflected, "will have to work on her." The very thought of her reminded him of how much he missed women. Not so much being married to a woman. It was the kind you could find in nightclubs and strip joints. That's the only kind he knew and felt comfortable with. Not that he was a chauvinist or selfish pig, but from his position, trained killer as he was, a woman could never hold equal or even come close to such a function. "Women," he pondered with a grin, "gotta love 'em."

At this time, little did he expect that one would emerge from the current extreme conditions, one that would challenge his very existence by the very sex; he had so little respect for.

THE PENTAGON

As quickly as Foster could, rushing along the corridor halls of the prestigious complex, opening and slamming doors, he checked up on coworkers and employees. With every day, it seemed, he was losing more people. Hallways, normally busy with office traffic and visitors, now were deserted. Today, there was nobody left. "Anybody here?" Henry "Hank" Foster, General, U.S. Army Command, shouted into the emptiness, but there was no answer. "Who can blame them?" he rationalized. Once the central bank quit printing money and paychecks did not show up in mailboxes or bank accounts anymore, the response of the people was swift. There was not even the postal system left to deliver the mail. All commerce and business in and around DC had come to a halt after the EMP strike.

First gone were the distant commuters living on the outskirts of town. It only took a couple of days for the service stations to run out of fuel or just quit selling it, and rightly so. Rioters took over the businesses, whatever they thought was of value. But some diehard employees, somehow, still made it to the office. Some came on motorbikes until their fuel resources ran out. Subways quit running the second the gamma and x-rays hit the electric and ground wires. Whatever other transportation running on fossil fuel did not fare much better. Robbers and muggers homed in on any and all target points. After that, everything that moved became a target. Break-ins followed quickly. Many people, decent citizens under normal living conditions, now, trapped without for food supplies, panicked.

It did not take much for decent people to realize that the once political and governmental hub had come under attack. Attacks launched came from many different directions. There were the criminal elements taking anything valuable. Next were the disgruntled, typically underappreciated employees out to cause damage and destruction, mostly for personal vengeance directed at the former employer. But, worse yet, rumors surfaced about gangs organizing, fending for an existence, especially after the food supplies ran out in stores and supermarkets. Many citizens went into hiding for fear of getting killed. Others sought refuge in the country with family and friends. The not so fortunate ones were left to fend for themselves. The city had turned chaotic. The common citizen had come under attack. It soon turned into "kill or be killed."

Foster, incumbent Four Star, Department of Defense, Pentagon, knew the conditions he faced well. He had turned powerless overnight. The technology, the science, the forces under his command, he regretted, were all gone. Only he and a few likeminded, hardcore career officers kept checking up on things. After many years assigned there, they looked upon the defense headquarters as their home. In a way, it was. For many, getting up on age, the Pentagon was a last career assignment. Many, abandoned by family members for whatever reasons, had nothing else to look forward. It was only a matter of time for those to succumb to an inevitable end. If age did not catch up with them, an assault would. In any case, they would become a target as long as they remained in the city.

Hank Foster was no different. The only thing that had kept him alive was the transportation he had acquired. It was a light armored truck he had checked out at Bolling AFB, located just across the Potomac River near Ronald Reagan International, or what was left of the once busy airport. He had even acquired his own personal body guard from there. Marines they were, hardcore, SEALs from Special Ops, Unit Six, the nation's elite fighters; nobody would dare mess with them. There was not a fighter tougher and more hard-hitting to combat, whether in hand-to-hand, weapons use, or armored support. With the state the nation was in, Foster had come under the personal protection of these elite fighters. That was the reason he was still here today. He felt safe walking his Pentagon in the company of the SEALs. But time was running short, even for Foster and his team. The city was being overrun. It was only a matter of time before they would be outnumbered and outgunned. He was thinking about taking leave from the city that had provided him a lifetime of career, pleasures, and security. Food until now had not presented a problem. The Pentagon had an ample supply of canned rations store away for emergencies.

The time was ripe. "Get your gear together," he instructed the SEALs. "We're heading out... west." He didn't have to extend a special invitation. He knew that everyone on the team was behind him, since most of the leaders had taken flight already.

Sporting a wide grin, his next in rank replied, "Just say the word. We're ready." The thought of leaving a city in shambles behind not only spurred a sense of adventure, but also gave them an incentive for building a new future elsewhere, perhaps a better one. All indications pointed westward. That's where most of them sought to make a better living. "Pacific, sunshine, sandy beaches, diving, and fishing," was on the young warriors' minds. In spite of the overpopulation everyone out west bitched about, between two major cities, San Francisco and L.A., were many open stretches along the oceanfront, inviting the prospectors. Although there might be rough patches of cliffs and reefs in-between, the region was declared open season for the warriors. "California," was the slogan, "get ready for us!"

CIA

"Screw this," Harry Carter, Chief of Operations, CIA HQ, Langley, VA, once the most powerful intelligence operative in the world, said. "Piece of shit." He vehemently raged at the headset as he tossed it across the desk. He was staring at the HAM set resting silently on the desk. Already, for days, he had exerted his patience on that "damned thing," trying to raise his agents. He was completely drained of energy, not just from the frustration of not getting in contact with the embassies, but more so from having to use this antiquated gadget.

He realized the nation was in dire trouble when the airwaves went silent. It took several more days to even get an initial assessment on the state of the nation. Information was only trickling in, spurts of data relayed mostly from special units carrying portables. It became obvious that all satellites went out with the first day. It took longer to get feedback from foreign offices on the global alerts issued primarily by NATO Europe. Other nations, more distant, knew something had transpired involving the United States, but were kept in the dark.

Carter, if he wasn't the hard-headed, hardcore son-of-a-bitch that he was, may have already panicked. But that wouldn't have been him. Short of the total blackout, he'd seen it all. The coup d'état, the takeovers, the overthrows, the attacks on governments— foreign mostly at this time—could well come knocking on U.S. soil. The only thing that had saved the nation's leaders, so far, was the fact that U.S. citizens were not used to attacking the government. Demonstrations, yeah, but a takeover—not likely. The dire lessons of killing and hardships learned from past wars and recent conflicts were still clearly on their minds, if not through direct involvements, but surely fed by the international news wires when they were still functioning.

For now, aside from the criminal elements roaming the streets, he still felt safe within the confines of the CIA complex. Military units from surrounding bases and posts were swift to dispatch defense units, not only for Langley, but for nearby Fort Mead as well to protect national security assets. It would be unforgivable if all the highly classified data and material fell into the hands of the enemy. "But," he questioned for the umpteenth time, "for how long?"

There was no guarantee for the safeguarding of America's intelligence properties contained in the uncountable databases and data vaults—not so much from the average citizen, but more from a foreign attack. With communication out, embassies turned silent, and agents not responding, Carter worried. "Who knows how long that'll last."

He worried for his future, for his family, for the agency, for the nation. "Gotta get hold of Foster," he muttered. "He'd know what to do." After all, the general had the entire defense arsenal at his disposal, or what was left of it. The thought gave him somewhat of a reassuring feeling. He reached for the headset to initiate the call no matter how frustrating handling the dated equipment was.

NORAD

Benjamin "Ben" Jackson, Commanding General, CINCNORAD, was frustrated. Never, in his entire career, could he remember feeling this helpless. The thing that kept him from completely losing it was the security of the Mountain. It would be a last retreat. In case of an imminent threat, provisions had been made to move him, his family, the staff, defense units assigned to this facility, and support members, on a last minute's notice, from the Peterson AFB housing into the secure sanctuary of Cheyenne Mountain.

So far, Colorado Springs and the surrounding areas had been relatively quiet. Rumors of attacks and takeovers coming in from other parts in the nation, in contrast, dictated otherwise elsewhere. Unbelievable as the rumors were, they flooded in from surrounding regions up north and down south, but mostly from the east. The west was pretty much protected by the Rockies. Not much of a threat was expected from there. "The east?" he questioned.

Visions of attacks from across the Kansas plains kept him up most nights. Rumors told about a major prison breakout at Leavenworth. "Inmates," he was told, "are organizing and on the move, and had already taken hold of the nation's wealth." As unbelievable as it sounded, he did give it credence. He had to. There was always a speck of truth to any rumor.

The only consolation he had when he thought about it was, "Let Fort Carson take care of it." With the many mission units, battle forces, tanks, and armament at the nearby fort,[4] he would boast, to his family and staff, "Let 'em try." Another thought hit him. *Bauer! Wonder what he's up to?* Last time he had heard from him was when Alex had been assigned a mission out west. "What was it again?"

Aah yes! It came to him. *SAC, WMD, B-2 loads dropped on foreign soils.* He also recalled the assistance he got from the civilian. "If anybody would know something," he figured, "it'll be him. Get me Bauer on the set," he ordered his assistant. *He'll know what to do.* Regardless of the man's status—being civilian, retired, and all—Jackson had gained great respect for the man. Somewhat relieved, he stormed from the war room bitching about the state of the nation, his command, the Mountain or what was left of it, and being kept in the dark. The call was waiting when he entered the privacy of his office.

The HAM for now was the only means to call, but it always took time to establish a connection. "Boy," Jackson grumbled, "did we ever fuck up."

"Jackson," he said gruffly after the call signal had been established and verified.

"Bauer...Alex Bauer," vaguely familiar, the voice announced.

"Yeah," Jackson replied, "how're things at the Castle?"

"Too quiet," Alex remarked.

"You're not the only one," Jackson stated, "can't get word in or out."

"That's basically the case."

---

[4] With a population of over 13,000, Fort Carson, a sprawling Army installation near Colorado Springs, was the home of the 4th Infantry Division, the 10th Special Forces Group, the 71st Ordnance Group, the 4th Engineer Battalion, the 759th Military Police Battalion, the 10th Combat Support Hospital, the 43rd Brigade, and the 13th Air Support Operations Squadron of the United States Air Force.

"What's your situation?" He wanted to know what was going on in the world. Maybe Bauer had some news. With the EMP hit directly over the central region, the Mountain and its external links were gone, incinerated. It would take many months to get things back on the air, if enough wires and cables could be located. Manufacturing, due the present conditions in the nation, was almost non-existent. Foreign nations, on the other hand, kept promising but deliveries never came true because of the lack of commerce and negotiable trade instruments: money, or the lack of.

"Took the time to upgrade my place," Alex informed him.

"Could need your help here," Jackson said.

"Send some transport," Alex suggested. "I'll be there."

"Tomorrow?"

"See you then." The call was terminated.

As promised, transportation had shown up early the next morning. Accompanied by several guardsmen, Alex was whisked from the sanctuary of the Castle and taken to the Mountain. Encountering local National Guard units along the way, blocking major intersections and inspecting travelers, reminded Alex of a war zone. National guards had been called up wherever possible. Availability and recruiting citizens was no problem. For now, it was the only occupation obtainable that paid. Payment was not in checks or money. Payment was in the form of food rations for the individuals and their families. Everybody seemed to want to join. There were more applications than jobs. People lined up to do just about anything as long as it promised a day's worth of handouts, as rationed as it was. Everybody was starving, but nobody complained. It was either that: move up north, or stay and slowly perish from starvation.

Although supply lines had been quickly established, the national food supplies from organizations such as the Red Cross and DHS ran out rapidly. Most of the supplies had been shipped out west early on to aid the fallout survivors. Farmers were ordered to release every bit of grain stored in containers and silos. The National Guard saw to it that orders were carried out. The central region fared better. People made connections wherever possible with local farmers. But the situation out east was more chaotic. Rumors had it that people were fighting to the death for scraps of food. With the way things stood, it would only be a matter of time before the central region would come under attack from eastern gangs.

Alex gave the general as much information he knew without giving away technology Foster had specifically authorized for his personal use.

"That's all I know," Alex reported.

Jackson had been intently listening. "Where'd you get the information?"

"Pentagon," Alex stated.

"Foster?"

"Yeah. Informs me of what's happening out east."

"Don't get any info from there," the general complained.

"Not surprising," Alex replied. "Government and military abandoned the region…moved out west."

"See what I mean?" Jackson complained some more. "Nobody needs the Mountain."

"Tell you what," Alex suggested after giving it some thought. "'Wanna join forces?"

"How can you help?" The general seemed doubtful about the capability of one man.

"Give me protection," Alex demanded, "and I'll provide you with Intel." What the general didn't know about Alex was the scope of his prior involvement with the defense structure. It had taken his entire career to build up the foundation of a survivable communication system. Only Foster was aware since he had provided the means. It was he who had put full trust into Alex. Only Foster knew of the full extent of Alex's capabilities, but it came with a price tag. "That's," he concluded, "how I get my Intel."

"Good enough for me," the general stated. "What's next?"

Alex gave him a general outline of his plans. He did not have specifics at this time, but made promises to keep the general informed. Indicating the visit was over, he promised, "Be back with the plan."

Jackson shook his hand with a hearty, "Good you're on board," then handed the visitor over to an escort. Alex went home with the comforting thought of having the protection he sought against any potential hostilities on the Castle. But more importantly, he already envisioned the use of the mega antenna farm sitting on top of the mountain. "Gotta get my hands on it," he thought. Once repaired, it'd provide him with a long-haul connection hop to microwave repeaters stationed in and around the central region. It would be his ears to the world.

GUANTÁNAMO BAY

Yusuf Hashim eyed him with varied suspicion. While sullenly leaning against the sturdy steel post shoring up the multi-layered barbed wire fence, the new face had casually sidled up to him. *Looks Cuban*, he thought. This was his favorite spot in the camp. It was his. Everybody in the camp respected it. After all, he was Yusuf Hashim. Fame had preceded his arrival. The year before, word leaked out that one of Al Qaeda's principle freedom fighter was due to arrive. He had put claim to this spot ever since first arriving in the camp along the Cuban shores. "How long has it been?" he surmised with indifference. He had lost track of the date. Either way, it did not matter much, one day was like the next. The only thing that changed around here was an occasional new face sent in from some fighting front. Al Qaeda, Jihad, Islamic extremists had undergone radical transformations in recent years. Where they used to be loosely-knit organizations spread out across the globe, today, although lacking the western weapon technologies, they made attempts to consolidate the forces under one command to better function.

At least from this vantage point, when the air was clear, Yusuf could make out the southern shoreline of the Unites States some ninety miles in the distance. *Key West I believe they call it.* He was desperately longing for the city he had called home. New York was where his family was. It was where his buddies lived. Although he personally had failed miserably in his actions, word had leaked out that the Jihad strike on the Northern United States had been successfully executed. From his family, he had heard nothing so far. He could only guess what the conditions of that mega city must be like without power, communication, food supply, and garbage collection. "Gotta find out," he promised himself.

The stranger finally spoke. "You Hashim?"
"Maybe," he responded with guarded caution. You had to be careful in the confinement of enemy territory. There were many spies—many informers—and many killers. "Who wants to know?"

Cautiously, with eyes nervously darting from tower to tower, he handed him a slip of paper. "Got something," the stranger offered then quickly retreated.

Yusuf stared at the scrap of paper. "Freedom is near," was all it said. He slid the paper between his lips and slowly chewed it to pieces. "What does this mean?" he muttered. "Could it be an escape?" His eyes immediately brightened at the thought with newly acquired hope. But euphoria did not last long. Reality set in once again with depressing thoughts. Nobody ever escaped from this place. "But," he encouraged himself, "just in case, I must stay alert."

Prisoners were held in small mesh-enclosed cells amid burning flood lights kept on by day and by night. Where in the distant past most prisoners had been Cuban refugees, prisoners in recent years turned out to be predominantly Muslims. Due to the unique cultural needs for the detainees, special dietary provisions had been allowed, with access to the Koran and prayer rituals. Outside of that, all prisoners were kept in isolation for most of the day, blindfolded when moving for interrogation, and forbidden to talk in groups of more than three. One hour was set aside for personal recreation. But time and recreation was mostly used up by hardened criminals and drug smugglers. Muslims were not much involved with sports activities and leisure recreation, not when in confinement.

Through cultural demands, as directed by Islam and defined by the Koran, much time was absorbed in personal prayer.

Following intense interrogation by the FBI, Yusuf had been moved to Camp X-Ray, his newly found home for an indeterminate period. Some of his fellow detainees had been here for years, some even decades; many were from Castro's criminal elements. There was a distinct dividing line between the two. Where one faction was prone to criminal intents only for personal gain, the other was in pursuit of freedom for the benefit of its people. In either case, all considered their individual cause as honorable, even though most crimes ended up in violence and even death.

Unbeknownst to Yusuf, his extraction had been in the planning for months. A plan had been devised purely based on surprise, for terrorist nations were keenly aware that nobody in their right minds would ever attack this closely-monitored base. The local command, while strictly enforcing detainment policy, was lacking rigid management. The basic sentiment was one of a residential prison contained within shark-infested waters to the north, and Castro's henchmen surrounding everywhere else. An escapee, if by chance one would have cleared the barbed wire fence, guarded towers and surrounding mine fields, would be offered two challenging choices. Neither was an attractive option.

For the planned escape, no cost had been spared by Jihad supporters to get one of their best fighters back and to free additional Al Qaeda members kept in detention. The day finally arrived when the assault was scheduled.

It began innocently enough. The day was like any other this time of summer, sweltering hot. Most prisoners had sought afternoon shelter within the shades of the spacious, white bleached tents. An occasional jetliner would pass lazily overhead, leaving familiar narrow streams of condensation trails in its wake. Including the guards, nobody paid it much attention. Even though the area had been declared "no-fly zone" in airspace charts, some enterprising commercial pilot, all foreign craft at times, ignored the restriction to let the passengers get a first-hand glimpse at the world's notorious detention facility. This gesture of international goodwill promotion, as always, was very much appreciated by the traveler.

On the island grounds below, it was the hour of prayer. The chanting, mostly ignored by the guardsmen but tolerated by fellow prisoners as eccentric behavior, was barely audible outside the shaded tent walls. Unofficially accepted as the mosque, dozens of Muslim inmates were gathered in the community tent. Prisoners of the Islamic faith were allowed this religious ritual once a day, not so much as to satisfy the inmate's demands, but to appease the U.N. policy makers. The change was met with initial resistance by the military and law enforcement agencies, but eventually accepted into the daily routine to the prison environment.

Amid the chanting, growing in intensity with each second, the cutting sound from chopper blades could be heard from the distance. This was nothing unusual because helicopters frequently landed at the nearby naval station. What was unusual was the type of craft directly headed for Gitmo space. Two menacing appearing craft of the Soviet Hind helicopter class simultaneously took control of the airspace directly over the prison camp, causing sudden turmoil among the confused prison guards and inmates.

Yusuf, as usual, had lingered at his favorite spot near the fence perimeter. He had spotted the dark dots in the distant horizon rapidly approaching at low altitude, skimming across the island's jungle terrain. His mind had been on guard since receiving the cryptic note days earlier. In an instant, he recognized the sign and rushed inside the mosque to alert his fellow detainees to get ready. Dodging back outside again, he took position near the fence while observing the unfolding action. What came next played out like a first-rate action film.

One Hind let go bursts from the wing-mounted rocket pods, completely destroying the two towers holding up machine guns. Both towers were incinerated and, with them, the sentries. The second Hind began strafing the compound after placing two precisely aimed bombs of the bunker buster type on top of the main building complex. They went off deep inside the command building and its guarded armory. The ensuing blast took out most of the steel-enforced detention infrastructure.

On Yusuf's command, dozens of the Islamic turban-adorned inmates began running from the mosque tent in the direction of the hovering Hinds, whose pilots kept the non-Jihad members at bay with fiery bursts from wing-mounted twin turret guns. The entire incident took no more than five minutes, with the rescued inmates rapidly ascending into the sky on the helicopters.

The assault had been initiated and executed with military precision even before an alert to the naval base could be issued. It was not until sometime later, when a wounded guard called base operations for help, that the rescue assault was reported. Immediately following, search craft from the nearby U.S. naval base were dispatched over the jungles of Cuba. The pursuit proved to be futile since international law prohibited U.S. craft from setting foot on foreign soil outside the perimeter fence.

With Yusuf now in command, over a few weeks the rescued members were smuggled through various terrorist friendly nations to eventually regroup in Jihad training camps.

THE SERPENT

In the sanctity of his Palm Jumeirah retreat, Hasan Hammad exclaimed, "Yusuf!" as soon as his friend stepped into the lofty foyer. "So glad you made it." He reached out to embrace his lifelong friend.

Avoiding the probing eyes of the famous commander-turned-leader, Yusuf whispered, "I'm sorry for failing your mission."

"Never mind," Hammad assured him. "We have great things to accomplish." He further stated, "What's past is past. We must reorganize our forces." Yusuf was invited to join Hammad on a recliner. "I need you."

After being served special amenities made up of figs, dates, and coffee from the Arabian Peninsula, Yusuf could not contain himself any longer. "What happened?" he shot at Hammad. He had been kept in the dark on national and world events throughout the entire detainment.

"This is what happened," Hammad began illustrating the events, "after you were captured in Colorado…"

"Sorry," Yusuf apologized again. "I failed you."

"Forget it," he was told with finality, putting the past behind. "The EMP strike was delivered as scheduled. With communication and power out, America became helpless like a wounded animal. When North Korea launched its missile, our success was assured. What I did not take into account was the counterattack by the U.S. It destroyed North Korea's capital city and, with it, most of their nuclear capabilities and technologies. I took over your mission from Denver."

"What about our forces?"

"I will come to that…the first cargo delivery went well. It was the second when I ran into resistance by the adversary. Alex Bauer is his name. My equal, I should say. Still do not know where he came from or what his position is with the infidels, but let me assure you," Hammad took an extensive pause to let the importance sink in, "you must watch out."

"Is he that good?"

"Best a warrior can be. Not only that," Hammad continued, "he has help. There is a killer team in the Central Intelligence Agency with a Scott Brooks their leader. He is another one to watch out for. Both managed to eliminate most of our forces, the U.S. cells anyway. But," he went on, "I had unexpected help. It came in the form of an entire military force."

"What?" Yusuf could not believe his ears.

"Cuba. It offered its entire defense forces."

"That explains it," Yusuf offered. "I remember the day when the Cubans mobilized. Everybody in the camp wondered about that."

"It did not fare well. The Americans got wind of our invasion. We were blocked by their submarine fleet."

"Most unfortunate."

"Never mind that," he said. "To make a long story short, I delivered the final cargo to New York. It went like clockwork until Bauer and his team interfered. Not only that," he added, "he almost took my life…several times."

"Incredible."

"The man must have a sixth sense. He always appears to be one step ahead of us."

Yusuf suggested, "Maybe his God," but immediately regretted it.

"You should know better," Hammad fumed at him. "There is only Allah," he proclaimed in utter passion. "And his Prophet is Muhammad!"

"Forgive me."

"Never mind." Hammad proceeded to tell his friend about all the setbacks with the mission he and his teams had experienced. He was passionate about it. What bothered him most was the missed opportunity to gain access to the free world. "With your help," he concluded the brief, "we must build new forces, new camps, recruit fighters. I have already initiated the new Plan. The North American continent is very vulnerable. It is weak. There is much fighting among them. The economy is depleted. They have no currency. They have no technology. There is no trade. The people are starving. The window of opportunity is wide open. It will," he cautioned, "not be easy. There is still Bauer and his team to deal with."

Hammad noticed his friend suppress a deep yawn. "Getting late," he concluded. "You need rest." Pushing his body up from the comfort of the deck space, he led his visitor to an airy guestroom and wished him a pleasant night. Happy to have his longtime friend back, he made an offer. "My home is your home."

The next morning Hammad, the disciplined warrior he was, was already up when Yusuf made his entrance. Briefed and updated the previous night about the past events, Yusuf had a clear scope on the trials Hammad and the Jihad forces had endured. He was invited to be seated. He could not contain his curiosity any longer. "What about the future?"

"I shall tell you…but first," Hammad suggested, "we eat. Then we talk."

After a customary Persian breakfast was served, enjoyed, and consumed, Hammad gestured his guest to the loftiness of the deck. "Insha Allah," Yusuf expressed in wonderment. "Like a mosque."

"Deserving," Hammad agreed, "eh, my friend?"

"Most admirable." It was there, watching the open expanse of space blended in with ocean and sky, where Hammad received most of his intuition. Whether through inherited intelligence, millennia of hardship endured by his people, or historical connection with his ancestors, it was this spot that inspired him most. Through divine intervention or other spiritual sources, he always suspected Muhammad himself was instructing him. It was this perception that provided the basis for elevating himself to the highest rank achievable in the Islamic earthly state of being, becoming the Prophet himself someday.

Comfortably and contentedly seated next to his friend, Yusuf was ready to listen. He was ready to pick up the earlier conversation. "What about the future?" he insisted once more.

Hammad was ready to include his friend in his quest for an awaiting destiny. "Let me tell it to you," he hinted with his customary grin.

After a considerable pause to collect his thoughts on the one element that would guarantee success, Hammad began to talk. "Ever hear of Tesla…Nikolai Tesla?"

Yusuf's face turned into a thoughtful frown. "Not to my recollection."

It became obvious to Hammad that he needed to explain the basics. He had not expected otherwise. Not to appear openly condescending, he thought quietly, *after all, who would have knowledge on something kept dormant for a century?*
"Tesla," he began, "was a genius in his own right…"

TESLA TECHNOLOGY

After researching the technology to no end in the past year, Hammad had obtained a pretty clear picture of this revolutionary European architect. "Whether it was an earthly vision, divine enlightenment, or just plain short circuiting in the brain, possibly due to an infantile illness," Hammad explained, "Nikola Tesla had something unique going." He took his time to share the acquired information with his trusted lieutenant. "Let me enlighten your senses," Hammad began with a patience Yusuf had not experienced in the past.

"Being a highly controversial figure for his time, Tesla must have been utterly frustrated trying to convince the science communities of boundless, and innovative, ideas, let alone selling them. Eventually, after emigrating to the U.S., he got his chance. It came in the form of grants extended by the war department. Not the ideal arrangement he had envisioned, but an opportunity nevertheless." Hammad then went into great details to explain most of the inventor's technology.

Personal inventions, as was the case with most inventors, were generally intended for peaceful purposes benefiting mankind, and not deliberated for destructive military and government applications. In an ideal world, this would be the case. In the real world, with most creations struggling for dominance, it became just another weapon for achieving a superior position. Whereas Tesla's visions were focused strictly on innovative communications, a means of transmitting voice and energy wirelessly, the war department saw an immediate application to knock out tanks, ships, and planes with lightning speed, in addition to more sinister renderings. With the menace from nuclear attacks by the enemy during the cold war and MAD[5] a constant threat, DARPA[6] scientists were searching for new types of weapons without the deadly aftereffects of fallout. It came in the form of HAARP.

The concept germinated from an RF technology already heavily utilized in transmitting radio waves across the Atlantic. Tesla's inventions went even deeper than that. "What if I could do the same with power and energy," he'd pose the question to himself. As a result, the modern-day microwave was born. Demonstrating the facts in the late 18th century, Tesla, often ridiculed by the scientific establishment, built a giant coil, supposedly generating ten million volts of artificial lightning, subsequently termed death rays. However, this inventor died with World War II into obscurity following a life in poverty without ever reaping the fruits of his lifelong ambitions, but the inventions lived on in the forms of klystrons, magnetrons, gyrotrons, and waveguides found in many modern-day technologies, whether used for peaceful applications or more sinister destructive exploits.

Since then there have been many eyewitness accounts from various parts of the globe attesting to the fact that the Tesla technology is very much alive. Numerous unexplained affects have surfaced in the form of expanding lightning, spherical glows, and RF

---

[5] MAD – Mutually Assured Destruction.
[6] DARPA – Defense Advanced Research Project Agency is the design and development branch for the defense department.

blackouts, to name a few, attributed solely to man-made phenomena. Aside from the ever-present conspiracy mongers proclaiming unconfirmed facts and figures, credence must be given to some of these unexplained phenomena created out of the Tesla technology with applications in super klystron, charged particle beam weapons, induction current, cosmic radiation, igniter coil, heterodyne effect, transverse waves, longitudinal waves, wireless power transmission, thermal energy conversion, ion propelled craft, and Tesla coil.

"Thence, while a brilliant man's dream for aiding mankind's relentless advancements has long since expired, the aspirations of his unremitting powers ambitiously live on."

After discussing technology, strategy, and approach for the next phase of attack, an exhausted Yusuf retreated to his private suite once more. "There's much to be done," Hammad reminded him. "See you early in the morning."

Alone now, Hammad sat by the balcony, watching night fall again over the Gulf of Hormuz. He was keenly aware of the swells of waves washing over the sandy beaches. The world seemed at peace. He knew differently. It was only the calm before the storm. A storm that would take months, perhaps years, to form, much like a hurricane, typhoon, or cyclone, depending on what part of the world his forces would inflict the devastation on. It would be a tempest, nevertheless.

BADLANDS

Rusty Norton, ex-penitentiary inmate Fort Leavenworth, head of all forces Badlands and elected leader of the Patriots, was currently headed for the assembly hall. Passing the main entrance to the heavily fortified complex, a sign proclaimed, "Welcome to Fort Knox!" It was a constant reminder of the stroke of genius he had exerted that had allowed the prison break at Fort Leavenworth. It could not have been worked out better. In the following swoop, with the support of the inmates, he had gained hold of the nation's most important fortification. Not only had he gained control over the nation's wealth stored and safeguarded here, but the best fortified military facility, and, as luck had it, a slew of support units including recently completed housing to accommodate his entire forces, grown, at this time, to 40,000 plus strong.

"How's that possible?" If the question was posed, Norton would be just too happy to sit down and tell the story to anybody that would listen. With the fort pretty well organized through his lieutenants—Duke Wheeler, aka Bad Man, in conjunction with the former prison mates, and his other trusted man, Brodie Elliott, Command Sergeant Major, 1st Armored Division, who without much convincing had joined Norton's forces following a brutal, but brief, combat exchange—he could not be happier. The present position he enjoyed as Commander-in-Chief for the entire mechanized forces, 1st Armored Infantry Division, 3rd Brigade, had elevated him to the military leader commanding the central region, the Badlands. In addition, due to popular demand, he had been elected political head of the New Nation. But the title to lead the new nation, at this time, was still under consideration dependent solely on the design of the new constitution, presently under development.

Located just thirty-five miles from Louisville, KY, Fort Knox[7] encompassed many acres sprawled across several Kentucky counties. The fort's population had seen tremendous growth in soldiers, family members, and civilian employees, not to mention former inmates from Fort Leavenworth, as of late. Above ground, several layers of security fences gave the facility advanced warning whenever a potential breach occurred. Below

---

[7] In reality, the defense parameters were impressive to any banking and depository system. To the outside world, the fort appeared only as ordinary headquarters building, but to the informed, the facility was ringed with fences and guarded. The depository premises were situated deep within, protected by layers of physical security, alarms, video cameras, armed guards, and the Army units permanently housed at Fort Knox. The force was complemented by Apache helicopter gunships based at Godman Army Airfield nearby, the 16th Cavalry Regiment, the 19th Engineer Battalion, formerly training battalions of the United States Army Armor School, and the 3rd Brigade Combat Team of the 1st Infantry Division, totaling 30,000 plus soldiers, with associated tanks, armored personnel carriers, attack helicopters, and artillery.

For added safety, there was an escape tunnel from the lower level of the vault, to be used by someone accidentally locked in. For security reasons, no visitors were allowed inside the depository grounds. This policy had been enforced ever since the vault opened, and the only exception was an inspection by members of the United States Congress and the news media in September, 1974, led by then Director of the United States Mint Mary Brooks. This was the saga of the fort.

the fortress-like structure were the vaults, lined with granite walls and protected by blast-proof doors weighing twenty-some tons. For the unauthorized, it was almost impossible to penetrate the fortification.

"Let 'em try." Bad Man, Enforcer to the fort's population, would attest when the topic of vulnerability came up. "Guys are a tough breed." He was referring to the armed guards commissioned for just one reason, to protect the gold no matter what.

That's what was presently on Norton's mind as he headed for the assembly hall. Today's session would not be an easy one. There would be much controversy. But it had to be done. He needed a solid constitution to proceed forward. Without it, it would only be a ragtag army, well trained, yes, but lacking a national structure, missing the political body. Personally, he would like to see a new policy instituted with strictly controlled voting. Otherwise, it would be just another repeat of failed democracy. And he did not want that. In contrast to democracy, he knew too well the outcome of such ruling power. It always ended in the same fashion: riots, takeover, coup d'état, followed with the death or incarceration of the leadership. No matter what the outcome, he planned to be around to enjoy the rewards of the newly created nation, his nation. He had earned it. He deserved it.

Stepping up to the podium, his mind was clear as he began. "Listen up." Norton hammered away with the gavel. "Today…" It was a lengthy introduction followed by the proposed articles for a new constitution. It covered the baseline for instituting and organizing a nation, much as it had been when writing the first articles back in 1776. Each article, when read, depending on its popularity by the attending voters, was either blessed by a Yea or rejected with a Nay. In addition, everybody interested for a position or post in the new government was able to have his/her say. The following debates were fiery at times, and, in the end, nothing got solved. The main body of the article read:

Article 1 – Legislative Department: Congress, House, Senate.
Article 2 – Executive Branch: Presidential Office, his Powers and Responsibilities.
Article 3 – Judicial Department: Supreme Court, Regional Courts, and Punishments.
Article 4 – Relations of States: Citizen's rights and protection of states.
Article 5 – Amendments…

It was at this point when the assembly fell apart. "Here we go again," Norton muttered, but his words were lost in the heated debates. "Democracy at work…gotta be another way." The whole premise for a new constitution was based on removing any and all amendments. There had been too many. The constitution before the collapse of the United States had been so diluted, it was the cause for its collapse. It was Bad Man that spoke up what many others were thinking, "Screw Amendments," he shouted into the ensuing melee.

"Just wait a doggone minute," Nelson demanded. He already knew reworking the amendments would cause a stir. It was the topic for many griping sessions in the past weeks. He had to come up with an alternative, but a workable one. Even he was at a loss for a viable solution at this time. Expecting nothing would get solved today he quickly left the hall headed for the base library, flanked by his lieutenants. What he needed was a political sense in direction. He hoped the history books would give him the guidance he needed.

SHAPE HQ BELGIUM

Reaching into the private recesses of his mind, Emmett W. Fletcher, Four-star General, Flag Officer, NATO European Command, thought, *Here's my chance*, in the quiet of his chambers. It was a thought that had been germinating in his mind more often than not in recent days. In the wake of the attack on what used to be the United States of America, he mulled over the idea. "The time's ripe." What he and everybody in the free world never could have imagined in their wildest dreams had happened, the Fall of an Empire. It came on so fast nobody had been prepared.

But the indicators, if one would have followed and analyzed recent political and economic trends, had been there, nevertheless. "But the dollar, gone?" he muttered, shaking his head in bewilderment. He still marveled at the phenomenon everybody, not so long ago, thought impossible. But there it was, visible to the whole world: the dollar standard, the world's commerce and trade instrument, vanished in one day. "Damned Jihad," he cussed, for the umpteenth time, but was quick to console himself. "Here's my chance...but, for that matter," he alarmingly stated, "everybody else's in the world." He knew, if he acted quickly, he had a jump on the rest of the world.

He made reference to the chaotic conditions that rippled through the globe. After the strike on U.S. soil, there was silence in the ether from the nations near and far alike. In the days that followed, he had been unable to reach the North American continent, the Pentagon, any military command with all the other forces under his immediate command. It was like a black hole had opened and swallowed up every kind of communication. It was not until days later when word slowly reached the European shores that something immense had transpired across the Atlantic.

The news came from a most unlikely source: Al Jazeera, broadcast out of Qatar. Once news broke, there was jubilation across much of the Arabian Peninsula. From there, it rapidly spread across the Middle East, India, Asia, Europe, and the Africa continent. Initially, most nations were stunned.

What followed the next day were stock market and foreign exchange crashes, much like a domino effect sweeping across the globe. With DOW Jones, NASDAQ, and S&P 500 exchanges gone, it was only a matter of hours for EUR, FTSE, CAC, AEX, OMX, Mexico, Brazil, Swiss, Nikkei, and Hang Seng before they collapsed. Investors, speculators, shareholders, private groups, individual investors, and every institution depending on profits for their investments not only lost everything they owned, but, to make things worse, with many depending on electronic statements, lost all their records and data. World commerce had collapsed within one business day with everybody in the world owing everybody else unimaginable amounts or nothing at all, if records could not be reacquired. The few fortunate ones, the ones not prone to gamble, the ones owning land, properties, gold, and jewelry, survived the crash. In spite of skepticism and controversies, they were proven the smart ones. They saw the trends.

Comments for years prior to that fact circulating among family, friends and likeminded individuals weren't too far off when stating, "It'll all end someday." For those, trade exchanges were just gambling houses on a grand scale. "No difference between Vegas and Wall Street," the comments went. "It's all gambling."

It took weeks for some nations to recover, many months for others. Some never did. Their banking systems were still shut down. Whatever cash was on hand stored in vaults stayed behind vault doors. Bank owners did not want to take a chance on completely losing everything. The public, the citizen, the common man did not fare so well. They were the ones required to fend for themselves. Forced from necessity, just like the olden days, was how barter got started.

But surviving was not what Emmett Fletcher had in mind. He had higher aspirations. His mind was on power, and opportunity presented itself on a grand scale. In one sweep, he had been presented an opportunity to take the power and claim it as his own. His immediate plan was to gain possession of all the military forces in Europe, by force if necessary. Invisible as much was, he had the power at his disposal. And that power came in the form of an entire fleet of submerged U.S. submarines. With no one in control on U.S. soil, he had asserted immediate command. "Get me SUBLANT Command on the line," he ordered his chief assistant. "And," he further demanded, "schedule a trip to Ramstein, Böblingen, Wiesbaden, and Naples." What he needed was to show his face at all of the NATO commands. For the U.S. Army, it was Wiesbaden. For the Air Force, it was Ramstein. For the Marines, it was Böblingen, and for Naval Fleet Headquarters, Naples, Italy.

"I'll get my hands on it all," he vowed. "I'll own the world." Visions of historic personages such as Genghis Khan, Attila the Hun and Napoleon swept across his mind. "I'll walk the Halls of Walhalla," he silently promised, "among all the greats!"

BRIAN HARRIS

It had taken him only minutes to arrive at the Baltimore docks. Today, he figured, would be the last time he would lay eyes on his beloved harbor. "Maybe forever." Although he had his doubts facing an uncertain future, the journey was necessary if he wanted to survive. To his relief, maritime traffic was back in operation, but from the names identifying vessels, shipping was mostly from foreign only registered ships. "All the better," he muttered. He noticed one vessel about to take to the seas over at the next dock. Gauging the distance, it was uncertain if he could make it there in time with its mooring ropes just released. Regardless, he had to try. Running with all of the strength he could gather, he gave it a shot. The ship had already left the docks when he arrived by the edge. It was now or never. In one motion, he tossed the duffel over the rail and jumped, landing hard on the deck just inside the rail. The fall had momentarily taken the wind from his lungs. Getting up on his shaky feet, he cursed, "Dammit." And there it was, coming from across the deck, the shouting from the ship's mate. "Hey, you!"

Between rubbing his ribcage, and collecting the duffel he ignored the caller, but not for long. The man was already by his side, demanding, "Get off my ship." He was furiously shouting obscenities. Avoiding the man's eyes, Brian muttered, "Typical sailor."

"What?" the mate raged with an angered face. Backed by a poised body, his fists were balled, ready to throw the stowaway overboard when Brian reached inside his jacket, pulling out a few silver coins. "I've got money," he offered. "See?" It seemed to pacify the mate. He backed off, then took the coins and carefully inspected them. "Haven't seen these in years," he grumbled. "Solid silver?"

More relaxed, Brian replied, "Damn right. Turkish, vintage."

"Okay, then. You can stay. Where you headed?"

"Texas."

The mate held out his hand, "Got more of these?"

"No," Brian lied. "Last treasure." He made a mental note to be extra careful while on the ship because he noticed the man's skeptical face when he turned and strode away, saying, "Stay on deck."

It must have been past midnight when Brian woke up from being rudely manhandled by what appeared to be three toughs. Sure enough, his fears had come true. He instantly realized he was being assaulted and robbed for his treasure. Still drunk from sleep, he staggered to his feet and tried to ward off the attack, but was kicked and punched. It did not take long. He was quickly overpowered. While Brian had kept up his strength with running and exercises, he was no match for the sailors, who were used to fights and brawls as a way of living. He was overpowered, frisked, and stripped of his jacket. "Dammit," he cussed when he saw them discover the sewn-in coins.

Beaten to the ground and hurt, Brian swore revenge as he watched them stalk off, tearing the jacket lining to pieces. What they missed was the revolver he had tucked away under the tarpaulin he'd used to cover up while asleep. There was not much he could do for the rest of the night. He needed daylight to identify the toughs before he could make an attempt to get the coins back. To distract his thoughts from his dilemma, he tried to enjoy the cruise as much as possible. Riviera Beach and Fort Smallwood were slowly passing by to the right. They brought back fond memories of the beach he used to hang out at with buddies when growing up. The vessel, once it reached the open waters of the Chesapeake Bay, made rapid progress. It was not long before they rounded Newport News, Norfolk, leaving Virginia Beach behind as they headed in a south-westerly direction. Under full power, he figured it would take a couple of days for the ship to get to Houston, his destination.

Brian did not sleep the rest of the night. His body hurt and his mind was churning with the formulation of a plan. Confined to the deck, he at least enjoyed the night sky. The sheer numbers of stars visible weighed down on him like a heavy blanket. He marveled at the strange sight. Back in the city, everyone stayed locked indoors during nights in fear of marauding gangs. Here in the open, at least, was a slice of beauty unlike any he had ever seen. He completely enjoyed the sight of uncountable stars set against the Milky Way. The ship released an occasional burst from the foghorn alerting nearby ships.

The night eventually came to an end. The vessel had just rounded the tip of Florida and was headed directly west towards Houston. "Should be there by nightfall," Brian figured. For now, he had more immediate plans. It was still early. The day had just broken over the eastern horizon. He was suddenly distracted by shuffling near the bridge. He reached for the weapon stashed nearby. It gave him assured confidence while edging closer to the sound. It was a group of maritime sailors, just finished breakfast. They were huddled by the bulkhead speaking quietly one last time before taking on their daily duties. Brian heard them speak a broken dialect. Although crews on these ships were made up by a variety of tongues, to understand what was said, each had some sort of English language skills prevalent in international commerce. The assembly seemed on alert. Their eyes were darting between possible hiding spots on the deck. Inching closer, Brian could now make out some of their words. "Dumb fool, carrying that much money…lucky us, and…how you gonna spend your money?"

"Whores," one voiced. "What else?" There was laughter and grinning among them just before they dispersed to their duty stations. It was enough for Brian. He had identified the faces from the mugging the night before. He carefully followed the one he thought was the instigator. Tucked behind some winches, he watched for a while, deciding on an approach. He needed his coins back no matter what. The sailor was getting ready to paint the rail. The newly restored sections were clearly visible. Painting was an ongoing task on ships. It served several purposes. One, it kept the vessel in shape. Two, it kept sailors busy. Three, it passed the time during lengthy voyages.

The sailor dropped the paintbrush the instant Brian shoved the revolver into his back. "I want my coins back," he demanded. At first, the man looked surprised. Upon further prodding from the gun, he shook his head, pleading ignorance. "I heard you," Brian replied to the man's reaction. The immediate effects of being exposed were painted across the man's face. Trapped alone, facing a gun, was a different situation than being in the company of a group. Right now, he was forced to deal with the threat himself. His buddies where dispersed elsewhere, but it did not prevent him from yelling out obscenities in hope they might hear his dilemma.

Brian's partial payback was to slap him across the head with the revolver. The man jerked and tried to run away, but Brian jumped on his legs, making him buckle under the added weight. "This is how it's gonna happen," he huffed. "You and I are going to walk quietly down to your quarters. Move." There was reluctance, but, shoved by the gun, he led on. The sailor must have realized Brian was of equal strengths and, without help coming his way, belligerence had turned to fear. It seemed he was an opportunist rather than a hardened thug.

Arriving in the berths below, it did not take long to locate the missing treasure. It was hidden away with the man's personal belongings. What gave the hiding place away was his jacket with the torn lining carelessly tossed into a corner. Waving the revolver in his face, Brian gave the man one fearful warning. "Next time you're dead." Regardless of the maritime consequences it might cause, he meant it. In these days of turmoil, one more killing would most likely go unnoticed for any legal repercussions, especially since most vessels had no legal jurisdiction in any one country. Judgment was usually rendered by the captain, on the spot, out at sea.

The incident went unreported to the captain. It was probably for the reason that no crew member was willing to lose his job.

The rest of the trip went uneventfully. As anticipated, the ship made landing late afternoon, and Brian departed for the next leg of the journey up north. This time, it would be on the road. He spent the night at a hostel near the docks. With coins back in his hands, it was easy to get lodging. Although he could not hide the treasure any longer due to the torn lining, his full confidence returned once more. Early the next morning, he sought out the waterfront. Loading docks, busy with hauling goods in and out on arriving trucks, would be his best chance to hitch a ride north across the Lone Star state. Sure enough, waving a few coins assured him the fare. The driver was a likable old-timer in the business of trucking for most of his life. As it turned out, he welcomed Brian's company.

The truck made good time on the way to Albuquerque, the next junction. It would be the parting point for Brian. The driver was scheduled to head for the Pacific coast, where most of the goods were shipped. California was still plagued by remnants from the nuclear explosion affecting the population. Since the contamination, there were never enough goods and medicines to feed and supply its poverty-stricken and sickened populace. But, due to its strategic position in the nation, protected from immediate threats, Pacific commerce was gaining hold once more.

Trucking along I-10, crossing the largest state in the nation, Texas, the trip seemed endless. During all of his travels, Brian had never been to this state. Between keeping the trucker company and napping, after many hours, the 18-wheeler suddenly slowed. Slightly dazed, Brian woke. He could not get his bearing at first. "Where're we?"

"Getting close to Juarez." The trucker gestured to the left. "See the creek?"

"Yeah?"

"Mexico's on the other side."

"The fence?" Brian marveled.

"Built years ago."

"Ah, yes," he recalled, "the infamous border disputes."

"Been there ever since. Spans the whole damned border. Look at us now," he grumbled. "Torn and ripped down at many places. Doesn't do anybody any good."

"Why do you say that?"

"Illegal good's smuggled into the country day and night."

"Like what?" Brian's curiosity was sparked.

"Guns, drugs, counterfeits…you name it. As long as you've got the cash, anything goes."

To assure he was still in possession of his treasure, Brian fingered the makeshift money belt strapped around his waist. With his jacket torn, he was able to fabricate a waistband from a piece of cloth he obtained prior to departing the vessel. Feeling the weight, he sighed with relief.

The gesture did not go unnoticed by the trucker. "Personal stash?"

"Got robbed once already."

"Can't be too careful." The trucker pulled up at the border crossing. "Gonna be search."

"Who?"

"Anarchists. Haven't heard?"

"Heard what?"

"They've taken over the southern states. Patrol all crossings."

"Thought it was only rumors."

"Take a look." The trucker nodded ahead. "Uniforms."

Brian could see it now. Squads clad in smartly-fitted blacks were directing traffic in and out the holding zones. Black boots, trousers, shirts, jackets, shades, resembling a time from another era not so distant. "SS," he proclaimed. Watching the border detachment in action reminded Brian of Hitler's personal security staff.

"Not quite as bad," the trucker replied. "But watch your steps. Confiscate anything that's of value. If you're caught smuggling, off you go to jail. These guys are ruthless."

"Any body searches?"

"Not if you've got proper credentials."

Brian relaxed. He figured the crossing was safe with his NSA identification.

"IDs," the guard barked through the window. The trucker showed him ID and shipping documents. They seemed to be in order. His gaze shifted to Brian. "You?"

Brian was about to lift his ID from the wallet when he froze. The plastic window normally holding his NSA card was empty. He was dumbfounded. "Taken on the ship," he muttered. "I was robbed."

"What's that?" The guard shot him a warning sign. "Better have some papers." A second guard suddenly appeared by the passenger side and practically ripped the door open. "Step down," he ordered. Brian was staring into the barrel of a shotgun as he hopped onto solid ground. The next second the guard was frisking him. "What have we here?" He had located the money belt, bulging with coins. "Move," the guard ordered, while kicking a cuffed Brian in the direction of the guard shack.

Brian had no choice. He made a feeble attempt to save the only treasure he had left. "Please." All the begging did not matter. Cuffed by nylon straps he was quickly taken away. He shot one last begging glance at the trucker, who had already been flagged on to cross the border.

The interrogation room was filthy. Nobody seemed to have any pride in keeping things tidy. His handcuffs were removed. Two uniforms questioned him. The interrogation was swift. According to the faction's rules he had committed a crime for smuggling contraband. "Undeclared coins," he was told after repeatedly protesting, "are illegal here." Off he went to jail. "Five years," the judge proclaimed with an on-the-spot sentence.

And that was how Brian Harris disappeared from the face of the earth.

SCOTT BROOKS

It was early morning yet. Scott Brooks, taking firm strides along the edge of the road, was headed out of town hoping a driver would stop along the way. It would only be a matter of time before someone was willing to pick him up. People in this area were always ready to help each other. Someday it would be their turn to need a ride, especially with the majority of vehicles being dated and frequently breaking down. Sure enough, he could hear the hum of an engine approaching from the distance. Stepping aside, he turned and waited. Two headlights approached. The truck rolled to a halt as the driver leaned out, shouting, "Where you headed?"

"Albuquerque," he replied. "Mind if I ride along?"

"For 'chure," he was told, "hop on."

They continued on Rt-90 out of Fort Huachuca, en route to Benson and planning to connect with I-10 East. Sandwiched in between the driver and happily chatting passengers, a group of day workers out of Mexico seeking employment on U.S. soil had crossed the Nogales border the night before.

Scott had to smile at the dialogue. He liked the Latino culture…or was it Hispanic? He was not sure what the correct expression was. It did not matter. He was always able to communicate. Spending so much time near the border, he and his buddies used to cross into Mexico many a night to have fun—especially Nogales, out of convenience reasons, with an occasional trip to Mexicali or Juarez. Everything seemed to be cheap there: the booze, the goods, the girls, whatever a man's pleasure. As long as you kept your nose clean while on foreign soil, and made it back on base without getting locked up for one reason or other, it could be a pleasant experience for any young GI. It didn't go smoothly all the time. As military life had it, after a few drinks, the boasting began, then came the challenging, followed by gauging strengths. It was always the same pattern, ending with a fight and getting thrown out or landing in jail. Fights, as frequent as they were, were always for the same reasons: girls. Like there were not enough out there for everyone, but a drunken mind could not rationalize.

He was enjoying the ride in the company of these pleasant people. Presently, the pickup took a turn east. They had just entered I-10. It would be at least a couple of hours before they met up with I-25. It would be the junction point for hitching another ride. The present journey would end in Albuquerque. Brooks had plenty of time. He kicked back in the seat and decided to take a nap.

Still foggy, Scott felt a tapping on his shoulder. "Estamos aqui, mi amigo," the driver announced. Torn from the realm of dreams, Scott looked up and saw that they had just arrived. It was a pleasant dream. He had been in the company of girls in one of the clubs he frequented with his buddies. Nogales, he believed. He blinked his eyes a couple of times to clear his still foggy mind.

Smiling broadly through a few missing teeth, the driver asked, "'Chu been dreaming? Pretty girls, eh?"

"Pretty girls, yeah."

"What 'chu gonna do?"

"Thanks for the ride, amigo," Scott thanked him and pushed a couple of silver dollars into the man's palm. "No," the driver objected at first, but took the coins when Scott insisted. "¡Buen viaje!" he yelled from the window as the truck drove on.

Brooks tossed his duffel on the ground, checking the environment, when his eyes caught the sign. "I-25," it proclaimed, "Albuquerque." He could not believe he had slept most of the way. Without a functioning watch, whether it was dusk, dawn, the sun and the moon now kept time. He contemplated how long it would be before another driver came along. It did not take much time. What appeared was an official sedan, government type, approaching from the south. The vehicle rolled to a halt. "Need a lift?" the driver asked.

"Depends," Scott replied. "Where you headed?"

"North," the driver indicated. "Santa Fe."

"Mind if I ride along?"

"Hop on."

"Thanks," Scott said, tossing the duffel on the backseat. At least it would take him closer to his destination. Because of his cautious nature, there was something that caught his eyes. It was the man's appearance. It seemed out of place for the environment. He decided to probe first chance.

"Where're you from?" the driver asked.

"Arizona desert."

"What's out there?"

"Same as here," Scott indicated. "Nothing."

"You military?"

"Sort of."

"Any more specific?"

"DELTA."

"Aah yes," the driver mulled. "Fighter, weapons specialist, killer elite."

Not exactly knowing what to expect, Scott eyed him with suspicion. He pulled the duffel close within reach. Just to be safe.

The driver apparently noticed the move. "No need for that," he gestured at the bag, "I'm not the enemy."

"Can't be too careful," Scott replied. He then noticed the tattoo on the man's neck. "What's with the bird?"

In an involuntary motion, the driver's right hand reached for the patch of skin on his neck. "Oh, this?" His fingers were slightly rubbing across the tattoo. "Condor."

"Secret society?" Scott had never heard of it.

"You might say that." The driver was talkative. There seemed to be something on his mind.

"Talk about it?" He wanted to know more about the so-called society. *Who knows,* he thought, *might even be interested in joining.*

"You cleared?" The driver was referring to the classified status many military and laboratory facilities operated within. Most employees required top secret clearances.

"DELTA…CIA," Scott responded. "Why Condor?"

"We're the watchers."

"Okay?"

The driver went on. He turned out to be full of information. He proceeded to tell Scott about the place he worked and the projects he handled at the Los Alamos National Laboratories.

Scott did not know much about the facility other than that it had been a nuclear weapons research center for the Manhattan Project and others, housing celebrated scientists with names like Oppenheimer, Teller, and Van Braun. What went on there now would be anybody's guess. He was about to find out. The more he heard, the more intriguing it became. *Gotta see this place,* he thought while listening to the driver.

Fifty minutes later they arrived at a heavily-guarded security shack. "IDs," the sentry demanded. Checking both credentials, it only took seconds to clear the gates.

After he parked the vehicle, the driver instructed, "Follow me." Scott kept pace with long strides to keep up with the man. They were headed toward a sprawling complex of buildings.

"Los Alamos," the sign proclaimed, "National Research Center."

NAPA VALLEY

"Another disgustingly beautiful day," Liz cheered into the morning dew as she stepped on the accelerator of the SUV. She liked the California-coined expression. In a state of prevalent sunshine for most of the year, people were looking forward to the annual monsoon season for a change. It was a time when daily rainsqualls would turn the brown and desolate country into a Garden of Eden, especially where she lived. She never got tired taking in the beauty of grapevines perfectly aligned in endless rows within the sloped hills of Napa, Sonoma, and the Russian River Valley, situated in the northern stretches of the Bay.

Today, as usual, she was in a rush again to drop the kids off at school. "Be good," were her parting words. Being the working mom, she was, raising children responsibly was a hectic life. Although she enjoyed the independence from marriage for most part, between managing a fulltime job, tending to the children's school activities, it could be overwhelming at times. When married, men never realize the true burden a mother carries on her shoulders. *Husbands,* she thought, *all the same.* Just because they were the primary Breadwinner they thought they could just prop their lazy bodies in an easy chair after a day's work and have the wife tend to their every whim for the remainder of the waking hours. Yet she felt slightly remorseful having these thoughts about a once beautiful marriage. Abruptly ending in failure, after many joyful years, she felt it was her prerogative to feel sad.

Leaving the schoolyard behind, her focus was on the morning traffic. Heading south on Silverado toward the city, Napa's mainstream traffic link, she took note of the billowing cloud formations up ahead on the horizon. Slightly worried, she shot a glance at the emergency radio mounted beneath the dashboard but only noticed the steady channel scans. By now, the otherwise static crackling emanating from the radio should have alerted her if the cloud formation had been fire related. Reaching for the mic, she decided, *Better check with Base.*

"Base One," she queried in her usual self-assured voice. "Any calls this morning."

"No emergencies," was the prompt response from the operator. "That you, Nine?"

"Affirmative."

"Why'd you ask?"

"Check the clouds out west."

"Standby." The shortwave speaker returned the usual static background noises.

She'd checked her work planner just before leaving home, and today she was on standby.

"Unit Nine."

"Go."

"Disregard clouds," was the response. "Chemtrails only."

"Chemtrails?" She deliberately traced the word between her luscious lips, wondering about the difference from contrails. Holding a private pilot's license, she knew all about contrail but was clueless about this new phenomenon everybody was bitching about lately. Trails appeared in all sorts of shapes and forms, from crisscross patterns to parallel streams of condensation, at times beautifully aligned against a blue, yellow, and red evening sky.

"Hmm," she muttered. "Gotta ask Dad about it."
After Liz reached home she geared up the HAM set placing his call sign on the ether.

Liz did not have to wait long for Alex to return the call. The message she left on his recorder was enough to perk his interests. "Chemtrails," he wondered. "What's she got to do with it?"
As cheerful as always, she answered, "Hi, Dad. Get my message?"
"Sure did. Now," he asked, "what's that all about?"
"I thought," she said, charming him, "if anybody knew it'd be you." Charm, she recalled, always worked to get what she wanted. It worked this time as well. What followed was a brief account of chemtrails[8] activities. He finished with, "That's all I know." As usually, he gave her more information than she asked for. When it came to scientific and technology facts, he knew the answers. But, she wasn't satisfied. She felt there was more to it than he was willing to disclose.
"What about the earthquakes, glacier melts, the floods, Dad?"
"Don't believe everything you hear. Mostly rumors initiated by conspiracies. If it gets too much for you out there," he suggested, "you can always move here."
"Thanks, Dad. Job, kids, their schools—they need me."
"They'll make new friends. They'd like it here. You did."
"We'll see. Love you, Dad." She hung up.

---

[8] Chemtrails: A new phenomenon has been observed by the public for a number of years from the Atlantic coast clear across the nation as far as the Pacific. First observed in the late '90s, aerosol spraying was strongly suspected as cause of the sudden appearance of what seemed to be manmade patterns of trails left in the wake of supersonic aircraft. In spite of persistent requests from the public and political members, admissions and disclosures have not been forthcoming from any government agency. All demands made by the public to this date have been denied as mere speculations and conspiracies. Following are some of the proposed speculations:

According to some scientists, the experiment was understood to be generated through chemical spray ejected into a specific test region for the purpose of observing the results of biological reactions from living organisms coming into contact with the chemicals. Moreover, numerous complaints have been launched by the public, as well as health organizations, to the cause of unexplained health issues by individuals affected.

Health afflictions have been reported ranging from skin damages to respiratory ailments and psychological instabilities. Official media reports have been very scarce due to the risk of ridicule by the news media and government officials. However, the phenomenon must be taken seriously since many regions have reported an unusual increase in health issues. Believers of this theory speculated that the purpose of the chemical release may be for global dimming, population control, weather control, or biowarfare, and claim that these trails cause respiratory illnesses and other health problems. At this point, it was all up to speculations.

TRACY BAUER

Although quite some time had passed since the EMP strike, Tracy was still residing at the Castle with her dad. The more time she spent there, the more frustrated she became. One day, she realized the reason. She was confined and, to her dismay, it was an involuntary confinement. After that, *time to move on* became a daily reminder. The only thing that kept her staying put was the promise she had made Dad. He had demanded that she stay until he decided the world was safe again. Unbeknownst to him, she would sneak away from the Castle in ever widening circles, going more frequently lately. Initially, it was local places only. A pub nearby had opened up for the townspeople. Rumors had it that it was a rowdy place. She had gone to find out for herself.

Showing up one evening, she found that the sign out front said, "Hell Hole." Stepping across the threshold, she immediately sensed trouble. One look inside and she knew why. The place's appearance held up to its sign and reputation.

"Look what the cat dragged in," and "What 'cha doin' here, sweetie?" were some of the remarks from local leering patrons. The place looked nasty. The floor was filthy. Walls were splattered with stains. The place, in general, was in shambles. And so were many of its guests. Not just rugged in appearance, but raggedy and smelly as well. Ignoring the calls, Tracy walked to the bar. "Beer, please," she ordered.

"Bottle or mug?"

"Mug."

Ten seconds later a mug slid in front of her. "Like the Old West," she mused. Another ten seconds more, a couple toughs sidled up to her.

"What brings you here?" one demanded while the other stared at her boobs. Not that she was advertising her shape; they'd been there since she grew out of puberty. She could not help it, she was just a shapely woman and she was proud of it. They accented her even more since she had started an extreme workout. Not only was her body well-toned, it was as hard as muscles could be.

"Fun."

"Well, well." He leaned closer and placed his hand on her back. "Look no further."

"What 'cha got in mind?"

With one hand clutching his crotch, he replied, "Wanna step in back?" Stepping back a few paces he leered in the direction of the restrooms.

It was such a lewd gesture she could not hold her tongue. "You don't have the equipment." She ignored his stare, shrugged her shoulders and grabbed the mug for another sip. She knew her insult on his manhood would turn on the fury in him. It showed in his face and posture as he advanced in her direction again.

"What'd you say?"

A defiant look cut across her face. She held her ground. It seemed to irritate him even more. The next word he spat at her gave away his intelligence. "Slut!"

"At least," she replied, "I don't have to prove my point."

"Hell, you won't." He took a hold of her wrist and twisted it out.

His face was so close she could smell his stale breath. "Not today." She spat in his face. "Not ever!"

That was all the abuse he would take. Next move was a slap to her face. But Tracy was prepared. She was sober. She was quicker. Much like a slow-motion film, she saw the hand lunge at her and ducked. With his momentum striking empty space, the patron lost his footing and twisted out. In a deliberate motion, she grabbed the mug and hit him across the face, leaving a deep gash. It would leave a mark for the rest of his life. He knew it as soon as his sleeve came up bloody.

"Fucking bitch," he screamed at her with the fury of a madman. "You're dead!" Out came a knife. It was one of the knives popular with hunters. Wielding it in front of her face meant he was serious. All she did was grin at him. It seemed to infuriate him beyond control. The next stab was directed at her face. He lashed out. Tracy blocked, then, with a twist on his wrist, made him lose his grip on the steel. The knife landed on the floor with a clang. He had not expected the reaction. Not from a woman. It stunned him for a second. "Damn you," he yelled out and thrust his full weight at her.

The fight was over as quickly as it had started. She used his momentum to knock him to the ground, punched him in the head once more, and finished up with a kick to the ribs. Sputtering, he lost his breath from the force. She deliberately faced the crowd. "Anybody else?" Tracy felt daring. It was an invitation some could not refuse. They came at her with pool sticks, bottles, and fists. It did not matter to her how many there were. *The more the merrier.*

There was a certain philosophy with the Chinese Kung-Fu martial arts Dad had taught her. It claimed that the more opponents a fighter faced, the easier it was for him to win. In other words, it meant the enemy was crammed in. There was just not enough room for everyone to get into the act. It was a strategy that would win her many battles to come. It proved effective here, it would prove her effectiveness in the future. Tracy took on one opponent at a time. Pool sticks thrust at her she broke in halve and used as Nunchakus, Chinese fighting weapon, on the opponent. Bottles struck at her she ripped from their grips, smashed it against the bar's edge, and used it as cutting tool. She had no intentions to kill. She was only interested in leaving her mark on the aggressor's body. It should serve as painful reminder in future confrontations. Within minutes, they all went down or wound up injured. The fighting turned out easier than she had anticipated. Aside from the moaning bodies sprawled on the floor, the place had turned silent. Without further resistance, she muttered, "Won my first round," and left the place. Passing by the many faces staring in awe of what had just transpired, she felt elated.

Over the weeks that followed, word spread about a killer woman. It even carried back to the Castle. When Alex heard about it he suspected Tracy. At first, he was furious, but after his nerves calmed down he marveled, and followed that with pride. "That's my girl," he boasted in the quiet of the Castle. He felt like some weight had lifted off his shoulders. He may not have realized it at the moment, but the protective bond he had all along for his daughter was finally cut. She was free to go. She was prepared for whatever would come across her path. He realized it would not be an easy path, especially not for what she'd indicated she had in mind.

From that day on, to test her skills, Tracy took many excursions, not just around the town, but to neighboring places as well.

"Just watch your back," Alex cautioned her whenever he would hear about another incident with an enraged female, a wonder woman, and a knockout to boot. For now, she lashed out with punches and kicks whenever it was payback time. She let her hands and legs do the work. And payback, with disorder, turmoil, and crime running rampant in the nation, was plentiful.

Rumors even had it that some parts of the nation were out of control and in complete anarchy. Even thinking about such opportunities fueled her spirits. It was a fighter spirit Tracy had taken on in the name of righteousness and justice. All she wanted to do was fight off evil elements and turn the clock back, so the next generation could enjoy a better future.

LISA (LIZ) BAUER

The turmoil from the fallout on the San Francisco region had somewhat stabilized in the past year. It was mostly due to the military presence taking root on the west coast. After abandoning the Eastern Sector, that region became vulnerable more frequently to terrorist attacks from across the Atlantic. News of it was carried across the nation mostly from HAM operators broadcasting regional events as they happened. Every time Liz heard about some new incidence she became more despaired.

With fallout shelters gone from the Golden State Park, Liz permanently moved back to Napa to be with her family again. "There's no way," shaking her head, Liz voiced her frustrations at her mom. It had become obvious. The nation was being splintered apart by competing factions. It became especially obvious on the eastern seaboard. But, that was not the only troubled spot. Troublesome rumors were surfacing from the nation's heartland as well. It seemed several factions had formed fending for their own agendas. And none of them, it seemed, had peaceful intentions. There were even rumors of Asian nations vying the Western Sector as easy prey.

"What?" Her mom was as complacent as usual. She seemed to have shut out the world. She appeared happy in her home, especially taking care of her grandkids.

Furious, as usual, by the very thought of losing her beloved Napa Valley to marauding bands or worse, foreign powers, she swore vengeance. "Not on my watch!" Not only her entire life, but the nation as a whole, had been dedicated to helping others and other nations. "And what do you get?" she fumed. "Nothing. Nada, nix, niet, not even a thank you or slightest appreciation." During such short outbursts, her inherited language skills jumbled together. Aside from English, she fluently spoke Spanish through her mother's heritage, German taught by her dad, and Russian, thanks to additional language skills acquired while at Stanford.

"Russian?" Her mom had had a verbal outburst when she found out. "But why?" To her mom, back then and now, Russia was still the enemy. Not to upset her mother's provincial thinking, Liz kept the thoughts to herself. Like many Americans, her mother thought a foreign language was not of importance. Her mom still questioned the purpose, "why, the whole world speaks English."

Dad had been more supportive. He was the visionary. With a career dedicated to travel to foreign places, it was only natural for him to have picked up the local languages. "Only way," he would explain to her, "to get confidence and trust from the locals." Aside from being a history buff, he was also very much involved in learning distant customs and cultures. It was thoughts like these when she missed him most. He had given her so much. Not only did he provide her the best of education he could afford, but, more importantly, worldly things to strengthen the body and the mind for a "broader vision." And it was this vision driving her now.

With the EMP strike followed by a nuclear attack nearby the previous year, Liz went into protective mode. Being a working mom raising two kids, protecting her children was only a natural instinct. With schools, recreation, sports, social living, and educational institutions destroyed, the nation went into survival mode. There was no alternative with the infrastructure destroyed. Folks throughout the nation had to learn to fend for themselves in order to survive.

With search and rescue as her career line, disaster recovery and survival became a natural thing to Liz. Much like Tracy, her sister, she was a survivor. "Tracy," the thought popped into her mind. "Wonder what she's up to?"

It had been some time since they had their last communication. Although everyone in her family owned an analog HAM set, airwaves were reserved to emergency and government calls only, making communication for the common citizen severely restricted. "Must give her a call," she promised herself. Reports she had received from Dad were not all pleasing. Apparently, with what her sister had to endure the previous year—the assaults on the nation, being taken hostage several times, air battles and other traumatic events—Tracy had taken things into her own hands. Liz did not blame her one bit. "Good for you, Sis," she cheered.

Although the nation had taken a severe setback politically, economically, and socially, there were new opportunities arising from the darkness. With government and military reestablished in the Western Sector, Liz was making plans. She would not let the present economic conditions get the better of her. She had to fight back. "But how?" She wasn't sure yet.

The opportunity came a few days later even without her planning. It came in the form of a call from Dad. "CQ…CQ…Lizard Three, report in." Lizard Three was the call sign Napa ground control had given her ever since she'd started using one of the local runways named the same for rescue missions. She immediately recognized the voice. "Dad!"

"First," he insisted, "how are the kids?"

"Fine," she lied. But she suspected he knew better. They were not fine. Nothing was fine. The economy, food supplies, finance—everything was broken. They both knew it, but it was one thing she had learned from him a long time ago. "Never complain," he would say, "unless you've got a solution ready." To her, it was a somewhat egocentric, but practical approach, she'd learned. It was a notion he lived by in his personal life and career as well. It worked for him. It worked for her. She only wished more people would stand by that philosophy.

"How about you? How are things out there?"

"Trying to survive," she replied. "Like everybody else these days." There was no need to explain or dwell on the situation. It was bad all around. The nation was in real trouble. And who knew better than Dad.

"You're not kiddin'." With a change in tone, he offered, "Listen, something's come up you might be interested in."

It quickened her breathing. Dad did not suggest anything unless it had merit. There was a halting silence at the distant end. It was her turn to speak. "Yeah?"

"Can't say much else," Alex cautioned her. "There's an opening with Foster's command. Interested?"

"Could you be more specific?" What he said had immediately piqued her interest. It could provide the change she had been contemplating in recent months. It could provide a much-needed direction change for her. For all practical purposes, careers were gone. Anything, any opportunity that could offer compensation in return was as good as gold. And gold was something she did not have. It was a commodity most people ran out of after personal heirlooms, mostly jewelry, had been traded in for food. When the finance system collapsed, bankers, fund managers, brokers, and everybody else was out to fend for themselves. Safe deposits and vaults were ransacked. It was anybody's guess who took it, but fingers were aimed at the proprietors.

Liz fell prey along with everybody else. Much of her earnings had been invested in savings, mutual funds, and other stock holdings. *All gone now.* With the dollar collapsed, nothing was worth anything. Paper money, bonds, certificates? *Worthless as toilet paper.*

Her dad's voice drilled into her brain. "Astronaut training."

That definitely caught her attention. "What?" She thought there was a mistake. With the nation in shambles, defense, missile launch, and space travel were the farthest things on her mind. "What are you saying, Dad?" She had doubts about his sanity. Had she understood right?

The kids, was her next thought. She could never leave them. *But on second thought,* she rationalized, *they've grown up.* Soon they would be on their own. This, his proposal, if it had merit, could be a worthwhile effort to consider. It could provide her with the sense of purpose she had been battling with lately. *Gotta give it some serious thought.* "Don't know, Dad," was her wavering response.

"Just think about it," Alex encouraged his daughter. "Will you? But," he reminded her, "Don't take too much time. Offer won't be up for long, just a few days at most."

"I'll get back to you," she promised. "My regards to Tracy and Rhonda."

"Will do. Bye now."

Time heals most wounds, were Liz's immediate thoughts as she entered I-80 South. Still early in the morning, she was presently headed for the Presidio. She hadn't been on the interstate in years. After Tent City had been dismantled in Golden State Park, the emergency shelters erected after the nuclear attack on San Francisco, there had been no reason for her to return. Working emergency shelters with nothing but terminal burn victims, she had had her fill of trauma for a lifetime. Although, after her return to Napa, she had tried to get back to her previous job—fighting fires, search and rescue—but that had been part of the past. She and many others had been recruited by the newly-formed defense sector created in the western region. With President Wilmot in office for an undetermined term, the new government was still under development. With General Foster headed up the defense sector, Liz was excited about the prospect of starting a new career, if there was such a thing these days.

After getting the call from Dad a few days ago, this morning she was on the way to see the general. Although it had taken an additional hour to round the peninsula via San Jose to get into the city, as the Bay Bridge was still an incinerated relic from the blast, she made good headway. Due to the lack of fuel, personal traffic was almost non-existent. With the nation in a state of martial law, she was authorized special coupons to purchase fuel for her vehicle.

Liz had taken the weekend to evaluate Foster's potential offer to her. "Astronaut?" She kept marveling. Even being considered for such a prestigious career was an almost impossible honor. "Why me?" She eventually came to the conclusion that Dad had something to do with it.

Alex, although he gave his daughters free reign to make their own choices, always had a personal vision for his daughters. All through their growing up years, she recalled,

Dad used to inspire them with stories from his travels. Enthralled by his adventurous feats, in spite of Mom's beckoning, it used to keep them awake late into the night.

He had given her the best education she could have ever hoped for. He had shaped her into the responsible adult she'd become. In all, he had shaped her body and mind into a cornerstone blessed by compassion, morality, and righteousness. It was these qualities she appreciated most this morning on her way to an interview that might or might not change the direction in her immediate future.

CASTLE ROCK

Alex felt like a prisoner, captive, and warden all combined into one. A prisoner in his own fortress, held captive by technology, and a warden protecting the property, which had turned into fulltime occupation. Over the months, there had been a number of infringements on the Castle initiated by what appeared to be a number of anarchical factions roaming the surrounding regions from the Kansas plains to the east and Albuquerque to the south. So far, he had been able to keep them from gaining entrance to his home. "If that's what the world's gonna be like," he'd comment to Tracy after another break-in attempt, "I don't want any part of it." Somehow, someday in the future, he planned to find out in person what the rest of the world was like. For now, it was safer to stick close to home. It was good enough to have eyes back in the skies once more, if only marginally, for a privileged like him. "Yes." He had earned it. He had worked hard for it.

His thoughts were interrupted by a persistent knocking from the front gate. Alex tried to ignore it, assuming it was yet another beggar or trespasser. But the knocking persisted. *Can't be Tracy,* he assumed, *she's got keys.* He knew she was out. She had left him a note. He finally surrendered to the annoying pounding. Headed for the entrance, he yelled, "Coming," then reached for the shotgun he kept by the entrance. Pushing a button, a series of deadbolts retracted almost magically. The steel enforced door opened to reveal a grinning face staring back at him.

"Mister Bauer?"

"Who wants to know?" *These days,* Alex thought with guarded caution, *can't be too careful.*

"You know a Brian…Brian Harris?"

"What…Why…Who are you?" he stammered. He had wondered many times what became of his friend. Alex stuck his head through the door to check if the man was alone, then briefly studied the haggard-looking stranger dressed in dirty, worn down clothes. "You alone?"

"I am. Got word," the stranger said, handing over a scribbled note.

Alex studied the hastily written line. "GET ME OUTTA HERE," the note read.

"Where'd you get this?" He immediately recognized his buddy's writing.

"Jail," the stranger said. "Juarez…Texas border. We were cell mates," he further explained. "Two years I did…Just got out myself. He's got another four."

Alex stared at the note again. It made a little more sense now. "You eaten?" He was appalled at the stranger's appearance, as gaunt as he looked.

"Not in days," he answered with a pleading look.

"Come in." Alex led him to the guest room. "By the way," he asked, "what's your name?"

"Jose…Jose Sanchez."

"Take a shower, Jose. I'll fix you something to eat." He showed him to the bathroom and handed him a fresh set of clothes Brian had left behind the year before.

"Thank you, sir," was his courteous reply.

Jose appeared thirty minutes later after a lengthy shower. Dressed in fresh garb followed by a hearty meal, the stranger was ready to talk. He unfolded a shocking story. In jail for greater than two years himself, he described the horrid conditions he and his cell mate

Brian, incarcerated a year ago endured. They had been contained in one of Texas' notorious border crossing prisons in the town of Juarez, just across from Mexico. Living conditions were atrocious. Filth, roaches, disease, and starvation rations were the daily norm. Beatings and solitary confinement was held at a minimum as long as the incarcerated behaved and cooperated, but many, after months and years in confinement, went crazy. Alex sat late into the night listening to the stories the stranger shared. He tried to picture the plight his friend was in. There was no easy way to comprehend and digest the suffering.

It was getting late and the stranger kept on yawning. "Tell you what," Alex suggested, "you stay here for the night."

The offer was readily accepted with, "I'll always be grateful."

The following morning, after Alex served him breakfast, the stranger bade him goodbye with a plea. "Hope you can do something for your friend." He added, on the way out, "He was a good cellmate and decent fellow."

"Don't worry about that," Alex assured him. "I'll get him out." He locked the gate after watching the stranger head for the interstate hoping to hitch a ride up north where his family lived.

Alex took some time assessing Brian's predicament. Since he had never been to prison, he could hardly imagine the conditions his buddy faced. He promised himself to get him out, no matter what it would take, and formulated a plan. An effective jailbreak took some planning, especially when you had limited resources. At this time, it was only him. With the ever-mounting chaos in the nation, he had lost connection with people that could help. Only thing he could do at the moment was plan. He collected some maps he had on hand and went to work. Days went by and he still did not have a plan.

Tracy came and went at her own discretion. She was always off on some personal mission. He lost track of her. Sometimes she would share her bouts with him, but with others she did not bother. Some days she would not even come home. Alex was becoming frustrated with her. He didn't know her anymore. Her personality had changed so drastically that she had almost become a stranger to him.

To his surprise, she showed up earlier than usual this evening. She sat with him after he prepared dinner. They even had a glass of wine together, which was a rare occurrence. They even shared the news, as limited as broadcasts were. She told him her latest bouts with drunkards. He relayed his encounter with the stranger and his dilemma of not being able to do anything about it.

At the mention of Brian, she suddenly perked up, proclaiming, "I can help." At first, he was skeptical. But when she explained what she'd been up to over the past year, her personal conditioning, combating in and around town, planning for a safer future for her and the nation, he was thrilled. He was greatly relieved to have an ally with a possible solution in sight. "There may be hope after all," he muttered.

Getting ready to retire for the night, she promised to help him form a plan over the next few days.

ISS

Current crew member at the International Space Station, Sergey Budenko, for the past thirty minutes, had worked up a layer of sweat from another vigorous run on the worn-down treadmill. A daily routine, there were a lot of other things he would have been doing, such as climbing local mountain peaks or sailing the prevailing winds of the Caspian Sea before signing up for this mission in space. But the treadmill would have to do for now. Floating off the still moving belt, he headed in the direction of the nearby snack counter to fetch a bottle of Alpine water. Refreshingly, it would replace the dryness in his throat and cool his core temperature.

Watching his action from this vantage point, Sergey had looked like a trapped squirrel in a cage, getting nowhere. Casually draping his already soaking wet towel across one shoulder, Yuri watched his live-in mate wiping his flushed face. "Good run?" Yuri Chenkov, Sergey's cosmonaut partner asked. It was more of a comment than an inquiry on his health. His mate never seemed interested in making conversation. He had tried his best to break the ever-present silence they've been subjected over the past several months.

With casual indifference Sergey Budenko replied, "Same routine and getting boring." With a swift push of his toes, his body tumbled across the service module, floating towards the shower stall. As usual, he kept the comment brief. Many times, he would not even bother to respond in a rather boring environment.

Boring was an understatement. It seemed the same dialogue between them repeated daily. As a matter of fact, Yuri did not know much about his space comrade. *Come to think of it*—in spite of the close quarters they had shared for months—*I don't know anything about him,* he thought. It could have been the isolated environment, an introverted personality, but, most likely, it was the rotation schedule. Recently imposed by the Russian Space Agency, they were forced to work twelve hour shifts to cover an upcoming test schedule. By the time the shift was over, each was too exhausted for conversation, or anything else for that matter. They were forced to share the same work space as well as living quarters, presently cramped within the limited confinement. Where he came from, the tundra, the wide-open grassland had seemed endless to roam. Although facing the infinity of space, as seen through the porthole, it did not justify his present confinement. He had dwelled on it many times. It was the only entertainment afforded in this potentially hostile environment.

Chenkov had just finished another busy shift and was looking forward to the break, but had to wait for Budenko to reappear. "About time," he muttered when his team mate floated nearby, freshly combed and dressed in workpants.

As he quickly squeezed by him headed for the sleeping quarters, not expecting a response, Yuri said, "Back in twelve." Once there, he securely strapped himself into the body hold to relax his tensed-up shoulder muscles. Glancing around the tight quarters did not help much for intellectual inspirations. He was dying for a much-needed constructive conversation but realized right from the start of this mission such luxury had to be shelved for the time. He compensated in his free time mostly by reading worn-out paperbacks and pondering inspirational thoughts.

His mind was still churning full speed from today's hectic schedule of tests and experiments. It usually took him thirty minutes to completely relax and fall asleep. Closing his eyes, he fell into a slight trance. His mind began to wander into the past.

Yuri Chenkov was born in the Caucasus, the southern reaches of Russia. Sandwiched in between the Black and Caspian Seas, the southern state of Georgia, his nation's popular vacation spot, shared its southern borders with Turkey and Iran. What used to be the vacation place for politicians and the elite of the USSR, and people of affluence, now was affordable to the working class. People were drawn to this state from just about anywhere. Since the breakup of the Soviet Union in the early '90s, most states prospered, especially underprivileged nations attaching themselves to become E.U. member nations. He was born into affluence, his mother a teacher and his father an upper-level party functionary in the defense ministry with connections to space aeronautics.

His birth advantage gave him a springboard into an assured career within the halls of the General Staff Academy, Moscow's prominent university and professional school for officers. Only the "best and the brightest" commissioned officers of all the Soviet Armed Forces were selected to attend this top-standing and most prestigious Soviet military academy. Students admitted to the academy ranked major, lieutenant colonel, and colonel. Yuri had the rank of lieutenant colonel when he entered the academy and was given the rank of colonel after graduating. Unfortunately, with the fall of the Soviet Union, prestigious positions were far and few between and came at a premium. It was this unfortunate change that redirected the course of his life from an otherwise celebrated career. Stuck for now, he contemplated a new direction for a career as soon as he completed the current mission.

Sergey Budenko, assigned commander, current space mission, renewed and refreshed after some twelve hours of rest, with some time on the treadmill to keep adept for space, squeezed his weightless body into the lightweight ops chair. The chair, weightless as it was two hundred fifty miles out in space, was not really necessary, but it provided a secure position for the body while working the terminal. In space, every move one made exerted a counter move. Unless strapped in, his body would propel in the opposite direction. Initially, especially during his first space flight, he had to adjust to the feeling of weightlessness. Once attuned, his mind took it as normal measure but, in contrast, adjusting the body was yet another challenge. It had to be exercised constantly to keep proficient. Otherwise organs, muscles, and bone density rapidly deteriorated. As standard equipment, each service module contained at least one stationary bike alongside a treadmill. More modernized amenities had been in the planning, but with the ensuing economic recession during the onset of the 21st century, nothing materialized. Although the ISS was a combined international endeavor, with the collapse of the United States it became obvious that space exploration had come to a standstill. Aside from occasional laboratory projects, initiated mostly from Europe and Japan, space expansion had come to a virtual halt.

Zvezda, Russia's ISS service module mounted directly to Russia's docking port on one side, and Unity, the command module at the opposite end, connected the Russian space platform to the rest of the space station, providing most of the station's critical systems. It rendered the station permanently habitable, adding life support for up to six crew members. Zvezda's computer handled guidance, navigation, and controls for the entire space station. Zvezda was located at the rear of the station according to its normal direction of travel and orientation. Alternatively, Russian and European spacecraft could dock to Zvezda's aft port and use their engines to boost the station back into its ever-degrading orbit. Power to the entire platform was provided by an array of solar panels securely connected through heavy-duty trusses.

Although the orbit, when viewed through telescope or with the naked eye, seemed fixed at approximately 250 miles, due to the gravitational pull from the earth there was an orbital decay greater than one mile per month. To compensate for the decay, periodic rocket boosts were necessary.

Like all occupied modules, Zvezda was pressurized. No space suits were necessary unless a task called for a spacewalk or transfer to and from the docking module. For the crew, it made life at the ISS somewhat enduring. Aside from the initial euphoric thrill of floating in space, the novelty wore off after some time and was replaced by the rudimentary demands of the mission.

For now, Chenkov and Budenko were the only two in orbit, interdependent on each other in every task and activity the schedule dictated. The upcoming test was a welcomed opportunity to break the otherwise tedious and repetitious work schedule. "Hope it'll happen soon," he muttered in the direction of Budenko, but as usually did not get a reply.

THE PENTAGON

"Alert…alert…alert," the calls reverberated through the endless halls from the River Entrance of the once prominent defense bastion. The contingent, presently occupying the Pentagon complex was shaken from another uncertain night of darkness. The situation in the once powerful seat of the nation, Washington, DC, was getting worse by the day. What had been the defense headquarters for over fifty years for appeasing the nation and the world had come under attack almost daily, especially during the early morning hours. Most of the advances were made by local terrorist factions fighting among each other for dominance of the nation's most colossal complex. As usually, "Hold your positions," Foster shouted initial defensive orders and after assessing the immediate situation, followed up with "Attack…attack…attack." It had almost become a routine mission sequence fending off the daily aggressors. The results were always the same. As soon as the alert was sounded, Foster's elite, the SEAL team jumped to action. It was this team that gave him the protective sense of dominance and superiority. He was still in charge. At present, it may have not been over the once flourishing nation, but holding his position over the complex was a worthy one, nevertheless. It was the only remaining place in and around the Beltway, holding that claim. Everyplace else had been ransacked, torched, and destroyed by attackers fighting for the city's dominance.

Hasting in and out corridors, one had to notice, The Pentagon did not fare much better. What appeared as solid infrastructure on the outside, once within, hallways and walls had been ransacked and stripped of its invaluable artifacts just the same. Items that used to be on display throughout the halls were torn from their mountings and carelessly tossed onto pickup trucks, then hauled off to be used for barter and trade. At the moment, this once prestigious complex now provided safety only for a small contingent of fighters under the command of Foster. With each day that went by, the situation was getting more and more critical. Roaming bands with eyes on the bastion were encroaching evermore. "How long you think we can hold out," one of his lieutenants was presently voicing his concerns. "Think we should abandon?"

"May have no choice," Foster responded. Holed up at Ground Zero, the once most prominent spot within the Pentagon complex, the general and his OPS team had been discussing alternatives for the immediate future. Ground Zero, once hosting a series of snack bars and restaurants, was running low on food supplies. Foster and his team had been living on the stored rations since taking possession. With no military support left in the region, it would be only a matter of days before they would have to fight one last stand with one of the many encroaching bands from the region. "We'll move out west," Foster said, after being forced into making a decision. "Tomorrow."

In the early morning hours, they gathered up what valuables were left and the remaining food supplies, loaded up the small armada consisting of one armored vehicle, one five-ton fuel tanker, one troop carrier, and a couple of attack mounted machinegun turreted Humvee he had acquired, and sped off before the city woke. "Where to?" The driver, a former, now defunct, SEAL operative asked.

He studied the map under the dimly lit dome light. "South," Foster replied. "Let's head for Richmond, then we'll take I-64 West, all the way into Kentucky."

"What's there?"

"Fort Knox."

"What?"

"I wanna see," he speculated, "if the rumors are true." Rumors about the takeover of the Fort and the gold the year before had spread across the nation. He needed to find out. He also had to know what the countryside was like. To sit idle in the city waiting for better times was not an option. Not for a man like Foster. His team, trained for action, felt the same. Presently on R-66 headed out of town, the small convoy was well on its way to Kentucky. Driving on, they encountered numerous checkpoints guarded by renegade rebels that, after spotting the armed contingent, quickly retreated into obscurity after assessing the firepower of Foster's mobile armada. Foster did not encounter much of a resistance, but it still took them two days to reach his destination. It was nightfall the second day the convoy was spotted by the security forces protecting the fort.

At Fort Knox, word was passed back to headquarters, reaching Rusty Norton's ears. Immediately, the fort sprang into action. He dispatched Bad Man, the Enforcer, to investigate. Life in and around the fort had become rather boring, almost stagnant, in the past year. Aside from daily skirmishes arising between the 1st Armored Division soldiers protecting the fort under Brodie Elliott's command and ex-inmates from the Fort Leavenworth contingency managed by the Enforcer, Bad Man, minor though they usually turned out, things were relatively quiet on this front.

On his arrival, cautious and unsure what to expect until he received a briefing by whomever was in charge of the fort, Foster instructed his team to be on guard. Flanked by Bad Man and several of his lieutenants he was led to the fort's HQ building's mission room. Waiting were Brodie Elliott and Rusty Norton. Although he had heard of Elliott on prior occasion, he had never met him. In contrast, Elliott was well aware of the Pentagon-residing four-star general's reputation.

Reaching out, Norton extended an invitation to the general. "What brings you here?"

Foster ignored the friendly gesture. "Rumors," he replied. He could see now that they had been true. Elliott stepped up. Being of lower rank, he was ignored by the general.

"What're your intentions," Foster challenged Norton, "about the fort?"

Norton ignored the gruff approach. Instead, he invited the general. "Have a seat."

Accompanied by a grunt, expecting an explanation, Foster settled into the comfort of the plush office chair.

With a nod of the head, Norton instructed his aide to offer the general a mug of coffee served piping hot. The room was rapidly filling with Norton's staff. Foster, within the heightening tension, savored the drink nevertheless. He was in no hurry to be put off.

In contrast, Norton, flanked by his lieutenants, seemed anxious to get rid of the uninvited visitors. But on further pressing by Foster, he eventually gave in and explained the reasons he was here, in command of the fort. He then described the events that took place right after the attack on the nation the previous year. He illustrated the opportunities presented during the ensuing chaotic weeks. He did not have to tell the general the present conditions here or in other regions. The rumors had been prolific. They had carried across every part in the land. With Norton being in charge of the fort and the surrounding region, the plains, Foster had to admire the battle advantage this once renegade soldier enjoyed. "Looks like," he said, not without admiration, "you've got yourself a Nation."

"That's the idea," the Patriot leader responded.

"What's your plan?" The general, in spite of the edgy situation, was genuinely interested. He had to know what intentions Norton had.

There was a hushed silence in the room. Then, after a deliberating pause, Norton stated, "Look at it this way," matter-of-factly. "You people screwed up long enough." A slight smirk shaded his hardened face underlining his remark. "Royally." He was watching Foster for his reaction.

Despite the disadvantage he momentarily found himself in, Foster displayed no visible signs. After all, he was a battle-hardened leader. Over the years, he had seen commands come and go. It was not the first time somebody had taken over a command by force. It would not be the last time. The problem he saw was one of strategic maneuver, one of intelligence, one of aptitude. *Does Norton have what it'd take to run a nation? Does he have his people's support?* A number of questions ran across his mind. "Guess," he finally consented, "time will tell."

Do I want to stay on or do I want to head out west? Those were the two most important questions that he had to consider at the moment. Right now, he needed a place to sleep, something to eat, and rest for him and his people. Tomorrow would be another day, perhaps another beginning.

Norton noticed the general's drawn face. Their talks had lasted late into the night. He was getting tired as well. In spite of the unwelcome guest, he graciously extended an invitation for the general and his contingent to stay the night, hoping the visitors would continue on their journey west first thing in the morning. "You can stay for the night," Foster was told. "We'll see you off on your way in the morning."

"We'll see about that," was his weary reply, uncertain what decision he'd make come morning. There was no sense in fighting over dominance. His small armored continent was no match for Brodie's army. He'd have to resort to diplomatic measures, his fortitude.

LOS ALAMOS

Months had passed since Scott Brooks arrived at Los Alamos. He still had plans to make his way up to Colorado to meet up with Bauer. But with banking accounts frozen, his job gone, no contact with his organization, traveling was not an easy task. One could not just pick up and get going. There were too many hazards along the roads. Bandit gangs had formed along many routes, robbing people for their possessions. For the time, it was safer to stay put. For now, he had found a home at Los Alamos, the once thriving national research facility.

After he first arrived, the driver who had picked him up by the roadside in Albuquerque had taken him to meet the head of the facility. "Brooks…Scott Brooks," he had introduced himself.

"Allen Spencer," the host identified himself. "What brings you here?"

Brooks was trying to figure out not just the man but the environment as well. Something did not add up. At first glance, the man in charge had a mysterious aura in appearance, yet his complacent smile was friendly and forthcoming. "Met up with your man down south. Gave me a ride. Thought I should meet you. That's what brought me here."

"Aah yes," Spencer replied. "White Sands…" His words trailed into a lingering pause. "Use the place to test technology. Where're you from?"

"Arizona," Brooks enlightened the man. "DELTA."

"Say no more. Not often do we get a visitor out here. Not these days." Spencer took hold of Brook's arm and pulled him along the corridor. "Wanna take a tour?"

"I'd love to." Striding along the halls to keep up with his host, Scott was about to enter a habitat most people never had. He tried to remember what he knew about the place. His host came to his aid and explained.

"Los Alamos National Laboratory[9] is one of several laboratories where all work is classified. Most projects are for nuclear weapons design. The laboratory's one of the largest science and technology institutions in the world. Also conducted are research in the fields of national security, space exploration, renewable energy, medicine, nanotechnology, and quantum computing."

"Impressive." Brooks said, after some halting thought. He had no idea about any of this. As a matter of fact, he, and what he suspected, most people never even question where technology was created and tested. It just showed up in the marketplace someday. If you were lucky, one or another newspaper or trade mag might carry an announcement.

In recent years, the laboratories had made intensive efforts toward humanitarian causes through its scientific research in medicine such as vaccines for the AIDS virus, theoretical biology and biophysics, breast and other organ related cancer, prevention for

---

[9] With approximately 9,000 employees and hundreds more in contractor personnel, in addition to DOE employees, LANL provided federal oversight of LANL's work and operations. Approximately one third of the laboratory's technical staff members were physicists, one quarter engineers, one-sixth chemists and materials scientists, with the remainder working in mathematics and computational science, biology, geosciences, and other disciplines.

outbreaks of deadly diseases, bio-fuels and advancing scientific understanding of renewable energy, to name a few.

"Where'd you get electricity, food, medicine? Thought research stopped with the collapse."

"Got our own generators and fuel sources. Food we grow. Medicines we produce. Just look around the valley. Rich on resources."

Moving from building to building, the cursory tour took close to two hours. Scott was highly impressed by the sheer number of people supporting the experiments conducted here. Coming from a non-scientific environment, being a fighter, much of what he saw was above his comprehension and interest. But there was one specific item that interested him: nanotechnology. He could see immediate value in it. *Gotta read up on it,* he promised himself.

"Question," his host prodded. "Where do you think you might fit in?" They had arrived back at the office. "Providing you've decided to stay." Spencer was eyeing him with anticipation.

"Gotta warn you," Scott said. "To be honest, I'm no scientist."

Spencer seemed to contemplate the response. Brooks had a chance to study the man further. There was a certain aura he perceived and wisdom he definitely sensed. It reminded him of prophetic images he had always been inspired by. *What was it? Aristotle, Da Vinci, Einstein. Interesting.* His eyes were assessing the man's features. There was this thing again he spotted. It was a tattoo on the man's neck, the bird. Same with the driver. *Condor?*

Spencer finally looked up. It almost seemed he had taken notice of the visitor for the first time. "Tell you what," he suggested. "You run my security."

With the mention of security, Brooks recalled some information that had surfaced not that long ago. It had been a stigma the laboratory had to deal with ever since. *What was it again? Yes, that's it,* he recalled. It was an incident with misplaced disk drives, followed by dozens of missing computers and something much worse. Several pounds of plutonium supplies disappeared from the nuclear materials inventory.

"Security?" *Now that's something up my alley.* "It's a deal," he agreed, followed by a handshake. "You won't be sorry."

From that day on, Scott Brooks once more attained a sense of direction. He felt useful again. He put his pending journey up north on the backburner, for now. After that, he had taken charge of the laboratory's security parameters. Nobody came in without proper credentials. Nothing left without his approval. He reworked the complex's entire surveillance system. It appeared that money was no object. *Why should it be?* he mused. *There is none.* He gained the respect of the science community and was feared by potential adversities. In practicality, with him in charge, the place had better security than it ever had.

FORT KNOX

The night had come and gone at Fort Knox, the current seat for Norton's and Elliott's armed forces, Badland Sector. Foster, in the company of his tactical detachment of SEAL operatives who'd arrived the previous day at the fort, had made up his mind. For the time being, he decided to stay put. He needed to assess Norton's capability whether he would be fit running a nation. As far as Elliott's mechanized infantry was concerned, he had no doubts. The man, a trained soldier, seemed to have his regiment under firm command. Besides, he seemed a dedicated national, republic that was, for his cause. He liked what he saw, so far, but still needed further assurance to see Norton and Elliott in action.

"What now?" Rusty Norton tore his eyes from the document he had been studying. It was taking up most of his time these days. With the collapse of the former government and the creation of the Badlands, it was up to him, he felt, to reorganize his new nation. Although the present parameters of the Badlands were still loosely defined, he needed a new form of government. "Government," he pondered on many an occasion, "another thing that needs change." At the moment, he did not have much of an idea of what his nation needed first or how to fix things. All he knew was that he liked the area he had staked out—the Badlands—and planned to make it a home for his people. His thoughts were interrupted by a disturbance from the compound's gate. Bad Man stormed in. "Word just got in," he blurted. "NORAD's been under attack."

Norton was startled. It was news he hadn't expected. The Rocky Mountain range, the western edge of his turf, had been relatively quiet for the past couple of years.

"Who says?"

"Informant from the Western Sector," Bad Man huffed. "Says it was a massacre."

Situated on the far reaches of his reign, the Rockies were an important strategic position he could not let fall into enemy hands. It would weaken his infrastructure and put his entire cause in jeopardy. "Get Brodie in here," he ordered. "Now!" He vowed to take immediate action. This was a more important issue than devising the new issues governing the Badlands. That would have to wait.

The command sergeant major entered the office seconds later. "What's up?" Brodie Elliott asked as he dropped his weight into one of the empty chairs by the desk.

"Got a problem," Norton said. "Take a detachment into the Rockies."

"Now that's," Brodie stated, "news I like." He had been edgy to get back into battle. It had been over a year since he'd been on the front, any front. It was not just him that was getting restless. His armored forces were even more so. It was getting more difficult by the week to keep them in line. Considered a frontier's environment, Fort Knox was not the ideal place to curtail an army the size he commanded. An army needed deployment. The men needed a sense of purpose, being soldiers. Although battle training was provided on a periodic schedule, it did not compensate for the real thing. They demanded action. That was what recruits wanted. Action. If an enemy could not provide it, the local townspeople would. But they, mostly being frontier farmers carving out a living, did not like it. Subjugation, oppression from government and military was the very reason the frontier people sought out new horizons. The news Brodie just received would be a welcomed diversion. "When?"

"Dawn," Norton stated. "Take your best trained division with armored support. Probe the region."

"Will do."

"And," Norton further instructed, "take it to the southern perimeters and get status back to me ASAP. I wanna know what's brewing down there."

Brodie jumped at the sudden opportunity. As he was about to take off, Norton stopped him. "One more thing. When you get back," he said, "we'll work out the borders." He had been contemplating about doing that all along, but something more important came up all the time. "It's too important to delay further," he deliberated. "Good luck with the mission." He was hoping the information had been exaggerated. He felt he had been caught off guard. He didn't like surprises. And this one definitely was.

"Gotta take control over the nation," he promised himself. "And quick." To do just that he needed directions. He tossed the historical document he had been reading when interrupted on the desk and left the office, walking across the courtyard in the direction Brodie had taken. He wanted to see firsthand what it took to energize and organize an army into action. The sound of armored activities reached his ears the closer he got. It was good to see his soldiers brimming with enthusiasm. Having been a soldier himself not that long ago, he completely enjoyed watching his men in action. Although highly energized, it took hours to get the gear and transport together. It was the first action deployment in his career.

Norton just added a thought. "Wait up," he yelled to get his attention.

"What?"

"Take Wheeler with you." He would be able to keep the criminals in line.

It had been more than a year since Norton's takeover of Fort Knox. At first, there was great confusion among the inmate escapees from Fort Leavenworth. Unruly by nature, it had taken many weeks to get the former inmates in line. Having been imprisoned, some for years, the difficult ones had turned hard core. Some would not adjust to the liberated freedom they had suddenly acquired. Those did not easily conform to new standards, new rules, and military type protocols. Not even Norton, who had gained respect from most, could easily manage those rebellious subjects.

With time, the fort was overflowing with insubordinate militants. Despite Bad Man enforcing tight rules, these subjects never conformed to a civilized and structured life. They were military derelicts trained to kill. In their minds, war was their destiny. It was these elite marines and ex-special forces that would spearhead an assault on the enemy, whenever necessary. Aside from minor skirmishes conducted mostly by roaming bandits, since there was no major conflict at that time to deploy the forces, they were completely disoriented during the calm of relative peace. And peace was something with which they were unable to cope. For this reason, they were always in trouble with authorities. To get a handle on the situation, Norton had initiated a military detachment unit much like the MP for enforcing rules and regulations. It was these subjects he interned for Brodie to transfer back to Fort Leavenworth.

Two hundred plus strong, in addition to the rebellious prisoners, the squadron got under way early the following morning. Elliott wanted to keep the mobile unit small to cover the distance in a relatively short time. Entirely motorized, they could cover the 560-mile trip west within one day, two at the most.

The convoy arrived at Fort Leavenworth by nightfall the following day. There was considerable commotion at the nearby town, Leavenworth, when the convoy arrived. To Elliott's surprise, the once prominent stockade was vacated. It seemed no one had been tending to the facility since the breakout the previous year. "Get me Wheeler," Brodie commanded. Bad Man promptly showed up minutes later.

"You're in charge," he ordered a somewhat surprised Enforcer. "Goin' to town." He had a plan and that meant his absence from the armored forces. To be safe, he took one of the light armored vehicles, rounded up a dozen of his trusted, and left for town. What he needed was the man that used to be in charge of the penitentiary. It took several inquiries to locate him this late at night.

"Russell Wilcox," was the name on the mailbox. Brodie knocked on the front door. It appeared the man had already retired as, when he finally showed up, he was dressed only in shorts and t-shirt. He was unhappy at being disrupted from sleep. "What?" He barked a rather gruff challenge.

Brodie studied the man for a few seconds. He was not what Brodie had expected from what Norton had described. The man standing in front of him appeared rather timid. He did not look like the commander that used to be in charge as a unit leader for the nation's most renowned penitentiary.

"You Wilcox?"

"Who wants to know?" His eyes were darting between the unwelcome visitors and armored vehicles idling nearby.

"Brodie Elliott." the command sergeant major announced. "First Armored Division, Fort Knox, Kentucky."

"I've heard about you…and your people taking the fort." His face turned grim. It seemed to remind him on bad times from the past. "You got my inmates."

"I need your help," Brodie ordered, "with the prison."

"I'm through with that!" Wilcox's demeanor worsened from resistance to defiance.

Brodie noticed something. He knew the symptoms too well. The nervous twitching, reddened nose, hardened facial features—all subtle indications of a man succumbed to alcohol. He didn't blame the man. Not for what he must have been through, prisoners taking his town, losing his job, and worse, losing an entire prison population. It could not have been an easy end for a once authoritative career.

"Listen," Brodie insisted, "you're still in the army. We can do this the easy way or we can do it the hard way. It's your choice." He was watching the man's reaction. "I can have you shot," he warned.

It must have driven the message home. Still undecided but making haste, Wilcox wavered. "Just a minute. Let me put some clothes on." In spite of the late hour, five minutes later Wilcox showed up, although a little disheveled on unsteady legs, wearing his prison uniform.

Brodie was pleased about having someone back in charge of the penitentiary. On the way, there he briefly illustrated the past year to a seemingly unaware, timid-turned prison warden. He also indicated the need to get the penitentiary back into an operational state as quickly as possible. "Can you handle it?"

"Damned right I can," Wilcox, who'd quietly followed the sudden turn of events, quickly turned sober by the unexpected intrusion, insisted. He seemed to have found a glimmer of hope for a new purpose in life once more. As soon as they arrived at the fort, Brodie handed over his burden to Wilcox. It had not been easy transporting the detainees. Once they realized they were on the way being detained at their former quarters, the penitentiary, many turned rebellious. No matter how much discipline they were subjected, it did not matter. They would remain mutinous. The only thing that kept a full-blown rebellion in check, for now, was a promise by Brodie to call them into action as soon as a fighting front was established. Whether it would materialize or not would have to be proven. He still had great reservations, ever, for throwing a killer detachment into a conflict or war, regardless of the brutality in action.

After one night's stay at the prison compound, the following morning Brodie and his military detachment got under way. He was very much relieved at having resolved the Knox insubordinate militant issue. He had gotten rid of the constant menace from these ex-prisoners turned renegades. Incarcerated at Fort Leavenworth once more, they were Wilcox's responsibility now. For now, it seemed, the Badlands had secured the means for detaining unruly soldiers unable to fit into society and the way of the military once more.

Next stop: Colorado Springs, NORAD Command.

THE SERPENT

"The world is changing," Hasan Hammad remarked to Yusuf. They were currently watching the news on Al Jazeera, broadcast from nearby Qatar Island. Born to Persian immigrants to the U.S., raised in New York, Yusuf was still amazed to be sitting here, surrounded by the newly developed paradise in the company of self-elect supreme leader, Jihad forces. Since his escape from Guantánamo detainment, Yusuf's life had taken on a new level of authority. With the planning Hammad had put into action there seemed to be no limitation to the expansion of the Islamic nation. The globe was theirs to take. The ensuing economic chaos was affecting most of the nations that had traded in the debunked U.S. dollars. Russia, China, and the E.U. immediately jumped at the opportunity to force their own currencies on world trade. But it did not solve global commerce. There was too much opposition from each of the super powers to align or even allow one currency to dominate over the others. To this day, international trade had yet to be resolved.

Due to this and similar issues, Jihad, under the cloak of confusion, had taken the opportunity to forge ahead and gain footing in many of the free world nations. It would only be a matter of time before it would dominate not only trade and commerce, but world governance as well. The foundation had been placed for the next phase of operation. "The world is ours for the taking."

"Destiny of Islam," Yusuf agreed in wonderment, "as promised by Mohammed. With you driving," he offered, "we are sure to succeed."

"What's the status with the camps?" Hammad had entrusted him with the development of new base camps by Al Qaeda, Jihad, and other radical allied factions around the globe. When Hammad had announced the new doctrine, recruits joined from all parts of the globe to be part of the expansion.

Initial conscripts were legionnaire volunteers, making up the core of the forces. To capitalize on their skills, Hashim had put them in charge of recruiting and training. It was those warriors that shaped the novices into fighters. Next were the seasoned lieutenants, the devout terrorists coordinating the global expansion efforts. On top of the chain of command was a select group of operatives, advisors to the executive panel selected by Hammad personally. It was these operatives that, in time, would be responsible for managing the various industry sectors around the globe. It was these experts that would be the key to his success. It was this team that would eventually run the Islamic nation proliferated throughout the new world, the world of Islam.

"The Arabian Peninsula hosts the majority of the camps," Yusuf reported. "Our Persian alliance partners pledged full support. Algeria, Libya, Egypt, and the Sudan promised to mobilize at a moment's notice. We even have solicitations from former Soviet nations whenever support is required."

"What about the E.U., Great Britain, Australia—what about there?"

"Too early to tell," Yusuf answered. "They have not yet decided what course of action to take. Some of the current member nations are still planning to secede from the E.U. Think they can fare better on their own. Besides," he added, "they still have a strong inherited Christian disposition."

After giving it some calculated thoughts, Hammad replied, "Well, I will give them special attention once we have conquered the globe." Yusuf could only imagine the intensity his leader would exert on those nations. They had been in control of the free world for too many centuries. It is their time now, time for the Jihad to instill Islamic faith on the world's people.

The grin on Hammad's face broadened just at the thought of it. "Infidels!" he exclaimed in a passionate manner. "You will pay restitution for eternity." Extending an invitation to Yusuf, he said, "Let's get the gear." He gestured at the gulf. "Wind's up."

Completely subjected under a different power—the forces of the ocean breeze—for the next few hours, they put world politics and dogma aside to fully enjoy the moment. As always, the time of windsurf power skidding across the ocean swells made them forget the troubles still ahead, if only for a short while.

TRACY BAUER

"Let's get outta here," Johnny Cox, the young GI, insisted. He had Tracy by the sleeve of her jacket, pulling her toward the exit door. They'd been out bashing at the nearby bar again, her favorite hangout—the Hellhole. The place had turned into a gathering place for the locals and nearby bases. Once Tracy had established her position among the owner and the customers, as the challenging combatant she'd turned out to be, attending patrons either liked her or hated her. The ones not in favor of her being there still carried marks on their bodies from earlier encounters with her. They'd learned the lesson not to tangle with Tracy. They'd received a taste of the silent rage she carried. Those were the ones that stayed clear of her whenever she showed up for a few drinks and games of pool. Most other regulars, including the proprietor, respected her buoyancy. With the help of the proprietor, she maintained the place for him in a somewhat orderly fashion among the restless society moving in and out of the establishment. After all, it was her place and she deemed to keep it that way.

As usually, rumors carried by travelers passing through were prolific. The east was under continuous attack from foreign nations trying to gain footing on American soil. The situation down south did not fare much better. At least the northern part of the continent was relatively quiet since the land was still heavily contaminated from the nuclear fallout drifting in from the west. Nobody wanted to talk about the central region. That part was subject to wild speculations. Although the western part near the Rockies was relatively calm, primarily due to the protective forces maintained around the Castle region, from the remnants of Fort Carson,[10] the Badlands carried the worst of stories and tales. Rumors had it that nobody came in and nobody left without a valid reason to be there. It was said the leaders, headquartered at the former gold depository, Fort Knox, made short process of everybody not conforming to the rules. Apparently, a new order had been put in place by the policy makers termed "New Republic," possibly a new form of government.

"Don't." Tracy resisted, yanking her arm free from his hold.

Cox was taken aback by her defensive reaction. Although he knew very well she didn't need his protection, he, nevertheless, felt the need to be the protector by her side whenever she had the desire to mix with people. Aside from her recent change in appearance and what he termed 'militant behavior,' he was secretly in love with her.

Johnny and Tracy met during one of her brawls at the bar. As with most of her visits to the troublesome establishment, she was challenged into a fight. The young and cocky infantry GI he was assigned to Fort Carson, like so many of the recruits, he thought he had the world by the balls. Especially after getting assigned his own helicopter, an Apache, heavily loaded down with sophisticated instruments and armaments, there was nothing that could stop his aggressive behavior. Not, until the day this awesome looking chick put his aggressive behavior in check. It was the day he grew up. Well, at least a little. The seasoned warrior that he was, so he thought after finishing basic training,

---

[10] Fort Carson was the home of the 4th Infantry Division, the 10th Special Forces Group, the 71st Ordnance Group, the 4th Engineer Battalion, the 759th Military Police Battalion, the 10th Combat Support Hospital, the 43rd Brigade, and the 13th Air Support Operations Squadron of the former United States Air Force.

where he excelled in combat techniques and other warring related face-ups, when he challenged her, it was an eye-opening experience he would not soon forget, if ever. Swollen faced, a couple of ribs bruised up by her lightning fast kicks, still dizzy from too many drinks, he fell in love on the spot. The chick's name was Tracy, he learned. After that, he followed her everywhere and whenever she would permit it.

This evening, as usually, she was unwilling to leave the premises. She was having fun in the company of the regulars. It was the only place nearby that provided entertainment. Also, Dad insisted for her to remain within the safety of the fortress, the Castle, she needed the open range to break out of the confinement. Hiding from the perils of turmoil was not her way of living.

For the time being, Tracy tolerated her newly acquired party buddy. He would watch her back and she his, when things got out of control. Not that she needed anybody for that. She mostly tolerated his presence to have someone to talk with. Whether he was sincere or not was not the issue. At least he paid her lip service when she felt like talking.

It wasn't that long ago, when the world was an open field in which to journey in and out. *Beautiful days,* she reminisced more often than not. She longed for those days. She needed those days. It was thoughts like it that gave her the inspiration to forge ahead. Today, for now, amid partially inebriated patrons, although she did not drink much, she felt she needed to keep her head clear from becoming foggy from alcohol or other enslaving substances so popular with the population. After a couple of beers, Tracy felt comfortable for the moment.

Ever since the nation turned turmoil, striving for a purposeful life by the once flourishing workforce had vanished. Many had taken to drinking, many more to drugs. Drug trafficking had escalated to the point of free trade. Smuggling was not necessary anymore. It'd become a common trade, especially across the Mexican border. Whoever had the means of buying the substances, as plentiful a variety as there were, would quickly develop dependency and addiction. The continent had become a playground for the pushers and the dealers of once illegal contraband, now accepted as a legal essence to life.

Tracy, as radical as she'd turned, knew the dangers of addictions. She did not want any part of it. Alcohol she could manage. Not so with drugs. She tried them once and lost her focus on reality. She wanted to keep a clear mind. It was the only way to maintain perspective in life, which had become a distorted reality for many.

"Tell you what." Facing Cox while reaching for the bottle of beer, Tracy said, "You teach me how to fly," she took another quenching sip, "and I won't pester you anymore."

"You're no trouble for me." His face turned cautious. Something was brewing in her and he did not like it. What he spotted in her eyes were reflections of compassion and hatred at the same time. Compassion probably for him, hatred for the world she'd been forced to exist in. Trying to reason out her remark, he was deeply concerned for what would come next.

"Fly what?"

Her face took on softness. "Look," she confessed, "I've not been the easiest person to get along with lately."

Propped against the bar rail, she turned to face him directly. Her eyes sought out his. He detected the suppressed emotions she'd curtailed. They held the full range of emotions of which a person was capable. For the first time he saw faint passion, kindness, empathy, and sympathy, mixed in with compassion, usually veiled by anger, fury, and rage.

"I want you to show me how to fly that damned thing." She purposely let the words sink in. "The Cobra." She knew her demand would bring forth an immediate reaction.

"Cobra?" He'd been bragging about his flying skills with helicopters. "Chopper pilot" was his MOS at Fort Carson, and he was trained on various types, from Bell trainers to attack crafts such as the Blackhawk and Apache.

"I don't have that craft." There was no such craft at the fort. As far as he knew they had been decommissioned years ago, and he said so.

"My dad has one." She grinned at him.

Cox was dumbfounded. "Your dad? Where?"

"The Castle." In spite of his reluctance, she proceeded to tell him what had been held dormant in her mind for the longest time. "I need to be able to go whenever, wherever…I'm not the innocent girl you know. I have clear direction—I have direction for what must be done. I have to do this. Nobody can stop me, not you, not Dad, and not the idiots out there."

He was mulling over what was just said. He'd had his suspicions for some time. *But this?* Her eyes were fixated on his. He could see the passion, the deep conviction. No matter what he'd say, no matter how much he'd resist, it wouldn't make a difference. Best he could do was support her passion.

"Okay."

"Okay?" She seemed surprised. "Just okay?"

As much as he disliked her demands, he replied, "That's what you wanted, isn't it?"

Seemingly relaxed, she said, "I need your full support."

He wavered several seconds before he committed. "Got mine…Think you got your dad's?"

"What?" Alex yelled out after Tracy told him her plans. He couldn't help it. He was taken by complete surprise. *My daughter flying?* And a chopper, to top it. He refused to accept it. Earlier that day she had brought along her GI friend Johnny Cox, whom he knew she'd been seeing for several months. *Moral support,* he had guessed. Not that she needed it. He knew she was quite capable of taking care of herself. *But a pilot?*

Ever since Brian had parked the craft it'd been sitting dormant on the hidden platform by the hilltop. He was faced with a dilemma. *What should I do?* he contemplated while studying her friend seated on the sofa while Tracy was pacing in front of him, expecting an answer. Despite his young age he seemed quite confident. *Perhaps he can rein her in,* he silently hoped. *She needs some protection.* He finally agreed, but not without fatherly advice. "Be careful. The craft's no toy. They're killing machines."

Over the following weeks and months, Johnny Cox had his job cut out for him. Tracy could not get enough. She took to the Cobra like nothing he'd ever experienced. It became her pet. Almost daily he would arrive at the Castle and take the craft aloft to explain instruments first, followed with simulated attack and diversion maneuvers. It did not take long for her to demand the controls, then the pilot's seat. From that day on, he became the copilot, really more of a tolerated passenger, to be exact.

Problem was fuel. All the flying demanded fuel, a lot of it. Alex solved the problem. He was able to negotiate with the nearby fort. Where Fort Carson used to be the Army's major armored proving grounds, now, with the military splintered into separate clusters around the nation, it had become an important post to protect the remains of military and government units in and around Colorado Springs.

Shortly prior to the devastating EMP strike, the fort had undergone a construction boom in 2007 and 2008 in preparation for the return of the 4th Infantry Division from Fort Hood, Texas. Due to the present political conditions then, this brought nearly 5,000 additional soldiers to the fort, but not without local controversy to the move expanding the Piñon Canyon maneuver site in southeastern Colorado. With the expansion, Piñon Canyon became the Army's largest single training area in the nation, about the size of the state of Rhode Island.

Many in the local civilian population had been opposed to this plan, because much of the land in rural areas that would be added to the training site was civilian-owned ranch land, and many current landowners were unwilling to be supplanted, regardless of the compensation offered. The Army's position at the time was that the expansion was essential for preparing soldiers for battle in ever growing theaters, such as Afghanistan, Iraq, and the Middle East in general. That, however, at present day, had become academic.

Today, this once controversial base had become the single most important site for protecting the region and the growing need for fuel sources.

"How's it goin'?" Alex asked after they walked in from the underground tunnel entrance after another training run. The tunnel had become a regular route for Tracy and Cox on their way to work. To Alex, it appeared like work. Each morning, dressed in flight gear after a hearty breakfast he'd serve, both would disappear into the tunnel and reappear hours later, covered in grime and sometimes torn fabric. Today was no different.

In her matter of fact way, Tracy announced, "Had a burnout." Where such a flight failure would be a major event in every pilot's passage, to her it was only a minor incident. She'd turned completely proficient. She knew it and Cox knew it as well.

In a way, Alex was proud of his daughter, but could not completely lose the feeling of danger whenever she went on a flight exercise. The hazards of flight were always there. *According to statistics, she is way overdue for an accident,* he'd mull but dared not speak it out aloud for fate might hear him.

In her self-assuring manner, she'd say, "Don't worry. I'm the expert."

Cox, reluctant as he was about her aggressive flight behavior, would always support her, no matter what. "She's right."

NORAD

Ben Jackson was playing at the Cheyenne Mountain Country Club, his favorite golf course, when his personal aid rushed up. "Sir," he said, "NORAD wants you." Although the nation may have already been in a state of chaos for more than a year, a game of golf was on the daily agenda in the general's life. It was the only pleasure left for his enjoyment. He was at an age where most pleasures such as a drink, vacation, smoking, and even sex had been removed as one damaging cause after another. *At least*, he pondered on occasion, *I still have healthy arms and legs to swing the balls.* The luxury he had among likeminded hobbyists was the safety he enjoyed. A permanent regiment of marine soldiers from the nearby fort was assigned to prevent unauthorized intrusion when at play.

After the terrorists took out the communication systems, NORTHCOM had decided on consolidating all local military command systems under one defense umbrella protected by Fort Carson. It was considered the only command with enough infantry forces and mechanized armor to resist most hostile aggressions. He was handed the receiver end of the tactical radio set always present for just such an emergency. Not happy with the sudden interruption, "Jackson," he bellowed into the mouth piece.

The caller, the daytime OIC on duty, informed him, "Russia's getting ready for a launch."

The general quickly paused to evaluate the situation and its possible implications. Although urgent, Jackson considered ignoring the call with an excuse, but, considering the state the nation was in, quickly thought otherwise. With NORAD rendered ineffective for most part due to the loss of the antenna array on top of the Mountain, he'd rather stay clear of Wilmot and his western allies than draw unnecessary attention. With defenses moved to the Western Sector, his position was already on shaky grounds. If it had not been for the support from his local advisor, Bauer, with his rational thinking, NORAD might have been lost already.

"Sir?" the caller reminded him on the impending sense of duty.

Although reluctant in handing the receiver back, he conceded, "I'll be there." It took only ten minutes to shuttle Jackson back to the command center. After all, although not detrimental to the nation's security at this time, it was his responsibility to monitor space debris circling the globe. With today's launch, unexpected as it was, for his nation had no support assets or resources for the once thriving endeavor, space exploration, there would be additional junk floating in space he had to account.

Watching the launch on the monitor feed provided by Bauer and his sophisticated equipment, the launch seemed routine. With the United States not participating in any of the space launches anymore, there was no schedule available to Jackson. But for record keeping sake, he had his staff kept track of launches and other space activities. Recent dockings were generally conducted at the Columbus service module or the European docking station. Today's launch was handled by Zvezda, the Russian service module, directly. It was rather unusual and he wondered about the deviation from the docking process. "Russians don't have a man in orbit. Or do they?" As far as he knew, it was only the Europeans and the Japanese with men in orbit. With the Americans, not a tactical threat anymore to the immediate space, the Russians had pulled out their crew months ago. His concerns were cut short by one of his commanders rushing into the command center. "They're at the doorsteps," he blurted out.

"Who?"

"Whole damned army."

"What army?" The general was dumbfounded.

"Badlands."

"Armored?"

"Heavy," reports from the outside indicated.

"Get me Bauer on the line," the general ordered. Since he did not have the means to fight off any intruders, and Bauer had pledged support, he figured he'd have to test the man's capability.

When Alex recognized the call sign he wavered at first, then thought otherwise. It might be something important. "Bauer," Alex answered.

The general had his usual gruffness, "Need your help," he said without much ceremony.

"What's up?" Alex was not very accommodating. He would rather not get involved with the egocentric general.

"Enemy's at the door steps," the general blasted across the airwaves.

"I'll get back to you," Alex promised as he did the last time.

"Now," the general insisted. "I need it now."

That, Alex thought, *is the least of my concerns.* He, nevertheless, conceived an action plan. *But first, the monitors.* To get the true picture of the danger, he had to personally assess the level of threat. He took full account of the intruding forces, watching their activities mounting against the Mountain.

For most part restricted to the Central Plains—the Badlands—Brodie Elliott and his forces had been pretty much isolated from the national turmoil. His primary responsibility was the protection of Fort Knox with its inherited treasures. He was somewhat surprised when Norton sent him on this mission. It would leave the fort undefended to unwanted aggressions for anyone to take over. But the remaining contingent in charge of Foster would most likely be enough to protect the nation's wealth. It had taken two days of easy and uneventful travel after leaving Ft. Leavenworth for his forces to reach the Rockies. Arriving late the previous evening, he decided to pitch camp near the Mountain entry. His plan was to have an audience with the head of NORAD command still reigning in the region.

The following day, with the war party on the way for the intended confrontation with the Mountain command, Brodie Elliot was sidetracked by a sound emerging in the distance. It was a sound he had not heard in ages. He grabbed a pair of field glasses to investigate the airspace. "What the fuck?" He could not believe his eyes. Now they all could hear it. Approaching fast was the chopping sound of a helicopter. Brodie shook his head in disbelief. "Craft," he questioned, "in the air?" He then watched the unusual craft configuration, he only recognized from old war movies, gradually descend on his forces. He ordered the driver to stop. "Hold your fire," he instructed his commanders, poised and ready to fire the turret mounted machineguns. "Let's see what's up."

The Cobra flared out nearby and settled firmly on ground. Seconds later, out jumped a passenger dressed in casuals. To Brodie's surprise, he seemed unafraid of his forces. "Identify," Alex demanded.

Elliott was taken aback by the briskness of this civilian directly facing him. For the moment, he ignored the demand because something else had caught his immediate interest. It was the female pilot manning the craft. In a somewhat defiant posture she held his stare through the visor. "Explain your intentions," Alex ordered.

Brodie broke eye contact with the pilot and shifted his attention to the man in front of him. He ignored the question fired at him but respected the direct approach. Apparently, from the aggressive demeanor he displayed, the man was not a stranger to conflicts.

"What's with the craft?" Brodie spat at Alex. "Where'd you get it?"

Alex, in command of the AH-1 Cobra helicopter, had firepower at his disposal he hoped the visitors would recognize. He stood his ground and firmly responded, "Not your concern." All he had to do was give Tracy the signal and the war party would face destruction.

"All things in my territory," Brodie insisted, "are my concerns." To back up his stated authority, he signaled his forces to immediate attention. In one swift motion, machine guns and cannons mounted on armored vehicles took aim at the Cobra.

Alex knew the dangers of confrontations only too well. It would take one slight move from an overanxious soldier to trigger a fiery exchange. He was not ready for that. He quickly countered the hostility. "Wait," he said. "There's no need for that." He needed more information. They both needed information. To defuse hostilities, he purposely stepped in front of the Cobra. "Explain territory," he demanded. It seemed to neutralize the immediate tension level.

Flashing a sign to his troupes to stand down, he said, "Brodie Elliot, Commander, 1st Armored Infantry Division, Badlands."

Alex welcomed the gesture and relaxed. "Alex Bauer. Commander, Castle Rock."

"Castle Rock?"

"Personal fortress nearby," Alex stated. "Explain your intentions."

Brodie decided to step up and defuse the tension for now. He was just as interested in learning more about this bold and daring rival. In a calming gesture, he faced Alex. "Let's not get hasty." Expressing a friendly gesture, he offered, "You talk, I talk, agreed?"

"Agreed."

He then led Alex to a makeshift tent nearby with Tracy still manning the idling Cobra. She kept the turbine up just in case of a fast exit maneuver. During the next hour both learned and came to respect each other's objectives and territories. Alex, in brief, delivered his position with the Mountain and Castle Rock. Elliott, in turn, pointed out his intentions in taking possession for his territory. The information passing hands would determine the future of their coexistence.

The way things stood for the moment, Brodie was invited to stay with a promise to get in front of Jackson, Commander, NORAD. Alex was pleased the way things turned out. In the advancing party, he had gained an immensely valuable ally protecting him and the territory east of the Rockies. From his perspective, in view of the present situation, it was more than he had wished for. Stepping back into the Cobra with a promise to inform NORAD command of Brodie's intentions, he muttered, "There's still hope for a nation."

The following day, after a brief report to the general, Alex, in the company of Brodie Elliott was summoned to the Mountain. The sentries guarding the entrance had been notified. They were immediately escorted in on arrival. The general, detesting the unexpected beleaguering by Elliott the previous day, appeared as gruff as ever. Viewing the visitor with suspicion, without extending any exchange formalities, "Make your statement," he ordered Elliott.

In view of the current situation, and the state of turmoil the nation was in, Ben Jackson had the Mountain entrance shut tight after his unwelcome visitor were inside the complex. "Just in case," he muttered to his aid. At this point, the general did not know nor had an idea what the visitor's intentions were. In either situation, depending on their demands and outcome, he had a strong bargaining power holding the continent hostage. As irritating the situation was to him, a semi-comfortable lifestyle interrupted, he made an effort to accommodate the visitors.

Ignoring Elliott, the inferior rank he was and addressing Alex directly, "Now," he demanded. "What's this all about?"

With a courteous gesture at the visiting commander, "Brodie Elliott," Alex patiently explained. "Is here to stake out the new territory."

"Territory? Explain," the general gruffed.

Elliott took his time to instill a solid self-composure before answering the abrasive Mountain commander. He needed to let the man know that he wasn't the only one commanding a sizable force. "I am here to assert the new territory."

"What territory?"

"New Republic."

"Under whose authority?" It was obvious that the general was getting impatient.

"Norton. Rusty Norton," Elliott stated. "Head of the New Republic."

Angered even more of what he heard, "Nonsense," the general responded with a negating wave of the hand. His face, reddened and contorted by the sheer thought of a hostile takeover would not hear it. This was too absurd for him after dedicating his entire life to a democratic form of governance. "Idiotic fool," he bellowed.

Elliott remained unwavering. He was about to direct the general with an ultimatum to comply with the new order or risk dire consequences. Alex, quietly standing by during their initial exchange thought it better to speak up before the exchange ended in a heated fight. Appeasing the general, "Please hear him out," he suggested.

"You need us more than we need you," Elliot opened the talks. Although reluctantly, it took some doing before the general submitted to the demands. He must have though over his present position and evaluated the consequences of a refusal to commit, when he replied, "Go ahead." He suddenly realized he stood alone at this national bastion for so many years. He had no direct supporting forces to impose his powerbase. Although Fort Carson was nearby, it was not the fighting force it had been at one time. Not only that, being a contingent based on open ranges, it had little use for the limited space and confinement of the Mountain And from a political position, there was no help forthcoming from the Western capital. He was alone. Alone and subject to any idiot wanting to remove him for his fragile position in protecting the once most prestigious fortification in the nation, the world.

With hostilities resolved, for the immediate time, Brodie was satisfied with the results. He planned to move on as directed by Norton, headed south come morning. Jackson, on the other hand reluctantly succumbed to the notion that he would be allowed, but managed, to continue his present none demanding lifestyle. "So be it," he consoled his immediate staff and himself. There were no complaints forthcoming. He felt that he had won the exchange what could otherwise have wound up in a hostile confrontation. For now, he was content once more looking forward to another of uninterrupted game of Golf.

BRIAN HARRIS

As he was dragged to the far end of the courtyard, Brian struggled against the forces exerted on his arms and shoulders. It was the day of his execution. Facing a detachment of armed soldiers, he stared into the barrel openings of rifles aimed at him. Breathing with extreme difficulty, sweating profusely, he could hear the blood pressure pounding against his inner ears. He was seconds away from a life cut short. In the salvo that followed from exploding gun barrels directly aimed at him, he could clearly see the bullets streaming for his heart, his body violently jolting from their impacts.

He had just relived the torture one more time, if only in a dream. In reality, the sound that created the nightmare was the jailer pressing his baton against the cell cages while pacing down the hall. It was measures like these to daily torment the prisoners aside from being the signal for wakeup time. Prison guards, to keep from complete boredom use tactics like it to aggravate inmates. Soaked in sweat like most mornings after a fitful sleep in the humid laden air this time of year, he reluctantly forced his body onto his legs to face another day of torture. The torture, as long as he behaved, was not so much the beatings and solitary—it was the idleness, the waste of a life held in confinement immensely degraded by the surroundings.

This morning was no different. It began with the daily shower, exposed to advances from cellmates on his body and mind. The body for sexual gratification, the mind for verbal abuse, anything was game from profuse cussing to threats on life, unless he complied with the personal invasions. Weeks had gone by since the release of his former cellmate. Brian had given up on any kind of rescue, but desperately clung to a glimmer of hope, nevertheless.

Breakfast was served, if you could call the slop dished out twice a day, served on tinplate, food. The only sliver of meat was the sight of bugs, struggling to stay afloat. They would be eaten just the same. Hunger pangs were always present, gnawing away what little fat was left on the body. Unlike some of the detainees, Brian had no family or friends in the area to care for him. He wore the same unwashed clothes he had on when he landed here. Unkempt and unshaven, he did not even know his appearance anymore. He suspected it to be appalling but nobody seemed to care in this hellhole. With mostly idle time on his hands, he gauged the time served by the lengths of his ever-growing hair and beard. His nose had gotten used to the stench emanating from him and the environment months ago. His eyes reminded him daily of his present predicament, staring at the walls confining the prisoners. The only sense of freedom he could experience was from above. The sky was clear for most of the year in this part of the country. What puzzled him was its silence. Not one aircraft ever flew by. The only explanation he had was that air traffic was still grounded. "But why?" he questioned after all this time.

Many months had passed after the strike on the nation. Something, some air transport, should have been restored by now. All he did was staring into space, hoping for things to change. There was no other activity that could take away the pain of injustice. Presently, the daily warning calls from the guard reached his ears. It was time for lockup after another day wasted in idleness. For a time, he ignored it. He was watching a distant bird enter his field of vision. Appearing as a speck, it headed his way. Almost a minute went by before he suddenly realized it was no bird at all. Then he heard it, the familiar sound of blades slicing into air. His heart almost leaped from his chest at the very thought. "Could it be?" His mind was already working on a possible rescue but he wasn't sure until he recognized the full shape of the craft. "Cobra?" he blurted out.

At first, he wildly gesticulated. "Over here." But then he had an ominous thought, making him dart for cover.

Two hours earlier, Tracy had made final adjustments on the instrument panel. Her destination was directly south. Alex had wanted to come along but had to remain behind due to the configuration of the chopper. It only sat two in tandem. Empty at present, the backseat was reserved for her love, Brian. "Get him back," Alex said one final time.

Shutting the canopy tight above her head, Tracy shouted, "I will." The next second, the Cobra lifted from the platform. To preserve precious fuel, she set the speed control at two thirds. It was enough power to clear the Rockies and still make it there before nightfall. Aside from the occasional up and down drafts from air currents she'd expected, the flight was uneventful since air traffic was almost non-existent. The Confederates, what was restored after the attack by Cuba, were running mostly supply shuttles to the West Coast, away from her flight path.

"Time to look for the place," she reminded herself. Cruising at eight thousand feet, Tracy was comparing the terrain below with the map by her side. The path was an easy one. For most part, she had followed I-25 directly south, guiding her way past Santa Fe, Albuquerque, and on to her final destination. Below, the sprawling city of El Paso, by the Mexican border, gradually crept into her view. It was time to descend. Alex had marked the precise location on the map Brian's cellmate had given him weeks earlier. Tracy went over the plan one more time then firmly took hold of the flight controls for the upcoming attack. Her strategy was set on pure stealth. Surprise would be solely on her side. Her right hand pushed the throttle to maximum power. Next, she forced the craft into a dive aimed at a spot indicated by the crosshair on the overhead HUD visor.

Tracy went for it at full speed. The walls of the prison were rushing at her. Five hundred…four…three…two…one hundred feet, the altimeter indicated. Seconds later she was on top of the compound releasing the first salvo. The forward momentum of the Cobra came to an abrupt halt from the recoil action of the miniguns. It was enough time to spot someone running for cover that looked like Brian, but she wasn't sure. With lengthy hair flowing in the wind and beard growths to the chest, most prisoners dodging for cover looked alike.

"Take this," she shouted over the pitching chopper blades, releasing another hail of fire into what she made out to be the guard towers. The pings from incoming slugs hitting the fuselage from returned firings immediately stopped. The towers, now ablaze, from the pressures of two solid streams of steel cutting into the infrastructure, crumbled seconds later. It paved her way into the compound. Executing several more attack sweeps, she kept strafing for the guards who, without tower support were fending for themselves wildly shooting after the evasive craft.

Presently headed for the center of the fenced-in field once more, she suddenly spotted one inmate rushing her way. Waving to get her attention, he kept yelling, "Over here!" A quick flare brought the craft to the ground. Tracy popped the forward canopy motioning him in. With blades still chopping, Brian rushed up, took hold of the frame, and jumped into the gunner's seat, ready for takeoff, "It's me. Brian." The attack was executed as she had planned. It took less than two minutes. Tracy was in and out, accompanied by a scraggly looking being she'd identified only by his voice.

"Welcome home," she shouted into the mic after he put on the headset. "I'll touch down once we're safe." Tracy kept the Cobra low until they reached the outskirts of town then settled in an empty field. Both jumped out, rushing into each other's arms. The embrace that followed was a happy one but missed passion: hers from the lack of it, his from a weakened body and tormented mind. After all, it had been ages since they were together. Both had to make serious adjustments to accept each other and the intimate individuals they once were. Five minutes later, the craft was back in the air headed for the Castle.

CASTLE ROCK

"She's back," Alex shouted into the quiet of the Castle. He had been on edge ever since Tracy had taken off earlier that day. It was one thing to step outside into a ravaged country not knowing what to expect, but it was another facing an assault on a prison, alone. He had tried to talk her out of it, but she had insisted. "Hope she's got good news." The radar he had installed had triggered the sensors. There were other precautions he had installed, more obscure, as well to alert him. At this point success was anybody's guess. "Should know in a few seconds," he huffed, rushing for the helipad.

"By God," he exclaimed. "You made it!" He dashed at his buddy for a welcome hug.

"Damned right we did." Brian beamed at Tracy, who only shrugged her shoulders as if she had just returned from another local outing. "Thanks to your daughter."

Alex was overjoyed. "Man…it's good to see you. Didn't think you'd make it. Come on in." He gestured at the remnants of what used to be his lifelong buddy. "Must be tired and thirsty. Look at you."

"Both," Brian replied. "I'm parched. Beer would be great, ice cold."

Looking at his buddy made Alex cringe. Brian appeared thin and haggard like he had never seen him before. If it wasn't for the rescue, he could have passed his buddy on the streets without recognizing him. Alex went to work as host. *Must have had a rough time.*

"Make yourself at home," Tracy invited him in then disappeared to her private quarters. Brian seemed too excited to be seated. He needed to talk. He needed current updates only Alex could provide. At first, he was slightly surprised at Tracy for not being very talkative on the flight back. He contributed it to the time they'd been separated, becoming like strangers. He vividly recalled the last time he'd seen her. *How long has it been?* He tried to remember. He couldn't. Not at the moment with his body and mind totally depleted of energy. Since, months have turned into years.

He was pacing the space, glancing at some of the familiar pictures and artifacts gleaning from walls and mantles. It brought back fond memories. They were the good years, the action years. It seemed a long time ago. Alex walked in, handing him the beer. "Welcome back."

They both took seats in the living room. Brian must have had something on his mind. His eyes were darting around the room before he blurted out, "What's with Tracy?" He was still disappointed from the flight back. He was unable to reconnect with her. She had seemed very evasive and, he suspected, to his regrets, that she might be in a relationship. *Who could blame her?* he justified her strange behavior. *With me having disappeared for two years.*

"Gotta be patient with her," Alex cautioned him, then described the transformation in his daughter. "You may not recognize her. Might not like it. Took me the longest time to accept the new Tracy."

"Tell me about it, and…" He paused. "Her flying a chopper. Who taught her?"

"Let me bring you up to date," Alex offered. He proceeded to tell him all the changes over the past couple of years. How she visibly changed, not only in character, but behavior as well. He passed on the many accounts of local barroom brawls, personal challenges, and confrontations with others, her growing into a worthy warrior in her own means. Brian kept shaking his head. As Alex had cautioned him, he did not seem to like it. "What's her plan?"

Alex's voice wavered. "Wished I knew."

"Can I help?"

"You'll have to talk to her. She doesn't listen to me."

"Will give it a try. Didn't like what I saw so far."

"You're not the only one. It's the environment. She keeps insisting she wants to change things going on in the nation."

"Don't think anyone person could."

"My thoughts. Now," he encouraged his buddy, "tell me about you. How'd you land in prison?"

Brian opened with, "Won't believe what's out east." He described conditions back home and why he'd decided to leave. He illustrated his plight on the road followed with the incarceration and prison misery.

"Unbelievable…incredible…amazing," Alex kept saying.

"Now," Brian insisted, "you fill me in on what's been happening in the nation. Don't get much news in prison. If at all, it's mostly rumors."

"White House, Pentagon, Government, CIA, all abandoned headquarters from DC to Maine. Without effective communication and with foreign forces pushing ashore, there's confusion everywhere."

"What about my Agency?"

"NSA? Gone as well."

"Military, national guards, law enforcement?"

"Most joined the Patriots."

"Tell me about it."

"It appears," Alex explained, "to be a new faction. Comprised mostly of ex-military trying to form a new way of life. They've taken over Fort Knox."

"Gold?"

"Yeah—nation's wealth—whole damned lot in their hands. Dollar's gone. Shut down the land—new borders—can't get through unless you join."

"That's it?"

"There's more—much more. Foreign forces trying to muscle in. Taken over seaports, plants, warehouses, stores, abandoned buildings—everything that's not occupied."

"What?"

"That's right." Alex was adamant. He was dead serious. "Don't know exactly who's doing the push," he explained. "But you can bet it's the Chinese, Russians, or Jihad."

"That bad?"

"Man, we're losing it."

"The nation?"

"The land. The whole eastern seaboard—gone."

"What about the government?"

"Fled out west—what's left—won't be long."

"What?"

"Before they're on our doorsteps."

"Here?"

"Yeah. Everybody wants the Mountain. Last stronghold west of the Mississippi."

Tracy made an appearance. She offered a refill on their drinks. "What are you guys talking about?" she asked, joining the conversation.

"Your dad filled me in on all that's happened." His eyes sought out hers but she avoided looking directly at his face. From her responses, he could sense a strange detachment between them, as if they have never been together. He was overcome by sadness. All the thoughts, hopes, and aspirations for her that kept him sane in the prison were slowly fading into emptiness. Her next statement confirmed his suspicion.

"You can stay until you get your strength back," she offered. "Dad?"

"Of course, you stay. I insist."

"Thanks. Don't know where else to go."

"Stay as long as you want," Tracy confirmed.

Brian sought out her eyes. "Can we talk?"

She moved up and pulled him by the arm toward the deck.

Alex gave them the needed privacy. "I'll be in the basement." It was where he spent most of the time, his command center. "See you in the morning," he said, biding them goodnight.

Brian and Tracy stood by the balcony rail in silence watching night fall. The moon was illuminating the wooded terrain, casting deep shadows into the foothills. For many, it would have been a romantic setting. At one time, it had been for them, but that seemed so long ago. They stood quietly for a while, gauging each other much like predator and prey. Brian wanted to blurt out *what the hell did you do to yourself.* He patiently waited for her to tell. For now, the female presence stirred almost forgotten urges within. Right now, all he wanted was a woman. He reached out for her. To his surprise, she let him caress her neck, then shoulders, and breasts. Long suppressed emotions began to stir. "It's been years," he whispered at her.

"Come." She led him by the arms to her room. As soon as the door shut, in one swift motion she kicked off her boots, dropped her jeans, and pulled off her blouse and panties, fully exposing her body. Brian followed her every move. He was awed by the solid body unraveling before his eyes. Where, at one time, she had been all female softness, now he was staring at what could only be described as Amazon, bronze in color, contours of a body builder, backed by an attitude of a warrior. He was bewildered at her boldness, but had no reason to complain. At the moment, he forgot his concerns about her earlier demeanor. All he could think of was ravaging her body. And he did. They both did.

There was no foreplay. Although he was at the brink of exploding his manhood, he let her drive the lovemaking. Passion would come later. For now, it was sex in its purest form, physical, brute, and raw all at once. Their bodies battered against each other, much like fighters wrestling for dominance. With one final thrust, Brian released all of the pent-up energy from his withered body, then collapsed on the soaked bed sheets, spent and completely out of breath. He lay there recollecting what had just taken place. As happy and as relaxed as he was, he wondered at the strengths and ferocity he had been attacked by from the once demure and reserved softness of Tracy. "That was awesome," he whispered at her. "Your body—you could have killed me."

"Like it?" She grinned at him.

"Where'd you get your strength?"

"Workouts—training—practice."

"Hate to be the guys on the receiving end."

"And they do," she responded with a mystical laugh.

"What's on your mind?" Brian was dying to get a handle on the woman he thought he'd known.

"Look around," she offered in a factual tone. "Country, people, mayhem—would you want our children to grow up in this environment?"

"Nobody does." He agreed with her wholeheartedly. "But what can one person do?"

"Watch me." It was all she'd say on the topic. They spent the remainder of the night in each other's arms followed by more lovemaking, but each time less violent. Tracy seemed to have boundless energy. Still overwhelmed by the radical change in her, Brian finally went to sleep totally exhausted, wondering what this woman had planned for the immediate future. At the moment, he had no care in the world. He felt secure.

"You need a shower," Tracy reminded him.

"In the morning," was his weak response, just before passing out into the first peaceful sleep he had in years.

CREW REUNION

There was knocking at the gate. It quickly escalated into banging. Alex reacted. "Wonder who that is?"

The three were seated around the kitchen table eating an evening meal Alex had prepared. Tracy bounded from her seat. "I'll find out." Although watchful, she hastened for the gate. These days, it was a rare occurrence for anybody to visit the Castle. But when they did, it mostly meant trouble.

Alex and Brian could hear the gate open and shut. It was followed by lively chatter. "Look what the cat dragged in," Tracy sneered. A hint of disgust was clearly painted across her face while leading the unexpected visitor into the Castle. Nobody could blame her. After all, it was she that took much of the visitor's insults while detaining her in the Arizona desert. Her memories were still vividly on her mind. Seconds later a familiar face was shoved into the room.

Surprise showed in all of their faces. "Well," Alex jumped up to greet the late intruder, "I'll be damned. Ole' warrior himself!"

Beaming with joy, Scott announced, "Greetings." It was an unexpected, but most welcome, event at the Castle. There, directly in front of them, in his living presence, stood the warrior himself, their former fighting partner Brooks. He displayed a humbleness they'd not seen in him.

"Where…?" Alex called out.

"South," Scott cut in without waiting for a response. There were many questions and answers that followed. He had his. They had theirs. At the end, it all boiled down to one notion: reunion.

Scott was offered a hospitality he had not had for some time. In response, he repaid his hosts and former fighter pilot partner, Brian, with a story they would not soon forget—if ever.

It had been many months since Scott Brooks arrived at Los Alamos. After he had been put in charge of security by Spencer, it took him several months to identify the weak spots in the facility. Systematically, he went through the gigantic complex, drawing data files on everything they had on record. He studied the building codes. He inspected every access to the complex. Next, he tested electronics for ID readers, finger print scanners, X-ray machines, security codes, and every other gadget in place to enforce security functions, many of which were dated. It seemed that there had been nobody in charge of enforcing IT effectiveness. Since every security aspect was managed by computers, the system was only as good as the weakest link in the chain of technology, which included operating systems, software applications, and individual access.

He developed a complete picture of the complexity at the time the EMP burst destroyed the systems. He needed to know how it all functioned before redesigning physical security. His intentions were to come up with a failsafe system with manual overrides. With electronic safeguards destroyed, it would provide a secure alternative. He was assigned a staff to assist. Manpower proved no obstacle. There were more resources on hand to satisfy his requirements than he had expected. Skills not required in certain areas were shifted to aid in security. Brooks shook up the entire Los Alamos facility to a point where he was hated. He didn't care. He was there to do a job. And he was proud of his achievements.

Once security was in place, next were policies and procedures. It concerned individual intrusions on personal lives, making him even more unpopular. By the time everything was organized and in place, everybody needed a break—even him. It was then when he requested time off. His plan was to finish a journey he had started many months ago. The time was now. Besides, although he appreciated the offer extended by Spencer to stay and remain in charge of the facility, he was a warrior at heart. He missed being on the frontlines. And he stated so.

"You know where to find us," were the parting words from his host and employer.

A few days later he was on the road once more destined for Colorado Springs, and, more specifically, the Castle.

The trip was uneventful. He made it in one day. Hitching a ride in a pickup, the journey took him from Santa Fe past Trinidad, Walsenburg, Pueblo, and the Springs, ending at Castle Rock. Only thing he'd remembered was an exit sign off of I-25 with a similar name to Alex's place, then to head for what looked like a tabletop shaped mountain. And here he was, knocking at a secluded gate blending securely into the surrounding terrain, the grounds of the Castle.

After knocking, he wondered whose face he'd encounter. He did not know what reception he would find. It was Tracy opening the gates. His doubts were dissolved when he watched her face change from apprehension to surprise followed by an extended welcoming hand, although reluctantly. "Well, well, if it isn't the jail keeper."

"Got a cot for a weary traveler?" He readily shook her outstretched hand with a grin.

Shaking her head, she said, "A cot I don't have. But you can stay." It was a play on words about the time she was restrained on a cot at his desert detainment center.

He accepted her invitation into the Bauer abode, surprised at the change in the once modest woman. What she projected, to his surprise, was buoyancy and complete self-confidence. There was something else that he sensed. Similar to a stalking animal, it was a calculating defiance accompanied by a personal challenge directed at him. He did not blame her. Being detained by force and then being taken hostage several times would anger any person. She led him into her home.

"Take a load off," Alex said, embracing the solid shoulders of this warrior.

Upon entering, Scott assessed the solidarity of the place with a nod of approval. "Quite a place you've got here. I'd sure like to see the rest of it."

"Later. What can I get you?"

"Got beer?"

"Tracy?" Alex shot a glance at her, and she promptly hurried to the kitchen.

He then noticed the third person idling off to the side. It took him moments to recognize his former Cobra partner. "Brian…Brian Harris. That you?"

"Yes. Yes, it's me," he said with a grin striding closer. "Been a while, hasn't it?"

"What happened? You look haggard."

"Been in prison," he reluctantly replied. "Sure, could have used your company."

"Prison, detainment, interrogation's my thing," he explained shrugging his shoulders. "But prisoner? Not a chance."

Minutes later, Tracy reappeared with the drinks alongside a tray filled with assorted snacks. Anticipating distant news carried by Brooks, although reluctantly, she joined the conversation in progress. Presently, he was explaining his whereabouts and encounters for the past years.

"Los Alamos?" Tracy asked. "What's there?"

"You've got to hear this," Alex told her.

Scott was telling them his encounters on the road that took him there in first place. "Ever hear of the Condors?"

None had.

"It's like this," he began. "Call themselves the Watchers. Don't really know where they came from or what exactly their intentions are. Only thing I know is," he explained. "They took possession of the nation's technologies."

"All of it?" Brian wondered.

"Every laboratory in the nation."

He then proceeded to tell them about the function and responsibility reworking security he'd been offered.

"Aah yes." Alex recalled the place. "Missing disks and plutonium."

"So, you've heard. Won't happen again," Brooks assured them. "Not with my security in place."

"Where were you back then," Alex hinted with a grin, "when they needed you?"

"You should know," Brooks fired back. "Chasing your adversary. Serpent, ever hear from him?"

"Not yet, but," Alex grunted with certainty, "as sure as my name's Alex Bauer, we'll hear from him sooner or later."

"I don't ever wanna see him again," Tracy cut in. "Makes me furious." A hint of rage was distorting her features from their normally relaxed gaze. Brooks checked her outburst then said, casually, "By the way, I like your looks."

"Don't mention it," Alex cut in. "Not the same Tracy you used to know."

"Noticed that," he offered with an approving nod. "What's up?" He seemed to be taken in by her appearance. "You sure look different from the girl I used to know."

"That's," Alex hinted, "something we've gotta talk about. But not today."

"What about you? How have you been?" Brooks addressed Brian.

"Been locked up two years." It was Brian's turn to tell his story.

"Glad you're safe," Scott said. More drinks were served and more snacks offered.

Getting up from the sofa, Alex said, "Let me show you the place." He indicated the hallway. "Follow me." He led them downstairs through several floor levels. It was Brooks' turn to be amazed. He seemed highly impressed at what he saw. "Always knew," he commented, "that there's something different about you and your clan." Scott took it all in with heightened expectations. Completing the tour, Alex guided his guest back the hall. "You can bunk in the guest room."

The room stayed empty since Brian had taken up with Tracy. Since he had nothing but the clothes on his body when he was rescued, his presence in her private chambers did not clutter her space. Tracy had provided him with sets of clothes borrowed from Alex. Although her general behavior displayed a certain distance between the two, Tracy seemed to tolerate Brian. She even remained at the Castle for the time being. Alex wondered about that. He knew she was seeing Cox, the GI from the fort, but did not prod her for it. He was just happy for his daughter accepting his buddy back into her life.

The next morning was the start of yet another bright and sunny day in the Rockies. Alex had breakfast waiting when Scott showed up. Tracy and Brian were not far behind. "Breakfast's ready." Aside from watching her shape, she still appreciated her dad's cooking. Ever since she had decided to take on the challenges of the warrior, her shape was not an issue. Just by virtue of daily workouts punching and kicking bags, in addition to other special training she took for target shooting, jogging, climbing sheer cliffs, and the barroom brawls, her body was hardened while still maintaining a feminine appearance.

"Tell us more about Los Alamos," she opened the conversation, taking a seat in the empty chair. After giving it quite some consideration the night before, Tracy decided to bury the hatchet, her acquired dislike she carried for Brooks, for the time being. "What's it like? What's going on there?"

"Barring classified restrictions," Scott replied, "I can tell you about the general gist of the place. Top notch scientists. Foreign influx as well, and that's where the problem lies."

"What do you mean?" Tracy asked.

"Affluent crowd sends their kids to the best institutions to study science."

"Princeton, MIT, SRI?"

"The ones." He went on, "Progress has slowed down since the collapse of the nation, but goes on, nevertheless, funded by affluent foreigners," he explained. "Most recent developments are genetics and chip implants."

Both Alex and Tracy perked up at the revelation. They had discussed the very subject on several occasions. Eager for hearing more on this science, "Tell me more," she demanded.

"Don't know all the details with me working security only," he openly admitted. "But they're making great strides—always looking for volunteers."

"There's your chance, Tracy," Alex blurted out. Not clearly understanding the comment, both Brian and Scott shot a surprised glance at him.

To emphasize his statement, Alex stood up from his chair. "Let me explain. Better yet," he gestured at the stairway, "let me show you."

"You go along," Tracy said. "I'll finish up the dishes." She was very familiar with what Dad was about to show them. They got up and followed him to the subterranean vault several levels below. First stop was the command room.

"Wow!" Scott exclaimed in wonderment. "Strategic command and control, military style."

Proud of his achievements and being able to afford the best in communications, Alex agreed. "Just about."

Scott was curious. "What does that do?"

Brian cut in to offer his technology skills. Gesturing across the room with an outstretched arm, "That, my friend," he said boastingly, "is ASAT downlinks. Right?"

Alex confirmed the suggestion. "Exactly."

"Tell me more," Scott insisted.

To avoiding further interruptions, Alex suggested, "Let me go down the line. This here," he explained, "keeps me connected to the world. Here we have frequency scanners for the entire voice, data, video, infrared, and ultra-violet spectrums. These are," he gestured at another series of racks staged against the back wall, "transmit/receiver units for satellites, communications, computers, downlinks, routers, bridges, hubs—the whole damned gamut." Alex was proud of his possessions. It showed on his expression.

"Satellites? Thought they took a hit with the blast," Scott said, slightly surprised.

"Not at all," Alex countered. "Military type hardening—entire Castle."[11] He didn't have to explain further. Both knew very well how much the government paid contractors for expensive EMP shielding. He could only guess where the funding came from to harden the Castle.

Scott pointed at what appeared to be an array of rack-mounted equipment flashing red indicators at him. "What about here?" he asked.

"That's," Alex explained, "the reason we came down here." Their heads turned to the entrance. Tracy had just joined the team. Nodding at her, Alex said, "You tell 'em."

She was eager to do just that. "After my implant," she started but was cut short by Brian.

"What implant?"

She ignored him for the moment. She'd deal with him later in private. "As I was going to say, after the implant," she explained, "this is what'll track and report on my passage. By passage, I meant journey."

There was more staring and bewilderment. It'd be incredulous to have a woman alone marching through the countryside, as hostile as the regions had become. "You can't be serious," Brian spat at her. He appeared gravely alarmed.

"Dead serious," Alex chimed in. "I gave up long ago trying to talk some sense into her, but will support her in any event." Although highly concerned for her safety, the caring father he was, he was proud at her fortitude, determination, courage, and strength all the same. He realized there was nothing else he could do to convince her otherwise. He'd sure as hell tried.

Scott was still mulling over the idea he'd just heard. It'd give him and the future new possibilities. And he liked it. "You know what," he said, "that's not a bad idea."

"What?" Alex thought he hadn't heard right.

"Implant."

"You too?" He was taken by surprise once more. "What's with you guys?"

Tracy had given the thought considerable time already, for months. To her, it would be the perfect solution for her plan. Aside from that, she'd get continuous data input from Castle command, satellite surveillance, and whatever news flashed around the globe. It'd require no reading. No dialogue. Only data streams and images fed directly into her brain. "Think about it," she insisted. "No equipment failure, no data distortion, no transmission delays."

"Count me in," Scott assured her.

---

[11] Hardening is the term used by the military for EMP protection. It required extensive, and very expensive and special hardware inclusion into every design aspect not only for the command and control center, but computer and communication equipment and interface connecting to the outside world. Where many government systems are hardened, commercial and civilian systems are not.

Brian, as much as he cared for Tracy, wasn't ready for such a dramatic endeavor. He still had his legs planted on solid ground. "Maybe later," he suggested. For now, all he wanted to do was support her in the conventional ways he valued: observe, support, and protect.

LOS ALAMOS

When Scott showed up at the Kitchen entrance the next morning, only Brian was present. "Breakfast," he was offered. "Could eat a horse," he responded. Looking around the room, "Where's Alex," he, in turn, inquired. "Making preparations," he was told. "Preparations for what?"

Brian eyed him with indifference. "Your trip." Turned curious, before he could question Brian any further, Alex and Tracy appeared in the kitchen. "You ready," Tracy asked her visitor who had just taken a piece of bacon off the breakfast plate. His hand poised in the air, "Ready for what," he asked.

"Implant." Tracy threw him a defiant glance. "Remember?" He clearly remembered talking about it the night before but did not think she was this serious. "Now?"

"I'll let you finish the plate," she said, then disappeared down the hall.

A question mark on his face, Scott shot a glance at Alex, "What's with her. What's the rush?"

Alex pulled up a chair alongside and said, "She's not the same girl you knew a couple of years ago."

"So, I've noticed."

"There's something I should tell you about her." Alex took a few seconds before he continued. "Her attitude towards you, me," he nodded at Brian, "us, life in general, has taken a dramatic turn after you incarcerated her. She hates everybody."

"Sorry to hear that. But," Scott explained. "You knew the circumstances."

"It's not only you. The Serpent had a lot to do with it."

"We all grew up with the EMP." It was Brian making the statement. "I don't know her anymore."

"Like I said," Scott justified his actions, "We were at war."

"It's in the past," Alex agreed. "You," he stared at Scott, "will have to live with it."

"What about the trip," he wanted to now.

"She's already at the controls waiting on you."

Scott gave him a surprise look. "She flying?"

"One of the best," Brian confirmed.

With Brooks as passenger and Tracy on the controls of her favorite toy, the AH-1 was presently being piloted south. It would be a relatively short trip along I-25 south for most of the way. Thirty minutes into the flight the town of Raton was slowly passing below. A partially folded map placed on his lap, Brooks was following the flight path. Although the airwaves were quiet for most part, both wore headsets to communicate onboard. "Head west," he instructed Tracy. The plan was to intersect with Taos and on to the final destination, Los Alamos. "Ten more minutes," he advised next.

Whenever she was behind the controls of this magnificent craft Tracy felt elated. It was a feeling of freedom she had not experienced since the time she'd chased after terrorists. "Wonder what ever happened to him?" she muttered.

"Who?"

"Serpent."

"Don't know…don't give a damn."

"Think he'll be back?"

"Maybe…maybe not. All depends on how bad he wants the nation."

"Don't think he'll ever give up."

Checking the terrain ahead, "Take it down," he said. "We're getting close."

Running parallel alongside E-502, a sparsely traveled road, Los Alamos airport just came into view. There had not been air traffic since airliners and military craft were grounded. As far as the national laboratories were concerned, technology advancements had come to a standstill. To the outsider, that was. What went on within was anybody's guess. Only Brooks, as limited as his comprehension was with science, had knowledge on that.

"Call in," Tracy suggested.

Brooks alerted the laboratory of their arrival. The head of the complex was waiting when they touched down. "Allan Spencer," he greeted her. "You must be Tracy."

"Sure am."

With a grin on his face, "So," Spencer said to Brooks, "couldn't stand it on the outside?"

"Not what you think," Brooks responded. "We need to talk."

Spencer led them to a chauffeured car. "That we will." It was light conversation from there until the driver stopped at a dorm-like quarters. Stepping in, Tracy was assigned a room.

"Make yourselves at home," Spencer offered. "Let's meet in an hour." He drove off with, "Driver will pick you up." Tracy and Brooks had enough time to settled in and refresh.

As promised the driver showed up an hour later, then drove them the short distance to the headquarters building. After passing security, they were led along a spacious hallway to meet up with their host. He was in his office accompanied by two of his trusted scientists. They seemed immersed in research talk upon entering. Right away, Tracy was impressed by the friendly atmosphere and the hospitality extended. A welcome table was set up along the window with a picturesque view into the valley. A framed, oversized regional map was mounted on one wall. It gave a clear overview of the vastness of the laboratory and its surroundings. Seated within the national forest, the complex of this scientific research facility sprawled out in every direction. There was more to it than Tracy had ever suspected. What was most striking was the buffet Spencer dished out. The spread was impressive, especially in an economy solely dependent on barter. There was meat. There were vegetables in abundance. Even fruits and desserts. "Where did you grow all this?" Tracy asked.

"San Luis Valley," he said. "Some comes up from Mexico."

"Mexico?" Tracy wondered. "How you payin' for it?"

"Technology."

"What technology?"

"In time," Spencer assured her. "Now, what brings you here?"

"Let me fill you in," Brooks opened the dialogue. "Tracy here," he gestured at her, "is the daughter of Bauer…Alex Bauer."

"I've heard the name." Spencer pondered. "Isn't he the one that launched the nuke starting the war?"

"Correction," Tracy jumped in, "stopped a war."

"Sorry," he apologized. "As you were saying?" He encouraged Scott.

"Tracy here…"

Scott proceeded to tell him about his visit at the Castle. Illustrating what Bauer had done with the place sparked Spencer's interests. Brooks explained the strategic position of the Castle with NORAD, Fort Carson, and the New Republic. Occasionally interrupting to clarify one or another point, Spencer listened patiently until the topic touched on the implant.

He questioned Tracy's intentions. "But why?"

"The implant? Let me enlighten you. You've got your lab. You have your people. You have security. Ever wonder what your children are saying?"

"Yeah," he admitted. "They'd rather be at Disneyland."

"I made my point." Tracy held his gaze while she studied him. *Typical scientist, or is he?* There was something that bothered her. It was something Brooks had mentioned a while back. *Bird or something?* "Aah yes," she remembered. "Condors." She made a mental note to ask him.

Spencer indicated the meeting was over. "Let's get together tomorrow. We can talk about it more."

"Fine." With Brooks leading the way, they left the office with a promise to be back. Stepping from the building, he offered, "Let me show you around. I wanna show you my accomplishments."

"Lead on." They were headed for one of the buildings. Security was tightly enforced wherever they went. He was eager to show off his sophisticated safety and surveillance systems. Although not the ideal conditions, without reliable electricity since the backup generators were mostly out of fuel or not always functioning, it was the best in mechanical design.

The following morning, Brooks was knocking early. He took her to an enormous building complex across the yard. Upon entering, overhead lighting normally illuminated by dozens of halogen beams had been somewhat dimmed to conserve energy. Even for the laboratory, fuel had become a commodity not easily obtained. Throughout the nation, battles were fought over ownership of oil pumps. Los Alamos did not fare any better. Scouts were sent out to secure whatever obscure rigs were still accessible. It was an ongoing struggle to acquire and then protect refined fuel sources.

Spencer was waiting to take the lead. He led them to a spacious, glass-enclosed laboratory section. "Future Lab," the overhead sign said upon entering. The place was spotless. Glass enclosed cages sectioned out the interior. An array of work tables, tilting platforms, reclining seats, spotlights, portable instruments, jars, vials, heaters, centrifuges, and everything else one could imagine could be found in the super modern research lab.

Off to one side was a small conference room with a table, chairs, and wall-mounted projector screen connecting laptop computers with servers and databases. Spencer invited them to be seated. He pressed a keyboard key. "Let's see what we've got," he opened the discourse. The screen came alive and up popped a series of X-ray images depicting the complexity of a brain. There was the skull, brain, face, ears, and other vital parts of the head. From the familiar contours, Tracy could make out a chimp's profile. "Looks like you've run some tests already," she remarked.

"We are ready. Are you?"

"We'll see," she hesitated.

Using a laser pointer, Spencer tagged several of the sections into one cohesive framework explaining the various functions. "Here," he went on, "you can see the chip implant at the base of the skull. Over here," he further indicated, "are connections with the visual nerves. And there," he focused on the temples, "receiver implants."

"What about vocals?" Tracy noticed all the elements except the mic implant.

"Won't be visible," he pointed out. "Nape of the neck. Micro switch's hidden behind the right ear."

"Ouch!" Tracy exclaimed.

"You right handed?"

"Yep."

"So be it."

Sporting a broad grin, Scott made the comment, "Don't get kicked in the head."

"Thanks for the confidence." Tracy shot a defiant glance at him thinking *not a chance*.

"What do you think?" Spencer had been watching Tracy's face for visible reactions. He seemed impressed by the focused interest displayed by his guest. He figured by now that she would back out from any such intrusion into the body, but he did not get any indications of that at all.

Regardless of the invasive procedure, she asked, "How soon?" Tracy had decided on the spot.

Spencer hesitated at her abrupt decision. He gave her one last chance to opt out. "No second thoughts?" He was seemingly impressed.

"You don't know this girl," Brooks stated. "One hundred percent warrior."

"Then let's do it. I'll schedule it first thing tomorrow. Don't know how long it'll take." With a gesture, he dismissed Brooks and Tracy. He spent the rest of the day with his lead scientist to discuss the delicate procedure, being applied to a human being for the first time. They had been waiting for this opportunity. Until now, experimental cases had only been conducted on animal subjects. Tests had proven promising, but without being able to communicate with animals, rendered inconclusive. He expressed his view to the staff. "Guess," he said, "tomorrow's the beginning of a new epoch in communication."

"Bring on the champagne," a member of the staff suggested.

"Let's wait 'til after the operation."

The surgical procedures went well. There were some adjustments needed to the transmitter and receiver equipment, but nothing major. The system was fine-tuned while Tracy was still on the operating table. Once adjusted, it performed well, as seen through the monitors. Spencer kept a close watch on Tracy to monitor her for any kind of adverse reactions. He was pleased to see she took to the implant well.

Only localized by anesthetics, Tracy was able to follow the procedure in full consciousness. "Now what?" she asked Spencer once the numbness in her face wore off. Tracy was anxious for a real-life test. The implant was still silent. Looking at her face and head told otherwise. "Swelling will disappear over the next few days. Bruises gonna take a couple of weeks," he advised her.

"Don't care as long as it works."

"You realize," Spencer stated, "that you're the only implant in the world." But the world outside the continent was buzzing with information. Data bits were passing through the ether in massive amounts, bombarding every conceivable technology design across a wide range of frequency spectrum. To filter out the intelligence for the implant, the range was narrowed to the EHF range. The implant Tracy had received was for voice, data, and video transmissions. It was the extremely high frequency, the 30 to 300 GHz range, ideally designed for a brain's sensitivity.

"I want it tested," she demanded. "Now."

"In due time," he told her. "For the time being, just listen. Get your ears used to white noise."

Brooks was impressed at the patience with which Tracy had endured the operation. Although as a fighter he was used to combating external threats, he cringed at the thought of internal intrusions on his body. He was lucky enough to have warded off serious injuries to his body from knife and bullet. He had never considered having an implant of any kind. But the way it went with Tracy, it would be something to consider. He contemplated the pros and cons in silence. He approached Spencer the next day. "Let's do it."

"Do what?" Spencer paid him full attention.

"Implant."

"You?"

"She needs a partner." And that was it. He'd made the decision.

Brooks was prepared for the operation, securely strapped to the table. Conscious but sedated, dreamlike, his thoughts were drifting. He was marching across the countryside facing a battle. Swarms of dagger-wielding fighters kept throwing themselves at him. Armed with only a knife he fought off one after another. He kept fighting on. Suddenly, he could hear a voice. Distant at first then, with ever increasing volume, it suddenly exploded.

"Testing...testing," Spencer's voice crackled in the earpiece.

He jolted from the dream, clutching both ears. "Pain," he yelled out in agony. He struggled to jump from the table, but was held back by the restraints. Lab technicians nearby rushed to the operating table, forcing his body down. He was shaking uncontrollably against the restraints until they snapped. His arms were free. In one violent motion, he reached down to unfasten his ankles. Freed, he threw orderlies out of his path and dashed across the room, headed directly for Spencer. Brooks grabbed him by the throat and viciously threw him against the wall. The orderlies regained their composures and rushed to Spencer's aid. It took half a dozen aides to keep him from inflicting serious harm to the head of the lab. Scientists, alerted that something had gone wrong, immediately shut the spectrum analyzer and pulse generators down. Once the source was eliminated, Brooks calmed down enough for Spencer to explain.

Apparently, the source generator had been inadvertently set to a high magnitude. The exceeded level, in turn, was amplified enough to drive the sound into acoustic feedback. Acoustic engineers, at one time or another, experienced the condition and were well aware of its implications. In many cases, at a minimum, it blew out speakers. That's what had happened to Scott's eardrums.

Mistake, Scott thought. He blamed himself for having the implant. "Get it outta me," he shouted at the lab coats clutching at his ears. He could not envision living the rest of his life with that damned implant. Brooks was ready to jump the techs again.

"Wait," Spencer suggested. "Hear with your brain," he was instructed, "not your ears."

Scott stopped struggling and, sure enough, he could clearly receive and identify sounds, although very distant. "Listen," one scientist advised. "There's an override switch implant in the base of the neck. In an emergency," Scott was instructed, "press down on the switch." He was shown a few more features, such as adjusting sound volume, tuning in frequencies, and selecting sound, video, and images. "Battery implant at the nape of the neck should last five years. By then," he was told, "you'll be ready for a technology upgrade."

Tracy was waiting for Brooks when he returned to the dorm. "How'd it go?"

"You don't wanna know…Need a drink."

"You mean," she pried, "the thing with the sound?"

"Ears are still numb," he complained.

She prepared a couple of martinis, then sat in silent for some time before opening the conversation. "Gotta plan."

It drew him from his private thoughts. "What?"

"Got any HAM sets in this place?"

"Equipment room." Scott grunted, then gestured, "Follow me."

He led her to the central section of the research building. Since he was in charge of security, he had access to all facilities. On entering, Tracy admitted, "Like the Castle." She let her eyes wander around the room and identified similar equipment to what Dad owned. Among it, she found what she needed, then made the call. "CQ…CQ…Castle Rock."

It was not long before Alex's voice answered. "Tracy. How's it goin'?"

"Went well…Listen, Dad, Brian around?"

"Where else would he be? He misses you."

"I know," she admitted. "Could you get him?" She knew he missed her. Sometimes she felt the guilt. She shouldn't feel that way, but couldn't help herself. Ever since she had a clear focus on her future and what needed to be done, Brian had taken a backseat to her plans. She still loved him, but—there was that "but" again. She didn't like it but had no easy answer. In her mind, the mission came first. Because of the extreme conditions in which she was forced to live, it had become personal. It was a mission that'd determine not only her future, but the nation's as well. Brian's voice interrupted her thoughts. "Tracy?"

"Need your expertise."

"Anything," he offered. "Just name it."

"ASATs. Backdoor access." She had known all along that the only effective means of communication support would be from the Castle and the satellites that were still functional. It would be these assets, belonging to the military that would be the carrier for sending and receiving signals. And, since he was part of the original design and development, she suspected that he'd have special access to the units.

There was an extended pause. She knew exactly what went through his mind. *Classified material...military defense...national security...Should I, could I, would I?* "Can't do it," he finally broke the silence.

"Why not? Damned system's not in use."

There was more silence, followed by, "Give me a good reason."

"The future!" If that wasn't good enough nothing else would matter. She knew he was deeply dedicated to the protection of national security and would never breach the defense code. But the present state of the nation called for extreme measures. "Well?"

"You've got it." He'd come to his senses.

"What?"

"My support...and whatever else you need. By the way...how did the implant go?"

"Well...and...that's the reason." She told him about the procedures, the testing and success. "Tell Dad what I need. Let me know when it's done."

"You'll be the first," he chuckled. "You coming back?"

"Couple days...Over." The HAM set turned silence.

BADLANDS

"This is my command," Rusty Norton insisted once more. He had been enraged ever since the defunct Pentagon armada arrived with Foster in charge, who had demanded control over the fort. He understood military ranking systems only too well. That was the reason he had gotten in trouble on first place, by disregarding the "Chain of Command." But this was when the military still had control. What he had on his hands was a militia, a complete contrast to a structured, now-defunct defense organization. He wasn't about to give in to anybody's demands. He had taken control over the fort, earned it, and decided to keep control. But he was no match for the lifelong experience of a proven battle commander, especially one with many honors and decorations.

"I outrank you," the general, ex-United States Army, insisted. "By several stars."

"Yeah, but," Norton countered, "I created this unit." He had fought for it and, besides, he would not resign the immense hostility he felt against the structured military he felt had done him injustice, regardless of the present conditions.

"Tell you what," Foster conceded. "You have full Brigadier command. I'll advise."

Norton mulled over the offer. It seemed reasonable. It just might work. It was something he could live with. *After all,* he contemplated, *everybody reports to somebody.* "Gotta discuss it with my commanders. It'll be up to them to decide. We uphold democracy."

"You know," Foster offered, "it'll be only a matter of time…"

"I know…I know all that crap. It's in every military history book." What Foster suggested was human fallacy. Nothing ever lasts very long, including government phases, no matter how much one might try. Norton left the office, advising him, "I'll let you know by tomorrow."

Early the next day, Norton showed up at the general's quarters. "Got your wish."

Foster jumped into action. "Here's what must be done. Immediately! We don't have time to waste." Norton was surprised at the general's urgency. From his perspective, during the past year, there had not been much alarm for a national emergency. New boundaries had been defined. Loosely yes, but defined nevertheless. At the Badlands, so far, there had been no threats or need to fend off intruders. On Foster's urging, nevertheless, he went into action alerting his troops. *Maybe it isn't such a bad idea with the general in charge.*

Using the map as guidance, "Jihad's on the move. They're pushing ahead full force. No nation's safe. Islam's on the rise," Foster reported. "And so are the superpowers."

"Superpowers?"

"China, Russia, India, E.U., Australia, everybody's juggling for position. With the dollar gone, our defenses destroyed, free world's up for grabs. Everybody wants domination."

"Australia?" Norton was surprised at that. They had always been a civilized nation down under.

"Not anymore. Been sidelined for too long, they feel."

"What about North Korea, Pakistan, Iran?"

"We took care of them…for a while anyway. Spirit of America. Remember?"

Norton, along with many citizens back then, had not been aware of the last retaliation act the Air Force had committed. Only Foster, his command, and trusted men like Bauer and Harris, the ones involved in the retaliation, knew about it. These nations did not have the resources necessary to pull off a major initiative. "We need to consolidate our forces. We need to defend what's left. We need a…"

"New Republic," Norton cut in.

Foster shared his enthusiasm. He bolted to his feet. "That's it!" He took the few paces to the map tacked against the office wall, took the black marker attached to a string, and waved it across the chart. "Here's where we are." He marked up regions he knew had been already occupied by the enemy. He encircled the territory he felt was the strongest concentration of national power then scribbled one word across the region, "Badlands."

"This," he proclaimed, "is gonna be the nation."

Norton seemed to be in agreement. The slogan carried out by his forces would be, "New Republic."

"What we need first," Foster summed up, "are boundaries locked down solid. Nobody comes in, nobody leaves without permission. I'll make sure of it…We'll make sure of it." He directed Norton to gather the assembly. He was anxious to present the new plan.

Twenty minutes later, his gaze swept around the assembly room. His eyes touched every face staring back at him. Briefly explaining the new direction, the nation must take, "The new policy," he summed up, "is a solid nation…strong boundaries…united citizens…protected and defended by the New Republic." It was his closing statement. It brought on many cheers. Next stop was the dining halls and bar rooms. "Celebration's in order."

"How long's it been?" Norton's first lieutenant cut in making reference to the creation of the nation.

"Two hundred-fifty years…almost..." Norton remarked. Much like after the completion of the first draft of the constitution, there was great jubilation.

THE SERPENT

The assault team had just been dropped off by the Long Island shores. Following a three days' journey they had arrived by cargo vessel from Jeddah via the Suez Canal, then shuttled to the American shore. A hurried assault, it had taken greater than an hour to deliver all of the cargo, vessel, and transport supplies. Although there was considerable noise created during the unloading, there had been no uninvited visitors from the island residents. With that, Hammad decided to camp out until daybreak. Surrounded by Yusuf and his lieutenants, huddled close by the water's edge near a place identified as Coney Island, he was discussing the next move come morning. Manhattan would be their first stop. He was anxious to step on the former grounds to check firsthand on the state of the once-thriving mega city. From what he knew, international trade there had come to a halt since there was not an accepted method for commerce. It would not matter. For reasons, he kept to himself at the moment, he planned to make Chicago the new world capital, Jihad's command center, not this city. But that was still some time in the future. For that, many hurdles needed to be covered.

"We settle here?" Yusuf asked the leader.

"Chicago." Hammad held steadfast. Chicago, after assessing the state of New York, would serve as his immediate military headquarters.

"Chicago. Why?" Yusuf had been meaning to bring up the topic with the commander but decided to wait for the proper moment. The moment, it seemed, was now. He had to try his influence, especially since he preferred New York as the new capital. After all, it was his former home. Having ready access to the world's oceans would make more sense. But it was not his to decide.

"I will tell you." Hammad pulled him aside. They settled on a wooden landing that used to be a boardwalk for a once prolific, but now deserted, amusement park. His gaze swept a seemingly well-constructed platform for weekenders to wander on. But the boardwalk was empty now. Shop owners, as far as his eyes could gauge, had abandoned their businesses.

"This city," he began, "is a dead town. It can only function with water, electricity, and..."

"I know…fuel," Yusuf cut in.

Hasan Hammad did not take well to interruptions. But with Yusuf, a friend since childhood, he made an exception. "As I said," Hammad carried on, "the city will not come alive for years, perhaps ever." He discussed the pros and cons with his friend as he saw fit. At this point, there were many more cons. "Perhaps sometimes in the future," he said, "we may make it our seaport. Let us get some rest. Daybreak will come soon."

"How will we get to Chicago?"

"We shall see by daybreak."

Hammad rose with the first rays of a new dawn. He found Yusuf studying the map and asked, "What do you know about upper New York?" The map did not show the entire eastern sector of North America. It was cut off below the Canadian borders.

"Why do you ask?"

"Waterways. Where does the Hudson River end? How do we get to the Lakes?"

"Two ways," Yusuf informed him. "By way of Albany or," he checked the map, "Saint Lawrence River."

"Which is easiest?"

"Saint Lawrence."

"Then," Hammad ordered, "let's go."

"It's not that easy," Yusuf cautioned. "It is very far. We don't have enough fuel to make the distance. There are no refueling stations."

"Then Albany it is."

"Not easy either. Erie Canals may be fortified."

"Impossible?"

"Not impossible."

"It is decided."

Without bathing accommodations, it did not take long for the team to get ready for departure. It was only a matter of stepping off to the water's edge, splashing cold water in the face, collecting blankets and eating utensils, tearing down tents, and moving on. Space on the speedboat was crammed with small arms and food supplies to accommodate the attack party. The craft carried them swiftly up the waterway, the entry point to the Hudson River. From there, lower Manhattan was only a ten-minute cruise. "Freedom Towers," Hammad directed the pilot.

"Eh?" The face carried a question mark.

"Trade Center," he spat at the combatant piloting the boat. "Idiot." Hammad had to remind himself that most of his crew had never stepped foot on this land before. *Hell,* he thought, *most can barely speak English.* But, it would not present much of a problem since many were educated. They would pick up quick on the language. He wanted to see firsthand what the Americans had done to the place since the 9/11 attack, his first assault on U.S. soil back in 2001.

Yusuf was first to jump from his vessel. "Remarkable!" he exclaimed. What used to be a demolished construction site, the last time he was here, was now a gigantic tower reaching into space. The first structure, Tower One had been completed. Projecting into the sky, it was iconic. Construction for the surrounding buildings Two through Seven were either close to completion or well on their way. Hotels, residential projects, financial centers, city parks, and many more buildings along Fulton, Church, and Broadway had already been erected. But today, ever since his recent assault, the EMP strike, construction had come to a halt.

"You sure?" Yusuf made another attempt to make this the new home. "Won't change your mind?"

"Perhaps," Hammad replied, "some day." He had seen enough. He was anxious to get going. "Get your team together," he ordered. "We are heading out."

The plan was to shuttle upriver as far as Albany, then head west to meet up in Buffalo, and onward on waterways to the Great Lakes with Chicago as the final destination. But that was days ahead, perhaps weeks. At this time, Hammad had no idea what would face them. He hoped to make rapid progress, but fate might not be on his side.

The cruiser left lower Manhattan in its wake, speeding north on Hudson River. Hammad and Yusuf were perched in front of the cabin, keeping their eyes on the city skyline as the boat headed north. Yonkers crept into view, then Riverdale, when something caught Hammad's attention. "There," he gestured to the immediate right, "I lost all my men."

"That's right," Yusuf recalled. "I've heard. Hillview, wasn't it?"

Hammad had bitter memories of the place. Although it had already been many months, the event was permanently burnt into his mind. He had been so close to victory when, all of a sudden, the beam from hell pierced from the sky, incinerating all of his men. It was there when he realized the game was over. The Plan, his plan, had been flawless until the day Allah, the almighty, intervened. He had not anticipated the act of divine intervention. It could not have been anything else. *How could it? Perhaps I have gone too far,* he had questioned.

It came on as a complete surprise. To his knowledge, there was no such weapon mankind had designed. But after some research, rumors had surfaced about a super weapon the Americans had been experimenting with. "HAARP," he muttered. "Perhaps some pulse weapon."

"What?" Yusuf thought he had not heard right. "Angels?"

"Not that kind of harp," he corrected. "Has something to do with the atmosphere." He proceeded to tell Yusuf all he knew about this so-called "super weapon. New defense against us…population manipulation…there is more to this than I know."

"Never heard of it."

"Nobody has…only rumors. Reason I am…we are here."

"The weapon?"

"That," Hammad explained, "and water."

"Water?"

"Yes. Water."

"I don't understand." Yusuf shot a glance at the leader. He could understand the quest for this weapon, as mystical as it sounded, but water?

"Think of it," Hammad explained. "You may not be aware, but the world is running short on water. Fresh water, that is."

"Thought it was oil?"

"We have plenty of that. It is the water I want." He had been studying the chart in his lap, presently showing the eastern seaboard with Manhattan in focus. He reached for and unfolded another map. It was one of the worlds. "Here." He indicated the Arabian Peninsula. "What do you see?"

"Desert…nothing but."

"What do you see here?"

Yusuf was trying to make sense from the contours on the map. His eyes captured the Himalayan divide. "Allah's abode?"

"Right," Hammad said. He was slightly frustrated that his first lieutenant could not see his vision. *But then,* he reasoned, *it is why I am in command and everybody in Islam will bow to me.* He kept the thought private. As long as he, and only he, held the answers, he would be revered. He would be revered at the highest post, as leader, as supreme commander, and, ultimately, as the messenger of Allah. *That, my friend,* he had hinted on one occasion to his only friend and ally Yusuf, *is my mission.*

There was one point he had not shared with Yusuf, nor his brethren or anyone else. And that was his drive for gaining control over the water. *Fresh water.* Only in recent years had geophysicists discovered the global state of water resources. One just had to look to central Africa, at Mount Kilimanjaro, to get the picture. Where this majestically perfect peak used to carry snow year-round, today it was barren. Similar warning signs surfaced at the Swiss Alps, the Ural Mountains, the Himalayas, and many more mountain ranges. Glaciers were melting at a disturbing rate without being replenished. *And the causes?* He pondered. *Global warming, climate change, solar influx.* It did not matter. The globe was doomed to destruction, unless intervened by Allah—or him.

Statistics had it that, at the rate the Himalayan glaciers were melting, it would only take another generation for glaciers to disappear. It not only impacted his homeland Kashmir, but entire countries, with India to the south and China to the north. India, the consensus was, would lose ninety percent of its population through starvation since the continent was solely dependent on this water for irrigation, cultivation, and drinking water.

China to the north, in contrast, would fight for this precious resource. The handwriting was there already. He suspected it to be the very reason the nation was gearing up its military might. The only difference was that he was taking the first initiative. "Now you understand? The world needs water." He folded the map over. "Here." He gestured at a specific point. "What do you see?"

"Water...nothing but fresh water." His gaze changed into a broad grin. Now he understood. What he was staring at was the Great Lakes. "Genius."

"Our destination!"

The trouble started as soon as they entered the perimeters of West Point.[12] They'd just passed a complex to the left the map indicated as Fort Montgomery. Other than it being a military academy, neither Hasan nor Yusuf had much information on it. All they could do was speculate based on the immediate resistance they encountered.

"Artillery," Hammad shouted. They needed protection, and fast. "Speed up." He was stunned in wonderment. What had rushed at them was a salvo of machinegun fire. Exploding water spouts right in front of the cruiser shot straight up, drenching the occupants with chilling river water. It was something he had not expected, not on U.S. soil. The pilot was quick to react, dodging water spouts right and left, exploding ever closer. There was no protection. He had to get away. Hammad considered turning back, but retreat was not an option. To achieve his goal, he had to forge ahead, to the Great Lakes. But getting there could be packed with many challenges. For now, he was fighting off what seemed to be the forces of an entire garrison.

A pair of field glasses pressed against his eyes, Yusuf planted his body on the stern. "Watch out!" he yelled.

"What?" Hammad reached for the glasses strapped to his neck. He could not believe what he saw directly ahead. Two inbound objects were slicing through the water. He

---

[12] The United States Military Academy at West Point Army was a four-year coeducational federal service academy located in West Point, New York. The academy sat on scenic high ground overlooking the Hudson River, 50 miles north of New York City. Rich on tradition, extremely prestigious, it was very difficult to gain entry into the academy, with admission limited. Graduates, however, were guaranteed to become part of the upper echelon in the Army's file and rank commanders.

identified them as fast attack craft. "PTs?" Hammad's eyes widened with surprise. How could that be? Craft from the past, here, now?

His confidence returned immediately when he considered the vessel below his feet. It was much superior. When Hammad made plans for the attack via waterway on U.S. soil, he'd had it specially designed. Although it had taken close to a year to build, it contained all the design features he had insisted on. He knew what he wanted. Knew what he needed. At the end, he got what he ordered and here he was, testing it for the first time on an enemy. The sheer thrill of what lay ahead brought bumps to the skin of his forearms.

The year previous, Milan, it was. At first, Hammad was unsure how an inland boat designer could effectively build a seaworthy craft. But Italy was known for its superior designs and construction for speedy and powerful vessels. After being told that money was no object it did not take much to convince the builder. Regardless of Hammad's abrasive and at times intimidating business approach, the builder was only too happy to accommodate the potential customer. "Can do," was his final response when the order was placed.

Although the specifications were to the extreme in speed and armament, the craft was finished eleven months later. Hammad recalled the design specs. They were from a craft he had seen in action not long before, an experimental British ship, the UXV built BAE Type-45[13], Daring-class destroyer. After witnessing the warship's firepower demonstration, he exclaimed, "That's it! Exactly what I need." From there on the task was easy. He paid a visit to the British builder. After negotiating a price, he acquired the craft's designs and headed for Italy.

When Hammad designed his master plan for an attack on the North American continent, he had considered a number of alternatives. Attacking by air was one. Attacking on water was another. Since he had no armed forces, attacking on land was not an option. His primary consideration for an air attack was the state of landing strips. In a nation void of commercial air traffic, and ground control as well, he chose to infiltrate via waterway. Once he had decided, he gave the design special care for what he needed. It would have to be a sea craft large enough to carry his assault team deep into enemy territory. The result had been a design to ward off every conceivable attack force. To achieve that, he had to get undetected to the continent. He suspected the shores were still

---

[13] UXV - General characteristics
Type: Multi-role attack ship
Displacement: approx. 1,200 tons
Length: 125 ft
Beam: 20 ft
Propulsion: Twin diesel-powered electric turbine engines
Speed: 52 knots
Complement: 12 marines
Sensors and processing systems: RFID sensors, infrared, radar
Armament: .30 caliber turret mounts front and aft
.50 caliber Browning machine guns bow mounts
155-millimeter cannons
Missile Batteries: Two, automatically guided

protected by a prowling and very effective U.S. submarine fleet. It was this fleet that kept the United States from completely disintegrating and falling into enemy hands.

Taking all factors into consideration, the result was a craft, although scaled down in size from its original blueprint to accommodate rivers and channels, exceeding the speed of every known sea vessel presently plowing the oceans. Not only was it "the fastest ship ever designed," according to the builder, it also contained an awesome array of firepower. Presently, he gauged the fast-approaching naval craft rapidly closing the distance. "Arm your stations," he commanded the crew who had already taken position. They were just as anxious to test the battle strength of this remarkable craft. Confidence and anticipation clearly reflected in their faces. Yusuf had taken the pilot seat, until now occupied by one of the lieutenants.

Hammad planted his body in the commander's chair. His gaze shifted between the view ahead and overhead mounted HUD display, watching the approaching targets being tracked by his navigation. Through the crosshair he could read the incoming telemetry, updating distance and direction. Watching the fast PT boats moving in he muttered, "Technology's come a long way." Then he reached for the controls. "Let's see what you can do."

He knew the UXV packed enough heat to ward off the attackers. On the foredeck, two automatic targeted missile batteries housed both surface-to-air and ship-to-ship missiles. Two .30 caliber turret mounts, one each at the stern and bow, would return enemy fire from any direction. Twin 155-millimeter caliber cannons along each side took care of what would be left of a threat.

Unlike the full-fledged British UXV, his craft was a modified version perfectly designed for speed, stealth, and assault. Seated swiftly in the water, the craft was propelled by twin diesel-powered electric turbine engines. It could reach 52 knots at full power, leaving most other craft in its wake. He gave it an appropriate name painted across each flank: "Eliminator."

Strapped into the command chair, to his right was navigation control, to the left, weapon select. This gave both pilot and commander ready access to the weapons. Hammad reached out to choose ship-to-ship arms. On-board radar already had a lock on the closest PT on approach. "Colors up," he ordered the crew. Up went the black skull and crossbones flag. Although it had been generations before, reading from historical archives, Hammad knew the attackers were not a force to take lightly. He was aware of the destructive fire power from the modified PT.[14]

He pushed the throttle to full speed. The sudden force lifted his craft off the water surface with only the turbo jets, hydrofoils, and rudder submerged. With nose tilted upward following the incredible thrust, the craft, much like in drag racing, shot forward,

---

[14] PT boats were a variety of torpedo-armed fast attack craft used by the United States Navy in World War II to attack larger surface ships. "PT" is the U.S. hull classification symbol for "Patrol Torpedo." PT boats, used in both World Wars, were built using the planing-type hull form developed for racing boats, achieving top speeds of 40 knots. They were designed to strike at larger warships with torpedoes, using relatively high speed to get close, and small size to avoid being spotted and hit by gunfire. Toward the close of the last war, a number of the craft were converted into PT gunboats by stripping them of all original armament except the two twin .50-cal gun mounts, then adding two 40mm and four additional twin .50-cal mounts. PT-109 was a boat last commanded by Lieutenant, junior grade, John F. Kennedy (later President of the United States).

accelerating to maximum speed. The G-forces exerted on the crew was equal to a jet fighter's. Within seconds, Eliminator shot past both PTs on approach. Hammad was playing with his prey. He wanted to have some fun. After all, with fire power at his disposal unknown to the attackers, he could relish the unequal match. Regardless of the PTs' firepower, they were no major threat as long as he kept moving. Water spouts were exploding from the river by the dozens. It reminded him of prior wars he fought but only on land. He was in a new element. He experienced a joy he had not felt in many years. The cat and mouse game, in this case with speeds to match the cheetah and antelope, was on. He became the hunter with the West Point forces the game. The game, once it began, threw more firepower and assault vehicles at him. They came in droves.

Warding off torpedoes and cannon fire, he took Eliminator into impossible jump, twist, and turn maneuvers unattainable by any other craft. Dozens more speed craft and power boats appeared from the grounds of the fort, which he readily identified as the Navy's own SEAL attack craft. He realized what he had entered was a waterborne flotilla like he had never seen. It was a force he would have to respect and avoid in the future. Allah only knew how many more such defense forces he would run up against.

This realization brought his spirits back to earth. Surrounded and chased by dozens of highly maneuverable enemy craft, Hammad decided to end the game. His immediate aim was the PTs. For that, he selected the ship-to-ship arms, the Sea Sparrow Missile. Radar had an automatic lock on the two boats closing in. He pushed the trigger. Both missiles fishtailed inches above the water, leaving steamers of white spray behind homing in on their targets. The impacts lifted the PTs clear out of the water, then disintegrated them in midair. A shower of debris rained down on other craft picking up pursuit.

"Yusuf," he commanded over the sound of the engines, "man the turrets." His lieutenant jumped onto his feet, rushing on deck to command the .50 caliber front-mounted Browning machine gun designated as M3. Hammad took one last visual around the boat's perimeters. "This is it." He took the craft into the tightest spin for which it had been designed. It virtually spun around its own center point providing a 360-degree turn. Securely strapped into their respective gunner seats, Yusuf and his crew unleashed an awesome fire power while rotating around the boat's axis, again and again. On command, simultaneous streams of fire shot outward, cutting everything above the watermark into pieces. PTs and SEAL boats, as quickly as they approached, were cut down, exploded by the shrapnel, only to splash into the chilling cool of the Hudson River until completely obliterated.

It would be the end of the Navy SEAL's once proud attack and rescue fleet on the Eastern Seaboard. The exchange did not last very long. It was over in minutes. Hammad did not linger to assess the damage. He knew the water-logged sailors would be promptly rescued by their own people. He had no plans for obliterating human lives that he confronted on enemy soil. He needed their respective skills and expertise for his own people. His objective was for converting all living soles to Islamic laws as soon as he had his hands on the nation, and the world. With the first attack over, Yusuf joined Hammad in the cabin and off they sped on the Hudson River toward their next destination, Albany, on Lake Erie.

SACRAMENTO

"Status?" President Wilmot demanded from his division secretaries. Like every Monday morning for the past year, the heads of each section gave his or her reports. On today's agenda were budget, crime, and border security. As usual, the heads presented their status on expenditures, revenue, law enforcement, and defense conditions. In spite of the drain of funding exerted on the national treasury, things were moving ahead, slowly but steadily. The new state was getting organized. It had taken many months, but it was shaping up. The former Pacific states California, Oregon, Washington, and Alaska had been merged into one nation, the Western Sector. Also annexed were Idaho, Montana, Wyoming, Nevada, and Utah under the same government. Unfortunately, Arizona, New Mexico, and Texas fell into the hands of the Anarchists. Although Wilmot had tried to prevent it, there had just not been enough military at his disposal. The one thing he could never figure out was why.

Why did the majority of my government and military desert me? Why did the people abandon the leader of the greatest nation on earth? It just did not make sense to him. It was this move that broke the nation apart. *What went wrong?* His advisors, however, the JCS, told a different story. They had the answers. They had the excuses. They had the just reasons for the abandonment. Their blame was on the "previous administration."

They were probably right. He had tried his best to run the nation. Then this thing happened with the EMP. Nobody saw it coming. The enemy snuck in under the radar. "That's what happens," he warned the nation on more than one occasion, "when a nation gets weak." Initially, when he ran for the presidency, he made it his platform. "Consolidate the forces...Bring the military back within the borders...Lock the borders tight...Patrol the borders...Revamp the dated silo system...Move into cyberspace...and more." They had the technology. They had the support from the people. "What went wrong?" It always brought his reasoning back to one denominator: complacency.

They were all at fault. The Senate, the Congress, civil service, commercial contractors, federal, state, city, all had turned complacent as a result of prosperity. Where the focus should have been on the borders, it had shifted to opportunity, money, and power. "We deserved what we got." Wilmot did not blame the individual. He blamed the system and himself. "Could have done better...should have done more...too late now."

And so, life went on. It went on for the government. It went on for the Badlands. It went on for the Anarchists. "Gotta do something about them," Wilmot kept insisting. Problem was, every time he made an attempt to negotiate and work things out, he and his emissaries were shut down. It always ended in quarrels and standoffs. He did not have the resources it took to eliminate the threatening forces. Consequently, to protect the new front, he decided to create a strong defense. What he had at his disposal was something no other nation had, that of HAARP. He would never let that fall into enemy hands. It would mean the nation's end. It would be his end.

"State your case," Wilmot ordered, vying him with distaste. It was the secretary for defense interrupting his thoughts. He was always at odds with him. Abrasive, smug, and selfish, the man was not a team player. It was him that inflamed his stomach ulcer, pushing his health to the limits. He had made several attempts to have him resign, but unsuccessfully. Somebody in the administration must be supporting the man. Consequently, it affected his wellbeing each time he showed up at the meetings.

"You know, Mister President," he insisted once more, as so many times before, "that piece of crap up there in Alaska has been sitting dormant for ages. Never gonna work."

"What you call crap," Wilmot fired back. "May be the only thing that might save your asses someday."

"Gonna be costly," the budget secretary intervened. "Treasury's depleted to an all-time low. Sector won't take on much more financial stress."

"I know all that," Wilmot agreed. "We've got to make some personal sacrifices. Spend less on personal comforts, etc. Do I need to say more?"

"Not a chance," the defense speaker countered. "I'm already living in the dump." *And so*, Wilmot deducted once again dismayed, *nothing will ever change.*

LISA BAUER

It did not take much for Liz to accept Foster's offer. Astronaut training, although it had never occurred to her, gave her the focus she desperately needed. For the past two years, much like most individuals, she had been struggling to make a living. It did not take much for her to make up her mind. She did not even bother calling her dad back to let him know. The following Monday, after securing several rationed fuel coupons to round the lengthy drive through the peninsula, 680 sought followed by 280 north into the city, she arrived at Foster's newly-occupied defense forces headquarters, the Presidio.

Self-assured this early morning, she entered the fort. The secretary directed her to the general's office. "Lisa Bauer." He beamed. "Good to see you. Glad you accepted my offer."

It was a welcome she had not expected. It put her immediately at ease. She was offered coffee, a tray of sweets, and even a "Cigar?" that she readily declined with a smile. "My only vice," he proclaimed. Although cigars had been unpopular for decades, the thick layers of smoke he puffed out did not bother her much. It reminded her on a time long past when Dad had puffed one of these occasionally. He came right to the point. "Guess you wondered," he opened the dialogue, "why you?"

"The thought had occurred."

"I need somebody trustworthy. Need a strong-minded woman. Don't put much trust in men anymore...always have an agenda." He took another puff on the cigar. "Smoke bother you?"

"Not at all."

"I've known your dad for ages. Your sister worked for me. By the way," he asked, "how is Tracy?"

"With Dad—Castle Rock." Liz knew about the working relation Tracy had with the general. Rumors had it there was more to it. Whether it was a fatherly instinct or infatuation by the general, there was talk. With Tracy, it was strictly career. She believed her sister. They had always been close and truthful with each other. Foster's face turned serious. "Since you accept the offer," he said, "let me fill you in on the mission. It's the most important one ever launched." Without getting into specific aspects, he briefly explained the when, the where, and why it was such an important mission.

"Yeah," Liz eagerly accepted the general's official explanation for the planned mission. "But," she questioned. "You didn't say anything about the purpose for your mission."

"That my dear," he patronized in a fatherly manner. "Is highly classified."

"Being part of the crew," she objected. "Don't you think I deserve to know? Should know?"

"In due time," he stalled. It ended the somewhat abrupt, but startling introduction.

It was not that long ago when space travel with the former United States had come to an end. If it had not been for the end of the Space Shuttle program, the attack on the nation would have ended the program anyway. All efforts predominantly operated and managed by the military, now had shifted to the private sector. The commercial zones from foreign nations picked up the programs. It had only been recently that the Americans, though secretly, joined the space effort once more. Although NASA officially had been rendered ineffective years ago, due to urging from the United Nations, it had accepted the tender as support unit to other nation's space endeavors.

Currently, astronauts were only trained to fly in the Soyuz launched from Russia. After the U.S. shuttle was retired, Soyuz was the only mode of transport to the International Space Station with training conducted at the Russian Space Agency, Star City. This involved assembly of orbit operations, extravehicular activities (EVA), robotics operations using remote manipulators, experimental operations, and ISS maintenance tasks. It was essential for astronauts to have an in-depth knowledge of ISS and its subsystems as well as operational characteristics, mission requirements, and objectives, in support of experiments on their assigned missions. The typical mission aboard the ISS normally lasted from three to six months and took about two to three years of specific training. It would give Foster and his team of scientists, engineers, and contractors enough time to design, fabricate, and integrate the necessary modification for his plan. What he did not, and could not reveal to Liz at this time was the super-secret mission he had planned. For that, he wasn't even sure it'd work. What it entailed was using HAARP, rather than it being an experimental atmospheric research facility exploring the full spectrum of radio and microwave capabilities in space, as it stood now, as a new weapon only tested on paper and laboratory environments. It would be a pioneering project of monumental proportions if he could get it to work as promised by the defense sector's planners. If successful it could mean lasting peace for everyone on the globe, if in the right hands, Foster's hands.

Today, Liz was months into the training program. "That's it," the command sounded over the headset, "you can breathe normal." Almost at the brink of passing out, another grueling day for Liz ended at Vandenberg. Under the cloak of secrecy, the once prolific launch center had recently been revived to conduct initial astronaut training. It involved indoctrination into the space program, getting the body in top shape, and preparing for space walks. For that, the facility offered a variety of chambers such as underwater tanks to experience weightlessness, centrifuges to test the physique, and more grueling devices necessary for space travel. Liz was exposed to motion sickness, orthostatic intolerance, and cardiovascular behavior during launch and reentry conditions. Without a space program on American soil, much of the mission training was performed elsewhere. For that, Liz would travel to Europe and Russia.

Space affects might sound straightforward to the non-indoctrinated, but in reality, each astronaut or cosmonaut had to be trained in every aspect of space flight, whether operations or technology. For that, training was conducted at the Columbus module training mockup located at the European Astronaut Center in Cologne, Germany.

Training was intense day and night. There had been days she regretted getting into the space program. In addition to operational functions, drilled into her was every conceivable engineering aspect of the spacecraft including propulsion, thermal control, life support systems, orbital mechanics, scientific experimentation, earth observation, astronomy, and more. It was not only one system she had to become an expert on. There were many.[15]

Whether it was a service module, critical life support facility, or emergency evacuation and exiting station, Liz had to become familiar with every aspect of functionality and operation whether domestic or foreign made. Everything was thrown at her from failure of a critical life support system, capsule depressurization, electronic failure, fire, to other life-threatening events. In addition, there was the need to train for hazardous events.

"What about weapons?" It was a legitimate concern with the state the world was in.

"Not part of the mission," the mission commander explained. The no-weapon policy was upheld. If there was no weapon accessible to the crews, fights breaking out would not cause damages to the modules. She was told, "It's a peaceful endeavor, after all."

Because of dad's rigorous martial arts training, Liz always thought she could hold her own in face-to-face combat. The assurance of a no-weapon policy put her concerns at ease. Soon, it would be her turn to be launched into space. Presently, she had to finish training at Vandenberg. Then, it would be off to Europe for advanced mission training. The space launch was given a tentative schedule, fortunately for her still months ahead. For now, she could still enjoy weekends spent with mom and her kids.

---

[15] Current ISS configuration:
Columbus—European payload and research facility.
Destiny—American research lab.
Harmony—providing electrical power and electronic data systems.
Pirs and Poisk—Russian docking modules.
Quest—Combined airlock to exit into space.
Tranquility—American made life support system for recycling wastewater and oxygen.
Unity—American built support station.
Zarya—Russian's functional cargo block.
Zvezda—Russian service module.
Recently added service modules: Kibo, Cupola, and Rassvet from Japan, Europe, and Russia, respectively.

ISS

As usual during regular scheduled working days, presently there were three cosmonauts on duty to perform the daily tasks. Although many were rudimentary, each represented a scientific research project, planetary or stellar observation, or just plain routine maintenance chores. With one half of the crew on duty, the second normally enjoyed a break. Today, however, the schedule called for all-hands. It was a special day. The arrival of a space flight was expected. It always caused a rare and deserving diversion to the crews. Following a docking, there would be greetings exchanged, presents handed out, and stories related from a number of cultures. Today's international space pool was comprised of a number of nations such as Russia, Canada, Europe, Italy, and Japan.

Life on the ISS had been going on routinely for many decades now with support from various space agencies. Scientific research was making great strides toward the possibility of living in space. It might yet take another decade or two, but explorations to Earth's planetary system would gradually be launched. After the successful moon landings by the pioneering astronauts and cosmonauts, setting foot on Mars was already within reach, perhaps in the Russian's lifetime.

Sergei Budenko and the crew, still under military command and control, were doing their part to assure the safety of future manned space explorations. Rumors were already circulating about shifting space explorations to the private sector. For the time being, however, commercial flights were still rare. They were mostly reserved for the rich and whoever had the money to spend on the extravagant grandeur to experience weightlessness for a brief, but memorable, thrill of a lifetime.

Many months had passed since the last Russian docking. Sergei Budenko had been more and more impatient as the months went by. Already extended several times to the confines of the space platform, due to budget shortfalls, he was anxious to get back to earth. The frustration became obvious not only to Yuri Chenkov, his shift relief, but the other members on the team as well. He became impossible to deal with. Short-fused and bad tempered most of the time, his comrades learned to stay away from personal contact with him as much as possible.

But that suited Budenko fine. It meant personal isolation. Though teamwork was always a critical factor in the perils of space, his provoking attitude gave him the space and privacy he needed for his agenda. It was an agenda only he and a few others on the ground knew about.

Now, almost daily, he would mutter, "Where's that dammed call." In the hidden recesses of his mind, he kept his hopes up for the day to arrive soon. He would not return to earth until his special mission was over. Those were the orders. The secret instructions he received from sources only he knew, all responsibilities had been placed into his hands.

Budenko had every right to be upset. He was overdue by many months for replacement. What he did not know where the reasons for the delays. Once again, he was floating from panel to panel. Crews learned quickly the easiest means to propel the body around the capsules. Not feeling gravity was one thing he appreciated. What effect it had on the body in the long term, he would deal with later.

He heard it at the same time as the other crew members presently on duty. It was the mechanical announcement generated by computers. "Alert…Alert…Alert…Oxygen leak." The alarms had gone off. It was not the first time this had happened. Leaks sometimes occurred during interlock transfers. But an alarm without a visible cause could be serious. His hand fumbled for the talk button on the headset. "I'm on it," he shouted. The master control indicators were flashing wildly. Because of the triple backup systems onboard, an alert usually triggered more than just one system. Budenko propelled his body from one space to the next. He was frantically searching for the leak. Other members on the crew fell in with the search.

Crammed into service module Zvezda, the crew had a backup option in the form of bottled oxygen and solid fuel oxygen canisters, a chemical oxygen generator system. It might appear complex when viewed for the first time, but it was a relatively simple system. Carbon dioxide, as well as other byproducts of human metabolism, such as methane from the intestines and ammonia from sweat, was removed from the air and body by activated charcoal filters. Other segments to the system were redundant functions.

Budenko inspected the immediate space around him. He was looking for water droplets or air bubbles floating in space. There were none. "Leak's hidden," was his immediate thought. Methodically, his eyes darted between connections, pipes, and tanks. One showed low pressure. "Got it," he voiced into the headset. Other crew members floating close by bumped into each other while they watched. Since space was limited, there was only room for one cosmonaut to work. Someone most likely had bumped against the primary tank and loosened an interconnecting seal. It took only a simple adjustment with the appropriate tool, attached to the tank, to tighten the seal ring. This time, the problem was an easy one. Others in the past had not been that simple. And it wouldn't be the last time. For now, the emergency was over.

As sudden as the alarms were triggered, causing immediate concerns to all onboard, as quickly it was over, but not for the individual. Heart rates, oxygen consumptions, and adrenalines were racing. It could take an hour or more for vital functions to return to normal. Regardless of the results, sometimes they were necessary, if only to keep the crews proficient.

CASTLE ROCK

Alex, presently in the company of Brian, was busy with monitoring the outside world at his command and control center deep inside the Castle. "Where's time gone?" Alex sighed. It seemed like a lifetime ago when he was assigned to DARPA, heading up development projects. He could vividly recall some of the innovative projects undertaken by the government. It all began with the development of electronic computers in the 1950s. But that was before his time. He did not get involved until later with point-to-point communication between mainframe computers and terminals, message distribution followed by packet switching, the modern-day Internet. Those were the days with Mark I, Merit Network, Telnet, AUTODIN I[16], and II, and eventually ARPANET,[17] the precursor for the modern-day Internet. At first, developed in the early 60s, highly classified networks to levels "Above Top Secrete,"[18] it was connecting the Pentagon with the White House, military command and control systems, Looking Glass,[19] overseas embassies, war

———————————

[16] The Automatic Digital Network (AUTODIN), conceived in 1962 by DARPA, took six years to design, develop and manufacture, and was implemented beginning in 1968 worldwide. It supported the DOD's communications needs for thirty years. Was superseded by the Defense Network System (DNS), an all digitally, remotely controlled information system in the late 90s. Administrated and managed from approx. thirty Automatic Switching Centers (ASC) interconnected and staged within the U.S. theater and its global allies, it provided the U. S. Navy, Army, Air Force, Coast Guard, NATO, other government agencies and industrial contractors with a worldwide, high-speed, automatic, electronic, data communications system through 24 hour operation. The system was driven by major special purpose computers (Mainframe) and their peripheral devices (front-end interface to communication and satellite devices), for on-line and off-line processing of communications data and other forms of digital data for AUTODIN.

[17] The Advanced Research Projects Agency Network (ARPANET) was an early packet switching network and the first network to implement the protocol suite TCP/IP. Both technologies, AUTODIN and TCP/IP became the technical foundation of the Internet. ARPANET was initially funded by the Advanced Research Projects Agency (ARPA, later became Defense Advanced Research Projects Agency (DARPA)) of the United States Department of Defense.

Packet switching was based on concepts and designs by Americans Leonard Kleinrock and Paul Baran, British scientist Donald Davies and Lawrence Roberts of the Lincoln Laboratory. The TCP/IP communication protocols were developed for ARPANET by computer scientists Robert Kahn and Vint Cerf.

[18] "Above Top Secret," is a misnomer created by the non-indoctrinated individual and perhaps somewhat mystical and overzealous intrigue projected by the public. In actuality, five levels of security classifications prevail: 1. PRIORITY; 2. NOFORN (no foreign individual allowed access); 3. CONFIDENTIAL; 4. SECRET; 5. TOP SECRET. "Above Top Secret" alludes to special Access clearances specifically authorized by an agency, organization, or classified project. There are numerous such special access requirements ranging from ATOMAL (Atomic), COMSEC, COSMIC, CRYPTO, EAP, ESI, NATO, SCI, SPECAT, SIOP, ULTRA among others more obscure and not so obscure. Each is compartmentalized to a specific project or mission with members scaled to the minimum number for project effort and mission requirement to maintain strict security.

[19] Operation Looking Glass was the code name for an airborne command center operated by the United States air force. It provides command and control of U.S. nuclear forces in the event that ground-based command centers were destroyed or otherwise rendered inoperable. In such an event, the general officer serving as the Airborne Emergency Action Officer on Looking Glass assumed by the authority of the National Command Authorities and would command execution of nuclear attacks. The AEAO was supported by a battle staff of approximately 20 people, with another dozen responsible for the operation of the aircraft systems.

fronts of Vietnam and Korea, and more importantly, Intel outposts in and around the globe. Ten years later, in the early 70s, ARPANET connected research laboratories with government institutions and major universities. Large businesses such as Bell, Westinghouse, and IBM were quick to follow. Everybody in the nation wanted to be connected, especially when the PC, Windows 95, and Microsoft NT came about. And the results, the modern-day Internet was born in the 80s. Although the Internet shaped the future world in communication, it was not the only project developed by DARPA. There were many more. Highly classified some eventually made it to industries such as space technology; ballistic missile defense and nuclear test detection; command, control, and communications; tactical armor and anti-armor programs; infrared sensing for space-based surveillance; laser technology, space-based missile defense; antisubmarine warfare; cruise missile; stealth aircraft; drones, armed and unarmed; robotics; microcircuits; medical instruments; and many more in future weapons and innovative technology designs.

"What teamwork that was," Alex Bauer proudly recalled. "Walking among the top brains in the nation." It was a time when people still respected the government for what it stood for: solid establishment, source of innovation, and trust. It was trust that allowed the emergence of programs, especially the classified ones. There was one such program that made the cut, the High-frequency Active Aurora Research Program, better known as HAARP. It began innocently enough as a communication and surveillance based project but essentially, like many of this type of program, through technology evolution and military demand, grew into a potential WMD.

"It's nobody's fault," Brian responded. "You can't keep a well-developed brain from conjuring up new ideas." He had been listening to one of Alex's griping sessions but didn't mind since his own ideas were along the same line of thought.

"I know. Life would be pretty boring without progress." At times, he thought the world may have been better off without the invention of the wheel. But then, we would still be living in caves.

"Heard from Tracy this morning? I'm worried."

Alex tried to calm him. "Brooks is with her." There was no real concern with him by her side. As a matter of fact, she was protecting him, Alex felt at times, especially since she'd gone through so much change. At least, she was an equal to him. It took him quite some time to make peace with himself about that. At first, he did not like the changes. But, after she laid out her reasoning, he understood. "This is no world in which to raise children."

"Say something?" Brian heard words but couldn't make them out.

"Nothing…just thinking." Alex felt for his buddy. *Without a job, without a sense of direction, spent his entire career on the forefront in technology—what's left for the guy?* He had no solution for him or for his daughter. He was just glad he could give him shelter. He'd been thinking about how to tap into his buddy's brain. After all, Brian was one of the nation's top software designers. But with the collapse of NSA and space science, there was not even a reason for him to get up in the morning. "Get you a beer?" Alex strode over to the refrigerator. He wanted to talk. He wanted to share an idea that had been germinating in his mind. It always helped to talk it out with someone. Alcohol was a sound stimulant for it.

"Okay." Brian seemed not himself these days. For most part, he'd been relying on Tracy to make decisions. But with her out, he felt at a loss in an environment that was not his own.

"I wanna share something." He tossed him the can.

"What?" It seemed to have piqued Brian's interest.

"Need to know the status on the MILSATs.[20] Orbits, transmit times, frequency, access codes, the whole works."

"You know," Brian countered, "that's classified."

"Don't give me that crap," Alex shot back. "Time's changed—you damned well know."

"Testy this morning," he said. "Aren't we?"

"Sorry. Didn't mean it. Thought you were on my side."

"But I am." Brian just brought up a caution sign. It was more of a reminder than anything else. He was well aware of the current situation the nation was in. But in the back of his mind he'd been hoping things would go back on track like before the strike. "Let's hear it."

"From what I read on the monitors," Alex started, "nobody seems in control of satellites. Not the NSA, not the military, and sure as hell not the government. Why not take control before the enemy or another nation does?"

"Explain."

"You get me inside and I'll do the rest."

"You mean," Brian pondered, "hijack the whole damned lot?"

"You've got it."

"You nuts?"

"Maybe so. But think about it." Alex allowed a minute to let his plan sink in. "Who'd be better qualified?"

"You may be right. Your skills, the equipment in the basement, the connection with NORAD, the antenna farm—you…we could own the world."

"Now you get it."

"I'm in," Brian nodded with a glimmer of enthusiasm Alex hadn't seen in years.

"There's still hope," Alex muttered.

"What?" Brian shot him quizzing glance.

"Nothing."

"You said something."

"Never mind. Let's get to work. Wasted too much time already."

"Be right back." Brian stepped out. He reappeared minutes later with a laptop clutched under his arm. He gently blew a layer of dust off the cover and slid the portable onto the desk. "Haven't used the damned thing in years."

"Here." Alex flung a sketch he'd prepared onto the desk next to the laptop.

---

[20] MILSAT – Military Satellite. This sophisticated, and hardened communications system provides the United States Department of Defense survivable, global, secure, protected, and jam-resistant communications for high priority military ground, sea, and air assets.

Shaking his head, Brian viewed it. "Must have stayed up nights to come up with this."

Alex shot him a smug glance. "Future form of communications." He picked off the pertinent points on the draft and discussed his theory. "Here," he indicated. "Orbits come around every ninety minutes, give and take. I need a continuous grid to sustain the global picture. That's where you come in."

Brian digested the words while assessing the plan. "I can do this." After several minutes of battery charge, the laptop had enough power to load the default application. It brought a strange grin onto Brian's face. "Hello. Haven't seen you in years," he muttered at the portable screen. Staring at them was the once so-sophisticated, highly classified NSA homepage in all its glorious colors. "Coming home, baby," he muttered.

Alex was touched to see his buddy back in action. Both sat up late into the night to get the plan into action. First, there were the hidden ports and scrambled passwords Brian had initiated years ago. He had a tough time remembering all. Through trial-by-error, it finally gained him access to the satellite units.

"Got it!" he exclaimed hours later, rubbing away the soreness from his fingers.

"What?" Alex was anxious to hear.

"I'm in." Gained access to the highly classified and sophisticated database backend, he could manipulate the targeting, tracking, and imaging application software to downlink data to the Castle's receiver equipment. Once they identified the specific frequencies Alex needed, it would be simple to retransmit data and images back over the Cheyenne Mountain antenna farm. It took two days to identify, manipulate, and finalize all parameters for Alex and Brian to have command and control not only over the military's satellite communications, but, more importantly, the ASATs, a major accomplishment.

"That's it," Brian proudly announced after he'd programmed the last unit in the global satellite cluster. "All we need now," he kicked back to let the enormity sink in, "is to test it. But for that we need Tracy." He then realized Alex's full scheme. It was for linking up Tracy with the global grid. *What a genius,* he thought. It never ceased to amaze him, the boundless capability of Alex. *No wonder,* he thought, *Foster let him do the things he did.* It had always puzzled him how much his buddy got away with, working with the Pentagon.

Alex didn't hear him. He was deep in his thoughts. "Need codes," he finally muttered.

"What?"

"Codes. Codes for everybody. Code names for everything. Wanna keep it covert—only us."

"I can program it in," Brian suggested. After he understood the purpose, he was in complete agreement. That part he liked. It gave them deniability if their plot was ever revealed. His hands were poised over the keyboard ready to enter. "Suggestions?"

"Take this down," Alex initiated.

LOS ALAMOS

Both sat at an outdoor picnic table enjoying the warmth of early summer discussing an uncertain future. Tracy had her ideas, Brooks his. With implants successful and operational, it still had to be tested for remote over-the-horizon functions. For that, they needed satellite input Brian had promised them days ago. For the time being, they were both on hold enjoying the valley below viewed from the hilltop. Tracy almost went into shock. At first, she punched him in the chest several times and slapped his face, yelling, "Bastard!" In one reflex action, she covered both ears. But the sound did not stop. It came from within her brain. Watching his surprised reaction, her fingers flew to the nape of her neck. In one quick snap of the fingers she shut the receiver off. Shaking her head, she rubbed both temples.

"What?" Scott yelled. He was still perplexed at her sudden outburst.

"You hear it?"

"Hear what?"

"Stinger…somebody yelled Stinger."

"You're hallucinating."

"Not even!" Tracy was sure the sound came over the air. Where the ether waves had been silent for years, suddenly there was sound, cohesive sound. Still shaken, her fingers hesitantly reached for the nape of her neck. With the tip of her index finger she gently pushed down. There was a slight click, then white noise ever so slightly. The implant was live. Minutes later she flinched again. But this time she was prepared. "Stinger, Black Knight, come in." It was a clearly familiar voice. This time she responded. "Dad?"

"Roger," the distant voice confirmed. "Just testing." There was silence once more.

At the other end Alex was euphoric. "It works," he yelled at Brian nearby. They both heard Tracy's response over the speaker. Brian seemed overjoyed. He had not heard the sound of her voice for weeks. "Tell her," he said to Alex, "to come back."

Alex ignored him for the moment. It would have to wait. For now, he needed to test the link. "You all right?"

"Fine," Tracy came back. "But next time," she chided, "give me heads up first."

"Sorry," Alex replied. "Where's Brooks?"

"Wanna talk to him? He's right here."

"Tune in on 33 GHz."

"What's with the Black Knight?"

"His call sign."

"Got it—33 Gigs. Black Knight." She cast Brooks a smug look. "You're on."

Scott pushed the micro button in the back of his ear. Another push and images appeared on the back of both retinas. Distorted at first, but seconds later they synced up. He could not believe his eyes. "What a view." He could see the world from above. It was from a bird's-eye view, the satellites'. He could make out the terrain he stood on as it panned into view. "Fabulous," he marveled. Only the slightest turn of his head would bring an immediate adjustment to the terrain ahead. "Just like a heads-up display," he muttered.

"Exactly like HUD," the voice responded. Alex had his focus on the monitor. He could follow each and every motion Scott's head made in the distance. "Put Tracy on," he ordered.

Scott gestured at her. "Your dad." She had been observing Brooks' interaction with the set. Apparently, Dad was giving instructions.

"Stinger," she responded after turning her set back on. Immediately, colorful images panned into view. It seemed like she was soaring high above. The view was spectacular. Every time she moved, the images followed. With each motion of her head the ground panned back and forth in complete synchronization. What she saw ahead and below was more than she had ever expected. It was a new world. It was a marvelous world. It very much reminded her of the diving experience in the Bahamas. The view was similar but with much more clarity. Not only that, she could adjust for distance. With a slight push on the micro switch, she could telescope the ground in and out. Gazing into the distance, she could read street signs miles ahead. "Marvelous," she gasped. "You did it."

"Like it?" Her dad's voice sounded pleased.

"Like it—love it," she echoed.

"There's more," Alex hinted. "Need you back here."

"Why?"

"Work out the strategy."

"Understood," she said. "Tomorrow…Over and out."

"No need for protocol," Alex replied. "Just switch the set off."

She followed his instruction. The world turned silent once more. Broadly grinning at Brooks, she said, "We'll conquer the world." Taking quick strides, she nodded at him.

Brooks followed. "What?"

"Laboratory."

Tracy led the way to track down Spencer. She had him paged on the intercom. It did not take long for him to show. "What've you got?"

"Implant's alive," she informed him. "Want a demo?"

"Let's see," he demanded gearing up the lab monitors. After adjusting some dials on the spectrum analyzer, he found the satellite link at 30 gigs. "Wow," was all he could mutter. He was speechless. "Hey" he called his lab team over. "Look at this." It had been several years since any had seen the spectacular views from above, the blue planet in motion. Depending on the zoom level of the satellite lenses, the focus was adjustable for near and far. "We've got eyes again," his principle scientist exclaimed. "What's next," Spencer directed at Tracy.

"Need a weapon."

"Whatcha got in mind?" He seemed perplexed at her request, but also knew how eccentric or, rather, extreme the woman could behave. After weeks in close association he had learned to accept it.

"Something new—something extraordinary—something powerful."

After some consideration, he said, "I think I know what you need. Follow me." Using the elevator, he led her and Brooks to an underground vault secured by heavy steel gates. Once inside, he gestured at the back of the vault. There, protected behind bulletproof glass, were shelves containing an assortment of weapons. Alongside handguns and automatic firearms her view struck what seemed to be things right out of science fiction. There were many such objects.

He reached for and deliberately opened one case in particular labeled, Top Secret. Within the oblong-shaped case an embedded object was embraced by a foamy contour. Handing her the weapon, Spencer prompted, "What you're looking for? Think you can handle it?"

"Whoa!" It was not every day Tracy was stunned. Between the palms of her hands, Spencer had dropped an object slightly resembling an automatic firearm. What made this one different from everything she had handled in the past was its weight and shape. It could not have weighed more than five pounds. Tracy caressed the contours of the weapon. Her fingers probed the shaped design. She could feel the coolness of the steel merge into her hands then traverse up and down the body. They became one, the body of flesh and the body of steel. A chill shot through her spine, making her shudder. It showed in her face.

"Like it?" It was a rhetorical question. Spencer could see her reaction. Her eyes had taken on a veil of darkness he had never seen in a person. It made him shiver. There was fury projected from her eyes, much like the weapon clutched in her hands. If there was ever a perfect match created between human and machine, this was it. He knew she'd found her savior.

Tracy cradled the firearm then weighed its design. She pulled it from the hip position and twirled it around the grip, much like gunslingers in the old western films. She was overcome with emotion. "What's it shoot?" she finally managed to say.

"Smart bullets."

"Huh?"

"Bullets smart enough to seek out the target." He gave her time to let the words sink in. "See the laser mount? It's what keeps the projectiles on target."

"This thing loaded?"

"Follow me," he gestured. They were headed for an underground shooting range nearby. "Let's find out." No sooner had he spoken then she pulled the trigger and let go a salvo against the backstop of the shooting range. Spencer's eyes followed the stream of bullets hurled in that direction. To his amazement, she had cut a perfect X-shaped image into the target. There was only a slight reaction reflected on her face. Spencer expected more. Most individuals to whom he demonstrated the weapon were startled. Not her. She remained unruffled. As he watched this woman in action, he thought, *I don't ever want to cross her.*

"Have it ready," Tracy commanded. "I'm moving out in the morning."

The following day, at dawn, Tracy boarded the Cobra and headed back home. There was work to be done. Although she kept the pending mission she was about to embark on to herself, there were details to hammer out with communication, support, and logistics with the home base, the Castle.

Not yet having a clear focus on a future, Brooks had remained behind. With his companion ready to depart for wherever plan she had, Scott suddenly felt himself being deserted. What he never thought possible was a feeling he had not experienced for a long time. He had grown fund of Tracy. As perplexing as it seemed, from the harsh treatment he received from her, he felt emotion. It was a new experience, emotions pulling him towards her. It fogged up his mind. It confused him. It affected his logical thinking. *What's in it for me* came to his mind. *What's the next step? Where do I fit in?*

For the first time in his life, he had no clear vision for his next step. To organize his thoughts logically, he jumped from his bed, got dressed, and headed for the lab. With her gone, he needed a new direction on life. He needed to assess his accomplishments. Striding along the halls his first stop was the security center. Security staff was actively watching the facility's perimeter monitors. It was his doing, his accomplishment. *What's left for me?* It was then when he realized his job here was done. He needed a new purpose in personal life, as well as in career.

He further questioned his presence. *If I stay, I'm secure. If I leave, I'm facing trouble.* At the end, he decided to leave. The determinant factor, he analyzed was adventure, and as of lately, a chance to see Tracy again. "Hell," he mused, "might even team up with her." It resolved his personal crisis. It determined his future. He was off for new adventures.

BADLANDS

"This is it," Rusty Norton said. As commander-in-chief and citizen elect for the Patriots, he made the final announcement to the tightly-formed cluster of lieutenants packed into the assembly room. For weeks already, ever since the return of Brodie Elliott's scouting party to the south, congressional debates had been prolific. Following his report on the Anarchists, with their renegade leader Derek Wallace controlling the region south of Route 66, it was decided to deal with that faction at a later date. As usually, gathered today were the battalion heads and group leaders from the ranks of the task forces, Fort Knox, KY. Progress, for coming up with a solution had been slow. Although the basic principles for a new constitution had been chiseled out, agreed on, and voted for and documented, specific articles were difficult to garner agreement on. The final vote still had to be cast by the citizens. Today was the day for the first vote. Already, a number of candidates had thrown their names into the political hat. "Some things never change," he muttered into the upcoming event of elections. Up to now, he had been able to curtail politics under his military command. But he knew those days were numbered. Whether he liked it or not, for better or for worse, he had to submit the nation under political ruling or fear for the eventual outcome, dictatorship. It was politics all over again. He hated it. But there was no option. No matter who'd be in command, it was only a matter of time before people demanded a change. *And so,* he thought with dismay, *the cycle begins again.*

To forge a new constitution had proved much more difficult than anticipated. What made it so difficult was deciding on how much to remove and how much to maintain from the original document. Foster finally stepped in. "Axe out all amendments."

It was as simple as that. From then on, things progressed rapidly. The basic elements for the new constitution were in place. It worked for the administration; it should work for the people. Refinements still had to be made, but, as once before, they would be included as necessary. The trick was to keep amendments defined as simple as possible. For that, the unified pledge was "The New Republic will see to that." The spread for such a promise could have wide range implications. But, based on the common census by the people, discipline was first on the agenda.

Henry "Hank" Foster, as many times before, held the solution. Head of the former Department of Defense, the Pentagon, he always looked at the common picture element first then selected the fundamentals necessary for a sound decision. Today, the accord was to decide on the final borders. Western, southern, and eastern sectors had been pretty much defined. The northern sector was still up to debate. Until that was resolved, the tactical forces were placed on hold. Ground forces, as patient and as difficult they had been, were battle ready. Once word was propagated about a pending mission, their enthusiasm could not be restrained. Tomorrow would be it.

The following day, the forces moved out, one by one. It was promised that simplicity would be maintained throughout every sector of the new front. At this time, it was only applicable to terrain since there was no air force. There were no naval forces either. Whatever happened to the submarine fleet was anybody's guess. It had remained silence ever since the EMP strike. All in all, the consolidated services were comprised of the 1st

Armored Division—close to 10,000 subjects sectioned into two brigades: Infantry Regiment and Tactical Assault Regiment. Each regiment was sectioned further into battalions, companies, squadrons, platoons, and patrols from leaders with Patriot rankings including Major General, Brigadier General, Colonel, Captain, Lieutenant, and Sergeants.

Moving out first thing in the morning with Rusty Norton leading all forces, and Brodie Elliott in command of the 1st Armored Division, was the Tactical Assault Regiment. It entailed light armored vehicles and Signal Corps with Armored Regiment and Corps of Engineers bringing up the rear. It was a formidable force with the leaders standing by to watch. Each would catch up within the hour to carry on their respective commands. Headed north for the moment, the forces planned to intersect with I-64 at Louisville, head west to St. Louis, then connect with I-70 on to Kansas City. At the pace, the regiment was moving forward, the first stop for the day would be St. Louis.

Advanced patrols had already alarmed the city's inhabitants about the movement. Provisions were hastily made to put up tents near the Mississippi River, along the route I-270 bypass. By nightfall, the entire town showed up to get a glimpse at the Patriots. Waving a newly designed flag, many volunteered to join on the spot. It held a new epoch for the nation. It was a flag appropriate to the new nation. It contained new colors many will fight for and many will die for, in the process of carrying and defending it. Everybody fight worthy was recruited. Word spread ahead: Join the "March of the Patriots." Food for services was the pledge. This promise alone was a God-given miracle to a starving population. Backed by a newly-defined constitution, it would be the first step toward a structured society.

The march had a two-fold purpose. It entailed recruiting soldiers but, more importantly, it would define the borders for the patriotic nation. At this point, only slight resistance was anticipated. The leaders were confident with that since no major conflicts had been experienced in the central plains.

Days later Kansas City was left in the march's wake. Next stop were cities and towns scattered along the Missouri River. More recruits joined up. The party eventually reached Denver, the western destination bordering the Rockies. Headquarters for this segment was established at the former Rocky Mountain Arsenal. Water was provided from the Derby Lakes nearby. From here, scouts were dispatched in several directions. One such scouting party eventually reached Castle Rock, some 30 miles to the south.

CASTLE ROCK

It was mid-morning. "Let me get that," Alex said. "You keep watch." They had been watching the monitors, which were, at the moment, trained on the highway a quarter mile out. When Alex did the security upgrade on the Castle, he had installed an elaborate surveillance system. It gave coverage of the access road, as well as up and down the hilly slopes. He had the foresight with the way things had turned out in the nation. Built into the mountain, the Castle was not readily visible from the road or casual passersby. One had to stumble onto the premises, climbing or descending the hillside to come across the Bauer abode. The one thing that possibly gave a fix on the fortress would be the reflection from the sizable panoramic window facing south. Alex knew the vulnerability but took a chance when he built it. He just could not live without visual access to the grandeur of the Rockies.

Alex and Brian, watching the distant traffic, surmised today was one such occasion of compromise since the convoy had turned on his access road. The reflection had been spotted by the patrol headed south on I-25. They identified the approaching party as troop carrier flanked by two Humvee light armored utility vehicles. Arriving at the driveway, out jumped a commander followed closely by his immediate staff Alex thought he recognized from an earlier encounter.

"Well, well," Alex greeted the party. "If it isn't the Badlands—friend or foe?"

"I remember you well," Brodie Elliott stated. "Man with the Cobra. Friend, I hope."

"Then," Alex gestured, "step up. What brings you back to this neck of the woods?"

"Got food? Sure could use a decent meal."

"Take a load off. Have a seat."

"Brian?" Alex gestured at his buddy at the kitchen. The visitors, a squad of lieutenants according to their insignia, seemingly relaxed at the invitation. Their welcome, armed and combat ready, was not always embraced with friendliness. These days, with the nation in disarray, there was always an element of distrust. Up to this point the convoy had encountered mostly friendly contacts, especially with the promise of food distribution. But, from what Brodie could make out, that was not the case here. The man of the house seemed to have his affairs in order with defense, supplies, and sustainability. He was thoroughly impressed with the host and the Castle once shown around the premises. Brian had prepared and served brunch then joined in the talks.

"How long you planning to stay around?" Alex inquired.

Gulping down the food, Brodie responded, "As long as it takes."

"Take what?"

"Stake out territory." He seemed to savor the breakfast Brian had served.

"The way I see it," Alex opened the negotiations, "you're on my land. And..." he was drawing specifics, "what is your land?"

Brodie, wiping his mouth clean on his shirt sleeve, pulled a well-worn chart from his back pocket. He pushed the dish aside and pointed out a specific region on the map. "Here," with an outstretched finger, he waved across what was identified as *Central Plains,* "Rockies in the west, Mississippi to the east, Great Lakes up north, and I-40 in the south. Those are the parameters."

"Why not take it all?" Alex felt anger.

It was a facetious challenge but Elliott ignored the dare. He gave his rational answer. "Outside of perimeters," he went on. "Too little resources. Places of interests don't matter. Not to me. My interests are the central corn fields with Kansas, Nebraska, and Iowa. Water supplied up north, Minnesota, Wisconsin, and Michigan…get my drift?"

"Don't want much," Alex replied, "do you?" He watched Brodie and his lieutenants for their reactions. He did not want any surprises like a forced takeover. So far, they seemed to be relaxed. "Tell you what," he said. "You take what you want. But I must warn you," he emphasized once again, "the Castle's off limit, to you and to everybody else. That's my condition."

"We'll see about that," Elliott replied. He had been watching the host. Apparently, he had pushed his limits. From here on it would only turn nasty if he pressed further. He did not necessarily want that. Not with this man. He had heard about Bauer's achievements. He was well aware of his connections with the Pentagon, with Foster. But he did have to make his point, especially when territory was at stake. Whether Bauer liked it or not, this region was his. Castle or not, it would be the perfect place to make his headquarters. "Expect my men by morning." Elliott shot a glance at his companions, stood up, and, with steadfast strides, headed for the exit. "Thanks for the meal."

Brian and Alex watched the party drive off, headed back north. Alex did not like this turn of events. Unless things changed drastically for the better, tomorrow would be the start of trouble. "What's the plan?" Brian was highly concerned. He also knew Alex would not put himself into a compromising position. He knew his buddy too well. He had to have a plan.

"Get hold of Tracy."

There it is, Brian thought, greatly relieved, *the solution.* Although he did not know what Alex specifically had in mind, the next day would reveal his plan. They headed for the command room to make contact with the lab to the south. "Stinger," the call went into the ether.

DENVER

Daylight was just rising over the eastern plains of Kansas. Judging by the cloudless sky Norton could tell, "It's gonna be a great day." The Mountain Mobile command base was already busy with preparations. "What's the status?" he shouted at Elliott over this morning's mobility. Following the briefing he got after Brodie's return from Castle Rock, Norton issued mobilization first thing for the morning. Like his battle commander, he could not let the Castle or anyone else dictate his initiative. A setback on his initial battle success would be a morale buster to the troops.

"Moving out," Elliott replied. The signal battalion fell in line first.

"Hop in." He motioned Norton into the Halftrack. Today's forces were small, but highly mobile. In formation was a company sectioned into squadrons with a couple hundred heavily-armed men. The command vehicle, a camouflaged M-1127 Stryker Halftrack with an armored shell, .50-caliber machine gun center mount and two .30-caliber machine guns each fitted along the sides of the passenger compartment, was a formidable vehicle in any event. Included in the armada were the AN/TWQ-1, Avenger air defense missile system, an M1117 Guardian armored security vehicle, and one 120 mm Dragon Fire heavy mortar mobile unit.

The convoy was headed south on I-225, expecting to intersect with I-25 in less than thirty minutes. From there it would be another thirty minutes to reach Castle Rock. Since each vehicle was equipped with hardened SINCGARS[21] systems wired to support multiple workstations with complete access through keyboard, video, and voice, the convoy was able to keep in instant contact with the Army Battle Command Systems mounted within the Bradley command vehicle. The configuration enabled the commander to perform all command and control tasks while on the move without satellite support. "Gonna be an easy win," Brodie assured Norton who agreed. "Lead on."

Because the interstate was sparsely traveled due to the shortage of fuel for civilians, the convoy made excellent time. But, as soon as it entered the Castle's access road, trouble began. The convoy came to a sudden halt because of an unusual sight. They were confronted by the Cobra helicopter hovering low directly ahead. It blocked their access to forge ahead. "Do not, I repeat, do not proceed." A female voice neither Elliott nor Norton recognized emanated through the headsets. Brodie was challenged and did not like it a bit, especially not coming from a woman. "You don't give orders. Not to me, and especially not the leader, the New Republic," he muttered into the roar of his advancing vehicles. "Identify," he responded, but was ignored. Maybe "Bauer's daughter," Norton cut in. He had heard rumors of a woman on the loose near the Rockies.

"What?" Brodie wanted clarification of what he'd just heard. "There's this woman," Norton explained. "Supposedly with a killer instinct. Nobody dares to tackle with her."

"Naw. Just rumors."

---

[21] SINCGARS (Single Channel Ground and Airborne Radio System) is a Combat Net Radio (CNR) currently used by U.S. and allied military forces. The radios, which handle voice and data communications, are designed to be reliable, secure and easily maintained. Vehicle-mount, backpack, airborne, and handheld form factors are available.

"We'll see."

Tracy had left Los Alamos a couple of hours earlier and arrived just in time to intercept the convoy. She had the vehicles on her monitor for some time. Looking over the convoy a few hundred yards below her she was calculating the odds. With the firepower armed and ready at the trigger of her finger, she was confident she could beat them but wanted to know the challenger's intentions first.

"Let me talk to Norton directly."

Norton switched to talk. Seconds later his vice was on the line. "What?"

"You may not realize the firepower in my hands. Just thought I'd warn you. I advise you to turn back. Your choice. Your move."

"Unless you're a complete idiot, take a look what's facing you." His upper body exposed through the top hatch, Norton turned to verify his detachment was still on track. All he had to do was give the command and cannons and missiles at his disposal would dislodge their destructive powers. And he did with the following command. "Arm Avengers."

Tracy could follow the closed-circuit chat ahead. If she resisted she knew what was in store for her. "What's your response?" Norton warned her once more. "Final warning."

"Do not proceed," she shot back at him again. The next move was now in Norton's hands who immediately gave the command. "Attack."

She saw the flash followed by a dark object headed her way. Impact would only be seconds away. Tracy reacted. Accelerating to full power, she took the Cobra into a steep climb, averting the incoming fish. The missile shot by inches from the fuselage. The battle was on. From here on, it would be skills and forces pitted against each other. Although much slower than a missile, the advantage Tracy had was maneuverability at close range. She was surprised that Norton had ordered a missile. It exploded into the near hillside. The RPG or 105 mm round would have done a better job finding the target at close up.

"Now it's my turn," Tracy shouted into the mic.

"Who says?" It was Norton's voice on the ether. "Take this." With a flip of the switch he released the second missile. Tracy was on guard. Again, she was able to avoid a hit. It infuriated Norton even more. They could hear him cussing through the headset. This time, she was prepared to return fire. Closing in to hover some 250 feet above the ground she had the Halftrack in her crosshairs. She let go one short burst on the Gatling guns. A solid hail of steel streamed towards the vehicle. Although she had notions to "shoot to kill," it was not her intent to kill soldiers. There were innocent lives at stake. It was only a warning. From above, Tracy watched the uniformed bodies jump from the vehicle and rush for cover. She took aim again and pulled the trigger. But, this time, her finger held steady for five seconds. It was all the time needed to completely incinerate the emptied Halftrack. Even from her distance she could see the awestruck faces staring at the destruction.

Alerting Norton of her intentions, "Your vehicle's next," Tracy yelled into the mic. Her next command would clear the air. "You wanna keep the rest of your men," her voice cracked like a whip in the sudden silence, "keep out. This is my territory. Negotiate?"

The response a second later was, "Standby."

Norton must have gotten the message. After a lengthy pause he summoned, "Negotiate," but silently promised to himself, *this isn't over yet.*

CASTLE ROCK

Tracy touched down on the helipad. Once inside, she was watching the monitors. It did not take long for the command vehicle to drive up. Guarded by lieutenants, out jumped Norton and Elliott. Alex met them at the gates. "Hello again," Alex greeted yesterday's visitors once more. His outstretched hand was ignored. The rebuff was an insignificant gesture, but it gave him a hint of the state of things. He was on guard.

"Your daughter," Norton poked Alex in the chest with his index finger, "just cost me a vehicle." There was restrained fury in his face.

Staring him down, Alex said, "Lucky you still have your people. Nobody's taking the Castle."

In one swift motion, Norton pulled his sidearm and shouted, "We'll see about that." Brodie reacted just as quick. Armed weapons were trained on Alex and Brian who had closed up alongside. "Now," Norton demanded, "let's see what we've got." With a slight motion of his weapon, he ordered both below. Alex knew exactly what the intruders wanted, to get their hands on his equipment. He could not let that happen. But for the moment he had no choice. Both were forced to the command center below.

Norton could not contain himself when he spotted the Castle's setup. There was communication equipment everywhere. He had never seen such a display of technology. "Where'd you get all this?" he marveled.

"Where've you been?" Alex did not know Norton had spent close to five years locked away in the penitentiary. He explained the state of his technology at hand. What he did not disclose was the super weapon at his disposal. That was a secret only he, Foster, and a few dedicated scientists knew. It was a weapon DARPA had been able to keep secret. When the EMP struck, whatever projects were in the midst of development at the time had been terminated. But, in recent years, under cover of secrecy managed by Spencer and enforced by Brooks, development at the LANL went on.

It had been several years since Alex had his first encounter with Spencer and his secret society, the Condors. When he approached Foster about it, the general essentially admitted, although reluctantly, his association with the laboratory. When further pressed he also revealed his participation with the development of a new weapon, a super weapon. "Not supposed to exist," he cautioned Alex. "Remember that."

Today, now, staring trouble head-on, Norton and Elliott had their sidearm trained on Alex and Brian. Alex could detect, from their faces, that they wanted their hands on the Castle even more. While Elliott kept Brian in check, Norton pushed his weapon into Alex's face. "What's it gonna be?"

Alex wavered. It was decision time. Freedom, he suddenly realized, did not come cheap. But possible death, his and his buddy's—he could not let that happen. He was about to challenge the standoff with personal combat when a sudden voice came from the doorway, "Drop 'em…drop your weapons. That's what's gonna be."

Coming silently up the staircase, Tracy surprised them all. "Dad…Brian?" She muttered. "What's going on?" What prevented Norton and Elliott from firing was not only the surprise, but the weapon trained on them. It was the first time Tracy threw Serpent Slayer, the weapon Spencer had given her, into action. "Only one in its existence," she recalled him saying when he offered it to her. It was an impressive sight, watching her handle the complex weapon capable of multi-fire various armaments.

Although Norton and Elliott were taken by surprise, they seemed to have composed themselves. It became obvious with Norton's challenge. "Count the odds," he spat at her. "Two weapons against one."

It did not deter her. "Mine shoots smart bullets." She did not have to explain further. All knew what it meant. The shape and size of the weapon clutched in her hands was enough of a warning. Although reluctantly, both lowered their side arms.

"These here," Alex gestured at the unwelcome guests, "want the Castle."

Staring at Norton, her stony face shifted into a wide grin. "Really?"

Norton was quick to respond. "Negotiate?" It was an obvious option for saving face.

"Got the message?" Tracy stepped up. In recent years, she had turned much more aggressive than her dad. "You leave the Castle alone," she insisted. "And you and your men are free to leave. Agreed?" Norton nodded, although hesitantly. "Agreed." Brodie confirmed his response with a slight nod of the head. Both realized, for the moment, unprepared, the odds with weapons was on their side. Next time, "we'll be prepared," he vowed in silence.

"Tell me," Tracy's face turned curious, "what's your agenda?"

After leaving Los Alamos, she had monitored the interchange between the approaching army and the Castle. Images fed by the satellites had kept her informed on the state of the growing hostilities. The true purpose for the attempted takeover was still up in the air. For now, Tracy had earned the complete respect from the uninvited visitors.

Alex motioned for the party to follow. He led the way to the den. "Have a seat." He checked with Tracy to stay guarded and headed for the pantry to prepare some sandwiches. He was barely aware of the subdued exchanges, mostly by Brodie and Brian. Tracy remained in silence. She had not been very sociable in recent months. "Wonder," he mulled over her sudden appearance, "what's on the girl's mind?" He was not very pleased with her mannish behavior. The attitude, the confrontations, the trouble she had been getting involved in lately was already troublesome. But one thing he was proud of was the commanding respect she was getting. He was still marveled at her, who, in just a couple of years, had gained an unsurpassed reputation as a single fighter. "Stinger," the code he bestowed on her, befitted her demeanor perfectly.

Alex returned, serving the sandwiches and refreshments. It eased the tension immediately. On a request, Norton briefed the Castle crew about the state of the plains. Alex did not volunteer any information on their planning and secret technologies on hand. Neither did Tracy reveal her plans. Brian mostly kept quiet. "What's your next move?" Alex wanted to know.

Norton responded, "We'll head north." Face set in a furtive grin directed at Tracy, "If you'll let us." Although guarded, Alex was pleased at the outcome. He listened to Norton's plans and proposals. Discussed was the March of the Patriots, the new constitution, plans for a New Republic, trade and commerce with focus on technology. "Whoever controls that," he speculated, "controls the nation." The session ran into the night. Brodie kept in touch with his infantry forces, whereabouts, and anticipated return. He put the convoy, what was left, on hold. Orders were to "Stand down."

It was past midnight when the party left the Castle with a mutual concession. "You clean up the countryside," Alex prompted the departing visitors, "and I'll keep this part of your territory clear." With an empathy placed on "your territory," Norton and Brodie seemed to be satisfied, for the time being. "Agreed." Although mellowed out by the drinks Alex had served them, both left hurried on somewhat wobbly legs.

"Now," Alex turned to Tracy. "Tell us about the lab, the implant."

FORT KNOX

Henry Foster was pacing the grounds. He had been getting restless, more so by the day. He voiced his frustration on more than one occasion. "Right," he'd agree on the place being the most secure in the nation. "But I'm gonna make sure." Although he had elevated himself to the command position, he was not happy strapped to the fort, especially with much of the forces presently on the move. Scouts came back almost daily, reporting on the progress of the party. Since the March of the Patriots was underway, there was no point for him to remain any longer. "Yep," he decided one day. "I'm outta here." Same day he gave notice to Wendell Nelson, Knox base commander.

"What?" Wendell Nelson hadn't been attentive lately. He had been burdened by too many commanders telling him what to do.

"You're in charge," Foster announced. "Base's yours." He had made his decision. His mind became focused once more. There was much that had to be done, but not from here. He had to move on to the new frontiers. "Military front out west." That's where he headed, come daybreak. First stop would be Castle Rock. He owed Bauer a visit. Besides, the two of them could figure out the best approach to his plans. Although Bauer was not getting paid for his services these days, "But who was? Nobody. Everybody owes everybody favors."

Getting transportation was not difficult among the fleet of military vehicles dead lined at the fort. An M113 Stryker, an XA-202 armored command vehicle, and a couple Humvee would suit him just fine. After all, the highest ranking general in the nation should not be caught driving alone on the highways. Next was appropriating drivers and a squad of guardsmen for protection. "Fuel could present a problem," his quartermaster cautioned. "Fort Carson's along the route." He was assured it was "Not an issue." The following day, the convoy moved out.

Wendell Nelson, Commander, Garrison U.S. Army, Fort Knox, KY, was highly relieved when the convoy went on its way. The past couple of years had not been easy for him. Ever since the prison break a few years back by the thousand-strong Leavenworth band, the forced takeover, Foster arriving and taking possession of his national treasure, his life at Knox had not been the same. There had been nothing but hostility ever since. At first, he tried to negotiate his way out. When that did not work, he threatened the mob with severe punishment. But all they did was laugh at him. Making it worse, they had ganged up on him and put him under house arrest, indefinitely. As time went on, he realized that there was no help on the way. Military, National Guards, regional law enforcement, all were dissolved. With communication out, there was no one to respond. The rebellion that followed splintered the entire nation into fragments.

At least, for now, with them gone, he was given back his job once more commanding the fort. He was proud to wear the uniform again. It gave him back the feeling of power, prestige, and status, demanding the discipline he deserved. He could still not believe his second in command, Brodie Elliott, had deserted the military constitution. With the 1st Armored Division taking over the territory, discipline enforced by the ragtag prison units, ex-convict Rusty Norton in command, he had been grossly outnumbered. The small contingent devoted to him and the former army command would not be enough to reverse the state. He realized that, but he had to give it a try. With the ragtag division gone, this would be the time to do so. It would not be an easy task. Most in the non-commissioned ranks had deserted the once glorious army. And commissioned officers were few. He had his work cut out.

General Nelson spent days and weeks convincing his once trusted. After that, in the company of his lieutenants, he spent every waking hour convincing his opponents to join his growing force. He was getting ready to stage a counter coup. What, who, and where, he was clueless at the moment. If the military could not step in to save the nation, he sure as hell would. Asserted to power once more, for now, he took possession of the strategic assets mostly consisting of mobile vehicles. Walking the ranks, presently making his daily rounds, he took stock on his inventory. Although lacking the fuel at the moment, the armored division and artillery brigade at his disposal was quite a formidable force.

There was the 1st Stryker Brigade combat team made up mostly of tactical forces. There was the cavalry regiment with its squadrons and troops. There was the 1st Field Artillery regiment with its brigades, battalions, and companies. Under normal military configuration, he would have tens of thousands of soldiers under his command. With the forces scaled down, he had to do with barely a thousand men and limited number of armament. But for the state the nation was in, considering the armored equipment he had on hand, it was still a formidable command. "Besides, he assured himself, "it'll be great bargaining power." He knew it would only be a matter of time before some command would come begging him for equipment and firepower.

Parading along the grounds, he gave his assets an initial inspection. There were M109A6 Paladins, self-propelled 155 mm howitzers to maneuver brigades of armored and mechanized infantry divisions alongside an M142 High Mobility Artillery Rocket System. There were M113, fully tracked armored personnel carriers, the backbone of the mechanized infantry units, largely known as APC. A cluster of M2 Bradley, the infantry's fighting vehicle manned by crews of three: commander, gunner/driver, and a squadron of fighting men. All in all, Wendell could not complain.

"Are you ready?" he shouted above the heads of the soldiers at the end of the inspection.

"At your command. Sir," was the unison response. Although Nelson knew he had enough military resources on hand to protect the Fort against possible intrusions launched from within the nation, such as from the Anarchists and roaming outlaw bands, he was also keenly aware that the garrison under his command could not sustain a war and major conflict. But for the time being, he had assured Nelson and Elliott he would lend his support to fill the ranks from fallen soldiers whenever, and wherever possible. He already had visions of vying a position under Foster's command at the Pentagon once it was in the hands of the nation again. His chest swelled with pride, he proudly strode among the lines picking out capable faces for a very much needed staff to fill the vacated ranks under his command.

THE SERPENT

Hasan Hammad had gained control over the lakes. It had not been an easy task. It had taken close to a year to accomplish. First, there was the naval encounter at West Point. Then there was the city of Albany. Heavily fortified to protect the local population, he and his crew had to fight their way through a number of estuaries and waterways to finally exit into Erie Canal.[22] To his surprise, waterway traffic was relatively scarce. "Must be fuel shortage," he figured. It affected him and his crew as well. He was running low on supplies. The 55-gal storage canisters in his possession were rapidly depleting. The battle for fuel was ongoing. It was something they experienced all the way through Syracuse, Rochester, and on to their final destination, Chicago. Hammad was amazed. He had no clue about the maze of canals and man-made waterways connecting the lakes. The map on hand did not clearly identify this complexity. He had to push and force his way in and out minor and major estuaries, getting to the final destination months later. He diligently kept tracking his path for future travels. On arriving, he had drawn a complete map of the waterway system.

As luck had it, he was able to get his hands on a Coast Guard icebreaker moored at a Lake Huron northern seaport. It would help with keeping the lake and waterway passages open for much of the winter.

Whereas many of the cities they passed presented obstacles along the conquering passage, it was nothing like the opposition they encountered in Chicago. As soon as it set foot on the lakeshore fronts, the scouting party ran into heavy resistance. It appeared the city had been warded off into small districts occupied by clusters of highly combative, competitive gangs fiercely protecting their territory. The fighting was mostly over food supplies. At this time, nothing was produced locally. Nobody seemed to work. "Thieves and robbers take everything," he was told, "in an ever-widening turf."

After only a short year, without maintaining upkeep, the city had fallen into decay. Supplies, whatever was not on hand, were readily appropriated by force from migrating trekkers seeking a new life up north. The exodus was heavy during the initial year, but fell off in time. Aside from food, fuel was the next driving factor. The lack of it was visible everywhere Hammad went. "I will have to see to that," he vowed to Yusuf.

---

[22] The Great Lakes Waterway was a system of channels and canals that made the Great Lakes accessible to oceangoing vessels. Its principal civil engineering components were the Welland Canal, bypassing Niagara Falls between Lake Ontario and Lake Erie, and the Soo Locks, bypassing the rapids of the St. Marys River between Lake Superior and Lake Huron, at Sault Sainte Marie. Maintained channels served the St. Clair River and Detroit River between Lake Huron and Lake Erie.

The Great Lakes Waterway was supplemented by the Saint Lawrence Seaway, which made the Saint Lawrence River navigable from Montreal to Kingston, Ontario. The Great Lakes Waterway had larger locks and deeper drafts than the St. Lawrence Seaway with the result that a number of lake freighters were confined to the lakes, being small enough to operate on the Waterway but too large to pass down the Seaway. This would become an important factor in Hammad's supply line across the Atlantic.

Hammad and his scouts encountered many casualties along the way. Entire families had been eradicated. Some were cremated by the survivors. Others hurriedly laid to rest by the roadside. Few were buried in grave sites. Trekkers kept pushing on, mile after mile, with one goal in mind: getting out of the city, the town, the region, hoping to make it north to less populated areas of Ontario, Manitoba, and Saskatchewan. For them, former city dwellers, it was a long struggle, especially making it through lengthy winters. But it was the only chance for many to begin a new life. Water was plentiful and so was food for those who had the means to track and secure local wildlife. Life was possible but it came at a high cost of human lives during the first cold periods. Many perished from diseases or starvation, but the struggle went on.

Over time, Hammad and his crew had built a stronghold on the lakeshore of Chicago, during which time a continuous stream of recruits was supplied from Islamic dominant nations. Most came up the Saint Lawrence to settle along the way. Many had never seen a body of water or a sizeable river. The country was wide open for settlers to the region. To the dismay of the local population, settlements sprang up much like in the pioneering days of the west. Hammad's plan was to gain control over shore land around the Great Lakes, the entry points to major tributaries with access to the Atlantic. A continuous stream of cargo vessels originating in ports like Dubai, Qatar, Bahrain, and Kuwait kept plowing through the Red Sea, crossing the Suez Canal into the Mediterranean, and on across the Atlantic to supply his needs. As far as the rest of the world was concerned, life, for most part, remained unchanged.

After the U.S. dollar had collapsed as the international currency, other superpowers like Russia, China, Japan, the E.U. and Australia had taken control over their respective regions. Global trade, at times, was cumbersome because no country had been able to successfully launch a solid world currency. Bickering about the currency issue was heard almost daily on world news broadcasts. EMP strike-exempted nations located outside the former United States had not yet been successful in forming strong alliances. Most nations were still struggling for stability. Northern European nations were more successful. They had created a "Northern Alliance." Asian nations such as Japan, South Korea, and Taiwan were in collaboration for industry, resources, and capital under the "Asian Alliance." Middle Eastern countries were pushing to get their hands-on resources in the former U.S. and previously controlled mineral wealth. Today, years into the mission, striding across the central plaza, Hasan Hammad was extremely pleased. In a friendly gesture, he gave Yusuf a brotherly slap on the shoulder. "This," he informed his friend, "concludes Phase One."

"What's next?" Yusuf, as much as he appreciated everything his commander did for him and the causes, such as gaining possession of the Great Lakes and establishing a new frontier, still yearned for the Big Apple, the place he grew up. Hinting on that thought once more, he said, "New York City…eh?"

"Nonsense." Hammad turned factual again. The sentiments he had displayed just a minute ago vanished. "Greater things await us."

"What could be bigger than America, waters, and new frontiers?"

"The world, my friend. The world is waiting for us." Hammad was already headed for the shipping docks. With a youthful jump, he landed on the deck of his marvelous speedboat. His mind was firmly set on his most treasured possession, Palm Island, his personal abode. It was there he planned to initiate Phase Two. What he still kept a secret and contained within his own mind was the essence of the second phase. It entailed forming a coalition of Islamic friendly states into a global force that has not been seen since the Ottoman Empire. It would be a force changing history driven by the course of Jihad the world would have to deal with, and very soon.

"Hop on," he gestured at Yusuf. "We deserve a break. We shall celebrate—but not here." With a determined gesture, he pushed the controls and gunned the engines, headed east, leaving Chicago in their wake. The new headquarters for the Jihad nation was in capable hands, managed by a select group of leaders personally handpicked by him. Eyes fixed straight ahead, Hasan Hammad, with his lieutenant by his side, took in the brisk scent of sea spray washing over his face. What lay ahead were challenges, exploitation, and adventure, all for a good cause, the cause of Islam. He was jubilant by the sheer thought of taking the world into his reign. He was anxious to have his name inscribed into the annals of history as the new Islamic Prophet, served by his devout, new converts, and the Muslim population around the world. "Allah is great," he shouted into the onrushing winds of the Great Lakes.

LISA BAUER

The astronaut training was brutal, in every aspect. There were times when Liz had second thoughts about the cause. When she confronted Foster, he would always put her at ease with comments like, "You can do it...stay with it...won't take much longer." She appreciated his pep talks but also knew hardship did not end with the training. The mission itself would be just as demanding. "At least," she'd console herself on those occasions of doubt, "I'll be doing something good for the country." It was more than many others could claim. Where much of the nation was struggling for survival, she claimed, "My effort's a peaceful one." So, she thought.

Foster made sure her acquired skills were on track. It was time to ship her out to the European and Russian camps. Mission preparedness primarily took place at the Yuri Gagarin Cosmonaut Training Center. The facility had fully-sized mockups of all major Russian spacecraft as well as the ISS main body. As for the ISS crews, cosmonauts were now assigned to Cologne, Germany and the Tsukuba Space Center, Japan for specific training in the various ISS modules. Although India and China were on the brink of space travel, their efforts might or might not be part of the International Space Station in the future. Both nations had been making overtures to put their own platforms into space.

Liz was looking forward at the new facilities and the chance at cultural diversity. Although her dad was born in Germany, she had never taken the opportunity to visit his land. Local events in growing up, her education, and raising the family had always taken priorities. Here was her chance to catch up. "Russia," she thought in anticipation. "Now, that's gonna be a challenge." Though it had been years since she had taken up that language in college, the upcoming trip would give her a chance to brush up on her language skills.

Upon arriving at Cologne, Germany, the first impression she received was that of organizational discipline. Every aspect of space exploration had been thoroughly worked out to its infinite details. Test facilities were immaculately spotless, meticulously planned out, and thoroughly organized—almost to a point of clinical conduct. The people, professionally as they conducted themselves, were always pleasant, forthcoming but strictly disciplined. Many extended invitations on weekends to either dine out at a local German restaurant, join in at a weekly Volksmarch event nearby, or to travel to Europe's popular tourist spots. She even had the chance to visit Dad's birthplace but, to her disappointment, no closely related family members were left alive. Aside from the clinical work environment during mission training she completely enjoyed the place the few months she remained.

Russia, on the other hand, was a completely different experience. Although there was not much of a language barrier for her, the Russian people's thinking, acting, and behavior were different from western societies. It took her quite a while to learn, accept, and then understand not only the cultural differences, but customary and personal attitudes as well. First off, she got the feeling of distrust. "Must be innate," she deduced. Millennia of hardship, centuries of isolation, and decades of wars must have left permanent scars on the people.

Working conditions were somewhat more relaxed. It must have been the dependency from confined living in capsules on the space station that developed a comradeship. What struck Liz the most was the strong Muslim influence in the architecture. Cathedrals, mosques, and churches were topped by the familiar onion-shaped golden and colorful domes.

Where the people may have been disciplined at the office, business, or job, in the evening, it seemed, the nation was out to enjoy life. Entertainment establishments were in abundance. In clubs, restaurants, and theaters, one could be swept up in the diversity of amusement, cuisine, customs, and culture. For Liz, it was a learning experience she appreciated to the fullest. Between Germany and Russia, she had the pleasure of enhancing her cultural horizons in ways she had not expected. But before long, the good life, the excitement and foreign impressions, eventually came to an end.

For the time being, Liz was sent back to her home base, Vandenberg. With the next space launch slipping for one reason or other, the flight was still months off. For that, when the time came, she had to return to Russia to join the cosmonaut team. In the meantime, she was able to spend time with her kids in Napa. For now, it was all leisure. She wanted her kids to remember the good times. There was always a slight chance she might not return from space. At least this way, she figured, they would have a lasting memory. But she kept thoughts like these to herself.

For now, although she had to report weekly to the secret Vandenberg space preparation facility, it was family time for most part.

ISS

A scratchy and somewhat metallic voice emanated from a speaker nearby. "Mission Control…Station Alpha, come in…come in." The tone sounded urgent, alerting the crew in command module Destiny. It was the ISS call sign. Half of the crew of cosmonauts on duty at the time heard it. The rest were on a standard twelve-hour break. In between space missions, workloads were rudimentary, but once a shuttle was announced the entire crew jumped into action. Although it was probably only a daily routine call, it prompted Yuri Chenkov to action.

"Station Alpha," he responded. "Go."

"Sergei Budenko. Urgent."

Not a routine call, he figured.

For most part, work was tedious and required infinite patience. To break the monotony, any call was welcomed. What made this call different was that it was name specific. Most times whatever cosmonaut was nearby would handle incoming. "Standby." Chenkov hastened to the sleeping quarters in the next module. To get there he propelled his weightless body forward using a hand-over-hand grip on the framework.

Budenko was asleep. "Wake up, wake up," the faintly familiar voice drilled into his brain. "Mission control…Urgent." Still drowsy from sleep, he unzipped both straps holding his body against the frame. Vigorously rubbing his eyes, Sergei Budenko responded, "All right—all right."

It was the call Budenko had been anticipating for months. It finally arrived. The faster he got the mission over with, the sooner he could return to Earth. Pulling his weightless body along the isolation tunnel, he wound his way to the command module. "Hold on." He could not pass by the restroom facility without stepping in. "Gotta go."

Chenkov, who followed closely, bumped into him. "No time."

"Can wait." Another minute would not matter, he figured. "Budenko," Sergei announced his presence when he arrived at the station, then listened intently. The call had been initiated from the city of Korolev, the Russian control center. In contrast, missile launches were initiated from the Baikonur Cosmodrome, located in neighboring Kazakhstan. Ending the personal call with, "Roger…Out," he motioned at the interlock. "We've got work to do."

It meant spacewalk. Chenkov was already headed for the interlock. Only too willingly, he followed Budenko to the prep chamber. Aiding each other with the help of a third cosmonaut, both slipped on the bulky spacesuits. It was a somewhat cumbersome task to don the suit, almost impossible for one person. Generally, a two-man operation, this was to ensure proper mounting and sealing for helmet, connections, and oxygen pack. Space was an unforgiving environment. There were no mistakes allowed. One slipup could mean instant death. Witness accounts illustrated on more than one occasion that it was not a pleasant experience to watch a body explode with blood splatter against the visor in an all too gruesome fashion.

Budenko was already headed for the interlock. "Ready?" One push of a button and streams of forced oxygen shot out from jets, filling the chamber. He entered the docking module by pulling the mechanical door lever from its interlock. The heavy steel door slowly swung open, allowing entrance. Chenkov followed. The door shut tight. Once both were secured, the process was reversed. Another push on the button expelled the oxygen. The chamber emptied. Both headed for the space exit lock. Again, the metallic clanking from interlocking bolts snapping open was accompanied by the swishing sound sucking the chamber dry. The green light turned on, indicating a secure exit into space.

With guarded care, fixed securely to a tethered lifeline, both made the exit floating into space, slightly pushing off the chamber frame. Connected securely to the outer rail of the space platform, there was no need for a jetpack. Slowly, both edged their way forward in the direction of the waveguide prominently mounted on the highly polished framework presently facing a brilliantly illuminated blue planet, Earth.

Budenko did not seem to notice the wonders of floating in space. He was already at work. It was different with Chenkov. The sight was spectacular no matter how many times he had floated in space. No matter what the mission call, he was easily distracted from the immediate task. To watch Earth slowly drift beneath the space platform was an unforgettable experience. The view was breathtaking. "Hey," Budenko's impatient voice sounded through the intercom, reminding him to the work at hand. Today's exercise was simple. "Unlock the waveguide from its transport position." Once the gear was freed from its bolted position, it could be manipulated from within. Although parameters for the upcoming test were accessible through onboard computers, the true mission was only known to Budenko. The rest of the crew still questioned the odd-looking monstrosity attached and mounted to the ISS module consisting mostly of highly polished, but maneuverable metal tubes.

The previous year, during the last ISS shuttle mission, the equipment for today's exercise had arrived from Baikonur, Russia's Federated Space Agency. Located in the far reaches of Kazakhstan, it was the world's largest land locked launch complex. Kazakhstan, neighbored by Russia, China, Kyrgyzstan, Uzbekistan, and Turkmenistan, also bordered the Caspian Sea. Vast in size, the terrain of Kazakhstan ranged from flatlands, steppes, taigas, canyons, rocky hills, river deltas, and snow-capped mountains to barren deserts. Subjected to mass deportation by Stalin in earlier days, Kazakhstan had over 130 nationalities including Kazakhs, Russians, Ukrainians, Uzbeks, and Tatars. It was this blend of ethnic and cultural diversity that allowed the prolific interaction of a multitude of nations. Considered to be the dominant state in central Asia, Kazakhstan was a member of many international organizations, including the United Nations, NATO, Commonwealth of Independent States, and the Shanghai Cooperation Organization.

It was this environment that provided the opportunity for many to slip unhindered into the country. Border patrols were vast and far in-between. Sergei Budenko was one such subject. Born in Afghanistan, he grew up during the war occupation by Soviet Russia. His mother, a devout Muslim, met his father, a major in the Air Force and aircraft pilot, during a prolonged hospital stay by his father after an injury sustained from a helicopter crash. Although Sergei grew up with his mother in Afghanistan, after his father's recovery, he moved to Kazakhstan where he entered the ministry's air academy in Astana, the nation's capital. From there, after graduating, it was almost a guaranteed move to enter Star City, Russia's prestigious cosmonaut training center. He arrived at the

T. RANDALL

space station on the most recent Soyuz TMA-17 space flight. The flight replaced the ISS orbital crew already in orbit for six months and delivered new payload and provisions.[23]

---

[23] In contrast to U.S. space shuttles, the Soviet space agency used a reusable space capsule launched into orbit by massively powered three-stage quadruple rocket boosters of the Soyuz-FG type. The craft, sitting on top of the boosters, consisted of three sections: orbital module, descent module, and service module for docking with the ISS. It was the service module that contained the equipment needed for conducting today's testing. With equipment manufactured in various countries including the United States, Russia, Japan, the E.U., and other allied nations, the Russian space flight carried the multi-national payload into space.

To support the many elements involved with every ISS mission, numerous organizations and countries were responsible for their respective sector. The Mission Rantrol Center was responsible to get the craft launched into space. The teams at the Operations Center were responsible for staying synchronized with Mission Control overseers and providing access to the resources required for payload operations, maintenance, assembly tasks, and support. Payload control was responsible for transferring instruments and equipment to the space station. Ground control stations were positioned around the globe, providing continuous monitoring along the flight in partnership with the Russian Space Agency, European Space Agency, National Space Development Agency of Japan, Canadian Space Agency, and Columbus Control Center in Oberpfaffenhofen, Germany.

CASTLE ROCK

"Saw you drive up." Alex beckoned the general into his home. He had been expecting him. It was not difficult to spot the convoy headed in his direction. The first indication was when Brian, who had been diligently watching the monitors, spotted military activity hundreds of miles out. Alex, with Brian's assistance, had the nation in his sight ever since the communication satellites and space surveillance had entered the hands of the Castle, with Stinger and Black Knight directly configured into the tracking.

"What brings you here?" Alex was curious about the surprise visit. He did not think Foster would make his headquarters here in the Rockies. There had to be a specific purpose.

"I'll get to that," the general replied. "But first," he said, "how'd you track me?"

Alex stepped away. He needed a second to calculate his response. He was not ready to share his secrets. Not to Foster, not to anyone else. Until now, only the Castle Rock team had been privy to the technology in his hands. But he also knew his longtime Pentagon friend was no dummy. If anybody was wise to him, it would be Foster. He needed time to think. He stalled. Instead, he offered, "Have a seat. By the way," he indicated outside, "your men can pitch tent on the mount." By mount, he signified the top of the hill the Castle was built into.

"Thanks." Foster switched the headset to "Talk." He informed his squadron via the SINCGAR. "Never thought I'd have to resort to this." He gestured at the dated comm gear. Without satellites and GPS, he was limited to line-of-sight communication. One thing the Castle had advantage over Foster was Cheyenne Mountain. It provided an antenna farm reaching far into the plains.

"Just like old times," Alex agreed. "Eh?"

"Hate it." Foster shrugged. "Whole damned mess we're in."

"We all do," Alex agreed. "Had to make serious adjustments myself. Hungry?"

Foster nodded in agreement. "Could use a bite."

"Your men have provisions?"

"They can take care of themselves."

"Okay then."

"Sure, could use a shower."

"Been in a Jacuzzi lately?"

"You kidding?"

"Follow me…Brian," he yelled from the hall, "could you fix something?"

"Right."

Brian showed up ten minutes later with beer and snacks. "Here we are," he offered. Alex gestured at Foster. "Help yourself. Hop in, Brian." The three were comfortably seated in a most carefree atmosphere at the Castle and perhaps the entire nation.

"You were saying?" Alex encouraged his guest.

As the most senior commander in the military forces, or what was left, Foster seemed slightly uncomfortable in the casual setting. It may have been the first time he ever conducted a briefing seated in a whirlpool. He shot a quick glance at Brian. "Can we talk?"

"He's cleared," Alex assured him. It put the general at ease. He was about to disclose something so sensitive he would only trust Alex with it.

"HAARP." Foster opened the dialogue.

"Ah yes," Brian jumped into the conversation. "Super weapon that doesn't exist. Funny you should mention it."

"Need to check on it," Foster suggested.

"Only check? Here's a chance," Alex encouraged the general, "to get our hands on it." Brian had his stare fixed on Alex. It had always been an off-limit topic whenever he brought it up. Today, it seemed, he might learn about it. As with most black projects, with every department compartmentalized, each program was restricted to the limited trusted personnel pool involved. With the nation in turmoil, Foster saw the opportunity to get his hands on this technology. But for that, he needed to be on location and that was thousands of miles to the north.

"What about HAARP?" Brian probed. It was not every day he had the opportunity for plunging into secrets he knew practically nothing about.

Foster nodded at Alex. "You tell him." It appeared he wanted to change the subject. "By the way," he asked, "where's Tracy?"

"Out, as usual."

His face showed concern. "Time like this?" He shook the head. He knew Tracy from years ago working in the Pentagon. He had no clue about the transformation she had undergone. "Lotta vagrants on the loose," he cautioned. "Shouldn't let her roam around on her own."

"You don't know her," Alex explained. It did not take long when the outside gate slammed close. "Speaking of the devil," Alex said.

Seconds later her head popped into the den. "Can I join the party? General!" she called out with joy. "What a surprise." Foster jumped from the tub. A few strides brought them close. She gave Foster a hearty hug. "Been a long time." Foster had closed the eyes to get the full feel of the embrace from the girl, the daughter he never had.

Although it was only a fatherly embrace, Brian looked on with a twinge of jealousy. He was not used to seeing others hug her.

The general opened his eyes to fully take in her presence. Looking her over, his face took on a look of concern. Shaking his head, he demanded, "What gives? The punkish hair, the outfit, your muscles?" He reached up to squeeze her biceps then gasped. "Whoa. Don't wanna mess with you, girl." Sporting a broad grin, he seemed genuinely impressed.

Tracy appeared more confident and self-assured than ever. "Been workin' out."

"Sure could use you," he offered. "Wanna come out west?"

"That's where you headed?"

"First thing come morning."

"Just might," she hinted with a promising smile. "Let you know."

Alex already knew where she was headed. He did not even have to think. It was something she had been waiting for, a purpose, a mission, a challenge.

Brian was shaking his head. It appeared he did not like it. As always, he was concerned for her safety. Although he was deeply attached to her, he realized not even he could rein her in. But he would always carry his love for her in his heart. It would have to do. "Turning in," he told her, stepping from the tub. "You coming?"

Ignoring him as he left, she replied, "Not just yet…you go ahead." She turned back to seek out Foster, who was leaving for the guest chambers to towel dry. Minutes later he emerged to join Tracy and Alex in the living room. Alex had prepared a late snack. Neatly arranged on the plates was his favorite spread: smoked ham and home-made butter on dark rye, garnished by pickles, mustard, and slices of Swiss cheese.

"So," Alex opened the late-night talks, "you're headed west?"

Foster took a hearty bite from a sandwich before he answered. "Only place for me," he hinted. "Government, military, defenses…" he explained between bites. "What's left moved west."

"You," Alex offered, "could retire and make your home here. We'd love to have you. Right?" He glanced at Tracy for approval, who did not commit.

"Not even close to retirement," he replied. "Not in these times. Tell you what I need," he explained. "A backup team I can trust." It was another invitation for Tracy to join his team.

"Whatcha got in mind?"

"With the Badlands on the move, the Eastern Seaboard in turmoil, the Anarchists taking over the south," he gestured, "I need eyes and ears."

"Way ahead of you," Tray cut in. "Show 'em, Dad."

Shooting a quizzical look at Alex, Foster did not know what to make of her comment. Alex shot a quick glance at Tracy. Inadvertently, she had made up Alex's mind, if and how much to tell Foster about the technology at his hands. At any rate, he got up from the chair and gestured for his guest to follow. "Come. I'll show you."

Brian stuck his head in the room. He had changed his mind and rejoined the party headed below. On arriving at the Castle's command center, Alex paused to let his guest catch up.

"Some technology," Foster marveled at some of the equipment. "Where'd you get all this?"

"You should know," Alex replied with a smug grin on the face, "paid for most of it."

"Aah Yes," he admonished, accompanied by a slight nod of the head. "Contractual support expenses, as I recall."

"…and, very much appreciated," Alex replied.

Rather than explaining, Alex said, "Brian." He gestured at the control console. "Show 'em."

Brian seemed to be in his world again. It was the world of secrecy and intrigue. Although NSA, his former employer, had been abolished, the former network guru had found a purpose in life at the Castle abode. He flipped a switch to turn on the wall mounted monitor. Seconds later, Foster was staring at the display screen.

He seemed stunned. "I don't believe it," he gasped. "Whole damned United States! Alive. In living colors." To him, no matter what had happened or what would happen down the road, North America would always be the U.S. He was born in this country. He would die in it, no matter what the Patriots, and everybody else in-between had in mind for a new nation. "How'd you pull it off?" He seemed marveled at the display and did not exactly know where data came from, but what he saw was good enough for him.

"With Brian's help," Alex explained. "We breached the defense net. Linked up what's left in space. Hooked together the northern surveillance grid."

"ASATs?"

"Mostly," Alex confirmed. "Among comm satellites."

"Sonofabitch!" Foster seemed enraged and euphoric at the same time. Enraged that someone had the galls to steal his space assets, but elated all the same to have the tools available he had missed so dearly over the past few years.

"There's more," Alex broke the moment. "Tell 'em, Tracy."

Foster shot a glance at her, indicating that there was no end to surprises.

A few paces later Tracy stood in front of him. She reached for his hand and placed in on the back of her neck. "Feel it?"

"Yeah." What he felt was almost imperceptible. It blended in perfectly with her upper vertebrae. "Do tell."

"Implants," she revealed with a sly grin. "VoIP."

"Voice-over-IP?" The revelation was incredulous. What made it profound was the genius in it. "Why," he marveled, "didn't anybody else think of it?"

"They did," Tracy insisted. "Sandia for one, Los Alamos for another."

Foster seemed perplexed. It clearly reflected on his face. Tracy said, "Shocked? There's more." She moved his hand to her jaw line and said, "Push." It immediately triggered the mini-switch. The monitor they were watching immediately switched from the shadows of space to the room they were in. Tracy slowly panned her head from side to side. With it changed the images on display, moving in synchronicity with her head.

"Data's relayed from satellite to implant and vice versa, then sent on to audio and visual synapses. From there, signals get converted to actual images and sound to eyes and ears," she explained.

"Over-the-horizon-radar?"

"Same technology," Alex offered. "She sees things satellites do."

"Come," Tracy offered, reaching for Foster's hand. With Alex and Brian in tow, he followed her up to the balcony where she gradually scanned over the horizon.

Foster was dumbfounded. It was more than he had ever anticipated. What he had just been shown were things directly out of science fiction. "Who…"

Tracy cut him short. "Ever hear of the Condors?"

"Yeah," Foster admitted. "But only rumors. Though it was only conspiracies."

"Not this time. Taken over technology," she explained. "Much of it existed for years but nobody developed it."

"Anybody else?"

"Two," she revealed. "Me and Scott."

"Brooks?"

"That's right," she replied. "Test cases."

"What now?" He was anxious to hear.

"Going with you," she volunteered. "Out west."

With Foster preparing for the road, as she had indicated the night before, Tracy was right alongside. Alex, standing by the gates, could see the glimmer of adventure in her eyes. They were dead set on the road ahead, west. In her mind, he could see, she was already there. As he waved goodbye, he reminded her, "Stay on the frequency. Coded transmission only."

Brian stood forlorn by the gates. "Bye, love," he whispered. "I'll miss you."

MARCH OF THE PATRIOTS

"Head 'em out." Elliott gave the signal as he watched his forces assemble into convoy formation. He then jumped behind the wheel of the command vehicle, next to Norton who was studying the map. The plan for the convoy was to first head north to Wyoming, continue on through Montana, then turn eastwards toward North Dakota, Minnesota, and Wisconsin with a final destination of Chicago, in the process embracing South Dakota, Nebraska, Kansas, and Iowa. "Shouldn't encounter much resistance," he advised Elliott, whose gaze shifted between the road ahead and the rearview reflectors, checking on the formation. Norton planned to stay on I-25 passing Cheyenne, Casper, Sheridan, and Billings, to eventually intersect some 500 miles ahead with I-94 East, the northern route to the Great Lakes. Barring unforeseen obstacles such as pit stops or unexpected vehicle breakdowns, they should make it there in a couple of months. Breakdowns were not showstoppers. Not with a tactical force on the move. The main objective was set within the target and timeline in accordance with military strategy.

As expected, the first few days went just like planned. As the convoy passed cities and towns, it left folks in their wake bewildered. Unsubstantiated rumors carried by farmers and townspeople were prolific prior to their arrival. "Enemy...Attack...Rape...Plunder," were some of the alert calls. But once the caravan arrived, they realized that the rumors were unfounded. In most cases the convoy arrived, stayed a few days, and headed out without much turmoil. Yes, there were incidents. But those were minor, generally created after a few glasses of beer or whisky by an aggressive soldier taking hold of a local girl, and then a fight would ensue with a gallant defendant. The soldier, although at fault, would come out unscathed because each and every hand was essential in the historic March of the Patriots. The direction was set. The quest focused on major towns. There was no purpose to proceed further north past Billings, Bismarck, and Fargo. Those were regions sparsely populated. They would have not much impact on staking out the central territory. Convoy, soldiers, and patriots alike kept forging east, toward Chicago. It was close to Milwaukee, WI, that the convoy encountered its first major resistance.

Progress along the way was pretty much routine. On arriving at a city or town, a special envoy was dispatched to seek out the governor, the mayor, or whoever was in charge. In general, the Patriots did not encounter much resistance from townspeople. They seemed to welcome a change in pace from their daily lives without power, communication, or trade. In some places water supply had been restored, primarily through gravitational flow. Life was on its way to recovery, although gradually.

First questions asked were mostly, "What's the state of the nation? Who's in charge? What about the White House? The Pentagon? Dollar?"

It all was sorted out during the first gathering in the town hall, followed by a promise to keep up communication. Fuel was the major obstacle. It was the reason why the economy had not recovered. Without power, drilling rigs were unable to work. Pumps sat dormant for the same reason. You couldn't just feed the crude back into the pump motors. It wasn't as simple. It had to be refined first. That took a lot of power. People learned to live through barter. For the unprepared, the first winter was an extreme hardship, especially in the northern regions. Keeping shelters warm without gas supply was a challenge. Many had no stoves to burn wood. Others had no access to resources, especially in cities. Living on modern conveniences had removed most people's pioneering skills. Trade, craft, and skills had to be learned, reacquired.

Entire industries had collapsed. And so had transportation, manufacturing, production, development, supply chains, inventory, and stock. Ammunition, canned goods, milk, bread, drugs, disposables had vanished from trading posts. If not hidden from the public, it was taken by force by marauding bands. Everybody was out for himself. Survival of the individual and family came first. Supporting neighbors was next. Small groups were formed within neighborhoods. It became necessary for warding off infiltrators. Neighborhoods shaped together, all for the protection of one's livelihood. Safety was of major concern.

Roaming bands were always searching for easy prey. They were caught up in the same predicament as the settlers: to survive another day. But for them, survival was acquired by force. The initial year was chaotic. But somehow, many survived. Starvation was prolific and so was epidemic. Misery was everywhere, caused by filth, lack of hygiene, decay. Decomposed flesh, exposed garbage, trash, and waste in many places were left unburied. Nobody wanted any part of it. It took many months, even years, to restore some sort of order. People in rural areas were quicker to organize. It was city dwellers that had the most difficult times. With all services out, sweltering heat in the summer and freezing cold in the winter made life unbearable. The first year, people died by the thousands.

Today, several years later, life had become more orderly. But trash and garbage disposal was still a problem when left to its natural cycle. First picked over was by the staving, then by scavengers, next by abandoned pets, and finally by rodents and maggots. Where the inner cities still struggled for survival, smaller cities and towns did better, to a certain degree.

In the countryside, following the initial struggle, people grouped together. Neighborhood watches were formed. Law-enforcing groups were elected. Mayors and city council were back in office, although on a limited scale. Though nobody wanted to be managed, leadership, direction, and guidance were necessities of life. Some people conformed, others rebelled. After the collapse of the nation, mismanagement became unacceptable. Townspeople saw to it. For now, greed, fraud, and corruption were pretty much under control. The law of the West saw to it. Justice was swift. Where in the olden days it was by hanging, in recent years deferred through courtroom debates, today it was by firing squad. The new order was enforced. Because of strictly enforced rules, the nation might have a chance to survive. The days of lengthy trials were part of the past. There were no costly delays, no judge, arbitrator, and lawyer debates, and no appeals. Judgment was fair, quick, and swift. Just like in the olden days.

CONVOY WEST

The Stryker, XA-202 Armored Command Vehicle and Humvee convoy commanded by Foster was well on its way headed west. It was their third day out. They had just passed Salt Lake City when a voice broke the silence. "Stinger…Crimson…come in." Tracy reacted. Her head snapped, alerting Foster. She repeated each message for him. Although Foster did not have the implant, Alex assigned the codename "Crimson" to him.

"Bandits ahead," the voice warned. As assured, Alex had been monitoring their progress. "Thirty miles out." He had given them ample warning. Back at the Castle, Brian had been busy trying to establish a satellite connection with the Western Sector. So far, he had not been successful. For now, Stinger was locked out from the grid. They had to rely on Specter to feed information via voice relay. Ahead, the Salt Lake opened up into ninety miles of barren wasteland. With field glasses pressed against their faces, they searched the distance ahead. There was no activity. Only the far-off contours of the Wendover foothills could be made out through the grayish blue haze.

Tracy activated the implant, but there were no images. "No feed," she reported back.

"No satellites…no repeater stations your area," Specter reported back.

"What about drones?" Foster was not happy and he voiced so. "All the money we spent. Dammit?"

"No hope there with GPS disabled."

"Watch out for the overpass. Skull Valley Road." Minutes later, the blockade came into view. What lay in waiting within the protection of the barrier was a group of vagrants holding up anyone on I-80 attempting to cross the salt flats. Using mostly M-16s to stop traffic, it was easy prey. Until today.

"Scout One," Foster ordered the Stryker. "Take the lead." What the vagrants did not anticipate was the firepower from the Stryker and XA-202. Trained on the target ahead were grenade launchers and a 7.62 mm Browning machine gun manned by the infantry squad in the back of the carrier, ready to fire. Once fire opened up, the exchange was short lived. Ten minutes later, the convoy was on its way once more, leaving casualties in its wake. Directly ahead, Wendover, Elko, Battle Mountain, and Winnemucca were passed uneventfully. It was not until the next day when trouble was encountered once more near Reno.

It was close to noon when Specter's voice alerted the convoy, "Trouble ahead."

"What?"

"Roadblock."

Twenty minutes later, the barrier came into view. "Toll bridge," a rudely-painted sign announced. "STOP all Traffic." It appeared a militant force had taken possession of the interstate. With Foster and Tracy in the lead, vehicle flanked by Humvee and Stryker, the convoy slowed to a crawl, then halted by the gate shack with lowered boom.

"Raise the boom," Foster ordered but his demands were ignored. With weapons at a ready, the entire toll force had joined the gate guards.

"One Humvee for passage," the gate commander demanded. It was the toll fee for the rest of the convoy to pass. Seemingly, he had already taken possession of the vehicle in his head. It must have been something he dearly desired. Tracy studied his face while he was talking with Foster. His eyes kept darting through the interior of her vehicle. It was obvious he was impressed with the electronics and armament.

"Not today," Foster snapped at him and stepped on the pedal, crashing through the barrier. It was enough for the toll road commander to jump into battle. Fiery bullets were hitting the convoy's protective shields all around. Foster, with Tracy on the passenger side, skidded to a halt fifty yards past the guard post. Next, they watched the Stryker take out the entire toll bridge: men, small arms, and all. Pieces were flying through the air and came crashing down on them. In one second, the path had been cleared.

Apparently, from what Alex's intelligence had gathered, a local gaming agency had taken command of the city of Reno. Everybody passing the region was subject to the locally enforced taxes. It was one of countless examples of how the nation had fallen prey within a land without federally enforced law and order. It was especially true near gambling cities. Folks there were so used to easy money that they had forgotten how to earn an honest income.

For the remainder of the journey, the convoy's progress was hampered by only minor skirmishes. These were mostly local and loosely organized gangs demanding payment for passage, especially along the infamous Donner Pass, the gateway into California. All were swiftly dealt with. The convoy arrived at the State capital a day later. Foster was ready to take charge over the Western Sector. But the State of California was not. There was no place for him at the State capital. It was a place reserved only for politicians. He would have to create his own post. It was Tracy who came up with a solution. "I know just the place," she offered.

"Yeah?" Getting rejected by the state's politicians, Foster had been frustrated. Although they were provided shelter for his mobile forces, it was only temporary. He had been set up at the rapidly expanding Travis AB nearby. Formerly a support base for transient personnel to Pacific assignments, it had become a strategic military base for troop movement, ground support, and logistics out west.

"Presidio," she said. "Perfect place for you…for us."

He was quick to respond. "But," he objected, "it's contaminated."

"Maybe not," she countered. "I was there after the blast. Presidio's located just west of ground zero. Fallout's carried east of the city by the jet stream. Should be safe."

"Well then," he agreed, "let's check it out."

The Presidio proved to be the perfect place. A real bastion, the place suited her as well. The foundation, built as a Spanish Fort in 1776, had held the place together through several wars. It had served as a support base during WWII as coordinating headquarters, deployment center, and training site for Pacific deployments against a potential Japanese invasion. More recently, it had lent support to the Korean and Vietnam Wars, as well as providing the Pacific submarine fleet with support.

"Our new home," Foster readily declared after giving the place a once over. Dosimeters still detected small remnants of alpha and beta particles on the ground around the fort, but not enough to be damaging to the human body. It was a different story east of Embarcadero, ground zero. There, readings shot up especially in and around former concrete structures. It'd take many more years before commerce and businesses would take hold again. For the time being, the once thriving Market Street business district, as well as cities of Oakland and Berkeley campus remained dormant.

SUBTLE WARNING

Last night, like many other nights, Alex Bauer had difficulty getting sleep. There were the days he just couldn't get any rest because of the gnawing muscle pains from past injuries on top of a never-resting mind. After lying in bed, tossing and turning for hours, he finally got up and headed for the kitchen. A cup of heated milk or cocoa always relaxed him. Back in bed, after more tossing and turning, the alarm clock on top of the nightstand read past five a.m. already. It was almost morning. Although he could have stayed in bed, due to a lifetime of conditioning as early riser, he got up and headed in the direction of the bathroom. Dawn already cast shadows through the windows, announcing a new day. Halfway along the hallway he passed a full-length mirror and caught the reflection of his body. He briefly stopped to inspect the shape. *Not bad at my age,* he thought while reflecting on his solid physique. He leaned closer and noticed the darkened shadows beneath the eyes. "Gotta get more sleep," he promised. Aside from that, he was happy for his good health contained within a well-toned body.

Satisfied, he got on to preparing the espresso machine for his morning treat. Where he used to enjoy the pungent aroma from the pure Columbian brand, since the EMP blast, he had to resort to the locally grown brands. It'd do for now.

His eyes caught the shape of the laptop computer resting on the coffee table. Hesitantly, he opened the cover. He knew once he got started the day would be spent seated in front of the damned device. But computers were his life. It was his lifeline to the world. The screen jumped immediately into action, but the applications took time to load. Waiting for the coffee to finish brewing, he moved over to the window to face the new day. It was still quiet in the early morning hours on the eastern slopes of the Rockies. He usually kept the windows open during the night to enjoy the gentle breeze of cool air sweeping down the foothills. He then noticed the sound of steaming water escaping the tank. It prompted him back to the kitchen. *Coffee's ready.*

A mug clutched in one hand, he turned the TV monitor, mounted on its sturdy entertainment frame, on. Where the set used to be tied into the major television networks, now, without news broadcasts capability in the U.S., he had it directly tied into the satellite downlink relayed from the Mountain to catch this morning's foreign broadcasts.

Flipping through channels he hardly paid attention. But there was one report that captured his interests. "A power outage struck several western Canadian cities yesterday, shutting down companies, affecting airport traffic, and blocking phone services in many areas." The announcer went on to list areas affected by the outage, ending, as usual, in speculation.

Ever since the attack on the World Trade Center in 2001 people in the nation had turned jumpy. It did not stop there. Other nations were affected as well. Terrorists became suspected for every emergency, for airline crashes, train wrecks, and shipping incidents. It was no wonder, with the growing threat exerted by radical factions rapidly expanding across the globe. Every nation had become a potential target. Unrest, riots, and resistance movements in many nations, had become an almost daily event. Where in former years the United States had policed and supported wars and conflicts on the international scale, to a certain degree, now, to the terrorist factions, it was open season. Terrorism had become prolific. Unrests and turbulences sprang up on every continent.

Absorbed by the news, Alex noticed a motion by the entrance. With a feigned smile, he acknowledged her presence. "Coffee's ready," he enticed her to join.

"Morning." Rhonda passed the den on her way to the kitchen. "Smells good." A minute later she squeezed her body on the sofa next to him. "What's new?"

It was then he gave her full attention. "The usual," he stated without showing much concern. "Power outages, food shortages, comm links down, crime and fighting everywhere."

Pulling her robe tighter around her shoulders, she huddled her body against his. Slightly disheveled from a night of restful sleep, she shot him a mellow look. "I'm so grateful for this place…and you."

It had been some time already since Alex reestablished a connection with Rhonda, who had been trapped at Peterson AFB with the EMP strike. Being strangers at this point, Rhonda felt uncomfortable moving to the Castle when he made the offer. With him visiting with her at the base frequently they became close friends at first, then became a couple. With the nation rapidly deteriorating, roads becoming dangerous, base being abandoned by its staff and support personnel, although months had gone by, he eventually convinced her to join him at the Castle.

Without the safety of the Castle, she had acknowledged many times over that "I'd be in serious trouble." Both knew it only too well about the fighting, crime, and marauding bands roaming near and far. So far, due to his foresight, Alex had been able to divert every potential assault on his home. Sometimes it worked by reasoning it out with potential intruders. Other times, he had to flash a weapon or, when things got out of hand, use striking force. No matter what the action, there would be no repercussion from law enforcement since it was virtually non-existent.

For the first time since his divorce from Annette, his daughter's mother, he was sharing his space with someone. Rhonda had become part in his life. He cherished her. The shared passion and love they felt for each other initially had turned into deep compassion and understanding. The feeling was mutual. He did his best to preserve the values. And, from all indications, aside from demonstrating an occasional womanly need, she did her best to accommodate his private space when needed. For all practical purposes, their relationship was solid. Both had similar interests. They respected each other. Aside from an occasional difference of opinion, Alex and Rhonda were in harmony.

GAKONA (ALASKA)

Facing his superior seated across the desk, "Wonder how long it'll be," Jack Owens stated, "before the world catches on." There had been speculations by the local people for some time about the causes of the increasing number of power outages affecting the state's power grid. The people in the state of Alaska considered themselves fortunate, having survived the strike on the nation years earlier. In actuality, it was their distance to the north that prevented the EMP burst from incinerating the region and their present location. The HAARP control station, being a shielded structure mostly located below ground, not much damage had occurred.

"We can only keep a secret for so long," the station manager replied. "Someone will figure it out and scream holy hell." Discovery would certainly mean the end of their career. There was a specific reason many citizens from the lower states sought refuge in the isolation of the frigid north. It was these individuals that thrived in the cold and isolation from civilization. Jack was one of them.

"Let's hope never." Following a disciplined career as Missileer at an underground missile silo years ago, Jack had been reassigned to this mission. Presently ranking captain, he knew there would never be another promotion. Not with the nation in turmoil the way it was. With only a skeleton staff on site, for the time being it was he who had to put up with the rudimentary tasks of more testing and compiling data on a relatively boring job. From a political perspective, he was clueless as to where his and his crew's efforts were ultimately leading. But from a mission perspective, it was to test yet another weapon. And even more dangerously, as of recent times, it was a weapon of mass destruction only he along with a handful scientist had knowledge and control over.

The computer operator assigned this shift was poised over the keyboard, ready to query the database. "Give me telemetry reading on the ozone layer," Owens ordered. To him, more important than the testing, was the critical significance of the ever-widening fissures in the northern ozone layer. Ever since the prolific testing had begun, scientists and researchers around the world had uncovered an alarming depletion in the layer. Supported with documented data, in spite of their voiced concerns, nothing seemed to be being done about it. The common excuse until now had always been attributed to atmospheric pollution, greenhouse gases, and climate change. "Little do the poor slobs on the outside know," Jack muttered.

The operator interrupted his thoughts. "Image's on the screen."

Jack inhaled deeply. "Damn," he gasped. "If this keeps up there'll be sunburns even at night." Although the operators chuckled at his remark, he was dead serious. Due to increased news coverage on the diminishing ozone, it had become common knowledge that the penetrating solar rays were the cause of skin cancer and other derma- and vision-related diseases. But within the test center, everyone was consciously aware of a direct relationship between their testing and the increase in global warming. There was not much Jack could do about it personally. He was only following orders like everyone else onsite. "It'll only get worse," he grumbled.

Deeply concerned, he strode back to the office, getting ready to prepare the report on the latest test results. Facing the safety vault, he dialed in the code to unlock a drawer, then reached for a folder labeled, "Top Secret." Leafing through pages of the classified document, he located the schedule for the next test. He glanced over the datasheet and prepared the monthly reports, compiled and channeled to his superiors. That accomplished, with both boots propped against the edge of the desk, he contemplated his past accomplishments that had landed him in this isolated base close to the North Pole.

Jack's staff included young recruits reassigned from missile silos located predominantly in the Midwestern regions of the nation. Following the EMP strike, with minuteman and peacekeeper missile fleets inoperative, the defense initiative was rendered ineffective. From his Missileer perspective, this mission assignment was not much different aside the location. Camouflaged within a lush green forest of the north, the high-powered antenna array protruding from the ground was barely visible. It blended in perfectly with the terrain. Being a no-fly zone for aircraft and completely isolated from civilization, the chances of someone stumbling on the facility was pretty remote. But the heart of the complex was yet another thing. Much like in past decades, until now it had remained concealed and buried below ground.

When Jack first arrived for this assignment, after giving the place an initial assessment, he was highly disappointed. He was under the impression he would have to manage what seemed to be a remote relay facility. Little did he know the true purpose for this place until he was handed the assignment file. "HAARP," the folder stated. Not until delving into the document did he learn about its true purpose. "Unbelievable. Incredible. Holy shit!" were some of his vocal expressions. Working on the forefront of political events, being part of the nation's prominent defense system, Jack had no inkling about something that was much greater than a nuclear warhead-tipped missile buried in a silo. What he read was a revelation he had never anticipated.

Completed in the late '90s by ARCO Power Technologies, aside from being the highly innovative and sophisticated Ionospheric Research Instrument (IRI) facility, most of its activity was generated underground. Aside from the antenna farm, only the support building was visible above ground. Although HAARP would transmit its high frequency radio waves in a narrow beam pointed upward, interacting with the ionosphere, potentially hazardous values of radio field strength would be present at ground level very close to the antenna farm. To prevent human exposure to these fields, an exclusion fence was constructed. Additional safeguards were built into the system to preclude any possibility of harm. Even aircraft detection radar was interfaced with the operations centers. It would automatically shut down the high-power transmissions should aircraft be detected flying en route or passing through the microwave beam.

Years ago, in the pre-EMP days, after heated and highly classified controversial meetings by opposing members in the Pentagon, Gakona had been selected as the ground-based HAARP facility. This site was chosen not so much for its remoteness, but for the ability to obscure the facility. The planners knew the site would eventually grow to immense size. To avoid unnecessary attention from any nearby community or big game hunters, the project plan called for a camouflaged and gradual implementation.

With his feet propped comfortably on the desk, Jack shot a periodic glance at the array of ZULU clocks mounted high on the wall. As usual, his eyes swept across the bank of synchronized timepieces. For now, he only had to contend with one, the "local" time. With nothing else scheduled for the day he anxiously awaited his shift relief. His thoughts were already in the support building above, which housed recreation, snack bar, and sleeping quarters for the crew. Looking forward to a cold beer to quench the dryness in his throat, he was counting the minutes before he could join into a game of darts or poker. After a shift rotation, as isolated as the place was, most of the crew couldn't wait to travel to nearby Anchorage for a few days of leisure in local establishments.

In this part of the world, for the casual observer, nothing much ever changed. Though rumors were persistent about something strange going on, conversations were usually centered on yet another newly arrived face suddenly showing up at one establishment or another. Curiosity held steadfast since the faces usually stayed on indefinitely. But this was Alaska. Outside of the usual tourist spots in Anchorage, Skagway, and Nome, arrivals were embraced and respected as new settlers.

Jack needed the break. He already knew tomorrow would be a brutal day. Advance notice a few days ago had forewarned of an upcoming critical mission. He had no clues about the details but knew it was the primary reason they had been testing all along. Something big was about to happen. He reached for the desk drawer to retrieve the combination code to the mission vault. Feeling slight uneasy, he muttered, "Just to be sure." He memorized the vault dials one more time necessary after the periodic changes of the code. He knew as soon as the call came he had to respond quickly. The success of the entire mission would hinge on his and his crew's readiness. In spite of his queries to visiting scientists, he had been kept in the dark for what was about to transpire. Nobody seemed to divulge information. Even the usual rumor mill had been absent. Briefing his shift relieve on the way out about tomorrow's critical mission, he muttered, "Guess we'll find out soon enough."

VANDENBERG AFB

It was a typical day in this mid-central coastal region in the sunny state of California. Light swells of green-colored waves, mixed with white sand, were gently rolling onto the mostly deserted beaches facing west of the fenced-in perimeters at Vandenberg, AFB. As usual, the sparse crowd of sun worshipers at the pristine beaches paid no attention of what was fenced in only a few hundred yards from the sandy beach front. Fog was still layered heavily this time of day, obscuring the countryside. But later in the day, after the sun burned off the remains of the mist, the colossal structures from missile launch towers appeared out of the gray, like gigantic robots displaying a menacing presence of a destructive technology.

Today, visitors could see an additional object clearly visible below the horizontal launch boom emanating streams of super-cooled hydrogen gases from fuel connection hoses still attached to the bottom of the huge missile tubes sitting on launch pad 3E. This was the only launch facility in the nation left. It was the missile testing facility for the dated, but still very effective, Atlas, Minuteman, and Peacekeeper missile defense systems. The ICBM sitting on the pad had been on standby for launch, waiting for the ground fog to burn off. With the fog gone, the pending launch became very visible to the crowd, who had not expected it. Especially not with the current struggle the nation was in. Although there was no official defense budget under the new administration, it had been quietly appropriated by the government to assure the security of the Western Sector. Development went on quietly with support from limited manufacturing and contractors.

It would be the first launch in years. Ground crews were preparing for the final launch sequence when the mission commander's mobile began chirping. Annoyed at the untimely interruption, he reluctantly reached for the gadget and immediately noticed the high priority number on the caller display. He did not have to listen very long to hastily pick up the PA mic.

"Hold…hold launch sequence," Blackwell shouted in a highly agitated, but commanding, voice. Clearing his throat, Lee Blackwell, Colonel, Vandenberg, CA, next ordered all personnel on standby until further notice. Checking the control stations on the monitors, he watched as his operators relaxed. Some took the idle time to rush to the nearby coffee service counter to refill their brown-crusted, empty mugs. As his own cup was empty, the same notion crossed his mind, but instead, he hastened for the executive office. Awaiting him was the mission support staff, prolifically speculating on the reasons for delay. He stepped up to a cluster of executives, who were demanding, "What's up?"

"Call from Eagle One," Blackwell stated. "Reports space intrusion and launch interference." Eagle One was the code name for the AWACS[24], airborne command post for his sector.

"What's the situation?"

Chewing on an ever-present cigar stuck tightly between his clenched lips, he further explained, "Mission Control spotted massive chemtrails activity." Although he was

---

[24] AWACS – Airborne Warning and Control System, designates as E-3, was a mobile, long-range radar surveillance and control system for air defense and battle management. Flying at medium altitude, its radar system could detect, track, and identify low-flying aircraft at great distances.

keenly aware of his disgusting habit from the distasteful staring eyes from subordinates, he didn't give a damn about anybody's opinion. He was in charge. And that was the only thing that counted in the career of the egotistical Blackwell. He did not care what people thought of him. He wasn't here to win a personality contest. He was here to run a mission. It was decision time. He needed answers. He needed an explanation for the delay. With growing impatience, he flagged down one of his staff. "Get me Edwards on line." He almost spat the order at the operator.

"Yes sir," was the snappy reply as the operator rushed to the nearest desk phone. "Right away, sir."

EDWARDS AFB

Gary Walters was having a bad day. It didn't matter that he held the top position as base commander at what he called, "a godforsaken dustbowl in the middle of the desert." What bothered him most was the ever-present daytime heat. He should have had no reason to complain for he was practically God here in this isolated facility. Being God, he should have been contented, blissful, and all empowering. Right?

Wrong. He had been assigned to this place for a third rotation already. The first time, long ago, was at the onset of his career. He couldn't even remember back that far. As a test pilot just finished with flight training, he had an entire lifetime ahead of him. At a young age, it did not matter much what assignment one held in the military. It could be some island paradise or a place in the remote desert such as this; it was all temporary. It really did not matter if you wasted a couple of years living at a desolate facility. Life at that age seemed endless. One had to live through it to experience the full breadth of ups and downs in a career.

It was no exception for him. What made his case somewhat different from the mainstream was the privilege of having been born into Air Force society through well-established family ties in a long line of military descendants. He came from several generations of military servants dating back to the civil war. His dad was a general, and so was his granddad, and, with the most recent promotion, so was he, for that matter. He'd held this rank since his last assignment here but it handed him some conditional strings attached to this place. He'd been looking forward to living out his career at the Pentagon, but that did not happen. Regardless of all the earned promotions and awards from a rewarding career, at the end, he felt like a scapegoat sent here.

"You're much better off in an environment you understand," was the excuse given by the last review board when a new star was attached to the lapel of his uniform. "You'd only be another four-star paper shuffler at the Pentagon. Consider yourself fortunate." It was the excuse given to him following another budget cut by Congress. He knew it, and so did the board.

Fuming under his breath, he responded, "Yeah, right. Lucky me." That was almost eight years ago. He was torn from his lucid thoughts by the ring of the phone. Slightly agitated, he hoped it would stop, but the ringing persisted. He reached for the phone. "What?"

The voice from the local base operator sounded urgent. "Call from Vandenberg."

"I'll take it," he replied. Any other time but today he might have ignored the call. He knew quite well they had a launch on the way. An ill feeling rose from the pit of his stomach. "Should have launched already," he thought while waiting to get connected.

Right away he sensed trouble. "Walters!" the booming voice sounded off. "What are you doing to me?"

Just as angry, he shot back, "What're you talking about?" *Who does he think he is?* He had recognized the voice immediately. The caller and he did not like each other very much, but had to tolerate infrequent and necessary interchanges during mission time.

"You let your crop dusters enter my space," accused the other. "You should know better, especially today, you bastard." The ranting continued. "You knew about the launch."

Trying to stop this verbal onslaught, Walters spat back, "Now you just wait a darn minute. Please, no name calling." He tried to keep his cool. "Calm down."

But Blackwell furiously continued, "Scrubbed the launch because of you. Wilmot will hear about this."

"Yeah. Why don't you take it up with him?"

"Would," was the angry reply, "but it's your people. Call them off immediately."

There was indifference in Walters' voice. "Can't do that," he replied. "Orders from higher ups." He knew his missions were a nuisance not only to him, but everybody else in the area. The public saw to that. The continuous outcries had every command on the West Coast jumpy every time the streams of white vapor trails appeared crisscrossing the Californian skies. He had no control over what everybody called a "phenomenon." Somewhere along the way it got coined by some newscaster and the term stuck. The ghost-like appearances were real. Been for years but nobody knew its purpose. Even he had no clues other than the persistent rumors for this or that reason.

From his perspective, it did not matter much what the missions were. At the end, it was just another experiment DARPA or whatever agency was conducting. He only followed orders. And they became more frequent, especially connected with the damned chemtrails. Like everybody else, he could only speculate. They were always classified—a need to know. What he provided were the craft. Testing had been going on forever, since the beginning of when this facility had been commissioned. It had been the very reason the base was built, in the middle of nowhere, away from the prying eyes of the public. DOD planners had selected the isolation in Death Valley for a special purpose. But that was before the ever-encroaching population. *Who knew back then?*

The base, strategically situated next to Rogers Dry Lake located within the Mojave Desert, was on a deserted salt pan with a hardened surface. It provided a natural extension to Edwards' runways. The large landing area, combined with excellent year-round weather, made it a perfect site for flight testing even though the lake was a National Historic Landmark. Not many visitors came here. It was only the occasional desert rat, discouraged from entering by the many warning signs surrounding the dry lakeshores prohibiting entrance to an unauthorized public. In the pre-EMP days, the place was buzzing with activities, including supersonic over-flights, in the process creating tremendous shockwaves that broke up an otherwise silent wasteland. Today, due to the lack of fuel, the base had turned mostly silent.

Many of the more valuable craft had been mothballed. Others, not as valuable, were left out in the open, exposed to the elements. Although partially preserved by the dryness of the region, the blowing sand was doing a job on the metal surface. Yet retired, still memorable were the once proud birds for their achievements. Many were remnants from notables like Chuck Yeager, Lt. Col. Henry H. Arnold, and test pilot Glen Edwards, with record breaking awards for speed, altitude, and the sound barrier. One could still imagine the sleek designs with crafts such as the Bell X-1, X-15, U-2, B-52, SR-71 Blackbird, the space shuttle, and, more recently, the F-35 Joint Strike Fighter and F-22 Raptor doing their supersonic flybys. But today, not even museum-worthy pieces remained.

"Walters! You with me?" The voice interrupted his thoughts. "What's your call?"

"Take it up with JCS," he offered. "Nothing I can do. Cancel the mission 'til someone sorts out the mix up."

"You'll hear from me," was the departing threat. Click...the receiver went dead. Walters could only imagine the irate Blackwell slamming the receiver into a well-worn cradle. *Sure, I'll hear from him, but so will the world.* He could already envision tomorrow's headlines in the local papers with the responsible agency spokesperson presenting yet another excuse: *"Vandenberg mission scrubbed!"*

PRESIDIO

General Foster, with Tracy as adjutant by his side, had been busy rebuilding the Presidio as their western-most situated defense headquarters. When taking possession of the Presidio, the fort had been abandoned because of nuclear fallout remnants. But, when checking out radiation levels with dosimeters, they determined the levels were acceptable for human habitation once again. Though much of the brick buildings had withstood the nuclear blast, the interior was in disarray. First on their agenda was fixing crumbled walls, then cleaning up the messy place. With the complex built in the 16th century, is held up well as a strategic Pacific outpost for the mission. Later, during several Pacific-based wars, it served the western seaports as support facility to the U.S. naval fleets. Now, under Foster's command, it appeared more as a tactical site then anything permanent. Cables, wires, desks and tables were arranged in a temporary fashion with a future goal in mind for Foster to eventually return to the Pentagon. How long that would take, at this time was anybody's guess.

First on the agenda was establishing communication links that had been damaged by the nuclear attack a few years ago. Next came fixing satellite transmitter relays to NORAD. Where physical wires had to be installed on the local levels in and around the Presidio, wireless connections were made by Alex using the antenna farm on Cheyenne Mountain.

It did not take long for the Presidio to flourish once more. Though limited as an effective military base, it was a well-positioned location for the challenges ahead. Foster and Tracy, backed up by a newly established support team, formed an effective tactical unit protecting the Pacific coastal airspace. Although water-based intrusions were expected, threat levels from the Pacific were considered minimal at this time. Most of the assault brunt on the nation was experienced on the eastern seaboard. The real reason for taking possession of the fort by Foster, at this time, was only known to him and Tracy, his most trusted lieutenant. Although civilian, she was indoctrinated into the army by the general to fall, maintain, and be manageable directly under his command.

"What's the status with the Castle?" Foster had stuck his head into Tracy's office. With her in the army, on the same mission platform since arriving here, he and Tracy had developed a close and interdependent relationship. Where in the past their association had been primarily on an employer/employee status, with Tracy in recent years gaining notoriety and recognition as a fighter, Foster had offered equal status between the two. Although she wore no military uniform, from a military perspective, he had assigned her the rank as Full-bird Colonel. Where at this time it was only a documented status, when on mission, it would become extremely important. With Foster's full support, Tracy's actions would be sanctioned not only by the general, but also by his subordinates.

"Working on it," she replied. Tracy enjoyed her superior position. She pulled rank whenever someone questioned her demands. By now, she considered herself "an old hand," among the troops. It reflected on her demeanor as well.

"Any word from Bauer?"

"Got his sector under control."

"Keep me posted."

"Will do." As usually these days, it ended their exchange.

MARCH OF THE PATRIOTS

The Patriots were on the move once more. Commanded by Rusty Norton with Brodie Elliott in charge of the 1ˢᵗ Armored Division, had arrived in Madison, Wisconsin after a long and arduous march for most of a year. By now, the once minor brigade from the garrison protecting Fort Knox had turned into a full-sized army. Though thousands of foot soldiers strong, transportation was still a problem. The shortage of military vehicles was supplemented mostly with commercial trucks, SUVs, and pickups. Fuel supply still presented a problem. Scouts were sent ahead throughout the countryside, confiscating everything closely resembling a 55-gallon drum. Country folks, the smart ones anyway, had stored up fuel for years, many with tanks buried beneath the ground, much like a gasoline station. Tankers would drive up once every quarter, replenishing supplies. But that was many months ago. Many had run dry since. There were no fuel tankers on the road other than the ones appropriated by Norton and his army.

It was getting dark already. The convoy had just entered the outskirts of Madison County. Norton, in the lead vehicle, was contemplating whether to stop for the night. Checking the map, the next major settlement was Milwaukee, about 80 miles farther east. "What do you think?" he checked with the driver. "Feel like going on?"

The thought of Milwaukee, hub of beer brewing, was enough for the contingent to continue on the way. Relaying his intentions to the rest of the convoy, Norton yelled into the mic, "Head 'em out."

Two hours later, flanked by a cluster of Humvee, Norton gestured from within the XA-202 armored command vehicle. He was trying to get Bad Man's attention where he was commanding the M113 Striker assault vehicle. The convoy rolled to a gradual stop just short of a sign mounted overhead announcing in large lettering: "MILWAUKEE – The City Welcomes You."

The vehicle drivers hopped from their cabs to gather around the lead. "Well," Brodie proclaimed, "let's see how friendly these folks are." Darkness had already fallen. The convoy needed a space to settle in for the night. Soldiers needed to get fed. Shelters identified. Fuel supplies replenished. It was the same process at the end of each day when on the road.

Norton called on Bad Man, the Enforcer. "Take your men and find the mayor." Since this was a major metropolis, he wanted to get approval from city management before claiming the place, if only for a day or two; otherwise it would cause unnecessary friction. For Norton, the march had been an educational one. He had gotten to know cities along the route he otherwise would have never visited. Since departing Fort Knox many months earlier, he'd left in his wake along the march headed west, among clusters of smaller towns, St. Louis, Kansas City, and Denver. From there, the convoy took a turn north headed for Cheyenne, Billings, and Great Falls. Arriving at the Canadian border, he decided to halt the advancement. There was no need to proceed further north. He had enough of a territory. Anything further would only jeopardize the acquired land. He did not want to make the same mistake as so many past conquerors. Usually driven by greed, once on the roll, a sizable army command did not always consider the ensuing logistics for supporting gained territory and just kept on going. But that, as history showed, would always be the downfall of a nation. Genghis Kahn, Attila the Hun, and more recently Hitler, if alive, along with other collapsed empires could contest to it.

It had taken several months to scout along the Canadian border. He decided to stay clear of that nation and only stake out the plains territory limited within an area that used to be the United States. Eventually breaking down its tent city, the convoy headed east toward the Great Lakes leaving Bismarck, Fargo, St. Paul, and Madison in their wake. For now, another major leg of the journey had come to an end. Over the years, the Patriots had gained popularity. After the seed was planted, there was no stopping the movement once the convoy got on the way. Ever since, citizens living within and along the plains boundaries were expecting the army. Many of the town's people along the route would readily embrace the advancing forces. Rumors proclaimed that there was a standing offer of "Food for Work," when signing up. After years of hardship and famine, it was a promise people would readily accept.

Bad Man and his scouts had just returned from the city. Unable to locate the city council he had returned empty handed. It meant Norton had to wait until morning. Spending a night along the roadside did not matter much. It was not the first time. There had been a number of times when his army had been refused entrance to a town or showed up too late at night for them to accommodate his soldiers. Despite the grumblings that followed such a refusal for gaining entrance to a populated settlement, Norton had a standing order for his army: no plunder, no raping, no repression. His March would be a clean sweep. Having never stepped foot in Milwaukee, not knowing what to expect, he gave the order, "Let's wait 'til morning." He felt his soldiers needed the break. Since it was summertime, the nights were pleasant for sleeping outdoors. Skies had never been more visible since the power grid went down. For many, it was a new experience. Most had never seen a starry sky. It was something only settlers had experienced in the early days of colonizing the country.

With the Promised Land, the city of breweries, within reach, Bad Man had a difficult time keeping the battle lines in control. The army had grown enormously in size. As was the case with every standing army, the soldiers were ready to fight. But, until now, other than local skirmishes, mostly among themselves, there had been no battles. Attention spans were short fused. Most fights were minor. Some resulted in on-the-spot disciplinary actions. Others, more severe, especially when a fatality was involved, would be sent to Fort Leavenworth.

"Don't give me any grief," Bad Man warned the most bothersome troublemakers. His warnings were generally regarded with respect. While he was feared among the men, he was far from being ruthless. In spite of the menacing appearance he projected—torn body garb loaded down with ammo belts, sidearm and semi tugged into belts, Mohawk haircut, scarred skin from knife-wielding fights—the man was just and righteous. All he wanted was respect. And respect he had once his men got to know him. Today, this close to the brewing capital, he made allowances. He, himself, could already taste a cool brew passing down a parched throat. "Can't wait getting my hands on a Miller," he proclaimed.

"Me too," were comments voiced by his trusted, closely huddled around the campfire. Speculations had been thrown around on how many breweries there were in the city. Words like Schlitz, Papst, along with beer halls and Oktoberfest were prolifically flung in the air. Unknown to them, it was Miller winning out the lead, through a number of commercial battles resulting in Miller Park as a brewing landmark in this northern region. Regardless, Bad Man was ready to march, taking the city by force, if necessary.

Early next morning, Bad Man and his scouts left for the city. They located the city mayor's residence. He was quick and insistent, setting up a meeting place. After word got back to the mobile garrison, Norton gathered his commanders. "Let's see what Miller City's all about." Driving East on I-94, they had just crossed the Zoo Freeway loop with the overhead sign announcing the next major connecting point: "North-South Freeway." It would be their destination. The city mayor had organized an early meeting for the arriving party. It did not come as surprise to him. It was something the city managers had expected for some time. Rumors were passed on weeks ago of an army headed in their direction announcing the "March of the Patriots."

The day Bad Man and his army marched into Milwaukee would be a landmark. After spotting the enormous complex of Miller Park, the brewery complex specifically, from his perspective, he came here to liberate the city. What made this place by the Michigan shores so valuable to him and his forces was not the climate, the lake, or the open spaces. It was the beer brewed here. The Patriots, the whole lot through all ranks, had become dependent on it. It was the dependency that made the city worth fighting for while time marched on.

There seemed to be an endless supply of beer, as long as there was water and hops available. The product was treated much like liquid gold. Once settled in, the consumption by the Patriots was restricted to only after sundown, it was rationed out daily. People with parched throats and symptoms of dehydration from drinking the night before would line up for hours, impatiently waiting. When the gates swung open, the onrush was much like a stampede rushing to get seated in one of the spacious halls. Where once the complex had been a well-organized machine, with raw materials feeding the boilers, fermenting in containers, followed with storage and delivery systems, today the process was still in place and functional, but the accountability for what was produced had gone by the wayside without electricity to feed computers and office equipment.

It was raw materials in, finished product out. "Out" meant from the holding tanks to the in-house tables. Whatever was brewed only made it to the army of thirsty soldier. At the end of the day, there was not enough liquid gold left to sell off to potential customers. "But that," Norton promised, "is gonna change." He realized the potential from the sales of this precious commodity. It would feed his army. He just had not gotten around to organizing a workforce to grow the hops and grain needed for fermentation, necessary technology to operate and produce the product, and supply thirsty customers at the other end. Intentions were good on all counts but when asked about the progress, the word on the Milwaukee waterfront was, "We're workin' on it."

The energy was lacking, especially after fighting off another hangover in the morning. At this stage in the life of Bad Man and his forces, the most important aspect was protecting the beer, the acquired lifestyle, and Milwaukee's waterfront.

Months had gone by since their first arrival at this magnificent lake pretty much empty from all shipping. Looking over the surface from the shorefront, during calm days, not a ripple disturbed the waters. Only an occasional spec drifting across the surface, usually a canoe or small boat, occupied by a local fisherman could be seen. Powered boats where still sitting idle in harbors collecting barnacles along the hulls.

It came as complete surprise when an armada of motorized boats made their appearance crisscrossing the lake. From the distance, it looked like a uniformed detachment they could not identify. When Norton was alerted, he quickly gathered a defense detachment made up of Elliott's forces together with Bad Man rushed to the shore for a closer look. It was their first sighting of strangers in the area. It only took minutes for the armada to beach at the shore front. Highly alerted and on guard, the Patriots, not knowing what to expect, Bad Man was ready. He was ready to defend his city. Poised for attack, M-16 aimed at the approaching party, he and his forces were ready to battle it out, if needed. But Norton, with Elliott alongside, was willing to negotiate. Negotiate what, still had to be seen. It all depended on what the foreigners had in mind. Regardless for what that would be, there would not be any concessions.

"Don't like it," Bad Man kept insisting. "Let me wipe 'em out." He was anxious to get this over with. He knew, and so did his men, that the only reason for anyone to show up here was for the beer. Their minds, as clouded as they had gotten from daily drinking, were made up. "No such thing," Norton insisted. "You…" he gestured at Bad Man, but paused, embarrassed. Norton was groping for words. If he had ever known it, he'd plain forgotten Bad Man's real name.

"Duke…Duke Wheeler," Bad Man said. "Told you before."

Shrugging a shoulder at him, Norton quickly conceded, "Sorry." He did not want additional friction with the enemy at their doorsteps. He was prepared to listen to what the visitors had to say. He would at least give them a chance to explain. After all, it was not very often an outside party would advance to these waters. One, tall, robust, and rugged in appearance, stood out. It was he that spoke. "Who's in charge?"

Norton, barefooted, only wearing fatigues, stepped forward. Steadfast to the core he declared, "That'd be me." He boldly faced the leader head on, demanding, "What brings you here?"

"Negotiations," was the ready comeback. He then introduced himself, to Norton's surprise accent free, "Yusuf Hashim. Commander, Jihad forces America."

Although astonished at the bold introduction, Norton retained his calm. "Negotiate what?"

"Territory!"

Flanked by his lieutenants Brodie and Bad Man, Norton responded with a cool, "You are on my territory!"

Bad Man, barrel chest and tough to the core, stepped forward. He could not contain his fury any longer and voiced his rage at Norton. "Kill 'em…kill 'em…Let me kill 'em." He was enraged at the audacity of this foreigner, demanding such a ludicrous claim. This was his territory. He had fought for it. And he would defend it at all cost. Norton immediately interceded. He did not want a war on his hands. He yelled back, "Put your rifle down."

Reluctantly, Bad Man stepped back with the rifle barrel lowered while Norton took the negotiation lead. He wanted at least listen to what the foreigners had to say. Also, he wanted the latest information from the outside world. It was not often that a foreigner made it up here to this isolated region. With satellites out, news was limited primarily to amateur radio operators. Reliable communication links had yet to be established. They could be years away, if at all. Without manufacturing capabilities, lacking organized schools and training facilitates, whatever knowledge and skills existed in the plains was applied to practical roles necessary to survive.

With a reluctant gesture, Norton invited the visitors to the Patriot headquarters center nearby. The following hours did not fare well. What the Patriots received form the unwelcome visitors were information on the currents political state on the world. "Just wait a damned minute," Bad Man, who had bolted from his chair, impatiently interjected. He was getting utterly frustrated listening to the boring interchange of political diplomacy. He'd rather fight things out fist to fist.

The visitor's attention immediately shifted his way when he voiced his anger. His frustration had swelled to a state of frenzied fury when he spat out his anger, "Nobody is waltzing in here to take away anything." He took a few seconds to compose the next words, "Not the military, not the government," while wildly gesticulation at the visitors, "and surely not you." Ready to fight, his drinking pals had also jumped to their feet cheering him on with, "Long live the Patriots."

There were several more of these outbursts when Norton decided to terminate the exchange with the rivals. Negotiations had gone nowhere. It became quite obvious that the intruder's intentions were hostile and final. Their departure was abrupt and quick with a promise to return. On departing, he sent Yusuf and his militants off with a final warning. "Next time," he promised. "You won't set foot on these shores."

"We'll see," was Yusuf's comeback. "Your days are numbered. It is our time to conquer the world."

"Let me kill 'em…let me kill 'em," Bad Man again shouted at Norton while rushing after the departing. "Stand down. Your time will come." It was an ominous promise by Norton who did not like it.

GAKONA

In a state of heightened anticipation, Jack Owens muttered, "Today's the day." He woke early to check on the readiness of the mission team. He could not afford any errors or slipups. A mission could be tested over and over, but when it came to the actual operation, it seemed like something always went wrong. It greatly concerned him. He finally came to the conclusion that it was human nature to falter under pressure. With today's mission, still a couple of hours out, he popped his head into each office cube to remind the department heads of the readiness brief. Still skeptical, but somewhat satisfied everything seemed to be on track, he headed directly for the control room. Swiping his card through the ID reader, the glass door opened promptly with a familiar swishing sound. Upon entering, he watched engineers and technicians, dressed alike in spotlessly white lab coats proudly displaying their name tags, were busy hurrying in and out of aisle ways.

Concern clearly showed on his face when he confronted the principle mission engineer put in charge for today's intercept. "Any issues I should know about?" he asked. A real professional, a highly dependable and always honest individual, though he had made it clear on a number of occasions that he disliked being here, the engineer was a man Jack could always depend on. "You're indispensable," was his usual response. Jack knew him socially. They had spent enough time together on weekends to Anchorage, hunting trips when elk and bear seasons were on. He knew quite well why the guy didn't like it here. But he was not the only one. There were others that desired to be someplace else rather than be stuck at this facility. It was not so much the remoteness of the place. Before being assigned here, they had all been excited for a chance to be in Alaska. It was the last sanctuary for the pioneering spirit many sought.

It was something else that bothered them. On arriving, it did not take much to figure out the true purpose for the place. Rumors were soon confirmed by the boundless tests that followed. "We are not stupid," Jack had been told on many occasions when the topic of assignment became the subject. After a few beers in one of the many social establishments frequented in the city, discussions usually escalated into heated arguments. He'd had to step in a number of times to remind them of the sensitivity of their mission. It was not always easy to calm them down. "Screw this…fuck that," were some of the outbursts he had to contend with. At the end, assuring them of the mission's peaceful intentions, they would always come to their senses. Nobody was willing to compromise a successful career or give up a highly rewarding job. Up here in Alaska, life went on pretty much the same as it always had. Water, food, and space were plentiful. It was different down south, all knew, about the trouble the nation was facing with pilferage, starvation, and killings the citizens were facing. But the sobering facts of the mission never went away. In contrast to wishful thinking, many suspected the true purpose for their existence here. It was to promote yet another destructive weapon.

"No issues," the engineer responded. "Everything checks out."

Satisfied, Jack headed for the elevator that connected the command capsule with the underground support structure. In deep thought, Jack had missed the elevator doors closing and opening moments ago, waiting for him to touch a button. He finally pushed the last button. It was the sixth floor below ground level to which he was headed.

Arriving a few seconds later, he stepped out into the wide hallway leading to the main generator building. He snatched a pair of earplugs from a small container mounted by the exit doors. Like so many times before, on entering the main hall he became fascinated by the immediate spectacle within a highly charged environment. When activated, the sound was horrendous.

Hurrying along the corridors, he was forced to sidestep to avoid colliding with busily chatting scientists and support engineers discussing last minute orders. Staffed by a remarkably skilled workforce, the atmosphere was bristling with emotional and physical tensions alike. He passed dozens of stressed faces displaying concerns, doubts, and even fears of personal safety. Where the facility had been designed for maximum protection against harm, a disaster could never completely be ruled out. There were many uncertain factors driving the unproven technology. While the underlying infrastructure had been successfully tested, the application for the weapon still needed to be tested and verified. Today was the day.

Stepping into the shielded, particle generator containment room prepared to release stored energy of billions of volts, Jack felt like being trapped in the midst of lightning flashes within a massive thunderstorm. He could sense the static energy sweeping over every inch of his skin, shooting waves of electricity up and down his body. Most times the turbo generators were running at minimum capacity, but today, they had been charged almost to maximum, awaiting discharge. Aware of potential and lethal danger, nevertheless, he was thrilled by the sheer display of this electrical spectacle, lightning-like energy beams were shooting back and forth between the highly polished initiator cages.

Pulling himself free from the mesmerizing effects of sheer power play, Jack headed for the mission room, which was staffed by a team of operators and engineers. "What's the capacity?" he shouted in the direction of the chief engineer.

"All charged and ready to test," the man responded. "Capacity's up at three billion." Jack pulled him by the sleeve into a nearby office and shut the door. It filtered out the overwhelming sounds. Both removed their earplugs. Suspecting something unusual was up, the man gave him a quizzical stare and waited.

"Listen," Jack started, "I need full power."

"What?"

"You heard me," he ordered. "Ten billion."

"Can't do it," a stunned chief responded. "Haven't even tested half that capacity."

Staring him down, Jack insisted, "If you won't, I'll get somebody that will. You've got no choice. This is not a request."

"I want it documented," the chief demanded. "I won't go down alone if something goes wrong."

"You'll get it," Jack promised. "Now do it."

He reluctantly agreed.

Even Jack had his doubts. Years ago, he had unremittingly committed himself to the cause. His entire future depended on the success of the mission. He held ultimate responsibility for its outcome. Like everyone in charge of every innovative invention before him, especially when unlimited powers were at stake, he tried to keep his emotions in check. "Damned those war mongers," he uttered with disgust. "Can't fail now," he reminded himself. When he realized the true purpose for the testing, based on the last mission report he'd retrieved and read from the safe, it was too late. He had already spent too many years managing this doomsday project.

"Now I know," the chief muttered.

"Know what?"

"The true purpose."

"Don't be naïve," Jack replied. "We've known the truth all along. I know how you feel. I felt the same but have adjusted to reality."

"I wish…"

"Never mind," Jack consoled his chief. "Wishful thinking won't get you out of this. You knew that."

"I've got nothing more to say," the chief sadly admitted shrugging his shoulders in defeat.

"Okay then," Jack stated. "Let's get to work." With that, he abruptly turned to enter the containment room once more. Reassured about today's success, he rapidly made his way through the many compartments of the underground facility. He worked his way through the primary power station, generator room, fuel bunker, converter banks, electron collectors, concentrators, igniter station, emission arrays, and wave guide passage, briefly chatting with the chief mechanics and operators on duty. He needed firsthand assurance that all elements were fully functional. He could not afford any malfunctions. He was assured readiness from each sector.

To make sure, he personally scanned the banks of indicators mounted alongside every major piece of equipment. There was the primary power station, producing AC voltage for the generators driven by diesel fuel supplied from the many underground storage tanks fed directly through pipes from the oil refinery up north. There were the banks of converter arrays, feeding the atomic collectors and concentrators to be passed on to igniter stations into wave guided tunnels, eventually making their way to the antenna array located dozens of feeds above. Specifically designed for the protection of the staff and to insulate the equipment from interference, each section was carefully shielded from the deadly rays.

Everything seemed functional, ready for operation. Though inaudible, he could clearly feel the electrical charges radiating though his body. Where the underground housed a deadly chasm of immense destructive power, above ground was the place where the powers were unleashed. Today was the day for testimonials of good versus evil. There seemed to be no end to man's destructive desires. This facility gave proof to that. With so much power in Jack's hands, he'd avoided a full-scale rebellion from the scientists by assuring a peaceful application once the system had been fully tested for its effectiveness. But that remained to be seen. His personal guarantee could be easily voided by the powerbrokers funding the system. The original promise for creating "free energy" had been proven a mere pipedream. Jack checked the clock. The local GMT read 0500 hours. It was time. He was needed upstairs. Back at the mission center, he received ready status from all stations.

The next step was up to him. Being trained in mission protocols, he fully retrieved today's code from the containment vault labeled "Top Secret – HAARP." He was keenly aware of the environment. The eyes of his teams were centered on him with heightened anticipation as he opened the mission folder. Prepared by Command months ago, it had never been opened by site personnel. For the first time, his eyes read its contents. In neat typesetting it contained mission time, target coordinates, and firing intervals. Expecting a ground-based target, he was completely taken by surprise when his eyes caught the coordinated target points for the trajectory path. "This is insane!" he exclaimed.

"What?" His chief scientist saw his reaction and reached for the folder. After glancing at the paper, he realized his fears had become true. "This is madness." All his hopes, all his aspirations for a peaceful future, had been shattered this very moment. He faced Jack directly and challenged him. "We can't let it happen."

Equally appalled, Jack turned to face his crew and said, "Folks." He paused to compose his thoughts and to quiet his nerves. "This is reality." To underline his statement further, he added, "Orders are orders. At 0600 we'll ramp up to full power. By full, I mean ten billion volts."

There were visible objections from the section heads. Hostility was written all over their faces. Nothing he could do. The die had been cast long ago. "After that we're on standby to receive firing orders from Vandenberg."

Where he and the scientists had assumed the test range would be the usual, Kwajalein Atoll, today's coordinates had changed. The target point was some six thousand nautical miles out. It read 13°31'01.63" N by 144°48'18.78" E, Elev-0. It suddenly hit him. "Guam."

It struck with full force. He had been there. He stared at the mission codes again. "It can't be." The place was heavily populated. It was not only a distant outpost for the U.S. Navy and submarine fleet, it was also the Pacific's vacation place for Asians.

"Can't do it. I won't," the chief engineer protested. "Gotta verify the orders."

Even Jack agreed. This was maddening. It was an annihilation of man. "To hell with orders," Jack decided. "I'm not gonna put a hundred thousand lives on the line. Not now. Not ever."

"Why," he pondered, "would they select a living target?"

It then dawned on him. *Force an example.* It was the only viable explanation Jack could come up with. "Pull the map up," he ordered the operator. All their eyes stared at the display screen. The island was clearly visible. "Zoom in," he ordered. "I wanna get the exact position." He was still puzzled at the elevation point being set at zero feet.

"Got it." For all to see, the chief engineer pointed at the specific spot display. "Tumon Beach. Doesn't make sense."

"Somebody wants a demo," Jack hinted. "Witnesses." It may not have made much sense to the uninformed, but to Jack it became clear. He vividly remembered the place and its vacation hotels. There were lots of them. Somebody wanted to demonstrate weapon effectiveness. Apparently, Guam had been selected for its remoteness and, if things went wrong, the place was isolated and distant enough that no one in the western world would care. He could only guess how much explosive power Vandenberg had packed into the warhead.

Jack was shaking with fury. "Sonsabitches," he cussed over and over. "As if we don't have enough trouble in the world already." He made an on-the-spot decision and turned to face operations. "Listen up," he called his team to action, "follow the orders." The final call would be his, but he did not share it with the team. Not yet.

After its initial design, there had been good intentions for developing the HAARP. It was for exploring the ionosphere with a potential capability to manipulate radio frequency in an already heavily charged ether space. In general, as designed by nature, the ionosphere provided a protective shield around the globe to filter out solar and cosmic rays. It protected Earth, with its fragile inhabitants, from being bombarded by lethal rays. Where scientists saw great potential for the benefit of mankind, many inventions wound up in the hands of policymakers. Although their initial purposes may have been equally honorable, they usually landed in the hands of the military to be used as weapons, also for the good of mankind.

The initial concept was relatively simple. It was to manipulate radio frequency. It could be achieved by heating the atmosphere directly above. Configured into a highly efficient synchronized array, it was capable of emitting billions of volts into the electrically charged space in ranges of between 40 to 600 miles.

In contrast to its design, decades later and most importantly for today's test, HAARP aimed to exploit the ionosphere for defense purposes, specifically, any hostile intrusion into American airspace. In theory, radio bursts sent into space should be received by the ionospheric layer, reflected back in focused concentrations, emitting a massive beam of energy that could destroy any electronic instruments in its path. It should, if all went well, neutralize the Atlas V, ICBM test launch scheduled from Vandenberg. In case the test failed, it would miss the missile rendezvous and allow the projectile to continue on its full path, only to detonate at the programmed targets. But that was not an option Jack and his team had anticipated. He could not fail.

Other important aspects to test HAARP were: ELF communications at extremely low frequency levels designated for aiding underwater communication. Over-the-horizon radar systems for providing early warning against incoming treats. Disturb hostile communication while protecting friendly military systems. Replace the electromagnetic pulse effects of atmospheric thermonuclear devices used in cyberspace against offensive and counter-offensive purposes. Cyber warfare was born.

"Intercept better be a success," Jack advised the staff. "Otherwise, there'll be holy hell to pay." His reference to the destination targets, the Kwajalein islands, and, if missed, the annihilation of Guam's population was clearly understood. To be clear, where much of the Vandenberg missile testing took place over the Kwajalein islands, a vast uninhabited region out in the Pacific, today, if the missile intercept failed, the charged missile would continue its flight path to Guam, a heavily populated island in the Pacific. Whether right or wrong, "Folks," Jack said, initiating the launch schedule. "Let's get hopping."

VANDENBERG AFB

One eye on the PDT clock and the other on the monitor, Lee Blackwell barked into the mic, "Ready to begin launch sequence." Impatiently pacing the floor within the protected LCC-A launch center he had been waiting for each operations section to indicate their readiness. It had taken years to recover and rehab the Vandenberg missile launch facility. Initially, there were heated debates about whether to rebuild in the first place. But not doing so meant relinquishing world space exploration leadership to another nation. Repeated attempts made by foreign nations trying to take the lead were unsuccessful at this time. The apparent reasons were the lack of collaboration between technologically-driven nations. Consequently, despite the limited budget available, the new Space Initiative kept struggling along until today.

From his vantage point, watching a cluster of monitors in the command bunker, Blackwell could visually check on every phase of the launch sequence. With only fifteen minutes left before launch, mission support sections called in their final checks. Software applications and computer data were continuously updated for readouts from ground control, as well as communications and remote satellite feeds, mostly located around the southern hemisphere. Other sequences were sitting idle at the moment, waiting for dynamically-generated input from target/destination trajectory and telemetry transmissions once the missile was under way. A pair of F-15E chase craft sitting at the end of the runway from the nearby Air Force base provided visuals waiting for liftoff.

Gazing at the clock steadily ticking down the final seconds to 0600 hours, the mission commander's voice picked up the launch sequence "...three, two, one, launch!"

What followed was the sound of liquid hydrogen and liquid oxygen rocket engines igniting. The tremendous flash and roar sending the ICBM on its way to its far-off destination could be seen and heard for miles. The liftoff went flawlessly. The Atlas V[25], aimed at the specific target six thousand nautical miles out in the Pacific, was on its way. Muffled through the roar of the burning rocket jets, Blackwell's voice could be heard.

---

[25] Atlas V – Atlas V was an active expendable launch system in the Atlas rocket family. Atlas V formerly operated by Lockheed Martin, is now operated by the Lockheed Martin-Boeing joint venture United Launch Alliance. Each Atlas V rocket uses a Russian-built RD-180 engine burning kerosene and liquid oxygen to power its first stage and an American-built RL10 engine burning liquid hydrogen and liquid oxygen to power its Centaur upper stage. Its relatively remote location and proximity to the coast offered an excellent location to safely conducting test firings of strategic missile weapon systems for Atlas, Titan, Minuteman, and Peacekeeper rockets, as well as to launch satellites into orbits.

Vandenberg was the only military installation in the United States that launched unmanned government and commercial satellites into polar orbit for reasons of safety. It was also the only site from which ICBMs were launched toward Kwajalein Atoll, mostly for conducting weapon system performance.

In 1972, Vandenberg was selected as the West Coast space shuttle launch and landing site, but had never been used as such. Space Launch Complex 6, originally built for the abandoned Manned Orbital Laboratory project, was extensively modified for shuttle operations. Part of the transformation was to the existing runway, which was lengthened to 15,000 feet to accommodate end-of-mission landings. When the Challenger disaster grounded the shuttle fleet, it set in motion a chain of events that finally led to the decision to cancel all West Coast shuttle launches.

"Missile's away." Anticipating eyes from mission personnel were either focused on the monitors or cast through the blast proof windows, following the flight path.

"So far – so good," he muttered from within the protective shield of the launch center as he watched the missile roar into the westward space. While his team was busy with analyzing data, making corrections, and watching the many monitors, it gave him a chance to remember past historical events. Where he had conducted many launches in his career, each gave him the same thrilling experience. There was still time for the actual test event. It would occur far out in the Pacific. At the present, he watched and waited like everybody in the operations center.

JACK OWENS

Jack Owens, presently awaiting the "Go" signal from Vandenberg had no scruples when it came to challenges, especially when new technology was involved. During the early '90s, just out of college and in search of a meaningful career, he came across an announcement made in *Aviation Week & Space Technology*, recruiting for engineers and potential scientists for the Department of Defense. Working for a commercial company then, he had several run-ins with upper level management. With several layers of management necessary to approve every minute task, the process seemed confusing to him. "On the one hand," he'd bitch to his coworkers, "they want you to take responsibility. On the other, you're micro-managed." Growing more frustrated by the year he was hoping to find a more structured environment. "Look no further!" he'd exclaimed when reading the magazine.

After reporting to a designated research and development sector in the defense department set aside for recruitments, he applied for the job and was practically hired on the spot. He took an immediate liking to the environment. Everything was right. Everything was organized. It would certainly reflect on his performance. The skills and knowledge he displayed did not go unnoticed by his superiors. He was encouraged to apply for ever-increasing career challenges. With them came a number of special clearances. One day he was handed an envelope stamped, "Top Secret." Curious about its contents, he opened it. It was a summarized brief on a project currently under development. When reading the contents, he was immediately interested. To his amazement, the brief went into great detail on the project termed "super-secret."

"How come," he'd asked himself, "nobody has ever heard of it?" Once he agreed to take the assignment with DARPA, it became clear from the onset. It had been classified to the highest degree.

Under the cloak of the department's total secrecy, dating back to the '80s, HAARP had been conceived, developed, and implemented. Recent advances in geophysical research, communication application, and computerization had led to substantial technological changes in military weaponry. Further yet, under the auspices of national security, the U.S. military was utilizing the "still to be tested technology" to strengthen control over its spheres of influence. Included in this endeavor was a proposed "revolution in military affairs," driven by a belief that while conventional armed warfare was still a necessary component of military strategy, the new priority was focused on quelling insurgencies, terrorist attacks, and social unrest overseas and at home.

As a result, HAARP was conceived as a possible weapon for national defense. In its simplest design, the major component of HAARP was a radio wave transmitter, utilizing powerful high frequency (HF) transmissions, and a variety of associated observational instruments, "to investigate naturally occurring and artificially induced ionospheric processes that support, enhance, or degrade the propagation of radio waves." Scheduled to be completed in the following five years, HAARP was presently running at about ten percent of its projected power levels.

While Jack was reading on with piqued interests, he tried to envision the ultimate benefactor from the program. "Serving mankind," as it claimed. But experience taught him that once the government got its hands on a project, the foremost reason was for weapons development. While the true nature for HAARP was conducted under the cloak of secrecy, word eventually leaked to the press. To satisfy the media and pacify the public, the true purpose was immediately suppressed by the government as "atmospheric ozone research," conducted in remote isolation in Alaska. In a 1993 Environmental "Impact Statement" addressing possible ecological impacts from HAARP, the Air Force indicated that the study of the ionosphere was being initiated "...*to better understand and use it to enhance communications and surveillance systems for both civil and defense purposes.*"

Opposition to the research project was immediate. Initial fear raised by HAM operators and airline pilots over possible disruption of radio communication was followed by environmentalists concerned over unforeseen radio frequency effects on animals and human beings. Soon, individuals and groups ranging from university students to followers of the paranormal voiced their criticisms. A few even suggested that this military technology would not only destroy communications, but might actually manipulate global weather systems and influence the ways in which people think and behave. Still, given the esoteric nature of the matter, public expression of this criticism was largely limited to the Internet and letters to the editor of Alaska newspapers.

Furthermore, in 1994, a series of articles appearing in the environmental publication *Earth Island Journal* brought wider attention. Shortly thereafter, HAARP was selected as an important chapter in the book *The Ten Top Censored Stories of 1994*. In response, the Air Force placed its own HAARP homepage on the World Wide Web, explaining the project's scientific goals and addressing criticisms raised in opposition. As public consciousness was heightened, more articles appeared in the press. Radio talk show hosts invited guests to present opposing sides of the issue; TV networks devoted segments to it; and, in Alaska, the legislature held hearings to learn more about HAARP and its potential environmental impact. There was more, much more. The report was comprehensive, not only from a technological perspective, but from prolific feedback by the public.

That was over twenty years ago. *The controversy had begun, and was still going strong to this day.* The question raised, "Why don't we ever hear about the project," by the public and concerned citizens remains unheard: the government manipulated news media never did a broadcast about HAARP. Therefore, the people are unaware of its existence.

Amid the hastened scheduling to get ready for the first missions test, Jack recalled distant but still vivid memories, the sole purpose for his existence. All of the public concerns, as limited and dated they were, today, came to a head. They were finally going to be put to the test. In spite of protests and concerns ranging from environmental impact to social implications, air traffic safety, wildlife hazards, international policies, and many more, today's test, he knew, would not put the public concerns to rest. Today's test would only add fuel to the environmental stress and public fears, if they just knew.

GAKONA

"We have confirmation from Vandenberg," the mission coordinator informed the interceptor crew. "Atlas V is on its way." Jack checked the clocks to confirm. "Right on time." They were watching a set of monitors hooked up to the Vandenberg space launch complex. Dawn was already breaking over the eastern horizon but to the west, this early in the morning the Pacific was still set in darkness, leaving a visually waning bright circle from the Atlas rocket burn in its wake. Locally, as Jack scanned the center with watchful eyes, he could see that most personnel were attentive to their specific mission segments. On the surface, everybody seemed calm, awaiting orders, but within, individual apprehension was growing to a maximum. At least, that was how he felt. He periodically checked with his section heads, seated intensely in front of their respective computer terminals. "Mission status?"

"Station One: Primary power…Ready at fifty percent."

"Station Two: Heater arrays…Maximum emission."

"Station Three: Ionic shield…Three, five, zero miles elevation and stable."

"Station Four: Atomic particle collectors…Ready and charged."

"Station Five: Igniter coils…Ready for discharge."

"Ground Station: Beam refractor…Standby and aimed on first target point."

For better or for worse, Jack was ready. Team's standing by. Systems set. Every ear was tuned into the automated missile announcement, recording the flight path in one-minute intervals. Gakona tracking lasers were bouncing their signals out to the Vandenberg-released ICBM, precisely measuring the rapidly expanding flight distance. Sophisticated software was at work computing the predetermined flight path. The target point was still twenty minutes out. The wait became intense.

Jack's mind drifted. He didn't like waiting—not for anything. He was an action man. He had no patience for mistakes or incompetence. When he took on this project, it had taken him months to weed out the slackers in order to get the solid team together presently supporting him. He was proud of his team. He trusted them. He could relax. To pass the waiting, he mentally went over each and every aspect of the system at his hands to assure success.

First, there was the ionosphere itself. It was the most critical aspect of the system. Who would have ever have thought that one day, mankind would be able to control nature itself? It was unimaginable. But today, the very foundation of nature was manipulated by Jack from this very center. It caused him immense concerns. He questioned a sobering notion entering his mind. *Have I become God?*

Jack's thoughts were momentarily interrupted by the computer-generated report. "Fifteen minutes to intercept." Perplexed by the very notion of his previous thought, he forced his mind back to the present. *Who am I? What have I become?* He had no rational answer.

Only minutes away, there would be an immense release of power. There seemed to be no end to creating the forces needed for reaching goals set by man. It was not that long ago when microwaves were invented. After that, it did not take long to achieve a workable gain of a million watts. "Look at it now," he wondered. "Not just billions, but already in the trillions." Technology somehow had leapfrogged ahead generations.

"Someday soon it'll be a Googol watt." He marveled at the very thought at this inconceivable number.

"Ten minutes to intercept."

Jack recalled the early days on the project. It was a technology that did not make much sense back then. Wireless signals he understood, but wireless power was another thing. He tried to recall all the elements used for the system. They were many. There was the klystron wave guide, induction current, igniter coils, heterodyne effects, thermal energy converters, and Tesla coil, all interconnected to generate the power necessary not only for heating the ionosphere, but also to create the charged particle beam for the awesome destructive powers to be unleashed shortly.

"Five minutes to intercept."

This is it, he thought. *Better pay attention.* "Final status check," he shouted at the team.

Stations One through Five all reported readiness.

"One," Jack commanded, "what's your power setting?"

"Seventy-five," the station chief shot back.

"Give me one hundred now."

"But," the chief objected, "we've never tested full power. Can't guarantee generators will hold up."

"I want full power—now!" Jack yelled at him.

"Okay," was the hesitant response. "But...?"

"No buts." Jack was getting irritated.

"Power station," he ordered his second in command. "Make sure he follows through."

"Not enough time," the man objected.

"Dammit, just go," he yelled with finality.

Time had ticked away rapidly during their verbal exchange. The clock had just passed the one-minute marker. Then ten seconds. With eyes fixated on the wall clocks, Jack initiated the final count down, "Three...two, one. Fire!"

They all felt it coming on. It started at the bottom of soles, then the ankles and the knees. It was a low rumble followed by a massive amount of power created by an array of generators. It felt like a magnitude six quake. It went on for several seconds. The station was rattled in its foundation until the initial pulse beam left the waveguide. As soon as the rumble subsided, a whooshing sound, gaining intensity, turned into a roar they had not heard or felt before. Some of the staff darted for tables and office desks to get a hold. Seconds later the incredible power display suddenly subsided.

In spite of the potential implications if the test failed, Jack was euphoric. "Dammit, what power!" But his glorious moment was short lived.

"Gakona!" The voice rattled over the Vandenberg PA system. "You asleep? What's going on? What're you doing up there?"

"What?" Jack fired back.

"You've missed the target point. You've got one minute to reacquire."

Jack was shaken. "Standby," he said, then flipped the switch to internal PA. "Where are you?" he demanded from his second.

"Almost there," was a hurried response. "Why?"

"We've missed the target," he fumed. "Give me status on power."

"Just a sec…almost there," the man panted.

"Hurry," he demanded. "We've got less than a minute." Jack was furiously pacing the floor waiting for the response. If he missed again, it would mean terminating thousands of lives. It came seconds later. "Ready," his chief reported. "I've got only seventy-five output."

"I told him one hundred percent," he screamed into the mic. "Damn him!"

Precious more seconds ticked away before the chief reported, "You got it."

"Ten seconds," Vandenberg PA announced.

Synchronized to the launch clock, Jack fell in with the final countdown once more. "Three…two…one. Fire!"

There was instant pain. It traversed from the ground into his legs then expanded up through the spine, culminating in the head. Every inch of his body was shaking. Everything in the room was shaking. His vision turned blurry. He was knocked off his feet and so were the others in the room. Although it felt like a real quake, there was something different this time. Living in this region quakes were nothing new. Where the general quake created a lateral displacement, in turn producing horizontal motion, the case here was that the displaced energy was a vertical uplift explosion. The results were devastating. From being squeezed in by strained walls under immense pressure floors buckled, doors became unhinged, windows shattered with shards of glass shooting across the room in every direction. Deep groaning sounds emanated from the support structure. Panic and fear were painted across the many faces.

On unsteady legs, Jack darted from room to room, conducting initial damage control from the awesome powers he had unleashed. Remnants from the superheated streams of pulsed particle beams released through the waveguides left signs of destruction in their wake. Further downstream, the microwave transmitters above ground took damages as well. Beyond that, a solid beam of energy cut through the heated ionosphere, leaving its heat signature in the form of concentrated contrails. From there, the energy pulse shot up three hundred some miles into space only to be redirected into a concentrated transitional wave seeking its programmed target. The result was a rapidly accelerating target headed for Guam obliterated in a burst of blazing destruction.

"We have a hit," Vandenberg PA reported. "Good work."

Jack rushed for the recording room. "Play the tape." He was anxious to see what the cameras recorded. He and the crews witnessed the force of power released for the first time. They watched in awe. "Such awful power," he muttered shaking his head.

When reviewing the sequence of tapes, *spectacular* was not the proper word. It was more like stunning, fantastic, and wondrous. But that was not all. The international space station recorded the event in its entirety. It would take hours for its telemetry data to be processed but it was expected to be exceptional.

Later that morning the western airwaves were buzzing with activity. Many foreign broadcasting stations carried the news:

"Early this morning, Vandenberg launched what observers believed was an Atlas V rocket booster into orbit. The launch was unsuccessful in as much as the missile blew up in mid-air over the central Pacific region. The mission," the spokesperson disclosed, *"had been scheduled to test newly developed technology for the rocket guidance system."*

No further comments were made on the rocket booster or payload. *"However,"* the announcer went on, *"a major power failure over Hawaii, including a number of mid-Pacific islands, was experienced at the same time. The cause is still undetermined as of this hour since there is only sparse information forthcoming from that region due to the blackout."*

The news was supplemented by commentators and supposed experts speculating on the various causes. Other broadcasts switched their video feeds to Anchorage, Alaska, who had reported an *"earthquake, magnitude 6.5, but only causing minor destruction to outlying towns. No tsunami is expected since the quake took place hundreds of miles from the Alaskan shorelines."*

It would take Jack and his crew days, perhaps weeks, of repairs to fix the damage caused by the test. For them who knew the true purpose for the test, it would make the coast a safer place. HAARP, after years of anticipation by the defense sector, had performed as expected. This time, it was for defending the nation. But next time, it may not be for the good of mankind. Only policy makers and a select contingent of operatives knew the true reason for what was yet to come.

NAPA VALLEY

Earlier that day, slightly annoyed at the slow pace at which her children were moving, Liz said, "Okay kids, let's go…let's go," trying to hurry them along.

"Still sleepy, Mom," her twelve-year-old son complained, rubbing his eyes.

"Next time you'll know better than to stay up all night playing games," she chided. "You knew we were leaving early." It was partially her fault. She had bought him the latest video game he had wanted. "I'll get you the game," she had promised after checking his last report card, "if you keep up grades." His grades had been slipping below the As and Bs he normally earned. After her promise, he had reapplied his usual energy to learning once again. It was not entirely her son's fault either. Hoping to get to the final playoffs, Coach had been pushing hard on the team to compete all season long. To his disappointment they had come in second. At least he had secured another semester of coaching. Where much of the nation was still plagued from foreign attacks, poverty, and shortages of every kind, the western sector fared much better due to the protection from Wilmot and supporting government. Schools, among other critical facilities, though gradually, had been restored to serve the public once more. Though only a temporary measure to curb back markets, there was even new monetary conscript authorized for the sector.

She had planned for this trip to Disneyland several weeks ago at the beginning of the school break. It was customary to take an annual vacation trip. Most times they wound up at summer camp nearby for a week since she was the sole supporter. Travel seemed to have gotten more expensive with each year. She had been surprised at how much the ticket cost had gone up to get into the world's most popular playground in Anaheim. Although somewhat limited on rides and entertainment, due to fuel shortages, Disneyland had just recently reopened after years of inactivity. Being the only adventure playground in the nation, after years of depravation, people flocked to the opening event.

Liz was loading up the last piece of overnight baggage into the luggage hold of her Cessna Skyhawk 172. She had decided on taking the kids there for probably a long time to come since she was scheduled to depart soon for Russia and her spaceflight. Finally seated behind the controls, with the kids securely strapped in, she made the final instrument adjustments. Selecting 121.7 on the radio dial, setting the altimeter to 35 feet destination ground reference, leaning forward, she reached for the mic and called in, "APC…LIZARD THREE."

"Come in, LIZ," the controller responded.

"Clearance request on 6R for takeoff."

"Where you headed?"

"Anaheim."

"Wish I could come along," he replied and gave her the clear signal for takeoff. Lifting off at 75 knots, she watched the ground quickly disappear beneath the canopy. Too early for sunlight, she was relying on instruments as they headed west for the coast. After reaching cruising altitude, her plan was to follow I-80 west to meet up with 280, then turn south toward San Jose and on to Monterey, where she could skim along the coastline past San Luis Obispo with Los Angeles as the final destination. She regretted that it was still dark. She would have liked to see Route 1 directly below, her favorite landmark, winding along the steep edges of the continental shelf. Driving the coastal route was beautiful enough, but seeing it from a Birdseye view was breathtaking. She never tired of watching the contrast in colors between well-groomed lawns, rocky brown cliffs, white breaking waves, and the deep blue of the ocean.

Looking ahead, for now she enjoyed the darkened sky illuminated by the stars from above and city lights from below. The Bay Bridge, with its crested lights but sparsely populated traffic bridging the peninsula twelve thousand feet below, was gradually growing out of the distance. She was glad to see that this major link across the Bay was under reconstruction once again after the devastation years ago. It was time to head south. It would take a couple of hours to reach their destination. Checking on the kids, she found they were back asleep. "Fine," she muttered over the hum of the engine sound. Adjusting her seat, she sat back to completely enjoy the flight in the quiet of the night.

Forty minutes into the flight Liz noticed the lighting display from Vandenberg some distance ahead. Dawn was just breaking to the east of the continent when she was suddenly startled by the brilliance of rocket bursts ignited on the horizon ahead. Awed by the spectacular display, Liz had just witnessed the missile launch from the best possible view. "Wake up, kids, wake up," she yelled in back. "Look," she shouted, pointing to the missile launch ahead.

Abruptly torn from sleep, her daughter asked, "What's going on?"

"Yeah," her son wanted to know, "what's up?" He was cranky about being woken up, but happy at the spectacle developing ahead, nevertheless.

Watching the brilliantly illuminated horizon in the distance, they were overwhelmed by the display of fiery streams left in the wake of the Atlas V rocket pushing its way rapidly into the upper atmosphere. It was breathtaking. "Missile launch," she informed the kids. "Probably Johnson Islands…another military test. Pappi used to work down there."

"Neat," her daughter said. Rather than the familiar granddad or Grossfather, as was customary in the old country, they called their granddad Pappi. Years ago, when she questioned her dad about the somewhat odd endearment, he told her, "I like it." Then he explained he preferred being called that after watching one of his favorite oldie films, "Popeye."

The second spectacle had just unfolded when the rocket shed its solid fuel thrusters. Much like an unfolding firework, the shells were burning the remnants of fuel while slowly descending down to Earth, leaving streamers of sparks in their wake. For the next several minutes the three watched the remaining rocket arching its way through the sky, slowly disappearing across the Pacific horizon. *Wonder what that's all about,* Liz thought. Soon it would be her turn to take to the skies. *Wonder what it feels like,* she wondered at her own space launch coming up soon.

CASTLE ROCK

Rhonda was somewhat surprised to find Alex slouched in the recliner at this early morning hour. "Getting to be a habit," she muttered. He was rubbing his sleepy eyes. His memory still foggy, he apologetically tried to justify the present surroundings. "Dozed off again." The TV had been burning all night. He was about to get up and join her in the kitchen when he noticed a news flash scrolling across the screen. The HAM set was busy with calls as well. Ever since the nuclear exchange with North Korea and the subsequent Al Qaeda attack on the nation, he had made it a policy to keep both the TV and the HAM set turned on. It gave him the added security of international wire services and amateur radio operators always on alert.

"Vandenberg, early this morning, launched what observers determined to be an Atlas V rocket booster into space. The launch was unsuccessful in as much as the missile blew up in mid-air somewhere over the central Pacific region.... The broadcast was quickly followed with reports from Alaska that had experienced a sizable earthquake.

HAM operators were already busy at work, broadcasting power and communication failures and alerting Alaska and Pacific coastal regions about a possible tsunami.

"Won't be long now," Alex speculated. Rhonda had joined him in the den. She had slept over, like so many nights since the beginning of their relationship. He was grateful for her company and hoped the feeling was mutual and lasting. One thing he had learned from her was to occasionally reinforce a need to strengthen their relationship. He had not realized how important romance was to nurturing a successful and lasting relationship. Still regretful, it had been the one thing missing from his former marriage. In spite of the fact that he was a successful communicator, career wise, he never had learned to share his inner feelings with his former wife and mother of his children.

He was aware of Rhonda's presence as she approached, carrying a mug of his favorite coffee in her hand. He briskly got up from the recliner to greet her with a kiss on the cheek and to gently slide both hands around her waist. He softly whispered in her ear, "Love you." Slightly startled, she reacted and returned his affectionate gesture. "Hear the latest news?" he said.

"What news?"

"Comm satellite's down in the Pacific…Alaska's been hit with another quake. Major one."

Nonchalantly, she responded, "Nothing new."

"Getting more massive each time," he explained. He had been following the outage trends on his sensitive monitoring equipment for months now. They seemed to be contained predominantly out west, but were growing in intensity. He suspected government policymakers were keeping the events low-key for reasons he could only speculate on. Life in recent years had been difficult enough just dealing with the enormous task of getting the economy back on track. "I'm concerned," was his final comment on the subject.

Rhonda, although still not sure about his obsession with all the equipment—the monitoring and the satellite feeds—made it a point to keep his feet planted on solid ground. "Don't take it too seriously," she said. She appeared more practical about worldly events.

Ever since she had become part of his life, Alex looked forward to her company. At first, he felt strange, having a woman around, but with the passage of time he'd come to accept her fully, realizing how much had been missing from his life. Now, in her presence, his life had taken a balanced turn. He could focus on tasks without being sidetracked by personal thoughts. The Castle was his sanctuary. It was the very source of his being. The safety of the place gave him the strength to maintain a sense of security. Even though he had retired years ago from the defense department and a colorful and fast-paced career, he felt he would never quit working as long as he could maintain good health and sound mind. "It's this combination," he would tell her, "that keeps a person going."

He felt invigorated this morning. It seemed as though the troubled news had given him the incentive he needed to start yet another adventurous day. Adventure was what his life was about. Although keeping those thoughts private to himself, he thought, *always has been...always will.* He had a compulsion for getting involved in events, especially when national security was at stake. It was his calling. His adult career had been dedicated to the cause of keeping his country safe, as well as protecting its people and family and friends. This morning's news reminded him of his daughter who was well on her way to the coast. *Time to check in with Stinger.*

He was about to proceed to his den to make the call but stopped pacing when his name bounced off the hallway walls.

"Alex," she had called after him.

"Yes, Rhonda?" he responded.

Always formal, she thought. *But that's Alex. Must be his upbringing.* Not that she minded the subtle formality, with which he responded when spoken to, but it made her feel somewhat detached from his very being. It was these times when she questioned their relationship. She probably made too much of it, she knew, but needed reassurance.

He hesitated in his strides, then thought better of it and turned to her. He did not have to wonder. He knew what she needed, they needed. He was always glad when she took the initiative at those times when he got carried away with the mission, as he called it. He always made up through passion. "Come," she gestured. "Sit for a while. Project can wait."

SAN FERNANDO VALLEY

Liz was still speculating about the purpose of the launch she and the kids had witnessed twenty minutes ago. "Time to check the map," she muttered. Comparing it to the terrain below, the San Fernando Valley was slowly panning into view. Liz knew this part of the state well from flying down here in the department's Twin Otter when helping out with fighting fires in the south when additional resources from the north became necessary. Dawn was already breaking to the east. It was time to prepare for the upcoming landing.

"How much longer?" her daughter's voice sounded from the backseat.

"Almost there," she said. "In time for breakfast."

Her eyes were concentrated on the terrain below, identifying landmarks, when her son yelled out, "Mom, what's that?" Liz jerked her head in the direction in which he gestured, Pacific horizon, just in time to witness, which appeared like a layer of waving sheets shooting out brilliant rays into space. "Aurora? Here?" An instant later, the engine quit. To make it worse, all instruments went dead as well.

Reacting almost instantly, her grip tightened on the controls. It steadied the craft, but only for seconds. Immediately, she had an ominous feeling. "We're in trouble," Liz muttered into the sudden silence. Only a whistling sound was heard. It was déjà vu all over again. The Cessna had lost hundreds of feet in altitude. Compensating against an imminent stall, Liz pushed the nose of the craft hard toward the ground. Without the hum of the engine, it was difficult to gauge the pitch angle. The only means for judging speed and direction was by the sound of air passing over the fuselage. The sudden quietness, all alone at twelve thousand feet, was an eerie feeling. It was too much for the panic-eyed kids. "Mom. Please don't crash. I don't wanna die." Liz dared not take her eyes from the horizon. She could only imagine their emotions. If it wasn't for the thousands of flying hours fighting fires she would have easily panicked. Instead, she took a deep breath. "We're not gonna die," she promised, then went through emergency startup actions. "Here," she shouted at her son. "Read the instructions." At first, he was perplexed, but a couple of seconds later he responded.

"Magnetos."[26] She punched the switch repeatedly without the slightest reaction. The engine refused to kick in. "Next?"

"Check fuel."

"Got enough. Next?"

"Throttle."

She had the throttle set at three quarter during cruising flight. Not to flood the carburetor, she pulled it to idle. It was part of the starting procedures. "Next?"

"Instruments."

"All out." She tried to start the magnetos again, and again but there was no response. The engine refused to respond. There was only one recourse left: emergency landing.

---

[26] Magneto – Magnetos are used to produce starter pulses of high voltage in the ignition systems of some gasoline-powered internal combustion engines to provide power to the spark plugs in light aircraft engines in the event of alternator or battery failure. For redundancy purposes, virtually all piston engine aircraft are fitted with two magneto systems, each supplying power to one of two spark plugs in each cylinder.

"Mom?" She could see the fear in their faces. Both son and daughter recalled their last encounter with engine failure not so long ago. If she could just identify the cause of the failure, it might save their lives. Then it hit her. "EMP!" *What else could it be? The rocket launch. The distant explosion. Followed by the engine failure seconds later. Had to be it.* At least now she knew. She could concentrate on the forced landing.

Most times, as it had in the past, the emergency had resolved itself. Flying through smoke and heat fighting forest fires, sometimes it happened that carburetors got clogged with cinder. Forcing the oxygen intake away from the fire zone usually cleared the obstruction. But that was not the case here. There was no fix for her dilemma. Her craft was on its way down. Liz knew where to look for possible landing sites. It was her personal policy to always know where to land. Without power to the engine and with instruments out the craft was coming down no matter what. In trying to get the craft started she had lost precious altitude. With instruments out, it would have to be all guesswork. At the present altitude, about eight thousand feet, she estimated, she had just enough time to seek out a landing strip.

"Mom," her daughter called from the back seat. "What's happening?"

Her son kept quiet. She was grateful for his courage. He was old enough to know the concentration it required to deal with an emergency. Mom, he knew, always had been able to solve the crisis. Liz always appreciated the confidence he had in her. But this time, the engine refused to budge. The thought just struck her. "Radio check." With frantic fingers, she grappled for the mic. "Mayday…mayday!"

Despite expecting an immediate response, the ether remained silent. Her call went unheard. "Radio's out," she muttered.

Her daughter's voice cut into her concentration. "Mom?"

"Not now!"

The ground was rushing dangerously close at them. At the present altitude, the craft was illuminated by the rising sun. But the ground level was still darkened by night shadows. It was difficult for her to penetrate the darkness. The pitch of the craft and the air passing over was her only connection with the craft. Not to stall out, Liz pushed the craft further forward. The horizon responded immediately. Fortunately, ground objects and landmarks gradually took on shapes.

The highway was her first choice. Her eyes sought out the bands of concrete now passing five thousand feet below. "No good," she decided. "Traffic's on the road." Next choice was an open field. She gave up on that too because it mostly showed residential. With years of population growth, she noticed in dismay, San Fernando Valley had become a crowded place. There were no open spaces, let alone a landing strip.

Visual was still difficult in the twilight of the morning hour. According to emergency landing instructions, suggested landing sites were the freeway, an open pasture, or a sandy beach. None was available here. Time was running out rapidly. With every wasted second the ground was rushing up faster. Because she only had one shot at the landing, she was frantically searching out an empty field, no matter how congested. To make matters worse, in the twilight it was difficult to spot potential power lines, protruding obstructions, and fence posts.

Then she spotted it. "Golf course," her mind screamed out. It was her only option. It would be a rough landing. Luckily, there were no tall trees in sight. Only groomed brushes and the greens were visible. There was no time to think anymore. The ground was coming up fast. From here on, her reactions would be driven by impulse. "Kids," she shouted. "Hang on!"

Hundred feet, Liz estimated. It was an altitude when ground effect took over. It was a phenomenon where the mind adjusted to ground speed. The craft was speeding up and so was the awareness of air passing over the canopy. The sound gave her an approximation for speed. *Almost time to flare out. Stay calm,* she assured herself, then a frightening thought popped into her head. "You strapped in?" she yelled.

Any answer, if given, was lost unheard. Another panicking thought popped into her head. This time it would be for make or break. "Landing gear!" In her haste to locate a landing site, she had completely overlooked lowering the wheels. In a last-ditch effort, she pushed the switch. "Come on…come on." Then she remembered the lack of power. "Manual," her mind screamed out. It was then she realized the full extent of the emergency. Her right hand flew to the manual override handle. Left hand tightly gripping the craft's controls, her right was frantically pumping the lever.

"Come on…come on…come on…" she pleaded. Ever so slowly, the gears came down into a locked position. But the drag it created drove the craft into an immediate stall. Realizing it, she forced the nose of the craft back down to regain precious speed. She was losing altitude fast. "Don't panic now," she kept saying. "I'll get us through it." It was her last chance of rational thinking. Her reactions were based entirely on instinct. She felt the crosswinds bucking the fuselage. Adjusting for drift, Liz sharply banked into the wind. The craft was severely crabbing sideways. *Must be fifteen knots crosswind.*

The terrain ahead rushing toward her was rugged. As soon as the wheels touched ground she flared out. A number of violent bumps followed caused by patches of sandy dips from the greens. "Mom," her daughter wailed from the back. In the process of landing, their heads had jolted against the ceiling. The craft bounced violently upward several times. Straight ahead a wooded area closed in fast. "Oh no," Liz yelled. On instinct she reached down, increasing flaps. The craft bounced up once more. It gave her the extra few feet to clear the obstruction before landing hard. Her next move was to push on the brake pedals. "Come on, brakes," she shouted in desperation. The craft finally slowed to a stop just before crashing into a tree line.

Short on breath and out of energy, she gasped, "Everybody okay?"

"Head hurts," her daughter complained.

"I'm all right," her son responded beaming with admiration for his mom. "Great landing!"

Coming through the emergency unscathed, with her son's confidence in her, Liz felt elated. She quickly unfastened her buckle and turned in the seat. "Let's see the damages."

The daughter looked fine but her son had sustained some injury. Brushing a hand over his forehead she could feel a bump forming and said, "A little blood."

Her hands reached for the emergency kit. "Let me fix you up."

"Don't worry," he assured her, wiping the blood from his forehead using the sleeve of his shirt. Liz was always amazed at the poise with which her kids reacted. There was never any whining or complaining. Now they could hear it. In the distance, there were sirens from emergency vehicles rapidly approaching followed by a team of early golfer carts. It had already turned daytime. The sun was glowing brightly out of the east.

Thankful for having survived the emergency, greatly relieved, Liz sighed. "Thank God," she said.

The team of emergency vehicles slithered to a halt nearby. Out jumped rescue teams headed their way. "Lady, you alright?" The early golfers crammed their way close to the canopy making comments, "Saw your landing. Great job. Impressive. Where you from?"

When spotting her children in back, "You kids alright." Everybody was helpful. It made the crash even manageable.

CASTLE ROCK

Alex opened his eyes to another cloudless sky. When he built the Castle, he had arranged the headboard against the wall with his head faced the panoramic window straight ahead into the Rockies. It was a view he cherished with each awakening. Laying there for several minutes his mind recalled the previous evening with Rhonda followed by a night of tenderness and passion. He reached over to her side to reassure their bond but was surprised when her space was vacated. He then recalled her last remark, "I have an early flight to catch."

This morning, as always when she was not by his side, he felt the loneliness sink in. He had gotten used to her living with him, although not fulltime, but whenever her busy schedule out west permitted spending a few days at the Castle. Invigorated by the sheer beauty of the view, he jumped from the comfort of the bed headed for the bathroom. Being an efficiency expert, subconsciously calculating each move, it never took him long to complete the daily morning rituals. As soon as he entered the hallway he became aware of a familiar resonance drifting through the ether. It always cheered him up hearing the sound of his daughter's voices. It was the HAM urging him to pick up. "CQ…CQ…Castle Rock…come in."

Alex recognized his eldest daughter. He had assumed that she was still in Europe for astronaut training. "What a pleasant surprise," he answered the call. "Thought you were still in Russia. Tell me about it. How're the kids? How're things in Napa Valley?"

She was quick to respond, "What Napa Valley?"

He immediately sensed something was wrong. "What's up. Where are you?"

"You won't believe it."

"Believe what?" He turned curious. Then she told him about the launch they'd witnessed, followed by the flash sometime later, then the emergency landing.

He was stunned. "You serious? Can't believe it!"

"Ask the kids," she said. "They're right here."

He was greatly concerned for their wellbeing. "They alright?"

"Hi Pappi." It was his granddaughter talking. "I'm fine. We're fine."

"Have to tell me all about it. You come visit me soon."

"I promise. Bye…" Liz assured him they were, letting them illustrate their experience once more.

He was truly amazed at his daughter's composure. "I'm glad you're all safe. How're you going to get the plane back to Napa?"

"Haven't figured that one out yet. Help's on the way. Gotta go, Dad." Alex could hear the sirens echo through the radio. Apparently, emergency vehicles were driving up to tend to the downed.

"Let me know if you need anything. I'm always here for you." After another though, he offered, "Think of coming here once your plane is fixed."

"I promise." She terminated the call with, "Thank you, Dad. My regards to Rhonda."

"You take care now," he said. "And take a break from flying." He was always concerned at her flying for a living, especially with his daughter's marginal safety records lately. This was the second time her craft had fallen from the sky, not to speak of the many more blowouts she may have had fighting fires. The thought alone made him shudder. With logical statistics dictating records, and he was an avid believer of statistics, it was not "if" there was another incident, but "when."

GAKONA

The place was in shambles. "Damages," Jack Owens ordered. Crew members were stumbling over debris scattered across the floor, mostly from the ceiling. He was handed a checklist by his mission chief. It said, "Damage Control."

"Nothing major…nothing we can't fix."

"What about generators, battery banks, power plant, wave guide?"

"All seem okay," he was assured. "Got maintenance working the facility."

"Fine then." Jack sighed, relieved. "Get me CONUS on line."

"Right away." What could have turned out as major disaster proved to only have caused minor damages to the building's interior. With the report in hand Jack verified the interior damages. It was mostly collapsed panels and broken duct work scattered amid broken glass from shattered windows. It would not take much time to fix but, until then, he had to shift control to HAARP backup command. Headed for his office, he noticed the desktop monitor shattered on the floor. "That's just great," he yelled. It took him a while to find a computer that worked. There was no response from the software. "Get me a connection," he yelled at the administrator. "That's all I need," he muttered. "Network's down."

There was backup to HAARP, but he needed a connection to the outside world. To gain access took the highly classified ULTRA clearance. Only command and a few privileged scientists had access to the classified global grid of this super-secret defense system. After many years of intensive research and testing by DARPA was completed, the operational burden had been turned over to the DOD. Aside from being used by several universities for atmospheric research, defense organizations took control over the weapons testing. Most other entities did not know it existed, especially the public.

"Try it now." It was the network administrator yelling at Jack.

He punched the enter key to pull up the homepage. "Working," he yelled back. His eyes darted across the grid indexes of other HAARP facilities outside the U.S. continent. Already a number of nations had implemented similar research facilitates. From the scientific perspective, they all shared their test results. That was not the case for weapons applications. Each country was out to develop their special application. Although they used various types of propagation methods, the end results were the same. Major facilities Jack was in collaboration with were CONUS—Backup, EURO—European Continent, PACR—Pacific Rim, SPAC—South Pacific Region, ASIA—Asian Continent, AFRO—African Continent, SAME—South American Continent, and SHEM—Southern Hemisphere. They were the official codenames for the checklist. Their physical locations were unknown to most.

There were additional sites projected for future expansion to the grid but all were presently still in planning or under construction. As for now, only five ground-based stations had been completed, primarily in the northern hemisphere. SHEM was still under construction and handled by the folks assigned to Alice Springs and Gila Down Under. For now, Gakona was handing over primary control to CONUS[27].

---

[27] CONUS – Military expression for Continental U.S. referring to the mainland region between Pacific coast and Atlantic coast.

He checked the status board for operational backup systems, then made the call. Seconds later an operator answered, "CONUS. What's up?"

"You've got primary," Jack informed him. "We've had some emergency."

"So, I've heard. What's the damages?"

"Maybe two weeks."

"Will do," was the response. "Anything else?"

"None." *Click.*

Jack was still fuming about the test. Although it had been successful, firing at maximum power without prior testing had been a mistake. He knew it, and so did everybody on the project. But policymakers don't see it that way all the time. They had their own priorities. What bugged him the most was that they just would not listen. They always had a different agenda.

VANDENBERG

The center was full of activity, analyzing and assessing telemetry data and intercept statuses. It became clear that the test firing had interfered with communications and power. Several satellites over the western Pacific had been disabled. Weather channels, flight navigation, and news broadcasts were screaming for data. Media analysts were busy with speculations. As usual, nobody was given prior warning of the missile launch. Officially, the outages were blamed on the failed Atlas V rocket launch.

The phone had been ringing all morning. Rhonda picked up. "Analysis."

"CONUS GRID," the voice stated. "Just wanted to let you know we have primary."

"Okay," Rhonda replied. "I'll update SKYGRID." *Click.*

She swiftly entered the new parameters into the keyboard and watched the array of monitors refresh the new tag IDs.

After the collapse of SPACECOM, due to her intricate knowledge in the defense system, Rhonda was offered the position of Mission Liaison reporting directly to general Foster. Although it meant being away from Alex for most of the week she had accepted. For the time being her plan was to catch a shuttle flight to Colorado for the weekends whenever possible. Alex promised to visit her likewise. She had been assigned to the Air Defenses Western Sector, operated and managed from Vandenberg. With space asset losses due to the EMP strike, what used to be the world's most powerful Air Force had never recovered. Whatever defense resources were left had been consolidated into one combined unit of national defense forces.

For herself, Rhonda was doing well, but would have rather had the job closer to home, the Castle. Ever since they had started a relationship, shuttling back and forth between the Pacific coast and Colorado was a cumbersome burden. Fortunately, after rebuilding many of their craft to flight status, she managed to hop a Confederate flight at least once a month to spend an extended weekend with Alex. Their relationship, as it had turned out, could not have been better. Whether it was the distance, the infrequent visits, or just the chemistry when together, so far it had worked out beautifully. Alex was just as pleased with the arrangement. Brian, during her stay at the Castle pretty much kept to himself. She felt for the guy not having a meaningful career other than assisting Alex. But, that's live, as limited as work opportunities there were in a still suffering nation.

As for her work, she had no complaints. With the world having been in disarray for a number of years already, more and more undesirable factions were rearing their heads around the globe. It was her task to track these elements. With only limited surveillance on hand, she was unable to cover the entire globe. At this point, the world was unaware of the true status of looming threats. Fortunately, Alex was able to help out. He had provided her with valuable data on many occasions.

A coworker stuck her head into the office. "Ready for lunch?"

She shot a quick glance at her, holding her off. "Just a sec." The HF transmitter had just alerted her of an incoming call. "Be right with you." She recognized the caller and picked up.

"Take a look at AFRO sector Delta," Alex advised her. "Unusual activity." She was well aware of his capabilities and the equipment setup at the Castle. It only took seconds for her to zoom in on the sector. "Interesting. I'll get back to you…miss you." Aware of the coworker lingering by the door, Rhonda said, "Gotta cancel lunch. Sorry."

In the basement of the Castle, poised in front of banks of equipment, Alex was watching the monitors scanning the desert wastelands in the Middle East. "Strange," he muttered over the hum of the electronics. He manipulated the zoom control relays linked with the satellites to take a closer look on the patch of wasteland. To get a sharper view, he moved up to the screen and muttered, "Never seen anything close to it…a trail leading nowhere." He could not make out if it was a trail, road, or tracks caused by a herd of animals, but the images did not show an oasis or refuge in the proximity. "Makes no sense." He switched the optics to close-up. The telescopic lenses in the sky adjusted to ground zero. Now he could definitely make out a road. He studied the terrain closely. It seemed manmade, paved, but covered up with sand and dust blown over by desert storms. "Could be an abandoned roadway, but…" his voice trailed into the quiet, "why hasn't data mining detected any sourcing? Software should be imaging timeline changes…makes no sense." He had closed in to the highest image resolution possible provided by the satellite but still was not satisfied. "I need a Hubble all to myself."

From the present view, he was unable to detect any movement, but knew there was life even on the globe's hottest places. In the past, he had been in deserts and was amazed at the prolific life from creatures of all kinds. "Brian," he called to get his buddy's attention.

"What's up?" Brian, since having made the Castle his permanent residence, had become Alex's specialty expert in most of the technical aspects in space. Where Alex took care of most of the ground based equipment and links, Brian took on responsibility for space assets that he knew best.

"What'd it take to get a link with Hubble?"

"You serious?"

"Don't know. Is it possible?"

Brian, at the moment did not know if he was serious or teasing him. "Need to think about it." It was a possibility he or anybody else, for that matter, had not thought about. He liked the idea. It meant new challenges to keep his mind occupied. *Problem is,* he was already contemplating the idea, *how do I get into the guidance system?* Since he had not been on the software development team for Hubble, it'd be difficult to break the access code. He had doubts whether anybody was still supporting the telescope at this time, to find out. *But,* the thought brought a grin to his face, *it can be done.*

GREAT LAKES

Alaska was not the only front where the fighting took place. Where the battle out west was for a super weapon the enemy tried to attain, the fight here was for the immense water resources, at this time still in the hands of the Patriots. After their last confrontation with the Jihad, it did not take long for Yusuf and his militants to reappear. This time, the terrorists showed up in force. An armada of a dozen speed boats made its appearance when the alarm went out, "Enemy on the horizon." This time, their appearance was not to negotiate. This time it was for taking and defending territory through force.

"Fire," Brodie Elliott shouted the command at his armored division dug in by the shoreline to defend the Patriot's territory. The first salvo fell just short of the rapidly advancing war party. It dispersed the onrushing fleet into several clusters swerving wildly to avoid direct hits. "Reacquire," was his next command. Although dispersed, the Jihad speed boats kept rapidly advancing. Brodie's next strategy was setting up for crossfire. Expecting to hold up their earlier threat made by Jihad, the Patriot fighting force was ready. Machine gun positions were dug in at both edges of the waterfront supported by the Striker forces with cannons and rocket launchers. The initial clash was quickly followed by advances from several fronts. Each time a speed boat cluster approached, it was successfully warded off leaving the dead and wounded in their wake.

Elliott's defense strategy seemed to work, for now. It was enough for the enemy to retreat to where they had come from. Elliott knew the enemy's home base just short of one hundred miles to the south, Chicago. "They're gone," he reported to the Patriot's leader, Rusty Norton.

"They'll be back." They all knew there would be many more clashes ahead. Both Norton and Elliott were well aware of the enemy's home base. They had discussed on many occasion what to do about the enemy on their doorsteps. Where Elliott's forces were primarily land-based, the Jihad had the advantage of having a well-trained fleet-based naval unit. Turning the periodic clashes into a battle front would mean taking his forces to the road south. For now, it was not an option. The opposing Jihad forces dug in at Chicago had grown to a sizable army outnumbering the Patriots. For that, "We need a bigger army," was Norton's assessment.

Until more troops could be recruited or a naval force implemented, for the time being, it was decided to keep warding off the enemy's advances whenever one approached by water. On the same line of thought, Norton figured the enemy was restrained to water-based assaults for similar reasons, not having enough land-based support equipment to fight their battles on land.

"Need more men," he determined. He knew where to complement his manpower and increase in armament. But, he also knew it would not be an easy task to get it from the source, that of Fort Knox and Wendell Nelson, its commander. For reasons unknown to him, he'd tried on several occasions but had always been denied his request for additional resources. To find out, he'd have to take a trip there but at the time could not break away from here with the constant insurgents by the Jihad testing his defense line. There would be many more of these and likewise clashes in the weeks and months ahead.

THE SERPENT

Too much time had passed for the Serpent's liking. Not that he had been sitting idle. The pace of his calling was not proceeding speedily enough. It was frustrating. Not much he could do about it. Although his Plan was pretty much alive, to assure non-discovery of his whereabouts by law enforcing agencies, especially Interpol, so far, he had been successfully protecting his identity. Keeping his birth name identity isolated from his operative identity known only to his mission commanders took care of that. Letting his lieutenants handle the fighting and logistics was his buffer. He had no indication that his identity had been breached.

Hammad considered himself fortunate. He could not have found a better location to carry out his Plan. Palm Island was the ideal place to headquarter mission command. Protected by a force of sentries and sophisticated surveillance systems in his abode, he was able to command all operations without detection and still pursue a lifestyle of luxury. He would hate having to subsist within a bunker confinement as did many of his comrades. At this paradise of leisure, he could easily blend in with the growing Muslim population. After the collapse of the United States, a severe economic recession followed in many of the nations, especially the ones heavily dependent on international trade. The very thought of one man bring an entire world economy to its knees made him gloat. It was his doing. He took a deep breath to savor the moment.

With Yusuf by his side, lying in the breezy shadows of the lofty balcony, his shaded eyes were lazily scanned the blue horizon off to the UAE shores. Created by the prevalent monsoons carried on top gentle swells of waves, the ever-present winds were pitching up foamy crests of white spray. He squinted to gauge the distance to the nearest shore. The waters off Dubai were relatively narrow at this point. Channeled between the Persian Gulf and ocean access he could make out the colorful flags flying atop the many freighters plowing the Strait of Hormuz. Adjusting the latest fashion frames resting on the bridge of the nose, he completely enjoyed his self-elevated status of supreme leader. He felt he was the only one deserving. After what seemed a lifetime of hardship, he had steadily moved up the ranks, aided by Jihad likeminded supporters. It had been a long struggle. In the end, especially since his attempted takeover of the fractured United States, he had been recognized by his wealthy supporters for his commanding skills.

Hammad should feel euphoric at his achievements. But this was not the case. He had much higher ambitions. His work had only just begun. He voiced his concerns with his trusted commander. "It is time to put the next phase into action." Nearby, the radio was receiving news from the ether. One in particular just broadcast captured their ears. Although broken up somewhat by distance, *American missile launch...Alaskan earthquake...massive power outages on Pacific islands.* He did not have to put two and two together to assume a connection between the events. It was the signal for which he had been waiting. Now it was his turn. "What's the status of your forces?"

"Teams are ready," Yusuf affirmed. He had spent two years getting the forces in shape and felt they were ready for action. All necessary technology and logistics were in place. With most of the world focused on rebuilding an ailing economy, conditions were ideal.

"The world has been quiet long enough," Hammad explained.

"Right," Yusuf agreed. "We are ready."

"Get your lieutenants together," Hammad ordered. "Desert Base Alpha—two days." Located in the Sudan, it was the force's primary training camp. He had carefully selected the site not just for its convenient access from here but because it was sanctioned by his nation. Because so many Muslims made it their home, its population and political structure was Islam-centric. There was a reason for all this. After all, "who else would spend a lifetime within the confines of extreme desert heat?" Where most of the western population had been softened with living in the comfort of climactically controlled dwellings with easily acquired conveniences, many Muslims still endured the hardships of living in heat, squalor, and deprived regions preferably avoided by an auspicious global population.

It was this environment that shaped the aspiration of the Islamic fighter in a world of global dominance presently only enjoyed by western cultures. With such thoughts in mind, Hammad reached for the voluminous folder placed on the table nearby. From years of use, the marked-up copy of "The Plan" was well worn. Revised several times over, based on the vision of hope and triumph he had promised his people, it was his creation. Ever since Osama had been taken out unceremoniously after living a life in obscurity in the caves of Pakistan years earlier, it had been up to him to carry on the cause of Islam. With airwaves still busy delivering the latest events over a failed Pacific missile launch, he grinned at his deputy. "Stupid people. Believe everything the media says or prints." He knew better. He knew the truth.

Just before the fall of the free world, Hammad had obtained a copy of the most sophisticated network and cryptographic deciphering tools. With these, he had been able to break into networks of governments and military alike. In addition, hackers and internet thieves were only too willing to provide their skills at breaking into secure networks and proprietary data vaults. The Internet provided a wealth of ready resources. One only had to ask for assistance. Where the majority of hackers had their own reasons, from bragging rights to vengeance, he fought for the Islamic cause. All he needed was the right weapon. And he thought he had found it. Only recently developed for offensive warfare, it was a weapon kept dormant for many generations. It was a weapon so destructive not even he had information on its full potential.

There were only rumors at first, which were then eventually substantiated by credible witnesses. "Leave it up to the Americans," he shared his thoughts with Yusuf, "to conceive another crazy idea." To him, it seemed that the nation of a quarter billion did nothing but develop weapons of mass destruction. Their destructive ideas seemed boundless. It could be new software for bringing a nation to its knees. It could be computers to manipulate finance and world trade. But, worse of all, it was most likely another destructive weapon used to manipulate nations by exerting immense pressure on their governments and their peoples. He was gnashing his teeth at the very thought as he collected his travel gear in preparation for the upcoming flight. "Let's get going."

ISS

"Fuck Soyuz...Fuck Baikonur...Fuck the whole damned space project." Budenko was furious. Outbursts such as now had become more and more frequent. In a way, he had just cause. When volunteering for the space program, he had signed up for one mission. Where the usual mission would take only weeks, this one had already passed months and turned into years. He had already been stuck at this godforsaken outpost for more than two. "Damned economy...damned politicians...damned ISS." Because of his gruff attitude his fellow comrades learned to stay away from him. It was not just the cussing and the yelling, his mood was also reflected in his appearance. Unkempt, unwashed, smelly, his body odor carried in the module. His faded appearance was a demonstration to the world: "Look at me...I've given up on society." Morale, no matter how hard the other crew members tried keeping it up, was rapidly waning. For all practical purposes, Sergei Budenko had given up on discipline, the mission, and the world.

In the tight quarters of space, to prevent morale erosion, strict rules and policies had to be adhered to. Because of the absence of privacy, discipline and respect for each other was foremost on the agenda. There was no, "I've had it." There was no, "I quit." There was no, "Goin' home." The mission was just that: the mission.

No matter how long and how difficult a mission, there was no out. Becoming ill, getting sick or not feeling up to it was unacceptable. Every waking hour of the day, each person had to carry her or his weight, metaphorically speaking. What made it worse was that gravity was absent after the spacecraft docked with the ISS.

Slicing thought space at a constant speed of 17,227 mph at an average orbit of 250 miles from Earth, each day in the ISS lasted only 92 minutes 36 seconds. With this short of a day, the sun was rising over the eastern horizon more than 15 times in an Earth day. An inclination of 51.6 degrees to Earth's equator was necessary to ensure that Russian Soyuz and Progress[28] spacecraft launched from Baikonur Cosmodrome could be safely docked with the station. The orbital inclination chosen was also low enough to allow American space shuttles launched from Florida.

Just as important to spaceflight were hygiene and crew schedules. Cleaning the body on the space station was an infrequent activity. Since the ISS did not feature a shower, crewmembers washed using a water jet and wet wipes, with soap dispensed from a toothpaste tube-like container. Crews were also provided with rinse-less shampoo and edible toothpaste to save water.

---

[28] Progress was a Russian expendable cargo spacecraft. Its purpose was to deliver supplies needed to sustain human presence in orbit. While it did not carry a crew, it could be boarded by astronauts when docked with a space station.

Progress was developed because of the need for a constant source of supplies to make long duration space missions possible. It was determined that cosmonauts needed an inflow of consumables (food, water, air, etc.), plus there was a need for maintenance items and scientific payloads that necessitated a dedicated cargo carrier. Such payloads were impractical to launch with passengers in the restricted space of a Soyuz.

There were two space toilets on the ISS, both of Russian design, located in Zvezda and Tranquility. These waste and hygiene compartments used a fan-driven suction system. To perform daily business, astronauts fastened themselves to the seat, equipped with spring-loaded restraining bars to ensure a good seal. A lever operated a powerful fan for the air stream to carry away the waste. Solid waste was collected in individual bags stored in an aluminum container. Full containers were transferred mostly to the Progress spacecraft, making periodic supply flights for delivery and disposal. Liquid waste was evacuated via a hose connected to the front of the toilet, with anatomically correct "urine funnel adapters" attached to the tube for both men and women using the same toilet, where it was collected and transferred to the Water Recovery System, where it was recycled into drinking water. Although the thought of impurity and aversion to such recycling, most space personal over time, accepted these practical applications, albeit necessary, as part of space living.

A typical day for the crew began with a wake-up call at 06:00 Zulu, followed by post-sleep activities and a morning inspection of the station. The crews then ate breakfast and took part in a daily planning conference with Mission Control before starting work at around 08:10. The first scheduled exercise of the day followed, after which the crew continued work until 13:05.

Following a one-hour lunch break, the afternoon consisted of more exercise and work before the crew carried out its pre-sleep activities beginning at 19:30 including dinner and a crew conference. The scheduled sleep period began at 21:30. In general, the crew worked a ten-hour weekday, and five hours Saturdays, with Sunday and the rest of the time reserved for relaxation.

Accommodations were limited to crew quarters for each member of the expedition's crew, with two sleep stations in the Zvezda module and four more installed in Harmony. The American quarters were private, approximately person-sized soundproof booths. The Russian crew quarters included a small window. Typically, the crewmember could sleep in a tethered sleeping bag, listen to music, use a laptop, and store personal items in a nearby drawer or net attached to the module's walls.

The module also provided a reading lamp, shelf and a desktop. Visiting crews had no allocated sleep module. For those crewmembers, a sleeping bag was attached to any available space on the walls. It was possible to sleep floating freely through the station, but was generally avoided because of the possibility of bumping into critical instruments and interfering with the working crew. Also important was ventilation; otherwise, an astronaut could wake up oxygen-deprived, gasping for air, because a bubble of exhaled carbon dioxide could form around the astronaut's head with unexpected, suffocating results.

Budenko was currently absorbed with the task on hand when his body jerked up as a result from the onboard radio signal action call. "Zvezda...Zvezda...come in." Body tensed with adrenaline flow, slightly surprised, he reached for the headset Velcroed to the console frame. Although he had not expected a call, it was the station's call sign. As far as he knew, no launch was scheduled for several more months. These days only routine call checks were made and they were on a scheduled basis. As usual, the call came from the Baikonur Cosmodrome ground station. "Budenko," he answered.

"Launch schedule expected. Anticipated arrival..." There was a halted pause by ground control to verify date and time, "ETA, five days...02:35 Zulu."

My shift, Budenko reflected on the docking hour. As always, he was looking forward to the extra activity. Life at the station, although busy during working hours, had become rudimentary, repetitive, and, to a larger extent, boring.

"Special instructions follow in coded sequence."

Now that's, his mind perked up immediately, *a new one.* In all the times, a new spacecraft had arrived to change crew and unload supplies, there had never been coded instructions. It meant a classified task—highly classified.

"Roger," he acknowledged. No further instructions were forthcoming. The call had ended.

"Well...well," he muttered in the silence of the capsule. "Let's see what that's all about." With a flick of his wrist he undid the body straps tying him to the seat. Reaching hand over hand, he steadily made his way back to the computer terminal where a text alert awaited him. A push on the key brought up the message. "TOP SECRET," it read. "BUDENKO EYES ONLY."

What followed was text expanding into detailed assembly and installation instructions for what appeared an unusual appendage designed for external operation. Studying the instructions, he thought, "New weapon, perhaps." But there was more, much more. And that something would take some planning. And it would not be a pleasant task. It might lead to death. He took a deep breath, capturing the full extent of the orders, then verbally exhaled, "The time is near."

Reading through the initial material received and stored in onboard computer databanks only accessible to him, he realized, he had much to study and learn for what was at stake. He had to become familiar with a technology he knew nothing about. It was something from the distant past—Tesla.

THREE MILE ISLAND

Much time had already passed since the last major event at the nuclear power plant. Although marauding bands from the eastern part of the state were a constant danger, Doug Olsen, with the aid of his dedicated shift supervisor Jim Ross, somehow managed to keep the plant in operation. Challenges were in abundance. Without a chance of ever getting replacement parts, Jim took it on himself to get necessary spares locally fabricated. Crafty people were only too eager, helping out just to keep the plant in operation. Without it would be doomsday. Scaled down to minimum power output to maintain safe operations, barely enough to feed the surrounding towns and a couple of cities, the plant had been off the grid ever since the last incident. The local townsfolk lend a hand whenever necessary to keep electricity up, although marginal at times, to their homes.

"Been in the city lately?" Doug asked Jim. They were taking a lunch break making conversation. They were not the only employees on site. There were others just as dedicated. Problem was getting food on the table. It had been a monumental struggle for most citizens in the region. As luck had it, for the employed at the plant, Quaker Farms nearby were at abundance. As a matter of fact, it was the only one prosperous in what was left of a once-thriving agricultural region.

"Nope."

"It's pretty bad," a nearby crew member cut in. "Crime's rampant. Wouldn't wanna go there unless it's family or relatively urgent."

"News is worse further east. I heard that damn foreigners have taken over Eastern Seaboard up and down the coast."

"Hell," another knowingly explained, "New York's been declared Western fashion hub for all of the Middle East."

"Wouldn't wanna live there anyway," someone else remarked. "Whole damned place turned Islam."

Doug finally voiced his open opinion. "The way I see it," he said. "For all I care, they can have it." That this was the common consensus was obvious from several nodding head. "Been a cultural melting pot for years."

They were interrupted by a security guard from the main gate. He gestured at the cafeteria entrance. "Got a visitor."

Their heads turned in the direction. Doug got on his feet. "Wonder what he wants." It wasn't everyday a stranger showed up at this place. It'd only mean trouble. He trotted his way to the office. A tall, well-built stranger was studying the map tacked to the wall when he entered. Guarded, Doug gave him a once over and said, "Who're you?"

"Brooks...Scott Brooks," the stranger replied.

"Olson's the name," he greeted the visitor with an extended hand. "Plant manager. What brings you here?"

"Los Alamos," Brooks stated. "Facility security's my expertise. I believe," he explained, "you sent for me."

"Aah yes," Olson recalled. "Been some time." He'd completely forgotten that he had requested the service. Back then, during the initial chaotic times, the plant had been under constant threat mostly from passing gangs. Since then, the countryside had somewhat stabilized. But the issue with security was still a problem. There was none.

"Care to join us?" he offered the visitor.

Back at the cafeteria Doug led him through the chow line. "Help yourself," he offered. "Food's good and plentiful. All fresh produce from nearby farms."

"You guys are lucky. Down south," Scott explained, "we've gotta fight for everything coming across the border."

"Border?"

"Yeah, border! Anarchists on this side. Mexican bandits on the other. Tax everything that's crossing. Cant's survive without it."

"Anarchists? Who's controlling them? Who's in charge?"

"Guy named Derek Wallace. Civilian-turned renegade."

"Sure, don't miss that," Doug stated. "Peaceful around here most times. Okay then," he opened business talks, "what's your plan?"

"Secure the plant. There are rumors about an attack. Strike may come from above. Hit will most likely crack the containment. Threat's real. Don't want nuclear fallout."

"I hear you." Doug and his crew were in complete agreement. He had visions of Badlands. From what he'd heard, blackouts were exactly the conditions that part of the country was facing. "Whatcha got in mind?"

"Mechanical locks, interlocks, mechanize the whole damned plant."

"What's it gonna take?"

Brooks was not committing to specifics. "Time," he stated. "And a lot of sweat. Shouldn't take more than," he paused, "six months."

"Then what?"

"I'll train your people. Hand-to-hand combat, knives, weapons…the whole gambit. All I need is capable bodies."

"There's plenty around here. People are fighting for jobs. Only way they get to eat."

"Good then. Got any quarters on site?"

"I'll make some available. When you wanna start?"

"Immediately."

"Tomorrow then," Doug sealed the deal. "Jim," he gestured at his supervisor, "put him up at your place for the night."

"Will do."

It took Brooks more than six months to get the facility secured. He had plenty of help. Problem was getting parts built. Unlike Los Alamos, this place was not set up for that. Processing machines had to be located. Materials bartered. Work negotiated. But Brooks realized people around here were willing to cooperate and made things happen. It appeared that this part of the nation was well on its way to building a workable future. For now, it was mostly agricultural, but with his initiative, manufacturing could be reestablished once more. It had been done before. It would be done again. It might be the only success for a future nation.

It all boiled down to one commodity: earthly resources. And minerals were getting scarce without mining. Without power, there was no chance to ever get back into the process. It was up to him to insure the plant was secured and kept producing power. For now, Brooks had found a new home.

THE SERPENT

Hammad had a clear vision for what he wanted. But in order to achieve it, it had to be accomplished in stages. For the immediate future, his focus was on securing water. "The rest of the word must wait," he muttered into the morning quiet. "But not for long." Although the major part of the Great Lakes region was under his control his scouts reported more frequently about a major push by a momentum gaining faction known as the Patriots. Apparently, they were expanding their centrally-located turf, identified as Badlands. Disturbing news was brought back about their advances, more so since the forces were coming in his direction. According to the scouts, it was a sizable force growing by the week from newly acquired recruits along their path. It would not be long before he had to face their forces. Hammad was in desperate need of more men. Recruiting additional fighters was not an easy task. Most volunteers were unruly and undisciplined speaking different languages. Many were typical street thugs, opportunists searching for easy money. Joining the Jihad was one answer. It paid well, provided adventure, and, most importantly, satisfied their fighting instincts. It was for this reason Hammad had recalled Yusuf, who had spent much of the time at the frontlines recently. He was his sounding board. When devising a plan, it helped him to verbalizing it with his trusted. Too much time had been wasted with recent clashes in trying to secure all the waterfronts. He had to press on with The Plan.

It was these concerns Hammad was presently dealing with. Passing his concerns on to Yusuf, he said, "A decision must be made."

"I agree." He agreed on most subjects. Yusuf was a capable fighter but had limited command capabilities. He was no match for his leader and he knew it well enough. He was quite content in the position he held as personal assistant and close friend to the supreme commander. His dedication had earned him the most sought out position of the Jihad followers.

"Now," Hammad insisted. "Immediately. We cannot waste any more time." His level of frustration clearly reflected in his voice.

"What is your strategy?"

"That is the dilemma I have to solve." Yusuf had no suggestions. He kept quiet. He knew pushing the subject would only irritate the leader more. Both sat silent, staring out at the Arabian Sea. Hammad was recollecting the years. He was searching for an answer. There was something that kept gnawing at his mind. It was a subconscious knowing that he had missed something, but could not identify the element. Digging even deeper into the recesses of his mind, it finally hit him. Bolting from the chair, he suddenly shouted out, "Of course!"

"What?" Yusuf was shaken from his calm. He watched Hammad pace the deck, muttering unintelligently.

Hammad then ordered, "Get me information. Everything you can find on recent missile launches."

"What regions?" He was unsure about Hammad's thoughts.

"Vandenberg."

"Right away." Yusuf hurried off.

Hammad kept pacing the deck. With every step, his thoughts were getting clearer. Although he only had a partial image at this time, all he needed was confirmation data to complete the picture. "It has to be it," he substantiated his idea. To expedite the search, he powered up the laptop, hoping it would provide some information. Normally, he did not miss the sources feeding the Internet, especially not since he had destroyed most of the network on the North American continent. But today, right now, staring at the computer screen, he realized once more the destruction of his making. After several hurried searches, he determined, "Not a damned thing." It was a time he was made keenly aware of technology. Not only had the western world invented the Internet, but it was they, that had developed, expanded, and managed the complexity of a system only Google understood. With the mighty corporation splintered into minor regions, the once prolific information source had been dramatically interrupted. Well aware it was his doing, he spat, "Piece of shit," and gave the laptop a kick and out it flew, over the deck rail, sailing into the winds. For now, he had to be content with waiting for Yusuf to return with printed matter.

Shortly after Yusuf returned with a stack of dated news periodicals, Hammad called to his attention, "There it is." Reading on, it confirmed his earlier suspicion.

"What?" Yusuf was still mystified at the outburst.

"Proof." What had caught Hammad's attention was an article printed several months ago following an event that had taken place over the Pacific. It gave the account of a failed missile launch over the ocean. Staring boldly into his face was the content of the article:

"Early this morning, NASA launched what observers believed to be an Atlas V rocket booster into space. The launch was unsuccessful in as much as the missile blew up in mid-air over the central Pacific region. The mission," a reporter disclosed, *"had been a scheduled mission to test newly developed technology for the rocket guidance system."*

As he read on, it was the second article that jolted his mind.

"A major power failure over Hawaii, including a number of mid-Pacific islands, was experienced at the same time. The cause is still undetermined as of this hour since there is hardly information forthcoming from that region due to communication failure."

The report was supplemented with: *Earthquake magnitude 6.5 that followed caused minor destructions to outlaying Pacific islands. No major tsunami is expected since the quake took place hundreds of miles from the Alaskan shorelines."*

"Alaska!" he exclaimed at a surprised Yusuf. "We must go."

"But why?" Alaska was a place he had never considered as a travel destination. Being desert bound for many years, he felt it was a cold, desolate, and miserable place.

"HAARP." What had struck Hammad was an incident he had experienced years earlier while trapped in upper Manhattan. Yusuf, at the time, was detained at Guantánamo. He would not have known. It was the weapon Hammad needed. He knew it then and he knew it now. "We must get our hands on this weapon."

"Weapon?" Yusuf was still in puzzlement.

"I will explain." As distantly as the event had taken place, Hammad clearly recalled its impact. He proceeded to illustrate the deadly account of his crew to Yusuf as much as he could remember. The only reason he had survived that dreaded night in New York years ago during his first onslaught on the United States of America, was the reaction he had witnessed on Bauer and his partner Harris, when all of a sudden, they had dropped their weapons. He could still hear the hollow sound of steel hitting concrete at the Hillview reservoir. He had not anticipated their moves but immediately followed suit once the weapon in his hand heated up. It had been too late to save his palms and fingers from getting charred from the heated barrel, but he was able to flee the scene amid the overwhelming forces from local law enforcement. Hunted down by the perpetrators, he had barely escaped the ensuing pursuit.

Their talks continued until dawn.

After only a couple of hours sleep, Yusuf was roused. "I need scientists, engineers, specialists," Hammad fired at him. "Get them from India, Europe, Russia or wherever, but make it quick. I only want the best. Make them offers they will not refuse."

"What about skills and experience?"

"Tesla, microwave, pulse weaponry."

"That may be difficult." Yusuf, as disinterested he was in technology, had at least an insight on the latest developments in the free world. What Hammad described was beyond the means of the ordinary engineering. It was a science held closely guarded that only few were aware of and less knew about, especially foreign subjects.

"Never mind," he was told. "Take your scouts to Alaska and explore. Find the facility."

Yusuf backed off instantly. His commander would fly into rage if he pushed on. It was up to him to get the details. "Three months," Hammad ordered. "I will give you three months to take and staff the place with our people."

"Not enough time," Yusuf protested.

"Get what you need to get it done." There was nothing more to be said. As impossible as it appeared, he had his job cut out for him and went to work immediately. Otherwise it would be his head on the chopping block. He made a mental list of the items he needed to accomplish.

1.   Acquire scientific personnel to study, modify, and test an unfamiliar system.
2.   Identify capable personnel to engineer and implement the underground complex.
3.   Organize the assault team from terrorists around the globe.
4.   Take over the facility in the globe's most remote region without any ground access to logistics support.

Everything had to be flown in over enemy territory. At this time, the task seemed impossible to Yusuf, but he had to make an attempt. "Three months?" Doubt was painted across his face as he turned to leave the commander, not sure of his destination.

"Wait," Hammad called after a puzzled trusted who stopped short.

"Yes?"

"Get me the precise locations of all of the HAARP facilities."

"What. There is more than one?"

"Need you to infiltrate every one of the places."

"How do you expect me to penetrate such secure facilities? I don't even know if and where they exist."

"Believe me," Hammad assured him. "They do, and..." he hesitated to let the enormity sink in. "Approach the scientists on location. Take hostages if you must. My orders are final. Now, go."

PALM JUMEIRAH

Several months had passed. Yusuf had just returned from his designated mission to Alaska. He was here to brief his commander of his progress. Rather than enjoying a well deserving break on the island from the frigid cold of Alaska, Hammad had other plans. It was early morning several hours into the flight. Presently, with Yusuf by his side, Hammad had a firm grip on the controls of the magnificent jet, ready to turn downwind. "Aah yes," he exhaled in somber admiration as he switched from autopilot, "Allah's paradise." They were seated in the plush comfort of a sleek Gulf Stream with their eyes darting between the horizon and ground. They were seeking out an uncharted place known as The Base, their destination. As part of the Plan, it had been his idea to construct secret facilities strategically staged around the globe in total obscurity. It had not been an easy task. As a matter of fact, it had been the most challenging undertaking ever in modern construction. It had put companies like Bechtel and Halliburton to shame, whose building methods were outdated by decades. But you could not blame them entirely for following the same blueprints over and over. They were behemoths in the true sense, unrelenting and unwavering on flexibility and established policies. "If it works, don't mess with it," was this type of corporate philosophy.

Building up an army faction of Islamic-minded recruits in support of his cause had been his design. His future plan was not religious-centric but rather political in nature as it embraced the entire globe. He had studied international politics thoroughly. He had considered every aspect of possible compromises to his Plan. To obtain its goals, it would entail creating a force made up mostly of industrial, scientific, and technology experts building up the new nation. The challenges could prove overwhelming. But there were ways for putting extreme pressure on nations to drive them into submission. It had suited history, and will suit him as well for achieving his goals.

They had taken off from Dubai a couple hours earlier, heading straight west across the Red Sea for the Saudi desert. The flight had been boring for most part, skimming over the seemingly endless wastelands of Saudi Arabia, with a final turn south over Egypt into the deserts of the Sudan, their final destination. Listless over the grayish-brown covered shades of the deserts slowly passing below, Hammad savored the moment. One had to be born into this environment to accept these lands. One had to be Arabic. He had not met one westerner yet that would bow to kiss the ground below, calling it home. Aside from comments made by travelers from the western world such as "Good God, the heat," or "How can anybody live here?" and "This must be hell," one only had to observe the rugged, cotton clad, turban bedecked individual happily residing within the vast, most unforgiving stretch in central Africa.

"Time," Hammad checked with his lieutenant, who shot a glance at the platinum Rolex tightly fitted against his wrist.

"6:23 am. Better speed it up," he urged. "Don't want to miss the window."

To Hasan Hammad this was paradise, especially now, with modern construction going on everywhere in the deserts. High-rises were sprouting up prolifically paid for with money mostly from the purses of the international investors. The general population had no idea how the wastelands had changed. Only the folks manipulating spy satellites had been wise. Hammad was keenly aware of dreaded spy birds up in orbit. They had made his life miserable. But, in time, he got used to their incessant orbits. "Someday soon," he uttered with vehemence, "I'll shoot them out of the sky."

Yusuf turned to face him. "What?"

"Nothing," he replied. "Just thinking."

Born to diplomatic parents and educated in Pakistani and Kashmir schools, Hammad was destined for the political world, but in his wildest dreams he'd never thought it possible to become supreme leader. After Osama Bin Laden went into obscurity first, and then suffered an unceremonious death, Hammad had been escalated into the very position to lead the Islamic cause. Although not anticipated, it was truly a blessing, considering the leadership skills combined with combat training and battlefield experience that he brought to the table. He would set a benchmark in Muslim society. "I'll go down in history as a great leader," he stated on more than one occasion.

To secure this promise had taken him years of planning and dedication. He thought he had found it in Shahadah, but warfare was not the answer to a lasting solution. He had to look deeper into the past to come up with an answer. He had found it by digging into history. History had become his companion. Studying western politics, cultural heritages, and warfare at Harvard in the '80s, he had become an advocate of the likes of Napoleon, Stalin, and Hitler. Aside from the fact that these leaders had fallen in disgrace with their respective societies, they nevertheless had been geniuses.

But with each one, there had always been one element missing to assure lasting success. It was the element of shock. It was the shock factor that was necessary to instill fear and terror. It was the fear of the unknown that kept the masses in check. He came to recognize this factor during his days at the university.

At first, he could not understand why the American could be so confident and self-assured for most of the year, but when April 15th came around, he panicked to beat a deadline. It made Hammad think: What was the IRS, who was behind it, what was its purpose? What would they do to the citizen, if one did not pay up taxes for the year? "Take away his freedom." He then realized how important this one commodity must be in their culture. Ever since, he had made it his instrument. It became his sword, a two-edged sword. One edge was to instill fear. The other was made for battle. It equated to the two sides of his very being. It had served its purpose for the Serpent. It became the enigma for Hasan Hammad, the leader they all respected but nobody had identified. His final thoughts as he prepared for the landing were, "Time to elevate my status to supremacy."

Both of their eyes were searching the distance. The desert finally was taking on contours. The outline of the complex was gaining shape. The craft approached what appeared to be a runway leading underground. It was a marvelous construction. A static sounding voice suddenly made its presence known. "Cleared for final." It was from ground control. "Runway Zero One."

"Roger," Hammad responded. They were approaching the last thousand feet when he spotted the runway entrance. "Clever," he muttered. You had to be at very low altitude and perfectly aligned with "Runway-01" to spot the huge gaping opening, studded by microwave and ground control antenna that could accommodate an entire aircraft. "Switch to auto," was the next command. Hammad followed the instruction and removed his hands from the controls. It was an uneasy feeling to have the craft completely guided by automation for final touchdown, even more so with the natural horizon replaced by camouflaged tarp and netting, rushing in on the speeding craft. The only view remaining was the white center-strip perfectly aligned with the decelerating jet.

"Magic Mountain," Yusuf remarked. It reminded him of a Hollywood thrill ride he had experienced as a kid many years ago.

"Magic Mountain?" Hammad did not understand.

"Disneyland. Hollywood." Yusuf boasted. "Must go there."

Hammad firmly pushed on brakes, slowing the craft to a final halt deep inside the tunnel.

The base commander came rushing up with both arms extended. "Congratulations." He welcomed the much revered, but feared leader with, "Perfect landing," then hurried his visitors along the underground pathway. "You are the first official visitor to the Base."

DESERT BASE ALPHA

It was an historic event. The entire force had assembled for the visitors. They had been ready for some time. Going underground had been no easy task. Logistics turned out to be more complex than anybody had imagined. Operational conditioning had proved just as difficult. Being trapped for years in isolation, emotions came to blows frequently usually winding up in fights. In spite of rigid punishment, discipline had weakened. Today, in the spacious, but crowded, command center, the atmosphere was tense. Commanders and squad leaders were crammed into the reception center, ready for the opening ceremony. The rest of the forces were packed in the many spaces and hallways. Everybody wanted to meet him. Unlike before, this time there was a face to the supreme leader.

He was deliberately taking his time on the platform. "Fellow comrades," he began. "I am Hasan Hammad, supreme commander, all Islamic forces." Stern faced, he began deliberating on the very reasons they had been summoned. During the next hour, he expounded on the changes of Islamic philosophy. "The days of the roaming Bedouins on camel backs, breaking and setting up tents, are over," was just one such example. He then delved into his Plan and explained why changes were necessary. "We must adapt to the world. Otherwise," he explained, "we will always be enslaved by the infidels." He made a promise to each individual on upcoming opportunities to become part of the new Islamic world. In closing, he emphasized, "Today, in the name of Allah," his eyes touched every one of his commanders to acknowledge their dedication, "we are making history. Now," he concluded, "make me proud."

His second in command took his place to address the assemblage. "For you newcomers," he said, "my name is Yusuf Joseph Hashim." He continued with the brief, "I am your mission commander." He then elaborated on highlights from the past years, successes as well as failures, concluding with the immediate mission at hand. "With the periodic shifts in a politically charged climate around the world, it will be necessary to maintain flexibility, covertness, and secrecy. As far as we know," he added, "the mission has not been compromised to this date. You will report directly to me…is that understood?" With a quick gesture at the next speaker in line, he turned the assembly over to the base commander.

Next up was Rashid Abu, Base Commander, Desert Base Alpha, Sudan, taking the lead for the technical briefing. He moved the laser pointer across the monitor screen, depicting the Saudi desert. "Here *we* are." He was indicating their present position on the underlying world map. "And there are our other bases." He commenced the presentation by pointing out other camp locations in the Sudan, Algeria, and Pakistan, well identified through various color-coded flags. "As you can see," he went on, "our main forces are concentrated in northern Africa. More bases are under development. Our African camps are permanent sites. They will be used to stage strategic thrusts while the rest of the camps are tactical support sites designated primarily for recruitment, training, and logistics."

Satisfied about having made the right choices on promoting his commanders, Hasan Hammad thought, *well spoken*, while listening to the deliberation. First off, there was Yusuf. At first, he was utterly furious with him when he had heard Yusuf had been captured in the Rockies at what ended in a failed hostage attempt during the assault on the United States. As it turned out, it had not been entirely his fault. The mission had been doomed to fail right from the start. Recruits were inexperienced. The forces had been too thinly spread. Logistics were not in place. And there was unexpected resistance popping out of nowhere in the most unlikely places. His face distorted with hatred every time he thought of him. "Bauer!" The visage was permanently imprinted on his mind. The man turned out to be the strongest adversary opponent he had ever encountered. Were it not for this infidel's nuclear retaliation on NKPR and Pakistan, the outcome would have been much different. *Where did this detested infidel appear from anyway?* he still pondered.

The reflection of this past failure still infuriated him. A nagging thought persisted. "I will personally take care of him…and his team," he promised with infernal hatred. Bauer's haunting caused him many sleepless nights, where he woke up in cold sweats, panting for revenge. With the United States, for all practical purposes, still shattered into unmanaged regions, he still had no clue as to the man's whereabouts. His fury incinerated once more. He would make it his personal mission to seek him out, claim justice, and destroy this detested opponent once and for all. "His time is near."

Because of one man, Hammad's entire plan had suffered. The result was a setback it took years to recover from. But it gave him the time needed to prepare for his next onslaught. This time he would be prepared. As his subsequent analysis revealed, the entire mission had been premature. He had not had enough of a force to see the mission through. Besides, operational support had proved inadequate with logistics not in place for a successful outcome. Following the failure, he had retreated to his covert sanctuary at Palm Jumeirah.

It took many months for the political dust he had caused to settle. He swore never to hurry into action again without all elements in place beforehand. After revising the Plan, he had pulled off what turned out to be the successful rescue of his friend detained at the world's most dreaded site, Guantánamo. He needed Yusuf. It was he that was familiar with the people, the customs, and the lives of the citizens of the former superpower nation, the United States of America.

With the presentation behind them, it was time for the local tour. "Very impressive," Hammad kept expressing with genuine approval. They had just finished the tour through the compact, but super modern, underground facility. Construction could have never been completed in the record time of two years had it not been for the ancient abandoned copper mine. Mines of this nature were abundant in this part of the world, with gold, copper, and tin mining dating back thousands of years. With the cost of minerals skyrocketing in recent years, revitalizing abandoned mines had made sense. It provided shelter to house the thousands of forces he was putting in place. What made it even more attractive, due to his meticulous planning, was that all activities so far had gone unnoticed by monitoring agencies. The outside world had noticed the construction, but it had been contributed to activities slated as mineral mining.

The solution had come to him two years earlier when revising the Plan. It was during one of his frequently occurring nightmares. It was a vivid vision. It held the solution for which he had been searching. It would not be without excessive costs, but his concerns for the enormous undertaking were quickly resolved by willing Saudi investors. Once he introduced his Plan, it was not difficult to gain their support since most were Muslim in culture and Islam by faith. There was one obstacle he had to overcome. Influenced by modern day comfort from the riches of oil, most were satisfied by a lifestyle of lavishness and luxury. It was impossible to convince a majority with an acquired attitude of, "Let's worry about that after the oil runs out."

That unperturbed, collective attitude was not good enough for him. He needed a steady supply of funding to pay for the rapidly-increasing construction costs. His vivid vision held the key. It turned out so simple. What he needed was ownership of unproductive mines that had been shot down and sitting dormant for decades. He acquired deeds for peanuts from owners who wanted to get rid of their barren mines. All he had to do was create a corporate vehicle to operate the business legitimately. For that, he went to offshore Bahamas. He had used their legitimate vehicles before. He would use them now.

Right from the onset the mines proved of immense success and wealth. With the demand of precious minerals on the rise, mining suddenly became lucrative once more. On the one hand, the mines gave him the resources needed to cover the cost for his expenses. On the other, utilizing the expended space for living and training quarters, it provided abundant room for his growing forces with nobody the wiser. It gave him the means to recruit, train, and prepare a distributed fighting force under the cover of legitimate employment. Where production was a byproduct from a ready fighting workforce, the main reason was militant training conducted out of sight of spy satellites. The project became a perpetually self-sustained, self-supporting work and the fighting force provided for its own expenses and logistics.

It could not have been pulled off prior to the collapse of the former United States with its incessant surveillance satellites. But, with the destruction of their sophisticated space capabilities, the plan had fallen into place. He took full advantage, not only for this place, but for many other cells as well. Where construction used to be confined to the cloak of darkness, it now could be conducted out in the open by underground and well-lit millions of candle lights.

Materials were purchased in quantities from Islamic-friendly nations. Construction engineers brought in from Saudi, Pakistan, and North Korea with promises of great wealth and prosperity were only too willing to sign up. Executive management was signing up from all over the globe. Their expertise was screened not only for operational and management abilities, but, more importantly, for individual skills in specific disciplines. Foremost on the list of requirements was brainpower and aptitude. It was Hammad's principle directive to recruit only the brightest engineers and scientists. It would be this force that would eventually control and manage the new world of Islam.

Later that day, the reward ceremony was in progress. Surrounded by his trusted and field lieutenants, in the comfort of the reception hall, satisfied the way things were proceeding, Hammad expressed his sincere gratitude and approval at Yusuf. "You've made me proud."

Yusuf, as humble and subservient as usual, admitted, "It wasn't easy, but we pulled it off." Thinking back on the many months since construction began, there had been challenges—many challenges. It was no ordinary task, going underground. Any miner could attest to that. In addition, since it was a pioneering project, this one needed special attention. What made it special was constructing a camouflaged runway, airport terminal, ground control, support facilities, fuel storage, generator backup, elaborate air exhaust ducting, passenger pathways, combatant housing, eating facilities, and water supply, not to mention waste removal. All in all, it was the complexity of constructing an entire public community, all underground.

The foremost challenge was the construction of an eight-thousand-foot runway. Built below ground, a fleet of dozers had been busy digging trenches day and night. As quickly as the trenches were dug, they were covered up with huge nettings of camouflage, blending in with the desert terrain. Walls were constructed from materials dug up, cement and gypsum added, and a ready-made casing was put in place to support the mine. The whole gambit was a conveyor type operation similar to subway constructions.

"What's your readiness to move out?"

Rashid Abu held steadfast. "Ready on standby."

Although Hammad was not prone to showing emotions, he nodded in approval, immensely satisfied. He was ready to move on. It was time to execute the Plan, a plan rehearsed many times over. The stage was set. All that was left now was the call for action.

The following day was action day. It was time for Hammad to disclose the initiative he had worked out for so many years. The projector was already primed with the world map. With laser pointer in hand, he began, "I will command the initiative." He nodded at his lieutenant and field commanders and said, "Yusuf will coordinate each phase. My first offensive is to strike here." The laser pointed at an Alaskan region identified as Gakona. "Attack force Alpha will advance on this base." He moved the pointer to the remaining markers, "Attack forces Bravo, Charley, Delta, and Echo will take the next four bases. It is of vital importance," he emphasized, "to acquire the Gakona base since the entire mission schedule is dependent on the success of this initial strike."

"Suppose we run against heavy resistance," one squad leader interjected.

"I must stress the importance," Hammad cautioned. "In case communication is disrupted, the lives of scientists and engineers must be protected at all cost. Since none of us have the expertise necessary, it is they who are needed to manipulate the target positions."

He went on to detail each mission segment and subsequent action item for a successful outcome of the operations as calculated by the Plan. "Code name," he reminded them all, "Shahadah." Although Shahadah had proven a failure during the last operation, it was the basis for the entire Jihad movement. This time, he concluded the presentation, "We will prevail."

"What's the status with the other atmospheric heating facilities?" he asked Yusuf.

"Sura and Tromso?" He was referring to two other HAARP locations within the northern hemisphere sited in Russia and Norway. He would need them for backup in case Gakona failed. There were more such facilities staged around the globe, but taking possession of these could wait. There would be a need when the time came.

"Will be ready by the time we need them."

"Dismissed," Hasan Hammad ordered with finality. He was satisfied with the progress.

Immediately, the place was buzzing with speculation and rumors. Strictly classified, only Hammad held specifics of the Plan, the operations, the overall strategy for purpose of success. It was of utmost importance to keep it this way.

There was one thing that still concerned him, the converting of the present operational functionality of the HAARP system to his needs. It was the reason he had recruited the scientists and engineers. From the design specifications, the scientists had dug up, although it had immense power generation capability, the Gakona facility was primarily geared for atmospheric research. What he needed was a weapon fed by just such a power. Gakona would give it to him. The challenge was converting the system, but "we can do it," he was assured. Bearing tedious details "Leave it to us," was the final promise from Yusuf's engineering pool.

LISA BAUER

Strapped securely into the tightly-fitted contours of the Soyuz-TMA[29] capsule hold, Liz became fully conscious of herself. The headset did not quite filter out the hissing sound from liquid nitrogen escaping the external fuel tank connections. There it was, the long-awaited countdown. She knew, one day, that the turning point in her career would come. Ever since taking up astronaut training, it had become the most critical moment in her life. All the built-up tension, anticipation, and anxiety of the past two years was compressed into a few simple commands projected through the media of the headset. It would be the last words she'd perceive while still planted solidly on earth. The long-awaited day had finally arrived. From here on out, all dialogue would be executed in space.

In her mind, time, minutes and seconds, were compressed into one single event horizon—timelessness. All of her senses were focused into one action scene in progress, unable to stop. The Go signal was only seconds away. Just in case, her mind was racing through emergency information extracted from the training manuals.

Countdown…liftoff…flameout…alert…evac…abort…event…action…emergency procedures, were the action scenes played out over the sound of rocket engines igniting with explosive forces. *Here it is, the long-anticipated liftoff.* "Three…Two…One…Liftoff." With rapidly accelerating G-forces pressing down on her body, her initial reactions were elation, euphoria, and exhilaration all compressed into one expression escaping her lips. "Oh, shiiit!"

Her mind was not the only thing rattled. Her body went through a similar reaction. First, she felt the vibration run through every fiber of her body from deep within her bones, shooting outward through tissue and muscles, emanating into every crevice of her skin. Her vision turned blurry. Seconds turned into minutes. Then, as suddenly as it began, the space surrounding her turned silent. Liz checked the onboard clock mounted against the capsule shell. What had seemed like a lifetime to her, in contrast, were only minutes. Within one fraction in time, the shaking, the G-forces, the trembling suddenly stopped. She was in space. All the pent-up tension left her body. Euphoria took over space and time. It would last for hours, even days, before the sequence of docking procedures became necessary. Until then, she, as well as her space companions, completely enjoyed the ride. It would be a thrill that would remain with her for life.

The following two days were pretty much routine. Although going by the book, there were many distractions with "Aahs and Oohs" shared between the multi-lingual space travelers. In spite of the recent collapse of the United States of America, English was still the preferred language spoken on international space missions.

Hours into the flight, after reading the voluminous mission checklist, Andrei Kubalev, Cosmonaut, Commander Soyuz Crew & ISS Space Platform, called, "Liz, status check." It was her responsibility during the flight to verify the onboard sensory

---

[29] Soyuz-TMA – Transport Modified Anthropometric*

(*) Anthropometric is the term for NASA specific human related traits and measures.

systems. Sensors, gauges, and readouts were taking up all conceivable cabin space. The instruments, though somewhat antiquated on Soyuz, the primary space capsule used as orbital craft after the termination of the space shuttle, were the external eyes into computers, instruments, and engines.

Liz was not the only crew member to check, monitor, and verify the capsule conditions. There were two other crew members onboard with similar responsibilities. Astronauts and cosmonauts alike were taught identical tasks at the space training centers. Training was so rigorous that any one crew member could take on any one of the tasks. It was the reason training took months and years to complete. Today, aside from the Russian flight commander, the other member was Mikhail Toporov. Just by personal contact with other crew members over the past years, Liz found that it did not matter what country one originated from; all members seemed to have similar traits. Although coming from various cultures, characters, spirits, and attitudes were generally in harmony. They were important traits for a space crew to function as an effective team. Space was a hostile environment. Unlike on Earth, one could not just walk away from a job. Here, one was set for the duration of the mission.

What struck Liz as odd halfway through the training at the Cosmodrome was an unexpected Russian crew change. The excuse given to her was, "Unsatisfactory performance." Apparently, both performances had not been up to par for the expected mission requirements. It had happened on a couple occasions before, but usually only during the initial stages of training. Replacing the crew late in the session was not a wise move, she had voiced to Foster. "Decision's not up to the American command," she was told. What troubled her most at times were inappropriate behaviors from the Russian replacement crew. They were not the likeminded cosmonauts she had come to appreciate. Kubalev and Toporov seemed somewhat disinterested in the general space exploration plan. They appeared more like conditioned fighters. Gruff, calloused, and short-fused in temper, they did not seem to care much for her or crew spirit. When she mentioned the upset, Foster shrugged it off. "Times are changing."

Aside from her concerns, her first space flight was an exhilarating experience. Between periodic mission checks, she enjoyed the little private times gazing out the porthole window. Earth, in its entire splendor, came into view. At the moment, Earth appeared slightly hazy. It was the effect of the layer of atmosphere shielding the globe. On the distant ground, she identified continents and nations, either from coastlines, geographic landmarks, or outlines of the continents. With the bare eye, no specific object was clearly visible. It did not matter. The color contrast between snowcapped mountains and deep brown earth was enough to simulate the pleasure senses.

By now, with the cabin pressurized, the space travelers had removed the bulky helmets, gloves, and boots and could, though limited on space, float freely within the sphere of the capsule. Between sighting Earth and getting glimpses of clusters of planetary systems in deep space, Liz made time to observe each crew member while at work. It would be important to her for knowing what to expect in personal reactions and emergency behaviors in case of an unexpected crisis. It was during emergencies when individual abilities became important. For now, she was content. Docking was still a day away. It was her time to sleep.

Liz did not know how long she slept. A persistent sound pressed onto her restful mind. "Wake…wake…wakeup…thirty minutes to docking." She was awake. Her eyes widened with astonishment at the closeness of the space station. Approximately a quarter-mile distant, the ISS, with solar panels unfolded in their entire glory, trusses holding together infrastructure, modules interconnected to the framework, appeared enormous. Aside from her breathing and the computer-generated calls of distance, "One hundred feet…fifty feet…twenty…ten…five, four, three, two, one, docking," dead silence prevailed, but not for long. It ended with a metallic clang.

As soon as the craft had merged with Pirs and Poisk, the Russian airlock module segments opened, and familiar sounds became audible. Each of the modules had two identical hatches. An outward opening hatch and an inward opening hatch providing a sealed and insolated path into the space station. Although narrow for the spacesuit clad crew, transfer went without problems. Pirs was designed to handle the Russian Orlan suits, providing contingency entry for the slightly bulkier American suits. The outermost docking ports on both airlocks allowed docking of Soyuz and Progress spacecraft, as well as transfer of supplies. A face suddenly showed up at the portal entrance. A broad grin was set on the face as the owner extended one hand to bid her welcome. "Kendrick…Kendrick Walsh." It was the American ISS commander. "You call me Kenny." Liz took an immediate liking to him.

More greetings were exchanged between the new arrivals and onboard crew. For the moment, cheers and handshakes took precedence over pressing tasks. The newly arrived were greeted with a hearty welcome. For the onboard crew, the long-awaited visitors brought a happy occasion. It meant word from home. It meant local and global news. And, more importantly, it replenished packaged goods with fresh fruits and vegetables vital for restoring deteriorating health in weightlessness.

Liz had arrived. The past couple of days had conditioned her body for weightless living. She was ready for space. She was ready for whatever exploits space and the ISS would hurl at her. Just before entering the module, she shot one last glance back at Earth. It was doused in another spectacular sunrise on the eastern horizon.

RIGA POLAR REGION

"Get your gear together." The mission chief squinted beneath his fashionable Eddy Bauer shades as he gave orders to the expeditionary forces based at this isolated polar region. "We are moving out." They had been assigned here three months ago under the pretense of leading an exploratory mission to the North Pole. Officially, their purpose was to study glacier melts and Nordic current flows due to global warming. "Holiday's over."

Amin Madani, mission chief and action officer, formerly Islamabad, Pakistan, had been handpicked by Yusuf for the mission. The team, mostly comprised of seasoned mercenaries recruited from camps in Morocco and Egypt, boasted a colorful past acquired during numerous conflicts following the dissolution of the Soviet Union.

Briskly moving within the midst of this endless expanse of a brilliant bluish-tainted ice sheet, shouting out orders, Madani felt exhilarated. Today, it all came together. Years of preparations finally had their payoff. Today was Day One. It was the beginning for the new world order for Jihad. He was not exceptionally thrilled at the prospect of living in a Muslim dominated world. "But, what the hell," he consoled himself, "one faith's like the next. All strive for world dominance." He had no part of it. It was their struggle, their cause. He had his. There would always be a place for him in one of the many desert outposts. He grew up surrounded by deserts. He was used to the heat and isolation. He could not wait to get out of this dreaded cold. With eyes burning from snow blindness, fingers and toes almost frozen, he complained, "Hell, can't take a piss without freezing my dick off."

So far, they had been lucky. There had been no inspections from the World Science Foundation or the U.N. to conduct periodic checks on the progress of their funded research efforts. Only once had a party, operated by the Finns from a nearby camp, paid them a visit, but the party was mostly interested in their Vodka supplies. After a night of heavy drinking and restocking their depleted Russian vodka, they had returned to their base the following morning with a hearty invitation to repay the favor.

The true plan, if discovered, would have caused immediate suspicion because of the equipment in use, consisting mostly of assault weapons type AK-47, RPG launchers, dozens of firearms, combatant wear, military type communication equipment, and grappling gear with hundreds of cases of assorted ammo. It was this equipment, hastily loaded on board at the ready for takeoff Black Hawk assault-type helicopters. The crafts had been maintained and prepared mission ready for weeks. It had been the base's principle activity to keep the craft flight ready for this day.

It had not been easy for the Jihad organizers to acquire such sophisticated craft. Only issued to the American military because of the innovative technology designs built into the craft, purchase was tightly controlled by the international trade commission. They all understood that. But, if you had a mission that required certain assets, "You must have it, no matter the cost."

Initially, the Russian rotorcraft was considered because it was readily accessible on the internationally organized black markets. They had the armament necessary for the mission but, when it came to range and speed, they were inadequate. The ground they had to cover was in excess of a thousand miles; the lacking Russia craft's capability was only hundreds. Speed was likewise disproportionate. Luckily, there was always someone willing to help out once you showed them the cash. Everything was available at a price.

Eventually, assembled from replacement parts, several craft were purchased, diverted directly from warehouses and delivery plants. "What's one more Black Hawk coming off the assembly line? Gov won't miss it," was the arms seller's attitude. Aside from specific mission requirements, the Black Hawk, UH-60 type, would give the assault team an added advantage. It would provide a cloaked cover for their initial approach to the final destination. Foreign military assets would have been suspicious right from the onset.

The day had finally arrived to abandon the ice-based camp that had been temporary home for the Alpha attack squadron. Aside from the pilots and backups, the squadron consisted of two dozen toughs, experienced and fanatical mercenary fighters conditioned by the many Jihad operations. It was a breed of fighters specifically selected to pave the path for the new world of Islam. The vision was supplemented by the promise to become future political leaders for the cause.

"That's it," Madani informed the lead pilot. "Take her up." The choppers had been warming up while the final gear was loaded and stored. Three craft were rapidly ascending off the permanent ice sheet, headed across the North Pole in the direction of Alaska. Once airborne, trying to locate the pole at this latitude was useless. The compass was aimlessly spinning around. To compensate, locking in on the magnetic pole directly below, navigation was linked to GPS. Madani briefly reflected on early explorers trying to get a fix on direction without the sun or moon to navigate. "Wonder how they managed?"

Holding up his middle finger, indicative to testing wind direction, was the comical response from one wise guy seated comfortably in back. Waving someone off was a newly acquired, somewhat lewd American gesture to the otherwise secular team of Jihad fighters, dressed in black combat gear. But in his case, it invoked prolific grunts and laughter.

ISS

There was a persistent tugging on her right elbow. Liz opened her eyes only to stare at the grinning face hovering two feet directly above. She had to blink a few times to clear her mind to the presence of space. The face belonged to Kendrick Walsh, her commander and American Crew Chief, demanding her attention. "Morning, sleepy head," he said with a smile. "Time to wake up," he charmed. "Breakfast's waiting." He then floated from her view.

Liz could not remember how long it had been since she had slept this sound. Enjoying the bliss of weightlessness, she remained there a few more seconds, motionless, then undid the straps holding her body in place. She wanted to linger some more, but the call of nature was pressing on her bladder. "Oh well," she muttered. "Time to tidy up." Tidy up was something as simple as folding the restraining bands onto the wall mount. One motion propelled her body in the direction of the space toilet. Module space was as crammed as she had experienced at the training sites. There was no wasted space at the station, no matter what the task.

The garment she had slipped on for sleep was light and comfortable. The space station was kept at a comfortable ambient temperature. The space toilet was practical and efficient in design. Floating in space, she undid her panties then positioned her torso onto the toilet seat. A water spray cleaned the body and facility for the next user.

The remainder of the cleaning process involved wiping her face with a chemically treated cleansing pad, followed by a couple of minutes brushing and massaging teeth and gums. "That's it," she muttered on the way out to face the world. Simple, hygienic, and quick, she recollected, "Just like home." Pulling and shoving along to reach the mission capsule, Liz approached the full crew, neatly bunched together, awaiting the morning brief. Serving as the mission and eating facility, six of the crew were seated on the specially designed table while the rest hovered in space nearby. Crews from the various space laboratories and foreign modules came together for the daily mission briefs. Food could be served at the table or at any time at individually assigned tasking space.

Being the only woman on board for the present mission, all eyes were directed at her for the moment. The full attention focused on her made her feel slightly uncomfortable. It was only a fleeting emotion before she received a hearty welcome from all. Embraced by grinning faces, most hands reached out to accept her into space. The solidarity in camaraderie gave her a warm feeling. Compared to American customs, the Russian crew acted somewhat reserved. The Russia she had experienced during training was generally forthcoming. Here, it could be the rigorous conditioning for space discipline.

"Lisa Bauer," Kenny introduced her.

"Call me Liz," she said with a smile.

Ground control had patiently awaited her appearance on the space monitor. "Your task," the Baikonur director's voice echoed through space, "is getting familiar with the modules and lab facilities." He went on to outline upcoming tasks scheduled over the next several days. "Schedule's very tight for this mission." He ended today's brief. "Enjoy the ride."

Liz was famished. She was ready for breakfast. It would have been great to sit at a restaurant getting served eggs, sausage, and hash browns as she did when dining out, but here she had to be content with processed food from a plastic squeeze bag. Everything was either liquid or paste. Heated to the appropriate temperature, the packages were tasty but without the customary consistency of real food. Not letting on her immediate discontentment, she gave the crew a "thumbs up," nevertheless. There was no chewing required. Between squeezing out another blob of semi-liquid and swallowing texture in between casual pleasantries, eating time was over in ten minutes. The crew quickly dispersed to their respective quarters and duty stations. She was on her own. "Get me if you need me," Kenny offered just before disappearing into one of the service modules.

On her schedule for today was indoctrination, getting familiar with her surroundings, and downloading upcoming activities on her iPod. Using her index finger, she pulled up individual parameter data on the American and foreign crews. Liz wanted to get specific personal information, especially on the Russian crew, to know exactly what she was dealing with. "ISS Crew[30]—Current and up to date status," the screen displayed.

Data, on most of the past and current space travelers, was usually extensive. For some reason, current parameters for the Russian crew were pretty sparse. Other than listing Kazakhstan as their base of operation, much of the data for personal history and background was missing. It troubled her. An immediate alarm flag went up, but she kept quiet for the time being. She had to get word to Alex and Tracy. But how, since all communication to Earth was monitored and relayed by Russian ground control stations? No information passed without getting filtered by their intelligence. Unfortunately, American Intel was ineffective, but word would eventually reach Foster via the Castle's monitoring system Alex had implemented. He promised to monitor her activities on ISS frequencies.

Liz, although treating everybody on the ISS with professional courtesy, kept personal contact with the Russian crew to a minimum. Her eyes were alert with her senses guarded. "Best I can do," she muttered, "for now."

---

[30] ISS Crew:
Andrei Kubalev – Cosmonaut, Commander, International Space Station, Soyuz Team, Moscow, Russia
Dieter Fuchs – Astronaut, Crew, International Space Station, European Union, Munich, Germany
Hiroshi Nagata – Astronaut, Crew, International Space Station, Asian Team, Nakashima, Japan
Kendrick (Kenny) Walsh – Astronaut, Commander, International Space Station, Houston, TX, America
Lisa (Liz) Bauer – Astronaut, Crew, International Space Station, American Team, Western Sector
Mikhail Toporov – Cosmonaut, Crew, International Space Station, Soyuz Team, Kazakhstan, Russia
Sergei Budenko – Cosmonaut, Crew, International Space Station, Soyuz Team, Kazakhstan, Russia
Yuri Chenkov – Cosmonaut, Crew, International Space Station, Soyuz Team, Kazakhstan, Russia

ATTACK TEAM ALPHA

The choppers were skimming across the jagged and desolate Brooks Range dissecting the Alaskan plains. In tight formation, they were rapidly homing in on the target. Leaving the Arctic Circle behind, they were headed straight towards Fairbanks. At this speed, it would take another forty minutes to reach their destination. Checking the map against the terrain a thousand feet below, Amin Madani could make out white-tipped Mount McKinley panning into view in the distance. The craft went full-out speed. Even with twin external mounted tanks along the fuselage, fuel was draining fast. There would be no refueling along their path. It did not matter much. There would be sufficient resources available once they reach their destination. For now, all that mattered was the speed to inflict surprise.

Checking the attack plan one more time, Amin Madani felt quite confident he would successfully pull off today's mission. They had trained for the operation many times over within the confines of a simulated HAARP site constructed in the wastelands of the Saudi desert. Madani took one last team count. He checked the gear of each fighter, hard-faced combatants clad entirely in black seated closely packed against both sides of the fuselage, twenty in total.

Satisfied, he returned to the command seat up front, pulled the spec manual from the pouch, and studied the craft's parameters one more time to assure nothing was missed. The book, provided by the manufacturer, listed the flight parameters for the Black Hawk's[31] payload, armament, and sensory capacities. Gazing ahead, he was searching for familiar landmarks he had marked on the map.

---

[31] General Characteristics
- Type: UH-60 Black Hawk
- Crew: 2 pilots (flight crew)
- Passenger Load: 20 troops
- Cargo Load: 9,000 lb.
- Power plant: 2 each General Electric T700-GE-701C turbo shaft, 1,890 hp each

Performance
- Maximum speed: 193 knots (222 mph)
- Cruise speed: 173 mph
- Combat radius: 320 nm.
- Range: 1,380 mi (1,200 nm.) with ESSS stub wings and external tanks
- Service ceiling: 19,000 ft
- Rate of climb: 700 ft/min

Armament (Guns)
- 2 each .50 in (12.7 mm) GAU-19 Gatling guns
- Equipped with VOLCANO minefield dispersal system

ESSS stub wings equipped with
- 70 mm (2.75 in) Hydra 70 rockets
- AGM-114 Hellfire laser guided missiles
- 30 mm (1.18 in) M230 gun pods

Sensory
- Rugged COTS Embedded Computer and Network Subsystems
- High-Reliability Data Networking Technology, COTS Products and Subsystems
- Day and Night Sight Systems, Barrel Inspection, Marksmen and X-Ray Detection

"Chatinaka River should be coming into view just about now," he muttered. "And there it is." It had taken him months of data mining public, proprietary, and classified computer banks to gather the information he needed for this mission. Being an open source app, Google had not provided much useful data. It only provided global terrain levels three through five. He'd had to dig much deeper into the annals of intelligence archives. Thanks to software geeks on his force, the tech-team had cracked code entries giving him access to the Intel networks. With that, he readily pulled mapping levels one and two from the imaging servers securely housed within agencies' vaults. The maps gave him the views he needed "down to the fence posts." Not that there were any fences along the route; rather, he was looking for pioneering trails and settlement signs. These were few and far in between in this part of the world.

Checking the map once more, he ignored the spot identified as Gakona located further south. Their target today had been tagged Fox One—the real site for the mission.

Conversations were muffled and brief amidst the chopping sound of the turbo-powered attack craft. Fighters wore headgear, comm equipment, infrared, and HUD display. Some were slouched in their seats, dozing. Others, to pass the time, were teasing back and forth. Those were mostly the new recruits. Seasoned combatants did not take time for chitchat. Madani, seated in the navigator's seat directly behind the co-pilot, continued checking route maps. They were close to the target. "Two minutes to touchdown," he alerted the team over the intercom. Twilight had already settled in for the day.

FOX ONE

"Sound the alert," Jack Owens yelled. He had just been informed by the operator about several objects moving close. Apparently, they suddenly appeared from over the North Pole horizon from an undetermined location. Jack rushed to the wall-mounted flat panel monitor to see firsthand. "Black Hawk," he identified the objects. He had seen them before but not for years.

"What's an attack helicopter doing here?" his staff wanted to know.

"Can only mean one thing," he replied. "Trouble."

The objects, three in count, had been tracked since DEW[32] picked them up thirty minutes ago. A quick run on the software trajectory indicated a possible flight path from somewhere in Europe. At first, nobody paid much attention until the flight had changed direction a couple minutes ago, headed directly for their base. Sure, they had the occasional unauthorized flyover by a curious hunting party wanting to catch a first-hand glimpse of the facility. It was understood that local hunting guides had known for some time but speculations were only rumored since hardly any information was available on the place. Light craft intrusions were largely ignored to give an appearance of inactivity. From the air, it looked like an experimental facility abandoned years ago. "Alert Vandenberg," Jack shot back at the operator. It only took seconds for the response.

"Vandenberg," the distant voice said. "State your mission." The operator handed Jack the secure receiver. "Fox One," Jack yelled into the receiver. "Unauthorized bogies closing in fast." Fox One, identified to the public as Gakona, was the classified top secret HAARP base.

"Standby." Vandenberg was taking calls like these almost daily. All deemed emergencies, they usually ended up being false alarms.

Worried and stressed by now, Jack shouted, "Come on, you idiots."

"Do not intercede," Vandenberg ordered. "We'll have Elmendorf take a look…stay locked down." The receiver had already turned silent by the time he was able to ask another question. Most of the crew had gathered in the comm center. Jack sought out his crew chief. "Get me base security."

Granted, Elmendorf was only a few minutes flight, but it would take time to alert and scramble out a couple F-15s. By then, a lot could happen. He checked the terrain monitors. They did not reveal anything other than the customary shadows from the antenna farm nearby. One had to know the antennas were there, otherwise they could have easily been mistaken for one of the pine forests customary around here. Aside from the colorful aurora suspended directly overhead doing their eerie dance, all seemed quiet at the moment. "Gotterdammerung," Jack muttered. The display reminded him of an

---

[32] The Distant Early Warning Line, also known as the DEW Line or Early Warning Line, was a system of radar stations in the far northern Arctic region of Canada, with additional stations along the North Coast and Aleutian Islands of Alaska, in addition to the Faroe Islands, Greenland, and Iceland. It was set up to detect incoming Soviet bombers during the Cold War, and provide early warning of any sea-and-land invasion. First line defense, it was part of the Mid-Canada and Pinetree northern U.S. defense parameters.

ancient gothic play he had seen in his younger years. For now, all he could do was wait for air defense to make contact.

The flight signatures on the monitors showed the approaching party already closing in on the facility. He could not contain himself any longer and yelled at the operator, "Get me Elmendorf." He ripped the receiver from the hand of the puzzled operator, screaming at the mouthpiece, "Elmendorf, come in, come in, you fuck heads." But no amount of shouting raised a response. All he got was the static generated from the aurora above. Scanning through the range of local frequencies trying to connect with the choppers, "Identify…identify…identify," did not return any response. Then, all of a sudden, the monitors turned dark. Almost in panic, he slammed the receiver back on the set and switched to intercom. "Attention all," he yelled at the crew. "Security breach."

What would be next was up to Elmendorf. There was still no response from Vandenberg. There were no sounds from fighters overhead. He had no fighting force. All he had were a bunch of scientists, engineers, and technicians on the grounds. He came to the only conclusion that made sense. "We're fucked."

ELMENDORF AFB

It was already getting dark over Alaska when the alert sounded from Vandenberg. Thomas "Tommy" Johnson, 3rd Wing commander, 11th AF ordered his crew chief, "Sound the alarm." The crew chief, Donald "Donny" Allen, 477th Fighter Group, studied the mission order just received and passed it on to the flight crews on standby. "Scramble two F-15Es over to Fox One."

"Roger that," was the response. Despite being an alert status calling for immediate attention, calls of this nature were routine. Being a remote place from the American mainstream, not much ever happened up here other than periodic Russian flyover into Alaskan air space. They usually came up from the Kamchatka peninsula for a quick intrusion into the outer Aleutians banks. On the lookout for quick action, Russian pilots were much like U.S. fighters, always pushing the envelope. By the time the incident was reported it had already passed. It was done all the time, not just between the superpowers, but also minor nations sporting an air force. It was what kept the fighting spirit alive.

Elmendorf Air Force Base was typical when it came to remoteness. It was not the only place. There were others stationed around the northern perimeters in Europe, Russia, and China. Combatants assigned here did the usual four-year tour, pushing up the ranks. "Gotta pay your dues," was the general consensus. For most soldiers, it was a stopover on their way to a more meaningful career in a more joyous assignment like Hawaii, Florida, or California, where there were people, entertainment, sun, and fun with weather always pleasant. Regardless of the assignment, the place was here to stay. It protected the nation from unpredictable, but worthy, adversaries in the power play of superpowers.

The call just received deviated from the ordinary mission in as much as the alert was sounded from the northeastern sector of the peninsula, in contrast to most alerts, which were generated from the west. Donny Allen took this mission command seriously. He gave it his full attention as he watched the F-15E wing scramble into the air. Seconds later, the afterburners kicked in, leaving black vortex streamers in their wake as the flight rapidly gained altitude. "Wonder what's up," he speculated. Although there was hardly any information available on Fox One, rumors had it that the site was the nation's most important facility in this part of the world. Because of strict security requirements at the site, nobody from his base had ever been there. His guess was as good as any for what activities took place there.

Ten minutes later the wing pilot reported via HF radio, "Fox One looks quiet." Seconds later, he added, "Choppers type Black Hawk on ground. Please advise."

"Hold your position," the order flashed out. Donny Allen switched to secure comm to make the next call. "NORAD," the distant voice acknowledged, "State your mission."

"Fox One," he advised Ops. "No contact. Repeat…no contact from Fox One."

His fighters did their job for surveillance. It was as far as he could go. He had handed the responsibility off to NORAD surveillance. The officer on duty there repeatedly tried to establish contact with Fox One. There was no answer. Frustrated at not getting any response, he switched to VHF, then UHF, with the same negative results. "Idiots must be asleep out there." Not much he could do from here other than watch the monitors for activity at the 65th parallel. "Wait 'til daybreak," he advised Elmendorf. "Then send in ground troops."

"Roger…Out." The F-15 wing made one last flyover before heading back to base.

ISS

Liz was startled when she felt the tapping on her shoulder. She had been engrossed with the flight computer, reading recent mission plans. Kenny Walsh was facing her, "Whatcha doin'?" She caught his eyes caressing her body, then openly challenged his gaze. She had noticed, on several occasions, the peek he had shot her when he thought she was not looking. Being a woman, she noticed everything going on within her space. Though a mom for years with a marriage ending in divorce, she did not forget that she was also a woman. Unlike others in her position, she did not dwell on the personal misfortune of family life turned estranged. Aside from personal issues with her kids, now in their early teens, her primary focus never shifted from her career. It did not mean complete isolation from leisure and pleasures. She just had not made an effort to return to the dating circles. Especially not with the past couple of years entirely devoted to astronaut training.

Isolated from the rest of the world, confined to tight quarters—crammed would be a more suitable term—Liz, was aware of the hormonal motivated energy emanating in space. Kenny Walsh was no different. During the training, although she had quietly wondered at times, the question about romantic interludes in space never came up. But now, she could feel his presence more than she would let herself admit. Not sharing her personal thoughts, she returned his gaze with a hinting smile. *Wonder what it would feel like. Come to think of it, nobody ever mentioned the possibility. Maybe it'd be a first.* The topic of sex in space must be taboo. It was not mentioned in textbooks, or the training manuals…and especially not carried in the news media.

Setting romance aside, she turned professional once more and said, "Got a question."

With a face turned curious, he replied, "Shoot."

"What do you know about the Russian crew?"

"Why do you ask?"

"Not the friendliest bunch," she commented. "Are they?"

"Well, it's not like we're on a social outing."

"Yeah, but," she protested, "our lives are dependent on each other. How can that happen when you don't know anything about each other?"

"Valid concern," he agreed. He then moved on to his assigned task. "I'll check with Foster."

Liz knew from past associations working at the space labs that Walsh had close rapport with the general. For now, she let the topic slide, but kept up a personal guard. Watching Walsh float off to another service module, she turned back to her task. Like most days, Liz was tasked to check on vital space equipment for possible alert conditions registered on computer printouts. As outdated as some of the modules were, they were numerous. Her mind was quickly absorbed by work demands once more. For the time being, her work was all inside the capsule. As excited as she was at the opportunity to float in space, spacewalks would have to wait. There had been no extra-vehicular assignments since she'd arrived here.

ATTACK TEAM ALPHA

It would be the last time Amin Madani laid out the action plan. From here on, the mission proceeded with utmost precision. It would follow the plan as it had been rehearsed over and over at the mockup back at base camp. "One minute to touchdown," his voice sounded through the closed-circuit radio. It was a final alert. The attack team jumped into action. The plan called for a night jump, taking the base by surprise. But, on second thought, Madani made a last call for change. The base, he assumed, probably had picked them up on radar by now. It would eliminate the surprise factor. Besides, it was still twilight over the Arctic Circle. Any approaching craft could be spotted. He took the position by the exit, ready to jump as soon as the chopper touched ground. One arm securely wrapped around an exit strap, he leant out to check the terrain below. The chopper was rapidly descending for touchdown, and the terrain panned into focus. "Allah," he sounded off when he realized the danger he had just avoided, "hold your position." Then "Good thing we didn't jump."

He had just detected the heavily camouflaged fields of thousands of spikes protruding menacingly from the ground. From a jump altitude, they would have entirely missed the transmitter arrays and most likely impaled many of his jumpers. Leaning out further to get a clearer view, he suddenly felt it. A sudden tear appeared on his right jacket sleeve. Then he heard the rapid-fire sound from below. Quickly, he ducked back into the safety of the fuselage. An instant later they all saw the streams of tracer bullets aimed in their direction from ground fire. They could hear the familiar pinging sound from metal hitting metal.

The pilot had spotted the ground fire. With a flip of the switch he armed the onboard weapons, then yelled in back, "Fire in the hole." The crew knew what came next and braced. An instant later the craft recoiled from the release of twin hellfire missiles. They watched as the AGM-114 laser-guided tubes sought out their targets, streaming to the ground.

"Hit," the copilot confirmed. Nobody expected otherwise. The AGM was one of the most accurate weapons in the attack team's arsenal. It was an incredible weapon. Aim and click was all you had to do; the laser guide did the rest.

An instant later, the guard tower below illuminated from the intense heat of the explosions. Large chunks of concrete and debris exploded upward in their direction. There were more impacts on the fuselage. "Damage report," the pilot ordered. He had taken the craft into a tight turn to avoid more damages. The crew quickly inspected the inside for holes and smoke. "All clear."

As soon as the craft reached twenty feet above ground, Madani ordered, "Ready to jump. Go...go...go!" It was a trained practice to hover while combatants slid down ropes. It served two purposes. One, it provided a speedy exit, and two, the craft was in a position to retreat the instant the last member made ground contact. Years of combat had proven the tactic successfully.

Madani, in the lead, was giving orders. With the guard tower eliminated as a threat it was easy to access the premises. He sought out the elevator shaft, but the heavy steel doors prevented entrance. "Explosives," he yelled. Shaped charges were hastily placed within the entrance frame. Seconds later they were set off. The entrance was clear. Half of the building entrance had been blown off. He sidestepped to make room for the combatants. "We're in," he shouted just in time. Seconds later, the sound of rapidly approaching F-15E sentries swooped in overhead. Their heat signatures would have detected ground activity. By now, ground fire had stopped.

Eighty feet below, in the safety of the command center, Jack felt trapped. He fully realized the vulnerability he and his people were in. It suddenly felt suffocating. He had to do something.

That something was taken from him in the form of an explosion from the elevator shaft. It had been initiated by the assault team now on his doorstep. The entire framework gave way, with most of the force discharged into the hallway. Debris torn from walls and ceilings flew at him with full force. He had enough insight to dodge under his office desk to avoid the fragments. Others were not so lucky. Many of his staff were caught on their feet and swept through the air from the explosive force. It would be too late for them. Death had come on suddenly.

Alarms went off everywhere. The pulsing emergency lighting created an eerie play of shadows. The wounded were crying for help. Everything was covered in gray dust. Survivors unscathed were stunned into silence. With eardrums fractured, most were too shocked to react. It was bedlam.

Jack pulled himself up by the tabletop, checking for damages. He patted down his body, looking for injuries. He could feel wetness alongside his temples. With the back of his hand, he wiped his forehead. It revealed only minor blood stains. Immensely relieved, he tried to make sense of the situation. "Thank God I'm alive," he muttered then took a quick assessment of the center. The sight brought on a sickening feeling.

In the ensuing turmoil, Jack realized his hearing was impaired. The tremendous shockwave had torn his eardrums. The immediate effect was a terrific ringing, to the point of making him nauseated. He was about to head for the hall to check on injuries of his staff when he was intercepted by another menace. Shaded in darkness, it came rushing toward him with insane shouts. His eyes fixated on the intruders, he quickly backed into an office space, but was stopped short by a dozen assault rifles launching at him. Dumfounded, he froze. The next second he buckled over after getting hit in the gut by blows from gunstocks. "Shadow people," he uttered just before blacking out.

DESERT BASE ALPHA

Hasan Hammad was presently touring the underground desert base. Immensely satisfied, with a grin on his face, he commended Yusuf. "You did well." Where Hammad had been organizing the offensive from Palm Jumeirah, his commander had handled the physical aspects for the bases. There were multiple. Where there were many mines throughout the regions of Egypt and the Sudanese peninsula, they were mostly owned by the Kingdom of Saud. After acquiring leases from the king, mining was in full swing. What he did not disclose was his real reasons acquiring the mines. When word spread, it attracted a great work force. Hammad made sure that workers were compensated for their laboring efforts. It set the stage for the future society.

He felt the subtle vibration in his pocket. It was the cell phone getting his attention. The caller ID identified a number. It was Madani. The call came from Attack Team Alpha. A text message followed. "Mission success."

"Casualties?" Hammad flashed back.

"Minor," was the response. "What are your orders?"

"Hold your position," he texted back. "Await further instructions."

Hammad prepared to depart. Phase One of the current mission had been accomplished with the assault initiative on HAARP. It was time to implement the next phase. For that, he wanted to return to his command post, the sanctuary of Palm Island. "Let's get out of here."

Yusuf readily agreed. He had spent too much time underground for his liking. His heart was not in the Arabian deserts. It was at the place of his childhood, New York.

The base operator was poised in front of the mission monitor. "Window—twenty-three minutes," he cautioned. Ever since the construction, satellite tracking had become mandatory. Yes, it was a nuisance. But keeping base activity undetected was of utmost importance for the success of the mission. Construction activity, as well as flights in and out, had to be suspended during over-flights. At this time, Hammad had no clear picture for how much the Western Sector was capable of, technology wise. All he knew was that most of the remaining military forces had been consolidated and were operating from the Pacific coastal regions of the North American continent.

His personal jet was primed and waiting at the end of the underground runway. Jet exhaust gases were funneled into a ducting system to filter out carbon monoxide expelled above ground. It assured clean airflow below ground and prevented asphyxiation.

Once boarded and seated in the cockpit, he pushed the twin controls forward. "Cleared for takeoff." It was ground control assuring a clear and undetected passage. The sleek 550 Gulf Stream rapidly gained speed. Seconds later the wheels left the covered tunnel entrance, rising steeply upward in an easterly direction. When it reached cruising altitude, the craft easily blended in with commercial traffic headed toward the UAE. Minutes later, the craft's transponder was picked up by Dubai air traffic control. Two hours later it touched down, minutes away from Palm Jumeirah.

PALM JUMEIRAH

Hammad had grown fond of the place. Although frustrated at times with his lieutenant, he had grown fond of Yusuf. He had turned out to be a true companion and worthy fighter. Not only did he expedite every need for the cause, he was also the best personal attendant Hammad could wish for. It was Yusuf that kept challenges alive. Hasan Hammad, in contrast, was a serious contender. Time with him was always prized. There were never enough hours in the day to accomplish the goals he set out. They had been working hard to get to this point. Hammad had to move quickly. The window of opportunity was open for only a brief period.

Preparations were setup for the next segment. His forces had been conditioned for years to see this day. Now, they were awaiting final orders. The time had arrived to bestow vengeance on the world. It was time for the final battle. It was a battle fought for the ultimate reward—a globe with all of its wealth, its resources, and its inhabitants. He had a clear vision for the theater of operation. It was to be a fight for world dominance. It was Islam against the Western society. Not for Islam the religion, but for Islam the new lifestyle.

Last night, they had been celebrating with the finest products grown in the region. Arabian coffee, French pastry, and dates were readily offered by the servants. Even alcohol made its round. Many had acquired the taste for it when abroad. It was Napoleon, aged twenty-five years, the finest. As always, Hammad, politely, but firmly, declined the brandy passed among his staff. To keep a clear head at all times, he did not take to alcohol as imbibed in western society or hashish as culturally accepted in Arabian society. Tonight, would mark a new beginning. Where conversations were lively among the guests, Hammad had his thought set on the new day, the battlefront. It would have to wait one more day. Reluctantly, he rejoined the celebration, wishing the night to end. Where others received party pleasures from food and drink, he in turn, received his from seeing his Plan in action.

It was early the next day. The air was still cool from the slight breeze sweeping in from the ocean. Hammad was ready to set his Plan in motion. "From here on," sharing his thoughts with Yusuf, "our lives will be spent on the move. Nothing is strategic anymore." Yusuf understood only too well. In keeping one step ahead of the adversary, operations had to be fluid. Nothing was permanent anymore. Base phones, websites, domains, registered links, calls—all could be easily traced. The cell phone invention was the answer. It was a most vital link for success. Without it the operation would be severely constrained. "Get me HAARP on the line," he ordered his lieutenant.

Though distant, the combatant's voice resonated clearly over the ether. "Madani."

"Status?" Hammad purposely kept the conversation short. There was always a chance of being discovered by foreign intelligence. For the plan to be successful he needed to avoid possible detection. Much of it was hinged on surprise.

"Fox One in control," Amin Madani reported. "Only slight resistance. No casualties. What's your order?"

"Expect hostile initiative from North American forces," Hammad cautioned. "Hold your position."

"Will do," was the response. Madani and his attack force had been busy orienting the HAARP weapon. There had been virtually no resistance from scientists and engineers. They were not prepared for battle with a nonexistent defense force at this underground base. HAARP may have been the ultimate weapon of mass destruction, but, at this stage, it was still in trial phase. Hammad shared the success with his staff. "Today's assault will shake them out of their passive mode." Brushing aside past thoughts, Hammad could only imagine the disorder he had caused to the complacency of the North American defense forces. It would only be the first of many such surprises he had in store for Islam's most detested opposition masses. From here on, it would be onslaught after onslaught, in rapid succession. He had the strategy cut out for his forces. Unlike his last initiative, today, now, logistics and support were in place wherever needed.

NORAD

"Any word from Gakona?" Ben Jackson demanded. The last information he had was from the F-15 flyover the previous night and that wasn't much. Edwards had recommended waiting for daylight to send in a ground team.

Furious by now, the general was pacing the halls. *Here I am, supposed to know what's going on in the nation and what do I know?* Completely frustrated, he answered his own question, "Diddlysquat." With a mug tightly gripped in one hand, he headed for the coffee counter, then changed direction midstream. Instead, he went for the bathroom. The sudden urge was greater than the desire to refill the cup. Besides, Doc had said, "Only two cups a day or you'll wind up in the ICU."

"Pisser," he silently cussed. *Here I am, finally making enough to afford the finer things in life and what does it get me? Can't eat...can't drink...and can't have sex.* "Forget it." *Nothing works anymore. The heart, the liver, the lungs, the plumbing...all shot.* He had been looking forward to retirement for years so he could live in leisure. The plan he and the wife had had was to travel the world. But now, with the nation in shambles and the world hating all Americans for letting the dollar collapse, he wasn't so sure anymore. It was difficult getting around. With gout in both ankles acting up, arthritic knees, an aching back, oversized prostrate and shortage of breath, who could enjoy going places. He was lucky enough to make it back and forth to the clinic for another load of medications. It wasn't quite that bad yet but, given another few years 'til retirement, it wasn't a rosy future Jackson was facing.

Back at his desk, he suddenly had an idea. "What was the guy's name again a couple years ago? Civilian, wasn't he?" he muttered. "Sure knew what he was doing. Baker, wasn't that his name?" *Mind's goin' too,* he scolded himself. *Down the drain.* "If anybody knows what's going on it'd be him." Although he disliked civilians for the most part, he liked the guy. "Can't trust them contractors, always wanting to sell things." *Nothing was ever delivered as promised.* He rummaged around the desk drawers looking for his address book. "Baker...Baker," he muttered. His eyes scanned across the pages, then he recognized the name. "Bauer...that's it!" He promptly established the call.

"Bauer," the other end responded seconds later on the HF receiver.

"Listen here," the general stated. "Ben Jackson up at NORAD."

"Ah yes." Alex immediately recognized the voice. Although it had been a while he still remembered the general. Egotistical, pigheaded, arrogant—*that's him.*

"Would it be possible to meet?"

"Now?"

"Yes, now."

"I'll be there. Give me an hour." *Click.*

It was a ten-minute hop on the chopper to the Mountain. Where he'd love to take the drive in the Beemer, roads were not safe for a lonely driver. Too many marauding bands were roaming across the lands. Colorado was no exemption. Reports came in daily about bands terrorizing homes, ranchers, and even fortified settlements. Patriots may be working out staked territory, but from the way things were going out east, borders had not yet been populated with support forces and logistics. Wars, although on a small scale, were fought. Alex checked the ground for landmarks. Since Tracy's departure out west, Brian, his faithful companion, was piloting the craft. The Black Forest, with its dark green colors, passed below the chopper. To the west, he could make out what used to be the pride and joy of the Air Force, the Academy. He could see human activity in the distance, but wasn't sure what group or faction had taken possession of the place. He did not care as long as they kept away from his abode. Although the nation was not entrenched in a world war, it had succumbed to a civil war that could last years. Alex knew from history that someday it would all be over. But until that time, they all had to make the best of the situation. "What do you think?" he asked Brian.

"What?"

"The war."

"Could drag on like it did with Vietnam and Korea. You know," he said, "we still have no peace treaty with North Korea."

"Doesn't really matter now. Does it?"

"Guess not." From their point of interests, Asia was too much removed to impact life here.

Ahead, the Mountain was coming up fast. He could make out the landing pod near the tunnel entrance. "Time to take it down," Brian muttered. The entrance they could see was heavily fortified. Being one of few places still controlled by the military, an armored marine detachment guarded the place.

As soon as the chopper touched ground, Alex hopped off the pods headed for the entrance. Brian followed after shutting down the engine. One sentry met up with Alex. "You Bauer?"

It appeared they had been notified of his arrival. A personnel carrier was waiting to take them inside. The general was anxiously waiting at the command center. They shook hands. "Glad you could make it." As he had in the past, Jackson completely ignored Brian.

"No problem."

"So, Alex," the brigadier began, "what have you been doing lately."

"Contracting with people out west," Alex explained. "Designing EMP protection to harden systems. Manufacturing's picking up in Silicon Valley. I give 'em the specs then inspect the finished products for you guys."

"Glad somebody's watching out for the nation," Jackson acknowledged with a sigh. "But that's not what I called you.

"Suppose not."

"I asked you here for a specific reason." He sounded somewhat mysterious. His body gestures reflected his state of mind.

"Figured that."

"What's goin' on," he let go the first salvo of complaints, "is that I get nothing out here. No information, no news, no word on the rest of the nation. It's almost," he took a breather, "as if I don't exist."

"Told you years ago," Alex reminded him. "NORAD's obsolete. With defense forces shifted to the Pacific theater, there's no need for the place regardless of fortification."

"What can I do? I get no support. Only thing that saves me is local ranchers. If it wasn't for them," he complained, "we'd have all starved to death."

Alex knew it was true. Out here, everybody had to fend for themselves. Fortunately, ranchers were sympathetic as long as they could get protection for their livestock and property. Many had taken in preppers and survivalists for personal protection. Otherwise, they would be taken over by the many roaming bands moving in and out of the region. It seemed like the entire nation was on the move. After metropolitan life collapsed, whatever citizens were strong enough to take flight had left the cities. Once stores and supermarkets emptied out, the only regions where the masses could survive were the plains. And that was where they headed. It was only the smart ones prepared for the chaotic situation that made it another season.

Jackson stopped pacing the floor to directly face Alex. "Any ideas?"

Alex gave him a report, as much as he knew from out west. He sketched out the geographical changes. He informed him of technology advances, as limited as they were.

Jackson's ears piqued at the mention of technology. He could not have imagined anything being developed by the flailing nation. *New weapons…new defense system…exotic super weapons?* "You serious?"

"Dead serious."

"Where does all this come from?" he wanted to know. "Are the rest of us asleep?"

"You may not have the need to know dealing outside NORAD defenses," Alex suggested. "In the free world," he explained, "development continues. Foreign nations have taken the lead since our nation collapsed. Not much left outside of Los Alamos and LLL. Take me, for instance," Alex suggested. "I keep up with technology, but also have the connections."

"But you're a foreigner," the general protested.

"So was Van Braun."

He eyed Alex with a sign of distrust. "Don't get it," he said. "Where're our people?"

"It may not be obvious, at times," Alex hinted, "but we are here. We are there," he said with finality.

"Just keep me informed," Jackson was ready to bid the visitors goodbye. "Will you?"

"Tell you what," Alex offered. "I'll tie you into my satellite feeds."

"You got satellite?" he shot back in pure astonishment.

"Don't you?" Alex joked. He knew quite well the mountain top had taken a hit, wiping out much of the antenna farm. He also knew Jackson had no funds or budget to rebuild the aging fortress. He and his staff struggled to survive, just like everybody in this part of the country. The reason they had not perished was because they were getting some protection from nearby Fort Carson, still occupied by remnants of a once mighty infantry force.

"When can I expect it?"

Alex was already sorry he had made the offer. *Here we go again,* he thought, dismayed. *Impatient as always.* "You'll know." He wanted to get away as quickly as possible before the general pried more information from him. He had no intention of sharing more, especially not when it came to secret technology.

"Keep me informed."

"Yeah, yeah." Alex left with Brian striding alongside keeping pace.

ISS

In spite of the heavy work schedule demanding all of her time, Liz could not put her personal thoughts about her brief encounter yesterday with Kenny behind. Every time he floated past her, she became aware of his presence. It was not that she disliked the thought of intimacy, though it had been ages since her last amorous encounter, but it distracted her. But over time, she was more and more drawn to him. Self-assured, tall and good looking, the astronaut he was, she could not help but take notice when he was nearby. Their interaction, it appeared, became more frequent.

It became evident in the personal interest he took in her activities regardless of his responsibilities with other tasks. He seemed interested in everything she did. In response, she would accommodate his queries with a smile, friendly nod, or warm touch to his shoulder. Sometimes she would even brush up against his chest. She began to have intimate notions about the man, but was secretly hoping for him to take the initiative. After all, they were in space. A place reserved for professional conduct at all times.

"Need your advice," she finally broke their silence.

Accompanied by a warm smile, he immediately replied, "I'm all yours."

Taking note of cosmonauts nearby, discreetly she motioned at the exit. He silently floated after her. Space was crammed within the service modules. Unless someone was on the radio, life was hushed. Personalities, for most part, had been trained to be considerate of each other. Boisterous and unruly behavior was not condoned. Aside from an occasional comment or friendly gesture, floating quietly in space was the norm when on duty. After all, without the daily interaction as lived on earth, nothing much happened in space to talk about as long as there were no emergencies or unforeseen events. Kenny and Liz went unnoticed as they left the capsule. Pulling her body hand over hand along the connecting tubes, she sought out the most private space on the station, the currently unoccupied Destiny, the American space lab. The lab was reserved for American space experiments, held dormant at this time. Most experiments were carried out by the European and Japanese space agencies.

Liz was waiting for Walsh to lock the hatch. Grabbing hold of the command console safety bar to steady her weightless drift, she approached the topic of her concern. "Can I trust you?"

Walsh's face took on a hint of concern. "Of course." The way he responded gave her a comforting feeling. She took a couple of focused seconds to study his face. A full set of hair, light brown, although closely cropped, gave him a look of commanding posture. Due to a fully toned body used to rigorous workouts extended by muscularly developed arms and legs, the preferred prerequisite for an astronaut, it was obvious he was in excellent shape. So far, she liked the traits he displayed. The only thing she was not sure of was his personal attitude, private thoughts, and level of trust. That she needed to explore. The time was now.

"I don't trust the Russian crew," she voiced her concerns. "They're up to something."

"What gives you that idea?" Walsh was slightly taken aback. Concern was clearly reflected in his face.

Liz immediately changed her position. She became guarded. To have him alienated was the last thing she wanted. *What if he...* Her thoughts trailed into a pausing halt before she went on. "I can't find any history on record."

Walsh responded, "You sure?" It appeared it was his mistake for not checking up on each crew member. In the past, it had never been a matter of concern because cosmonauts had long-trusted and established track records.

"I can't be sure," she said, "until I speak with Foster—in private."

"That," he replied, "may not be possible." They both were well aware of the monitoring processes to which the space station was subjected.

"Gotta get a hold of him somehow."

His body had tensed up. It turned from initially social to present concern. "Don't know how we can accomplish it."

She was happy to observe that his response was positive. Her trust-basis for him strengthened. For what she needed to do, he had to be totally on her side. There was no room for compromise. If her intuition was correct, both of their lives could be in danger.

"I'll figure something out," he said finally.

She looked him straight in the eyes. "Glad I can trust you."

Without breaking his gaze, his voice almost to a point of whisper, he took hold of her hands. "Trust," he said, "is not the only thing I feel for you." It was out in the open. He had taken the initiative to break their professional bond. With eyes locked in an emotional embrace, he was waiting for her response.

The next move was up to her. She could either accept or reject his gesture. Whatever she decided would determine their future association. She knew she had to make a decision. Her mind was racing through a spectrum of emotions, from rationality to reality. There were the children. There was her career, the current mission, the confinement of space, the company policies. But there was also the long time spent deprived from passion, romance, and love. All of her pent-up emotions and feelings, suppressed for so many years, suddenly merged into one intense force. The woman in her won out. Closing her eyes, her hands gently reached out for him. Their lips met ever so gently, their hands were probing each other. Then, in a sudden burst, both bodies exploded into passionate embrace.

Liz felt his hands caress her body. First it was her neck. His fingers were touching her skin ever so slightly, then slowly moved on to her breasts, caressing the sides first, then the upper part, the lower part, and gradually her hardened nipples. She liked the touch of his hands. It was a sense she had not felt for more years than she could remember. She did not pull away. She longed for more. Her body arched into a bow. Her senses ached for him. She could feel his hands caressing the insides of her legs. The sensation was overwhelming. It bought her senses to a boiling point. Probing for zippers, she undid his flight suit. Then, tugging at his shirt, in one swift motion, she ripped it from his body. She kissed his shoulders then his chest. Almost subconsciously, her hands moved to his shorts. She pulled them off. Unaware of his actions, her sweater came off. Both lost their hold on each other. It was enough for their bodies to drift apart weightlessly in the capsule.

If only for a second, reality ruled once more. Both realized their present state. It did not matter much. The human instinct had taken over. With bodies heated and emotions blistering, both grasped for each other. Motions taken for granted on earth, in space, without gravity, became a struggle. Floating, pushing off ceiling and walls, their two bodies finally came together again, clinging to each other in an embrace of desperation, merged into one. And there they remained.

Again, it was not easy to move. Her legs clutched around his with arms interlocked as well, she felt the intense senses from his hardness pulsating into her body. It was sheer bliss followed with ecstasy, then rapture she could never have imagined. In the silence of space, they were two pulsating bodies surrounded by equipment, gear, and instruments. A deep moaning escaped her lips, imperceptible at first then, with ever growing intensity, slowly rising to full force. Almost simultaneously, Liz and Kenny's bodies, with senses stressed to the limits, finally exploded within each other. Liz could hear one final scream echo within the isolated chamber. She realized it was hers. Then both of their bodies were drained of energy. The only motion was two lungs gasping for air. Space had turned silent once more.

Overcome with a deep sense of fulfillment, almost to a point of passing out, feeling nothing but total bliss, Liz clung to his body. She wanted it to last forever. She felt his hands caressing her. It slowly relaxed her body. Her lips were moving. She opened her eyes to his. Words were emerging from within. "Thank you," they whispered. Both their bodies relaxed to a state of exhaustion. There they remained, floating through space without a care in the world below.

Still locked in silent embrace, Liz did not know for how long, a deep sound groaned into her ears, distant at first, but rapidly growing into an exploding force. Seconds later with a metallic clang, the compartment door bolted from its hinges. With an ear-piercing crash, it bounced against the framework.

Floating close to the ceiling, Liz and Kenny reacted instantly but it was too late. Partially undressed and disheveled, both stared at the barrels of two semi-automatic weapons aimed at them by two of the Russian space crew. Stone faced, determined to pull the triggers at the slightest resistance, the faces belonged to Mikhail Toporov and Sergei Budenko.

Liz was shaken. "Weapon?" was all she could stammer. Kenny was dumbfounded. It clearly showed on his face. There had never been a weapon authorized on the space platform, ever. It could mean possible obliteration if a bullet were to penetrate the metal shell. Without wearing the protective spacesuits, the crew could perish in an instant, exposed to frigid cold and emptiness of space, if the shield were to be breached. The pressure difference and lack of oxygen would explode body and brain into instant death.

Liz struggled upright to confront the assailants. Bracing her body against the bulkhead, she was ready to defend herself. But the weightlessness prevented her from reacting effectively. Next, she felt a blow explode to the back of her head. It was so violent it sent her sailing across the crammed space. In an instant, *I knew it,* flashed through her mind before blacking out as her head slammed against the steel structure of the service module.

FOX ONE

Jack was slouched on a park bench. He could feel the gentle touch of the sea breeze on his face. He was watching the waves slowly rolling in from the open ocean. He thought he recognized the place but wasn't sure. "Looks like Pismo Beach." It was his favorite spot. He was counting waves. Sure enough, number seven was slowly building up. It was larger than the rest. It broke against the shoreline, drenching his body. He was gasping for air when he realized somebody was splashing water in his face. It made him jolt from the comfort of the dream. In spite of his clinging to the ocean scene, reality set in once more. He must have lost consciousness. He slowly opened his eyes and stared into a sullen foreign face persistently slapping his wet face.

"What," he started to protest, but quickly recognized the shambled environment. His ears were ringing, his head hurt, and breathing was difficult. Watching him gasp for air, Madani suggested, "Collapsed lung. We'll take care of that."

Slowly rising on one elbow, Jack sputtered, "Who are you? What do you want?"

"In good time," was the indifferent response. "First," the foreigner insisted, "we gotta check you out…Need you alert."

"What for?"

Jack was still hazy from the blast. "Later," the commanding words seeped into his brain. "Get your people together. Operations only. Mission room. Now!" The scene at the underground command center was more than Jack could presently comprehend. On unsteady legs, Jack was dragged by two combat clad intruders across the hall. It slowly dawned on him: *shadow people.* Now he remembered.

He was propped against a wall. Somebody strapped an oxygen mask over his face. He felt the pressure pumping against his lungs. To his relief, normal breathing slowly returned. He could think clearly again. Rationality had returned. *What's going on? Who are they? What should I do? What can I do?* His mind was searching for answers, but no solution would formulate. The apparent leader returned and approached Jack. "Amin Madani," the man offered. "This is what I need you to do."

"Who are you guys?" Jack stammered.

"We have taken command of Fox One. You will instruct us on the use of the facility."

Still shaken, Jack scrambled to his feet, protesting, "Hell I will. Can't do that!"

"Can and will," Madani commanded.

Jack was forcefully pushed into a chair. "You can make it easy for your team," the stranger demanded. "Or we can make it tough. Your choice."

"What do you want?"

"Ops charts and firing sequence."

"Can't have it." No sooner had he spoken the words than Madani had pulled a semi from his waist and leveled the weapon at the chief scientist. With a gun barrel pressed against his temple, the poor man's face turned ashen with fear.

"What's it gonna be?" It was an ultimatum.

When Jack wavered, he saw intense fury well up in the leader's eyes. Apparently, the guy was not used to objections. His eyes were filled with rage. Unless Jack was willing to sacrifice his friend's life, he had to submit to the terrorist's demands. "All right…all right," he pleaded.

With great reluctance, he led the way to the mission safe. His hands were trembling with fear and anger. It took him several tries on the cipher lock before he was able to open it. He reached for the mission folders, then hesitated. There, placed in the containment of the safe, he stared at a pistol. Madani must have seen the reaction and shoved the semi into his face. The choice had been made. All he could do was comply with the terrorist's demands. Jack submitted to the intruders, although very unwillingly.

The JTRS[33] wireless suddenly interrupted with a high-pitched squeal. "What?" Madani responded. It was a call from the squad leader above. He listened intensely for a few seconds. Apparently, his flight crew had just gotten word that an advance team was approaching from Elmendorf. Radar had picked up a craft, what appeared a cargo plane, according to the signature, headed in their direction.

"Five minutes," was the impending warning.

"Take defensive."

"Roger." It was the order for his attack team to go into action. Jack was off the hook, for the time being. It gave him precious moments to hopefully come up with a plan. He needed to protect not only his crew, but the facility as well. His mind began to churn.

---

[33] The JTRS was a family of high-capacity tactical radios that provide both line-of-sight and beyond-line-of-sight C4I capabilities to war fighters. This family of radios covered an operating spectrum from 2 to 2000 MHz, and was capable of transmitting voice, video, and data.

ELMENDORF AFB

"Check your gear," Hector "Heck" Rivera, C-130 Squad Leader, barked over the roar of the twin turbo engines. He was instructing the paratroopers, a dozen strong, seated along the craft's fuselage, to get ready. Approaching the target at 185 knots, it would take another five minutes to arrive. The C-130 troop carrier from the 477th fighter group had been dispatched forty minutes earlier. Dawn should break by the time they reached their destination. Unfamiliar with the specific target, 3rd Wing HQ command had decided on daytime recon. The detachment was a mix of seasoned soldiers and new recruits on their first reconnaissance mission. You could spot them by the edginess of their body motions. Though trained to stay calm, the excitement of an upcoming fight usually won out. What gave the tension away was the repeated heavy breathing taking in a deep lungful of air. It helped increase body vitality. It usually worked. It calmed the nerves, increased blood circulation, and, most importantly, generated insulin flow. It was the insulin that got the soldier through the pain of battle.

The flight crew up front reduced the twin engines to let the craft descend to the desired jump altitude. The crew had been forewarned that it might be a tricky jump for there was not much open space in this heavily wooded part in the region. The target slowly crept into view a couple of miles ahead. Rapidly approaching the target, the pilot took the craft into a wide turn to check for possible drop zones. Eyes on alert, scanning the horizon, the copilot warned the crew chief, "Not an easy jump." He could only make out one small clearing near a building he assumed was the objective of today's flight.

"Target in sight," the pilot reported back. Both home base and onboard radio systems were tuned to the same frequency. The copilot switched on the ten-second alert system. The rear cargo gate slowly opened. The jumpers could feel the after-draft turbulence tugging on their uniforms.

The onboard klaxon sprang into action. Accompanied by red, flashing strobe lights, eerie shadows were painted against the rear compartment walls. "Five seconds," the squad leader's voice reverberated. Braced against the opened cargo door draft, jumpers were holding on to chute straps. Dawn was just breaking.

Craning over the cargo door, the crew chief's jumpers spotted something peculiar. What appeared to be pine trees rushing past both sides of the craft, converging in the craft's wake, turned out to be an antenna farm. But that wasn't what alerted Rivera. It was the streaming rocket plume rapidly accelerating in his direction.

In the cockpit up front, concentrating on the drop zone, the pilots were unaware of the impending danger. What alerted Rivera was the red, flashing warning signal pulsating on the instrument panel. His body reacted instantly. He shouted, "Incoming…incoming…brace yourselves!" Reacting on instinct, due to years of combat missions, only the seasoned fighters sought protection. The rest of the team stood frozen, unable to move. In a split second, an AGM-114 Hellfire laser-guided missile entered the craft's exit ramp. A fraction of a second later it exploded against the bulkhead into a huge fireball, ripping the C-130 apart. Pieces of metal were slicing through the air, severing limbs and body parts on impact.

"That's it," the Black Hawk chopper pilot said, watching the exploding craft nearby. They had been hovering in the shadows of the antenna forest, waiting for the approaching recon team dispatched from Elmendorf. The pilot was well aware of the devastation the weapon would cause. There would be no survivors. There was only one solace to the dying: it was instant. A few more lives had been expended. Lateral damages, the casualty report would indicate. To the command they were only numbers and figures, but to a soldier taking orders, it was a life cut short. At the end, it was the young paying the price. Only the young were willing to lay their life on the line.

"Recon One," the voice went out. The Elmendorf operator kept repeating, "Come in…come in." Base Ops was trying to raise the C-130 cockpit without much success. Not getting a response, the alert call went out. "Craft down." It forced the base into action.

Base commander Thomas Johnson had just arrived at the office. "What's up?" he demanded. He had received the red alert on his HF while enjoying morning breakfast at the officers' club café bar. He was an early riser. Early morning was his favorite time of day. This way he could catch the morning roster and listen in on the news. It would get yesterday's business out of the way before the base came alive. It also gave him time to reflect on personal things. Two more years at this desolate place, he figured, and "I'm outta here."

"Don't get me wrong," he would voice his personal opinion at an occasional Friday dinner party. "Alaska's a beautiful place for the woodsman, grizzly, and sasquatch," he'd explain. "But give me a beach, sunshine, and bikinis anytime." It would always bring a chuckle to the table, with the exception of his wife, who would generally frown. Except for a couple of months during summer, Alaska was a cold place. Then, when you thought it'd warm up, it turned humid—extremely humid. And the mosquitoes. He'd rather not think about it. "Must be getting old," he'd remark. In his younger years, he used to be full of vigor and unpleasant things did not bother him as much.

Excited to experience new places, he had been looking forward to the next rotation. After an assignment to the north, available to him would be places like Rhine Main, Germany; Anderson AFB, Guam; and Hickam AFB, Hawaii. Now, that was a duty station he'd enjoy. He was looking forward to the outdoors. He couldn't wait to get his hands on fishing and diving gear. For now, it was Alaska. An alert tone just triggered the HF scanner. "C-130 down," the dispatcher announced. "Lost over Fox One."

He quickly reached for the radio. "Repeat!"

"Gakona, sir."

It was a place most knew existed but nobody talked bout. If there was one hidden place on Earth, this was it. "Get a couple Apaches out there," he ordered. "And report back immediately." Losing a troop transporter was unusual. These craft had been around for half a century and were considered the most reliable craft in the air. With a, near-zero loss track record, it was the service's workhorse. Shaking his head in disbelief, he could only hope the crew and combat team had somehow survived in the rugged terrain.

ISS

"Liz…Liz…wake up." It was a soothing voice that brought her around. Liz blinked a few times then opened her eyes to strange surroundings. She stared into two sets of eyes, one that of Hiroshi Nagata, Japanese astronaut, and the other belonging to Kenny Walsh, who was holding her head between cradled hands.

"What? Ouch. My head…it hurts." She reached back for the source of pain and felt the swelling. Her fingers came back bloodied.

"Lie still," he comforted. "You took a nasty blow." Hiroshi was busy pressing a towel against the injury.

Her eyes slowly adjusted to the semi-darkened environment. "Where…"

"Kibo."

"Experimental Module," Hiroshi explained. "We've been taken prisoner."

Liz gazed around the space. Her eyes captured a modern and well-organized space laboratory. The place was more spacious than she had anticipated. Cages, trays, and microscopes were neatly arranged into rows of experiments. The space was saturated with more instruments and gear used for university-sponsored projects. There were even lab animals floating within the confinement of cages. She could make out mice, birds, and even a couple Rhesus monkeys amid a colorful flora of plants and vegetation.

Walsh made an attempt to keep her calm. "Listen," he said. "It seems we're safe for now. The Russian crew turned out to be Jihad. Don't think they're the ordinary killers. Families probably held hostage like us."

Liz thought she hadn't heard right. "What…how?"

Kenny shot a glance at Hiroshi. "What'd you think?"

"I agree," he replied. "Didn't see the killer instinct." But his assessment would prove him dead wrong not too far off.

Aside from the internal pressure pushing against her skull, her mind began to clear. She was fully conscious. Her eyes were focused on Kenny. Then she remembered. The blackout, the passion, their lovemaking, but the moment had long since passed. Although the feeling of elated satisfaction still lingered within her body, the present situation demanded her full attention. Her eyes shifted between the two. "Any plans?"

"We have two choices," Kenny stated. "Stay put and comply with their demands," he shot a gaze at Hiroshi, "or fight our way out."

"Negotiate." Hiroshi seemed to hold steadfast to a diplomatic solution.

Liz agreed with Kenny. "Gotta fight. Gotta stop them before they can cause more damage."

To her, the current situation only added to the overall misery of an already oppressed nation. Conditions on Earth might already be beyond repair. It might be too late for the free world to remain a free world. More and more rumors surfaced about a possible takeover by Islam. Their agents and brokers were infiltrating every rank of society throughout the continents. According to recent statistics, Muslim faith and secular reliance had gained majority in many nations of the free world. And now, it had even infiltrated the space station. *What'll it be next?*

It suddenly hit her. Her eyes widened with the revelation. "We've gotta get out of here!"

Her outburst was so alarming that both Walsh and Nagata shot her a distressed glance. Both had question marks on their faces.

"It's an attack on the nation," Liz shouted out. "What else could it be?"

"Now, now," Walsh calmed her, "let's not get carried away."

But Liz insisted, "Don't you see? The platform…perfect weapon!"

Both of her companions stared at her with doubtful eyes. She could read it on their faces: "She's gone mad." But her thinking was focused on information her dad had shared. At the time, it did not make much sense, but fitting the pieces together after the cosmonaut attack, it became clear. Most of the world had been lulled into complacency. Even Dad had said so during the lengthy discussions they had on world politics. There were other things he had said. Things so alarming even she had to question them. Not his sanity, although it may have sounded as such, but the perils of it. "Dad," she muttered into the isolation of space. "You were right."

"Right about what?" Kenny asked.

"Ever hear of HAARP?"

He shook his head. "Rumors only," he replied. Nagata's face returned a blank stare. Obviously, with island isolation and cultural differences, Japan had taken a different path. Science and technology to them was more important than weapons research. Advancing in many sciences, the nation had taken a monumental leap where many other nations had fallen behind.

"Explain," Kenny demanded. "I wanna hear more."

PRESIDIO

Highly energized, Tracy unfolded the classified High Pri message just in over the SCI[34] net. What used to be the nation's uppermost classified comm net, SCI today had scaled down to a dedicated link accessible only within the Western Sector. "Don't believe it!" she exclaimed. Generated by Echelon, the Intel watch list read:
ALERT STATUS: HIGH
PRIORITY: IMMEDIATE
CLASSIFICATION: EXTREMELY SENSITIVE
TOPIC: COMINT
ORDER: NEW ID
SUBJECT: UNKNOWN
LOCATION: SUDAN
LINK: POSSIBLE JIHAD
SOURCE: VOICE PATTERN RECOGNITION
MATCH FOUND: GAKONA...HAARP...FOX ONE...
REPORT: END
NNNN

The communiqué caused her to immediately react. She punched the intercom button. "Give me video on Sudan," she ordered, then waited for the screen to switch sectors. Seconds went by without a change. Highly irritated by now, she punched the OPS button. It directed the shift operator into her office. "Step in here," she ordered. "Now."

"Ma'am?"

A newly assigned operator, he lingered by her desk, shifting from one leg to the other. She sensed reluctance mixed with in with uncertainty. "What's your name?" she lashed out at the bewildered young man.

Groping for words of justification, he stammered, "But...but." She knew what he was about to say *can't do it...not authorized.*

"Don't want excuses," she demanded. "Just do it."

His head lowered toward the floor much like a beaten dog. The operator abruptly turned and headed back to his duty station. She had been well aware of his reaction. *Am I turning into an emotionless bitch?* She had not planned on sounding this stern, but early on, she had decided to maintain a professional distance from coworkers. It served two purposes. First off, it kept coworkers from prying on personal matters, and second, it maintained discipline just like military policy. Her lingering thought vanished as soon as the monitor sprang into action.

With space assets still sparse, no one was authorized to dedicate an entire satellite to one specific target. Space birds were appropriated by the new congress with one stipulation: shared assets across organizations. Along the same lines, they demanded strict accountability. Ever since the Western Sector took responsibility for space assets, Tracy, as much as everybody else working within the defense sector had been frustrated

---

[34] SCI – Special Compartmented Intelligence is the highest classified data communication network dedicated mostly to the Intel community.

to no end. She would have to address the issue when the time came. The time had come sooner than she had expected.

She was jolted from her thoughts by the ringing of the phone. Picking up, she answered, "SPACECOM."

It was an irate voice. The caller was very familiar to her. Screaming through the receiver, an outraged Western Sector director demanded, "What the fuck's goin' on over there? You tying up space assets?"

She placated his charge by pleading innocent. "Don't know what you mean."

"Just had an urgent call from NWC,"[35] he explained, highly outraged. "Give me an explanation, and make it good."

Not to divulge the decision she had made minutes ago, she innocently stated, "Satellite's malfunctioned. Working on it."

"Let me know immediately," he directed, "the second the problem's fixed."

"Yes, sir. Damn," she muttered with a grin on her face. "I'm getting good at this." Her mind briefly reflected on her personal changes. Thinking back, she had not always been like this. There was a time when she was as timid as the rest of the lot, but, "if its politics it takes, I'm in the game." It was a game of power play. And she liked it.

Tracy was brought up in a home devoid of deceit, deception, and egotistical behavior. When growing up she could not recall one occasion where someone in the family was caught lying. That word was not in the family's vocabulary. It was only after entering the working world that she'd realized people were not always honest. It seemed that the higher up the rank one went, the more dishonest people became. "Politics," was her explanation. Commercial and government alike, it was a world of politics. She'd quickly learned that, in order to get what you needed, one had to lie. One had to cheat. One had to steal. Although the scale varied between occasions, those were the terms. She'd struggled for the longest time to control her emotions, but, at the end, saw it necessary at a time of crises and needs. Today was such a need.

With her eyes focused on the Sudanese region, her thoughts wavered from the present to the past. Images of unfinished business crept into her vivid mind. The elusive, scarred-faced images still stood clearly out. "Could it be possible?"

First, there had been the kidnapping. Then the chase, followed with retaliation by both sides. It was a time when she grew up from her sheltered life to the spoils of the real world. It was a time she met with the extreme. It had also been a time for romance and love. It was when she met Brian. He was the love of her life. In spite of the pressing mission, a tender smile swept across her face. She made a subconscious motion for the phone to try to call him, but changed her mind. This wasn't a time for sentiment. The present called for action. Personal issues had to wait.

The operator stormed into her office, interrupting her thoughts. "Ma'am," he gestured at the monitor, "take a look at this."

"Fox One?" The secure COMINT relay from NORAD jumped into action. Her workstation was configured to switch seamlessly between Intel agency networks. Apparently, MILNET had picked up intelligence coming from Alaska indicating that all communications from Fox One had been lost.

---

[35] National Weather Center.

"I'll take it," Tracy directed before waving him on. Switching the monitor to internal net, she put a query string into the database. Immediately, warning flashes pulsed across the screen. "Classified DOD…DOD eyes only." Carnivore[36] had located information she queried on Fox One but denied her access. Furiously, she picked up the HF receiver and dialed a direct number.

Two rings later Foster's gruff voice cut in on the secure line, "Crimson."

"Stinger," Tracy charmed. "Need a favor."

His voice immediately changed tones. "Here we go again." he grumbled. "What's it now?"

"Need access to Carnivore."

"Not possible," he replied. It was his privilege to allow or deny access to the nation's most classified database. There was information stored to which only he had access. The world was better off not knowing some of the information he kept strictly secret.

She deliberately stressed the next words. "Fox One."

The line turned silent. It even stopped his breathing. Apparently, her words had struck home. She gave him a few seconds. *Must be thinking*, she surmised. *Must not be every day anyone demands that kind of information.*

"Just can't stay away from trouble," he chided. "Can you."

She put the burden on him. "Just doin' my job."

He succumbed to her charm once more. "Okay," he said. "Keep me posted."

"Thanks." *Click.*

Tracy was very much relieved. "Went better than expected," she muttered. She liked the fact that she got what she wanted, and, to top it, she had placed the burden on him. It was something Dad had taught her.

"In a crisis situation," he'd instructed her, "always put the burden on the opponent, no matter what the cause." It was one of many rules he had shared with her. She had seen the list of gambits he had compiled over a lifetime of challenges. There were many. Next time they talked, she reminded herself, "Need to ask him for a copy."

---

[36] Carnivore – Carnivore is the name given to a system initially implemented by the Federal Bureau of Investigation analogous to wiretapping. Later renamed to Digital Collection System, it was segmented into three packages including Carnivore, Packeteer and CoolMiner, referred to as the DragonWare Suite.

ISS

"Alpha One…Alpha One…come in…come in…urgent." It was Baikonur calling the ISS. Mission control demanded the space crew's immediate attention. Apparently, Russian mission command was receiving conflicting commands from the space station. Their Ops software applications had detected what seemed to be conflicting command data on the monitoring systems. Minutes later, a high alert was issued to all Baikonur personnel.

For the past hour, at the far end of the space station, disputes had erupted. Crammed into Zvezda, the Russian service module was the Russian space crew. Four in numbers, they represented the majority on the station. Toporov, mission chief, and Budenko, long term space occupant, were busy preparing for the pending mission. While only the cosmonauts were privy to the true mission at hand, the combined effort from all aboard was required. Presently, Toporov was feeding new parameter data into the onboard computers. Budenko was busy coordinating trajectory and target points.

Andrei Kubalev, Soyuz Commander, was held at gunpoint. The assault came as a complete surprise to him. Dedicated cosmonaut that he was, he had been on the space platform numerous times before. He had not seen it coming, the takeover. He was currently mulling over his predicament. *How could they?*

"Imbeciles…idiots…traitors," he yelled at Toporov. The outburst made his position clear. It earned him a slap in the face with a 9mm Strizh.[37] The sheer weight of the weapon, Russia's newly developed military issue replacing the popular, but dated Makarov, left a deep gash in his face. He immediately lashed out. "Give me that," he shouted at Toporov. That just created more anger in the Jihad. It earned him another slap in the face, even more forceful. Rivulets of blood floated off in space. For the moment, he remained still.

Unable to comprehend what had just developed, Yuri Chenkov, who witnessed the violent outburst, was undecided on what steps to take and lingered nearby. He had never expected such treachery. Much like Kubalev, he was a dedicated cosmonaut. He also tried to resist the takeover effort. Toporov moved forward, confronting him. A heated exchange erupted between them. Chenkov did not want any part of the plan and said so over and over. "Nyet…nyet…nyet."

Completely frustrated and distressed by now, with one swift push against the bulkhead, Chenkov propelled his body in the direction of Budenko. He needed to get his hands on the radio. But Budenko saw him approach and reacted quickly, warding off the advancing body. They grappled for the receiver. Budenko fought him off with a blow to the chest, sending Chenkov into the opposite space. Toporov was waiting for him.

Sailing across the capsule, Chenkov landed hard against some equipment mount. It momentarily stunned him. It had knocked the wind from his lungs. He desperately gasped for air, then turned and came face to face with the adversary. Directly aimed at his face, he boldly stared into the barrel of the Strizh.

He was powerless. *Or am I?*

---

[37] Strizh is a 9-mm automatic handgun similar to the Glock design, manufactured and issued to Russian military personnel in 2012.

The crew was paired off even in opposing forces, in numbers anyway. Chenkov sought out Kubalev, the commander. With a flip of the head he tried to get the commander's attention. The gesture was returned with an imperceptible nod. *At least,* he thought, *I'm not alone.* He trusted Kubalev. A student from the old Cosmodrome school, Kubalev was a righteous man. Although superior in rank, he had always respected his fellow cosmonauts. Chenkov struggled to comprehend the change in direction the mission had taken. There was an ominous foreboding surfacing in the Russian service module. For now, both were biding time. But time was not on their side. Time was working against the mission they had set out.

FOX ONE

"Status on ionic shield," Jack shouted across the OPS center. He could feel the very foundation strain under full power. The heater coils had been pumping out maximum energy into the beam refractor. Ever since yesterday's attack on the facility, he and his team had been kept hostage. The attackers had an easy victory without a significant defense force in place. Since nobody carried arms on Jack's team there was practically no resistance. What small fire power was available had been stored away in the site's armored locker. After all, Fox One, up to now, had been a test facility in an extremely remote area. An assault on the station had been the farthest thing from his mind. Using HAARP as a defense weapon was scheduled farther down the road, once all elements had been tested and evaluated.

Earlier in the morning, after a couple hours of fitful sleep, Jack had been rudely awakened by the attackers. He was ordered to gather everybody. Once assembled in the mission room, the leader identified as Amin Madani held an operative speech. "We have taken over your site," he stated. "It is purely for political reasons. If you cooperate," he stressed, "you will be treated fair. We are in complete control. We control not only this station, but we have control over your nation as well."

That revelation was a bombshell. Jack had stopped breathing and so had everybody else in the room. As incredible as it sounded, he had to give it credibility. Although it might be an exaggeration, NORAD, SAC, or Elmendorf should have contacted them by now. But all communication was absent.

"What do you want from us?" Jack demanded. "We're only a NOAA[38] test facility. We have no harmful intentions."

"You will see in due time," was the only reply. The next command was issued an hour later. The order was clear. "Separate your team. Two groups: scientists and engineers."

Jack resisted. Splitting up his team would only weaken his position. He was quickly overruled by an automatic pointed at his face. Although it might be a bluff, he could not take the chance of anybody getting killed. He complied. Trained as Missileer, he had the world's largest weapons at his disposal, the ICBM, but at the moment, no matter how launch and silos were prepared for an attack on the land, it was meaningless to his present situation. There was nothing he could do about it. The entire defense posture needed to be reworked. He made a mental note to check with his command once he got out of the jam he was presently in.

"Engineers man controls," Madani instructed. "Scientists," he gestured across the hall, "conference room. Now."

"Controls?" Jack pleaded innocence.

 The National Oceanic and Atmospheric Administration (NOAA) is a scientific agency within the United States Department of Commerce focused on the conditions of the oceans and the atmosphere. With the help of observational satellites, NOAA warns of dangerous weather, charts seas and skies, guides the use and protection of ocean and coastal resources, and conducts research to improve understanding and stewardship of the environment.

"Primary power…heater arrays…atomic collectors…igniter coils…beam refractor," Madani rattled off. "You know the rest."

Jack was dumfounded. How could the enemy have intricate knowledge on the workings of HAARP? The most super-secret operation in the world.

"I," it took him several seconds to compose himself, "refuse your demands."

Flanked by two of his lieutenants, Madani dragged Jack into the conference room. "Come." The next thing that happened was beyond his control. The scene developed in rapid action. Facing the first scientist within his reach, Madani lifted a semi-automatic and shot him between the eyes. The man collapsed with the back of his head blown off. Blood and brain matter was splattered through the room. There was no display of emotions in the leader's eyes. There was no sign of remorse. To him, it seemed an act of justice. No more—no less. The sacrifice was one dead body. It demanded instant respect. It was that simple of an act.

Jack could not react fast enough to safe his man's life. When he did, he earned another blow to the face by the intruder's weapon. On wobbly legs, he was shoved back to the mission center. Pale faced, sickened, and still in shock, from then on Jack followed orders. At this time only the ionosphere layer directly above was being heated. *Maybe things won't be so bad,* Jack thought. He was listening to the muffled voice from Madani communicating with someone on VHF radio. "61 north by 149 west…3-mile pulse radius."

Jack mentally calculated the numbers. He was puzzled. They seemed vaguely familiar. Within minutes his fears were confirmed by the final orders. "Coordinates 61°15′05″N 149°48′23″W." It instantly hit him. "Elmendorf!" What he did not immediately understand was the path of destruction his weapon was about to unleash. There was only one path the particle beam could take. *Via the ISS.* When his brain assimilated the thought process, his face instantly turned green with fear. "My God," he muttered. "Space crew." His eyes veiled with fury, his head jerked at Madani. "No way," he refused. "I'm not giving the order."

Out flew the weapon again aimed directly at his temple. "Can and you will." In spite of the immediate order, Jack refused. He weighted his life against his crew's, the space station crew's, and the target destination he knew would amount to many lives. "Never."

Madani hesitated. It became obvious that he was evaluating his position as adversary commander. His thought processes were clearly reflected in his facial features. Whatever thoughts hurried through his mind reflected a hint of quizzing, determination, then rage. Jack and his crew could clearly read it in his face. He'd made up his mind. He needed to eliminate the immediate obstacle, Jack. It was here when the chief engineer stepped forward with, "Take me."

"So be it," Madani nodded and pulled the trigger. In a quick motion, he had shifted his weapon at the engineer and shot him point black in the temple. With all eyes trained at the man, he collapsed without a sound escaping his lips. He was true to his lifelong dedication. Serve mankind with peaceful intentions. Unfortunately, his dreams and wishes did not come true in his lifetime. Jack, who'd followed the unpredicted execution of his friend and protégé, relinquished any further resistance. Silently, he succumbed to all further orders initiated by the enemy. He suddenly realized, with each refusal to cooperate, he would lose yet another of his friends and team members.

Keenly aware of the awesome and destructive energy he was about to unleash, between clenched lips he passed the order on. He could already envision the super-heated plasma beam from a pulsed particle generator shooting through the waveguides. Jack and his crew, at this time, were unaware that the ISS had been taken hostage as well by the enemy. It was from there where the particle beam, amplified to its full strength, guided by the final coordinates, would be reflected back to Earth toward their target, obliterating everything in its focused target sight by a burst of blazing destruction.

Madani's trained operatives took positions near the engineers to assure his orders were executed. One final check on the watch assured the leader the precise position of the international space station. Counting down the seconds, Madani gestured at his operatives when zero point was reached. "Let's see what this baby can do." Living many years among the western society, and enjoying every aspect of its culture, habits, and conveniences, he had also acquired much of the jargon spoken. Words such as jerk face, Peckerhead, and baby had become a natural aspect in his vocabulary.

Each sector indicated readiness when he issued the final command, "Fire." Amid suppressed breathing, there was dead silence. Then all felt it. It was a low rumble at first. It was quickly followed by pulsating waves released from massive energy banks shaking the center at its foundation. Rapidly building up in intensity, a whooshing sound followed when the beam reached its maximum strength of concentrated obliteration.

Madani, in direct VHF communications with Hammad at Base Command, immediately lost the connection. He was subjected to a temporary blackout. He was puzzled at first, then realized it was due to his firing. The fury he had unleashed neutralized all frequency waves nearby. He would get the signal back as soon as the destructive beam was shot down.

Jack and his team were terrified. It clearly reflected in their faces. They could only imagine the destructive firepower just released hoping the target was missed. Hope was quickly shattered when the next call came over the speaker, "Success." The cheering followed by Madani's team only confirmed Jack's worst fears.

ELMENDORF AFB

3rd Wing Commander Tommy Johnson was steaming with anger. "Get a Raptor wing in the air and," he ordered, "make it snappy." He was extremely furious about the loss of his assault team. Although the lost men had been assigned from the 477th fighter support group, they were ultimately under his command. He was responsible for every activity that took place at the airbase. "I'll teach them a lesson," he fumed. "Whoever those bastards are." He quickly got sidetracked by his action call when the base came alive.

A wing of three Raptors in tight formation left the tarmac, headed directly for the runway. It gave him the chills each time one would barrel down the strip. Being the nation's most advanced combat fighter craft, he never got tired watching these magnificent fighting machines take to the air. He still recalled how stunned the nation had been when the craft was announced by the Air Force.

After the F-117 Nighthawk had been introduced to the world in 1988, he had thought it could not get any better. He never thought he would witness yet another technology leap in aircraft design in his lifetime. "Where do they come up with the ideas?" he speculated. "Guys at the Skunk Works must be geniuses...or just plain bored."

To counter the gaining Soviet air superiority back then, the U.S. Air Force required a new fighter craft primarily to replace the aging F-15 Eagle. The F-22 Raptor, the military's fifth generation fighter plane, had been on the drawing board as far back as the mid-80s. It was a highly controversial craft with its quad-wing design and fly-by-wire computer controls. To achieve superiority above everything currently flying in the air, a number of requirements had to be incorporated for stealth, maneuverability, air-to-air combat, ground attack, electronic warfare, and signal intelligence. After many design changes, the craft was finally commissioned into service in 2005.

As was the case with many U.S. military and DOD defense assets, new technologies needed to be proven. And what better way than in battle. Since there had been no recent conflicts involving the United States, today was to be the first opportunity to put the technology to work. He watched the proud wing of three crafts take position at the tarmac, ready for takeoff. Although he tried instructing NORAD to monitor and manage the craft, he was unable to establish communication. *Decision's mine,* were his final thoughts.

In addition of losing base communication, the airwaves had also been silent to its outlaying duty stations. "Damned technology," Johnson cussed like so many times in recent months. It seemed communications had been breaking down more frequently for one reason or another. Following each incident, he had the electronics team investigate, but never had been able to pinpoint the true cause. "Something's up," he had complained to his superiors on more than one occasion. The only response he would get was a shrug. It got to a point where even his amateur operators were complaining. There had been times when the ether was silent for hours on end in the northern hemisphere. No one ever came forward to explain the strange phenomenon. What he and nobody else knew was that, this morning, another HAARP initiative was taking place.

The initial concept for HAARP had been for energizing the upper atmosphere to conduct frequency testing and its global implications, but more recently it had been designed as the new defense grid. Supposedly, but highly unofficially, it would become a defensive/offensive weapon to annihilate any intrusion and threat entering the North American air space. It was what made the super weapon such an effective defense. It was this interdependency that the adversary so desperately wanted to get his hands on. Verified on design paper, the theory still had to be proven in space.

The technology, shelved after Tesla's death, had been gathering dust in the secret libraries only to surface years later. Under development once again, but this time for more sinister purposes, today was the day to finally test the weapon, not for its intended purpose by the inventor, to harness nature for sending wireless power through the ether, but for another destructive means aimed at mankind. Tommy Johnson, like everybody else in the defense grid fighting for the safety for the nation, his nation, was kept in the dark guessing about yet another power or communication outage. "Damned politicians, damned government, damned technology." At the end of his frustrated outbursts, as usually, he forgave the technology inventors because they provided him with a job not many could glory in, but had a difficult time doing the same for the political elements.

ISS

As he was each day, Munich-born German astronaut Dieter Fuchs, representing the European Union, was alone as usual, conducting laboratory experiments at Columbus, the primary research facility in the space station. Out of the entire space crew he was kept the busiest with projects. Due to the isolation between the lab and service modules, unaware for most part, the only time Fuchs came in conduct with the rest of the space crew was during dinner hours. Columbus, centrally located within the ISS infrastructure, was the generic laboratory for biological and biomedical research with pending quantum physics research scheduled in the near future.

The Columbus module was a spacious capsule. Being of recent design, additional space had been acquired by relocating vital services through external mounts and accesses. Though Italian in blueprint, Columbus was managed and controlled from DLR, German-based Aerospace Center, and CNES, French-based Toulouse Space Center.

Having earned a physics degree at Max Plank, Fuchs was a dedicated scientist. Presently busy with vials, dishes, bacteria, and viruses, Dieter was in his element. In heightened excitement, he was anxious to open the super-cooled container that had just arrived with the last Soyuz space transport. He was about to open the lid when his eyes caught the prominent red warning label. "Achtung!" it proclaimed in German. "Gefährliche Giftstoffe!"

Surprised at the unexpected warning stamped on the critical shipment, he secured[39] the container gingerly to the table. "The suit," he muttered to himself. Reading the warning was enough for him to fetch the protective garb. It would not only protect his body from contamination. The Velcro-strapped boots would give him sure-footed steadiness stepping across the lab floor. He headed for the locker unaware of a destructive beam originated from the Alaskan region emanating and rapidly expanding in his direction aimed at the externally mounted waveguide.

It was at this critical junction when the violent jolt shook through the laboratory. Without warning his body slammed against one side of the bulkhead. For a second, everything turned blurry. Immediately, from the sheer force of the lateral violence, he knew something had gone awfully wrong. Pushed against the wall, he felt his body weight increase tenfold. Unable to free himself from the wall, he was stuck there, bonded. Then, he felt the tremendous weight disappear just as suddenly as it had set on. A puzzled look came over his face. Seconds later it turned to fear. In an instant, he spotted some spilled dishes from the container broken into pieces, floating next to his head. The contents had torn free, bounced against the wall and spilled into many droplets, floating through space right in front of his face.

Realizing that he would die if just one drop touched him, in one swift motion he propelled himself toward the control console. He punched down hard on the alarm button prominently mounted on top of it. A high pitch alert went immediately out through all sections of the space station. Mounted against ceilings and exit doors, a series of klaxons

---

[39] In space, most objects are fastened with Velcro tape to prevent from floating off.

triggered, creating an ungodly sound never before heard in space. Pulsating red lights turned on in every service module, including JEM, Leonardo, Destiny, Unity, Rassvet, and Zvezda.

Up front at the Russian service module, Toporov and Budenko were bracing themselves. They knew the impact from HAARP would shake up the station. What they did not know was the magnitude of power generated for this impact. With maximum energy rapidly expanding in their direction, Zvezda jolted violently. The station took the full brunt of the energy released by Gakona. Though the energy was focused into a narrow beam aimed at the waveguide, the refractor impact pushed the space station from its orbit. Budenko desperately tried to cling to the control console. He had to guide the target direction of the beam. To accomplish that, he had to insert a series of parameters into the guidance system via the keyboard. With the acceleration and shaking, he had a most difficult time. Seconds later, he managed to punch the last data into the onboard computers. With it, the beam of destruction was on its way to its ground target.

With the sudden acceleration, the three other crewmembers sailed across the module. Their bodies slammed against the far end of the wall, knocking the wind from their lungs. Chenkov, pressed against the bulkhead, took the distraction to an advantage. Pushing hard on his feet, he propelled himself back in the direction of Budenko, who was momentarily distracted with the controls.

Chenkov, approaching from behind, reached for Budenko's neck. Vice like, hands clasped around the Jihad's neck in a stranglehold, he hung on, using all the strength his body was capable of, but he was no match for his combat trained opponent. With a swift twist using one arm, Budenko freed himself then turned, pulled the Strizh from the waist, aimed, and fired. It was an automatic reaction by the trained fighter but had missed its target. The immediate threat at hand had superseded the intended outcome.

Unable to get a grip to steady his body, Chenkov, slowly floating in space, watched the next scene unfold. While his mind reluctantly accepted the inevitable, his brain desperately struggled to prevent the unavoidable. Almost in a trance, his eyes watched as the fiery flash escaped the gun barrel followed by the 9mm slug on its way to cause his instant death. His face had just enough time to change from surprise to shock. It held a mask-like impression for seconds before relaxing into eternal bliss. Chenkov did not feel the impact. The last thought he had was that of his soul gently floating into space, seeking out eternity. His body hovered in midair when Kubalev gently moved up to brush his eyes closed. He then pulled the expired body of his dedicated comrade towards the exit, temporarily strapping it to the wall mount.

Kubalev, ISS commander for the mission, deliberately headed for Budenko. Disregarding the weapon aimed at his face, he punched the Jihad infiltrator in the face. The action propelled his body in the opposite direction, where, with a dull thud, the commander landed against the service module's wall. Budenko followed the commander. A fight ensued between them. Barehanded and unmatched with the Jihad's fighting skills, Kubalev was quickly subdued. He was taken prisoner, securely strapped against the bulkhead.

Restricted in the confines of Kibo, Liz was about to give Walsh a brief lecture on the facts of HAARP, as little as she knew, when all of a sudden, the capsule took a tremendous jolt. Sounds none of them had ever heard emanated from the connecting trusses and framework. It sounded like the infrastructure was tearing apart. Struts, frames, bolts, and nuts creaked under the tremendous strain from sudden expansion. Explosion-like, the entire structure was reverberating. It shook the surrounding spaces into blurriness, resonating through every inch of the space station. It seemed to last forever but was only the beginning. Then the HAARP effects set in. They came on gradually but rapidly, expanding exponentially. It was a lateral motion causing a sudden strain in positive gravity.

Whoever and whatever was not securely tied to the framework was thrown against walls, equipment, and instruments, bouncing off in every direction. Although the ISS was slicing through space at greater than 17,000 miles an hour, the added forces pushed the platform from its programmed orbit. It had gained miles of apogee distance before the automated, solar-powered retro jets kicked in to slow the acceleration. Liz, Walsh, and Nagata's bodies, within their confined space, were slammed into the barriers of the Kibo capsule. Pushed against the far wall, the breath had been pushed out of all of them. Liz, very familiar with changes in G forces from years of fly-by-seat firefighting flight time, composed herself first. "We're in trouble!"

It seemed like an eternity before Liz, Kenny, and Hiroshi recovered from the sudden impact from the energy burst. Liz reacted. She headed for the module exit. Her plan was to reach Harmony, the station's main node connecting with Kibo. But the exit was blocked. No matter how hard she pushed and pulled it did not budge. Kenny and Hiroshi came to her aid. Regardless of their combined strength, their effort was in vain. It seemed jammed from the other side. Since none of the exit doors on ISS had security locks other than manually manipulated interlocking systems, a tool must have been used to jam the door or the framework was twisted from the impact.

They were trapped. But for Liz, fighter as she was, the realization was not good enough. With years of search and rescue in her past, she had learned that there was always a way out. The "way" came with training and experience. First thing on her mind was, "Tools!" But her search for a workable solution proved unsuccessful. There were no tools robust enough to pry through the exit door. To punch through the reinforced, negative space-pressure designed steel would have required a jackhammer. And that, with space travel at its infancy, was not an option. There was no bypass. Contrary to her immediate thinking, there was an escape. It was space itself. She spotted it. It was an opportunity clearly visible through the Kibo porthole. There, closely mounted by the edge of space, was Canadarm-2, the Canadian supplied secondary robotic arm. A remotely operated maneuverable robot, it was an auxiliary system maneuverable from within Kibo and Destiny. But Destiny, the American service module, was not accessible from space. It was a service module interconnected between Harmony and Tranquility. Fortunately, one possible access to the arm was from Kibo, their present location.

Liz was already headed for the interlock. Attached to the framework was a locker containing three spacesuits neatly fastened by support hangers. Both Walsh and Nagata carried a startled look on their faces when she beckoned. "Help me with the suit."

Walsh was quick to respond. "No!"

Nagata, rushing to her side, also objected, "I'm going!"

But Liz, placing one foot at a time into the spacesuit, was already slipping the rest of her body into the protective suit. "Not a chance," she objected. "This one's on me." Her eyes, and gestures as well, underlined the single determination on which she was about to embark. "Just get me to PMA-3." Her immediate destination was the pressurized mating adaptor connecting with Zarya, the Soyuz docking module. It was through Soyuz docking Liz was planning to free herself from the Kibo confinement. With all the training, she had on the ISS, individual blueprints were permanently etched into her mind. She did not need a chart or diagram to find her way around the station. Rigged for mockup on training grounds, possible emergency evacuations were simulated over and over by the crew.

Walsh was cautiously manipulating the external robotic arm. He maneuvered it as close to the Kibo docking exit as he could without damaging the surface. He was ready. The arm was waiting for Liz to exit.

Nagata helped Liz through the interlock. While he turned the inside, she, after the gate shut tight, secured the lock to exit. The interlock opened. Liz hesitated. *Where's the tether?* There was no strap to secure her body. Reluctantly at first, she carefully stepped into space. The feeling was overwhelming. Space was too much all at once. With shaky hands, she clung to the service frame.

Liz inhaled deeply to calm her quivering nerves. Suspended in freefall, she lingered for moments. Space, as unforgiving as it was, was waiting for her next step.

"Take your time." It was Kenny's assuring voice over the headset that helped. The radio, primary audio and video communication link for crew members, kept her connected with the ISS. She wavered. Then, after taking a deep breath, with one determined push Liz shoved her body toward the robotic arm. Free of all ties, she floated through space. Seconds later, her hand caught the robot's arm but, to her horror, slipped off. She had lost her hold on the polished metal.

Walsh and Nagata watched in horror through the porthole as she lost hold of the platform.

In desperation, with one swift motion, she flung her body in the direction of a tie wire. It would be her only chance to stop herself from floating off into space. Her fingers caught hold of the wire. It stopped her forward momentum but slammed her body hard onto the platform. Gasping for air, she felt the impact on her ribcage. Hurt, bruised, and aching she clung to the platform. She remained there until her fear-stricken breathing subsided. Then her eyes caught both of the crew's "thumbs up" gestures through the porthole. Reassured once more, Liz prepared for the next step, the impending emergency evac.

CASTLE ROCK

With coffee mug in one hand, Alex made his way down the stairway, then on to the basement. As usual, he was up early checking on alarms and equipment status. All seemed normal. The HAM radio was relentlessly scanning through the ether spectrum. On every sweep, it would briefly lock on to some station that was communicating. His ears were tuned in to the Castle call sign. There was none this morning. But, somewhat surprisingly, there was increased chatter on the HF radio rack mounted nearby. He looked up frequency and information source on the locator chart. It was a relay hub between the ISS and ground station somewhere in Eastern Europe. The signal must have bounced around space and reflected back by the ionosphere. "Hmm," he mimicked the hum of the equipment, "another Soyuz launch."

His face quickly changed from curiosity to one of compassion. His thoughts reached out at his daughter Liz. *Wonder,* he reflected in the early morning hour, *what you're up to.* He was well aware of her passing over the Castle region approximately every ninety minutes. Since the last space launch, he'd followed the path of the ISS, many times clearly visible through his binoculars on cloudless days. There was a slight creak on the floor behind him. He turned to check. Rhonda had joined him.

She moved up close by his side. "What's the matter?" she asked. "Miss your daughter?" She gently placed one hand on his shoulder. With the other she massaged his furrowed forehead. It always seemed to have a calming effect. Not that he was a callused person. He just had a passion for work and technology. She had learned that early on in their relationship. At first, it used to bother her. She thought she had made a mistake getting involved with this seasoned man. He seemed to care more for his electronic world than he did for her. But over time, she had found out otherwise. He was just as attending and passionate with her. All she had to do was prod for his attention, and that she did often.

His eyes displayed concern. "Something's about to happen," he whispered.

In an understanding gesture, her hand slid down his chest then past his waist. "Why, Alex," she chuckled, "again so soon?" She noticed his eyes shift to her face but his mind was somewhere else. For a brief moment, not quite understanding her meaning, his eyes lingered on her face, then broke into a knowing smile. "That's what I like about you," he chuckled. "Your sense of humor."

His absentmindedness was a distraction she could tolerate. Outside of that he was the model friend, attentive partner, and passionate lover. She would have liked more than just friendship, but each time she brought up the subject of a more permanent state he retreated into his shell. "I think we have a perfect relationship," he would politely rebuff her advances. "Don't you?" It usually followed with a calculated rationale that always made sense. It was his way of reminding her of what seemed most practical, even preferable—a life in harmony. She had no real reason to complain. It was just her womanly instinct for taking ownership of the man.

Gently kissing his forehead, she chided him into reality, "Getting a bit paranoid, aren't we?"

"Why won't people take me seriously?" It was a quiet response. "You do, don't you?"

Appeasing his concerns, she said, "Of course. You're always right." She had to remind herself of his intuitive qualities. His psychic ability always amazed her. He'd demonstrated on numerous occasions how dead on he was at predicting things.

"I'm not psychic," he would correct her. "Just assuming logical deductions."

Studying his face, she realized again how deeply she loved this man. She could not think of a life without him. A hint of tears began to form in her eyes. From beneath her stained eyes she felt his gentle touch on her arm, "What's the matter, sweetheart?"

"I'm just happy." Reinforcing their bond always made her feel better. Wiping away the tears, she gave him a pat on the shoulder, turned, and headed upstairs preparing for her departure to the west coast once more. Spending a weekend with Alex always rejuvenated her energy. It was time to return to her duty reporting to Foster for another couple of weeks.

With her gone, Alex lingered on. As he took his time to check over the banks of sophisticated sensory equipment, he noticed a red alert signal emanating from the spectrum analyzer. He pushed the print button for a hardcopy and reset the alarm. A few paces brought him to the printer. He tore off the status graphs. The sheet confirmed his earlier suspicion. "Thought so," he muttered.

It appeared the ionic particle layer at the upper atmosphere had changed again. "Gettin' to be a habit," he griped. Then an ominous foreboding crept into his mind. He could sense some tragic event was not far off. "If I could just pinpoint the source," he grumbled. "Could do something about it…but what?" He was not sure.

His eyes swept over the sophisticated sensory equipment for additional alerts. No other alarms were present. It did not calm his stretched nerves. In recent weeks, alerts had come up more frequently. That alone did not bother him as much. What had been more alarming were the frequently occurring radio blackouts with the usually reliable HAM equipment. "Somebody's messing with the ionic shield." With that conclusion, he left the seclusion of the equipment room.

Alex was keenly aware that somebody or something was destroying the protective layer of the ionosphere shielding the globe from cosmic rays. The shield, fortunately for mankind, provided a twofold guard. First, it protected man from destructive solar rays. Second, the shield allowed radio communication on Earth to exist. To analyze a possible cause, he vividly recollected the science behind how it worked from his college days.

A broadcast transmitter stationed on the ground sent a signal into space. The signal bounced against the ionic layer and was reflected back to Earth, where it was received by any distant receiving station. The station either retransmitted the signal to a repeater for further propagation or modulated it to public radio found in private homes. It was how AM and FM signals were broadcast for cities and outlaying towns. It worked for voice, sound, TV, and data feeding radio, HAM, and other communication equipment within the specific radio spectrum from 50 to 1000 megahertz.

Breaking away from his analytical thoughts, Alex decided to head back upstairs. Back in the recliner he tuned the HF receiver to world broadcast, trying to catch the morning news. It was a habit he had become dependent on. Most of the news came in from European stations. It gave him an unbiased input normally omitted by the national media broadcasts. One had to tune into overseas broadcasts to get current news.

While his eyes were focused on the locally published weekly paper, his ears kept listening. Suddenly, something caught his attention. His head perked up in the direction of the receiver. *"We just received a news wire that there has been a disaster in the Alaska region,"* the anchor announced. *"Please stay tuned..."*

Alex's senses immediately tuned to the forthcoming details. *"This station just learned from KFAR Fairbanks, Alaska,"* the newscaster announced, *"that all communications with Anchorage have been severed. We have no further information available at this time. Please stay tuned. We will keep you up to date as soon as information comes available."*

Alex was highly alert. "That's just great," he huffed.

He had known something was up. For some time, already he'd had a gut feeling that something big was going to happen. Today, his intuition was confirmed. He was still in deep thought when a burst of alarms hit his ears over the remote monitor. He immediately broke away from the news and rushed for the basement.

As soon as he entered the equipment room he spotted the source. Every possible alarm had gone off. Where in the past with previous microwave test shots only an increase in freed energy particles was recorded, this time it was different. Receivers and spectrum analyzers had gone wild. Printers were spitting out data streams and graphics. Struck with awe, he tore the sheet from the printer. "Rhonda," he yelled out. "Take a look at this." There was no response. He'd forgotten she left earlier to catch a flight to the coast.

Visions of devastation from not so distant events came into his vision. He remembered the destruction in San Francisco only a few years ago. Hoping the equipment was in error, he muttered, "This must be wrong." Abiding by his better senses, he already knew the results. Testing the equipment to confirm, he reset the alarms. Seconds later they were on again. Taking layered samples from various slices of atmosphere, the sensors were recording real-time data. In amazement, he stared at the data. The figures were incomprehensible. "What's it mean?"

Brian hearing his buddy's outbursts, hurried below to join Alex. They could not believe their eyes. According to the readouts, enormous amounts of energy had been released into the atmosphere. "Impossible," he muttered over and over. He knew no sources outside the sun could generate the amount of energy hitting the ionosphere. Then, it suddenly hit him. "HAARP!"

"You sure?" Brian had his doubts. "Maybe a solar burst."

"Not a chance. GOES-15 Satellite would have warned us from a coronal mass ejection."

"You may be right."

ISS

Manipulated by Walsh from within Kibo, clinging to Canadarm-2, Liz felt the motion exerted by the robotic arm. Donned in the bulky spacesuit she felt her body slowly move through space towards Rassvet, Russia's cargo module, her immediate destination. Attached to it was Zarya, the now-abandoned service module replaced by the modernized and more effective Zvezda[40] currently in possession by the Russian crew. But Zarya would give her entrance through Pirs and Poisk, Soyuz's interlocking access ports to the station. Once there, she would figure out a plan.

Presently, Zarya came within reach. "Get hold of the entrance hatch," Kenny's voice drilled into her ears. He was using Kibo's closed circuit radio to communicate. He had selected a dedicated frequency isolated from the rest of the station. Not to interfere with the station's ground command, it was a low power frequency utilized specifically for localized, external space activities.

All she had to do now was reach out to get ahold of the interlock hatch. A slight push landed her there. Clutching the framework with one hand, she tried to maneuver the opening hatch. It was not that simple. Without solid footing, every move she made was countered by inertia working against her body. Moving the hatch counterclockwise caused her body to rotate in the opposite direction. One hand clung to Canadarm-2, balancing her body, while the other pulled on the hatch cover, frozen in place following years of inactivity. She repeatedly pounded until it suddenly gave way. The lid snapped open ripping her body with it. Grappling for a hold on the interlock, she managed to get a solid grip on the hatch with one hand. Next, she struggled against the ripping force on her arm, wrist, and hand. Desperately clinging to the hatch cover, straining with extreme exertion, she managed to grab hold with the other hand and shoved her way through the porthole. She shot a quick glance back at the Kibo porthole. Kenny's face stared through

---

[40] ISS Configuration:
Russian orbital segments/modules:
    Zarya – "Dawn" First ISS module providing orientation control, communications and electrical power
    Zvezda – "Star" Service module, containing stations critical life support systems and living quarters
    Pirs – "Pier" Docking module
    Poisk – "Search" Airlock module
    Rassvet – "Dawn" primarily used for cargo storage and as a docking port for visiting spacecraft
U.S. orbital segments/modules:
    Harmony – Utility hub providing electrical power, electronic data, and acts as a central connecting point
    Destiny – Primary research facility for United States payloads
    Tranquility – Contains life support system to recycle waste water for crew use and oxygen supplements
    Unity – Passive connecting module was the first U.S.-built component of the Station
    Quest – Only U.S. airlock hosting spacewalks for both United States and Russian segments
International orbital segments/modules:
    JEM – Japanese Experiment Module
    Cupola – "Dome" Seven window observatory, used to view Earth and docking spacecraft
    Leonardo – Multi-purpose Italian research module
    Columbus – Primary research facility for European payloads aboard
    Kibo – Japanese laboratory, used to carry out research in space medicine, biology, and biotechnology

the porthole window, filled with worry. It quickly changed to relief when he realized she was safe. He gave her the "thumbs up" signal. Once inside, Liz shut the latch.

She was on her own, smothered in darkness. The chamber was pitch black. Liz groped along the wall to locate a light switch. "Light switch's to your left," Kenny instructed her over the closed circuit. Her gloved fingers located the set of switches and buttons. "Found it," she reported back.

From here on, keeping a connection with Walsh, Liz gave a running account of her every move. "Flipping switch one." It brought on a slight humming sound. *At least the battery works.* "Switch two." Although very dim, the instrument panel lit up. It was barely enough to illuminate the interior but she was able to read the control labels. One button read, "Interior lights." One firm push doused the internal cabin with bright lights. "What's next?"

"Oxygen," Kenny's voice shot back. The silence of space was suddenly broken by the sound of oxygen rushing into the chamber. It was safe for her to unlock her helmet. One twist removed it from the seal. She could breathe freely once more without the restraint of the portable tank. Without helping hands, removing the suit always proved a challenge. It took almost ten minutes to free her body. *Next...the task.*

Using extreme caution, Liz slowly advanced toward Zvezda at the far end of the passageway. In a subdued voice, she gave Kenny a running account. "Hatch's open...nobody near the exit." She carefully pulled herself close to the edge of the entranceway. "I see Budenko by the console." She was about to enter the module when her vision caught a new scene. "Wait...Toporov's got Kubalev covered."

"Clarify," Kenny ordered.

"Toporov has a gun on Kubalev." Liz then described the immediate scene in the service module. It appeared Budenko and Toporov were bracing for the next HAARP onslaught while holding their commander in check. Kubalev, victim of the hostile takeover, seemed to be held hostage. From the expression on his face she could only deduct what was next. Their bodies seemed braced for impending action. Liz was absorbing the immediate environment when Budenko shouted a warning, "Take hold!"

With Toporov training his weapon on Kubalev, the scene ahead of her suddenly became blurry. Then Liz was slammed hard against the service wall. Almost to the point of blacking out from extreme Gs, the pressure suddenly subsided, but not for long. Her body was slammed against the bulkhead next. Extremely blurry eyed, visions of utter destruction shot across her mind. *Oh my God,* was all she could muster. What she experienced was HAARP energy pulsing. After each devastating pulse, because of the concentrated energy beam released at her capsule, the space station was forced farther and farther from its orbit. With each shot fired, the drifting target in space had to be reacquired by the ground station before releasing the next energy burst. Manipulated by Budenko, using the waveguide for directional control, the end result was annihilating vital strategic ground commands 250 miles below the targeting waveguide. She could only guess the devastation the beam would inflict on earth.

"Tracy, Dad!" her mind screamed into space when a Strizh tumbled across her vision. It was a startling motion turned into an unexpected aid in her favor. One push propelled her body after the weapon. She was not the only one after the Strizh. Knocked from his hands by the jolt, Toporov too was after the weapon. It was then when the capsule crew detected her unexpected intrusion.

Budenko, startled by her appearance, in one quick move pulled his weapon from his waist, aimed, and pulled the trigger. The shot went wild. The bullet pierced the framework, then deflected off, imbedding into an oxygen tank. Pressurized air exploding into the cabin forced Budenko and Toporov to seek cover. Liz dodged for cover using the sudden confusion but kept her weapon trained on Budenko, holding him in check. Kubalev, off to the side, realized an instant opportunity to escape. One push propelled his body toward Liz. He reached for her arm and quickly pulled her through the exit hatch. Once outside the service module, he slammed the lid shut. With the piece of steel jammed into the hatch, he ensured it stayed tight. The Russian-turned-Jihad crew was trapped.

"Follow me." Liz, with Kubalev in tow, advanced through Zarya, gradually making their way back past Unity, Destiny and on to Harmony, the primary command module to free Walsh and Nagata. It was the only other place aside from Zvezda to manipulate the ISS platform, which was currently spinning out of control. Using the Soyuz's rocket jets, currently secured to the service dock, it took Liz and Kubalev hours to stabilize the ISS and return it to its pre-assigned orbit. It took care of the immediate problem. But they faced a much bigger problem. It was a problem none of the crew was capable of solving. The Soyuz was out of rocket fuel. They were unable to return to Earth. The space crews, antagonist and protagonist alike, were trapped.

ELMENDORF AFB

He never got tired watching these magnificent fighting birds, the Raptors, lift off the runway. Exhilarated by the sheer spectacle, Tommy Johnson muttered, "There they go." A pair of binoculars pressed against his forehead, he'd followed their flight path from the tarmac down the runway and as they rapidly disappeared in the sky. Only the ascorbic smell of the JP-4 fuel lingered on. He filled his lungs with the waning fumes. Much like an addict, he marveled, "Aah."

He loved the smell. It reminded him on his younger years going to the drag races. There, he used to hang out by the starting tree to be closest to the exhaust and the roar of engines emitted from dragsters, rails, and funny cars. It was pure ecstasy. You could not only hear and feel energy, you could even see it. It was the sheer power of mechanics taking hold, and it was what got him started in the service. Still in college then, he would drag his school buddies to see the races. To the consternation of his dad, he'd decided that "Automotive is my calling." Dad wouldn't hear of it. His dad had other plans. He'd already paved the way for Tommy to follow the same career. "Gonna be Air Force," he'd proclaimed.

Eventually, he'd listened to his dad's rational. With his parents' sacrifices for his attending private schools, four years at the academy made sense. Colorado Springs was a nice place, especially with what it had to offer. Climbing cliffs, hiking Pikes Peak, canoeing the Arkansas River, and gliding on thermal drafts from the Rockrimmon Foothills kept him busy for many years. Fighter training in Texas after graduating gave him the commanding perspective he'd needed. Never commissioned into battle, he eventually wound up here in Alaska, hoping to eventually get back to Colorado for retirement. But that was still a long way off.

Tommy Johnson had been following his wing's progress. "Target's up in three minutes. Advise when visual." Prior to takeoff, the center bays of each Raptor had been loaded with one 1,000-pound GBU-32 and two AIM-120C Advanced Medium-Range Air-to-Air (AMRAAM) missiles. Side bays and on-board cannons had been configured for possible air-to-air and air-to-ground attacks. Originally, when the Raptors were commissioned, they'd been somewhat mislabeled with the prefix "F" for fighter, whereas an "A" for attack craft would have been more appropriate to accommodate both air and ground spheres. But old habits were hard to break. Pilots much preferred the fighter status. Although the A-10 Wart Hog had earned its status among the elite fighting craft in the Gulf War, pilots considered attackers as second-class citizens.

With the wing in the air, he forced his thoughts back to the present. He had a problem on his hands, a big problem. It wasn't the only intrusion he'd had to deal with in the past. Hot shot pilots out of the Kamchatka region were buzzing him all the time, especially out west in the Aleutians. Sending out a couple Raptors would usually force them to retreat, much like dogs with tails clamped between their legs. He knew from experience they were only testing him. It was a chase, a cat and mouse game both sides played. This time it was the Russians. Next time it'd be him. Today, the Russians wanted to learn the combat capabilities of the F-22s.

Back at his desk, the intercom was tuned in to the crafts' frequency. He could listen in on the chatting crew receiving ground commands. It used to be him sitting in one of the craft. In his time, it had been mostly F-15s. He'd never been checked out in the F-22 Raptor. The craft was commissioned after he'd been forced to ground duty. He'd missed his chance, not only for these marvelous birds, but for space exploration as well. A hint of melancholy swept across his mind. The sadness reflected on his face. He'd give his right nut to be thirty again. He dearly missed the hands-on, but it still gave him a thrill to listen in on the cockpit. Entirely guided by computers, with afterburners pushing into the upper layers of the stratosphere, he could almost feel the G-forces on his butt. Flying mostly on fly-by-wire autopilot, he could just kick back and enjoy the scene. A fleeting notion replaced the sadness he'd just felt. He had to smile by the very thought. "Look, Ma, no hands."

It was to be his last thought when the ground in and around him incinerated in a pulsing burst of unimaginable energy. He would never realize his dream of looking at the Rocky Mountains again. There was no brain matter left for thought.

VANDENBERG

After spending another enjoyable weekend with Alex at the Castle, Rhonda had just arrived back at Vandenberg. She was at her desk once more following another relaxing weekend spent with Alex. Ever since they started living together, her life had taken a turn for the best. Rhonda could hardly remember the time, or did not want to be reminded of the daily drudgery spent as career woman at the Mountain. Back then, she thought she'd have to spend the rest of her life alone. It was not until Alex came into the picture that she had begun to flourish.

Sitting in front of the monitor, checking her facial contours reflected on the screen, her mind was on such pleasant thoughts when the door to the office flew open with a bang. Popping his head through the door, short on breath, the operator yelled, "Lost Elmendorf!" His head disappeared as quickly as it'd appeared. Rhonda could hear him slam one door after another, informing everybody on the floor. To make things worse, rapidly blinking alert tags had popped up all over the monitor screens. The image alerts were all concentrated near Anchorage. Stored, maintained, and compared between previous and present imaging scans for the purpose of recording and plotting geospatial changes, GEO sources instantly plotted the marks.

After a few keystrokes on the desktop computer to rehome satellite cameras, the images immediately brought up Alaska region map. Authenticating the topographic changes where real, Rhonda could not help but exclaim, "I'll be damned. Entire base's gone." Comparing last and present scanned images, the fact that the airbase was there one second and gone the next only enhanced her fears. Rhonda kept zooming in and out from bird's eye to ground vision, hoping the original terrain would reappear. Unquestionably, Elmendorf, the town as well as the base, was gone, annihilated from the globe. Googling adjacent landscapes did not show any lateral destruction. "What would cause such devastation?" she asked herself. Then it struck her. She recalled the talks she and Alex had only recently on the subject matter. Her body froze. Her mouth became parched. She swallowed hard. "Alex was right. HAARP!"

A series of functional GEO satellites placed in orbit by the European Space Agency years ago were patiently scanning the globe along the longitudinal grid. Their original purpose was to pick up and record the rapidly waning ice shelves. Scientists became aware of the melting polar caps but were unable to follow the rate of the changes. Over the years, images taken from satellites showed the alarming rate with which polar ice was disappearing. To identify the possible causes, scientists were building bigger and better computer models while politicians keep insisting the warming trends were "due to cyclical climate changes." The headily debated causes on the topic were still up in the air. At this point, it was anybody's guess as to what was causing the rapid melting. Today, it was not glaciers plotted against the imaging lens, it was Elmendorf, one minute there, the next gone.

Rhonda reached for the receiver and punched the button to connect directly with the newly organized defense headquarters at the Presidio.

"Foster's office." It was a voice she immediately recognized as Tracy's.

"Hear about Alaska?" Rhonda shouted.

"All over the map," Tracy shot back. "Been trying to raise Anchorage, but all comm links are down."

"What's your best guess?" Rhonda wanted to know. If anyone knew anything it would be her.

Admitting to nothing, Tracy implied, "Something we've been working on." Regardless of Rhonda's personal relation with her dad, outside of Foster and the LLL scientists, the project didn't exist. She wasn't going to compromise that. Not to anyone, but the Capitol bearing down on her had to be pacified. "I'll handle the bureaucrat," she went on. "You take care of technical."

"What about surveillance?"

"Stay with it," Tracy ordered. "Until we hear otherwise. Jihad's primary suspect."

Hanging up the phone, Rhonda confirmed, "Got it."

PRESIDIO

Tracy switched to Intercom. "Meeting in five minutes," she announced then hurried for the command center. Taking a stand at the podium, she watched an apprehensive staff staring back at her. About to begin the briefing, she was being interrupted several times by local news reporters arriving and hastily setting up equipment. It gave her additional time to organize her thoughts for the ad hoc news conference. Aside from a nation already in turmoil, the topic she was about to disclose, she knew, would hit the media like a bombshell.

Foster, as head of the defense alliance for the Western Sector, until now had been able to suppress the technology that had suddenly surfaced into the open. Today, it was on the forefront of all major wire services. Where rumors had been circulating among the military about a super weapon for years, evidence substantiating the fact was practically nonexistent outside of DARPA, who'd developed it. Cloaked in secrecy under the guise of "black project," Tracy was preparing for the unavoidable onslaught ahead. She'd been volunteered by Foster to speak to the press.

The room was packed with reporters highly energized with pending questions. Holding up her palms, Tracy warded off the anticipated onslaught of questions. It was time for her to speak. She deferred all questions to later. "We may have a major crisis on our hands," Tracy started. It got their immediate attention. "This morning," she stated, "our satellites picked up an event of massive destruction in the Anchorage vicinity."

"Got family in Anchorage…Brother works there…Oh my God, my husband," were some immediate interruptions. Turned into a major defense sector after the collapse of the Pentagon, naturally many had relatives and friends there.

"We'll deal with that," Tracy consoled the concerned. "We believe," she went on, "that Elmendorf Air Force Base has been affected. At this time," she further informed the reporters, "until a ground team is on location, we have no confirmation other than marginal satellite images. Tactical advance teams have been dispatched but," she cautioned, "because of the remoteness, it will take some time for them to report."

"What about…" Questions were shot at her from all directions.

She deferred most of these. "I'll let you know as soon as I have more information."

She was anxious to terminate the press. "That's all I have at this time," she said, as she hastened back to the security of her office. One push on the implant connected her instantly with the Castle. "Specter," she whispered into the ether. "Need help."

Seconds later Specter's voice was on the air. "Go."

"Need damage report," Tracy demanded.

"Standby."

Although it'd been some time since they last talked, coded protocol was strictly observed over the ether. To keep the implant technology from possibly falling into the wrong hands, their personal liaison could never be compromised. Where Specter relayed real-time surveillance video data directly to Stinger, she, in turn, was able to act on the information accordingly. Response time between satellites and implant receiver only slightly lagged behind due to the turnaround distance and propagation delay. For all practical purposes, as long as the implant was active, her brain was connected with instant over-the-horizon images of any spot on the North American continent. She had visual.

The devastation Tracy perceived was horrific. Most of the Elmendorf AFB appeared to be in ruins. It seemed that most of air traffic control, tower, and support structures had been incinerated by the pulsed energy beam. Once sleek looking jet fighters and bombers parked on the tarmac and hangars were now only charred alloy skeletons. In just a few seconds, the entire fighter fleet had been eliminated. It appeared the enemy was in control.

Scanning over the damaged terrain made Tracy's blood boil. Personal, traumatized memories from the past surfaced. Distant clashes and conflicts with the enemy seeped into her mind, stirring far-off images. The full impact of suppressing emotions for so long became instant reality. She knew what had to be done. And it was up to her to deal with it. The time had come for which she'd been training and preparing, for so many years.

At the other end of the implant, the link turned quiet. Specter was waiting. He imagined the reason for her present silence. *After all*, he thought in the quiet of the Castle, *she's been persecuted too many times to let the assault go by unpunished.* He was ready to lend her his full support, no matter what her intentions might be. He finally broke the silence. "Your thoughts?"

"Will get back to you," was her only response.

From the tone of her voice Alex could only guess what might be in store for the enemy. He was glad to be on his daughter's side. He knew from recent years the damage she was capable of inflicting on an opponent when enraged. In this case, a still unknown adversary.

"Keep me posted," was Specter's final command.

FOX ONE

"Status," Madani demanded in his usual crusty voice. He was used to commanding with instant results. Interrupted by the blackout brought on by the particle bursts, he needed a link with the command base. He had ordered his electronics team upstairs to test and repair any damages.

"Link's working," someone finally called down.

Madani picked up the receiver with the first ring.

"Yusuf," the familiar voice demanded from the distant end. "State your conditions."

"Phase Two activated," Madani reported. "Target destroyed."

"Hold your position," the voice came back.

"Will do," he acknowledged, "what…"

"Standby one," Yusuf cut short. There was a halting pause followed by an imminent warning. "Falcon One," it warned. "Bogies coming your way."

"How many? How soon?"

"Standby." Several seconds of ETA calculations passed before the voice came back. "Raptor wing, count three…six minutes."

"Confirm incoming, six minutes."

Although he had not expected an immediate response from the enemy defense sector, Madani was prepared. He jumped into action by forcing the engineering team to cooperate. At gunpoint, he ordered, "Target points three. Pulse scans five hundred yards. Distance 110 miles. Altitude six thousand. Acquire."

Understandably, there was resistance from the engineers. Nobody made a move. They had been ordered to terminate people from their own ranks. Whatever the targets, they were friendly, but orders were specific. It was either them or the approaching targets. It was an individual decision each had to make, to live or to die. As is the case with most people, each tried to prolong their individual life. There was hardly ever an exception, unless someone stepped up to a heroic action. But that was usually reserved for the trained combatant. Engineers, on the other hand, were not trained for such tragic action. With support from the scientists, they were the operands behind the frontlines. Today, that had changed.

Madani made one more attempt to shake the team into action. Pointing his semi at the next individual's head, he demanded, "Alright, what's it gonna be?"

They knew it wasn't a bluff. They all had witnessed the brutal actions executed by the terrorists. The threatened engineer begged for his life. Another came to his rescue, promptly stepping up as spokesman. "What are the orders?"

Madani turned to wave the semi at the team. "Take your positions," he threatened one last time. "You…you…you, over there." Although with great reluctance, the team fell into rank.

"Let's crank it up," he commanded. "We don't have much time." Five precious minutes had passed with the standoff. The Rapture wing would be above unloading their loads in less than a minute, he calculated. He could feel the reluctance from his captured. Flanked by his lieutenants, firearms pushed against the reluctant engineers, the team was forced to their respective stations.

In rapid succession, once more, Madani called out the HAARP initiation process: "Primary power...Heater arrays...Ionic shield...Atomic collectors...Igniter coils...Beam refractors." The team rapidly fed the new coordinates into the computer system. The uplink command stream sought out and locked in on the fast approaching targets. With only seconds left before their destruction, he shouted the orders, "Fire!"

RAPTOR WING

With the wing approaching the perimeters of Fox One, the wingman's voice came alive. Donald "Donny" Allen sounded extremely urgent. "Elmendorf...Elmendorf...come in...come in," the wing lead yelled. He repeated the call again and again but there was no reply from home base. He sounded highly distressed when no response came forth. Waiting for orders, he finally yelled, "Target's in sight."

For the most costly and advanced craft in the Air Force arsenal, final orders were initiated and coordinated from base command. Pilots were only authorized to make decisions as a last resort. Most orders were initiated by computers and directly handed off to the wing lead. Humans could not think fast enough to guide the all-automated superior craft. Flight paths were initiated and calculated by onboard computers according to pre-programmed battle scenarios. Since computers were not capable yet of making rational decisions, the final mission could be overridden by base command based on dynamic target conditions.

Unaware at this time that the base had been obliterated minutes earlier, clutching the tactical radio in desperation, Donny yelled into the mic, "Dammit. You asleep?" There was no response from base. The Elmendorf transmitters remained silent. Unable to get mission confirmation from base, getting close to the target, he desperately selected a range of dedicated backup frequencies on the radio, "Nothing."

There was, however, new chatter on the ether. It was distant but audible, nevertheless. The voices seemed to be initiated by HAM operators located on the Pacific coast handing off current events. Tuned in on the sound, he finally made out the words, "Elmendorf destroyed." He was dumbfounded. "Base's gone? You hear that," he queried his wingman.

"Sure did," was the response. "What'd we do?"

Flying in tight formation only feet apart, the wing was almost on top of the base. "Guess it's up to me now," he muttered. "Open bomb bays." Not having any info on depths or shielding for the underground facility, he needed a visual pass to acquire terrain and target. The plan was to drop the load in sequential succession directly onto the plotted target point. The final pass registered with the onboard laser guidance system, getting a precise fix on the ground target. Newly recruited pilots, as his wingmen were, it would be their first active combat mission in these marvelous craft. There was elated excitement from his wing. With the exorbitant cost involved in sophisticated weaponry, it wasn't every day a pilot had the opportunity to drop a bunker buster in real time.

Donny's fingers gently moved the joystick for a left bank. The craft instantly responded. Body tightly strapped into the seat, he felt the pressurize flight suit counter the G forces. With his head slightly tilted into the bank, he spotted something from above. At first puzzled, his face contorted into a grotesque mask from what he'd identified. Puzzled for an instant, he knew it wasn't a laser aimed at him. It was something much fierce. It was pure energy charged with pulsed particles.

It started as a tiny speck in the upper atmosphere. From there, it rapidly increased into a fiery energy beam headed his way. Combat trained as he was, he quickly reacted, but not in time. The beam was traveling at light speed. It was too fast even for his action-trained brain. He cussed in silence as he realized his life would be cut short from an unlived future that could have been, but was erased an instant later.

The HAARP beam lasted only a fraction of a second before it sought out the next target for more destruction. It'd burned a hole straight through the craft, which might have survived for an emergency landing, if it wasn't for the immense heat shooting through the fuselage. The craft acted as a perfect fuse, in turn igniting the armed payload securely mounted in the craft's belly. The resultant force was an explosion tearing painstakingly-fitted rivets violently from their anchors, allowing every piece of structure to explode outward in a brilliant fireball at lightning speed, killing everything in its path of destruction.

The end result was atomic fusion on the molecular level, incinerating all solid matter into pure energy. Unlike a nuclear blast, this force left no lingering radiation to harm nature and left no traces of evidence for a likely identification.

HAARP,[41] the ultimate weapon, was at work. It struck effectively, traceless, clean, and perfect for its makers. Problem was, it was in the wrong hands.

---

[41] HAARP – By design, the heart of the HAARP system was its transmitter array fed by a cluster of large power generators creating billions of watts of power. The limitation, however, was that it was fixed, pointing in only one direction, up. Although the system produced immense power, it did not have the flexibility needed as a weapon. The conversion plan conceived by Hammad entailed numerous aspects that needed to be achieved in a very short timeframe. According to the scientists he solicited, numerous segments had been reworked, including the antenna array, waveguide system, microwave-generated frequencies, beam deflectors, telemetry processing, target acquisition, and computer software, in creating the ultimate weapon for the Serpent.

ISS

The strobe light effects triggered earlier by Dieter Fuchs in Columbus, were nauseating. The sound was deafening. Liz, aided by Walsh and Kubalev with access to the central computer system in Harmony, the ISS primary module, was looking for the source of the alarm. "Let me." Kubalev insisted on handling computer inputs. They decided to let the Russian cosmonaut operate the computers. It'd take an expert to localize any authorized or unauthorized activity on the central control system. It'd free up Liz, Walsh, and Nagata to defend the space station.

It did not take long for Kubalev to track the source of the initial alert. It seemed to have come from the European space lab. "Columbus," he readily identified the source. Kubalev was able to silence the alert condition.

Liz was already headed for the exit when the insane alarms turned off. "I'll check it out."

With Hiroshi floating closely behind her, Kenny called after her. "Wait up."

Shaking her head at Kenny, Liz insisted, "You stay. Gotta protect Kubalev."

There was always a chance the Jihad crew would free itself. One only had to apply ingenuity to find a way out of an involuntary confinement. Liz knew that too well. Shoving her weightless body expertly along the main passageway, she could see the European lab just ahead. She cautiously made her way to the capsule. There was no porthole to see inside. She yelled into the headset mic, "Dieter," and kept banging on the entrance gate. "Open up!" Frequency transmitted in the capsule or passageways did not carry very far.

There was no response. Switching the headset to main, she called out, "Andrei, what's the status with Columbus?"

"No activity," the computers indicated.

"Entrance's blocked," she reported back at him. There was one other way in. Liz was faced with another spacewalk to make her way to Canadarm-2 once more. Extending the hydraulic arm would carry her to the external payload hatch. But this time she knew what to expect. With help from Kenny, this time slipping into the suit proved effortless. Five minutes later she was by the exit.

The Canadarm-2 platform was already waiting for her at the Harmony node, her transfer station. Again, she used the interlocking compression system to exit into space. Though damaged with pressure leaks, the compressors were still functioning. Within seconds, the chamber was filled. It emptied just as quickly after pushing the activation buttons. The exit port opened. Two testing steps brought her body into space. Again, as with her first spacewalk, Liz halted momentarily. Another cycle of daytime had just begun. Her eyes took a few seconds to adjust to the brightness of space. A slight push on the Harmony frame propelled her body the short distance to the robotic arm. Clinging to the platform, again, Liz was overwhelmed once more by the infinite view into deep space.

This time, though in better control, a feeling of euphoria still came over her. She was overcome by space sickness once more. Years of simulation testing did not compare with the actual experience. It was overwhelming. Her eyes were fixed on distant Earth slowly scanning across her vision. She could almost reach out and touch precious Earth. One push away from the robot arm and her body would propel toward the blue planet. It'd be sheer ecstasy. In her present state, similar to envisioning a mirage, she suddenly realized her mind was playing tricks with her. Her body would shoot by the planet, only to end up floating into eternity.

A faint voice was drilling into her brain. "Liz," it whispered. "You okay?" From inside, Walsh remotely had moved the robot into position. He sensed something was wrong. She would not respond. "Liz," he called to get her attention again. "You alright?"

"Fine," she finally answered after being reminded of her present mission. "Just enjoying the sight."

"Open the hatch." He had manipulated the robotic arm close to the Columbus hatch.

"I'm on it." Normally the space shuttle would dock here, at the European service module she was now facing. With a twist on the external entry lever she opened the hatch, allowing her entrance to the module. Another twist on the inside shut the hatch. Inside, in the safety of the space station once more, a few overhead pulls brought her into the Columbus module. Landing by the porthole, Liz spotted Dieter Fuchs cowering at the far end of the lab. Banging on the glass immediately got his attention. With a frightened look on his face, he fiercely shook the head. It was an urgent warning for her not to enter the module. Liz gestured at her headset. He responded by moving to the console controls. There, he reached for the radio receiver to take her call.

"Nein…Nein…Nein," he kept insisting over and over about her entering the module. "Giftstoffe in der Luft."

Liz knew enough German to realize the danger of poisonous substances in the air. From her position, she could clearly make out the mess in the module. The jolt the station took when the weapon was initiated must have affected the lab experiment. "Let me in," she insisted. "I can help." How, she did not know. But, from her experience with laboratory experiments, she knew there was usually a means to neutralize toxic agents. All she needed was to get her hands on the proper agent. Every lab had the means to cope with emergencies, no matter how lethal.

Entering would expose her to the same substance. But she was protected by the suit, which would prevent her from direct contact with the lethal substance. "I can help," she kept insisting. It took forever for him to be persuaded. Dieter moved closer to the entrance hatch. "Finally," she muttered into the headset, letting Walsh, who was intently listening, know he was about to cooperate. Following more pleading, he finally opened the hatch. Liz faced a shaken Dieter. From the expression on his face she knew there was little hope to save his life but she wouldn't let on to it. With encouraging gestures, she pulled him toward the lab table. His breathing was laborious. His speech was impaired as well. The poison must have damaged his lungs, throat, and esophagus.

Searching frantically for the cause, Liz tried to identify the substance to which he had been exposed. Facing the unfortunate victim, she yelled, "Wo ist das serum?"

After he realized there might be a slight chance of hope in saving his life, he desperately motioned at the object floating through the capsule. "Dort." Liz moved to the object Dieter had indicated and gently reached for the broken Petri dish. Reading the letters almost stopped her heart. Printed in bold lettering was a biological agent she had heard of but never thought to ever face in real life. "Ebola!"

Liz recollected the many conversations she had with her dad. It was on more than one occasion that the topic of biological warfare came up. At the time, when she was young and inexperienced, the severity of the topic had not sunk in. It was only later, at Stanford where she studied nuclear science and other majors, when the almost forgotten memories had surfaced to the forefront. Even now it was difficult for her to grasp what science conjured up in the many laboratories spread through the globe. What she faced was the deadliest of all deadly viruses created by man. It was not only the most lethal living organism ever discovered. It had also been genetically manipulated and altered to be the ultimate weapon of mass destruction for man and animal. Locked away and kept classified in the bowels of USAMRIID,[42] the government's principal research institute at Fort Detrick, MD, this lethal substance should have been destroyed years ago. The thought alone of anyone using the substance as weapon infuriated her to the utmost.

She had been reflecting on the past way too much. Liz suddenly realized Dieter was closing in on her. "Dieter," she called out. "Was machst du?" Backing up, her hands went up to rebuff him. Although she felt immediate remorse, she could not afford to let him get close or even touch her. There was panic in his eyes. "Listen closely," she said. "I will come back for you. I need you to keep calm. Do you understand?"

He reluctantly backed off. He shot her a quick nod that he understood. She asked, "Is there an antidote on board?" He did not answer. His eyes held steady on hers. They were only filled by a silently pleading. All he did was shrug his shoulders.

"Stay back," she ordered.

Liz felt deep compassion for the young man. On his first assignment in space, his life was only beginning. If there was no antiserum on board to counter the lethal disease, his days would be running out shortly. As far as she knew, there was no cure against Ebola. She could only hope that Fort Detrick had the foresight to develop and maintain an antiserum. If not, it would be the perfect weapon. "God help us," she prayed at the thought.

On exiting, Liz hurried directly for Tranquility to scrub her spacesuit, if only with water and liquid soap, infected in the contaminated lab. She needed information on the virus, and fast.

---

[42] USAMRIID – U.S. Army Medical Research Institute of Infectious Diseases. With four Bio-safety levels, it is the largest containment laboratory in the United States. Once a biological warfare and bio-weapons facility, today, it is mostly used for infectious diseases research such as Ebola, and newly emerging viruses.

SACRAMENTO

"Gentlemen...Gentlemen," George Wilmot, pleaded for the third time. "Order...order please." He was highly annoyed at the conduct of the panel members. "Whatever happened to respect and discipline in this country," he muttered at his aide while courteously watching the selfish behavior displayed by his staff. Today was not the time. The nation was under attack. He needed immediate action. Pounding his fist on the table to emphasize his frustration level, he finally shouted, "Silence!" That gained him attention. The room finally calmed.

Today's emergency panel was called to session by the national security advisor, Henry "Hank" Foster, who was hosting the panel. Org heads, meeting at the presidential situation room, were the principle forum to host the National Security Council. Also attending were the heads of state, defense, central intelligence, the Chief of Staff, and the White House counsel. Under normal conditions, additional members were called to represent foreign affairs, foreign intelligence, the attorney general, the secretary of treasury, and law enforcement, but today public and international affairs were not given much consideration for the emergency at hand. Besides, most offices had been drastically scaled down since the attack on the nation. Many of the previous offices had been either eliminated or abandoned.

Focus today was entirely centered on national defense and what to do in case of an attack on the nation's infrastructure. To have an entire military base wiped out was bad enough. At this point, nobody had an idea for what might follow, but all indications pointed at more trouble on the horizon. "Hank," the president gestured, "you've got the floor."

General Foster had arrived minutes earlier. It'd taken him a couple of hours to get there from the Presidio, his customary office. The Bay Bridge, already under construction for two years, would take at least another three to complete. For now, he had to take a ferry across the Bay into Oakland to get to the mainland, and then it was another hour by road to Sacramento. "We assume," he began the deliberation, "that Jihad's behind yesterday's attack. We received reports from the ISS, that the space station was used as reflective platform to redirect and focus the HAARP energy beam on selective ground stations."

"What?" The outburst came from the Chief of Staff. It was too incredible to think the highly classified research facility was in control of the enemy. "Impossible." Infuriated, his eyes sought out the head of National Security, screaming at him, "How could you let this happen?"

"No Intel," was his short and defensive reply.

"What makes you so sure it's Jihad?" the White House counsel quickly intervened. They all knew the limited state the nation's defenses were in. To avoid a shouting match, he refocused on the emergency at hand. "It could be Al Qaeda."[43]

---

[43] Jihad (Islamic struggle or Holy War) – is the term used relating to the use of physical force in defense of Muslims against oppression and transgression by the enemies of Allah, Islam and Muslims.

Al-Qaeda, (The Base) – is thought to have been established by Osama bin Laden. Where it was a loosely held network of terrorists, it gained recognition with the attacks on the World Trade towers. Although, there were

"Believe me," Foster insisted. "It's Jihad."

"I don't like to point fingers," George Wilmot indicated.

"With due respect, sir," Foster was adamant, "it's diplomacy and political correctness that's got us into this mess in first place. I'm sick and tired of pussyfooting around the true issues. Let's call it for what it is. There are too many terrorist factions already hiding under the cloak of Al Qaeda."

"What's the latest statistics on that?" the president wanted to know.

The director for intelligence, CIA, jumped in. "Latest figures show 150 hostile factions operating in various nations. We, the U.S.," he explained, "identified and carry 50 factions on our list. Hell, our nation's number one on the terrorist hit list from Iran."

"What?" The news just heard caused quite a stir among the politicians. Outbursts such as "Crazy…stupid…bastards," echoed through the hall. The fact that it was, could easily be proven.

"Never mind," the president called out. "Let's get back on track. Do we have any claims or demands yet?"

"Nothing so far."

"Could be good news?"

"Not likely," Hank replied. "According to the latest finds," he went on, "Jihad has expanded operations across a number of Islamic nations throughout the African continent, but, I must warn you," he emphasized, "that we haven't much Intel on any of their bases.

"It appears," he further explained. "that Jihad, over the last couple of years, has been able to increase their militant strength into a sizable force. At this time, we don't know their strength or locations, because we still don't have operational satellites."

"What's the delay?" the president asked.

"Budgets," the White House counsel cut in.

"Who's here from the accounting office?" Looking around the table, he didn't recognize any representative from that office. "Anybody? Why weren't they notified?"

"Budget shouldn't be the consideration in a national crisis," the counsel defended.

"You're right," the president agreed. "Let's not waste time with bickering. Hank?"

"Doesn't look good," Foster responded in his usual abrasive but assertive mannerism. "As long as we don't have global coverage," he firmly stated, "we are vulnerable on all fronts." Hank Foster was a man of few words. He'd grown out of the combatant environment serving mostly fighting fronts where time was critical and a commander gave orders.

"Go on."

"Our communication infrastructure could be in danger again," he cautioned, "not to mention the power grid. Once that shuts down, it'll affect power, utilities, and all industries and services. You know the score. Just ask people out east."

"Badlands?"

---

many terrorist groups worldwide sprouting up from local and regional conflicts such as ISIS, Taliban, Mujahideen, al Qaeda is generally the term used to identify Muslim based revolutionary activities.

"Among others. We've all lived it a few years back."

"How likely is the threat?" the president asked. "What's our SIOP status?"

"Haven't even made any attempts to evaluate," the Chief of Staff cut in. "Don't have a plan."

"What's the problem? Be more specific." The president was highly concerned for a possible attack on the nation whether initiated by jihad, al Qaeda, or any other terrorist group.

"Doesn't work," was the harsh response. When the Single Integrated Operations Plan was put in effect, it was thought of as an all-encompassing solution to an emergency front. They were wrong. When tested, it proved to be littered with holes. The SIOP had been developed decades ago. It'd been refined over and over to cope with national emergencies of this nature but the world was rapidly changing. And so were the threats.

Enforced by the National Guard or military defense forces and involving anything from a biological attack to military invasion and natural disaster, the SIOP spelled out every single step the government must take in case of an emergency. But every test so far had failed miserably. The problems were always the same: immense traffic congestions, resistance by the citizens against abandoning their homes, logistics support failure—including food supplies—medical, emergency, and many more irresolvable issues when trying to move the masses out of cities.

"Any recommendations?" George Wilmot demanded. There were none. "How about you?" he demanded, targeting the chairman, the Chief of Staff.

"What about me?" It was not the friendliest of replies.

"Defense...surveillance...satellites?"

Everybody on the table already knew his response. "I don't have all the answers. We can only try our best with the resources we have." The cost of building new and improved satellites was enormous, not to mention incorporating EMP protection into computers, communication, and telecom assets. "We are not prepared," he stated, "to fend off any major assault on the nation."

"What're our weak points?" the Secretary of State interrupted.

Foster stepped up to address the audience. "I'll give you the most likely scenario." He then reached for the laser pointer and ordered the operator to bring up the emergency action procedures on the screen. In rapid succession, the projector painted the nation's communication grid, overlaying the newly constructed New Republic map. "Most likely attack point will take place from the Atlantic Coast. Since that sector is the most disorganized, we are most vulnerable there. New York City for sure, Chicago, perhaps, Washington DC is chaotic. Enemy's been pushing on those border lines. To make things worse," he further iterated, "incident reports indicate a major push from Arabian nations from across the Atlantic. As you know," he emphasized, "we have virtually no effective defenses there."

"What about the subs, the Patriots?"

"Subs are ineffective. We've got no communication means to contact them. Word has it the entire fleet's been taken over by NATO, Europe."

"Meaning?"

"We're defenseless from across the oceans."

"What about the Patriots?"

"Created a pretty effective borderline along the Mississippi. Guy named Scott Brooks' holding up defenses."

"Hear he's pretty brutal."

"You're not kiddin'." Foster took a pause then underlined the statement. "Glad he's on our side. I'll let him take care of the eastern sector. Rest of the nation, with satellites out…God only knows."

"Foster," the president cut in. He was getting frustrated with nothing but complaints. "Suggestions?"

"Okay, folks." Hank was prepared to educate the assembly on how bad things really were. He had to shake them out of their sheltered environment. What they did not know was knowledge he had of the outside world. It was a world banded against what was left of the fractured United States.

"Fact Number One: Jihad infiltrated ISS. As far as I know," he stated, "they're in complete control. Hell, you all witnessed Elmendorf's destruction."

"Fact Number Two: Jihad's taken control of the Eastern Seaboard. For all practical purposes, the whole damned sector's Muslim settlements. Come from far reaches of the globe to establish footing on American soil. Industry, infrastructure, transportation, power grid, communication, all under foreign control. Big Apple's their favorite spot for shopping and entertainment."

"Who's behind the push? Who's organizing it all?" There were rumors to the fact, but Wilmot wanted it out on the open.

"Don't have a confirmed identity. Could be the Serpent. Could be somebody new. Don't know at this time. Been following western ideals. "Clarify ideals," Wilmot interrupted. "Keeping religion segregated from politics, seems like," Foster explained. "Still have a long way to go aligning the rest of their secular factions. But," he emphasized, "they're taking over the globe in big strides."

"Fact Number Three: With our satellites aging and falling from the sky, our defense is virtually nonexistent. Other than reaching over the Pacific, we have no defense system. And," he stressed, "with the ISS fallen into enemy hands, our advanced warning shield has turned ineffective."

"What about you? Where'd you get information?" It was the Secretary of State demanding an answer.

"Classified!"

"Bullshit that!"

Foster's face scanned over the room. He made it a point to capture the eyes of all of the attendees. "What am I supposed to do without a budget?" He sought out the face of the specific complainant. "You haven't exactly kept up with collecting taxes," he reprimanded the top executives present, "have you…any of you." His face turned towards the president who acknowledged with a short nod of the head.

"That all?" someone shouted above grumbled and unhappy outbursts.

"It's only the major issues. There're many more. Just ask your president." Not addressing the head of state by full title was not meant as an insult. Everybody knew it. The newly formed government was much more informal. Wilmot wanted it this way. It gave him direct access to his ever-grumbling department heads. Aside from that, the present Capitol facility would not sustain an increase in staff or expanded organization.

Without a currency in place, no other nation was extending any credit to aid his nation. The once revered U.S.A. had, in an instant, turned into a third-world nation.

"When's it going to end?" one functionary asked.

"As soon as we get support from some sympathetic nation," Wilmot explained. "For now," he stressed, "we're on our own." He stood up to adjourn the assembly, then approached the general. "You going to stay for dinner?"

"If you insist." He took the luxury to accept, knowing his defense perimeters were in very capable hands with Tracy at the Presidio, and Rhonda at Vandenberg.

"I insist."

Foster only knew too well Wilmot was trying to pump him for information. After a well served dinner accompanied by wine and after-dinner brandy, information slipped too frequently from lose lips and mellowed minds.

WORLD COUNCIL

Located at the south end of Manhattan, the skies were clear and smog free around the U.N. complex this morning. It used to not always be this way. There had been a time when the area was covered feet deep in incinerated dust and debris from the collapse of the World Trade Center. It had taken years to clean up the city and to rebuild. Many debates waged before the U.N. council to make a decision where the new headquarters should be located. In spite of the many invitations submitted for locations such as Singapore, London, and Paris, the final choice had been New York once more. The rationale was simple. Everybody in the world was drawn to what used to be the hub of trade and commerce with the European world. People just liked to be at this once thriving metropolis.

The usual blue layer of suet and haze found in a mega city was absent. Since the collapse of the nation, there was hardly any fuel left for personal use. One had to know somebody or pay exorbitant costs to obtain this precious commodity. Gasoline, the limited production there was had been severely rationed to government and emergency vehicles. For the same reason, street traffic was near to none existing. Today, a special session was called early in the morning by the head of the U.N. Daylight already had broken, but for many members it was considered the middle of the night since they had gone to sleep only a few hours ago. Entertaining, socializing, and partying kept many members up all hours of the night. Political networking was first and foremost on the collective agenda. For most part, it was this environment where global resolutions were made.

Trying to establish calm and order in today's emergency session, Sanjid Rahman, general secretary for the United Nations, was swinging the gavel. "Order…Order please." Following yesterday's mysterious events in Alaska, the assembly went into emergency session. The nations present demanded answers. Accusations were flying back and forth, mostly directed at the Western Sector of what used to be the United States of America. Since the attack had taken place on American soil, it was only too convenient to pointing fingers in that direction. Still unexplained was a logical reason not yet identified. In contrast to past conservatively quiet sessions, today was bedlam. Swinging the gavel violently again and again, shouting from the top of his voice, "Order," he finally achieved some attention. Minutes later, the assembly finally calmed down enough for him to commence.

Composed, he began, "I have called today's emergency session to determine the cause of yesterday's incident in which an entire Air Force installation on American soil was obliterated." He went on to describe as many details as he could, received from news clips from local and international wire services. Speculations, as usual, were already flying rampant, generated by the usual conspirators: cyber fanatics, warmongers, and antagonists of all kinds. The rumors cast were thriving while governments kept silent.

He made an attempt to seek out the American council members, but most of their seats were vacated. Only one representative had made it to the assembly. He had missed the earlier warning call from his office and showed up by mistake. It was he that, at present, had to take the brunt of the accusations. "What is your position?" Sanjid Rahman demanded from the assembly head, directly seated across the conference table.

Leaning back to distance himself from more verbal onslaughts, the head of the American council stated, "We have no comments at this time." He left the flourishing speculations up to each member, and with good reason. He was clueless. Stalling for time, he was sweating it out until his people sorted things out. Yesterday's deliberate hostile act came as a surprise to him and his nation. The assembly continued throughout the day without as much as a simple resolution. At the end, members left utterly frustrated to rejoin the next day.

PALM JUMEIRAH

In his lofty magnificent mansion fronting the sandy beaches on the Persian Gulf, Hasan Hammad was leaning against the ornamentally designed balcony deck. Yusuf was nearby, beaming with joy. Obviously relieved, Hammad glowed at his trusted lieutenant. "Phase One accomplished." Yusuf had flown in the night before from the Sudan base to brief his commander. Depending on each other ever more over the past years, cultivating their friendship, they had been drawn even closer. A bond of trust had developed between the two. They had become a unit with an energy completely focused on the missions ahead. Nothing else mattered. Yesterday's surprise attack initiating Phase Two had been enormously successful. From indications carried by the news services, the attack came as complete surprise to the western world. Rumors and assumptions were prolific. Many nations were clueless as to what had transpired. The North American continent and its border allies were the only ones with an inkling of what had transpired. But only a closely-knit group of scientists knew the real truth.

"I think our success calls for celebration," Hasan suggested. "What do you think?"

Yusuf was slightly taken aback by the very idea. "I am not used to celebrating." He hadn't celebrated an occasion as far back as he could remember. His life had been solely dedicated to the cause, the Islamic cause, where there had been no room for such frivolous notions. Sure, there were the wealthy Emirates everyone knew about, taking junkets to cosmopolitan cities like Paris and London for unlimited spending trips, but as a whole, the Arabic nation and general population was kept poor. Whether achieved through obedience or discipline, it did not matter. The old adage, "Keep 'em pregnant and barefooted," still held true in the society. It was this purity he had been fighting for. He was a true Islam believer, follower of the Koran—disciple to the one and only Prophet, Muhammad.

Hammad gently pulled him along by the sleeve and suggested, "Come, I'll show you." In big strides, they descended through the lofty abode, headed for the basement storage. On entering, he indicated the rack-mounted surfboards neatly stacked against the wall. Directing Yusuf to an assortment of Mistral Racers, he suggested, "Take your pick." The sight of these streamlined sporting objects invoked distant, but fond memories in Yusuf. They reminded him of his college days filled with fun windsurfing California's beaches. Long Beach, Laguna Beach, Sunset Beach were still vividly on his mind. Ever since windsurfing was introduced among the young and fearless, he had been an avid windsurfer. It was a sport dependent on wind, just as demanding as surfing the waves on Hawaii's North Shores.

It took only minutes to assemble the gear, don a wetsuit, and rack up the sail. Hammad took the lead. With his board clutched under one arm, he was the first to the beach. His friend hastened after him. As soon as the board touched water Yusuf could feel the wind press against the seven-meter, tailored fabric. Tightly holding onto the boom, reining in the sail, he held on as the rig accelerated rapidly at an ever-increasing speed. Scanning the horizon from behind a pair of fashionable shades, he could make out busy sea traffic ahead. The azure blue tint of the shallow Persian waters perfectly blended in with the cloudless sky. Reaching for the harness, he hooked up to the boom and leisurely leaned back to enjoy wind, water, and speed, the ultimate in pleasure for a surfer.

Prevalent monsoons at these waters for most of the year generated only shallow rolling waves with the occasional white-tipped, foamy crests. The cooling spray against the skin was a thrill for any wave rider. Thankful to be so alive, Yusuf yelled at his leader, yards ahead, "Heaven on Earth!" Today, here and now, life was truly paradise. He finally understood what his friend had been trying to tell him for years. "Paradise is not the afterlife. Paradise is on Earth. You only have to find it. If not, then you create it."

After hours of riding the waves, the evening was slowly breaking. Completely exhausted, they arrived back at the mansion. With colors changing from yellow to orange and bright red, growing enormously in size just prior to sinking beyond the calming waters of the gulf, the sun was just setting in the west. Once the remnants of brilliance sank beneath the horizon, nightfall came on quickly in the tropical region. It was a time where land and water temperatures became balanced. The air came to a rest. Construction activities from a financial boom experienced in recent years shut down for the day. Hidden sounds became audible for a brief span until the night's traffic noises picked up.

It held true for the two shadowy figures lingering in the twilight, silently overlooking a sea of luxuriously illuminated domiciles and pleasure yachts. It was a place for the rich, the famous, and the not so famous. Although his body had been driven almost into exhaustion from the day's surfing, Hasan's mind was very much awake. He was an action man, equally attuned to the body as well as the mind.

Propped leisurely against the rail of the balcony for the second time, Yusuf demanded, "What's the next move?" He waited minutes for a response.

Hammad had been contemplating in silence for how much he should, and how much he could, divulge from The Plan—*His* Plan.

He carefully calculated his next words. "We must," he began with halted deliberation, "change the fundamental doctrine for our cause."

Yusuf instantly became alert. "What do you mean?" He did not like the unexpected.

With unwavering determination, Hammad insisted, "Let me finish." He had been appraising the proper time to tell him, and the world. He knew quite well that there would be resistance, harsh resistance. It would be a true measure for their friendship. Not only would there be immense opposition from his lifelong friend, but public outcry was sure to follow. The Prophet's devout followers' principles would be tested. There would be rage through the Islamic nations. Even under ideal conditions, it would be almost impossible to align Arabic nations with new principles in secular practices. But it had to be this way. Otherwise, the entire Jihad cause would be in vain. It was of utmost importance; Yusuf would have to understand. For this, Hasan had to pick the right timing to disclose his doctrine.

"We must," he picked up the thread, "integrate democracy into the Islamic way." As expected, the reaction from his close friend and devoted soldier was fierce. As soon as the most detested word in the Muslim language "democracy" left his lips, a completely infuriated Yusuf abruptly turned and stormed from the balcony spitting out one word, "Traitor!"

"Hear me out," Hammad yelling after him, demanded.

"Traitor," Yusuf vehemently insisted. "How can you do this?"

It was a reaction that demonstrated the conviction of a passionate soldier. Outcries from the nation would be just as infuriating, he realized, perhaps even more violent. There would be riots. In a calming tone of voice, he said, "Let me explain." He then carefully evaluated each word. "I love you like a brother but," he went on, "there are certain measures necessary I cannot do alone." He was searching for a reaction in Yusuf's face. "I need your help."

"I don't want any part in any *democracy*," Yusuf emphatically insisted. "I despise everything it stands for. I will never tolerate and subscribe to the 'Infidel's Society.'"

Again, rage was building up in the face of this once devout soldier. Seeing such a negative reaction from his closest friend gave him a true sense of what was in store once he released his doctrine to the nation. He carefully selected the next words. "We must forge ahead together."

Hammad could not afford to lose his most dedicated and trusted disciple. Keeping a wary eye on his friend, he remained quiet for some time to calm the tension, then deliberately explained his reasoning. With one hand, gently on Yusuf's shoulder he sketched out the basic foundation of The Plan. With great details, he illustrated the most prominent particulars, ranging from fundamental Islamic philosophy imprinted in the Koran to the necessary execution of new policies that must be initiated and put in place. The entire success hinged on the surprise attempt of Phase Two. It was the plan that would subsequently pave the way for Phase Three. The timing was right. The time was now. He had to prepare his lieutenants for total conviction. He had to prepare a nation to break long practiced traditions. He was changing the course of history.

First off, Hammad had to convince his lieutenants that the past could not meet the modern changes of time. Life was too demanding for inherited customs, culture and beliefs. Traditional life, trade, and commerce put too much of a burden on his people. For that, the current conditions and timing for global change and confusion could not be more perfect. His nation was already gaining momentum. Under his leadership implementing a new order, he'd see to it that under the rules of Islam, the new world would be a world of great wealth and prosperity. It would be his world, his globe, his planet. The mechanics were already in motion. All he needed now was to convince his people and gain unwavering support from his forces. But, there was something else more pressing at the moment.

"Get ready for departure," he ordered a somewhat surprised Yusuf the following morning.

"Where?"

"China."

Yusuf did not question his leader any further. After the evening before, he did not want another argument on his hands that might lead into a personal battle. He was still not completely convinced about his leader's political intentions for his much beloved nation, Islam.

BEIJING REPUBLIC OF CHINA

At first, Hui Wong, party secretary, had been very upset after being so rudely awakened in this early morning hour and vowed disciplinary action to whomever was responsible. Labeled "Classified" in bright red lettering, titled "Urgent," it had been delivered by the defense ministry very early this morning. Rubbing his bleary eyes still veiled from sleep, he couldn't remember the last time he had been so rudely awakened from the deserving sleep a person of his age required. Under normal circumstances he had several levels of subordinates that usually handled the daily political affairs. Unlike many other nations, the chain of command protocol in the People's Republic was strictly enforced, followed by the book. Here, rules and discipline were still very much imposed and respected.

But reading the brief handed by his personal assistant somewhat calmed his edgy nerves. After a cup of Oolong, his mind was slowly clearing up. What he read did not make sense at all. There must have been a mistake in the clarity of the intelligence. Someone in the ministry should have been aware of unusual events taking place in Alaska. After all, his naval fleet stationed around the arctic waters was to be aware of the Americans and their military activities. He had his reasons for staying alert. Rumors had reached the Chinese homeland recently of unusual atmospheric events taking place, defying every explanation by his scientific community. In spite of Chinese intelligence and surveillance, nothing had been uncovered that would constitute suspicious activities by the Western Sector and its allies. Dismayed at getting caught unaware by the Americans, he muttered in anger, "We have become complacent. Where are our agents?"

China was very aware of the American capability to design and develop innovative technologies, but from all reports received, their combined economic and military efforts, at this time, were geared toward replacing disabled communications and utilities knocked out by North Korea and Jihad years prior.

Rereading the brief several times over still did not make much sense. He kept staring at the bizarre words printed on this morning's report.

"...Late yesterday, as reported by UPI and other international news agencies, an unusual occurrence transpired in the southeastern region of the Alaskan territory. It appears that one of its strategic defense positions has been obliterated by some as of yet unidentified weapon or system. The defense ministry is currently investigating this bizarre and possible hostile act. Satellite surveillance has confirmed the alleged data.

"The former United Stated and the United Nations have no comments on the situation. Further reports will be forthcoming as soon as they become available."

"Who delivered this?" he demanded.

"Special envoy," he was informed. "Requesting your presence at Party Headquarters."

"General Assembly," Hui Wong, ordered his personal assistant. "Now."

"Yes, Mister Secretary," the assistant replied, then rushed out of the office to inform the ministers of the emergency session.

It took more than thirty minutes for all ministry heads of state to arrive. In the meantime, Hui Wong took the time to study the faces seated directly across from him. Impeccably dressed, clean shaven, but hardened in bearing and posture, he scrutinized their cultural heritage. *Arabic,* he concluded. *This could be interesting,* he thought in silence. The last party members were finally seated. He was dying to hear what the visitors had to say.

With a gesture of his hand, he invited the apparent leader of the visitors to open the session. "What is it you desire?" he demanded. The spokesperson introduced himself as Hasan Hammad, representing the Arab nation. "We have come," he opened the session, "with intentions for creating an Arabic-Sino axis."

Immediately, the sound levels in the assembly hall increased by several magnitudes. Disregarding the visitors, dialogues between the members were flying. Personal outbursts such as, "Ridiculous, preposterous, idiotic, outrageous," uttered in Chinese, could be heard across the table.

His aging body poised back in the lavishly upholstered office chair, Hui Wong waited for the leader to continue. It became obvious to him that the panel's reaction presented a great challenge to the visitors. That in itself was not unusual. It was not every day that a radical movement asked for what could be considered an act of war by the rest of the world. What was unusual and extremely bizarre was the fact that the request was made by an unknown representative of the Saudi Arabian kingdom. The kingdom, until now, had been pretty much left to its own affairs. There were reasons for that. Reasons that spelled out "Oil."

Although the name Hammad immediately struck an accord within his memory reaches as the leader of the Jihad faction, he had never regarded their actions as a direct threat to his nation. Today might prove otherwise. Although most wire services about foreign terrorist activities were heavily censored in his nation, news reports eventually leaked in over the prolific Internet. Just the thought of this spider web made his blood boil. Because of it, much of the ancient Chinese heritage was rapidly disintegrating.

With gavel in hand, pounding the table to regain composure, the secretary demanded, "Quiet, please. Let the emissary speak their grounds."

"Yesterday," the visitor announced, "we took hostage what was formerly the United States of America." The leader appeared to enjoy the bedlam that followed. The scene that followed pretty much looked like an anthill colony suddenly disturbed by some invading horde. It took several minutes of gavel swinging and threatening shouts of disciplinary action to finally quiet the assembly.

Like his ministers, the secretary was outraged. "What on Earth are your demands?" He was undecided about whether to detain these preposterous visitors or just have them thrown out of his country. He had never regarded the Arabic nations as equal to the eastern and western worlds and hearing the idiotic announcement was unorthodox, to say the least.

"We seek only one demand," the leader mandated from the agitated assembly, "and that is economic equality and cultural acceptance by your nation."

"What gives you the authority to demand such ludicrous declaration?"

"Our power was demonstrated yesterday over Alaska." Again, the Chinese assembly went wild with speculations. "We have," the foreign leader proceeded, "in our possession, the most advanced weapon system ever devised. It is a weapon much more powerful than all the nuclear arsenals in your possession." As before, the chairman watched him savor the moment of perplexity and confusion once more. The declaration finally revealed the true purpose of the visitors. It was an act of hostility not experienced since WWII.

Shouts of protests and objections arose from every direction. Suddenly, the doors burst open. Armed security services streamed into the conference room. It was the ministry's security force, alerted by the unusual outbursts. Standard precautionary procedures dictated having a detachment stationed nearby. Today, it was deemed necessary. Aside from the current disorder, the final proceedings would probably end up in similar fashion.

Wong violently slammed the gavel on the tabletop. "Order...I demand order," the party secretary shouted over and over. He was forced to get up, gesticulating violently by flailing both arms in the air to calm the assembly. "What are your specific demands?" he challenged the leader after the assembly had calmed down.

"We demand your neutrality," the leader insisted. "Complete neutrality in our global maneuvers. We have initiated strategically positioned measures to acquire certain resources."

This is no ordinary pushover, the secretary instantly assessed the spokesman. *This individual's highly educated and knows what he wants.*

"Furthermore," he continued his demands, "we need access to your resources."

"Resources?" Hui Wong finally lost his composure. "I cannot," he stressed, "and will not submit to such demands. We have hardly enough to sustain our own economic growth." It was a bluff he had used in many negotiating instances before. It was mostly with the U.N. to justify his country's incessant consumption from already strained world resources. But, this time, his response did not work with this outrageous, but worthy, opponent.

"You have Siberia," was the unyielding counter. Research into global mineral resources had been one of the principle issues when he prepared The Plan. Hammad had expended extensive investigative efforts into the world's raw material reserves. It was the driving factor behind his mission. Now, it was up to him to convince the Chinese to enter into an alliance with him against the Russian empire.

It was then that the party secretary realized he had walked into a trap. He desperately tried to salvage whatever was left for a negotiating hedge. His nation had eyed the vast expanses of the Siberian tundra on more than one occasion in the historical past, but had always been rebuffed by the Russian empire, almost always by force.

Power struggles over that wealthy stretch of the Asian continent had been going on for centuries. But now, with the implied ultimatum, he had an ominous foreboding about the future of his nation. With the self-assured team of emissaries in his lap, he suspected the entire Muslim nation had already formed an alliance against the free world.

He already anticipated the answer with his next question. "What is your ultimate objective?"

The answer was steadfast and unwavering. "Islamic world dominance."

This time, the unexpected revelation shook the Chinese assembly to its very core. There was instant bedlam. Fists were pounding on tables. Threats were thrown at the unwelcome intruders. Some members even had to be restrained by the security detachment from starting fist fights with the visitors.

Amid the shambled halls of the ministry, Hammad enraged the situation even further with his next demand. "We will obtain our objectives regardless of your position." He was puzzled by a nation that could appear so stone-faced to the outside world without exhibiting internal emotions. This cultural trademark made negotiating so much more difficult. This, nevertheless, did not matter since he had complete control of the world's most lethal weapons system. He had not come here to negotiate. He was here for absolute submission.

The secretary, trying to curb his emotions and his party member's reactions, was stalling for time. "You will have immense resistance from the Russians. They will never submit to your demands."

"This is," Hammad commanded, "where you will support our cause. You will deploy diplomacy with your Russian neighbors to achieve our demands for neutrality."

"We will do no such thing." It was too preposterous to even think on such terms. *This lunacy must be stopped. And it must be stopped right now,* he thought, utterly repulsed. Chinese history was ancient. His country had been cultivated for millennia, dating back to where the rest of civilization was still nomadic, especially neighboring Russia. China was a proud and prosperous nation in spite of the many aggressions exerted by Mongolian, Tartar, and Ottoman conquests. It may have not appeared as such during recent times with the Mao regime submitting to the demands of the common people. "Why can't the world just leave us in piece?" he fumed.

To avoid further exasperation and perhaps incarcerated detainment by his host, the leader promptly stood up, collected his lieutenants, and departed with a final warning. "We will demonstrate to you and to the world the pointlessness in resisting our efforts. Our objectives will be obtained either through peace or by force. The choice is yours."

RUSSIAN FEDERATION

Since the collapse of the Soviet Union, the Russian Minister of Defense was the nominal commander of all the armed forces, serving under the president of the Russian Federation, in whom executive authority over the military was vested. In this capacity, the minister exercised day-to-day operational authority over the armed forces. The General Staff, the executive body of the Ministry of Defense, implemented the instructions and orders of the defense minister. As was the case with the former United States of America, the Russian president was the commander in chief. By constitutional decree, this was an important factor to the modern regime. It provided protection to the echelon membership, the politicians, and safeguarded the government from being ousted or overthrown. From a security perspective, the president would have instant access to his forces regardless of political or military issues.

Government members of the Russian Federation, early in the morning, had been called to an emergency session. In attendance were the chairman, the deputy chairman, and the majority members of the federal ministries. The Federation had been bombarded with news flashes of yesterday's attack on Alaska, their troublesome neighbors. Today's topic was the reason of the cause for the destruction, HAARP.

On the podium representing the federation was Nikolai Chernoff, Deputy Chairman for Foreign Affairs. As such, he organized the work of the government, headed the meetings of the government, regularly conferred with government members, and made decisions on current issues. Today was a day of great concern, not only for the political leaders, but for the citizens of the nation as well.

The head for national security had taken the stand. "There are numerous HAARP facilities like this in the world," he explained. "Alaska, Norway, Australia, India, Brazil, Puerto Rico, China, Peru."

Hearing the nations called off by name, Chernoff tried to maintain a calm demeanor but could not contain himself any longer. "I must ask you," he yelled into the silenced hall, "why not Russia?" The very thought of his nation having missed another opportunity was too much for the deputy chairman. "Why not Russia?" he repeated. It did not help much. He was shouting by now. "Where are our scientists?

When HAARP was initially commissioned in the early 1980s, there were three facilities in existence. Today, it seemed every nation was staging to get a share of the technology. Although highly classified, the parameters of the systems were contracted out to private institutions in most cases. Where HAARP was still considered an atmospheric research project, the superpowers, as usually, had other intentions.

The head of the scientific research community stood up and haltingly approached the pedestal. He seemingly avoided the caller's penetrating stare. A wad of printed paper in one hand, he motioned to be allowed on the pedestal. Appointed lead, he had the courage to speak up to at least try to justify the scientific community's position. "Mister Chairman," he stuttered into the reverberating echoes of the last speaker, "may I explain?"

The scientist was not extended any courtesy. "Make it good," he was instructed. "No excuses."

"We do have such a facility," the slightly composed but still shaken man began. "Our researchers have achieved extremely interesting results regarding ionosphere behavior. They discovered the effects of generating low-frequency emissions at the modulation of ionospheric current." Getting some confidence back, he further explained the specifics of the technology. "At the beginning…"

What would follow was a twenty-minute dissertation read mostly from research papers. The deputy chairman could not contain his impatience any longer. He jumped to his feet and shouted, "Get to the point, you fool." The unexpected outburst visibly shook the speaker. It also jolted the assembly into attentiveness. Red faced and completely irate, he demanded, "I want facts…facts."

In an apologetic gesture, the scientist pressed on. "There are no facts. The facility has been dormant for years. We have requested…" he paused to muster up more courage, "begged for budgets, but nothing was ever forthcoming."

"Enough with excuses," the chairman thundered at the frozen assembly, shocked by his harshness. "From now on," he bellowed, "funds will be made available, even if we have to extort them from the citizens."

In a fleeting gesture, he dismissed the assembly and ordered a select group of functionaries into his private chambers. He was still fuming from the lack of intelligence he had about what was rumored to be the world's future super weapon. He was totally caught off guard on another missed opportunity. "What will it take to catch up?" he demanded when the group was settled. "And…" his eyes sought out each and every one present, "no leaks." He could not bear to become a laughing stock for other nations that had decades more development on their side for the HAARP technology.

Next in his focus was the still confused scientist. "Give me," the chairman demanded, "the current status on the facility."

Ten minutes later, with the aid of the resident technology team, the wall-mounted widescreen monitor sprang into action. Painted across the screen within the wild steppes of Siberia was what seemed to be an overgrown farming pasture. Although extensive in size, visible only was a cluster of antennas protruding from the ground. What came next were dated images followed by a set of research parameters outlining the location, technology, and purpose.

The head of the scientific research community stepped on the podium once more explaining with the help of a laser pointer: "As you can see, the Russian HAARP is located approximately 430 miles directly east from here, Moscow, in Russia's central area near the city of Nizhny Novgorod, Sura, as it is known, used to be as powerful as the Alaskan HAARP. But, in its present state, as you can see by the images on display, Sura appears quite seasoned."

The condition of the current facility was clearly visible. On display was a cluster of slightly rusted antenna surrounded by neglected grassy grounds. In grid formation, there were straight rows of 20-m antennas protruding from an area of approximately ten hectares of land. A complex the size of a country shack sat in the center of the field with its emitters used for studying aural developments in the atmosphere. Where research there was prolific at one time for Russia's scientific community, today the once busy facility was vacated. The Russian HAARP has been neglected far too long for the scientists to catch up with the advanced technology developed by other nations.

Chernoff was fuming. He had seen enough and promptly interrupted the scientist, "How quick can we ramp up to make Sura operable?"

"Months," was the wavering reply. "Perhaps years." He was about to justify the time by explaining the need to refurbish, upgrade, and implement new technologies into the system but was cut short. "Enough excuses. You are dismissed. You all are dismissed." He then strutted off vowing that, "Heads will roll."

UNITED NATIONS

"United Nations," the newly hired receptionist announced in a courteous manner. "How may I help you?" Civility was the trademark of this highly visible organization, prominently located in central New York, fronted by the East River. Situated across Manhattan from the infamous trade center, every department of this remarkable complex was built to resolve and support world troubles ranging from extreme political disputes to more tolerable humanitarian issues caused by hardship. There was no other place on Earth where cultural connections were so much in the forefront and interwoven into world peace accords. The whole premise of the organization was to create an ideology in humanity that might never be achieved, but also, to a lesser extent, to maintain an environment of coexistence and cooperation between the many faceted nations on earth.

"Secretary General's office," the distant caller demanded in a somewhat rude tone of voice. "Immediately."

Slightly taken aback at the gruff caller, the office secretary replied, "He is in session. Can I take a message?"

"No messages," the caller insisted. "I want you to connect me with the session immediately. Everybody must hear what I have to say."

Unsure how to proceed without additional help, she put the caller on hold. "Just a moment, sir." Calls of this nature were very rare outside of the occasional bomb threat initiated by an irate citizen. But those callers were only interested in voicing their frustrations to anyone picking up their call. This call seemed different because the caller demanded to speak with the head of all nations, the secretary general. Not to disturb His Eminence, and unsure what other functionary to call, she dialed the secretary's office for cultural affairs. In an unsteady voice, she proclaimed, "Sir, I have a caller on hold demanding to speak with the Secretary General. Can you take the call?"

"I'll handle it," was his assertive response. Switching back to the caller on hold, the parties were connected. Curious about the undeniable urgency, the receptionist switched the phone to conference to listen in on the caller "...demand immediate sovereignty for the Palestinian nation. It must be sanctioned by all nations including Israel. You will have twenty-four hours to comply. No exceptions! An example of our seriousness will be demonstrated tomorrow regardless of your decision. We mean business."

Barely a second went by before the secretary for cultural affairs stormed into the receptionist's office, yelling, "Get me the Israeli Foreign Office...Now!"

The Secretary General was immediately notified. An emergency session was called within the hour. Unaware of the gravity of the urgent situation, disgruntled members trickled in slowly. The assembly was finally called to session three hours later. To the shock of the attending members, the Secretary General revealed the nature of the threat.

Initially, there were mixed feelings of doubt, hesitation, and uncertainty about the validity of the call. Accusations and counter-accusations were flying back and forth between suspected nations harboring terrorist factions. It was difficult to keep the session under control. As usual, there was an abundance of blame to go around without any resolution in sight. No consensus could be achieved under such circumstances, which placed many nations at risk for being targeted, in case the threat was for real. When the session finally adjourned twelve hours later, nothing had been accomplished.

Because of the severity of the threat, all U.N. nation members were advised to stay home until further notice.

The burden to act was on the Secretary General's shoulders, nevertheless. It would be a heavy burden. The warning, or ultimatum, if true, had been undetermined and could target an individual, a group, or a locality. Back in the solitude of his office once more, the Secretary General prayed, "I hope to God that it's only a hoax."

Staring across a sea of skyscrapers, he could not bear another blow dealt to a nation like the one he had witnessed within eyesight on September 11, 2001.

ISS

A new dawn rose over the fast approaching horizon at the International Space Station. Although each orbit only took ninety some minutes, ordinarily the crew was allowed to rest eight hours at a time. But, because of the hostile and deadly environment on the station, Walsh and his crew divided the sleeping period into short shifts. Kubalev and Walsh were presently on duty, with Liz and Nagata scheduled for a rest break. Unfortunately for Kenny and Liz, after the terrorist takeover on board the space station their intimate relationship had fallen apart. Under the present circumstances, sentiment and romance were put aside. Liz desperately needed a break. But, under the present circumstances, with the Russians threatening the crew and Dieter dying, she had to press on. She was about to head for the lab again when Walsh caught up with her, "Liz," he yelled after her. "Wait up."

"What's up?"

"Know anybody named Specter and Stinger?"

Liz hesitated. The words he'd mentioned had brought her to full attention. "Maybe," she muttered.

"Just received word over HF," he continued. "Global warning issued for an all-out attack on the North American continent."

Liz's face turned ashen. Regardless of her promises to Dad, she had to take Walsh into her confidence. He needed to know because it involved the space station. She removed the holding straps and pulled him into the far end of the capsule for added privacy. "What I'm about to tell you can never be shared with anybody else. Promise!"

Startled, his face changed from curious to alarmed. "You've got my word."

She had hoped to never have to reveal what she'd learned years ago. Stern faced and shaken to the core, her voice trembled as she told him.

Liz had just entered the astronaut training program. "Please, Dad," she'd wavered. "Don't!" Liz did not want to collaborate in the secrets her dad had dwelled in for a lifetime. Secrecy, from the onset of his career, had become part of his existence. Where he took to it naturally, she, on the other hand, had severe reservations about being part of man's devious inceptions. Life was difficult enough for her already without it. Stressful at times, yes, but relatively simple. Her dedication was to her job and raising her children. Secrecy, in her mind—although she was sensible enough to realize it might be necessary for governments, covert operations, and security reasons for nations to exist—was something unwanted. Under the pledge of severe duress, she'd finally agreed to hear him out.

Walsh was getting impatient at her wavering. "Tell me."

"You promised."

"Go on already. The suspense is killing me."

"There're only five people…six now," she corrected, "that know about it. There's Specter, Stinger, Crimson, Black Knight, you and me." She watched a perked-up face and mind churning in anticipation. She then told him about the implants, the satellite relay via her dad's over-the-horizon technology, the newly established cyber command headed up by Foster, and the future plans for the Western Sector. *There's more...much more*, she thought, *but for now, this is enough for Kenny to digest.*

All he could stammer repeatedly was, "Wow!" His face told the story. It showed utter amazement. Liz knew it'd take him time to absorb. It had for her.

"Nobody else knows," she reinforced his promise. "Not the government, not the foreign sectors, and definitely not the enemy."

"I had no idea."

"That's all I have to say...for now."

"There's more?" As incredible as the information just laid out was for him, he kept shaking his head, clouded over with doubts.

"In time," was all Liz would reveal.

A frightening thought just popped into her mind. "Dieter!" She looked at Walsh. "Fuchs...How's he doing? How's he holding up?"

"Been talking with him on the intercom. He's scared to death and anxiously waiting for you."

Unloading the secret weight, she carried for years just dropped on an unsuspecting Walsh, her mind clear and revitalized, Liz rushed for the computer and said, "I promised a solution for the virus." Two keystrokes later, Google, a classified version from the public sector, the onboard search engine popped up on the screen. Her next entry on the search window was: "Ebola."

Seconds later, at her fingertips was the complete set of data available on the deadly virus. She sifted through pages of displays. "This isn't going to work." There was too much information to process for reaching a viable solution, but she had no choice. The data she had to absorb was the following:

Ebola – Best known as viral hemorrhagic fevers viruses. First recognized in Zaire in 1976, the virus has been linked to an alarming increase in number of outbreaks. Fatality rate is 92%. Most recent outbreak, 2012, Uganda and the Congo...*This is bad,* Liz thought.

Symptoms – The virus is characterized by an acute flu-like illness often associated with internal bleeding. Agent is highly infectious via the aerosol route making it attractive for terrorists...*Even worse.*

Signs – Being a viral hemorrhagic fever agent, it primarily targets blood vessels, producing internal bleeding. Symptoms include fever, aches, exhaustion, low blood pressure, severe shock, and bleeding from the eyes. Advanced stages include impaired nervous system, liver and lung damages, deafness, severe internal bleeding, kidney failure, black blood vomit, and other life-threatening symptoms...*Terrible.*

Possible Causes – Exposures to rodents (Arena virus, Hantavirus), mosquitoes (Rift Valley fever virus, yellow and dengue fever viruses), or even slaughtered horses (Rift Valley fever virus, Crimean-Congo virus). To identify the virus, laboratory tests are required. Testing can only be conducted at the CDC in Atlanta or the U.S. Army Medical Research Institute of Infectious Disease at Fort Detrick in Frederick, MD. *Here we go again.*

Treatment – Treatment for viral hemorrhagic fevers is largely directed at easing the discomfort of the symptoms. Victims benefit from being placed in a hospital setting immediately. Air transport is not advised. Sedative and pain-relieving medications are helpful, but aspirin and similar drugs should not be given because of their tendency to make bleeding worse…*That's just great!*

Caution: Doctors are advised not to use IV lines or catheters because of bleeding problems. Specific treatment with ribavirin has been used and is currently under investigation as a therapy for Lassa fever, Hanta virus, Crimean-Congo, and Rift Valley fever. Treatment is important if begun at once. Ribavirin, the only known medicine, has poor results against filo and flavi viruses.

Liz had seen enough. She felt terrible. Any chance for Fuchs to survive was slim. But there was a slight chance if she could analyze the specific agent he had contacted or at least get her hands-on Ribavirin. Unfortunately, the broken vial was not agent specific. The label only read, "Ebola."

Encased once more within the protection of the bulky spacesuit she made her way to the lab. On entry, she found a horrified Dieter cowered in one corner. "Dieter," she called to his attention. "Listen." In spite of the bad news, she tried her best to give him hope. "Is there Ribavirin on board?"

He momentarily hesitated then said, "Think so." Although his voice was shaken, his face reflected a glimmer of hope. Already too weak to move, he gestured at one of the lab cabinets. The viral effects appeared to have already taken hold of his body. His face was extremely flushed from fever. He had been swallowing hard, trying to keep from vomiting. Dark, brackish blood was already seeping from the corners of his mouth.

Liz reminded herself of the urgency. *Better hurry.* Too much time had already elapsed searching for an answer. Floating in front of the cabinets, her eyes frantically scanned the container labels. She lucked out. Sure enough, one of the labels indicated its contents: "Ribavirin." The next challenge would be getting the syringe needle into his arm. Her gloved fingers struggled desperately with the delicate instrument. "Need your help," she indicated at the syringe. It took several tries, with him helping to direct the needle, to finally shoot the lifesaving serum into Dieter's body. For now, all they could do was wait.

"Liz." It was Kenny on the headset calling her attention. "What's happening?"

She was quick to reply, "Dieter may live."

"Need you here," he responded back. "Immediately. Something's about to happen."

"Now what?" *Always another emergency,* she huffed. "On my way." Dieter seemed to have fallen asleep. There was no way for her to check his pulse through the heavily-insulated gloves. She had to assume it was sleep. Accompanied with the consoling thought of possibly having curbed the spread of the Ebola virus for the time being, the danger might be isolated to only one service module, that of Columbus and the interlock.

"Next," she muttered. "Decontamination!" For that, Liz had to make her way to Tranquility, then the PMA.[44] "Need help."

---

[44] Pressurized Mating Adapter-1 (PMA) connected permanently to Zarya, the other was used to allow the space shuttle to dock to the space station. In earlier times, the ISS remained unmanned for years, during which time Mir was de-orbited. In 2000, Zvezda was launched into orbit. Preprogrammed commands on board deployed its solar arrays and communications antenna. It then became the passive vehicle for a rendezvous with Zarya and Unity. As a passive "target" vehicle, the Zvezda maintained a station keeping orbit as the Zarya-Unity vehicle

She knew Walsh was busy someplace but did not know his whereabouts. "Where are you?"

"Destiny," his voice echoed back.

"Pick me up at the shuttle interlock." It was an interlock not used anymore since the space shuttle had been terminated. That end of the space station had been dormant ever since. Most docking efforts were localized to Zarya and Soyuz, Russia's capsules located at the opposite end. Although Harmony and Destiny were the station's preferred modules space-wise, the Russian crew conducted much of their activities in those capsules. It was the location in which the Jihad crew had been entrapped.

"Roger." It would be a while before she would be picked up and transferred via the Canadarm-2 external robot.

---

performed the rendezvous and docking via ground control and the Russian automated rendezvous and docking system. Zarya's computer transferred control of the station to Zvezda's computer soon after docking. Zvezda had added sleeping quarters, a toilet, kitchen, CO2 scrubbers, dehumidifier, oxygen generators, exercise equipment, plus data, voice and television communications with mission control. This enabled permanent habitation of the station.

SACRAMENTO

It was past midnight when his personal aide rushed into his private chambers. "Mister President, Mister President, sir." George Wilmot was rudely awakened. Following the Elmendorf incident in Alaska hours earlier, the new seat of government had been swarming with military department heads and droves of frantic reporters. Questions had been flying through the air all day with "any further news?" and "what's the latest?"

Rubbing his weary eyes, he jumped from the bed on unsteady legs to open his chambers. He had been dreaming. It was always the same scene. The stage was usually set in or around the enormous battlefields of Gettysburg, his favorite place whether awake or asleep.

Where his predecessors, their families, and presidential staff in the past had sought out relaxation at Camp Davis and Long Island retreats, he, in contrast, preferred to spend time at the colorful and rich historical sites in the Pennsylvania forests located just above the Maryland state border. Stumbling across the stony, yet very much alive, regimentally delineated battlefields, festooned by functional, but capped off, cannons, piles of geometrically arranged cannon balls, and erected memorials with regiment commanders and soldiers' names hewn in solid granite was a vivid memory. Yet, all had fallen into the hands of the enemy, the Jihad. Muslim territory now. He hadn't set foot on the historic site for almost a decade and could only guess the condition it was in. Foreign powers, after a takeover can be very destructive to a nation's historical heritage. Jihad, as they had demonstrated over and over had little respect for such values.

Now, seated by the edge of the bed, his personal aide handed him a set of casual dress clothes to wear. He quickly donned the items before being ushered to the command center. The place was buzzing with executive and second chain of command members.

Satellites, however marginal in operation, were feeding data onto the wall-mounted monitors. "What've we got?" the president demanded.

"Our intelligence information, but not yet confirmed," the head of this morning's emergency session explained. "Jihad has demanded complete submission of all U.N. member nations." He paused to let the enormity sink in.

Somewhat callused in recent years from the ever-present unpleasant news, he demanded, "Where did the Intel come from?" With him, intelligence surveillance had always been a sensitive issue. In spite of its supposed intrigue, he had always detested cloak and dagger secrecy.

"Presidio…General Foster, sir," was the prompt response.

"Get 'em on line," he ordered.

The familiar image of the general popped up on the screen. "Already present," Foster stated.

Somewhat surprised, but equally pleased, the president said, "General, how much time have we got?"

"Twenty-four hours, sir," Wilmot was advised. "Beginning yesterday morning."

"Then what?"

"Regardless of the U.N. or our position," Foster explained, "an example will be made by Jihad."

"That puts it up for this morning?"

"Yes sir," Foster replied.

"What's the threat?"

"Don't know. We're monitoring for unusual activities, but have not been able to identify the threat or source."

"What's your best guess?"

"Still unconfirmed. Al Qaeda or Jihad," Foster surmised.

"Who do we have for the Jihad faction?"

"All we know," he was told, "is that there's an emerging leader known as 'The Prophet.'"

"Any idea," the president demanded, "who this new leader might be?"

"Not at this time."

"What's next?"

"Wait for their demands." Foster's image faded with the last words.

Wilmot muttered a silent complaint. "It never ends." Like most executives in charge, he hated ultimatums, especially ones like this. It had all the indications of being factual. There was not much else he could do at the moment but wait for their next demands. With the annihilation of Elmendorf, the previous day, the nation was already in a state of panic. He could not let this happen. It'd be too much for his people, the citizens, to bear.

THE PRESIDIO

Earlier that day, as usual, Tracy had been busy monitoring the global skies. Ever since receiving the micro implant in her brain, watching over the globe had not only become her passion, it had turned into an obsession. There was not much that escaped her watch. Once the aftermath from the onslaught on the United States had settled, economy, commerce, and life in many of the other nations had returned to business as usual, except for the New Republic and Western Sector. Free enterprising nations, it seemed, fared better than oppressed or deprived ones. No matter the calamity or disaster, the enterprising spirit prevailed. Some always exceeded others whenever an opportunity presented itself.

Whenever her thoughts touched on opportunity, her privileged fate surfaced to the forefront. Even a couple of years ago, in her wildest dreams she could not have imagined the way her life had turned. After getting beaten down a number of times by a most ferocious adversary, an inner rage had surfaced that she did not realize she was capable of. Whatever may have been the cause, it sure did not come from her dad or mom. For most part, she remembered that her growing years were spent in harmony. "Look at me now," she muttered. "Hunted turned killer."

In a way, she was thrilled about the changes destiny had brought out in her. *Or was it opportunity?* There was no turning back. Her cause was the future. And that was where she concentrated all of her pent-up energy. Initially, it was pure loathing, focused on only one element, the Serpent. Now, unaware of the Serpent's whereabouts, her focused hatred had turned into open aggression against all evil. Her entire energy had shifted to the global cause of tracking, hunting, and eliminating the ever-growing threats fashioned by bad elements. Factions were sprouting up all over the planet. Some localized, others regional, it was a fight for world dominance she could not allow. She realized now that her fight was for the preservation of all nation's cultures, customs, and traditions, with an exception to perhaps one, that of Islam. She feared, once those values were lost, the world would be a desolate place barren of individual heritage.

Her thoughts were suddenly preempted. "Stinger," the voice drilled into her brain. "Report."

Specter demanded her immediate attention. In spite of their occasional differences in ethics and morals, mostly mandated by her, her ties with him were inseparable. After all, he was her dad. He was Dad, Specter, the link between a nation at risk and a world in imminent peril. Although she would prefer operating under her own identity, and taking credit, for that matter, he demanded strict protocol enforcement of the communication code. "Dangerous elements," was his rationale. And as always, he was right. She respected the rigorous discipline he forced on her.

Her response was short. "What's up?" For security reasons, they had to keep their dialogue short. Technology, although crippled since the EMP attack, had not stood still in other nations. Development had become even more sophisticated in the free world. She was a typical example, with the integrated voice circuit implanted directly into her brain. *What'll be next?* The possibilities were limitless. *Probably thought processes.*

"Possible enemy strike on military and government commands. Have Crimson warn Sacramento…must evacuate…immediately." Alex hoped the sometimes-pigheaded politicians would listen. If not, it couldn't be helped. "Did my job." It all depended on how much clout the general had with the president.

"Got data?"

"Standby," Alex instructed her.

The warning was clear. "Stay clear of strategic positions." Specter was always right. His instant access on surveillance was uncanny. With the foresight, he had years ago when building his fortress, the Castle, implementing the personal command structure, initiating secured surveillance and tracking capabilities equal to NORAD, there was no other place on Earth with his ability. Being Tracy, Stinger, she respected every bit of it. He was her backing, he was her support, and, most importantly, he was her protector.

"Stay clear," was all that needed to be said. It was an imminent warning. The rest was up to the cause already initiated. Time would tell. And the moment in time was imminent. From here on, all she and the world could do was wait and see. The decision was not up to her. It had already been set in motion by an adversary she still had to identify.

The warning was set for Noon, EST, 10:00 AM MST, and 9:00 AM PST for the anticipated menace to be unleashed. Still unknown to the world, it would come in the form of a firestorm like nothing that had ever been experienced since mankind was created.

CASTLE ROCK

Minutes later, Specter's voice cut across the ether once more. "Stinger…Report…Report immediately." Tracy was known to shut off the implant. Since the warrior she turned out, he allowed her the occasional privacy. He understood her needs for it quite well. But this was too important. He had to get in touch with her again. He still could not quite imagine his daughter's drive for wanting to be on the front line. On the one hand, he was proud of her dedication to the cause for freedom, but, on the other, he was always concerned for her safety, as every father would be. "Stinger…Report." This time his concern was for Rhonda, especially her since her place was at Vandenberg, another potential target. He was still uncertain whether the threat by Jihad was for real or only a bluff. At this time, neither he nor anybody else in the nation knew the status of the HAARP facility.

"Go." Even though Tracy had her visual implant turned off, she could feel the slight vibration from the audible ping command. Much like the now defunct cellular devices, she was able to adjust the sound, mode, and visual levels for sensitivity. Since no one else but her and Brooks had the implant, as far as she knew, for now she knew it was her dad. *Brooks,* the thought just entered her mind, *must check on him.*

"Immediate contact with Rhonda…make her take the next available flight here…very urgent…insist…no exception," Specter urged. "Maintain visual. Link's established." Tracy had a direct connection with surveillance satellites, Western Sector. From here on she could monitor activities directly without relay delays.

"Confirmed."

"Over." The transmission with Specter ended.

At least, he thought, *she takes me seriously.* She never questioned his commands. Like video, his sensors recorded information whether on the wire or wireless. As long as satellites picked up a data stream, he'd know it. His computers listened in on key elements just like Intel organizations. It still puzzled him that the now defunct NSA organization had not reactivated. The only difference between him and them was the scope of operation. He did not have but a fraction of the manpower, data storage, and surveillance capability. Where the NSA used to hoard infinite data capacity, he had to scrub most of it.

Alex also knew he wasn't the only ground station picking up data. There were a number of nations listening in on the ether. The advantage he had was Stinger, his daughter that nobody else had for processing instant data and real-time decision making. Another thing, as long as their identity was coded and undisclosed, the rest of the world could only speculate on who they were. Radio triangulation would point towards Cheyenne Mountain which was fine with him. It was a natural decoy for where data and information was fed to and from the Castle.

Fifteen hundred miles to the west, Foster was mulling over the ultimatum. He needed confirmation. "Tracy," he called her office. "Get in here." Seconds later she stormed into his office. "Got problems," he announced. He held in his hands a report just received from the U.N. Since the United Nation's headquarters were on American soil, it would be prime suspect for a target as well.

"What've you got?"

"Need surveillance."

Tracy hurried to the control console to initiate the command sequence. Pushing a series of keyboard buttons brought up the global satellite grid on the big screen TV mounted against the office wall. Another selection zoomed in on the Western Sector. The next image was dynamic. Her implant went remote. The images began panning across northern America. From here on, her implant relayed data received directly to the screen. Both could observe events initiated from the ground or over the horizon, no matter where. The screen kept painting image after image as the satellite swept across the northern sphere. When one unit went out of reach, the next would pick up the link. As long as the satellites were operational, data would be available. It was how Brian had connected the grid. "Brian," her thoughts fleetingly touched on him but instantly reflected back to the present reality.

"Ingenious." Foster could not help but confess his approval.

"Look at this," Tracy gestured. Her focus was on the outer reaches of Alaska. She had detected ground activity at Fox One. Ever since Alex had revealed to her the super-secret installation, it had become a frequent focal point with her.

"What do you make of it?" Foster's gaze sought out the camouflaged arrays of antennas. "Maybe the enemy?"

"Could very well be," Tracy agreed. Her facial expression suddenly changed. An urgent thought had stuck her. She'd almost forgotten Specter's appeal. Headed for the office exit, she said, "I'll be right back." From here she rushed back to the command center reaching for the external headset. Mic pressed against her lips she switched to HF transmission. "Vandenberg…Vandenberg…Rhonda, come in."

Seconds later, a familiar voice from the launch site responded, "Hicks."

"Return to Castle Rock," Stinger orders. "Immediate! Specter's instructions. No questions!" There was a halting pause.

Rhonda's response was wavering. "Can't."

"Listen," Tracy insisted. "Your life's on the line."

There was another pause. Tracy could hear the breathing on the other end. She could only hope Rhonda would be sensible to the warning. "I'll try."

"Don't try. Just do it!"

She then hurried back to Foster's office to find him presently on the HF radio with Sacramento, "…get the people out …immediately." He looked up when she entered. His voice was weighed down with concern. "For once," he muttered, "I hope they will listen."

Unable to suppress her own views, she opted, "Not so sure. Politicians, remember." There wasn't much more that could be said about the pending events. The alerts had gone out. It was up to the government to act on them.

Back in Castle Rock, Alex also had his focus on HAARP monitors. He was watching intently for any ground activities. At the moment, the only visible objects he identified were a wing of Black Hawk attack helicopters sitting at idle. He tried to capture the moment while staying one step ahead of the enemy. To do this, he needed to get to the source of the imminent threat. While his eyes kept watching the surrounding terrain, his mind kept gnawing at some missed elements. It was the menacing technology itself. The answers he knew were hidden in the faint recesses of his brain. The hinted knowledge slowly surfaced to the forefront of his cerebrum. It suddenly dawned on him. It all boiled down to one element. "Microwaves."

It was many years ago during the early days in his career when microwave, with radar, and electronic technologies were still taught in schools. He tried to remember the specifics but had forgotten much of it. Using the internal search tools on his computer server, almost instantly, the data was painted across the display. He read:

Microwave as a technology source had been around since the days of the vacuum tube. Specifically, a microwave device operated on the ballistic motion of electrons in a vacuum under the influence of controlled electric or magnetic fields. Primary elements included the magnetron, klystron, traveling-wave tube, waveguide and gyrotron. Depending on the desired application, the beam could be modulated for communication or pulsed as weapon.

Scientists at Bell Laboratories made some fundamental advances in the transmission of microwaves during the early 1930s. Incidentally, researchers at Stanford University developed a new microwave generator known as the klystron. Shortly after, in the '40s, the wave-guided klystron and cavity magnetron were brought to the United States in a famous "Black Box" by a British team. All became key elements in a wide variety of radar systems developed by the Massachusetts Institute of Technology. Microwave detection and communications systems have had a role in American life ever since, with the application best known to the public as microwave oven. More obscure was that microwaves made live television possible from space and transmissions between continents. The technology was also essential for weather operation of commercial and military aircraft as well as intercity telephone traffic.

Bell System was the first to impact radio communication in the United States by means of repeater stations between New York and Boston during the late '40s. Similar devices were used in satellite operations beginning with the launch of Pioneer 3 in the late '50s. The discovery and development of semiconductor devices and oscillators during the '60s developed the market for consumer and industrial applications in microwave technology. Further innovations were made, relieving ever increasing congestion within the electromagnetic spectrum through the invention of the hollow pipe in the '70s, capable of carrying 250,000 simultaneous conversations over long distances.

Separately, the U.S. military explored microwave technology but for their own purposes. In this case it was for a potential weapon with the enormous advantage of being totally silent and imperceptible, unless an observer happened to stand nearby or in the line of fire of the energy beam, in which case the blood in the body started to boil.

The electromagnetic pulse, or silent killer, was quickly expanded through the development of devices that generated EMP without the need for nuclear explosions. Such devices could be deployed for use against enemy command and control centers and against aircraft in order to produce vital failures of electronic equipment needed in communication. A derivative of this program was HPM (high-power pulsed microwave), a system producing intense, extremely short pulses of microwave, which, through experiments, quickly powered up to one thousand megawatts and beyond.

Ever since, microwave energy had gained important military applications capable of penetrating the body, putting all organ systems at risk. Also exploited were effects on the central nervous system for its immediate debilitation to audio and other sensory properties, producing sledgehammer effect dealing with terrorist groups, crowd control, security breaches at military facilities, and antipersonnel tactical warfare.

Alex, presently staring at the HAARP facility, suddenly made the connection. He had a horrific thought if it would materialize. But, at the moment, he had no idea if the enemy had his hands on the weapon. He could only hope it wasn't the case.

FOX ONE

It did not take much imagination from the operators, engineers, and scientific teams to figure out what had transpired. They had followed the Raptor wing approach on internal monitors provided by Doppler radar and microwave receivers through the world's largest antenna farm ever designed and built. Jack Owens was devastated by the destruction he had to witness. He'd rather be dead than have to go through another episode of destruction. He could never live with the burden imposed on him by his captors. He had to devise a plan.

He had been contemplating for hours when his plan took root. By nightfall he could not sit still any longer. He carefully approached the section heads of his teams to present the plan. He had to get to the weapons cache without being detected. He could not do it alone. It was the only hope he would have to get the automatics and semi-arms into the hands of his team. He laid out a short but effective strategy, hoping most of the enemy forces would be asleep. Cautiously, he moved to his office desk to retrieve the key to the storage facility. At last, in possession of the key, he deliberately moved to the predetermined location to meet up by the armory.

He checked on the assailants. Aside from prolific snoring, it was quiet. Most were asleep sprawled on floors. A couple near the elevator, guarding the exits, was chatting in Arabic. Jack's team was nervously waiting for him to show. Indicating the section heads, he handed out the automatics. "You…you…you," Jack whispered in the quiet of the night. The rest received semi-arms and everyone was handed a clip of ammo for their specific weapon. He could feel tension and fear growing in the corridor among the teams. The lighting had been subdued for the night. Pacing along the hallways, the shadows from his silent warriors played out against the walls like an old-fashion puppet show. Dispersing in different directions upon entering the control room and office spaces where most of the enemy force was located, the shadows, with a sudden burst of energy, turned into reality.

It was the only chance Jack had. Surprise was on his side but killing was an act he had never anticipated, neither anyone else on his team. Sure, there were emergency plans filed away in computer folders. There were sophisticated evacuation instructions as well. But nobody had ever thought of printing out a copy or bothered to read the instructions. "Who's got time to read?" used to be the common excuse. This evening, the results were obvious. None of Jack's team had any fighting experience. He knew it, but it was their only chance to survive. He knew only too well that there was no other option for his team but death. If he could get lucky, through sheer surprise action, the intruders might be overpowered.

He flagged the team to fan out, to spread in different directions. Then it happened. All of a sudden, the shooting began. One had tripped over a body sprawled asleep in a corner of the control room. Rudely shaken from sleep the terrorist immediately realized the danger. He yelled out to alert his comrades who immediately charged into battle. Shooting started from all possible directions. The firing brought down numerous targets in the rooms and corridors. Screams of pain were heard from both sides while the fighting continued.

When the shooting began, Amin Madani was hosting a strategy session by the exit shaft with his lieutenants. He immediately jumped into action during the first sounds of gunfire. Reacting on instinct he ran along the halls to reach the command center. His battle-trained mind was already working out a fighting plan. *Should have put a tighter watch on the hostages,* was his self-reprimand. As soon as he reached the firing scene he realized the damages. Sprawled along the floors, casualties were piling up from both sides. He counted several of his men down. Fury welled up against their attackers.

A few paces later he was greeted by a hail of bullets. Seeking protection behind a partition, he came face to face with Jack. For a halting second, both faced each other in silence.

Madani knew the weaknesses of non-combatants. There was always a halting indecision. He could read it in Jack's eyes. His trained battle eyes watched for the next move. An instant later he recognized the glimmer in the man's eyes. He watched the fury well up in this honest soldier's eyes and instantly knew the answer. He had seen it many times in close combat. The instinct for survival took over. The only difference between the two was combat experience and who pulled the trigger first.

Jack's legs buckled before he had a chance to aim his weapon. Mortally wounded, his shot went wild. It only took a fraction of a second for him to realize that it was the end. The final glimmer of recognition quickly faded into the bliss of eternal salvation. His life and death decision had been made by a speeding bullet launched into his brain.

In spite of being a Jihad commander, Madani felt sudden remorse for the adversary officer, but worthy and righteous opponent, nevertheless. He reached out for Jack and took hold of his arm, slowly aiding the dying body to the ground. Watching Jack fall halted the resistance attempt by his colleagues. Amin Madani's team swiftly rounded up their weapons. That was last night.

Facing a despondent operations crew, Madani demanded, "What's the battle status?" The death of Jack Owens and several of the crew was still vividly on everybody's mind. The terrorists had taken back full command. As before, the system operators had been ordered back to their stations. Each was closely watched by a member of the Jihad. "Ready for the next target?"

"Ready." With a nod of the heads, the ops team assured their readiness.

Madani should not face any more problems from within the bunker. A final check assured him that each operator was covered by one of his people. He was in a position to concentrate on the mission once more. He reached for the HF receiver.

A voice immediately responded to the call. "Desert Base Alpha."

"Fox One…all secure." He had complete command over HAARP.

"Final coordinates," the caller commanded. "Ready to copy?"

"Copy," he assured the distant end.

"Execution time 12:01 PM EST…Target points multiple." What followed was a series of coordination points:

Target coordinates: 34° 45' 20.50" N – 120° 37' 20.35" W – Elevation 185 ft.

Target coordinates: 38° 34' 36.12" N – 121° 29' 36.05" W – Elevation 121 ft.

Target coordinates: 37° 47' 55.95" N – 122° 27' 58.30" W – Elevation 177 ft.

A whistle escaped his lips when Madani recognized the targets. Targeted for annihilation were Vandenberg, Sacramento, and the Presidio. He had studied the global positioning grid and knew many strategic locations from memory. Indications were that the entire Western defense grid would be eliminated. By inserting the parameters into the HAARP system, the trajectory software sequentially programmed the ISS refractor mirrors to be sequentially aimed at each target point. In destructive succession, HAARP would take out primary command and control systems as well as military air defense forces.

Madani was mesmerized. "If that's just a demonstration," he muttered under his breath, "I'd hate to think what he has in mind for the rest of the world." Again, he was very much impressed with the ingenuity of his leader. All he had to do now was wait for the ISS to appear over the horizon.

During the remaining hour Amin Madani and his crew were occupied with final mission preparations. Using terrain maps for the appropriate sectors, he verified each target point for accuracy using mission coordinates received earlier from half way across the globe. Relay satellites were positioned awaiting final instructions. The first pulse stream from the source was focused on the initial target, then redirected to the successive targets.

The antenna array forty feet above was currently fired up to heat up the ionospheric layer. Ion sensors imbedded in low-orbit satellites confirmed the layer expanding and dissipating over the Western region. The resultant opening punched into the atmosphere would allow the microwave-produced energy beam to shoot through the ionic layer without getting diffused. In the final moments, there was no sound. The firing crew held their breath. The moment could only be equated to the first atomic test shot many decades ago.

The control center was charged with emotions. The final minutes were ticking away. The wall clock registered 12:01 PM EST. Instruments indicated system readiness. Directed straight at the orbiting ISS, with the crew on standby, Madani was ready to release the first burst. One final check on the clock was immediately followed with the first command: "Beam One—Fire."

The initial indication was that of a serene scene. Every motion was frozen in time. It was dead quiet in the center. But, a second later, a low rumble could be heard. It came from the depths. It grew out of the bowels of earth. Within seconds, the sound charged into an immense energy field, touching everything nearby. Every particle in the surrounding space was affected. Instruments, equipment, air, skin, surfaces, and bodies acted like empty capacitors induced to high voltage charges. The instruments, calibrated as they were to take maximum power, pegged out. The ambient air, supercharged with static particles, went wild. It pulled hair straight up from the skull, turning petrified faces into grotesque caricatures. In an instant, the place had turned chaotic.

The first pulse initiated by Madani reached the waveguide at lighting speed. The results created an inferno very much like an atomic explosion but without the gamma ray contamination effects. The energy beam grew in intensity beyond what anyone had ever imagined. It overwhelmed all human sensory input. It could only be described as being trapped within a Tesla cage surrounded by high-voltage pulsed lightning with its electromagnetically supercharged static pulses tugging on every part of the environment and humans alike. These were the senses perceived by anyone caught close by. What went on inside the cage and waveguides could only be described as the total destruction of all life forms. From there, the concentrated beam particles shot straight out to hurl its energy toward the ISS refractor guide. Captured by the highly polished waveguide and reflected back to Earth, the beam sought out its programmed target, but not without leaving its mark on the space station, which was violently forced from its calculated orbit once more. The full potential of this devastating weapon was only limited by its power fueling the system. Today's energy level provided by the system was ten billion watts, an unimaginable figure for anyone to comprehend.

"Recalculate!" Covered by Madani's team, although reluctantly, the light motion from a semi was enough to spur the operations crew to comply with the next commands.

"Beam Two—Fire!"

"Recalculate!"

"Beam Three—Fire!"

The pulses were fired in quick successions. Each time the beam was recalculated to the new position of the ISS and target point.

Vandenberg took hits across all launch pads. Support beams began to melt as soon as the energy pulse hit the steel. It was a meltdown unlike seen before. Entire steel supports and infrastructures collapsed into a heap of molten iron. It was an eerie sight for people watching from the distance at nearby Lompoc, Santa Maria, and as far away as San Luis Obispo, to see the launch towers' majestic presence one minute, then gone the next. It was a grim déjà-vu reminder of the crumbled Twin Towers for many.

The Western capital presidential seat did not fare much better. Fortunate for the president and the first family, they had taken the earlier warning serious and evacuated from the premises. The new White House and command centers took the full force of the concentrated energy pulses. Pumping holes ten feet wide left empty voids to a depth of fifty feet, leaving only blackened remnants of crumbled brick and ashes from the destructive force.

The Presidio did not fare much better. The main building that used to be Foster's tactical command and control center was obliterated. The general and his support staff would have to seek out a new HQ with fresh accommodations if he would ever want to remain in this part of the nation.

For all practical purposes, Hammad, Yusuf, Jihad, with HAARP control in the hands of Madani, had achieved the initial stage of Phase II, obliterating the remains of further resistance from the once proud and thriving nation, the former United States of America. With HAARP completely in his hands, he was already calculating his next move, the globe. In order to achieve that, Hammad knew, he had to initiate an example by force on the U.N. Since it was the seat for world council, he needed to instill mortal fear into its members. But there was a problem.

He realized months ago that his super weapon, HAARP, could not reach the east coast from its Alaska location. For that, he had to alter the position for the beam's relay station, the ISS. To achieve that, the ISS had to be dislodged from its present orbit to a new height. It took his scientists not long to come up with the necessary parameters. To accomplish, the required altitude level was attained with the last three firings. It jolted the ISS from earth orbit enough to be set for the next assault. He could seek out targets on the eastern part of the continent, up to now unattainable over the horizon. With the backing from the other HAARP locations staged around the northern hemisphere, he was set to give the nations of the world an ultimatum.

SACRAMENTO

It was just before noon, when "Hurry, Mister President…please hurry," his aide urged. What used to be the showcase of governing at the former White House, now, relocated on the western frontier, was a far cry from it. Ever since the transfer of the political seat, each and every day brought on another crisis. "What is it now?" Wilmot demanded. He was especially irritated since it was a weekend and he and the family had planned on spending a couple of days at the Angel Island retreat. The presidential limo had just driven up to collect him and his family members for the all-out emergency.

Life for the president used to be well organized. Every minute detail for the head of state was laid out for the day. Meetings, visits, and speeches were scheduled down to the minute. For emergencies, logistics, transport, and exit stages, practices used to be flawless. Today, here and now, every situation turned chaotic no matter how big or small.

Minutes before he was disturbed, the White House had received the call from the Presidio with Foster alerting the staff of a possible assault on Sacramento. The political seat was still in uproar from the destruction at Elmendorf only the day before. Facing the first lady, shaking the head the president complained, "Never ends." At least he did not expect any resistance from his wife. She totally supported him in all decisions.

A woman with great patience, she responded, "I know. Terrible times."

The president nervously queried the limo driver who was receiving the hurried passengers. "Where're we headed?"

"NORAD," he was told. The decision was made following a warning of the imminent attack. Although limited in selection, a number of alternative sites were available depending on severity, sphere of threat, and anticipated duration. For safety reasons, the vice president and his advisory staff would follow in a separate transport.

"What?" the President uttered with incredulity. It would mean vacating his responsibilities not only as commander-in-chief, but to the citizens as well.

"Travis is expecting you." It took thirty minutes for the limo to reach Travis AFB. About to board the craft, headed for the Rockies and Peterson AFB, his aide rushed up once more to inform the president, "Sir. Vandenberg and The Presidio have just been hit by HAARP."

The president's face turned ashen. He could not fathom the loss of Foster if anything had happened to the general and his staff. He was his eyes and ears to the nation, and the world.

"Any word?"

"Communication's out," he was informed. "No contact."

Extremely agitated and concerned for the safety of his family, and the nation, he fumed. "That's just great. What about VHF, UHF and satellite backup?"

"Already in motion," he was advised. "But there's more. We've just been informed the White House's been struck by a beam." Bounding to his feet, Wilson's head hit hard on the roof. Apparently, he had forgotten he was still seated in the limo. "Not possible," the president yelled out in pain. "What about my people?"

"Don't have details," he was informed. "Strike's been confirmed by many observers. White House's been leveled."

THE PRESIDIO

It was a couple minutes' walk from her desk to the cafeteria located in the next building. Taking long, hasty strides, Tracy was in a hurry to get back to her desk. Lately, it seemed all she did was eat on the run. A half-finished ham sandwich wrapped in tissue clutched in one hand, the other holding on to a can of soda, Tracy had just returned from the snack bar as she chewed on her last bite. Back at her desk, the sensors on her implant vibrated an alert. It was Specter.

"What's up?" she responded.

"You," was the imminent warning. "Need you to get out of there…immediately."

"But why? I can't leave my post. We're in a crisis situation."

"Sensors indicate HAARP's gearing up for another attack. Your station could be in danger."

"What?"

He sounded highly distressed. "Been getting alerts across the spectrum." He pleaded again with great urgency. Almost to a point of yelling, he urged, "Want you out of there right now."

In spite of the demanding urgency, Tracy wasn't shaken. These days everything was an emergency. "Right." It was a pacifying response before breaking the voice connection. Her visual was still tuned in on the space above.

"Stay on visual…" were Specter's trailing words.

Still, she was concerned about what he had said but couldn't just leave her station. Not in a crisis situation, especially not with comm satellites conspicuously dropping off-net. She was short staffed to begin with. For once, she could only hope Specter would be wrong.

Her mind was still distracted by the call when the warning took effect. Much like a kaleidoscope, it came on in vivid colors sweeping across her vision. She could almost smell the ozone in the atmosphere. Images directly ahead, as well as peripherals, became distorted. Light waves streaming towards the Earth began to split up into individual spectrums to a point where it made her dizzy. The pain in her head became too intense to focus. It affected her very being when a thought suddenly struck her, "Implant." On instinct, her fist reached in back of her nape and punched down hard. The action shut the implant down. And just in time, otherwise it would have been fried along with her visual and audible nerves. Immediately, her eyes and brain reverted to local vision. She was disconnected from the space grid.

An instant later, she felt the physical impact. Space, air, and the environment surrounding her began to vibrate. She could feel the energy build up all around. Her vision suddenly blurred. The ground began to shake violently beneath her feet. Her body was heating up, almost to the point of exploding. The blood within her veins began to boil. Seconds later, the force hit her with full intensity.

Time turned into slow motion. She could see each act one frame at a time. The hallway blast doors were torn from their hinges, hurled violently in her direction. A surge of wind rushed by her head filled with flying debris. Her body was lifted from the floor and violently flung through the air, where she landed against the far end of the lengthy hallway. It knocked the air from her lungs. Her limp body crumpled to the floor, where she passed out with collapsed lungs. What saved Tracy from the deadly projectiles was the blast door landing on top of her body. Resting against the inside of the building frame, the steel stopped just short of crushing her.

The assault was over in three seconds. Following the dead silence, groans emerged and call out for help began filling the halls. Tracy regained consciousness. Struggling desperately, gasping for air, she tried to get up but couldn't move. Her legs were pinned to the floor by the heavy steel door. She moaned out in pain. But it went unheard amid the groaning and devastation. Her body succumbed to the veil of unconsciousness once more. It was a blessing for her. One cannot imagine the terror pressing on body and mind when struggling for life's most precious commodity, air for the lungs.

On waking, it seemed like hours before Tracy was located by rescue. In reality, it had only been minutes. With legs pinned to the ground, her body was limp. After one quick look by the recovery team, checking for pulse and testing for breathing, they rushed on. She'd been determined terminal.

Foster had been desperately searching for her. He himself had sustained a number of injuries. A cursory check on his body and limbs revealed only surface damages. Although bloodied from top to bottom, looking monstrous in appearance from baked over ashes and caked debris, his body still functioned. The only thing on his mind was, "Please Lord, don't let her die."

In the years that Tracy had been working for him, Foster had developed a deep fondness for her. It wasn't so much a romantic sentiment, although that was a notion he had never ruled out, but he was practical enough to realize that romance with a woman half his age was mostly wishful thinking. The fondness was more of a mentor and counselor on his part. Tracy was more of an object he had come to treasure. Since his failure in marriage many years ago, Tracy became the only thing he had left to live for. She was his inspiration, giving him the inner strength to go on fighting for his cause. It was a cause worth more than material things and selfish ego. It was a cause to carve out a future and pave the way for the next generation. It was this treasure he so desperately tried to preserve.

"Find her?" the booming sound of Foster's voice echoed through the halls.

"Woman?"

"What?" He shouted back. It was here when he realized his eardrums were busted. He couldn't hear a thing above the awful ringing in the ears. The lip movements on the rescue worker gave him the hint he was understood.

"Yeah, woman!"

"One buried under the blast doors," one rescue member gestured while rushing to the next scene.

"Please…please, let her be alive."

He headed straight for the blast doors where he stumbled on her trapped beneath the steel. Checking for vital signs, Foster realized she was dead but refused to accept it. He sank to his knees, sobbing. Although his mind was numb, his heart went through emotional stages he had never experienced. Emotions swept from grief to regret, then on to fury and rage. Beneath it all, there was a deep affection and love he had not felt before. It was that feeling that brought him out of the grief.

My Tracy dead? He could not let that happen. His mind cleared up. "Tracy," he stammered over the intense ringing in his ears, "don't you die on me." With the back of his hand he wiped the tears from his eyes and face then, using both fists, he began pounding first, then pushing on her ribcage. "Breathe," he yelled at her. "Breathe, dammit!" He kept it up for minutes until he was pulled from her by a rescue squad.

"Give it up," he was told. "She's gone."

But he refused to accept it. "No!" Foster struggled. The team hurried on. Foster went back to work. He started pressing down on her chest again followed with deep resuscitation to the lungs, when all of a sudden, she let go a scream. Where it may have sounded like a scream to her, it appeared as a deep groan to Foster. Her lungs had been emptied from contracted chest muscles, collapsed lungs. The persistent pressure to her lungs supplied from his resuscitation was enough force for the diaphragm to fully inflate into the chest cavity. The result was an abrupt oxygen surge, allowing air into Tracy's lungs once again.

She was dazed and confused, expecting Dad. But, after recognizing the familiar face, her expression gradually turned from panic stricken into a wide grin. "General?" The ordinary sound of breathing had returned once more.

Averting her eyes, he nodded his head.

"You crying?"

"No," he lied. "Tears of joy."

PALM JUMEIRAH

Palm Island, predominant seat of the Muslim nation, for residents and visitors alike was growing by leaps and bounds. More and more of the manmade islands sprang up. As long as growth and expansion was maintained in an orderly fashion, Hasan Hammad had no complaints. What he was mostly concerned about was maintaining the value of the lifestyle of the privileged, and he would see to that. There was one way to assure that: maintaining acquisition costs at a premium. They would have to be so high that only the affluent would be able to afford the purchase. In due time, he promised himself, "I'll acquire all assets, such as the Marriott, the Hilton, and even the Trump Towers and force all foreign investors from the islands." For now, he was enjoying his status as leader.

A new day was rising over the eastern horizon. Hammad and Yusuf were seated on the lofty balcony waiting to be served breakfast. It would be a light serving as customary in the region. Where Yusuf was used to the western eating habits, Hammad had never acquired the taste for a solid breakfast such as ham and eggs. He was satisfied with only a handful of figs and nuts served with tea.

Euphoria from yesterday's HAARP attack success had slightly worn off by now. It was back to business again. Where Hammad was ready to move on to the next phase, Yusuf was still bothered by unfinished business. He was not satisfied by his leader's answer about the changes Islam was facing. He was prompting again. "What about the nation?" Yusuf asked. Still outraged at his leader for suggesting the preposterous new doctrine, "Imagine," he thought quietly, "democracy." The most detested word to his culture's language. He forced himself to remain calm while in Hammad's presence. Elsewhere, he would have killed somebody by now. Someone had to pay for the rage he felt.

"What nation?" Hammad was well aware of the tension built between them since their last argument. He had to make his commander comprehend what was at stake. If he could not make him understand, the rest of his forces would resist just as violently. Educated in the western world in political science and economic trade, Hammad had a thorough understanding of the ways of free trade and enterprise. That was why the free world had been thriving for the past century while his nation had not been able to emerge from the dark ages. Neo-political distribution was living proof. Statistics did not lie. Where eighty five percent of the world's nations were populated by Muslims, less than twenty-five were of Islamic faith. *That,* he vowed, *is going to change.*

Hammad would make sure of it. It was up to him now to make his nation understand and follow new rules, *his* rules. After some consideration, he responded, "We have no nation." He would have to carefully formulate each statement to ascertain acceptance of the new ruling by his people. *This,* he thought, *will be a good test, to make my friend understand.*

"Pakistan, Iran, the Sudan, Palestine," Yusuf responded. "That's what I meant." He had never considered moving to any one of these nations. His home had always been New York City, where he grew up, but in recent years he had been forced to camp out in the deserts. Jihad had become his home.

"Think about it," Hammad persisted. "We always had one final aim."

"Jerusalem?"

"Right," he settled. "We must liberate Palestine from its Judea heritage. We must make the Mosque our world Capital."

"But…"

"Please hear me out," Hammad adamantly insisted. "In order to achieve this goal, I will tell you what must take place." He took another calculated pause then continued in a firm tone of voice, "First, we must separate faith from politics." Yusuf did not take it well. "What?" He was preparing to jump at his leader again, but was stopped. There was total rage in Yusuf's face.

"No interruptions." Hammad raised both of his palms at him to ask for quiet, then continued. "This will permit the many religions to coexist side-by-side. It will be the only means to obtain our aim. It has worked for Christianity, it has worked for Judaism, and," he reiterated, "it will work for the Islamic nation. You must understand that people do not tolerate genocide and ethnic cleansing in the free world. And it is the free world we must conquer."

He let the enormity of his statement sink in. Watching his comrade's face, he could see the anger well up again. "Second," he continued. "Our government must rule with democratic principles…"

As he had expected, another outburst followed. "Never!" Yusuf had bolted from his seat. His actions clearly reflected on the state of his mind.

"Let me finish," Hammad yelled at an irate subordinate. "Listen! It is important to let the people participate in future events. Tribal warfare," his shouts elevated to a crescendo, "to gain possession of land, does not work anymore in a nation confined by borders. Free land for our tribes to roam and settle is waning rapidly. It will be history soon."

Yusuf could not control himself anymore either. "But there is…" he spat back in utter frustration before settling again into a more civilized exchange. "What about all the deserts?"

"Most deserts have been taken by the oil companies." Although the thought of it made Hammad's blood boil, he kept his calm. "Besides," he continued, "we will not be confined within the wastelands anymore. Our time has come to expand. This brings me to the next principle." He reached for a glass of orange juice to wet his parched lips. "We must decentralize governing, at least for now, until political Islamic assurances are guaranteed. We must let our people participate in world affairs, not only in the United Nations council, but, more importantly, in every nation on earth.

"What about command and control," Yusuf demanded. He could not fathom his people gaining political independence in each nation only to let cultural blending and non-sustainability destroy his people's customs and cultures. He recalled the historic fall of the Ottoman Empire only too well. They had tried the same policies before but wound up in failure. "Their world dominance was short lived."

Hammad, watching his lieutenant still wavering, insisted with absolute determination. "I," he emphasized with strong conviction, "will obtain that privilege. I *will* become commander in chief."

"What will happen to our Mosque?"

"Secular ruling will be limited to Islamic practices and will not change. But," he insisted, "it will be isolated from governing the nation. Political leaders will emerge to manage our people, which takes me to the next ruling. Once we obtain population majority, Jihad must disperse across all nations. It will take time, but eventually it will be achieved. It may take decades, perhaps even a century, to get us there. But," he assured his comrade, "it is our destiny. It is the divine destiny pledged by Muhammad and promised by Allah, our Creator."

"What about opposition from world councils? Other nations striving for world dominance?" Regardless of his leader's confidence, conviction, and planning, Yusuf still had doubts that their monumental efforts could be achieved. "What about them?"

"Not to worry. They will follow."

"But," Yusuf made one final attempt to object, "you have failed before."

Hammad reached out by placing one hand on his lieutenant's arm to assure full confidence, "One must keep trying," he answered. Although he did not want to be reminded of his past failures, he was not here to justify himself. Not to his friend, nor to anyone else. For Yusuf, he conveniently ignored the challenge. For anybody else, he would have dealt swift justice. "Even the scriptures say not everything is without failure."

Yusuf had not sought of ideas to this magnitude. *Guess I will always be a servant*, he thought with dismay. But he was elated enough to accept his leader as The Prophet, leader of the Islamic nation, ruling and governing Jihad and Muslim nations.

Hammad put the receiver in its cradle. Expecting nothing else, he had just been rebuffed by the head of the United Nations. Yusuf, who had been listening to the conversation just taken place via the speaker phone, although there were many questions on his mind, he opted to remain silent. He still had a difficult time in trying to understand his leader's initiative. He felt like a beaten dog with a chattered, once devout secular mind, trying to make sense out of it all. His commander was relentlessly pushing ahead with the Plan. Time, it seemed, was the driving factor. "Warfare is our destiny," Hasan Hammad reminded his lieutenant one final time. "Allah has spoken!" There was no more time to waste with explanations and sentiments. From here on out, any dialogue would be strictly mission oriented. He knew precisely what needed to be done. Negotiation efforts had failed. He had not expected otherwise. Any future blame for his cause would be placed into the hands of the United Nations. His responsibilities had been absolved from all international repercussions. His conscious mind suddenly gained the clarity he had not felt since conceiving the original Plan. "We must proceed to the Sudan," he decided. "Desert Base Alpha."

"Insha Allah! May Allah be with us!" Yusuf muttered into the serenity of the mansion.

"Tomorrow," Hammad finalized. "A new beginning awaits us." At present, for one last time, both appreciated another spectacular sunset. Night had broken in over Dubai and the Palm Islands. Propped against the rail of the balcony, they were taking in the beauty of their land once more. It was a time of day when the prevalent winds from the gulf slowly turned into a gentle breeze, cooling off the island sand. "From here on," Hammad muttered into the calm. "It will be nothing but destruction and devastation." Losses would be heavy to nations, to communities, and to his people. There was no stopping now. Phase Two already had been set in motion. Thoughts for the immediate future were set aside.

It was time to make preparations for an early departure. Both moved inside to pack up a few necessities. Hammad's eyes briefly lingered on the well-worn mission plan placed on the coffee table. Determined for action, he reached for the voluminous document, then thought otherwise and tossed it carelessly into the suitcase. There was no need to check the mission. He knew every step by heart. Every action element had been permanently carved into his brain. He already knew what tomorrow's headlines would read. *"Jihad declares War on the World."*

With that reassuring thought in mind, he stepped out on the balcony, once more absorbing the sounds of paradise. Although the immediate environment was quiet, his mind could not rest. He was quietly recollecting the day's events. Ultimatums had been assigned. Targets taken out. Deadlines issued. Measures set in motion. There was nothing to stop the upcoming sequence of events. With his trusted friend by his side, he pondered. He was free to turn the remainder of his energy to the principle causes of his very being.

"What's the next step?"

"Taking hold of the world's resources." It was the first time he saw a joyful beam on Yusuf's face. The following morning, at daybreak, they were headed for the private landing strip. Minutes later, the sleek G550 Gulf Stream took off toward the skies. Their first stop would be Desert Base Alpha. It would be a brief stopover to present final attack plans to his forces and assign the most capable lieutenants to command the multiple sectors necessary to assure complete success for his conquest. From there, Hammad would proceed on to the most important sector, the eastern regions of North America, the Promised Land. A land blessed with rich soil, infinite minerals, and most important of all, fresh water.

NORAD

Alex had promised the brigadier he would get his command center, NORAD back to full operations. To achieve this, he spent most of his waking hours at the Mountain. First, it was getting the antenna farm back into operation from the devastation many months ago. Several maintenance crews were dispatched. One climbed up the cliffs to the top to assess damages. Another was testing interconnectivity between transmitters and receivers. The next, and the most critical one, was to inspect and repair internal damage to computers, databanks, monitors, sensors, and other equipment essential to NORAD's operations.

Initial radio signals received, although marginal and fuzzy, were encouraging, nevertheless. Apparently not all steel towers had been destroyed. All were scorched, but some of the more robust structures were still standing and intact. When questioned by the brigadier, Alex summarized, "Good news and bad news. What do you want first?"

Jackson had no patience for game play. He didn't want to hear excuses. Short fused, he demanded, "Spit it out."

"Antenna farm's salvageable. Internal cables to the top, fried. Need to be replaced." He thought carefully before giving him the next report. Either way, he was on the hook. It was his responsibility to get it fixed. At this point, he had no idea about functional spares kept in storage. "In-house equipment," Alex paused a few seconds, then said, "marginal at best. Most interfaces are fried."

As usual, Jackson's response was gruff. "What are you waiting for? Let's get hopping."

Alex had an edge up. His lifelong experience had allowed him to acquire skills in analysis, troubleshooting, and repair of different computer and communication systems, which gave him an advantage over many specialists trained mostly on one system. Trained on one system, superiors expected them to stay with it as long as it stayed alive. But after some time, the job became mostly rudimentary, then boring. When Alex recognized the trends, he would switch career paths. It would give him opportunities on emerging designs in a runaway age of technology and information exchange.

Government systems normally designed for a maximum lifespan of ten years were still in operation after twenty, thirty, forty, and more years. There was a saying within the technological and engineering turf: "Don't mess with it as long as it works." Most technicians adhered to this adage because there were dire consequences within the ranks if something was broken and interrupting operations. In such cases, everybody in the chain of command was breathing down your neck. You were directly held responsible for any failures you'd caused. In many cases, it would limit career advances.

It was not long before Jackson's footsteps rang in the halls once more. "Get ready, people," he instructed his commanders. "President's arrived."

Even Alex was surprised. "President?"

"Whole damned White House," Jackson responded. "Staff and all."

Air Force One, what used to be the pride of a presidential air fleet, today was nothing that came even close to it. Since most modern aircraft and airport landing systems were disabled, a C-130 craft now carried the presidential markings painted on both sides of the fuselage. Presently touching down at Peterson Air Force Base after a laborious flight from Sacramento, the president with his advisory staff and family were ushered to nearby helicopters on standby waiting to take off. The party was hastily boarded and immediately whisked away to the nearby Mountain entrance.

Arriving there, they were picked up by a staff bus, disappearing into the tunnel headed for the safety of the steel doors. A quarter mile into the tunnel they arrived at a spacious holding platform. From there, they were quickly escorted by impeccably dressed MPs through another entrance toward the main complex. Their first time here for most members, the presidential party was in awe of the sheer size of this underground city. In spite of the grave national emergency, one had to stop to admire the enormity of this place, chiseled from solid granite rock. The president was no exception. Even though years ago he'd been given a brief about this place as part of the defense related indoctrination into office, words could not describe the enormity of the place when experienced firsthand. He fleetingly recalled the film illustrating this marvelous place.

Although, there were several other underground facilities built more advanced at places such as Mount Weather and Raven Rock, today, those facilities were in the hands of the enemy, and the Badlands at best. They were not accessible to the New Republic. As a matter of fact, there was nothing secure enough out west to accommodate the presidential party. Since the entire defense system was centered between east and central regions, the West Coast had never been considered as an alternative to the Mountain.

Called Cheyenne Mountain after the Native Americans that lived here, it was no ordinary mountain. It was the primary warning center for air, space, and missile threats to North America. A serpentine road from the nearby town of Colorado Springs led the way to the first security checkpoint entrance. Prior to 9/11 there used to be periodic tours into the Mountain where non-cleared visitors could have a rare glimpse at this highly-fortified facility, but these had been discontinued for security reasons. The tunnel, located at 7,500 feet altitude, going inside was a journey in itself. Everything was designed to survive a nuclear attack or other apocalyptic related events.

The city was built inside a mountain, accessible from three entrance tunnels with the main from the east. The north and south accesses were both inaccessible for road traffic and used for utility support and emergency exits. Entrance was gained past blast doors built of solid steel, each weighing twenty-five tons. The complex was primarily built to house the military and its staff for thirty days in isolation with all the food and water needed to survive. Passing a maze of hallways with one leading to the command center at the main building, the entire complex sat on thirteen hundred gigantic steel springs to absorb the shock in case of a direct nuclear hit.

Power was fed by six enormous generators fueled from a 510,000-gallon diesel fuel tank backed up by 4,000 batteries to supply emergency power to all facilities. Water was collected from a natural spring inside the mountain. Air was circulated to remove any chemical and biological or radioactive agents. Interconnecting pipes were made of flexible material to bend in case of a blast, as were connection mountings.

Holding the complex together were 110,000 bolts drilled into the rock to prevent the structure from caving in. All of this was designed to support the two hundred men and women of the American and Canadian military that had to survive in this sprawling, but primitive military community close to two thousand feet beneath solid rock in case of a national crisis. Aside from a number of recreational facilities like the gym, pool, and other support functions, a number of storage facilities contained the tons of canned foods necessary to sustain the operation.

The command center was the central nervous system for Cheyenne Mountain with a mission of integrated tactical warning and threat assessment to detect and deter threats to Canada and the United States. The people were also on the lookout for man-made or asteroid objects in space, in addition to monitoring all civilian air traffic within North American airspace. Information gained was from a network of radar systems and satellites staged around the world, as well as sensors and detection systems with the motto of "If it's in space, it will be detected." In case of a space intrusion or hijacked plane, interceptor fighters were immediately dispatched from the various military bases staged around the nation into the air for acquisition, pursuit, and resolution, as stated in mission manuals.

With the presidential party settled in temporary living quarters, the commander in chief was at once given authority over the command center. He was immediately led to the infamous War Room to meet up with the assembly already impatiently awaiting his arrival. After introducing his ops staff, he then called on his dedicated civilian lead busy working nearby.

"Alex Bauer, Mister President," Ben Jackson introduced Alex.

"Ah yes," the president acknowledged Alex. "I remember...Saved the world from catastrophe a few years ago?"

"Was nothing," Alex replied with diminutive modesty.

"Modesty," George Wilmot responded. "I like that. But you deserve a lot of credit."

"Thank you, Mister President."

Turned businesslike after reminding himself of the urgent national crisis they were all facing, Wilmot demanded, "What've you got?"

Jackson did his best to explain to the president as much as could remember of the state of the nation Alex had reported and described to him earlier. "With most backup command centers immobilized, the nation had been decentralized. The Mountain was the only practical facility left to hold the nation together." He went on to explain, "Given, spread across the globe among allied and foreign nations there were a number of strategic and tactical mission commands remaining. But yesterday's attack was directed against the free world. With strategic North American command reduced to one facility, the rest of the forces were commanded by tactical orders shared by military units, Intel agencies, and law enforcement, and are not structured or in position to take the supreme command."

Terminating introductions and formalities, the brigadier motioned Alex in the direction of the command center. "We've got a crisis at hand." Alex was well aware of it.

BADLANDS

It was hours into the flight. Only the quiet droning of the craft's twin turbo jets was heard. Aside from the cockpit crew up front, there were only two more passengers present in the cabin. Both wore combat fatigue. It was not an ordinary camouflaged uniform issued and tailored as was customary for the combat zone. This one was specifically customized to impress a new order upon a conquered nation. To make a lasting declaration for supremacy, Hammad followed the unwavering footsteps similar to the once world renown dictator Hitler. The difference was the cut and practicality of the garb. Weighed down with packets of ammo belts, semi-automatics, and provisions of force, the uniforms were tailored to suit the present environment and combat-centric demands. Where Hammad wore the insignia for the supreme commander, a four-star general, the battlefield command for Yusuf was that of brigadier. In either case, should something unfortunate happen to the leader, Joseph—Yusuf—Hashim would take over.

Presently gazing out the G550 Gulf Stream's portholes, both were craning in their seats to get a look at the ground view slowly panning across their field of vision. "Take a good look, my friend," Hammad pointed out. "Our new battlefront." Following the ping of the overhead alert signal, both fastened their seatbelts, preparing for the imminent landing. Coming up fast, what used to be the nation's most prolific airport now looked like a battlefield. Though much of the debris from crashed airliners had been removed from runways, leftover wreckage was clearly present. Midway Airport had become a foreign-occupied port. Where O'Hare used to be the busiest airport in the nation, for strategic reasons Hammad had chosen Midway as his private hub. It gave him direct access to the Chicago shores. Initially disputed by competing nations for landing rights, Hammad had declared this port as his own. It did not take long for competitive nations to withdraw. Today, with Islam on the move for world dominance, no nation was prepared to oppose the demands made by their leader.

The personal jetliner was flaring out for final touchdown. The cargo it carried, mostly weapons and supplies, was quickly unloaded into waiting trucks. Staffed with security forces for personal protection, flanked by personnel carriers, the convoy headed toward the eastern shores of the city without obstruction or interference. The foreign presence of Hammad's forces was highly dreaded and feared by local resistance factions previously occupying the region.

Over the past years, since the land had been fractured, there were many skirmishes for space and turf in and around the Great Lakes region. Everybody wanted to secure this great source of water. But, the stronger force, that of Jihad, as had been the case in recent years, won out. The convoy sped along Stevenson Expressway, crossed Armour Square then turned into Lake Shore Drive. After making a sharp left headed north, what used to be Monroe Harbor frontage came into view. With the arrival of armored forces, the harbor had quickly turned into a Jihad garrison. The convoy had arrived at its destination.

Space was ample for setting up headquarters. There was no shortage with shelter on and along the shipping docks. It was a haven made for inland trade. Once the water supply had been secured, dealing with the rest of the world would be part of the next phase on Hammad's agenda. For now, he was dealing with the situation closer to home. His newly found home. As soon as the convoy settled in, as was usually the case after his absence, reports came in from the surrounding areas about an increase in fighting. It was always for the same cause, gaining possession for shorefront ports.

After the briefing Hammad just received, he spat on the ground. "Damn Patriots. I must teach them a lesson." It was not the first time he enforced discipline and would not be the last. He was well aware of threats from the Badlands leaders. He had been forced to deal with them on a number of occasions. Up to now, he had been successful in warding off their advances. "You deal with it," he instructed Yusuf. "Take whatever forces you need." Hammad had enough on his schedule just dealing with local issues. "One more thing," he reminded the battle commander. "Under no circumstances will we lose the Lakes."

Yusuf understood. "Promise," he assured the leader, otherwise, it would be his head.

During Hammad's recent absence from the region, to his dismay, two battle fronts had developed. Local thugs were pushing up from the south with the Badlands forces marching in from the north. The 1st Armored division, with its heavy equipment, was a very formidable force. He had to deal with it first. The one thing in his favor was that the enemy was coming to him. This way, he did not have to waste exorbitant logistics and precious time chasing them. It would be mostly hand to hand combat. Luckily, he had unlimited supply of mercenary volunteers willing to fight.

It took two days for Yusuf to get underway. Not knowing what to expect once he left the area, he organized a sizable scout party consisting primarily of attack boats shipped in from across the Atlantic. As part of his effort to expand across the globe, Hammad had acquired whatever craft he could get his hands on. With the former U.S. fleet, for all practical purposes, inoperative, he was reaching out to other nations, such as Italy and Argentina, for water craft. In time, he had acquired an armada—somewhat dated, but seaworthy, nevertheless. Because of the isolation and difficulty of ocean access, the craft had to be of limited size, weight, and capacity. They had to be easily transportable to get up the Lawrence River. With Atlantic access in his control, light sea craft could easily reach the lakes.

Yusuf's current path took him north along the western shorelines of Lake Michigan. Two hours into the trip, the tips of Milwaukee's high-rise buildings gradually grew on the distant horizon. The armada under his command, skipping across the swells, was rapidly approaching the city built on beer. *What a shame*, he thought, *all gone by the wayside*. Even in his younger years, his college days, he had never acquired a taste for this popular drink.

"Wham! Kaboom!" Unexpectedly, directly in front of the boat, spewing tons of water into the air, a shell exploded with thunderous force. It was a sound he immediately recognized. Two, three, four more shells exploded in rapid sequence with equal force. Weaving in and out of the water spouts, the pilot reacted accordingly, and so did the others in the craft following in tight formation. Yusuf quickly realized it was a salvo designed to slow the convoy down. It was a warning delivered from the shores. With the accuracy of howitzers, he knew some of his boats would be flying through the air in splinters by now.

Searching the shoreline through binoculars, he spotted the source. As he thought, it was the heavy armament from the 1st brigade he had encountered on several occasions in the past. So far, he had always managed to outrun prior assaults. But today, with strict orders from Hammad, he had to face the threat head-on. Then he spotted it. It was a white flag someone had raised by the shores. Somebody wanted to negotiate. On the other hand, it could be a trap. He had to take the chance. With a swift gesture toward the shores, he headed in. Following his lead, the armada was right behind in tight formation. Throttled to cruising speed, he cautiously approached the armored forces waiting by the shores.

"Only a matter of time," Rusty Norton had proclaimed earlier that day. He and Brody Elliott were discussing the future. They, amid a swarm of soldiers, were enjoying a morning swim in the waters by the lake. While the weather was nice, it was a daily ritual to clean body and garments of the daily crud collected in and around the city. Waste management was virtually nonexistent. What little there was, considering the prevalent circumstances, was limited to piling up garbage in the middle of major intersections. It was the most practical solution. Dumped daily from neighboring dwellings, the piles had grown gigantic. It provided a two-fold solution. First, it attracted rats and other vermin, making them easy prey to shoot for the meat, and second, whatever morsels remained edible in the piles were scavenged by the homeless.

Ever since they had landed here following the March of the Patriots, the forces under his command had developed a semi-comfortable existence in and around this fine city. Milwaukee—surrounded by huge bodies of waters, Lakes Michigan, Huron, and Erie, situated close to the Canadian border—had been relatively safe from domestic and foreign invasions until Norton, Elliott, Bad Man, and the 1st armored division had arrived, taking the city by force.

"What?"

"Sooner or later," he picked up on his earlier thought. "Someone else is gonna get the idea."

"Breweries?"

"Exactly."

When Norton and his army had first arrived, he had a difficult time keeping his soldiers in line, if one could call the motley forces soldiers. Though the core of the 1st armored division was trained fighters from the former U.S. Army, the majority of the forces had been recruited along the way during the march. Everybody fight worthy, including men, woman, and children, were taken in. Only the sick, the elderly, and the farmers were left. Securing farmlands along the route, a small detachment remained to ensure a constant food supply to Norton and his men.

It had taken close to a year during the march to get the borders established. The Badlands, as it was called, served the region well. It was exactly what the Patriots needed. The whole premise for the movement was to regain lost values so diluted over past generations. With many principles gone over the course of the former nation's growth, it was the loss of morals that brought the United States of America to its knees.

To reestablish principles, morality, and ethics once more, Norton created the Badlands along with a new constitution. To uphold this constitution, severe discipline and order was enforced. The best man for it, as he had proven himself many times over, was Bad Man, the henchman for the new territory. But one man alone could not control all sides of the borders. Because of its limitations, many holes remained for the enemy to slip through. It was this weakness that was a constant cause of fighting along the borderlines. It was a problem Rusty Norton still had to solve.

"Alert…Red Alert!" The call resounded up and down the immediate shoreline. It was a call everybody dreaded. It was a call that grabbed everybody's immediate attention. It meant the enemy was at the threshold. Heads went up immediately, searching for activity across the horizon. They retracted just as quickly with the sound of outgoing explosives streaming overhead toward their targets. All were only too familiar with the sound of shells going off. The morning serenity was suddenly shattered. Soldiers were hurrying out of the water to get to their posts. Commands were shouted. Orders issued. Gestures made toward the horizon. All eyes were locked in on the advancing, what appeared sizable, amphibian war party.

Bad Man, in his usual solid strides, was pacing along the sandy waterfront. He met up with Norton and Brodie headed in his direction. A pair of field glasses was passed around the leaders to quickly identify the intruders. "Jihad," Norton proclaimed after a few seconds' search. "Whole damned lot." It was not the first time he had encountered the adversary. They could not be readily recognized by their distant features and weather-beaten skin tan. It was the black Jihad flag flying from the mast that immediately identified the war party. Under international law, talks, or whatever term one wanted to use, negotiations had to be honored. Though civilized, it would not be a happy occasion.

"What do they want?" It was Bad Man verbalizing everybody's thoughts. Clad in combats wearing the customary headgear befitting Arabian customs, he was ready to pounce on the foreign looking lot.

Striding toward the water, Norton assured him, "We'll know soon enough. And, keep your mouth shut. Don't wanna start a war."

"Why not? Let me kill 'em."

"Let's find out what they have to offer." The visiting war party had advanced as far as their boat keels would allow. With engines throttled to idle, a white flag was raised. A dingy was launched. Several shapes hopped in and shot off in their direction, beaching minutes later on the sandy shores. Jumping into the shallow waters, a detachment of four men weighed down with heavy ammo belts and AK-47 semis waded onshore. "Greetings," was the welcome offered by the apparent leader.

"I'll give you greetings," Bad Man stormed up mouthing off but was held off by Norton. "Shut up. Take them to the assembly hall."

UNITED NATIONS

The representative minister from the Sudan emphatically insisted, "Not our responsibility." In spite of his repeated denials, all eyes were glaring at him and his representatives. He sat there, leaning on the enormous table defiantly defending his nation. "Preposterous," he accentuated once more at the accusation of his nation of harboring terrorists, staring at the Secretary General of the United Nations.

Glaring back at him, the secretary general demanded justification for this latest atrocity committed on the North American continent. Today's heated issues were solely centered on yesterday's attack on the White House. By now, most nations suspected the Sudanese either supported or were directly involved in the Jihad-initiated attack.

The Western Sector emissary cut in. "We have documented proof to the contrary." This bold statement seemed to have shaken up the delegates. All heads flew in the speaker's direction when he continued. "Our investigations revealed Jihad training camps clandestinely staged around your deserts. Furthermore," he stressed, "we have reason to believe that these camps are sanctioned by your nation."

The Sudanese representative was extremely angered. He jumped from his seat. "Please," he declared with determined resolve, "the desert is a big wasteland. We cannot control every covert activity that is taking place in our vast backyard. For all we know it is *your* nation conducting unauthorized activities."

The Western Sector representative kept silent. He realized he had already exposed too much. The whole world knew that his nation conducted global surveillance, but consenting to it was yet another matter. Many nations spied on each other. It's what kept one abreast of political shifts. Unstable nations needed to be monitored. Political takeovers could happen in a moment. It was the duty of a technological advanced nation to keep informed. These were the thoughts going through his mind. He made an attempt to defuse an already tense atmosphere by expressing his thoughts with trained diplomacy. "We are here to solve a problem of Biblical proportions. There is not time to quarrel."

The secretary general was about to commence talking when the telephone set in front of him began blinking. He pushed the connect button, then reached for the receiver. It was the urgent voice of the office secretary. "I have yesterday's caller on the line one."

An initial hush fell over the assembly hall. "The terrorists are on the line." Hearing that, the quiet was quickly followed with calls of reprisals. It forced the Secretary General to profusely rap the gavel on the massively polished conference table to demand quiet. "Order...Order please." His action was so violent that the water-filled crystal on the bench cracked.

The assembly hall turned into a hush once more. He pushed the connect switch and immediately recognized the caller's voice. He did not give the caller a chance to speak. "How could you put the American citizens in jeopardy?" he raged into the receiver. "You endangered not only the lives of the free world leaders but innocent people as well. I demand immediate restitution."

The response was unyielding. The harsh voice proclaimed, "You were forewarned. What is your consensus?"

In response, the Secretary General raged on, "We have no consensus. You will be held responsible for your actions with dire consequences." He then stated further, "All nations have aligned against your demands."

A calculated challenge followed. "All nations?"

"All free nations!"

"You mean all capitalistic nations."

"You realize that you have placed yourself into a position of unremitting annihilation," the U.N. leader insisted. "Your irresponsible fight for world dominance will be squashed. I demand you immediately cease your aggression." He tried his best to force the Jihad leader to the peace table, but also knew from their radical past that it would be a fruitless effort. In face of the grave situation, the head of the U.N. tried his best to maintain the world peace.

"The bargaining power is on our side," the voice persisted. "You have no options to negotiate." Listening intensely to the language interpreters, the assembly had turned silent when the caller concluded with a final order, "You have made *your* choice. Now it is *ours*." The line went silent.

The assembly in session immediately sprang back to action. It took again minutes before it was brought under control. The only order the Secretary General was able to issue was, "Session adjourned." His voice had weakened with the caller's last remarks. *There's no hope now,* he thought with remorse. There was no reasoning with unrelenting factions. The responsibility was now in the hands of the Americans. Giving the American representative a gesture to follow, he abruptly stood up and headed for the exit.

"What is your decision?" he queried the once leading world delegate.

"We brace for attack," the American delegate replied. "It's not the first time our nation has been confronted by lunacy."

CASTLE ROCK

Alex felt tense. He was waiting for Rhonda to show up. He wasn't sure if she would heed his warning. Even if she decided to act, there was still the problem of transportation. Flights to and from the West Coast were marginal, to say the least. After the military's fleet of craft had been disabled with the EMP strike, only a few Confederate craft could be salvaged after the Cuban air battle. Whatever craft had survived the invasion attempt where severely damaged and had taken months to repair. Though flight worthy for most part, in their antiquated fashion, the Super Fortresses along with a fleet of C-130 cargo craft were the only means the New Republic had at its disposal. Where shuttles to the western region were prolific, travel to the East Coast was almost nonexistent within nation. That part was completely in the hands of hostile factions. Although an occasional private craft could be spotted in the air, nobody in their right mind would cross the airspace over the Badlands. That part of the plains was controlled by the Patriots. What made it even more dangerous was an army of ferocious killers was on the move. The War Dogs were patrolling the borders. Word had it that anybody caught illegally entering the Badlands was executed on the spot. Prolific rumors held that there was no mercy, no clemency extended to infractions.

The B-17 Flying Fortress touched down on the runway. Despite the emergency situation the nation was in, Alex, for the moment forgot all about it. His eyes closely followed the descent and touchdown on the tarmac. It was always a splendorous sight watching this magnificent bird in action. He'd decided to meet her flight. "So glad you're here." He embraced her in a pent-up desire. Her commuting to California was not his first choice. He wanted her to retire. He wanted her so much by his side. Alex realized more and more how much he depended on their companionship. He had spent too many years alone. Ever since he had stopped traveling, he had been isolated into seclusion. Not so much by choice as by present circumstances.

"What's so urgent to call me off the job?" He had sensed a slight resistance when they embraced, but shrugged it aside. But now, with her response he was certain. She'd resented the emergency call. "They need me there."

"Not anymore," he said. "Vandenberg's gone. Wiped out."

"What? When?"

"Taken out by HAARP. Right after you left."

"Oh my God." She was stunned. "The people. My friends?"

"You haven't heard?"

"In transit. Remember?"

"Sorry. Thought you'd heard." The rest of the way to the Castle was spent mostly on assumptions, theories, and speculations. There was not much else to talk about until the next day when the ultimatum was supposed to spring into action. Ever since the announcement by the U.N. secretary general about the pending ultimatum by Jihad, newswires had been prolific.

Arriving home, "Sure could use a drink," Rhonda suggested.

"I'll fix us one. Martini?"

"Fine." He returned balancing two martinis. Rhonda was seated by the coffee table. She seemed in quiet thought, reaching out for the glass he offered. "Why's Tracy's not here?"

"You know her," he hinted. "Always got her own agenda. Nobody's telling her what to do, not even Dad." He lifted the glass for a toast. "Cheers." Then he explained, "Foster refused to let her go." They both knew Tracy had become indispensable to the general, and him to the Western Sector.

"I'm not important?" He sensed she was playing with him now.

Good, he thought, *at least she's relaxed.*

Alex gently took her hand and offered, "I need you here by my side. It's the only way I know you're safe." She leaned forward to deposit the glass on the tabletop. He could read it clearly in her face. It had turned from curiosity to concern. She was waiting for an explanation. It was time to explain. Pronouncing each word deliberately, he said, "Tomorrow. The world's gonna change." He then leaned back to let the importance of the announcement sink in.

It immediately got her attention. She sought out his eyes, then quickly responded. "What? What do you mean?"

"There's a major buildup by Jihad forces. Troop movement are reported in Europe, Africa, and Middle East. I think," he emphasized, "there's gonna be an all-out assault on the world."

"You sure?" As incredible as it sounded, she always gave him credit for his acquired knowledge. The words she had just heard were frightening. It reflected in her response. "Like there's not enough turmoil already. Must there be more tragedy?"

"See for yourself."

He turned on the TV monitor. It connected the set with a dedicated channel to the racks of computers in the equipment room to the outside world. A second later, the TV screen popped into motion. Dynamically fed data streams were scrolling across their vision with information transmitted from Qatar. It was an independent broadcasting station with direct links to Jihad. Rhonda listened in awe of what she heard. *"...demand immediate sovereignty for the Palestinian nation. It must be sanctioned by all nations including Israel. You will have twenty-four hours to comply...No exceptions. Regardless of your decision, an example of our seriousness will be demonstrated tomorrow. We mean business!"*

Rhonda's face had taken on a frightened look. Her expression deepened even more when Alex warned, "That's not all." He could see her chest heave. She was taking in full breaths of air to prepare for more. The station had been broadcasting the warning to the world ever since he woke up this morning.

"Wait...here it comes..."

"The bargaining power is on our side," the voice proclaimed. *"You have no options to negotiate..."*

She'd heard enough. "Ultimatum," she queried Alex. "You believe it?"

"Got to," he insisted. "News has never been wrong. You see," he explained in earnest, "Jihad always forewarns its pending actions."

Rhonda knew that she was stalling but needed affirmation, nevertheless. As the saying went, *misery loves company* sure held true. She, like most people in the nation, was not prepared for more disasters. But, if the information was true, it would truly be Armageddon. For that, mankind was never prepared. The severity of the warning suddenly took hold in full force. Her mind clouded over filled with deep compassion. A great feeling of empathy came over her for the people of the world. "What are we gonna do?"

Alex saw the change in her face. He got hold of her arm and guided her gently out to the darkened balcony, away from the news broadcasts. "See the stars," he gestured toward the heavens. "They'll be there tomorrow. Sun will come up as always. Future will be there. Castle's gonna survive. And so will you and I—I'll made sure of that."

His assurance seemed to give her renewed confidence. *After all,* her thought went, *the Castle's survived this far.*

FOX ONE

The air was laden with blue layers of smoke drifting across the room. Slouched casually around the mission table, one of the lieutenants questioned his comrades, "Wonder who's behind it?" No one gave him an answer. It seemed all were busy with their own thoughts and issues. There was only the occasional shuffling sound of combat boots grinding against the concrete. A cough or two was audible here and there, more from habit than irritation. Smoking was one of few pleasures available to the Jihad warrior. Reading their faces, the general mood seemed to be contentment. Aside from a few isolated oppositions against the hostile takeover, a forced dominion over the local research and operations team, the attack had gone well. Until now, it appeared that fate was on the Jihad side. After all, who would expect otherwise with the world's deadliest weapon in their hands?

Madani was quietly listening to speculations going back and forth. With the question directly aimed at him, he finally spoke. "Your guess is as good as mine." If anyone would know, it would be him. "All I know one named *The Prophet* is running the show. Took over leadership after Bin Laden died."

"What about headquarters?" the warrior pressed on. "Where's it located?"

Madani explained. "Faction's spread around the globe. Al Qaeda's been splintered into many sectors. Each sector's divided further into cells all operating independently. There's no need to have a central command headed up by one commander. We are not fighting one common front," he emphasized.

"Why was the change in command not heralded as deserving to a fallen leader?"

"Western world did not want the once famous leader become a martyr."

"So," Madani was questioned again, "Nobody really knows who is in charge for our cause?"

He was about to enlighten the fighters about the emerging leader when the conversation was terminated by the tactical radio cutting in. "Fox One…Fox One…come in." It was Desert Base Alpha.

"New target data," the voice commanded. "Ready to copy?"

"Execution time Noon, 12:00 PM EDT."

"Target points—Multiple Coordinates.

    One: 40^0 45' 02.08" N, 73^0 58' 06.78" W, elev. 41.

    Two: 40^0 42' 42.48" N, 74^0 00' 47.22" W, elev. 19.

    Three: 40^0 09' 25.34" N, 76^0 43' 22.85" W, elev. 295.

    Four: 40^0 09' 19.37" N, 76^0 43' 22.62" W, elev. 295."

There was deep silence after the last code was read. Amin Madani gasped after checking the chart for coordinates. "This is major." He could not believe what he had just heard and jotted down. The coordinates identified United Nations Headquarters, N.Y. City; New World Trade Center, N.Y. City; and Three Mile Island, PA with two target points. "Get me the Eastern Seaboard map," he ordered.

Not clear what just happened, the lieutenant gaped. "What?"

"Dammit!" Madani exclaimed. "They are taking out the entire eastern hemisphere." He knew New York City only too well. It was the global center for the United Nations headquarters. *Not only that,* he thought utterly bewildered, *New World Trade Center?* He was completely perplexed. Then it hit him, "Sonofabitch." Slapping both of his upper thighs with his flattened hands, he bolted straight from the chair yelling, "Insha' Allah." He could not believe his eyes. They were taking out the new trade center building just rebuilt. "Ultimate insult." It would be an offense the leaders of the free world had never experienced. It would be a warning to the entire world, "Islam is taking control." Then there was the Three Mile Island, nuclear power plant. Although he remembered the previous assault on the plant not so long ago, he virtually knew nothing about it. All he knew was that it'd contaminate many of the eastern cities.

"What does that mean?" His band of terrorists was surprised at the sudden outburst from the normally coolheaded commander. They were eyeing him for an explanation.

Madani explained, "Tomorrow. The world will be ours."

"That means no infidels. Can they do it?"

"Not they, idiot—Us!" Madani checked his wristwatch. Somebody just handed him the chart. He needed extract and verify the targets. "Yeah," he confirmed with a grunt. "Just what I thought." There was great admiration cut across the many faces. "Clever. Listen up, people," he called his team to attention. Checking the clock, "We've got thirty minutes. Get cranking."

The attack team jumped into action. While Madani had ops program the new coordinates into the computer with the help of a resisting HAARP team, his men initiated the firing sequence. Under threat of losing more members, the team had no choice but to comply with the new orders, although unwillingly. They did not want to lose more of their fellow scientists through additional execution examples. Thirty minutes later the system was ready on standby.

Jack Owens's dead body had been removed from the control room. Covered up by a tarp, he was resting nearby the generators on an old army cot. Putting his soul to rest, some teary-eyed, spirited coworker was giving him the last rites. "May God be with you for eternity."

It was all they could do within the hostile environment. Burial had to wait until he was moved above ground, whenever that might be. The place had been quiet for a couple of days until this morning's orders. They had hoped that the crisis would be over, but it appeared to be only wishful thinking. Readiness orders were relayed through all sections with final count. "One minute to fire."

"Give me a ten second countdown," Madani ordered into the tensely charged atmosphere. The air was getting stale. He hoped to get out of here soon. He wanted to join in with the main mission forces he knew would be unleashed. All their eyes were fixated on the mission clock. His voice was synchronized with it, initiating final countdown, "Ten…two, one, fire."

Madani was mesmerized once more by the sheer power surges generated by the destructive technology in his hands that followed. "The ultimate weapon," he muttered, just as the beam began pulsing away. The explosive forces displayed on the monitors at target points were just as devastating as watching nuclear bombs going off. But his charges left no deadly residues. Other than immense damage to local infrastructures, his weapon came off clean. There were no damaging shockwaves, deadly x-rays, or radiation burns. It was a clean weapon.

"Should be grateful." Madani couldn't help but make the comment. It was justification enough for him. It might have been true for the survivors outside the target ranges. But, from within, the case was just the opposite. Everything and everybody was incinerated.

The resultant destruction would not be graceful.

"Fuck it," he verbalized his thought. "Not my problem."

One of his lieutenants approached with, "What now?"

"Now we wait. We wait for new orders."

The new orders would be solely dependent on the response from world nations. Regardless of their positions, as humanitarian and charitable as they might be, the predetermined cause executed by Jihad, supported by Al Qaeda forces, would be carried out. The end result was payback for a thousand years of Muslim injustice. Injustice to a nation patronized, manipulated, and suppressed by the free world, European monarchies, and Asian dynasties dating back to the medieval days.

It would be a world led by The Prophet. Madani launched the radio message he had prepared to the bristling ether. All it said was: "Mission accomplished. Allah' Akbar— God is great."

UNITED NATIONS HQ

Hui Wong, United Nation's party secretary was worried. He could not remember a night when he did not get any sleep. Last night was the night. His nerves were on edge. He could not quite come to terms with yesterday's ultimatum received by the terrorist leader. What made it even worse was that the caller did not identify himself or his faction. At this point, all he and the U.N. assembly knew was the treat of an imminent attack on the world. Since there was no specified target declared, every important facility had to be considered as primary aim for destruction, most likely on the eastern seaboard, his section. He could not recall any other worthy target left out West since the Capitol, Vandenberg, and Foster's headquarters had been destroyed a couple of days prior. A thought just occurred to him. It was still early. He had to be sure. He initiated a call to his personal aid to verify that all members had been notified. "Nobody report to the office today. Repeat, nobody," he panted. "Is that clear."

"Understand. Nobody."

The confirmation put him somewhat at ease. "Can never be sure," he muttered. Since today was an unexpected break from the daily routine, he thought he'd take a late morning stroll to the nearby waterfront. Dressing casual for the occasion grabbing hat and leash, he fetched his pet dog Fifi and left his domicile. He wished his wife was by his side. But it was not the case. He had sent her back to China following the first warning by the terrorists. Heavy hearted about yesterday's call, he reprimanded himself for not being more diplomatic with the caller. Considered the most diplomatic emissary on the globe, negotiating, pacifying, and appeasing every troubled nation on earth, he could have done better. He sincerely hoped there would be another call. But in the depths of his mind, he knew it was only wishful thinking. The message was clear, "Complete submission to Islam or face essential destruction."

As incredible that it may sound with the world facing a complete takeover, the indications were real with HAARP in the hands of the enemy. "Blasted weapon," he uttered. "If it wasn't for that, the ultimatum could not have happened." His dog sidled up to him to let his owner know he wasn't alone. He could sense the demise he was in. He underscored the personal connection between man and animal with a quiet yelp. Hui fished for his heirloom timepiece to check the time. It read 11:58 am. From habit, since it was an ancient family heritage, he had to manually wind the spring. And he did so. It was then when Hui Wong saw it. It appeared as a tiny piercing beam out of the upper stratosphere. Even though it was noon with the sun at its highest zenith, it was blinding his eyes. His heart almost stopped. He collapsed onto the bench. Craning his head upward shielded by his hand, he followed the pulsing beam to its target. It aimed directly for a very structure he'd just left. The United Nations building—Seat of his beloved province within a nation under attack. "My God," he whispered. "Beginning of the end."

The devastation did not stop there. The beam, as rapidly as it had struck the U.N. building reacquired its next target, the newly erected Trade Tower. It was too much for him. He was awestricken. He never felt so sickened. The guilt of failure he felt was overwhelming.

Watching the main building of the once proud peaceful complex disintegrate nearby was almost too much to bear. Tears welled up within, sending his loving passion for world-peace through every sense of emotions. There was nothing else to do but return and assess the damages. Already he could hear multiple sirens from fire engines headed his way. Office workers on their way to lunch were following the sound of the sirens nearby. Black smoke was billowing up in thick clouds obscuring sights and senses. Acrid scent permeated the air seeping to the ground. Even Fifi began sneezing and wheezing. He stood and watched the HQ building collapse into itself. He knew it would be the end of his career, perhaps the end of a once free nation.

WORLD TRADE CENTER

Before the news wires could even finish the "News Flash" alert of the U.N. building being under attack and in flames, the next Headline already announced the newly constructed One World Trade Center under attack as well. It was 911 all over. People, wherever, dropped what they were doing tuning in on the news, rushing to windows, or hurried in the direction of lower Manhattan. The thought of being under attack once again was too much for many of the mega city dwellers, to bear. *New York City,* the newswire broadcasts went over the ether, *late this morning came under attack. It was a direct result of an ultimatum call received yesterday by the U.N. Secretary General...*The report was quickly followed with the usual speculations and opinions from so-called experts on international affairs. Rumors, as usually were prolific and rampant.

What made it even more of a tragedy was that the same World Trade Center, the Freedom Tower had been destroyed only a decade ago. It was an unbelievable act of hostility. At this point, nobody had any inkling on what faction may be responsibility for this atrocious act or who claimed to be responsible. But that changed quickly. First it was rumors. Then, the call came. "Jihad."

Everybody with a television screen watched in utter fascination at the morning broadcast. Mesmerized, the screen switched to the One World Trade tower, now a smoking skeleton of its former iconic magnificence. Suddenly, a faceless voice appeared over the gruesome scenery. The leader of the terrorist faction spoke in almost perfect English. "To the peoples of the former United States of America, I am talking to you today to inform each and every one that your nation has been taken over by a new government. As of today, your nation is in the hands of Islam. You will report directly to me. I am your new leader. I am The Prophet of Islam. The new order will be strictly enforced by Jihad. I have chosen Chicago as the new capital of this nation. It is from here where your nation will be governed. It is here your representative-elects will be received. It is here, you will pay tribute. It is from here, new laws, rules, and policies will be issued. Following are the new rules as inscribed under the laws of Sharia:

"All religions practiced other than Islam are banned.

New dress code will be issued under strict law of Islam.

It is forbidden to wear western style suits, dresses, and foot gear.

The women's body will be covered in accordance to the Hijab dress code.

You will adhere to prayer rituals practiced five times daily as dictated by the Koran.

Individual property rights will be revoked and governed by rule of Sharia.

The Koran will be your new bible. No exception.

"Specific rules are forthcoming as soon as the new government has been elected and is organized. The governing rules directly related to the Five Pillars of Islam are:

Prayer, ritual, and warship

Taxation, transactions, and conducts

Fasting, beliefs, and purification

Marriage, morals and manner

Justice, rights, and punishment"

"These are the rules compulsory by your new government, that of Islam. Non-compliance will be dealt with quick and swift under the ruling of Sharia. I have spoken—Ruler and Prophet of your new nation. May Allah prevail."

The nation was stunned when the announcement was broadcast over TV, Radio, and News channels. Rumors and conspiracies were quick to follow. Every citizen in the nation, upon hearing the broadcast went through a series of primal emotions that of bewilderment, bedlam, followed with utter rage. It was here where the impact of the present confusion and demise were experienced to its fullest extent. Individual reactions were so severe that it caused uproar from border to border.

Alex and Rhonda were intently listening to the broadcast. "Oh my God," was her initial reaction. Alex was not shaken at all. Although it had a sobering effect on him, "I warned them, didn't I," he responded.

Tracy, presently in the care of General Foster kept shaking her head when hearing the new order, "Not on my watch," she kept repeating. "Not on my watch."

Rusty Norton, Patriot leader Badlands in the company of Brodie Elliott was intently listening to the broadcast. Both knew something like it would happen sooner or later unless the nation could be salvaged by either him or the leaders of the Western front. Since neither was presently capable to accomplish the impossible, their patriotic efforts were newly inspired. "Now," Norton said, "we have an agenda." The news gave him a clear and precise direction on how to proceed from here on. "No matter what," he asserted, "gotta drive the vermin from the land."

"Our land," Brodie agreed. "Let's get to work." They had their work cut out when Bad Man stormed in, "You hear. You hear it?" He was outraged to his physical limits. "I'm gonna kill 'em. Gonna kill 'em bastards," he kept yelping. "You send me there, you hear." With spittle flying across his present space, shaking a fist at Norton, he insisted. "Calm down," Norton pacified the outraged fighter. "Nobody's going anywhere. Not at the moment. We need to build a strategy," he maintained. "And that takes time."

"Ain't got time," he shouted again. "Ain't need no time. I'm ready now." He would not listen to reasoning. And justly so. Diplomacy was a word unknown to him. It was fighting he truly understood. And fighting it would be. It was the only means to avenge the present peril his nation was in. "Please," he begged. "Let me go." It took hours to calm him down. Eventually, he was promised "hands on the enemy" as soon as a battle strategy could be hammered out.

THREE MILE ISLAND

Earlier the same day, Doug Olson was headed south on River Road in his RAM pickup as he did each weekday. Most times these days he was the only one on the road. Not having to pay much attention to traffic, he could let his mind freely wander. As usual, it sought out better times. It was not that long ago when his life was pretty well organized. Job, wife, two beautiful children, home almost paid for—what more could a working man ask for? Life was good, especially living in Middletown, surrounded by rolling hills centrally located in the state of Pennsylvania. Quiet, mostly rural, the path to his workplace was a convenient drive. If one wanted a more metropolitan flavor, just 10 miles to the north was the city of Harrisburg. South of the plant was Lancaster with its substantial Amish and Quaker populations. Like many of the small surrounding towns in this part of the state, all had a rich agricultural heritage.

Aside from the setting, it had not always been this calm. There were times not just his town, but the entire region had been in jeopardy. He could still vividly recall the first time the plant had an accident. It was back in March of '79, a Wednesday he believed, when the accident occurred. A couple weekends prior, as many of his coworkers did, he had just seen "The China Syndrome." It was a film that shook up everybody in the station, and the nation. As a matter of fact, it was the cause of the government halting all further nuclear plant construction. To make things worse, two weeks later almost the identical disaster happened to his plant.

Since he had just started the job he had the pleasure of working the graveyard shift. Newly hired, inexperienced on the system, it was a few hours after midnight when the alarms went off. He was awestruck at the spectacle that followed. There was not much he could do other than follow orders in a well-organized turned chaotic environment. What followed was a sequence of errors caused by some workers. They tried everything from resetting alarms to recycling pumps, releasing valves and turbines, but nothing seemed to help. It was not until hours later and pages after pages of simulation testing that he noticed a peculiarity. Things just didn't add up between the indicators and computer readouts. Using his prior experience on the nuclear sub, combined with logical thinking, he finally detected the problem. It was a stuck valve not getting reported because of a burned-out indicator. *Imagine,* he recalled, *one third of the nation almost annihilated for a $2 miniature bulb.*

That was the first time Doug Olson saved the plant. The resultant recognition he got was a promotion to shift supervisor, a sizable pay raise, and daytime work hours.

The second time he saved the plant was not that long ago. But the end result was much more dramatic. It caused the shutdown of much of the nuclear reactor complex. Ever since, he and a skeleton crew were stationed just to keep the cooling system operational to feed nearby towns with marginal power. Their only requirement was to check on the proper flow of cooling water through reactor cores. It was that which worried Doug this morning as he turned onto the Three Mile Island's access road.

Gazing out the pickup window to check the Susquehanna River water level did not ease his ill-begotten feelings. Water levels in the Pennsylvania rivers, for the past decades, had been gradually receding. He could only guess the cause—population growth. The same dilemma was experienced all over the globe. That's what worried him. As if it wasn't bad enough already with the nation in turmoil, splintered into hostile factions. Fending off marauding bands from taking over the nuclear plant had become a constant threat not only here, but elsewhere as well.

He was only too grateful for the security Los Alamos had provided. With Brooks in charge, he couldn't have asked for better protection. At least, within the containment walls, the nuclear contaminant seemed relatively stable. As long as there was cool water to feed the fission rods, in case of power failure, thanks to Brooks, neutron extraction could be handled through mechanical manipulations. The plant within had become relatively safe. On the outside, it was a different story. Marauding bands were continuously testing the plant for breaches. Everybody wanted to get their hands on power. In this part of the country, it was power that had gained value as most precious commodity.

What worried Olson mostly were the recent rumors about these attacks. Where the plant was pretty well protected from the ground, it wasn't so from the sky.

He arrived at the entrance gate. Glad to have made it to work without an incident, "Well," summing up his thoughts, he muttered, "another boring day."

It was close to lunch time at the power plant. Employees, as was the case in most regulated industries, had a circadian mindset about taking breaks on the job. Lunch was not an exception. Most workers had their eyes set on the clock close to noon. Jim, his pal and shift supervisor, was taking quick strides past the "Management" office entrance. "You coming?" he asked.

"Be there in a minute," Doug called after him. "You go ahead." He was presently in conversation with Brooks, who had stopped by to make another revision to the "Process and Procedures" manual. Designed many years ago, the manual was grossly outdated. It was too advanced for the present mode of operations. Written for a fully automated system, it proved almost useless for the manual parameters the crew had to work with. Some of the primary control parts were burnt up with the EMP strike. Without printed circuit manufacturing and with foreign nations unwilling to help out, Doug and Brooks had to do with what was locally on hand. And electronics had no part in it, other than solid state alert signals fed to control panels. At least, it generated rudimentary alerts in case of mechanical failures. Cooling systems on primary (contaminated) and secondary (none) circuits were under manual control. And so were the "just-in-case" flood gates Brooks had installed. "Guess," Doug motioned to the hallway, "it's lunchtime." Brooks was about to get on his feet when it happened.

"What…" Both their eyes caught it at the same time. The instrument panel suddenly lit up. Accompanied by a deafening explosion, it turned to a flaming red from all the indicator bulbs, then just as quickly shut off. Doug was dumbfounded. And so was Brooks. Their eyes almost blinded from the display, Doug lunged for the control board. "Not again!" he yelled at Brooks who had rushed to his side. He had experienced this condition once before. "EMP!"

"Manual override," Brooks shouted back. But his orders fell on deaf ears. The crew had already left for the cafeteria. The plant was only in the hands of the two. Capable? Yes, but extremely shorthanded. Fortunately, neither Doug nor Scott had to resort to reading the manual. They knew all the necessary steps by heart. The manual could not have saved them anyway. The energy being forced on them was beyond any human control.

Next, both felt an intense heat wave emanating from the direction of the containment towers. "What's happening?" It was Brooks screaming at Doug, who had lunged for the manual override but stopped short. His entire body was bristling with static electricity. His generally groomed hair was standing on edge. The clothes he wore were smoldering, emanating the acrid scent of burnt fabric. He tore off shirt, trousers, and sneakers to save from getting burned. The strike was over in seconds. Remaining was a gaping hole into the skylight where the roof had been. The only sound remaining was from pieces of brick and concrete tumbling to the floor. He'd seen the results of such an attack before. He clearly remembered the buzzing sound just before the impact. It only took him seconds to assess the damages.

"Let's get outa here," Doug yelled back. "Boiler's gonna explode."

After the dust had settled, what remained was a pile of concrete rubble. Seconds later, the cooling tower exploded with nuclear-like force, shooting lethal blocks of concrete projectiles outward in every direction. The high voltage towers, along with reactor and turbine buildings, administration, control room, generators and backup systems, and cafeteria were all incinerated. The reactor cores, as luck had it, were buried under megatons of debris. Fission material, slowly melting its way into the earth, contaminated from neutron emission, would be active for many years to come. The Quaker State, what used to be the nation's showcase in farming, agriculture, and conservatism, would be inhabitable for just as long.

Brooks and Olson where the lucky ones. They had enough time to escape the ensuing inferno, partially by a quick reaction followed with the help of an air rush throwing both from the building. Landing in a field nearby, the chaotic conditions just seconds ago turned an eerie silence.

After the dust had settled, Where Doug was forced from a devoted and dedicated career he so dearly enjoyed, Scott, on the other hand was forced to seek new horizons. At this stage in life, he had two options to pursue. One was to return to Los Alamos, the other was joining the Patriot forces. Evaluating his present location, he chose the latter because it was the closest. Besides, his work as head of security implementation at the laboratory was practically completed. Work here was so abruptly terminated. He had an ominous feeling that other nuclear power plants in the eastern regions would be destroyed just the same. He did not want to stop and assess the damages. It would be a futile effort with the nation thrown in renewed turmoil, to contain the escaping nuclear contaminants without an army of MOP and cleanup equipment.

He left the region empty handed wearing only the cloths he wore, headed north where it would be safer.

ISS

Clinging to Canadarm-2 once more, Liz was exposed to the unforgiving elements of space. Walsh manipulated the robotic arm. Getting the arm close to the interlock, he slowed the motion to a crawl. A few more minutes and she would be back in the safety of the station. In her case, safety was relative. It was confined to the man-made miracle of science. Liz still marveled at the ingenuity of man to even have the first thought of joining the stars, of going into space. That, in the sphere of the universe's existence, was only a blink of an eye. *What?* her mind quickly calculated, *fifty some years ago.* Liz caught a last glimpse of the marvel before signaling Walsh for reentry into the space capsule. She was ready. "Ten more minutes to day break," Walsh's voice came back. "Let's wait." Transfer, compression/decompression, and decontamination would be safer during a daylight cycle. She did not mind. It gave her so much more time to enjoy the beauty of the blue planet, Earth. If at all possible, for safety reasons, most spacewalks were conducted during daylight hours. Nocturnal activities in space, although illuminated with floodlights, were always risky business.

Reaching out into space, Liz enjoyed the galactic view one more time. Overwhelming as it was, the scene reminded her so much on being stretched out in the seat of an IMAX theater, absorbing the magnificent sound and view. It was hard to describe. The panorama contrast in the dark was spectacular. Viewed from this distance directly above, the home planet was an enormous object. Situated directly below, perpendicular to the space station gradually passing beneath, the coastal outline from continents slowly panning into view could be readily identified. Some parts were covered by clouds, mostly cumulus, others clear from any obstructions. In the dark, with glowing city lights reflected by the ground, you could make out the populated areas. Where most of the globe was lit up and easy identifiable, the North American region was almost invisible without power for electricity. Liz could barely imagine the struggle people there had to endure in the frigid winter. Her view slowly scanned across the visible sphere of earth.

Her serenity was suddenly broken by what appeared as a tiny, a burning speck growing out of the dark. Her senses perked up. From the outline of the coastal shape, she could make out the region as central Alaska. The lit-up speck attracted her attention. She pulled up the protective helmet visor to get a clearer vision. It would prove an unfortunate move. The immediate action that followed was too overwhelming for her mind and body to react. With her eyes focused on the distant light source, she watched as it suddenly grew into an intense beam. Floodlight like, the source shot straight in her direction. On instinct, her body reacted. Her hands grasped for the access hatch, but it was too late. The beam hit the ISS at light speed.

"Not again!" Liz yelled into the emptiness of space. Her voice drifted into space without being heard. Inside the space station, the vibration of her voice was picked up by Walsh, Nagata, and Kubalev. There was enough time for the team to brace against the onslaught. But for Liz, there was no hope to be saved.

In an instant, her feet and arms were torn from the robot's boom and platform. When the beam entered the waveguide mounted nearby and was reflected back to Earth, as it had previously, the sheer energy forced the space station from orbit again. But this time, the extremely narrow beam of concentrated energy leveled on the ISS at maximum force of 15 billion watts was devastating. Trusses that held the space station together tore apart with an equal magnitude in reactive force. The delicate solar panels reaching into space to catch sunrays were torn off their mountings, and so were the HRS[45] radiators.

Seconds earlier, when Liz screamed into the headset, Kenny, Hiroshi, and Andrei, inside the capsule, at the time occupying Harmony after recognizing the extreme danger, were unable to react in time. Their bodies were hurled through the capsule's confinement only to violently slam against the module walls. Without the protection of the bulky space suits, they took the full brunt of the force leaving them breathless. Fighting for precious oxygen to survive, their bodies turned and twisted in agonizing movements, on the brink of blacking out. The agony of air escaping unchecked from the lungs can only be imagined by someone that had experienced the condition.

It took what seemed to be endless minutes of desperate struggling to get air forced back into lungs. The intake of oxygen preempted all other thoughts and actions from the struggling bodies. Fortunately, the oxygen generating system within Harmony held steadfast. Kenny was first to respond. With the station forced out of orbit, using extreme muscle strength, he propelled his body off the walls in the direction of the system controls. Getting hold of the console, his fist drove down hard on the retro controls. Immediately, he felt the G forces on his body diminish but not fast enough. It would take time and many more miles for the ISS to settle into a new orbit.

Next, he rushed for the porthole. He could make out the outlines of the spacesuit against the brilliance of the sun rising over the horizon. "Liz," he repeatedly screamed into the headset, but there was no answer. With the strike diminished, the ether had fallen silent. Worse yet, all communication seemed to be out. Lips quivering with fear, voice broken with grief, eyes moistened from tears, he kept repeating, "Liz," over and over. But it was in vain. Aided by Kubalev and Nagata, he finally calmed down enough to regain his composure.

Kubalev was shaken up as well. "We'll get her back," Kenny consoled his fellow astronaut. Nagata was already on the computer, pulling up emergency procedures from the onboard database. Fortunately, because of the strict specifications for space-based designs, the "hardened" equipment held out. Backup power had automatically taken over. The ISS had stabilized for the time being, and so had Liz. But her body was floating in the loneliness of space, out of reach from any help.

At the same time, the station was hit by the beam, in another segment of the ISS, Toporov and Budenko were busy with the waveguide controls in Zvezda, the Russian service module. Still trapped in the capsule from their earlier shootout with the American space crew, both tried to cope with the unexpected development. Because of the extreme secrecy observed for the capability of HAARP, no data was available on the true impact

---

[45] Heat Rejection Systems – The photovoltaic systems collected the warming solar rays. The heat rejection system kept the ISS cool during its daily orbital cycle with temperature changes ranging from minus 250 to plus 250-degree Fahrenheit, a five-hundred-degree difference.

force exerted as weapon. Both jihadists turned cosmonaut were unprepared for what was about to develop.

With the incoming beam at full power, as was the case with all crew members, Toporov and Budenko's bodies were slammed against bulkheads. The result was prolific profanity flung at the creators of the weapon. Both kept cussing out everybody from the Balkans to the Pacific. With nerves on edge to the breaking point, it would take them hours to calm down. Things would have been easier to tolerate with some tobacco and a little Vodka on hand. But that commodity was not allowed in space. Not yet anyway.

Toporov composed himself first. "Get hold of yourself," he spat at his comrade.

"Fuck you," was the immediate comeback. If Budenko had access to the weapon he had lost earlier to Liz, a shootout would have been guaranteed. But without it, only their fists were flying, although mostly ineffectively. Without gravity to keep the body steady, hand-to-hand combat in space did not work. Every action from a body in motion caused an immediate counter action. Floating in space, the body always headed straight for the opposite direction, consequently drifting apart from the opponent. Unless strapped in and contained to a hold, which conversely defeated the purpose of a fight, the physical struggle was mostly ineffective. With every punch thrown, both opponents kept drifting apart. Budenko finally solved the problem. In one swift motion, he got hold of a strap floating nearby, wrapped it around one of his and Toporov's wrists and began punching away.

Beaten to a pulp, exhausted to the limits, the fight eventually ended in a draw. Nobody lost, nobody won. "Truce…truce…" Toporov panted. Both agreed to stop the fight, but did not stop Budenko from lashing out to land another punch. The fight was on again. It lasted until Budenko became aware that something was wrong with the capsule. Taking a break from the fighting, he quickly noticed their bodies revolving around the confined space. It dawned on him. It was not them. It was the capsule spinning out of control. He tore loose from the wrist strap to catch a glimpse out the porthole.

What he spotted gave him the shock of a lifetime. Zarya had broken free from its Destiny mountings and was now freely floating in space. He immediately knew the consequences. There was no chance for rescue. They would be floating in space from here to eternity. *Unless,* his pulpy, beaten face took on a slight glimmer of hope, *help comes in the form of a shuttle type spaceflight.* But it was months, perhaps years, away. "We are fucked," was his final comment to his cosmonaut comrade. Toporov agreed in silence. It was either beating each other to death or starvation setting in. In either case, they were doomed.

Confined to the Columbus Lab, Dieter Fuchs did not fare any better. Terrified at first, when the insane acceleration finally slowed he regained his composure, tremendously weakened and mentally destabilized. He realized a disaster had happened, but to what extent was anybody's guess. He was in no shape to react. His body was thrown around the capsule, first to one end, then the opposite, finally landing against the ceiling. Drifting weightlessly, it really did not matter the position a body was floating in, after the initial disorientation, the mind gradually adjusted. But, taking the terrific jolt that he did, floating became extremely nauseating for Dieter. Without an external porthole, he had no means to orient his body. Enormously weakened from the earlier accident, exposure to the lethal virus, his body tried to cope with the added stress. It would prolong his sickness even further.

Unanswered panicked calls on the intercom did not ease his disparity. Trapped without power, communication, and food at this time, all he could hope for was someone coming to his aid. Until that time he was susceptible to starvation, extreme heat and cold, and more detrimental, the isolation of space. It was thoughts like these that harbored in his mind until he took the time to assess the internal damages the lab had sustained. As if it was not already stressful enough, a new shock painted across his face. Vials, Petri dishes, microscopes, and lab mice were scattered across the lab, floating in space. Driven by compassion, he gently reached out for the white-furred animal drifting past his face. He was about to collect it and place it back into the wall-mounted cage when he realized the animal was already dead. The expression on his face quickly changed from compassion to grief when he discovered the real damages caused by the strike. "I am a dead man," was all he could muster up in the isolation of his confinement. Days would go by before his lifeless body was discovered still clutching the furry little animal. The Ebola virus had taken its toll once more on both the lab animals, as well as Dieter, whose promising life had been drastically cut short.

When Liz was torn from the station, her body was the only object remaining in the station's former orbit. Without tether, torn from the capsule, she now tumbled freely through space. She tried hard to keep her calm, but it wasn't easy. The sun had just disappeared beneath the horizon. It would take at least ninety minutes for it to reappear again at the opposite horizon. Until then, space had turned dark with only the distant stars giving off their pale light. She tried to get someone's attention by calling out, "Walsh, come in…anybody, come in." There was no answer. Space remained silent. Liz finally gave up after she realized there was no communication with the crew or the station. And without a repeater or HF transmission via the station, her voice would not carry all the way back to Earth.

"Keep your cool," she instructed herself in-between taking in excessive amounts of precious oxygen. "It's not the first time you've been stranded." But this was the ultimate example of being caught up alone and isolated from life. Her body shuddered with the sheer realization. She suddenly longed for company, any company. Even the company of the enemy would be better than this eternal loneliness. Her mind began to drift.

When the magnitude of her plight set in, Liz reminded herself to get a grip on reality. To keep her sanity, she created images. What appeared from the recesses of her mind was a familiar face. "Dad," she muttered. At least she had company in this loneliness. She began talking with him. "There's a way. There's got to be. Dad…Think!" When there was no response, her own mind churned for a way out. "Think, girl, think!"

Her mind kept drifting in and out of reality. Childhood images swept in front of her vision. They were playing catch, her sister and her. They were laughing. Those were the happy times…the innocent times…times without burden…a time for play. She was a child again. "Dad," she would call for his attention. "Why…why…why…?" Her mind was like a siphon. It would absorb everything he'd throw at her. And there was a lot. No matter how trivial or challenging, he seemed to have an answer for everything. He was her living encyclopedia.

She recalled. The first weeks after birth was emptiness, much like the present surrounding space. Then, she gradually came to know a happy face. It was the face of her mom, filled with love and admiration. Occasionally, the face would change. The new face was also filled with smiles, but there seemed to be wisdom rather than love. It was this face that gradually filled her with knowledge, knowledge of life. It did not stop there. He showed her things. He'd demonstrate everything, from her first attempt to ride the bike she'd received for her sixth birthday, to skiing, skating, diving, and, of course, martial arts. But that was many years later, years ago.

Presently, with her body drifting through space, she vividly recalled each and every segment of growing up. There were the happy times, then the not so happy ones when getting hurt. At the end, she grew into an adult, into a woman taken over by career, marriage, followed with divorce. She thought she knew it all, the knowledge of life. But there was one thing he'd never taught her, and that was how to escape her present plight of aimlessly floating through space. "How could he?" she justified that one single element she so desperately needed now. "Dad," she screamed into the empty silence, hoping for an answer. "Where are you?" She waited for the answer, but there was none. His image gradually faded into nothingness. She was back at the sober reality of her plight.

With each time the sun rose, in the distance Liz could make out the fragmented sections of what once was the space station drifting slowly apart from each other. Torn to pieces, it looked nothing like the once proud shape the world had come to value and admire. Billions of dollars, years of labor getting the hundreds of thousands of pieces created first, then manufactured, tested, and finally launched into orbit, were now ripped apart at the seams.

It would have been understandable if it had been destroyed by an internal accident, a solar event, or even through cosmic cataclysm, but to have it destroyed by a manmade incident, caused by anger and resentment over political and secular differences? "Unforgivable!"

Rage she'd never known slowly took hold on her. Maybe it was a good thing. Maybe it was the ingredient needed to spur her mind into action. Perhaps, looking through the eyes of rage was what she needed to clearly see what needed to be done, what had to be done, now, this very instant. Her eyes shot to the oxygen gage fastened on her wrist. It indicated that she had used up almost half capacity. It came to her. She suddenly had an explosive idea. "What if I use the remaining air pressure from the tank? Could it work? Will it work?"

As far as she knew, it had never been tried. As a matter of fact, it had never even come up as a rescue option. "Worth a try…Either way, if it fails, I'm doomed." Her oxygen supply would run out in less than thirty minutes. It might be just enough to propel her to the nearest capsule, drifting farther apart with every second. She made her decision. "Let's do it," she instructed herself. "But first, must slow the tumbling." She was able to slow it by repeatedly throwing her arms above her head. The sudden action gave her body the extra dimension she needed. Although miniscule in space, the ensuing reactive force gradually slowed her body mass. With eyes fixed on the nearby space debris, she cheered into the emptiness of space. "It works!" With the rotation slowed to an inching crawl, at least for now, she could get a solid fix on the nearest space module.

The next step would be the most critical. It would decide whether she was to live or die. Her breathing, although erratic at times, returned to almost normal.

Her mind was made up. It was churning with final calculations. Her eyes fell on the wrist-mounted meter one more time for the remaining oxygen. "It's now or never!" A few more seconds and several degrees of body rotation, and the external air hookup-connection centered at the midsection would be in position. For the experiment to succeed, the connector had to be precisely positioned in the opposite direction from the space module. After one final directional check, an eerie cry escaped her lungs, "Now!" At the same instant, she tore the outer seal from the space suit connector. If it weren't for the helmet the yell alone could have propelled her off into space. Anxious seconds went by, then, breathless with exuberance, she shouted, "It works…it works…it works!"

But her cheering was short lived. It quickly vanished the closer she drifted towards the capsule. It was Harmony she was shooting for. Being the most robust of the modules, it would be her best chance, her only chance. The trouble, aside from another night cycle descending on her, she realized, it was not aligned with her course. It had slowly drifted off on its own path. Panic set in once more when Liz realized the only hope for survival was slowly drifting by. "No, you don't," she yelled at the passing shadow tumbling through space only feet from her grasp. She could almost touch its surface. "Get over here, you bitch," she yelled in desperation. "Now!" But no amount of screaming and yelling would bring her closer. Any chance for rescue had suddenly vanished. "No! No! No!"

Liz was devastated. All her optimism, all her aspiration, and all her hope was shot, vanished, forever. She began to sob. Tears freely floating across her visor clouding her vision. She did not care. Life that she so dearly cherished ended in space, here and now. "Sorry, my precious daughter. Sorry, my dear son," she grieved in the blackness of space. It was too dark for her to see the oxygen dial strapped on her wrist. Time would not matter anymore. Only minutes would remain. Preparing for the inevitable, her gaze fell on the distant stars. There was Orion and the Big Dipper, amid all the other constellations. Her eyes slowly shifted farther. They finally locked on the Milky Way. The sight was grandiose. Viewed from space, it was especially spectacular without being obscured by layers of smog and dust particles as on Earth. A sudden calm came over her. Liz prepared for the end.

She was in this terminal setting when something rubbed against her shoulder. Still night time, on instinct Liz reached for it. The touch was solid. Her fingers grabbled for it. Her hands got a solid hold on it before she realized it was a mess of torn cables and wires trailing Harmony. "There's life after all!" she yelled out.

It took only minutes to inch her body up the cables on toward the capsule. The life-supporting oxygen was running out fast, escaping into space. Without oxygen, her energy was failing rapidly. She was unable to pull up the external interlock. In one last desperate effort, she banged against the hull, then fainted into nothingness, succumbed to the inevitable, death.

It was some time later. Liz did not know how long because her mind had already shut down when her eyes caught a glimmer of light. It was the slight motion from a shadow. Next, it gained shape. Then the shape turned into an object. It was a face staring at her. It was a grinning Walsh by the opened hatch, quickly pulling her inside the protective shielding of the interlock. The hatch slammed tight. The chamber filled with oxygen. She could breathe once more. She was safe. Liz was home again.

DESERT BASE ALPHA

With jet engines winding down, the craft came to a halt. Yusuf jumped from the copilot seat to greet the crew. It seemed the crew was anxious, showing off their efficiency with servicing the craft. He knew as soon as he stepped off, their world would change forever. Hammad leaned back in the cockpit seat, watching the refueling process. He was taking his time. He was collecting his thoughts. His thoughts reached back in time. It was long ago. Thousands of years have passed since. It was so long ago that only history books contained specific accounts. But for him, every detail was imprinted in his mind. Growing up as devout Muslim, the Koran and Muslim history was all he read. It was a world of dreams, a world of great riches, and a world of roaming freedom for his people. The time had come to regain the dream. The time was now. He was ready. Yusuf stepped up to inform him, "The troops are ready." Hammad pushed himself off the pilot seat, taking deliberate steps, savoring the moment. Gazing at the crowd, he could make out the many anticipating faces cheering at him, all reflecting yesterday's successful strike against the infidels. They seemed ready for action.

Desert Base Alpha was built as the primary command and control center for the upcoming missions. The base was manned mostly by commanders and an immediate support staff. The main thrust of his force was positioned throughout the African continent, spread over a number of secluded base camps. The planned offensive was commanded from here, but coordinated by regional cells placed into position years earlier. Although heavily concentrated in Europe, auxiliary cells had been staged around the globe supported through European managed satellites.

The leader was hurried to the command center. All eyes were focused on him when he entered. Looking over the many expectant faces he raised his right hand to salute his forces. Slowly, with a calculated gesture, his lips formed the words that would launch an epic of time guaranteed to be recorded in the next chapter of history. Right arm raised into a fist, his face turned into a broad smile when he shouted out the announcement, "Shahadah."

Hands flew up everywhere. Soldiers were jumping and cheering wildly with joy. Shahadah was the battle cry for days, weeks, and months, to come. It set in motion forces suppressed for eons. Once the initial cheering subsided, Hammad waved for his lieutenants to join him at the mission table. Projected from one wall of the desert-based headquarters onto a display of multimedia screens were a number of globally indexed charts indicating attack positions. Tagged in green were the Jihad forces. Red outlined immediate target points dominant for the American coastal zones. They were places where most of the communication centers would be located. Yellow designated supply chains. Black designated Jihad HQs and command and control centers.

Yusuf gestured at the cheering crowd. "They are ready." There was more cheering when Hammad stood up to approach the podium. His forces were driven into ecstasy. The display was enormous. It was fueled by a thousand years of frustrations endured through oppression, repression, and hardship. Today, the Islamic nation would be liberated. It would be the beginning of a new epoch. Indicating to calm the cheering, Hammad lowered his outstretched arm. The cheers lasted for at least another minute before they subdued. The hall finally turned silent.

"First," Hammad opened the speech he had been waiting to deliver for years, "I need to express my gratitude to all of you for your dedication to our cause." He took the time to assess the renewed cheers from the floor. Witnessing it gave him the power surge he had so desperately sought for years. Where, in the past it might have been wishful thinking, the ecstasy, the display facing him today had turned into reality. His emotions were caught up in the moment. A shadow of great pride swept across his face, widening into a broad grin.

"Next," he had to shout to be heard, "I am your supreme commander, taking on the free world." Again, the crowd went wild, fueling his ego even more. Although Hammad normally did not tolerate such outbursts, here, due to the monumental occasion, he made allowances. *After all,* he thought in the midst of the turmoil, *this is an epic event.*

Had he allowed it, the cheering would have gone on for hours, possibly turning into fury. He could not allow an outbreak of passionate rage. It would alert the enemy. He knew only too well that it was the character of Persian blood. Aided by Yusuf, they eventually brought the turmoil under control. He was finally allowed to continue. "Comrades," he gestured at his battle commander. "You all know Yusuf Hashim. He will now lay out the strategy, his position, and your roles for the upcoming battle." The sea of faces shifted to the battle commander. Hammad returned to his seat. Exalted in silent pleasure, he watched the expressions on the many faces. Through distinct cultural features, he could easily identify the many nations represented here. While mostly Arabic in nature, there were many mercenaries recruited from various other countries. He could make out features from Europe, Asia, India, the Pacific, and as far away as the southern hemisphere. Black, brown, yellow, and white faces were exuberantly following the words Yusuf presented.

Pointing at the world chart, Yusuf opened the session, initiating the attack sequence. "Here," he indicated, "is where our primary forces are stationed." Waving the pointer across the screen, he went into great detail to illustrate each segment of the attack.

"What about the infidel's military forces?" one lieutenant wanted to know.

Expressing great confidence, Yusuf said, "Surprise will be on our side." After a slight hesitation, he warned, "Of course, there will be resistance. The free world will demand retribution but their countermeasures will be uncoordinated. And above all," he put emphasis on the next words, "we have the ultimate weapon in our possession, HAARP."

Again, loud cheers went up across the room amid profanities against the free world such as, "damn the infidels…crush the sinners…down with the democratic mongers." Each time the most hated word "democracy," was spoken, it was promptly accompanied by spitting and spewing. Democracy, in the minds of the jihadists, was the archenemy.

As a last act, he assigned his lieutenants to their designated battle zones then cheered a final departure message. "May Allah be with you." Catching up with Hammad, they quickly took their seats in their aircraft and departed the base for the last time. Although his combined forces were mostly invisible, they were trained and battle ready, hidden in secluded caves and training camps staged across the globe ready to move out on a moment's notice.

In the days and weeks that followed, wherever there was resistance, the American military forces were swiftly suppressed. Jihad assault teams had been stationed near strategic battle fronts in Central America, Cuba, Venezuela, and other off-shore locations with support from dormant cells located through the nation and across the surrounding borders from Canada and Mexico. A contingent of trained commanders were skillfully coordinating the battle efforts using tactical voice equipment ranging from JTRS to HAM sets and mobile phones wherever operational. Whereas most satellites along the equatorial belt and southern hemisphere were still functional, it was the northern regions where the grid had been taken out with communication marginal at best.

It may not have been obvious to the western world that Islamic nations had been on the increase for decades. Muslim people spreading throughout the globe had been prolific. Under the cloak of general world population growth, they conveniently blended in with newly created communities, settlements, secular sects, and ethnicity sectors within rapidly expanding third world zones. The stage had been set decades ago, but not activated until Bin Laden had taken the cause into the field, ironically funded by the American taxpayer, to help in the destruction of its once proud nation.

1ST ARMORED DIVISION

It had taken Brodie Elliott and his 1st Armored Division three months to get his forces battle ready. Spending years of inactivity at the temporary headquarters established at Milwaukee, mostly drinking beer and fighting each other for the good of the nation, his men were grossly out of shape. It took repeated orders and threats from Norton to do just that. "Get your men in shape or I'll have you replaced." It took some time to reestablish authority, discipline, and order. Everybody, without exception, was forced back into basic training much like initial recruiting. Training was brutal. For the young, it was easily managed once the body got used to the rigor of basics and the forced intake of added calories, complemented with enforced rest. It was not so easy for the seasoned warrior. Set in ways and complacent in lifestyle, they were used of having their way. Women recruits were easier to deal with. They took orders more readily, spurred on by incentives for carving out a position among the ranks of soldiers. It was especially inspired by that figment called Stinger making headlines throughout the regions. Considered a myth in the early days, but with reports mounting, pretty much confirmed her legend. Each time a new rumor surfaced, though unaware by Stinger herself, the response was enthusiastic among the woman population.

Even hymns were created after her legendary battles. "We are the warriors…Our day has come…Victory is ours…"

At times, with conditions pressing on a populace, it might only take the smallest seed to be spurred into flourishing. In this case, female recruits signed up in droves. A new army was being amassed, that of an entire division managed by women, for women. As was the case with each new creation, it needed a label. And so, the "Red Brigade" division with Big Red as commander was born.

It was this division enduring the brutality of basic training to get battle ready. The seasoned warriors came down hard on the new all-female division. It was a direct threat on the established soldier, but Elliott was relentless in getting bodies shaped up for battle. Their first challenge, it was decided, would be the fight for HAARP. It would be a make or break condition, setting future trends for the women soldiers. Short on military training, in need of armament, lacking in command support, with men unwilling to compromise their positions with the 1st, the Red Brigade more or less was on their own. Spirited, full of vigor, after two months of hardship, the all-female division was ready for the rank and files.

That was six months ago. Today, deployed in the wilderness of Alaska, they were facing the harsh reality of the first battle ahead. "Move…move up." Big Red ordered the loosely held, all-female battalion into tighter formation. "This is no picnic."

It would be the first battle for every recruit in formation. While anxiety showed on many of the young faces, once the battle perimeter was identified it was quickly replaced by determination. Shots rang out the minute the Red Brigade division stumbled from the wooded regions surrounding the HAARP perimeter. Unfamiliar with the terrain, hindered by lack of communication and air support, roaming the vastness of Alaska as was the case here, the sudden confrontation with the facility came as surprise.

"Down," the voice of Big Red echoed through the woods. "Everybody." The sudden, unexpected confrontation called for an ad hoc battle decision. Checking the map, taking a few minutes to assess the area, assigning section squadrons, the command was ready for battle. In spite of the heavily-wooded terrain, numbers were in her favor. From their present perspective, the scenery ahead blended in perfectly with the density of the surrounding forest. The HAARP antenna farm was indistinguishable from the woods. That's how camouflaged the site was. Only on forging their way closer could they identify the forest of antennae. What the soldier faced were rows and rows of steel spikes jutting vertically up, aimed at the sky above. It was a wondrous sight for any firstcomer. "What's it do?" was the question shot at Big Red. "Are we fighting over metal sticks?"

"Not sticks," she quickly educated her lieutenants. Her face pulled into a grimace. "It's this shit," she cussed, "that caused all the trouble in first place."

Suggestions that followed were prolific. "Burn it down…Tear it out… Shoot it from the roots."

"Idiots," was her silent response. With all squadrons in place surrounding the perimeter fence, Big Red gave the command. "Attack."

Earlier in the day, Muhab Sadek, commanding the HAARP facility, was shaking his head to clear a troubled mind. For days reports of an advancing army were carried back by his scouts. He had desperately tried getting more information from his battle command out east. Completely isolated, without satellite or radio communication, he was subjected to a total blackout. It had been this way ever since his last attack. But that was months ago. Ever since, he had been clueless of current state conditions, as well as the rest of the world. Only occasionally, when the ether was favorable, did he receive scattered information over VHF and UHF antennas poised on top of the support building.

Dug in near the building entrance, prepared to ward off any possible intrusion, his squadron of mercenaries lay crouched around the perimeter and waited. His lieutenants, their field glasses trained on the dense forest surrounding the facility, could hear the advancing army, but not identify it until it broke out of the woods. It was then he gave the orders. "Fire at will."

It appeared his men took the advancing army by surprise. There was an initial confusion, followed by a rapid retreat, but not before he and his men spotted something highly unusual. They were stunned by what they saw. From beneath the helmets of many of the fighters protruded the flowing hair of women soldiers. Highly perplexed, questioning the sighting, Sadek muttered, "Must be a mistake…I'm hallucinating." Shaking his head, dumbfounded, he promptly asked his lieutenant, "What do you make of it?"

Equally perplexed, the bewildered response was, "Women…Whole damned army."

CASTLE ROCK

More time has passed since the United States of America had been fractured: first, from the nuclear exchange initiated by North Korea; second, immediately following the all-out attack by Jihad; third, the prison break at Fort Leavenworth; fourth, the hostile takeover of Fort Knox; fifth, the forming of the Badlands; sixth, the fall of the former government and military; and seventh, the splitting up of the north American region. The severe economic setback that followed had traumatic effects on the lives of a once powerful nation. Upholding the constitution, as promised by the forefathers, had proven futile. Because of the extreme hardships placed on its people, it did not hold together.

"What now?" Tracy prodded her dad into the conversation. Where Alex was generally a quiet person, almost to a point of introversion, she could always find a trigger, provoking him into the philosophical discussions she so dearly treasured. It was more than that. In recent months, a feel of entrapment had come over her more often than not. She felt trapped by the Castle, trapped by the situation, and more so, trapped by the loss of their only defense rendered useless, HAARP. With it gone, she suddenly felt exposed. It was a helpless feeling. Months had already passed since the Presidio was destroyed by the enemy. At this time, Foster, along with the president, and herself, were clueless as to who kept initiating the attacks. The only sure thing was that it would not end here. All surveillance indicated that Islam was on the move. Middle-Eastern news media carried propaganda almost daily, threatening the free world with more things to come. To make things worse, much worse, after the monumental announcement by the supposed Islam leader, taking control over the nation, people quickly realized that their worst fears came true. Jihad openly took hold over the nation with all of its doctrines, customs, and ruthlessness, especially within the populated regions, the Atlantic coastal cities. From here, the Islamic forces gradually pushed its way up and down the coast, as well as inland. At times, fighting was fierce. Foreign brutality was felt everywhere there was resistance. Many of the outlying regions did not, and would not submit to the oppressors. Beheading, the cruelest of all executions to the western world was the ultimate outcome. It was swift and merciless. It fueled the battle morals evermore within the nation's borders, as well as externally, the rest of the world.

According to recent reports, world leadership consensus had it that free world nations had already lost their majority statuses. Muslim population has taken the lead not only in trade and commerce, but, even more significantly, in technology as well. Tracy, as usual when she was prodding Dad, waited patiently. She gave him another minute to respond.

"Don't know," Alex finally broke the serenity in the den. "Let me give you my take." After another drawn pause, he began his usual semi-monologue. "All indications," he explained, "on an eventual collapse were present all along, especially to the historically informed reader. Even prior to 1776, before the constitution was formed, there had been historical data to contradict a permanent and everlasting nation. Our forefathers knew that it was only wishful and conceited thinking, but regardless, an attempt had to be made for a new form of government. It had worked for two hundred plus years, a remarkable duration by any means for any nation, for any people. Consequently, the former period ended, paving the way for a new cycle. Successful or not," Alex emphasized, "it would not matter."

"It is said that no nation is created to last forever. The need for mankind to expand is too great. Man cannot be contained for very long. It is in man's nature to seek out new horizons. It is what progress is all about. It is the way of creation. It cannot be otherwise. Or else," Alex explained further, "life becomes one of stagnation. And that would be the collapse of civilization. We may consider ourselves fortunate, having been planted in an ever-expanding universe. It is this expansion that allows life to flourish. It works on a small, as well as on a large scale. It is this horizon that gives mankind the incentive to strive, to excel, to build, to prosper, and to expand with time and distance. Technology is only the means to aid in the ever-increasing speed of expansion. But," he emphasized, "at the end, as sure as the cycle of nature repeats itself, it will make way for another beginning."

Like so many times before, encouraged by her dad's wisdom, Tracy felt energized once more. He had the uncanny skill to bring out the best and worst in a given situation. It was a gift not many had. It was the result of a lifetime of analysis work. It was here where an individual acquired the skills to analyze not only both sides of a conditional state, but all sides as well. It was a rare quality to achieve what her dad had. He'd spoken his piece. It was up to her to pick a new topic. For now, she decided to give him a break. She suggested, "Up for a match?"

Right away he knew what she wanted. Getting on his feet, he motioned to her. "See you at the gym." Working out had become a daily routine. For the most part, it would take the edge off of boredom.

With Tracy unable to return to work to her once prominent position in the intelligence agency, the NSA, as well as more recently, the Western Sector, like thousands of others she found herself without a career. The only factions that were thriving were the Patriots, formerly known as the Republic; farmers large enough to repel the marauding gangs raiding for food; newly created, likeminded splinter groups prowling across the land in search of unclaimed land; and finally, what was left of the once powerful military. The remnants of it had been pushed to the shores of the Pacific. It was the land nobody wanted because of its contamination from the nuclear hit. To this day, some regions still were uninhabitable. It was these circumstances that Tracy and many others were facing.

They had been sparring for close to an hour. After landing another solidly planted kick to Alex's ribcage, Tracy mocked him from between clenched teeth. "Gotcha."

"Hey!" he exclaimed. "That hurt." Getting short winded, he ended their sparring for the day.

"Give up?"

"Let's take a break."

Tracy could have taken another few rounds, but realized her dad needed a break. *After all*, she considered, *he's getting up there.* At her age, anybody over forty was "up there." Regardless, she totally appreciated the things he taught her.

"Yeah," he reluctantly admitted. "You beat me." Concern showed on his face more frequently lately. More often than not, his daughter had taken control over their sparring. Averting his eyes while squatting in the Lotus position, as they usually did after a bout of matches, his thoughts were troubled. *She's getting to be a menace,* he thought in the quiet of the gym. *Wonder what motivates her?* He had his concerns about her, but had not approached the subject yet.

Tracy, his once precious daughter, in recent months had become more and more reclusive. *Gotta find out what's on her mind.* With that thought he made a first attempt to approach the subject. He had to know what had brought on the change. Not wanting to alienate her and their close relationship, he gave it considerable thought. Finally getting up enough courage, he opened the topic. "Tracy, what's been bothering you? Tell me what's on your mind."

"What do you mean?" Surprise showed in her face. "I don't understand."

He made another attempt. "Tell me I'm wrong. But lately it seems," he took a brief pause to assimilate his thoughts, "like you've been preoccupied with private thoughts. Thoughts I may not like."

"What are you saying?"

"Well…" he paused. "Your face, your attitude, your demeanor's giving it away."

"What?" She challenged his gaze for several seconds.

"Is it your hatred for the Serpent? Is it the punishment from Jihad? The new Islamic order? Is it me? You can tell me." Alex hoped he would finally get some straight answers.

She took a deep breath then said, "Dad, it's not you. It's because of what's happened over the past few months. I've decided to make some changes to my life. Job," she took a calculating pause, "for all practical purposes, is out…nonexistent, as you well know."

"Job, career," Alex responded. "Believe me. I thought about that." He did not like what he'd just heard but continued anyway. "It's a new beginning," he explained. "It'll take time."

"How much time?" she challenged. "No government, no military, instability all around? We're fortunate we don't live on the east coast. Muslim living forced on everybody. I will never wear a veil or Hijab and Jilbob. I'd die first."

"Just don't know."

She shot him another defiant look. "See what I mean?"

"Yeah, but," he cautioned, "you shouldn't take the law into your own hands."

"That's exactly what I'm doing." Gazing into his weary eyes, she explained, "How many times did you preach to us to hold our own, to stand our ground? It builds strong character. Remember?"

"Strong character," he replied, "yes…but anarchistic? No!" He had observed her change from a once rational person into what he could only categorize as someone with a 'killer instinct.' He had seen that trade too often in recent years. He could only equate her present behavior to what Brooks and the other DELTA killing elements had displayed. And he didn't like it. He did not like it at all. Not with his daughter.

"Dad," she attempted to put him at ease, "you worry about the wrong things. I'm on your side…always have been…always will."

"Then what's with all the sparring…the aggression…the hostility?"

"Focus the mind," she proclaimed. "I wanna fit in with the new society."

"But it's all chaotic!"

"I wanna survive."

"You're safe here at the Castle."

"What?" she violently objected. "Spend the rest of my life in confinement? Not a chance."

"It'll not always be this way."

She made an effort conceding with, "Dad…you cannot guarantee it." After a brief pause she went on. "I, however," she exclaimed with deep commitment, "can!"

Alex suddenly realized he had lost his once precious girl. It was time for him to accept she had grown up. "I've reached my limits."

"What limits?"

He explained, "In order to move forward, I can no longer teach you. By that, I mean," he went on, "that you'll have to solicit new skills. Skills I've never learned, those of the Assassin. I'll help you get in touch with people that can help."

Tracy kept silent. She seemed to mull over what was just said, then changed the topic. "Anything from Liz…anything?" It had been months. Last word anybody got from space was about the HAARP attack. Ever since, all communication had been out from the space station.

Alex wanted to give her assurance and said, "Workin' on it." It was all that needed to be said. He and Brian had been spending much of their waking hours trying to figure out a means to get an uplink established with the ISS. If anybody could do it, it would be him. Although governments had more technologically advanced communication equipment, Alex had the ingenuity to make it happen. As long as something was logically possible, he would find a means. But this time, he was stymied like everybody else living under the sun. No amount of query from any ground-based support station, so far, had any luck in getting a response from space.

For some time already, news reporting services had given up on the ISS crew. Life support only lasts so long without getting replenished, especially the food supply. There were other, more pressing, concerns, like that of onboard power. Without power, the heating and cooling systems would be rendered inoperative, consequently making life on the capsules, whatever little was left, impossible. With temperature swings from minus 250° to plus 250° every ninety minutes, it would only take a few earth cycles to destroy the occupants.

Tracy noticed the despairing look in her dad's face that he'd carried for months and offered, "Need help?"

"As a matter of fact," he conceded, "I could use your help. Follow me." He was already headed for the basement and gestured for her to follow.

She knew where he was headed. It was the command center, his private sanctuary. "Be there in a minute," she called after him. She wondered about Brian. It was getting to be late morning already and he still had not shown his face. *Must be sleeping in,* she supposed. *Don't blame him.* After the collapse of the nation's satellite grid and the abandoning of NSA headquarters, his life, for all practical purposes, had become meaningless.

Today, after listening to her dad's reasoning, she decided to light a fire under his butt. Ever since her forced return home from the West Coast, he had been very accommodating to her. There was nothing he would not do. In spite of the current economic shortcomings, his love for her was still as uncompromised as ever. But, regardless of the current state of affairs, she wanted to kick some meaning into his life. If anybody could do it, it'd be her. Those were the thoughts on Tracy's mind on her way to the bedroom.

Expecting him in the room, she was somewhat surprised not to find him in bed. "Must be in the basement," she presumed, then headed below as well. But he wasn't there either. "Seen Brian this morning?"

Alex was preoccupied with his world of wonders, setting up equipment. "Sure haven't," he responded. Slightly concerned by now, Tracy muttered, "Be back in a minute." She decided to look for him. It wasn't Brian's habit to just disappear without letting her know. Moving with quick strides, she hastened back to the sleeping chambers. It was there that she noticed the envelope tacked by the mirror. Spotting the object so prominently on display made her worry. In one swift motion, she tore it from the frame and opened its flap. It was a letter written with painstaking intent.

"Tracy, my dearest," it began. *"I am writing these lines under great duress. I hope my decision to depart today will be easier for you to accept when I say 'I love you.' No matter what happens, that will never change. Lately, however, I've felt deeply depressed and inadequate just sitting around without any real purpose in life. Despite being together full time again, like when we started our promising future so long ago, I have realized that it'd only be for a short while. I'm beginning to realize your needs, as well as my own. There's more to life than being trapped in the Castle. Nobody knows how long the current turmoil will last. Could be months, could be years, maybe a decade. I, as well as you, need more than this present confinement. We both need space. You more so than I. Because of the way I feel, have felt for some time, I've decided to break out of my shell and at least give both of us a chance to regain a purpose in life. There is more to it than being trapped in one place without knowing for how long. I'll at least give it a try.*

You can believe me when I say, 'I've given it much thought.' Thoughts were the only thing I had left for years. At least you have a purpose, solving the world crisis working closely with your dad. I, on the other hand, have no tools to work with. Mine have been destroyed along with my career. It is that what I'm looking for, another meaningful purpose for both of us. Until such time, I'd only be in your way. We well know what that is: Hostility, retribution, and vengeance on an enemy that may be too overwhelming to tackle with the few resources and limited access from the Castle. It's only a matter of time, my dear, before you'll take to the road as I did. I have not abandoned you. I want you to know that. It's only temporary, and I dearly hope you forgive me.

Love always, Brian."

A WARNING

After reading the goodbye letter Brian had left, Tracy felt a deep sadness. It wasn't so much for his departure, it was for a failed relationship. She blamed only herself. It was she and she alone. The once beautiful relationship had gradually disintegrated into a means of acceptance, an acceptance for each other rather than love and devotion. That part seemed to have been lost long ago. She could only contribute it to the living restrictions both had been subjected. Although deeply troubled, with him gone, she was free to act without any given consideration of a loved one. Despite the deep sorrow she felt from losing him, she forced her mind to the present. "Well," she muttered, "So be it." She desperately needed to resolve issues that had been gnawing on her mind, chiseling away at her very existence. Presently seated on the shaggy carpet in lotus fashion with her back propped against the wall, she wore a headset, testing the mouthpiece clipped alongside her face. Her immediate thought was to record her personal disposition, her frustrations and private feelings on pent-up matters. They were of personal concern rather than of general opinion. They were issues that would lay the foundation to her future. At the moment, unsure how to begin she hesitated. Several attempts later, her thoughts became clear and focused for what had to be memorialized.

Months before, it had started as a tiny seed. In time, the seed germinated, eventually culminating into a cohesive pattern. The pattern was soon shaped into a substance she felt she had to embrace. And that she did. It would not only shape her body and her mind, it would also sharpen her focus. And the focus was set on the immediate future. It'd be a time that would leave a benchmark and her legacy for future generations to come. But that, at this point, was for history to decide. For now, Tracy was only concerned with getting information recorded. It would be information she could retrieve from time to time to fuel her aspirations. After taking one more deep breath, her mind was clear. Her eyes were focused. Her lips were moving in accord with the words pouring from her. It would be a warning for things to come:

"With the end of the Cold War," she began. *"The major threat of adversary superpowers using nuclear weapons diminished, so we thought. There is, however, always someone else to take the lead. Because of what we are, mankind will never be at peace for long. Although many nations continue striving for lasting peace, others will never align. The struggle for dominance will continue as it has for eons. Where one nation may fight for more space, another will fight for ideology, or, worse yet, religious causes. Americans, living in a democratic nation, have learned to live side-by-side with a multitude of religions, seculars, and orders of faiths. The people of the United States have proven that many factions can coexist.*

"The reason our democratic nation has been successful is because of a simple rule: keeping state separated from church. Where the state is run by government and politicians, it is not greatly influenced by religious causes. It is our choice to live in a paradigm based on the principles of freedom of speech and liberty established by our forefathers.

"Contemptuous nations should study the constitution of the United States to learn what it'd take to coexist among many diversified faiths and cultures. There is a strong reason why this constitution was created. After all, its

designers themselves escaped persecution. We can only hope to control acts of aggression with the help of science and technology, hopefully in collaboration with likeminded nations. A nation's people, culture, and borders are important for the preservation of identity and freedom, regardless of political structure.

"There may come a time when nations may unite under one global government with the purpose of effectively managing crime and aggression, but in the process, we will lose individual identity. For that, organizational readiness should be the nation's highest objective for warding off terrorism, hostile confrontation, and crime on humanity, which cannot always assure success. In cases of emergencies, crisis management will take over to resolve the situations whether from natural causes, hostile aggressions, or fanatical factions. The government has the power to eliminate any conflict, unless its interest and effectiveness has diminished. At those times, especially when a nation is caught off guard, the government and military may prove ineffective in defending the nation.

"Causes for this, the ineffectiveness, may be complacency, insufficient funding, mismanagement, greed, or just plain corruption. It has been written on many accounts that power corrupts people. There is no exception to the rule. It affects all sectors and ranks of society. It is in these times when an individual, a warrior, a leader may emerge and take charge to organize and combat the threat. What may be an act of desperation, fending off an unequal force, determination is sometimes enough to thwart the aggressor.

"It is important to protect the nation's borders, even though it may cause the occasional conflict. As with crime, terrorism is expanding with population growth. It is here to stay. The only recourse we have is to manage its means effectively. With the expanding threats, entire new industries have been created, demanding an ever-increasing resource in manpower cost, and expenditure. The cost of freedom is high. To keep this freedom, we all have to share a growing awareness for the preservation of a free world. After all, we have vast regions of space open to explore and to populate.

"Each level of threat, at a minimum, must have an equal or greater counterforce to sustain itself. Sometimes, the effectiveness of power needs to be demonstrated. Success can only be accomplished by example or by show of force. If the adversary attacks, a counterstrike becomes necessary. If that proves ineffective, retaliatory power must be elevated to strike home, as many times as it takes. In the process, lives will be lost. At the end, the aggressor, if defeated, must pay. The spoils must fall to the victor. And that," her mental energy drained, Tracy concluded with finality, *"is my pledge."*

CASTLE ROCK

When Tracy entered the command center Alex was busy with the racks of computers. Hunched over a stack of printouts, he seemed completely absorbed. It was an all too familiar scene. Recollecting her childhood, it was the place she would usually locate him, working on one piece of gear or another. It was the place where he had taught her the basic wonders of electronics, mathematics, and history. It was also the place where they would spend hours discussing worldly things from politics to philosophy. It was the place where she had learned about the OSI stack, the intricate workings of the software model. It was the place where he had showed her the inside of the computer box and how everything fit and worked together as one unit. When she got tired of listening and learning, he would reach for the board and they would finish out the day with a game of chess. A sigh escaped her lips, thinking of those innocent days. She had quietly paced by his side when he took notice of her presence. A teardrop had landed on the paper, leaving a wet spot. He lifted his gaze from the table to study her face. His expression quickly changed from surprise to concern. It had been many years since he saw his daughter with tears in her eyes.

"Brian?" he said.

All she could do was nod. The letter in her hand was slightly jittering from unsettled nerves. Through here teary eyes she tried to make sense of the draft in her hands. She handed him the letter Brian had left behind.

"Tracy, my dearest," it read. Alex kept reading on. He was not surprised. He had known the tension had developed between the two for some time. When he realized the strain, he kept quiet. When it came to relationships, it was best to stay out of it. Personal issues normally had to be resolved by the involved parties. Even though a family member or friend meant well, the true issues where generally hidden. All he could do at this point was lend his support through her difficult times. At the moment, there were more pressing issues he had to deal with. It was with his eldest daughter. It also provided a distraction for taking Tracy's mind off the sorrow she must be feeling.

He reached into the toolbox and handed a tool to her. "Here," Alex offered. It was a wire cutter. It was one of those small tools for stripping insulation off wires. He gestured at a bunch of cables neatly strung along the wall and said, "Cut the tie wraps."

Shaking her head, she briefly stared at the tool and turned to head upstairs to her private quarters, but then changed her mind. She decided to stay and lend him a helping hand. *It'll take my mind off of Brian. Besides,* she reflected, *Dad can sure use her help.* In the recesses of her mind, she hoped that there still may be a chance for her sister to have somehow survived. Even though all indications dictated otherwise, it was the human nature for hope that inspired the person to keep the spiritual connection with a loved-one alive. Her fingers went to work on the wires and cables. Alex was busy with some sketches he had developed. She knew his tenacity for solving problems. Although the chances may be slim for any survivors on the space station, she knew he would never give up trying to establish a connection.

Both worked on assisting each other with cutting cables, splicing wiring, and soldering connections to contacts in made-up circuit boards. It proved a challenge, fabricating electronic circuitry. Alex being a scrounger from the olden days had many spare parts on hand.

They had been quietly working as a team, with Alex making an occasional correction to the sketches. It had been hours when Alex broke the silence. "What do you think?"

Tracy studied the sketches. Her eyes shifted from the table to the setup, comparing it with their work. Like so many times in the past, she realized once more the genius in her dad. He had accomplished on the fly what would normally take weeks or perhaps months to manufacture. The results were right there staring at her. "It'll work. Has to."

"We'll find out in a minute." Alex took extra time to verify their work. In-between nods of approvals, he kept assuring himself of success. With a final gesture, Alex was satisfied. "Let's test."

What Alex had accomplished in only a short time, due to limited hardware resources, was a complete bypass to the satellite tracking equipment. Marginal as it was, operating across the North American continent, he had designed a direct link. Although, because of its predestined orbit at a speed of 17,000 plus miles an hour, the access time with the ISS would be limited to only a few minutes from the Castle, six at most. Providing there was still a receiver in operation 250 some miles out in space, it would be enough to make contact.

It was a tense moment when Alex flipped the power switch for the first equipment in line, the multiplex modem. The unit immediately responded with its internal self-test then, seconds later, the green-colored ready indicators turned steady. "So far so good," Alex muttered above the hum of the equipment. In the utility room, they could hear the backup generator kick in on occasion to recharge the battery banks providing power to the racks of electronics and gear.

He flipped another switch to connect the next gear. "Alright," he said with approval when it passed the test. One by one, they checked the rest of the equipment necessary for establishing the link. With the last gear working, Tracy could hear an audible sound escape from her dad's chest. It physically released the pent-up tension from his body. "Think we're ready?" It was a rhetorical question just to break the silence in the room.

She intently listened for a signal, then said, "Think we've got something."

"What?" Alex increased the volume on the amplifier. He could hear it now. Though distorted and limited in signal strength, there was definitely sound coming through the speaker. Slightly discouraged, only white noise generated by the cosmos was audible. "At least," he confirmed, "the equipment's working."

Where, in principle, the system was performing, it still needed much improvement. For that, Alex needed components he had to scrounge up from other equipment in his inventory. The alternative was salvaged parts from the outside world, which was almost impossible to get his hands on. For now, he was content that the system was functioning. What he needed now was to rig the transmitter to the right frequency to ping the space station. That, however, would be a challenge which, at this time, he did not know how to succeed at.

Many hours had slipped away building a link. "Come," Alex gestured at Tracy, "we'll finish up in the morning." It was late into the night when they headed for the kitchen, famished. Tracy prepared an early breakfast while Alex poured a glass of wine for each. Sitting by the table, Alex raised his glass at Tracy for a toast. With a solid promise, if ever so slight, he captured the moment. "Liz," he toasted. "We'll get you back to Earth."

Tracy, just as wishful about her sister somehow having survived emphatically agreed, "Hang in there, sis."

MILWAUKEE SHORES

Tensions were high. Flanked by the Humvee with Norton in tow in the XA-202 armored command vehicle, Bad Man led the way in the M113 Striker. Their destination was the headquarters building located a few hundred yards distance from the Milwaukee shorelines, the Bradford Beach House up North Point Park. On arrival, the Jihad party was escorted to be seated at the somewhat plain, but spacious, conference table centered within the hall. Preceding their arrival, word had spread among the Patriots about the Jihad scouting party, prepared to negotiate. The hall had filled up rapidly with the Patriots. As always, Bad Man had his hands full with keeping the forces at bay. Most of the Patriots were ready to pounce on the visitors, especially since rumors were circulating wildly that it was the terrorists responsible for all the misery and hardship caused on the nation. Norton pacified Bad Man about the current uproar. "Let 'em have their day." He was in no hurry to break it up. It was better to let off steam on the Jihad than among each other. There had been pent up hostility for too long amid the nation against the stealthy killers. Norton was ready for whatever the demands.

To mellow the tension-filled air in the hall, vast amounts of beer were served. Norton, seated directly across the table from the visiting party, "Here," he offered Yusuf a freshly-filled mug of beer. "Enjoy."

Yusuf studied the insignia on the mug for a while. His eyes were centered on the former Miller emblem, now rebranded "Freedom Beer." He slowly shook his head and said, "I don't drink alcohol." He knew it would be an insult, refusing the offer. As in most cultures around the globe, when an invitation was made to open negotiation, refusal of such was a direct insult to the host. While Norton was taken aback he was also educated enough about the Arabian world to know about their culture and customs forbidding alcohol. Bad Man, on the other hand, was not. Getting on his feet he deliberately approached Yusuf. Foaming at the mouth, he flexed his muscles and, in a wide sweeping gesture at the stunned visitor, demanded, "You will drink the beer willingly." He then paused to catch his breath and threatened, "Or I'll make you!"

Yusuf and his party immediately jumped to their feet reaching for their weapons. Due to being outnumbered by the Patriots, Norton had allowed the visitors to retain their arms. It was a mistake. He realized that negotiations were not getting off the ground well. He bolted from the chair and pulled Bad Man who, although reluctantly, returned to his seat. "Calm down," he ordered the Enforcer, shooting a conspiratorial wink at him. "We'll deal with ethics later." He wanted to let him know this was not the time or place.

At Bad Man's outburst, Yusuf's lieutenants where ready to protect their leader. If it had not been for Norton's intervention, the standoff could have exploded into a nasty battle. Grossly outnumbered by the Patriots, the outcome would have been clear. They would have been massacred. But Norton would not let that happen. He was enough of a leader to allow anybody their say. The time had come to be serious. He gestured for the visitors to take seats once more. They reluctantly complied. The hall went quiet. Not that it mattered much one way or other, the people were interested in hearing what the terrorists had to say.

It was Yusuf's turn to speak. "You may not be aware," he began the deliberation, "that the world is at war." Prolific outbursts followed. Renewed accusations were flying across the table such as, "It's you," and, "we'll make you pay," followed with, "we'll kill every damn one of you." Bad Man was doing most of the irate shouting.

"Regardless," the Jihad warrior continued after the turmoil calmed, "we *will* take the world." The resultant accusations were flying back and forth without much getting accomplished. It was here when Norton stepped in, yelling into the uproar, "Quiet or I'll throw you all out. I mean it." He was getting sick of his people's undisciplined interruptions. He wanted to hear what the Jihad had to say. In a warning gesture, he ordered Bad Man and his battle commanders to take position by the tables. It was a measure necessary to keep further outbursts at bay. With an inviting gesture, he promised Yusuf, "Go ahead. Say your piece. There won't be any more outbursts."

Yusuf Hashim, in a self-assured manner, was able to begin his delivery. His voice carried through the hall as he described the current world situation with its uncertainties, instability, and upheavals exerted by many nations. "It appears," he suggested, "that every suppressed nation on the globe wants to be liberated." He also illustrated in its details the new order his supreme commander was forcing on the world. "The Muslim nation," he iterated, "will be liberated to freely occupy nations in Europe, Asian regions, and the former United States. Furthermore," he stated, "this will include all of the nation's assets and mineral resources such as fossil fuel, agricultural production, and," he insisted with finality, "water."

No sooner did the last word leave his lips than the hall broke into bedlam. Battle cries were heard. The atmosphere was charged with tension and outbursts calling for, "Death to Jihad...Down with Islam." There were more shouts with not so pleasant language.

Norton had hoped for a peaceful or more favorable outcome in terms and had not expected such an indictment on the world. The revelation of the Jihad's declaration even affected him. His nerves were shaken to the core, but he held himself in check. There was not much to say but people expected him to speak. He stood up and steadfastly held eye contact with Yusuf. He was ready to state his position. It would be brief and final. What was just revealed was that Jihad forces were already set in motion. He did not care what action the rest of the world would take. But there was no way he would ever allow his nation to be taken over by a foreign force, especially not the new territory. "You know," he conveyed to his visitor, "it means war."

Yusuf was prepared and countered with, "I expected no less." He then signaled to his scouting party that the negotiations were over. He stood up and made his way to the exit. Bad Man had to use all of his persuasive strength to contain the Patriots from jumping on the visitors. At the end, the Jihad party returned unhindered to the waiting sea flotilla they had arrived in. Both hosts and visitors knew the next steps that would follow. It would be an all-out war for his precious resources. Not only that, it would be a religious war none had ever hoped, expected, or envisioned having to fight. The battle was imminent. Brodie had remained quiet for most of the negotiations. To him, the talks were mostly political in nature. Regardless of the outcome, he, and his regiment were ready on standby at a minute's notice. "May the battle begin," steadfast, he said. "Wherever it may be."

As soon as the visitors had left Norton gathered his commanders. It was high time to form a battle strategy. With the enemy at their doorstep, there was not much time to waste. Though the visit was unexpected, for some time now, Patriot scouts had been reporting alarming border incidents. On top of it, wire services carried similar news. It was always the same reports: "More Muslims arriving daily at the eastern ports."

From a battle-ready perspective, Norton had a big dilemma on his plate. Without an organized military command, a working National Guard, or local law enforcement, and, worse yet, with undisciplined Anarchists and other factions roaming the plains, his Patriots, although a sizable force, were in no position to protect all their borders against any intruding power. Something had to be done. *Immediately!* With the imminent danger, there was no time to waste. He called his forces to order. The time was set for 18:00 pm.

LISA BAUER

Two hundred fifty miles out in space, Liz had survived the most traumatic episode in her life. The anguish, the torment of floating away from the safety of the capsule, the agony of having faced death would take days to settle her stretched nerves. Eventually, with support from Walsh, she would regain her former self-assurance. The imminent threat of death in her wake, she could focus on the future, as paltry as it might seem. With Kubalev in command, Walsh by her side, the core of the space crew, although reduced to three, was in charge once more. It was assumed that Nagata was trapped within Kibo[46], the Japanese experimental module. Dieter was yet another story. For the time, he had to fend for himself, if he was still alive. There had been no communications with them. It was time to take stock, to make an assessment of the seriousness of the environment. Torn apart at its very heart, the major parts of the space station—modules, trusses, and solar panels—were separately speeding through space. Some parts of the debris were trailing dozens of yards away, connected only by chafed cables and frayed wires. Harmony, the main capsule, aside from severe leaks and torn off equipment floating freely in space, seemed intact on the interior. It was this disarray the crew had to tackle first. Without a fix for the escaping air, it would only take hours for the oxygen supply to completely deplete. Without compressor backup and with battery banks severely hindered and life-giving solar panels ripped off, unable to provide energy, trying to find a bypass would be the first task on their agenda. It would be a difficult task without computer software and database information. But, with several creative thinking heads at work, the human mind would find a way.

Liz, still slightly unsettled from the traumatic experience of facing death, asked Walsh, "What's the chance of getting to the solar panels?" Huddled together by the porthole their eyes swept across the immediate space, searching for a solution. Their object of focus was visible dozens of yards away floating in space. If there was any chance for survival, it would have to be through some of the debris floating nearby.

"We need an extension," Walsh decided.

"And a long one," Kubalev added. He was already busy searching for suitable objects. Any object long enough would do, but it would mean leaving the capsule. It would mean floating without support functions from within. They all knew the risks involved. Going outside was necessary for survival. With only one space suit still functioning, it would be a draw of the straws.

Liz and Walsh joined Kubalev in the search for a possible object to build a life supporting, lifesaving tether line. Harmony—tube-like in design with 14.5 feet in diameter and 23.6 feet overall in length, with every conceivable space taken up by equipment, racks of instruments, supply boxes and waste bags stowed behind racks—did not have much space for moving freely. The search, as thoroughly as it was conducted, proved fruitless. Something as simple as tearing a bed sheet into strips tied together would have sufficed, but there were none. Nothing seemed workable or long enough to produce a lifeline.

---

[46] Kibo or JEM – Japanese Experimental Module used for laboratory experiments in space.

"Need a break," Liz said. Hours into the search, the three gathered back at the command console. Despite there being no gravitational pull exerted on the body, any physical activity spent caused the body eventually to wear itself down. Exhausted and frustrated, it was time to approach the problem from a different perspective. For now, it was time for a snack break.

"Take five," Walsh said. The break was welcomed.

"What's for lunch?" Liz jokingly inquired to break the tension, but already knew the answer.

"Pouched potatoes," Walsh came back. "What else?" Here in space, everything was contained in pouches. Liquids, solids—it did not matter what the flavors were, after the fresh fruit supply from a crew change ran out, it was all pre-packaged food, mostly tasteless, but food nevertheless. Intravenous vitamin shots and pills had been tried during the initial space flights, but were abandoned after physical examinations. There was too much loss in bodyweight, especially after a prolonged flight. From then on it was pouched food. Nobody ever seriously complained. Every astronaut and cosmonaut knew what was expected once they arrived in space. Life was limited for pleasures. Activities were confined to working tasks, exercising on the treadmill, and resting strapped against the bulkhead. After some time, the body and mind became used to the weightlessness. Dreaming of sleeping in one's own bed, enjoying personal space and privacy, eating a solid home cooked meal, was never far from thought.

The meal consumed by the crew now was for pure survival. In between squeezing semi-liquid food into his mouth and voicing suggestions, Walsh picked up the conversation. "We need a different approach. It's useless to search for an object that doesn't exist." Liz readily agreed. Kubalev had a rather primitive suggestion. "Tie ropes together." Where it may have sounded like a good idea at home, here in the emptiness of space, there were no ropes. While Walsh and Kubalev were tossing ideas around, Liz kept silent.

There was something about the statement made by the Russian cosmonaut that kept gnawing at her. *What was it? Come on,* her instinct encouraged her. *Think of something.* Then it dawned on her. They might all perish in the process, but anything would be better than sitting idle only to expire without trying. She was dying to share the revelation with the other two and said, "I've got an idea."

Walsh and Kubalev looked at her hopefully. Unable to restrain his curiosity, Kenny demanded, "What?"

"May be dangerous," Liz explained. "But worth a try."

Walsh could not contain himself any longer. He practically shouted at her, "Speak up, woman. You're killing me."

"Wires!" Liz blurted out.

"Wires?" Walsh and Kubalev were dumbfounded.

"We cannot destroy the only power support we have," Kubalev shot back at her. It had dawned on him as well, as Kenny, what she was referring to. It was the electrical wiring strung all along inside the walls, flooring, and ceiling of the module, tying together every piece of electronics. It would be inconceivable to cut out power, electricity, and communication. The problem was, no matter how desperate the current situation, they could not exist without the power feed to the heating and cooling systems.

The utility cycle was necessary for their survival. Without it, they would either freeze or burn to death within the hour, depending on the wrecked craft's orbital cycle, or suffocate from lack of oxygen.

"It's not gonna work," Walsh objected. They all knew the implication of going without life support or power in space. With the solar panels torn off, there was no way to get power to Harmony.

Liz instructed them, "You're missing the point."

"Okay," Walsh conceded. "I give up."

"Green wire," Liz announced with a grin. "Green-wire ground."

She watched their faces light up in recognition. "Dammit, Liz," Kenny roared at her. "You just may have saved our lives."

Kubalev, some yards away, pushed against the wall and propelled his body toward her. As reserved as Kubalev was, he caught her by the arms and gave her a tight hug. It was the first one by a Russian since she had landed in space. Both tumbled against ceiling and opposing walls laughing with joy. "You!" in his broken accent, he exclaimed with the broadest smile he could muster. "Are Angel!"

Walsh caught up with them at the opposite end of the capsule. Already on the job, he ordered, "Need diagrams."

Liz rebuffed him, "No need to waste time. We just pull." Although startled, the Russian joined in. The task became easy once they located all the fittings and outlets. With the help of standard tools—a Phillips, a cutter, and a pair of pliers—the three went to work cutting and pulling whatever looked green within the mountings. The effort paid off. At the end of the task, spools of coiled-up wires floated through the interior, waiting to be tied together into one continuous lifeline, whatever length was required to reach the solar panels. But it came with a price. The new danger they faced inside the modules was keeping away from any object that could cause an electrical spark. Without green wire protection, the entire electrical system became vulnerable to a spark-induced explosion. The chance had to be taken. It was their only way out of an otherwise deadly dilemma.

With most of the pent-up tension gone, Kenny, laughing out loud, called after her, "You are my hero."

In spite of the grave situation, she corrected him, "Heroine!"

Kubalev was as ecstatic as well. Blushing, Kubalev exclaimed, "Love you." They knew it was only a rhetorical outburst of joy. Back home, he was solidly married to a fine Russian fighter pilot wife who had been patiently worried for his return to Mother Russian soil.

Liz posed the question. "Who'll have the honors?" Whoever was tasked with exiting the module only had one shot at the difficult charge they faced. It would be the first time anybody had ever tried to exit space tethered to only a fragile, single wire. "Let's pull straws."

"No such thing," Walsh vehemently protested. "You've done enough. I'll go."

"I'll go," Kubalev insisted, moving up close.

"Never mind," she protested, "I know space best." Although junior among her companions, Liz, on this flight, had been in space the most.

"Don't argue," Walsh insisted. He was already collecting the coils of wires, headed for the interlock. Handing him one end of the wire, he instructed Kubalev, "Hold this." He had already securely tied one wire end around the inside of the interlock hatch handle.

Next was stuffing Walsh into the only remaining space suit. With two more sets of hands to help don the suite, it only took ten minutes to accomplish this cumbersome task. The next hour would determine how successful their endeavor would be.

TRACY BAUER

Tousled, not having taken a shower yet, Tracy was on her way to the kitchen, then changed her mind and headed for the basement when Alex was not there. Watching her dad at work always gave her the confidence that the nation, someday, would be back on its feet again. Though he was a genius when it came to mechanics and electronics, she suspected there were many others like him in the nation. Otherwise, who would have invented, produced, and implemented all of the technological wonders in the world? One man just could not do it all. He just finished making one final solder connection to a printed circuit board.

Wearing a light sweater, dressed in casual jeans, she greeted him, "Morning, Dad. Whatcha doin'?"

"Ready to try," he said.

"Finished already?"

"Yep." He sounded pretty self-assured.

"What…" She was about to inquire about the fix, where he found the parts and more, but changed her mind. Knowing better, she did not want to distract him from the immediate task at hand. Besides, without the benefit of a hot cup of coffee she was not prepared this early in the morning to listen to tech-talk. She knew enough to recognize the equipment and gear packaged into the racks of electronics he had just finished. "Muxer," she commented into the coolness of morning, inspecting the gear with a nod of approval, "not bad."

What Alex had done was cannibalize, tech lingo for borrowing components from other equipment either not needed at the moment or with a lower priority. Since it was difficult to come by parts, and because of the current urgency, he took to this method for the fix. The box he had just reconnected was a multiplexer, a unit capable of shooting various types of signals into the ether. "Yeah," he endorsed her comment. "Let's see how it works."

Tracy stooped over the equipment, holding her breath in anticipation. If it worked, Alex had performed a miracle. If it did not, it would be back to the drawing board. In either case, they had to find a means to rescue her sister or, at least, establish a link with her. She was ready. "Go."

As soon as he flipped the power switch, indicators turned on associated by a steady hum emanating from the box. "So far so good." Both watched for the few seconds it took for the electronics to complete their internal self-tests. The results came back positive. It meant the basic unit was ready to fire.

From here on, Tracy followed each and every move Alex executed with heightened expectation. Perhaps someday it would be her turn to fabricate something on the fly. On the front face of the box was a selector knob patiently waiting to be manipulated. Inside the box was a series of frequency generators ready for transmission. Using the knob, she watched him dial up different frequencies. Each time the selector locked in on one, he pushed the transmit button. The action caused the signal to be shot into space. Much like underwater sonar rippling through water, here, when the signal bounced off any metal reflector, such as the remnants from the ISS, it was returned. The readout monitor returned both frequency and distance with each ping.

The trick was homing in on the right target to establish a comm link. For that, Alex used a remote tuner, directing an external antenna mounted on top of the Castle. Where an automated process would resolve a target fix within seconds, Alex's manually processed signal could take hours and days to get a response, if ever. All they needed now was to find the precise azimuth to ping the space station. "Could take a while?"

"May take forever. May never work," he responded while sending another signal burst into space. "Unless capsule transmitters work."

It was something she didn't need to hear. Where she was greatly concerned for her sister, something else had been gnawing at her for some time and confinement at the Castle would not be the answer. She had come to a decision. "Dad," she broke his concentration. "We need to talk."

Alex stopped working the dials. He gazed at her for a moment, then exhaled with a slight groan. His face was set in an expression of reluctant acceptance. It was apparent that it did not come as a surprise to him. He had been expecting *the talk* for some time now. Ever since his buddy Brian left he had expected her to break out from the safety of the Castle. Though Alex was in a solid relationship with Rhonda, he had gotten used to his daughter by his side. It was the closest he had been to having a family life.

"I know…I know." Reluctantly, he conceded, "You've got to go."

She watched him study her face. "Will you be alright?" There was an undeniable sadness in the depths of his eyes. They even turned teary. She knew how hurt he would be with her leaving. It was not so much the departure he dreaded. It was her vengeful nature and ensuing actions he feared would expose her to extreme danger. But he kept silent. He understood there was nothing he could say or do to persuade her otherwise.

He finally broke the silence with a deep groan and said, "You do what you have to do."

Close to tears herself, with a deeply felt compassion she had not sensed for a time, she whispered, "You too. Get Liz home." She then hurriedly turned and left the basement. She did not turn back. She did not want him to delay her departure. Her mission was clear. Where Dad had to bring back Liz, she had to bring back Brian.

"Wait," She heard him call after her. It was a pleading outcry. It made her stop in her tracks. "Wait up." Alex, in a sudden revelation of facing utter loneliness had second thoughts. It made him change his mind. Rushing after her he declared, "Coming with you."

Tracy was dumbfounded. "Really?"

"Can't let you be out there on your own. Too dangerous."

"But Dad," she said trying to instill reason. "Need you here. Need your backup. We've talked about it." Her words reminded him of reality once more. The reason he'd build up the Castle with all of the surveillance equipment and links to her implant. "You've gotta stay."

Alex knew she was right but refused to surrender to the inevitable. A time of action flashed past his vision with him on the frontlines he so dearly missed. The planning, anticipation, confronting the enemy, success and failure, it didn't matter. All it mattered was the action. But then, he realized he did not have the ruthlessness and vigor he had once for taking down the ever-expanding enemy. Her words also made him realize it was her turn now, the next generation to take his place. He could not have asked for a better replacement. He'd trained her for this occasion, though unintentionally, for years. He knew she was ready to face the world. "But alone?" The fact was hard for him to accept. But he knew it was true.

"You're right. Will miss you. Now go before I change my mind."

"Bye Dad," she said kissing him on the cheek."

"Bye Girl. Love you."

Upstairs, collecting the duffel from the bedroom that she had prepared days ago, Tracy took one last look around the Castle, then hastily left the security of the gates in her especially souped-up Humvee she had acquired from one of the soldiers at the nearby Carson base. Almost a year ago, at the first opportunity, Tracy took possession of the vehicle. It happened after an incident at a local bar when she was confronted, like so many times before, by a young GI who insisted he could arm wrestle her to the ground. After being warned of her skills by some patrons, who cheered him on nevertheless, he insisted anyway. He did not take them seriously. The bout was over in less than ten seconds. He challenged her two more times with the same results. It was here when she insisted on the keys. He refused, then turned belligerent.

What followed was natural. He challenged her to a fight. That was also over in seconds. With him on the ground, she stooped down, fished the set of keys from his pocket, collected her black leader jacket from the barstool, and said to the owner, "Take care of him."

Over the next several weeks she made a number of upgrades to the H-1 Hummer, military version. Modifications to the vehicle included hardening of communication gear and making it combat ready. First, there was the engine. At a local shop, assisted by a couple of friendly mechanics with promised compensation in beer and otherwise, she had the block chafed off with cylinders bored out to obtain almost double the engine power. On top of it, she installed a twin turbo unit fed by the hot exhaust gases from the manifolds. Spinning at 100,000 rpm when kicking in, the fiery unit quadrupled the vehicle's power output. Transmission was in fair shape. All it needed was a good tuning. With over 1,200 roaring hp on her hands, the vehicle performed better than anything else on the road. It was the perfect vehicle for a perfect being, a killer machine for a killer woman. She even gave the Humvee a label she felt appropriate for its design. She named it Stingray. The final touches were fiery red, painted serpent tails streaming off the hood, spitting fire and sparks when the turbo kicked in. It was the personalization the vehicle needed. A dual-header, with eight individually shaped exhaust tails mounted diagonally against the engine compartment, breathing in life-giving oxygen through its air scoop intake, prominently protruded through the center of the hood. Heads turned when she made passage on any given road, not only at her, but at the wheels under her as well.

Today, Tracy left the safety of the Castle confronting the enemy and hoping to track down Brain. Presently accelerating the supercharged Humvee, 6.6 Liter TURBO charged, DUROMAX/V8 engine, propelled by an Allison/1000 5-Speed transmission, to the max, Tracy vowed over the roar of the engine, "Judgment Day is near!" Speeding on her path north on I-25 toward Denver, she cut east on I-70 speculating what would be waiting over the horizon.

ISS

With the air pressure leak in the Harmony module and batteries rapidly running low with virtually everything shut down to consume as little energy as possible, time was running short for the space crew. With breathing, already being impaired from low oxygen supply, Kenny Walsh was the only member with a functional tank. But that would not last long. The portable pack on his shoulders fed the Orlan spacesuit, whose oxygen supply, on a full tank, only lasted 6 to 8 hours. By that time, the rescue mission would become futile. Harmony would have turned into a grave for Liz and Kubalev. The Russian, supporting Walsh's exit from the module, stepped back from the interlock. Liz was poised by the inside hatch to control the exit. Since power was out, the transfer latches had to be handled manually. Walsh, in spite of the bulky spacesuit, turned one last time, bidding farewell. Waving his partially raised arm in a clumsy motion he said, "Wish me well."

From here on, the green wire coil clutched tightly in one hand would be his only lifeline with Harmony. To free both hands, necessary to maneuver the jetpack, he flung the coil over his shoulder, opened the exit hatch, and stepped into space. His breathing accelerated dramatically with the first step. The sound was clearly audible to Liz and Kubalev on the onboard intercom.

Liz was greatly concerned about him. Though it was not his first spacewalk, it was a walk of death if his efforts failed. She said, "How you doin?" Anxious seconds went by before the crackled response came through the headset. In-between shortened breaths, he replied, "All right. I guess."

"Take your time," Liz cautioned. "Only got one shot." Much like the oxygen tank, the jetpack carried on his shoulders had a limited amount of supply. With each push on the triggers, the jets propelled him closer to the solar array. He had to be very careful not to overshoot or else precious fuel would be lost, never to be recouped. Inching his way closer, through the wide-angled view he was able to truly assess the damages HAARP had caused to the space station.

He gave a running account. "Won't believe this," he illustrated as close as he could. "Looks like a junkyard out here. Columbus's drifting off into space…already miles away and so is Kibo."

"What's the condition of Kibo? What about Nagata? Any sign of him?"

"Negative…blown apart…no possible survivors. Poor fellow. May he rest in peace." The anticipated loss of a crewmember, though his body was not visible with the experimental module torn to pieces, weighted heavy on Walsh and Liz. Walsh pressed on. "I can see Zarya and Zvezda not far off. Seems they survived. Not much damage."

There was an extended break in conversation when Liz cut in, "Walsh?" She was worried about him. "What's going on?"

The damages must have been worse than expected. "Trying to identify bits and pieces."

"Yeah," Liz threw back a warning. "Just don't let me hang here."

Within the crackling of white space noise, he promised, "Try to do better…here we go…Tranquility's tumbling wildly…Leonardo, Unity, Kepler…forget it."

Liz could not contain her anxiety any longer. "Panels?" It was those, this whole effort's success depended on. "What about the panels?"

"Think we may get lucky…drifting. Not far off. With a bit of luck," his breathing had somewhat calmed, "I think I can get to them…changing direction." There was another suspenseful pause, then, "Here we go." Noting but silence followed.

Precious minutes went by with Liz yelling, "Walsh…Walsh what's happening?" There was no response. Only silence prevailed. From their vantage point, the porthole, Liz and Kubalev could only see a small portion of space. Between dawn and dusk, the light and dark cycles changed every ninety minutes. Not knowing Walsh's whereabouts, the suspense was killing them both. But no amount of audible prodding would return a response. Liz kept muttering over and over, "Something's happened."

All Kubalev would respond with was, "I know…I know."

There was nothing she or the Russian could do but wait. But wait for what? Liz's mind was churning for an answer. Frantically, she kept thinking of alternatives to their plight but could not come up with a solution. Oxygen in the capsule was running dangerously low now. In spite of reduced physical activity, they had to pace themselves. With pressure, already at a suffocating level, each movement became an effort.

And so, each second, every minute was ticking away into hours. In spite of the heavy insulation encasing Harmony inside and out, after nightfall, in the darkness, the temperature fell to below freezing. After sunup, it became sweltering hot. The cycle repeated over and over with the terminal end coming on fast.

Almost a quarter mile out, drifting away from Harmony, torn between being awestruck by the beauty of space and bewildered from the gloomy destruction he faced nearby, Walsh inched his way ever so gently toward the torn sections of solar arrays and radiator panels still connected to mounting trusses, if only partially. "If I can make it there," he continued his monologue. "We may have a chance. Problem is," he surmised within the deadly silence of space, "will the wire reach."

Although the inside of the Orlan suit was a comforting temperature created by the circulating oxygen pack, pearly drops of sweat had formed, impairing his vision. He had no means to remove the moisture. With a subconscious motion of the hands, on several occasions he had tried to wipe his face, but his gloved hand was blocked by the helmet. Between dealing with obscured vision and trying to locate a connection point to tie the wire, he was becoming frustrated. He had inched his way as close as he could without damaging the spacesuit on the torn fragments of the trusses. Jagged edges and torn pieces of metal were protruding from every part of the framework. It was a nightmare. His fear, split between getting the spacesuit ripped open, exploding in the process, and losing the green wire from his grip, was almost beyond his ability.

He huffed into the mic, "One more push on the jet trigger and I'll make contact." At this stage, he was unaware that communication was cut to Harmony. Regardless, he kept up the monologue. "Dammit," he yelled out in sudden fear. "Wire's too short." After releasing the last propulsion stream his body jerked violently. He lost his grip on the last loop of wire, unraveling to its end.

It may have been from fear, it may have been sheer panic, but in the last fraction of time he was able to recapture the wire end. He held on for dear life. When there was no response from the module, he realized communication had cut out and he still had a way to close the distance. *So close,* he muttered into the silence. He gauged the remaining distance to the array of panels closest to him. It was still a hundred some feet. He had to bridge the gap in one way or another. To steady his frayed nerves, he took several minutes before making even the slightest move. After taking one deep breath of air, using extreme caution, his fingers gently pressed down on the jet triggers. There was one final puff, then nothing. The jet fuel tank had run empty.

"Damn you," he yelled into the silence of space. "Give me another second." It would have propelled him to the nearest truss. Without the means of propulsion, they were doomed. "At least," he muttered with a comforting thought. "Liz and Kubalev are safe." It then dawned on him that they were trapped in the same deadly situation. "My God, their oxygen!"

Struck with panicky thoughts like this, he tried staying calm. He had difficulty facing the end. Hopelessly trapped in space and in the dark—night time had taken over—Kenny felt cut off and completely isolated. He was waiting out the end. At the moment and without daylight, he could not make out the oxygen dial on his wrist to read how much more time he had left. Then he noticed something. A spark of hope emerged out of nothingness. "Could it be?"

He waited to make sure. He hoped it was not just an illusion. In the dark he could not gauge his surroundings. He had to wait until a new daylight set in. How long would it be? He had no clue how much time had passed since the last sundown. Counting to sixty, passing the unbearable tension, he gave himself a minute, then another, followed by yet another, and many more. He did not know how much total time he already spent drifting in space. Then, with hope and oxygen almost expired, the life-giving rays from the sun gradually appeared over the horizon. And there it was, close enough to the touch, directly in front of his face, the solid frame of the starboard end of the solar trusses. Still in disbelief, he slowly reached out to touch its presence. He wanted to make sure it was not just an illusion. He felt the solid touch of metal. It was real. In one swift motion, he wrapped the wire end still clutched in his hand around the beam. His mind turned euphoric, but there was no way he could share the good fortune with the space crew.

"Liz," he bellowed into the mic. "We made it." But there was no answer. Space, as vast as it was remained silent. "Oh God," he muttered in desperation. "I'm too late."

TRACY BAUER

"Stinger…Stinger, come in." It was a call from her dad using the dedicated code. He was probably testing the comm link. Since living at the Castle for the past several months, she had hardly used the implant. She would have forgotten about it if it weren't for the slight pressure beneath the skin by the nape of her neck where miniature control switches were buried. One set was a power on/off switch. Another enabled volume changes. It was this set behind her ear that she turned on. There was no indication for volume level. If inadvertently adjusted too high, the sound level could damage her inner ears. *Click.* She put her mind at ease. The electronics were adjusted to normal level.

Her fingers rubbed against her chin alongside one jawbone where the microphone implant was located. "Specter," she quickly responded. "Go."

The implant worked as designed. She put her mind at ease. From here on, it was Alex leading the way. He had already activated the over-the-horizon imaging technology. The implant would allow her to recognize distant objects and events such as obstacles and roadblocks in real time. Transmission carried the visuals from the ground to the nearest satellite in the 450 miles range, then relayed them through hops and beamed back to earth to three receivers. One was located at the Castle which was fed to a monitor, the second at her implant, and the third to Brooks. When she pinged him, there was no response from Brooks. At this time, with only three individuals accessible to the technology, as far as she knew, chances for a security compromise were slim.

Specter could see she was headed east on I-70. Unless there was an urgency or danger ahead, Alex gave her free rein. Tracy chose to be free of obligations not only to her dad, but with anyone. She preferred it this way. It would leave her mind clear to act spontaneously and uncluttered of responsibilities. He was as direct and precise as they had agreed to keep triangulation from possible detection to a minimum. "Destination?"

"Kansas."

At least he knew her immediate path.

"Stay connected," were his final orders. This way, he would be able to feed live data into the implant. Although satellite coverage was still marginal, the international space consortium had made big strides in replacing damaged units. Fortunate for her and Specter, as it allowed them full visual coverage within the North American perimeter.

With the implant tested and operational, her vision focused ahead. Virtual images appeared from the distant horizon. "Amazing technology," she mused with a broad grin. It reminded her of the HUD[47] display a fighter pilot used for making instant judgment decisions when in pursuit of the enemy. The lower part of the images provided a direct view to the horizon. The upper portion went beyond and over the horizon. "Marvelous," she emphasized the wonders once more. Specter, monitoring the set at home, received the same images. For him, satellite imagery had always been part of his job but he could not imagine the live feed into a brain.

Almost eight uneventful hours and 520 miles into the first leg of her journey, Tracy had just left Topeka in her wake. "Another 60 miles," she muttered over the steady hum

---

[47] HUD (Heads Up Display) – Overhead Display designed into many modern war fighters.

of the engine. An hour later she arrived at the outskirts of town. "Kansas City," the overhead sign proclaimed.

About the same time Specter was on the link. "Intentions?"

"Gonna bed down for the night."

"Next contact 6:00 AM," he instructed. Both agreed to break the connection for today. Unless an emergency dictated otherwise, Tracy demanded her personal privacy, especially during nighttime hours. At the distant end Alex being a light sleeper, was never far from radio equipment. He had engineered several connections into a remote alarm carried with him or placed near the bedside.

The overnight stay was uneventful. Kansas City, while situated in the fringes of Badlands territory, was relatively quiet after dark. It was mostly farmland cultivated by farmers and landowners. They worked hard and for long hours, supplying "The Plains" with food and other provisions.

Tracy was up at first daylight, even though she was up talking with her host and his family half the night after being fed a homemade meal while listening to her mission and planning the journey. Her host refused any kind of compensation or payment. While she did the talking, the others did the cheering. Tracy could see it in their faces. Her news from outside was a fresh breath of air to the locals. After a light breakfast and some snacks for the road, she bade them goodbye with a promise to stop by on her return.

Next stop would be St. Louis, then on to Indianapolis. By the end of the day she had cover as much distance as she had the previous day. At this point in her journey, Tracy did not have clear focus on any set destination. That part was still an open subject. The general route she plotted was east through Columbus, in what used to be Ohio, past Pittsburg, formerly Pennsylvania, and on to New York, her eventual goal. It was the place where she had almost died during the EMP strike. It was a place she could readily identify with. It was a place of unfinished business. It would most likely be the place she'd find Brian. For the moment, it was her mission. Aside from that, known only to her was a much greater motivation. Though still germinating in the recesses of her mind, once she recognized the familiar environment it would surface to the forefront.

Deep in thought for the moment, high-rise buildings had suddenly encroached on her vision. She checked the map by her side. It was St. Louis, Gateway to the West, built along the Mississippi River. It was the first time she had come face to face with the actual Gateway Arch. She fleetingly recalled a rich history recorded from the pioneering epoch. "Good place to stop." The rumblings in her stomach reminded her it was time for a lunchtime break. Striding toward the Arch after parking the vehicle, Tracy watched a young couple munching sandwiches close by. The girl waved her over. "Wanna join us?"

Tracy was delighted by the invitation. "Be glad to."

"Emma and Buck," the girl cheerily greeted her with a gesture at her husband. It turned out to be a young couple on their honeymoon. They had also been watching the archway. Tracy enjoyed the sandwich her gracious hosts from last night's stay prepared. For now, between watching the prominent structure and light conversation, Tracy was content, but she noticed a slight unhappiness in the woman's face. "Why the sad face?"

"We wanted to go to Niagara Falls for our honeymoon but the place is off limits to travelers. Roads are blocked. We were refused passage."

"Tell me more." Tracy was surprised at the news.

Emma gazed at her husband then released a string of complaints, freeing some pent-up frustrations. "Damned foreigners!" she cussed. "Destroyed our country and took all our wealth."

"What about the roadblock," Tracy prodded.

It was here that she heard what she had suspected all along. The nation was severely exploited by invading forces not yet identified. Where rumors were prolific about foreign influx into the nation, primarily on the Eastern Seaboard, because of poor news coverage, particulars were not available to the general population. It seemed like the outside world was getting footing in the once powerful nation. With a forlorn look in her eyes, she explained, "We tried to get to upstate New York. They won't let us cross."

"Cross what?"

"The river."

"Mississippi?"

"Yeah."

"Who's stopping you?"

"Anarchists. Only let people in but nobody from here can cross."

Tracy needed clarification. It seemed incredible what she was just told. "You mean you can't get east from here?"

"That's right," Buck chimed in.

"We'll see about that." Tracy was ready to get on the road. She was anxious to find out herself about the river crossing. The rage she'd suppressed for so long began to surface from the pit of her stomach. "You finished with lunch?"

"Where we goin'?" Fear showed in Emma's face but Buck readily followed Tracy's determined strides, pulling his bride along.

Tracy was defiant. "New York! It's where you wanna go, isn't it?"

"Yeah, but..."

"Hop on," she gestured at her vehicle.

Buck took one look at her Humvee and said, "Awesome." He wildly shook his head with a broad grin on his face. While Emma took a seat in back amid all of the electronic gear, Buck, rubbing his palms in anticipation, claimed the seat up front.

Tracy extended her hand across the steering wheel and formally introduced herself, "Tracy...Tracy Bauer," then firmly stepped on the gas pedal. In an instant, the Humvee leaped off the ground only to bounce back yards ahead with tires burning rubber on the paved concrete. "Hot damn!" Buck yelled over the engine roar. Tracy shot the vehicle east, headed directly for Poplar Street Bridge, their immediate destination. Just like the couple indicated, coming up fast was a road barrier blocking her path. The horizontal boom was lowered. Tracy not to damage the vehicle stepped hard on the breaks. Several uniformed sentries bolted from a guard shack in front of the Humvee, wielding AK-47s.

Taken completely by surprise, Tracy shouted out, "Ragheads?" She was stunned by the faces staring down at her and her passengers. There was nothing but loathing emanating from their faces. Apparently, they did not appreciate being called such a derogatory remark. They knew about the label placed upon their people. It was a time when many of them were tribal dwellers living in desert tents. The once oppressed culture, today, it seemed, had become liberated from ancient customs and culture.

"Look at them," Buck practically spat out the words. "Taking our country."

"Told you," Emma muttered from the backseat.

What appeared the group leader, with his guardsmen ready to fire at them, ordered the occupants, "Out." Not putting her passengers in jeopardy, reluctantly, Tracy stepped from the vehicle onto the pavement.

"IDs!"

Although expired years ago, since there was no government or federal enforcement on identification and renewals, Tracy handed over her ID to the sergeant. He studied the card for some time, then gestured his fellow sentries to keep a watch on the vehicle and quickly disappeared into the shack. Tracy, in her intuitive way, immediately was on guard. Years ago, with having been taken hostage, she had learned to trust no one. She watched the sergeant pick up the receiver from the wall-mounted radio equipment. He was on the phone several minutes, then returned. She knew right away from the expression on his face that there would be trouble. Concerned for the safety of her passengers, Tracy, rather than taking flight, decided to wait for the outcome of what the guardsman had to say. Being fearless, she was also curious. Sensing an ominous feeling, Tracy stepped back into the vehicle. Ready or not, the next few seconds would decide her actions.

The sentry stepped up by her window with menace written all over his face. "You Tracy Bauer?" he confirmed her identity. She knew right then and there that her cover had been compromised. There was no knowing what his next actions would be. Not waiting for a potentially treacherous outcome, Tracy acted. In one swift motion, she ripped the card from his hand, threw the shifter in reverse, and stepped on the accelerator, yelling, "Get down."

The vehicle accelerated backwards in the direction they came from. Getting past the barrier, Tracy spun the vehicle into a 180 degree turn and careened back to safety. Checking the rearview mirror, they were not being pursued, but the metallic impact of a dozen slugs boring in back of the vehicle confirmed their intentions. "Told you," Emma repeated her earlier warning. Where Buck was ready for more action, she appeared shaken. For now, they were safe.

Slowly driving on, her passengers gradually recovering from the dangerous encounter, Tracy evaluated their choices. She was furious that their journey east had been interrupted. The roadblock was fortified too heavily, not by the Anarchists, but by a foreign force. An alternative path had to be sought. She fished for the map. It had been tossed under her seat. She handed it to Buck and said, "What's the next crossing?"

He intensely studied the map. "Let's see." His index finger was tracing along I-70 north. "Up ahead is Eads Bridge. No…no good," he muttered. "Only a biker crossing." Tracy had already identified the bridge passing by to her right. "Martin Luther King's up next. Then McKinley, further north."

"What else?"

"Only one bridge left," he nodded ahead. "270 crossing way up north."

She had just passed a stretch of empty lots to the left. The sign indicated, "College Hill," when the interstate suddenly took a turn west, away from the Mississippi.

"No good," Tracy muttered. "Wasting too much time." She turned the vehicle into an empty lot by the waterfront and said, "Stand by." She stepped from the vehicle, headed toward the river. It left her passengers with question marks on their faces. Away from earshot she made contact, "Specter."

"Go."

"Got a problem," she flashed back.

"I know...Watched you on the monitor. What's your intention?"

"River crossing," she indicated.

"No good here...All bridges blocked. Take direction north or south...Only options."

"North," she decided on the spot.

"Okay then," Specter's voice trailed off. "Keep connected."

From her vantage point, Tracy could see Buck intently watch her. He was waiting for her to return and asked, "Who you takin' to?"

"Just thinking out loud," she said but didn't think he bought it. He still eyed her with suspicion. From her passenger's perspective, for all they knew, Tracy could be a threat to their wellbeing. It didn't matter much. She just did not want to have to explain the implant. It was nobody's business. It'd only jeopardize her mission. She could not let that happen. "Wanna see the Falls?"

That cheered them up. It also took their minds off the present dilemma. "Niagara Falls," both cheered in unison. They did not have to say more. Tracy was already headed north toward Davenport. Unfortunately, it would be country roads all the way. There was no major link leading directly to the Great Lakes without crossing the Mississippi. As suspected, Specter confirmed her assumptions along the route. Next stop would be somewhere along the western shores of Lake Michigan. She hoped to make it by nightfall.

ISS

Liz and Kubalev were silently drifting within the perils of Harmony. After Walsh had left the capsule, they had lost track of time. To preserve the remaining oxygen, he and Liz had positioned themselves close by the interlock. Each moving effort had become a laborious task. There they waited for the end. It was Kubalev who expired first. He lost his hold on the handles he desperately clung to when death set in. His body gradually floated free and so did his earthly spirit. Kubalev, Russian born, like so many who had lost the little faith bestowed on him by his parents during the Cultural Revolution, was not a religious person. He did not believe in Heaven and beyond. For him, his present position was about as close as he could come to his Creator. Liz lost hold on reality shortly after. Her mind kept drifting in and out of consciousness, body weakening by the minute due to lack of oxygen, it was only a matter of time, perhaps minutes before she would follow Kubalev into death. During the waning moments, what little there was left, she was reliving her life just as the last grams of energy stopped supplying blood to her brain.

"Hurry up," the voice of her sister, two years younger in age, kept drilling into her mind. Liz had overslept again. Being a child, filled with never-ending vigor, devoid of energy after another endless day's play, she was barely able to drag her exhausted body to bed as she did every evening, drifting into soundless sleep. Slightly startled, rubbing the remaining sleep from her eyes, she recalled yesterday's plan for the family to go on an early hike. It was a day she always looked forward to whenever Dad came home from another lengthy trip abroad. As usual, he had brought back a load of the latest electronic gadgets he had purchased at places such as Itaewon, Seoul, and Akihabara, Japan. To her, the names were meaningless. To Dad, they were the technology heavens on earth. Between Korea and Japan, these were "must stop" places for any traveler to Asia. Internationally known marketplaces, shoppers could find everything manufactured under the sun, from the latest model radio and stereo equipment to most advanced television and computer models. What made it especially attractive were the unforgettable discounts at which the goods were sold. At better than half the cost sold elsewhere, it was no wonder that these markets were the world's most popular places.

Dad, being a male, was clueless about the wants and desires of a little girl. For this reason, there were no dolls, handbags, or pretty dresses among the presents. It was always another electronic and entertaining wonder. Consequently, the daughters grew up without a dollhouse, Cabbage Patch, Hugga Bunch, or Barbie dolls. They grew up with the practical knowledge of computer parts, components, and items used to fix and enhance whatever was broke. He thought that was important.

Hurriedly getting dressed, she already had her backpack waiting by the exit. She was the last to jump in the family car, ready to take to the road. Today's hike was at their favorite place, Waldo Canyon, a lengthy winding path leading into the hills along I-24. It would be fun for the girls, prolifically chatting along the way, hop-skipping here and there, chasing ghostly images, only to have a picnic at the distant end of the hike. Trekking back in late afternoon would be more laborious with spent energy, but worth all the fun just being a wholesome family.

Images from her childhood such as these were rapidly passing through her fading mind. She did not want the outing to end, because she could see into the distant end of the canyon. There was only darkness. Liz became afraid. The sky was also darkening. She could hear thunder approach over the hills. There was lightning. The thunder grew louder. It persisted with its deafening pounding. The pounding turned hollow. She could feel the vibration pushing against her forehead, reverberating into her brain. Unwilling to yield to the sound, her mind was drifting in and out of terminal unconsciousness. Reality and the drive to live finally won out. She opened her eyes. Adjusting to a hazy focus, her vision gradually moved to the porthole where the pounding originated. It took seconds for her to recognize the helmeted face of her astronaut partner only inches away, staring at her across the safety glass.

Thirty some minutes earlier, hundreds of yards away in space, during another ninety some minute day/night cycle, after finally linking up with the solar trusses, Walsh, one hand clutching the wire end, careful not to lose the green wire, it took him close to fifteen minutes to make the connection. Without tools, it was an almost impossible task. Gloved and sweaty within the bulky suite, his fingers kept groping for a bare metal connection. He finally managed to wrap the wire around a frame several times to secure the connection and with one trust jammed the wire end into a metal clamp and not soon enough.

The sun was already rising again over the horizon. It was the signal for him to hurry back to the capsule and away from the wire. With the remaining solar panels getting heated up again by the sun, heat being converted to electricity and transferred to the wire, he was afraid of getting electrocuted. Carefully not to lose his grip on the wire, he grappled back to the capsule just in time to be safe. It was here when he faced Liz at life's end. It took all of his remaining energy to yank the interlock to the open position. He pushed his way through, locked the hatch, and pulled the inside hatch open. Closing it shut, hoping it would be his last spacewalk he propelled his body forward to where he had left his companions.

"We did it!" he exclaimed in the safety of the module but his exuberance quickly faded. A shade of panic swept over his face when he realized the terminal state she was in. He wildly shook her body and frantically yelled, "No you don't. Don't you dare leave me!" He was petrified at the thought of living out the last days in space alone.

His eyes frantically darted around the capsule, looking for something, anything, to bring her back to life. Trapped in the spacesuit, the only containment preserving life-giving oxygen, he pulled her body to the storage bin. His hands were tearing through the cluttered jumble of bagged waste, used garb, and spare parts. Then he spotted an item he immediately recognized, an emergency respirator. It was an item supplied for space travel in case of disaster. It was a simple item especially designed to connect with the spacesuit for situations like the one they were presently in. Walsh tore the item from its mounting and connected it to his Orlan suit. He could hear the passing sound of oxygen escape through the hose. Then he quickly connected the mouthpiece and forced the mask over Liz's face. At first, her depleted lungs struggled against the sudden surge, then, with an explosive force, she sucked enough oxygen into her lungs, jolting life back into her brain once more.

Her body reacted. It struggled against his solid grip. She tried tearing free. It took all of his strength to contain her from injuring him or herself. Against the struggle for life, Liz finally opened her eyes and recognized the environment. Memories came flashing back. Reality set in again. She found herself back in the space capsule, staring at the affectionate eyes of her suit-clad space partner. A wide grin came over her face when she recognized his presence.

Walsh again checked the meter on his wrist. Time was running out for both of them, and so was his oxygen. "We've got work to do." He pulled her back to the interlock. Getting hold of a wire stripper from the supply cabinet, with her in tow, he fashioned a connection to the internal power grid. It was this connection that would allow them to live on. The green wire that was used to secure the solar trusses to Harmony Walsh now used it to bring power back to the capsule. One more tightening with a screwdriver, and the connection was made.

After watching him work, Liz took the chance to test it. Chances were a static spark could trigger an explosion. After all their work, it would be the end for both. She took one deep breath and removed the oxygen connection from the suit. A push against Walsh's bulky body propelled her in the direction of the control panel. Unsure whether to activate power, she hesitated but there was no sure way other than throwing the switch. Walsh made the decision for her. In a labored breath, he yelled "Throw the damned switch." She flipped it to "On." There was an indication of light, however dim. But there was a hum. It was the backup generator kicking into action. The load supplied by the solar panels, gradual at first, then with increasing force, surged into the internal system. Harmony was back in operation. The lighting came on all around. The oxygen worked. And best of all, the static sound from the cosmic ether was feeding the radio with its crackling noise. But, to Liz and Kenny, at the moment, it was a melody of life. They felt safe once more.

Only seconds had passed when the familiar voice from Baikonur ground control echoed through the capsule. "ISS…ISS, come in…come in." The same words had been broadcast over and over for many hours. Where the ground crew had given up all hope earlier, the automated recording continued to send out the transmission. It would continue indefinitely or until someone at ground control shut off the transmitters. For now, it was only a one-way link. With comm electronics disabled in Harmony, the world was still unaware of their conditions fighting for survival.

Walsh, with the help of Liz, slipped from the bulkiness of the spacesuit. His body and vision were freed once more from the confinement. Liz watched his face break into a broad grin. In the bliss of the moment, having survived the emptiness of space she planted a passionate kiss on his lips. He was startled, but returned the fervor, kissing her back. Taking a deep breath of life-giving oxygen, this time from being short on breath from the lengthy kiss, *maybe,* she thought in the quiet of space, *there's hope after all.* Her thoughts were on a possible relationship in the future.

Having an unobstructed field of vision again, Walsh detected the lifeless body of Kubalev floating against the far end of the capsule. He rushed to the cosmonaut's aid but Liz pulled him back by the sleeve, shaking her head, and said, "Too late."

For the space crew, now dwindled down to only two, there was work ahead. Permanent connections had to be fashioned between Harmony and solar trusses. Internal equipment had to be checked out. Computers and software tested, and most importantly to Liz, a downlink feed to the Castle had to be reestablished. *Dad,* she thought in the revived security of space, *I'll make it back after all.* But it would be some time before that dream would come true. They were not yet out of hot water. Harmony, a module without docking connection, would be a challenge for any space flight to dock with. But man, with its ingenuity and the aid of science and technology, would find a way. As was always the case in space, time was limited. There was already another peril waiting around the corner: food supply. What remained, though vacuum packed and safe from getting spoiled, would only last a few weeks, perhaps a month if restricted to severe rationing. Limiting activities, she could stretch her caloric intake, but with Walsh being almost twice her bodyweight, she wasn't sure how he'd cope with severe rationing.

For now, no matter what came across her path, Liz felt she was able to tackle any and all obstacles. With her spirits lifted to new heights, grateful Dad had taught her the intricacies of computer technology, Liz went to work on the database software and electronic gears, assessing the safety of the space capsule and how to prolong their limited life sustaining resources.

TRACY BAUER

It was late afternoon when Tracy, Emma, and Buck, her lively passengers, arrived at the outskirts of Davenport, IA, the rest stop for the day. Getting here using mostly country roads had taken longer than expected. It was a tiresome drive with countless bends and turns, sometimes only dirt covered treks connecting with another secondary road. Slithering to an abrupt halt at the first inn along the roadside, Tracy, begging for shelter wearily inquired, "Got rooms?"

"Got silver?" was the comeback.

Tracy openly reached into a pouch she wore around her waist, pulling out a few coins. "That enough?"

The host studied the coins then replied with a satisfied grin, "It'll do. Can't be too careful with all the forgeries." Since the country was still plagued without a national currency, values and monetary standards had returned to zero right after the economic collapse. But it did not take very long for traders, merchants, and the entrepreneurial spirited to devise methods for bartering. Items necessary for survival such as food, fuel, batteries, and soap, the most sought-after items could be acquired through barter. Other costlier items such as shelter, weapons, ammunition, and livestock were yet another challenge. Most people did not have the necessary silver and gold for that.

Because of it, more and more potential buyers would pull a weapon and just run off with the stolen merchandise. Law enforcement, unless it could be found, was close to non-existing. Without pay, officers quickly gave up, staying home to take care of their own family and loved ones. Some regions fared better than others. It all depended on the wealth and resources of a specific section of land. Other precious possessions were agricultural lands, animal and dairy farms, feed stores, and hothouses growing vegetable and other plant life desired by humans and animals alike.

Tracy, despite flashing gold and silver coins out in the open, was not worried. In most cases, her general abrasive demeanor was enough to keep potential muggers at a distance. Occasionally, where an assault was inevitable, it would take her only one or two swift and stunning punches or kicks to subdue the mugger. As a matter of fact, since it kept up speed, agility, and fighting proficiency in her path of vengeance, she preferred such confrontations.

For today, all were tucked in at the coziness of the inn, entertained by the host and his wife, who were dishing out meals in exchange for news from the heartland. Tracy and her passengers were only too willing to accommodate the hosts since it meant free lodging for the newlywed honeymooners. Though it would be a delayed arrival, they had grown fond of the idea of spending some time at the once popular falls. For now, they were grateful to be in the company of the warrior woman protecting them.

The stay at the inn was restful and refreshing. Early next morning they departed for Chicago. Traveling would be much quicker since she could stay on I-80 East, a major link to the city. They would be there way before noon. Travel went without a hitch, but trouble began as soon as they arrived at the city's major thoroughfare, I-294, the Tri-State Tollway. The path was barricaded with heavy fortification enforced by what appeared to be a foreign militia. After Specter shot her a warning, "Look out for trouble ahead,"

Tracy spotted the barrier miles ahead. Because satellite coverage at this level of latitude was marginal, Stinger decided to rely on Specter for distant visuals.

From the vantage point up close, the scene looked much like a war zone. From the north, east, and south, military type vehicles and troop carriers passed in and out of the immediate region. Alarmed at the unexpected disorder, Emma gestured at Buck. "What's that?"

"Looks like military to me," he replied.

Tracy ordered her passengers, who intensely kept their eyes on her, "Stay put." She had already jumped from the vehicle. With assuring strides, she headed for the guard shack for a closer look. Gesturing at a disappearing Tracy from the back of the vehicle, Emma asked, disconcerted, "Where do you think she gets her confidence?"

Buck turned to face his bride and declared, in a determined tone of voice, "Don't know…don't care." He gestured at the interior of the Humvee. "Just look around." His eyes captured the valise stashed in the back of the driver seat. Stretching his body to reach the bag, he could no longer contain his curiosity about the black leader duffel. "Wonder what's in here?"

"Don't," Emma warned. "It's not ours."

Already pulling the zipper open, he joked, "Don't be a pussy." A second later his face turned from curious to stun. His eyes caught something he had not expected. His hand had already reached for the object of his probing. "Dammit," he huffed at her. "Look!" His eyes still marveled when the firmness of steel gripped his arm, ripping the weapon from his hands.

"Not a toy," Tracy warned, shoving the weapon back in the duffel.

Emma reproachfully said from the back, "Told you."

Rebuffed and feeling embarrassed, Buck wanted to know, "What'd you find out?"

Used to military presence working in and around the Pentagon for many years, and not too perturbed at the unexpected barrier, Tracy edified her passengers. "Jihad forces."

"What?"

Surprised at such an ignorant response, Tracy asked, "Where have you been?"

"We are simple rural folks," Emma explained his obvious ignorance.

"Never mind that," Tracy assured them both. "I'll get you to the falls. But first," throwing a glance at her watch to check the time, "gotta find out what's goin' on in the city. You game?"

A squad of guards was firmly planted by the shack, barring entrance to the city. Several cars were ahead of her directed either to drive on or to turn back. With Stingray driving up it was her turn now. "Where're you headed?" the guard in charge demanded. Tracy had decided to take the direct approach. The worst that could happen would be that she was forced to turn back. Firm and confident in her usual demeanor, staring down the guards, she replied, "City." Already she detected hostility from the guardsmen. It may have been her attitude, rebellious and defiant as usual, or her appearance, but it put the sentries on alert. Their automatics immediately came up, pointing at her. "Where in the city?"

Throwing a nod straight ahead, she replied with indifference, "Navy Pier."

The guard seemed to change his interrogation tactics. His curiosity shifted to the vehicle. He asked, "What about the Hummer?" He spoke English but with a broken accent.

Her face turned even more defiant. "Like it?"

It must have provoked a certain curiosity among the guardsmen. Chatting among themselves in a foreign language that Tracy identified as Farsi, they circled the vehicle and carefully inspected the interior through the windows. One spotted the black duffel bag in back. "Out," he ordered Tracy. With another gesture at the valise, he ordered, "Open."

Tracy caught Emma's eye and covertly shook her head. To open the bag, revealing its contents, was the last thing she wanted. Stepping out alongside the vehicle, Tracy opened the backdoor to reach for the bag and said, "Okay." The sentry stepped back, giving her space. In the meantime, observing their comrades milling around the Humvee, the rest of the guardsmen from the other lanes had joined in with the chatter. One of the sentries, a rather vicious looking individual, was pacing around the vehicle nodding and grinning at his cohorts. He had taken a liking to the Humvee. His right hand was gently stoking the steering wheel. He came to a conclusion and said, "Like! Must have." He shot a quick glance at his comrades, who on cue raised their automatic weapons, pulling both remaining passengers from their seats.

It was the danger signal Tracy had anticipated. She knew what would come next. The question passed through her mind, *who wouldn't want a souped-up vehicle that I am driving?* Not only did the fiery red painted vehicle attract everybody on the road, the air scoop and external headers gave away its power.

What followed next was action exerted on instinct. In one continuous motion, Tracy yanked the duffel from the car, stepped back to give her and her weapon some breathing room, pumped the slide to chamber the first round, and shouted, "Enough chitchat." With her left palm, she warned her passengers, "Down!" and pulled the trigger. Body turned rigid with legs solidly planted on the ground, forehead furrowed, with both hands cradling the weapon, it was an attack many a fighter would come to know in the future.

The guardsmen were too stunned to act. By the time they realized the danger, it was too late. Peril had struck already. Her aim had been lethal. One after one, bodies collapsed around the Humvee. It was the combination of training, fighting skills, and the weapon, giving her the advantage over anyone else she would encounter blocking her path.

Her body relaxed once more. Pacing around the vehicle, she muttered into the massacre, "First payback." Her eyes sought out the honeymooners, who had taken cover the second the shooting started. The event took less than ten seconds. Sprawled around the perimeter, the body count was eight.

Shaken to the core, her passengers hovered near the embankment. Tracy heard Emma mutter, "Told you so." Both appeared frightened, not only from what had just happened, but the consequences as well. They agreed; they did not want anything more to do with this killer woman.

"Ready?" Tracy beckoned them back to the vehicle. She was ready to go on with the journey. Shooting a hastened glance at her husband, Emma decided, "Think we stay here for a while." Taking a step forward, Tracy beckoned to them. "Come on. I only slay the enemy."

She gave them both a minute to make up their minds. After all, they had been nice, keeping her company. After discussing pros and cons, they apparently decided it was safer to travel with her than on their own. "Where we headed?"

"Docks." It was a common place for the city folks with time on their hands for fishing, loitering, and observing. She needed information on Brian's whereabouts. This time, there was no one by the guard shack to block their entrance. For now, her passage was open. How long that would last would be up to reports about the slaying by the toll road. The Humvee was enough of a deterrent, allowing her passage at other checkpoints.

After they arrived at the Navy Pier asking questions, Tracy handed out Brian's picture. At the end of the day there was no one that'd recognized the face. She decided to stay put another day. It'd give her a chance to examine the inner city. Since none had ever been to Chicago, Tracy did not know the conditions here, how safe it was or how much trouble they'd encounter. Emma and Buck readily agreed to stay close to their protector.

It had turned dark in the meantime. City and streets began to fill with shadows. The night dwellers started to arrive. People began to show up everywhere. Since the majority of them dwelled in the dark already, it did not matter where one spent the hours. The home, the streets, the docks, it was all the same. Although personal safety was on everyone's mind, there really was no safe place in the city. Housing was vulnerable to break ins. Streets to muggings. The few shelters some Samaritan groups had made available were noisy places overrun with derelicts, thieves, and robbers. Nobody was safe. Not even the criminals. They were fighting and robbing from each other. Such was urban life, disorganized, frenzied, and chaotic. It was the reason many former city dwellers had left years ago, resettled into the hills and by lakesides up north where settlements were sparse. It provided a safer life for the family but also meant labor and hardship. It was a magnitude better than getting killed off in the city by muggers or dying from starvation and disease. As a result, many small settlements popped up in the wilderness, cultivating land mostly up north across the border that used to be desolate and unpopulated.

Tracy did not desire any parts here either. But it was a place for making connections, obtaining information, and confronting the enemy. The enemy seemed to be everywhere. Her problem was identifying friend from foe. As culturally jumbled as this metropolitan area had turned, it would be no easy task. She had to let them come to her. For that, she'd already put her plan in action. Killing off an entire guardsmen squad would definitely attract the attention of the enemy. All she had to do was sticking around and provoke an attack. Then another attack and another, until the invading forces got tired, leaving the shores. But with only a one-soldier army on the attack, it could take years.

Though miniscule, something persistent spurred on her drive. Tracy considered herself much like a raindrop. If unrelenting enough, over time, it would gradually chisel away even a granite mountain. Time, as youthful as she was, was on her side.

ISS

Kenny and Liz spent many waking hours testing and fixing damaged gear. The general conditions were not too bad. Most life-giving sources seemed to function. The problem, she detected, was to the interface. When Harmony and the other modules were torn apart from the last HAARP blast, interconnecting wiring mounted against bulkheads and inside paneling was torn off. Damages were mostly physical to the interactive system, and the ones she identified were numerous. First and most critical was the communication interface. Whereas internal electronics to the radio gear and computers seemed to be in working order, the connections to the external antenna systems took the biggest hit. Without a voice link to Earth, ground control and monitoring stations around the globe had no way of knowing their plight. For all they knew, the folks below had given up hope of survivors on the ISS. There were other damages to fix, but those had lower priorities. There was the water replenish, oxygen filtering, system stabilization, and more. Though it had been filtered and re-filtered, Liz and Kenny were forced to drink their own urine. The same was true for the oxygen supply. Here again, the air was pulled through similar filtering processes. The space modules were designed for the recycling process, but filters had to be replaced periodically to clean drinking water and oxygen.

Breaking the silence after many hours of working, Liz said, "We're lucky it wasn't an EMP burst." As devastating the HAARP pulses were, they did not have the destructive forces on electronic circuitry.

"Right," Kenny answered. "We'd be in serious trouble." From the initial inspection, most comm and computer gear was functional. If that had been damaged, there would be absolutely no means to reestablish ground link. It might take some time to repair the broken interface connections, but both hoped eventually establish contact.

It was just as critical that they stabilize Harmony. Without equalizing jets keeping the module stable and on course, it had been aimlessly tumbling through space. Unless the dilemma could be rectified, there was no hope for rescue. No spacecraft would be able to dock. It was this dilemma Liz and Kenny were desperately trying to figure out how to solve. The tumbling presented two problems for them.

The first, in a way, was to their advantage. The tumble provided a certain amount of gravity, a minute amount, but it was gravity nevertheless. It was a force both had not experienced since leaving Earth. Rather than be tied to weightless netting during sleep and the occasional break, each could enjoy the sense of almost being back on Earth. It pushed the body against the padded bulkhead allowing for a more comfortable rest. It also energized body tissue and muscles to their advantage. It slowed the atrophy effects.

The second problem was more severe. It was a distraction from their work when focusing at a task on hand. The surroundings, as well as the objects, kept rotating around their vision unless securely strapped to the object. They solved the problem by one steadying the other's body while they performed the repair.

"Hold this," Liz instructed Walsh as she fixed another broken connection.

Kenny wondered, "Think it's gonna work?"

Liz assured him, "It has to. We've got no other choice." It was this sort of dialogue that kept their spirits up. Though their romantic relationship had been rekindled after the desperate rescue effort, the present urgency for restoring operational functions to

Harmony was agreed by both to be more important. The many tasks kept them from pursuing any personal desires.

Like so many times in recent days, Kenny asked, "How's it coming?" He had just taken a break to refresh. That in itself, even under ideal conditions in space, presented an issue. Flushing a toilet or using recycled water for cleansing the body clean was a daily challenge. With the automatic functions disabled, it had to be performed manually using disposable diapers and wet wipes. For the average adult, the lack of hygienic functions was dismal. It did not do much for one's self-esteem, let alone the other people around. But, for the astronaut with months and perhaps years of space related living, as long as on-board systems were working, it was acceptable.

Liz was just tying up the final connections between the radio and a fabricated antenna. Earlier, when searching for extra wiring and realizing there was none left, an idea struck her. "Why not?" she exclaimed.

The outburst startled Kenny. "What?"

"The antenna."

"What about it?"

Ignoring him for now, Liz muttered, "Thank you, Dad." Along the practical training she had received from Alex during her growing years, dormant knowledge kept surfacing, it seemed, whenever she needed information. Something had just struck her like lighting. "Of course!" All she needed was short pieces of wires. For that, she could always cut a piece from some damaged circuitry or stowed away spare parts not essential at this time. It would not take much time to fabricate the necessary bypasses. Sure enough, she was able to put together some electrical bridges between the radio gear and the green wire connecting Harmony to the solar panels.

Walsh was not the electronic expert she was and impatiently demanded, "Share a little of your excitement, will you?"

Liz, too absorbed with the potential solution at the moment, shot him a slightly annoyed glance, but reminded herself of their interdependency. She immediately adjusted her attitude and replied, "Of course." She then explained her theory. Where the green wire connection provided the basic power from the solar panels to Harmony, the same wire could also function as the signal carrier from the space capsule to the ether. "It's done on Earth all the time."

"Brilliant." He understood.

She did not have to explain much further. AC home wiring was used many times, especially in outlying areas, to carry radio frequency. Where power wires acted as basic carrier, voice frequency was carried in both directions.

"Voice over IP?"

"You got it."

It was the connection she needed to the outside world. The signal could be picked up either by satellite or ground station. *Perhaps,* a wishful notion crossed her mind, *Dad will hear me at the Castle.* But it was not the Castle that had sent the first signal that was received after successfully testing her solution. It was a pulsating sound pushing its way into the capsule. It was a repetitive sound, taking only seconds for Liz to recognize. "Morse code," she shouted at Kenny. She identified the signals made up from dots and dashes: ". . . - - - . . .," alternately repeating, "..... -.. .--."

Even Kenny recognized the signal. "SOS – HELP." It repeated several more times then went silent. Liz was puzzled. "Wonder who sent it?" The signal could have been generated from anywhere. Until identified, it was only a call for help. Since there was no signal generator on board, there wasn't anything Liz or Kenny could do, but tinkerer as she was, she'd find a way.

For now, fixing the radio equipment had higher priority. Getting it repaired, Liz realized, would take some doing. It would not be as simple as rigging up the external antenna. For that, she needed miniature replacement parts or, if she got lucky, to locate a spare set. Unfortunately, there was only one radio on Harmony. She had to find another means to communicate.

Realizing the plight, they were facing, Walsh had an idea. "What about the Morse code?"

"That's it! Look who's the genius now," Liz burst out at a grinning Kenny.

Again, it was her ingenuity that applied a fix. It did not take much effort or time to fabricate. Though only makeshift, all it took was a bare piece of wire. One end was soldered to a terminal strip on the backside of the radio gear, and the other end, shorting out the transmit line, did the trick. The rest was simple. Using the Morse code chart that she pulled up from the onboard computer, with a bit of skill all she had to do was repeatedly tap the lose wire end to the signal path to generate the minute sparks necessary. It worked the first time. The tiny sparks created pulses. The pulses transmitted to the wire. The test pattern came through on the radio receiver loud and clear. From here on, the signal was fed via the green wire into space. "Time to report in."

CASTLE ROCK

"Stinger...come in." There was no answer. *She must have turned the implant off,* Alex assumed. Slightly disappointed about not getting an answer, he finally gave up, muttering, "Gotta try later." With Rhonda gone again, supporting the rebuilding of the damaged defenses on the Pacific coastline, Alex was left alone once more. Alone and feeling deserted, he was busy in the basement command center. Sitting in front of the monitors, as he usually did during his waking hours, his thoughts were suddenly interrupted by a signal shooting across the screen. His eyes caught a glimpse of an unexpected data stream on the monitor screen. It was a pattern he had not seen since the early days of his career. Suspecting it was only blurry vision, to confirm the signal, he switched the speaker on.

Where his transmitter was sending continuous ping signals over the airwaves, hoping for a return signal from space, there had only been static from the ether. Staring at the monitor, there was only fuzzy static filling the screen. He shook his head, muttering, "Must be seeing things."

"There it was again." This time he knew it was a distinct data pattern, but it went by too quick for his eyes to capture. His ears detected a modulated tone. His body straightened into a rigid posture while he kept his eyes locked on the screen. He hoped it would repeat and prepared for it. He leaned over to the printer to switch it online. This way, he would capture the data. He did not have to wait long. Even before his eyes could detect the next pattern, the printer was already pushing the data onto the paper. He could not wait for the printer to finish and tore the sheet as soon as he could to identify the message. It read, "SOS – HELP."

Dumbfounded and highly curious at the cryptic message, he suspected something was wrong with Tracy's implant. He pinged her again. "Stinger...Stinger...Come in."

This time, there was a response. "Specter...Go." It was Tracy's familiar voice.

"You sending Morse?"

"Negative. Why?"

"Somebody's pinging the ether...Just got an SOS."

"Liz!" It didn't even take a second for Tracy to figure it out. "It's Liz!"

Still skeptical, he agreed nevertheless, "You may just be right."

"Got a Morse generator?"

"No," he said. "But I will rig one."

"Let me know as soon as you make contact," Tracy replied. Ecstatic that there was a glimmer of hope her being alive, she was dying to talk to her sis. *How long's it been?* It felt like years had gone by since the time they had said goodbye.

"You'll be the first to know," he promised. "End transmission." The ether went silent. They kept communication as short as possible. With Tracy on her path of vengeance, and Alex keeping up a lifeline, neither could afford to be compromised. As long as there was no triangulation intercept by outside listeners, they felt secure. Alex, with all of the sensitive snooping equipment at his disposal, thanks to the budget Foster provided him years ago, would know the instant they'd been compromised. His scanners would lock in on any scanner searches.

Glued to the monitor, minutes turned into hours without another transmission. Alex used the wait to test the signal generator. Though dated and not used in decades, it seemed in working order. What he needed was to program a data pattern into the software. He gave it some thought before transmitting the text he prepared and uploading it into the computer. Next, he activated the transmitter, watching the patterned stream pass the monitor into space. He could easily make out the code. It read, "Castle Rock...Castle to ISS...Respond." From here on out, the data stream would repeat until Alex would shut it off.

250 miles out in space, Harmony was just about to complete another path around the globe. Watching through the porthole, directly below, broken up by puffs of clouds, was the bluish breadth of the Atlantic. Gradually panning into view up ahead, as expected every ninety minutes, Liz could make out the eastern coast of North America through a hazy horizon. Also visible was the broken-up ISS debris circling the orbit nearby.

Walsh was busy handling the manual wire task. It was his turn. They had decided to switch position after each orbit to operate the code generator. One would handle the transmission while the other monitored the radio receiver. It was a tedious and tiresome task on the wrist constantly manipulating the wire to generate the code. So far, only the transmitted echo was fed back through the radio. The same process was repeated hour after hour.

Then, all of a sudden, there was a signal. Liz did not think she'd heard right. Barely audible, there it was again, a woodpecker type signal. She yelled at Kenny, floating close to the interlock by the green wire connection, "You change the code?"

"Negative."

Her heart took a leap. Liz shot a glance out the porthole to get her bearings. Harmony was closing in over the Rockies. Slightly north of Pikes Peak on its present orbit, there it was again, a distinct, identifiable pattern. "Castle Rock...Castle to ISS...Respond."

Unable to contain her joy, almost to the brink of ecstasy she shouted at Kenny, "Got a response." Startled, he had missed what she'd just said. He let go of the transmit wire and turned in her direction. "What?"

"Got a signal."

"Where?"

"Castle Rock...Dad."

It took a second for it to sink in. His frustration from trying to establish contact with Earth quickly changed to a grin. He was ecstatic. With one quick push against the bulkhead he propelled his body over to Liz. She caught him sailing through mid-air and pulled him close. Overjoyed and overcome with emotions, both clutched each other in a cheery embrace. Though weightlessly floating through space, Liz felt like an enormous weight had been lifted from her shoulders. If they'd been standing on solid ground, Liz felt certain they would have jumped up and down with joy, but due to the gravity of their situation, Liz urged, "Quick, send the signal." It would only take minutes before they would be out of range again.

"ISS to Castle...Alive...Liz and Walsh."

It only took seconds for a response. "Thank God."

Responses back and forth were slow until Alex modified the software to accept direct keyboard input. A semi-solid link was established. From here on, at least there would be communication. Rescue, if ever, was still far off. In the meantime, Liz reported the current condition of the space station, requesting urgent rescue.

Alex promised to do his utmost to get a rescue mission on the way, but could not confirm a date or the means to accomplish that. He was already on the radio, making contact with Foster out west. In the meantime, no matter how difficult and frustrating the wait would be, with each orbit there was communication between Castle Rock, Baikonur, and Harmony.

For the Western Sector, headquartered on the Pacific coast, it was a renewed incentive for stirring up interest and funding for a defunct space program. Although marginal, funding trickled in from unexpected sources. It seemed, as in the past, that the Pacific region was leading economy and technology trends once more.

The world, with each orbit around the globe, was watching and waiting in hope of an expedient rescue. Lisa Bauer and Kenny Walsh, potentially trapped in space forever, had won the hearts of many nations.

"Help's on the way," was the worldwide promise initiated from broadcast stations, individual multimedia devices, and Twitter accounts near and far. But, for Liz and Kenny, the struggle for survival was not over, not by a long shot.

TRACY BAUER

Presently driving east on Chicago's I-290, Tracy headed straight for the piers. Driving inner city streets took almost an hour to reach the destination in-between evading periodic roadblocks set up along the way. After the first stop she was warned that, as long as she kept the speed down, she wouldn't be bothered by the guardsmen. Regardless, she kept the assault rifle close at hand. Buck, the nosy person he was, kept an ardent eye on the weapon. Tracy could see him peek at the weapon frequently as if he already owned it. She couldn't blame him. After all, there was nothing like it elsewhere in the world. It had been specially shaped and fashioned by Spencer according to her specs at the lab.

He could not contain his curiosity any longer. He gestured at the various parts protruding from the streamlined stock and kept asking, "What's this…what's that? How come this…why that?"

"Don't bother her," Emma kept insisting. "She's driving."

Unless Tracy gave in, she realized he'd keep on pestering her forever. "Triple action weapon. Primary, 10mm pulse rifle…Secondary, 30mm grenade launcher…Tertiary, 12 gage pump action shotgun."

"What about this?" He gestured at the external accessories.

Pointing at the various parts, she explained, "Combination sniper rifle, grenade launcher, shotgun, electronic pulse controlled…Laser spotter scope…LED cartridge counter…fire selector switch…ejection ports…high explosive armor piercing ammo…multi round magazine stacks."

Impressed beyond words, Buck did not have much of a comment other than, "Wow…wow…wow." He was completely taken in by the technology. He had one final question. Actually two. "Why Serpent Slayer?"[48]

---

[48] Serpent Slayer – Tracy's combat weapon:
Triple Action Assault Weapon
1. Pulsed Assault Weapon 10mm Caliber – Primary
   - Muzzle velocity 850 m/s
   - Maximum range 2,500 m
   - Maximum effective range 750 m
   - Cyclic rate of fire 1,200 rpm
2. Magazine-fed 30mm Grenade Launcher – Secondary
   - Gas operated, electronic primed
   - Maximum range 210 m
   - Maximum effective range 35 m
   - Cyclic rate of fire 15 rpm
3. Pump Action 12 Gage Shotgun – Tertiary
   - Manual Pump Action
   - Automatically fed cartridges
4. Rifle weight without magazine 3.5 kg
5. Full magazine
   - Primary 125 rounds
   - Secondary belt-fed
   - Tertiary 10 rounds
   - Firing weight fully loaded, 5 kg

"Cause it spits fire and lightning."

"Can I?" He was dying to finger the steel.

"No."

"Put that thing back," his bride insisted. "It frightens me."

"Don't be a pussy."

Tracy could not help but grin at them patronizing each other. They were simple folks from a simpler time. But that was the past. Though they bickered at times, she was glad to see a dependency between the two. *They'll be okay,* she mused. *They'll make it.*

The rest of the day was spent by the piers. There was sea traffic, a lot of it, but, from the looks of them, mostly foreign sea craft occupied, it seemed, by crews from the Middle-Eastern region. "Muslims," Tracy assumed.

Buck was baffled as well. "What are they doin' here?

"Water," Tracy believed. "Nothing else."

"Water?"

"Think about it." She then explained, "Muslims, Islam, Jihad, whatever you may call it, has enough open space. Wasteland, desert, desolate places, that's all—but no water. You may not be aware that world population is running short on freshwater."

"What? Look at all the water out there." His arm swept along the Chicago waterfront.

"Let the woman talk," Emma cut in. "I wanna hear."

"That's right. It's all that water everybody wants."

The dark of night had broken in. Tracy suggested, "Let's find something to eat." She looked smart. Heads turned wherever she stepped foot. Dressed in her tailor-fashioned, leather-made overcoat, pulse weapon slung over her right shoulder, hidden beneath the coat, taking long strides, she led the way. Her target was Michigan Avenue, which, according to rumors, had turned into an amusement district. One more corner and they had arrived. Amusement was an understatement. It was a spectacle. This was more like a carnival. With the honeymooners in tow, the closer she got the noisier and more vivid darkness had turned. It seemed the entire city was out on the streets, not only loitering up and down sidewalks, but taking over streets, hallways, and passage ways. Everything was available for barter from fast food and contraband to prostitutes, blatantly sold out on the open. All was up for sale, that's how desperate life had turned. Where it might have been sheer survival in the first turmoil years, the district had turned into what might be the largest marketplace in the world.

After years of depravation, not only did the honeymooners marvel at the goods and services sold, but Tracy as well. People seemed to have adjusted to poverty with the simplest means of living. One thing was noticeable from the onset. There was no obesity. *Maybe,* Tracy considered, *the economic collapse wasn't such a bad idea. At least it made the nation a healthier place. But was it worth it? Depends where you live,* she supposed.

The brilliance in setting reminded her much of past travels to Shinjuku, Tokyo's Pearl City entertainment district, but this was in no way as organized. That was where it stopped. Beneath all the lighting where trading took place, it was more like Manila, Bangkok, and Mumbai City. Here, everything went. It was a place to barter for food, alcohol, goods delivered from farmlands, fish from the lakes, and everything else produced, fashioned, and sold under the sun. There was even a large influx of foreign-made artifacts, especially from the Persian region. The Arabic language was heard everywhere. You could easily spot the foreigners clad in traditional Muslim garb.

"Dragon Palace," one prominent overhead sign announced.

"Let's check it out," said Tracy.

Everything was fine with the Honeymooners, especially since Tracy was footing all the bills. Her every suggestion was readily returned with a couple of eager nods. Buck and Emma had become fond of their host. They felt safe in her company.

On entering the palace, Tracy, in one quick swoop, assessed the environment. It was a cautious habit from years of unexpected encounters. Looking around, waiting to be seated, there were only few tables and stools to accommodate the fast-paced services. People hurried in and out of the food section as fast as the services allowed. She stubbed her toes against a table leg occupied by one person only. He looked up, seemed to assess her and, after a pause, invited her and her guests, "Care to join me?"

"Sure," Tracy readily accepted. They gladly occupied the three empty seats.

The lone patron introduced himself, "Bill Bailey."

"Like the song," Tracy mused.

"I get that a lot," he countered. "New to the city?"

"You could say that."

"So, what brings you here?"

Scrutinizing him to assess his sincerity, Tracy volunteered, "Passing through. New York's the destination."

"But why?" Bill said, appearing startled.

"Why not?"

"All the fighting, the hostilities, the struggles getting there? You'll get killed."

"I'll take my chances."

"May change your mind after I tell you." He raised his beer mug. "But first," he toasted, "let's drink." After several noisy gulps, he slammed the mug on the table with a jarring clang. The thirsty customer Bill Bailey was, Tracy ordered another brew for him. It made him even more talkative. "Let me tell you why not," he started to explain, then went on to tell them his story.

Apparently, from what he told them, everything east of the Mississippi had been claimed by the Muslims. They were in control of the Eastern Seaboard including major cities like Boston, New York, Philadelphia, DC, and Atlanta, as well as Chicago.

"The truth," he proclaimed, emphasizing his story by downing it with another mug of beer. As incredible as it sounded to his guests, it might be true. If it was factual then Tracy had her hands full trying to make it east. During the course of the conversation, she swept Brian's picture across his face and asked, "Seen this man?"

"Don't know the face," he proclaimed. "Too many folks in and out the city."

Tracy believed him. He changed the subject to local issues. He asked, "Hear about today's incident?"

"What?"

"Entire sentry squad wiped out."

This bit of news jerked the three to the present. Emma and Buck were throwing meaningful glances at Tracy, who projected a self-assured grin. "I'll drink to that." Their glasses went up in unison as well.

"It's all over town," Bill proclaimed. "Woman did the killing. They're looking for her."

"Is that so?" Unable to suppress a grin, Tracy further asked, "Who?"

"Al Qaeda…Jihad faction," he underscored his statement. "That's who…made Chicago its headquarters." Explaining further, he told them about the state the city was in, who controlled it, what was taking place, what was prohibited, what was tolerated, and what was allowed. "Islamic order has taken roots in the region."

Hearing that made her blood boil. She'd heard enough and said, "Time to clean house."

The statement did not go unnoticed by her company. Her mind focused on the mission, Tracy got up, collected her valise, and headed for the exit, trailed by the honeymooners, making their host guess what he had said wrong. All he could do was raise his mug high over his head, yelling after them, "Thanks. Have a nice trip!"

The revelation was unexpected to Tracy. As a lone person on the attack, regardless of the technology and weapons at her disposal, she felt she was not prepared to take on an entire invasion. It would take some serious planning. She needed help. The thought kept gnawing at her mind for the rest of the evening. What followed was a fitful sleep.

Early the next morning it hit her like a lightning strike. "The Patriots." It was the answer.

Since the last accounts after the March had them settled on the shores of Lake Michigan, they were within easy reach from Chicago. Just a few hours north from here. Her direction was set. Tracy was already in the driver's seat when the honeymooners showed up. "Where we headed?" Buck wanted to know.

"Milwaukee."

"But," he protested, "it's the wrong way."

"I'll get you to the falls," she assured him. "May take some time, but I'll get you there. Consider this your honeymoon, for now."

Emma was grateful. "Thanks."

Buck was not. "Don't mention it."

THE PATRIOTS

Norton was flanked by Bad Man and Elliott. He was just about to step off the sidewalk into the street, headed for the congressional assembly scheduled for 6:00 PM, when he was almost run over by a crazed driver. There was a woman behind the wheel of a fiercely painted H-1 Hummer. Jumping back to the curb saved the party. Being military, he recognized the model immediately. What he could not understand was a civilian having possession of it, and, what's more, what seemed to be a souped-up version with headers, air scoop, and the trimmings of a hotrod. Bad Man was irate. He raised his fist and chased after the mad woman. Wildly shaking his shotgun, he yelled after her, "Hey! Come back here, bitch."

Bad Man, always ready to fight, had already leveled the 12-gage pump action, his faithful companion, at the speeding off vehicle. To their surprise, the Humvee slithered to a stop fifty some yards out, backed up at max speed, and almost ran him over again. For the second time, he had to jump for safety. "Lemme kill her…Lemme kill her," he barked at Norton, who still marveled at the girl, waving him off to stand down.

"Maybe later," he promised a crazed Bad Man. For now, he was interested in what the woman was all about. On guard for maybe getting run over again, they stepped from the safety of the curb, approached her cautiously, and said, "What's with the rush?"

Bad Man, by his side, foamed through the open window. "Crazy bitch!" he yelled at her. "I'll kill you."

Staring daringly into his face, undeterred by the man's crazed outbursts, Tracy stepped from the vehicle and boldly demanded, "Where can I find the Patriots?"

Norton, pulling Bad Man away from the vehicle proclaimed, "You're looking at them." Brodie Elliott, who was a bystander through the hostile exchange, stared at Tracy and took a couple of steps forward. He knowingly gestured at her. "I know you."

She also seemed to recognize him, then replied, "Colorado…Castle Rock."

"Years ago," he recollected. "Didn't recognize you. Changed quite a bit, haven't you?"

"Things change," she stated. "And so, do people." It was an acceptable statement to Elliott and Norton, but not to Bad Man.

"You almost killed us," he insisted again.

Not being the slightest deterred by this brute of a man, she grinned at him. "Don't be such a baby. I know what I'm doing." He was ready to pounce on her, or at least give the bitch a punch in the face to regain his respect. Norton held him back, "You can fight later. We're late for the meeting. Care to join us?" He invited her with a gesture to follow.

Tracy turned to instruct the honeymooners, "Stay here. Don't go anywhere." Both were still shaken from thinking they were getting shot and readily agreed in unison, "We won't."

The assembly hall, "War Room," as it was called by the Patriots, was as rowdy as ever when the party entered. But this time, as soon as Tracy was spotted, with all eyes aimed at her the hall immediately turned silent. Between grunts of approval and nods of admiration only subdued muttering and commenting was heard. With an unusual gusto

Norton opened the assembly. "We have a guest." He willingly stepped aside to give her space at the podium and offered, "Tell us about you."

Not used to such unexpected welcoming courtesy, Tracy took a few seconds in silence preparing her thoughts. She opened with an introduction by saying, "The name is Bauer, Tracy Bauer," then, over the next fifteen minutes, described her journey. "Where I am from…" she went on, relating the conditions in the mountain reaches of the Rockies and the general state of the central and western parts of the nation. She illustrated as much as she dared without jeopardizing her mission.

She also described the conditions in and around Chicago, but that seemed to be nothing new to the Patriot commanders. Reports came in daily from the south. What was more of a threat were accounts received from the Atlantic coast, though mostly rumors. "It is my mission," Tracy said in conclusion, "to ward off the enemy and invasions with or without your help."

Norton invited her to be seated next to him and stated, "We know about the enemy. What we didn't know was its size. Not until yesterday."

She was curious. "What happened yesterday?"

"Yesterday," Norton informed his guest, "we were given an ultimatum." He further explained the accounts delivered by the Jihad commander, Yusuf, which were the grounds for today's emergency assembly. They spent the next few hours postulating, hypothesizing, and theorizing on how to best deal with the advancing enemy. Followed with enthusiastic cheering, the assembly was adjourned to the nearby Freedom Brewery.

Norton and Elliott, accompanied by Tracy, adjourned to more private quarters. What followed was a roundtable session, hammering out a defense strategy. Relentlessly, pros and cons were passed back and forth between the respective leaders. Tracy was the sole warrior with a solid promise of being backed by the Patriots. There was no question that an attack was imminent. The question was when and where. Spies and forward spotters deployed by Norton in recent weeks came back with only sparse reports. They had not been able to infiltrate or penetrate the enemy's forces.

Since the 1st Armored Division was not a tactical force, but due to its size was strategic by nature, they decided to build and hold the line at the Mississippi River. To assure success for holding up the defense perimeters up and down the river, it was decided to demolish all bridges with the exception of one. It would be the Poplar Street Bridge at the St. Louis crossing, which would be heavily fortified. Without air and sea coverage for fending off the enemy, the sole success lay in the hands of the Patriots, supported by the armored heavy equipment. Holding the line at the river would be much like trench warfare. But this time it would be manned by water-borne craft under the command of Rusty Norton with the support from Brodie Elliott's 1st Armored Division.

A thought had just occurred to her. There was something else Tracy needed accomplished. "One more thing," she said. "We must take back HAARP."

"HAARP?" Norton was surprised at the news. "Thought it'd been destroyed."

"Only the waveguide," Tracy clarified. "Ground station's still operational to full capacity."

"How're we gonna do that? Don't have forces out there."

"Get in touch with Foster," she advised. "He'll have a battle plan ready for you. Just remember," she stressed once more, "get it back." Tracy, after a night deserved rest, with a promise to keep in touch, prepared for departure. Bad Man, after regaining his calm, shook her hand in a peaceful gesture and bade a, "Farewell," as he watched the Humvee speed off, headed east along the Lake Michigan shorelines.

Tracy and her passengers were back on the road again headed into enemy territory. It was her decision. Besides, she was determined to keep her promise to the honeymooners. With Specter in the Rockies guiding her and Foster out west, perhaps she could stay ahead of unexpected surprises.

"Where we headed?" Again, it was the nosy Buck by her side. With him and his innocent bride seated in back, the trio made its way towards her final destination, New York, by way of Chicago, Cleveland, and Buffalo, with a stopover at Niagara Falls to appease an overdue promise. "Leave her alone. She's driving."

The Humvee team did not encounter any serious confrontations along the way since their path was along a sparsely populated Great Lakes. Without fuel, fishing fleets, smaller seaports around the lakes had been abandoned. It was not until farther south when they observed an increase in foreign influx. For now, the three enjoyed the freedom along a stretch of land that used to be part of an independent, solid nation that already had fought once for independence. It seemed history kept repeating itself. The souped-up Humvee with Tracy, honeymooners, and Serpent Slayer by her side kept forging ahead, attracting attention wherever they went.

THE SERPENT

Hasan Hammad had chosen Chicago, the once thriving metropolis, to be his command center for one specific reason. It was for the unlimited supply of water resources from nearby Lake Michigan. What made the location so desirable was not only the one lake, but five in all. With climate change on the rise and ice glaciers melting at alarming rates, water supplies around the globe were dwindling. Whether the phenomenon was real or merely proclaimed by geophysicists, the occurrence was visible all around. It was happening in every mountain range on the globe. Hammad had recognized the dangers decades ago. All he had to do was take a trip to the Nile, Ganges, or Yangtze to be reminded. Same was true with the Colorado River when he crossed it years back during the battle for California. Since then, things had gotten worse, far worse. Water shortages were experienced everywhere. People were demanding justification.

Yusuf and his scout party had just returned from up north. "What have you found?" He was curious to get a first-hand report. Until now, Hammad had been content with the initial stake at the lake he had claimed. But it was time now to secure the rest of the shorelines. He had his eyes set on the city up north, Milwaukee. The only reason he had not put a claim on the city earlier was because of its heavy fortification by the dreaded infantry forces called the Patriots. It was time to deal with them. "Spoke with the leaders, a certain Rusty Norton and his lieutenants, Brodie Elliott and the one they call Bad Man."

"Bad Man?" The name sparked a curiosity.

"Yes," Yusuf confirmed. "He must be watched. Primitive and ferocious, he cannot be negotiated with. Our commanders are no match for his physical strength."

"We shall see soon. But first," Hammad shifted the topic, "locate a woman they call Stinger."

Rumors had been floating around the ether about a woman on the warpath against Jihad. Apparently, it was a coded call sign picked up by several of his monitoring stations. "I've heard of it. But I believe it is only myth and legend."

"Nevertheless," he was ordered, "check it out. Put a recon squad together. Unless we capture her," he argued, "it will be bad for the morale of our forces. It may jeopardize our mission. We cannot afford further delays. The window of opportunity is open. The time is now. It may not stay open for long. For all we know, other nations may have their eyes on the Lakes. There are scouts along the fronts. We do not know how many. We must prevent rumors at all cost. We must stop Stinger."

Panting and out of breath, Hakim Massoud, First Lieutenant, U.S. Cell Central, Chicago, came bursting into the private chambers. "Commander," he huffed. "We have more attacks."

"Calm down," Hammad ordered the overzealous lieutenant. "Explain."

"Reports just arrived from the city about more killings."

"Who's doing the killing?"

"The one they call Stinger."

Rumors-turned-news enraged Hammad. He ordered Massoud, "Call group and squad commanders to meet. Immediately."

Although Hammad was not much for rumor and gossip, the new reports might have truth to them. He had to consider the possibility as factual. Though it would distract from his pending mission, he was giving it highest priority.

Thirty minutes later, Hammad was surrounded by his field commanders. Since he had reassigned most commanders to the new headquarters, Chicago, most were in easy reach. He was familiar with most. Currently present were his most trusted commanders, Antarah Radi, Mission Commander, Jihad, Central Sector, Chicago, IL; Bandar Malik, First Lieutenant, U.S. Cell Alpha, New York, NY; Hakim Massoud, First Lieutenant, U.S. Cell Central, Chicago, IL; Yusuf Hashim, Commander, Al Qaeda/Jihad, U.S. Cell Alpha, New York, NY; Tariq Amman, First Lieutenant, U.S. Cell East, Washington, DC.

It was a select cadre from the best and most proven of his trained warriors. Aside from years of battle experience, what made them the best of his breed were intellectual levels, judgment, achievements, and on-the-spot decision-making abilities. While Hammad was overall supreme commander, upcoming battle judgments, whenever necessary, needed to be made on a local level. This was especially true with ineffective communication channels in the northern part of America. Since he could not be present at all locations and times of conflict, he had hand-picked the men presently surrounding him.

A few could not be present. They were still assigned to designated sectors around the globe in addition to the Sudanese training camps. "We have a problem," Hammad opened the emergency assembly. He explained the urgency confirming rumors about the enemy infantry preparing for battle and the one they called Stinger. He could not afford to let the woman slip from his hands, if she existed. She may be a vigilante on a path of vengeance. He could not allow that, especially not from a woman. In the history of Islam, from what he knew, there had never been a woman leader. And there would be no room for it now. "She must be stopped."

Earlier that day, after leaving Milwaukee, Tracy and her passengers were headed south on I-94 along the shores toward Chicago. "Hand me the folder," she ordered Buck, seated in the passenger seat. Eager to appease her, he rifled through the glove compartment and handed her a folder containing several charts. "Take the wheel," she ordered.

Reaching out to grip the steering wheel with his left hand, again, he was only too eager to please her. Emma, in the backseat, kept a wary eye on him. It freed Tracy's hands to study the printout in the folder. She held the paper close to her face to keep the information private. It was the Al Qaeda watch list Alex had provided. It not only listed the locations for Jihad cells in the country, it gave the names, addresses, and descriptions for active members as well.

Several cells had been identified at the lakeshores along her current path. Tracy stopped three times. When striding off, each time she fetched Serpent Slayer and kept it hidden beneath her coat. Minutes later, she reappeared as self-assured as ever. In the meantime, her passengers were up for speculations about her brief disappearances. "Wonder where she's goin' this time," Emma would wonder.

"Taking a pee, I suppose."

Shaking her head, Emma would respond, "Don't be an idiot. Young woman like her only goes a couple times a day, morning and night. Besides, she's not an ordinary woman. There's a plan for every move she makes." After the third disappearance, she showed concern. "I'm worried."

"Don't be a pussy," Buck condescended just as Tracy reappeared from her last spree. Gunning the engine, they were back on the main road. There was a slight difference in her appearance this time. Both honeymooners noticed specks of blood splattered on top of the coat.

Wiping his left hand across her jacket sleeve, Buck hinted, "Got something on the leather." His hand came back slightly smeared with blood. He did not say anything else. But Tracy was certain both passengers' minds would be churning with questions. It showed on their faces. She kept silent, wishing they would never have to find out about her quests, as vengeful as they were. After all, it was a personal vendetta she waged against an enemy that had caused the demise of her, the nation, and its people.

Over the past two hours since leaving Milwaukee, Tracy had been able to annihilate three Jihad cells. It could have also been Al Qaeda or other factions. It did not matter. The list Alex had provided not only spelled out persona parameters, personal IDs were attached with printed pictures and all. It was a recent list compiled by Foster provided by international Intel. Where the list provided names and places, they were still a hidden enemy.

Confronting the enemy face-to-face, each time she confirmed the IDs on the list. Afterwards, she felt relatively safe since local law enforcement was almost nonexistent in the Badlands. Her task was above local laws. Her mission was to get the land back whole for a people that deserved to have their nation back. This time, it would be the law of the land, by the people and for the people.

The last confrontation had just taken place after leaving Chicago in their wake. It had been her last stop in the central sector. As before, after verifying the location, she had entered a local mosque. It was during the noon hour. As she'd expected, the local congregation, bowing on their knees to give praise to Allah, was unaware of her entry.

What the parishioners noticed the next time their heads came up was a woman propped up by the prayer wall, holding an open book in her left hand. It was a copy of the Islamic Holy Bible she had lifted from the pedestal. In bold lettering, the title page read, "Qur'an," known to the western world as Koran.

Everybody took notice of the unusually defiant woman dressed in a fashionable, but daring, combat uniform. Where some of the faces turned inquisitive, others turned alarmed. The prayer session came to an abrupt halt. Though Tracy had noticed a number of assault weapons, the customary worn-down AK-47 planted against the entry hall, nobody in the congregation moved. It might have been the situation, it might have been her stance, cradling the Koran, but the many faces were poised, waiting for her to speak.

And speak she did with a direct quote out of the Qur'an, verse 2:244. *"Then fight in the cause of Allah, and know that Allah heareth and knoweth all things."*

Where the general worshipper was still perplexed at the unexpected intruder, as soon as Tracy cited verses from the Koran, several of the bearded, Kurta clad males jumped up on their bare feet, rushing for their weapons placed against the worship hall. It was a desperate act. It would be their last.

In one swift motion, Tracy dropped the coat, swooped up Serpent Slayer to waist height, and cut down everybody reaching for a weapon. Upholding her vows, she spared the innocent worshippers who had cowered, wailing, against the carpeted floor.

Tracy took stock of the dead, checked off their names from the Al Qaeda list, and, as before, declared, "Do not harbor the enemy." With a deliberating gesture just before departing, she closed with, "Never forget, you are guests in my land."

CANADIAN WILDERNESS

"Get your gear together," Scott Brooks, group leader for the advanced scouting party, urged. "Time to head out." It was early. The morning dew was still clinging to the underside of foliage, making for a chilly dawn in the dense Minnesota forests. They had been waylaid in this part of the country for *who knew how long,* Brooks contemplated in the early morning hours. Time had passed, much like in the rest of the nation. Without an organized schedule or calendar, many had lost track of the exact day of week, week of month, and month of year. It did not matter much to Brooks and his crew. They had adjusted their lifestyle to the time of season. Living on the land, surviving off the land, and bound by the land, one lived and struggled through the seasons much like early settlers. It was the life of the prepper, the survivalist, Scott Brooks and his crew had chosen. Following the march of the Patriots, headed up by Rusty Norton, their path took them way up north into Huron Territory. Settlers he and his party had turned. It was a difficult choice, breaking from their carefree acquired lifestyle of hunting and fishing. Abound with animal life, fertile soil with trees for constructing log cabins, the region was a hunter's paradise. What's more, there was an abundant source of clean, clear freshwater. Opportunities were endless for a small group like his.

Brooks had been toying with the idea leaving this sanctuary for quite some time. Was it his young age, was it the exploration spirit, or just plain boredom? He could not clearly identify the reasons. There had been quite an out roar when he had called his team together the other day. After he had laid out the plan, there was much disdain from everyone. Most of the members had made this their home. Away from the struggle the rest of the nation faced, here, life had been good and plentiful.

Over time, with more and more survivalists joining the Preppers, the original dwellings grew into a sizable settlement. There was a growth in population. With it came added problems, social problems. People began making rules. Laws were created and enforced. Educational systems built. Life had come full cycle once more. It was here when Brooks became secluded. He began feeling suffocated by the growing and encroaching settlements.

He knew it would not take many years before the place turned into a town, then a city. It was a natural process created by people. Numbers created security. Entrepreneurs were born. Technology followed. Industries were created, followed by more laws, politics, and, eventually, government control. The modern lifecycle began all over.

Scott could see the writing on the wall before it even began. It clouded his mind. He needed to get away. Here, he was only wasting his life away. It was then that he realized his calling. "Control growth, manage the growth, and protect it at its onset."

At least it would keep him moving and from becoming stagnant. It would provide challenges. The world was open to explore. The world was his for the taking. "I'll be the harbinger. I'll be the messenger for a nation crumbled. I'll put an end to the invasion." He had not quite figured out how to go about doing that, but he would recognize the means and opportunities when presented.

Today, Scott Brooks and his squadron of former CIA assassins-turned-hunters were on the move.

The reaction was obvious. The common consensus was, "Why?"

Brooks gave himself some time to respond. After some contemplating, the answer came to him. The place was too isolated. Being a young and determined warrior, he could not let time pass by without being part of mainstream life. Regardless of prevalent conditions with the struggles and hardships to the south, his instinct was gnawing at his conscience. In the privacy of his log cabin on quiet nights, and there were many, an inner voice kept prodding him into action with, "Get your act together."

After the constructing log cabins, gathering food supplies, adjusting to the local lifestyle, it was not an easy choice. Problem was, there was no entertainment in the wilderness. Aside from the hunting and killing game, there was no recreation. But, most of all, there were no women for personal companionships. "Who's with me?"

A number of the settlers were willing to join him. It was enough to form a small scout detachment. The rest would remain behind to protect the settlement. "Ok then, get your things together." With a promise to return with women for the left behind preppers, the detachment made final preparations for the journey the next morning. Backpacks were stacked, M-16s shouldered, with some preferring sidearm slung by the side. The team took off, headed south. Left behind were several 55-gallon drums of diesel fuel Brooks figured they did not need where they were going.

Since it was a late start due to loading up and leaving Thunder Bay behind, Brooks figured they would make it to Duluth by evening. From there, the path would take them along Lake Superior down and across to Madison and on to Milwaukee.

"Milwaukee," some of the guys wondered. "Why?"

"Place 1st Armored Infantry Division was headed last," he explained. It was also confirmed through rumors carried by the occasional hunters passing through on their way north. It would be the most likely place to meet up with Norton and Elliott. If not, next stop would be Fort Knox, the infantry's home base. Traveling mostly on country roads, it took two days to reach their destination. "Where the fuck have you been?" where the first words out of Norton's mouth. Brooks was not the least bit affronted. He could understand why the Patriot leader was upset. It'd been many months since they parted.

There was a time, not that many years ago, when Scott Brooks felt at a loss. It was right after the EMP strike. He and his teammates had been pretty much isolated from society. Assigned by the CIA to the DELTA team in the Arizona desert, his job back then was hostage interrogation. Then came the day when communication suddenly went dead. Scott Brooks had left for the Pacific coast but never returned as promised. The team had remained behind until the food supplies run out. After a forced march, days later the crew arrived at Fort Bliss, Texas. Reporting in, the crew was ultimately attached to the post's intelligence center, tactical operations. With the nation split up into various sectors, the crew decided to abandon the military to join the Patriot movement. It was here, were Brooks eventually reunited with his team.

Headed north on I-25, not much later they arrived in Colorado Springs just in time to witnessed the encounter with the strange looking AH-1 Attack Cobra and Elliott's 1st Armored Division. Laying low out in the protection of the Black Forest, they watched the standoff with the Castle team. Following Brodie's negotiations and peace treaty with the owner of the Castle, Alex Bauer, it was then when Brooks and his team joined Brodie's regiment to eventually wind up at Fort Knox and Rusty Norton. That was many months ago.

On his arrival today, right away, he noticed something unusual was going on here. From the harried activities, it seemed Norton and the Patriots were getting ready to head out. There were certain signs obvious to every military man when troops were preparing for the road.

"What's up," Brooks wanted to know.

"You're just in time."

"Yeah? What's goin' on?"

"War's goin' on. That's what," was the hurried reply. "Come morning we're headed out." In a definitive gesture, he invited Brooks to follow. "Join me." He was already striding toward the command headquarters. In the meantime, Brooks' team sought out and joyfully reunited with former military buddies from years prior.

Pacing alongside Norton, keeping up with his long-legged strides, he asked Brooks again, "Where have you been the past years?"

"Northern fringes, Lake Superior."

"Canada? Thought they tightened borders."

"Government doesn't care. They've got enough land to accommodate everybody seeking refuge. As a matter of fact," he explained, "they welcome their southern neighbors, especially with what's happened to the nation. Don't want foreigners on their land, especially not Jihad." He then went on and made the offer, "Ever need a place built," he said, "let me know. I'll build you a fine cabin."

Norton ignored the offer. "Reason we're headed out," he explained. "Jihad declared war on us."

"What?" This bit of news sounded ludicrous to Brooks. While he maintained his cool, a hint of loathing swept across his face. Facing imminent Islamic takeover was intolerable. He could not bear the thought of seeing himself dressed in Arabian attire, growing a beard, and bowing to Mecca five times a day. He even became more enraged at visualizing the beauty of the American girl covered from head to toe in a veiled garb, perhaps even being mutilated by her husband.

"Islamic force's on the move," he was warned. "Already taken much of the eastern shores. New York, Boston, Philadelphia, all lost to foreigners. It's up to us to stop 'em."

"What's the plan?"

"Have a seat," Norton invited Brooks to the table. They had arrived at the assembly hall, which was already packed with military troops.

When he saw his commander getting ready to speak, Bad Man yelled out, "Quiet!"

"You all know the reason we're here," Norton opened the talks. He then went on to explain the mission ahead, their destination, and the anticipated battle strategy. Brooks' patiently absorbed what was said, then wanted to know, "Why anticipated?"

"Don't know what to expect. All I know," Norton stated, "is that we better hold our ground or we'll be in deep shit." Unlike previous world battles fought, in case of failure, now and here was no battalion, brigade, or division that would come to his aid. There was no Army, Air Force, or Marine lending support for the fight. It was solely up the 1st Armored Infantry Division to defend the central plains and lakes.

The talks, heated at times, went into the night. Brooks heard enough. He sat back and contemplated his possible participation. One thing, he did not want was to get attached to

Elliott's division. He and his platoon were too much of an independent group to be ordered around by some war college trained commander. While deliberations went on, large quantities of beer were served late into the night. At times, Brooks was lulled into drowsing. His mind was drawn between paying attention to the present environment and pulling away to the past, trying to come up with his own solution to the pressing issues at hand.

THE PAST

Scott Brooks, growing up along the American–Mexican border, unsure whether to cross or stay behind, hesitated by the creek's edge, the borderline, while his playmate Julio urged him on. "Hurry—hurry up." As always, his mind screamed, "Yes," but his body kept him planted on solid ground. The other playmates had already arrived at the other side of the border and were waiting for him to catch up. Playing by the creek was fun. Sometimes they were chased by border guards, but most of the time nobody bothered them. After all, unlike grownup smugglers, they were only kids at play. Through his childhood, he seemed to always be the last to arrive, and rightly so. Where most kids freely hopped and skipped their way through the day, Scott always fell behind. When he complained to his mom, she would console him with one or another explanation. "You're born this way. Nothing anybody can do." And life went on for Scott Brooks, born in Nogales, Arizona, just across from the Mexican border.

Eventually, at age six, he entered first grade. It was from that day on that all the misery began. It would last for many years. Brought into this world by hard working, but poor, parents, his imperfect body did not match a very alert mind. It was not until much later when it was confirmed from a first visit to the local doctor that their son was born with scoliosis. Deformity was nothing new, very often contributed to unsanitary conditions, especially among the economically deprived. It was an accepted condition by the grownups, but for the individual afflicted, it was no easy matter. Considered an unjust penalty by God as punishment from one's previous life, it greatly affected the child's behavior, mannerism, and performance. Regardless of justifiable reasons, the punishment upheld a lasting imprint on the inflicted person's character. Most grew up timid, insecure, and complete lacking in self-confidence.

This was the case when Scott entered school. From then on, it was nothing but daily harassment by school bullies. Enduring the mental and physical anguish in silence, his character took on that of retribution, deepened year after year. By the time he left grade school, whatever inherited understanding and compassion he was born with had been beaten from his body. It was at age twelve when his dad died from an unfortunate automobile accident. Fortunately for his mom, he had left a sizable life insurance in her name. It was the first time there was money in the family.

It was not long after when she took her son to seek medical advice about his chronic complaints about his back. After a cursory examination by a general practitioner unable to help, the doctor referred the child to a clinic that could. That's where he finally landed, the University of Arizona Medical Center, Tucson, AZ.

Fortunate for Scott, the physician on duty examining his spine was a neurological specialist. He promised he could fix his back but also cautioned his mother an operation would be expensive and intensive with rigorous exercise schedules to follow. His mom assured the specialist money was not a problem. Shortly after, Scott was scheduled to undergo a medical procedure to straighten his spine. "It'll be a lengthy and painful process," his mom was advised. "But, at the end, he'll be pain free." For Scott, pain was part of his life. Most importantly for Scott, he would be able to walk like a normal person.

It was all Scott had to hear to readily agree to the procedure. The procedure, a posterior fusion, was intense. It involved a lengthy incision on his back and use of metal instrumentation to correct the curvature. It called for a spinal fusion in addition to metal implants, which involved a combination of rods, screws, hooks, and wires, over time straightening his spine. The operation itself lasted a grueling eight hours, but to Scott, enduring weeks of bed sores was worth it. He could finally walk upright and, most importantly, pain free. Once healed, there was a new world to explore for a boy born into pain and shame. Sports, games, dating, and unlimited amounts of experiences were awaiting him. Carefree about adult responsibilities and future plans, Scott spent the next years having fun.

The ingrained hatred against bullies and tormentors, however, although suppressed, prevailed within the deep recesses of his mind.

Time had passed quickly for Scott Brooks as he tried to catch up with life's virtues. Before he knew it, he was an adult, and with that came obligations and responsibilities. When his mother encouraged him to seek out a career path, the unspeakable happened. The nation had been attacked and torn apart at its very roots, terminating any kind of career planning. Scott was caught up in the aftermath of the economic Armageddon. Overnight, his career plans had waned to nothing. It was then that he ran into a group of mercenary operatives at the nearby desert town of Tombstone.

Scott immediately knew he had found his calling, especially when they revealed their mission, covert operatives DELTA forces, CIA. It was a dream-come-true for the once timid and aimless youngster struggling through an unkind and sometimes cruel childhood world. He signed up immediately. From then on, he was an equal player with money to spend. But luck did not last long. The nation had been attacked and torn apart at its very roots, terminating every prospect for further advancement. There was none. With the economic collapse and destroyed nation, the fortunes he sought had to wait. It came in the form of a chance meeting. With the once glorious organization, CIA, abandoned and the DELTA team splintered into a directionless squad, Brooks took to the road. He was headed north.

It was there that he ran into the man that had turned around his life, Dr. Allen Spencer, head of Los Alamos Laboratories. Reworking plant security had given him another chance at a career. Once put into place, however, being an opportunist, plant operations seemed too boring a job. He sought out something more challenging, one that would provide him with action. It did not take long. It came in the form of his former combat partner, Alex Bauer. He took to the road. It was Castle Rock he was headed. It turned out to be a reunion but also a rather short visit with his friends Alex and Brian.

Along the route Scott Brooks sought out and teamed up with his former DELTA teammates. Weeks went by, then months and years, in the wilderness of the Canadian backwoods. In recollection, the years spent there was worth the cause. It had formed a close bond between them. They came to depend on each other for life and death. They considered themselves reactionary survivalists, with everybody trained in weapons marksmanship, experienced and skilled in carpentry, fishing and land cultivation. A new faction was born: The Preppers.

It was these Prepper groups making up much of the nation's uncultivated land. Whatever was necessary, not only surviving disasters, but making a comfortable living without the customary multimedia, entertainments, and games, was provided by the land.

Living through the first winter without the benefit from cultivated grain, vegetables, and fruits was tough, but meat was plentiful. Making it through the first cold season living on protein only did not seem to have much of an adverse effect on the body. The Eskimos had done it for eons. The second season was much better after the seeds took hold in the fertile soil. From then on, bread was baked from the grain and whiskey was distilled. Vegetables and trees began to bear fruit and life was good.

Whenever meat provisions ran short, a hunting party would go out to replenish supplies. More and more, the team came to depend on Brooks. He seemed to have a knack for hunting. Each time out he would come back with his shoulders loaded down by fresh kill. Most times, regardless of severity in weather, there was a deer slung around his neck in addition to hare, geese, and fish carried in both hands. "Wonder how he does it," his huntsmen buddies would speculate. They did not know that Scott Brooks had endured a life in pain and depravation throughout his growing up years. After a mended spine, he spent all of his spare time strengthening his body and muscles. Working relentlessly on limbs and muscle groups, after years of unrelenting training, the end result was a body supported by superior strengths.

Bones, once brittle from inactivity, became steel like. Muscles began to form where once there was only weakened tissue. Growth turned into strength. With strength came power. Power promoted exercise. Exercise initiated training. Training generated speed. His boundaries in strength and speed seemed nonexistent. The reaction even affected his eyesight. He would spot and recognize objects before anyone else could. Animal like in instinct, speed, and endurance, Scott Brooks was revered among his peers like no other. He was prone to be a leader. It was this quality that came in handy for Brooks whether it was for hunting, building, or fighting. For all practical purposes, he had turned super-soldier.

In the early days of settlement, it was the pioneering challenges that kept him busy. Recently, after wilderness life became routine, he no longer had anything challenging to look forward to. He had to break out of the current environment. It was time to move on. All he had to do was look at the surroundings. Log cabins had gone up and grown the initial settlement into a small community. It wouldn't stop here. He had seen enough.

For Scott, though he was a human phenomenon among his troops, with life relatively comfortable in the Canadian outback, he realized there was something missing from is life. He had become more and more restless in recent months. Stepping outside the log cabin that morning, he suddenly realized what was missing. "Challenges."

THE PATRIOTS

Scott Brooks was an early riser. He was an action man determined to get most from a waking day. The first shimmers of lights were barely flexing the horizon across the Great Lakes. He liked stepping out while it was still dark. It gave him the full breadth of the night skies. All he had to do was look up to get a feel of the immensity of a cosmos bearing down on the insignificance of mankind. Though he measured his personal skills on and above the average man, each time his eyes captured the immensity of the Milky Way and stars beyond, his mind and body became overshadowed by sheer humbleness. "There's got to be a creator," he reasoned into the quiet of early morning. There was a time not that long ago when he was devoted to the scriptures. It was a time when he prayed for a healthier body. "Perhaps," he thought, "my prayers worked." A touch of shame came over him for not paying more tribute to the Almighty, if there was such a being. "How soon we forget." His mind fluctuated between the rational thinking man he had turned into and the faith he had been taught by his parents and priests. More often than not, misgiving thoughts such as "Man or God?" troubled his mind. Achieving superiority among mankind in recent years, he felt that man was striving to become more of a Creator. But gazing at the stars this early made him question his reasoning. Once again, he became overwhelmed with a feeling of insignificance. Although man had tinkered with creation for some time, it would take a long time for him to ever truly create at the immensity of the universe, if ever.

Slight sounds began appearing all around him. It was then he realized the world was waking up to yet another day. "Wonder what today will bring?"

Norton had quietly sidled up to him, catching the tail of his whispered words. "Your guess's as good as mine," he stated. "Ready to move out? By the way, I've got an assignment for you. Ideal mission."

Brooks' interest piqued. "Yeah?" He was looking forward to a change after years in the complacency of the Canadian backwoods.

"Get your squadron together to hold off the enemy from crossing the river."

"Mississippi?

"Yeah, Mississippi."

"Why there?"

"Perfect borderline for the plains," he explained. "Great Lakes up north to the gulf south. Border's gonna be locked tight. Nobody crosses without a purpose. Don't wanna inherit the same problems the former administrations had. This is the land of the Patriots, and don't let anyone forget it."

"But the bridges," Brooks objected. "There're many."

"That's my job," Norton explained. "I'll blow them up. Every one of 'em, but one."

"You serious? Which one?"

"St. Louis crossing."

"Gateway? Let me think about it," Brooks stalled. He did not want to rush into something he might later regret. The offer sounded okay but he needed full support from his squad. At least to give them notice.

A voice emerged from the semidarkness. "No need to." Bad Man had quietly joined and overheard the offer. "It's my territory." He had wedged his muscular body between them and stared Brooks down in his typically brutish manner.

Norton gestured at Brooks. "You heard the man." Brooks did not like orders. He never did. He had been ordered around by everybody while growing up. It was up to him to give orders now and he stated so. If there was a problem it'd have to be solved here, right now. "Get out of my face," he defied Bad Man.

"You'll have to fight for it," the Enforcer challenged. It appeared he wasn't going to let this snot-nosed fledgling muzzle in on his territory.

Norton realized a fight for dominance was imminent but stepped in regardless. He pacified his lieutenant. "No need to fight. Enough space for everybody."

Brooks felt it would be the best time to hold his place. He had been holding back for years from demonstrating his skills on other than hunt wildlife. He stepped forward deliberately, sizing up his opponent. It only agitated the man more. Taking up the challenge, he backed off to give himself some space. With a sly smirk on his face, he shot a quick glance at Norton and challenged, "He wants to fight? Let him."

It enraged Bad Man even more. In one determined motion, Bad Man ripped his well-worn shirt from his body, stepping in ready to throw a first punch. Norton, unwilling to interfere further, let them have their space. In the meantime, word had reached the living quarters about the challenge. Both proponents and opponents of Bad Man rushed up, forming a circle, drawing a perimeter for the pending fight. Side-bets were placed and money exchanged. Aside from stated differences between the two, it would be purely a measure of strength to demonstrate to the world who was the better man, the usual cause of a fight.

Much like in a boxing rink, both men assessed each other by staring their opponent down. Bad Man had one watchful eye on Brooks and the other on the Patriots. He wanted to make sure everyone was present when he delivered a lesson to this outsider. Provoking his opponent, he made overtures of shadow punching by feigning and dodging blows. It was nothing but intimidation tactics.

Brooks, realizing his challenger's intentions, only grinned and smirked at Bad Man's antics. He just stood there in a casual stance, waiting for the first real punch. It came seconds later. Self-assured, overly confident and used to brawls, Bad Man threw first. To Brooks, it was an act of slow motion. It took an eternity for his fist to reach his face. The speed of which he was capable, he side-stepped the punch with casual deliberation. The missed punch left the man off balance, but he quickly regrouped for the next advance. Following a dozen more ineffectively thrown punches delivered with brute force, Bad Man not only lost his breath, he was losing his patience. His followers could see the mounting frustration in his eyes. For the first time in the ex-con's life, he realized he had no chance ever to land a punch. Brooks was just too quick. With a smirk on his face, Brooks just kept mocking his opponent, begging for another, then another, punch.

It was enough for Bad Man. He let out an animal-like scream and threw his entire weight against a smirking Brooks. This time, Brooks did not budge. He held his ground. The result was 280-some pounds of moving mass slamming into his steel-like fist extended from a body solidly planted to the ground. The Enforcer buckled much like a sack of potatoes, hitting the ground hard.

Wheezing from the wind getting knocked out of his lungs, clutching a throbbing chest, he was desperately gasped for air. From his facial expression, it might have been the first time Bad Man felt pain. He made several attempts to raise his beaten body but gave up, succumbing to the pain. There was no further incentive to get up. He had been beaten fair and square. Perhaps not fair, but it wouldn't matter. There were enough witnesses for him to lose the confidence he'd enjoyed for so many years as bully. Bad Man had met his maker. He would never be the same. From here on he would always be second best unless he decided to challenge Brooks again.

It was Brooks' turn to be revered as the best man. He had won the battle without even trying but his true fighting skills taught, trained, and practiced by the DELTA team still remained hidden. What nobody on the outside knew was the CIA's special program created to produce a next generation fighter. It still had to be proven in battle as a new fighting force. For now, it would remain that way until Brooks was confronted by a worthy opponent. He wasn't sure when, but the time would come when he could gauge his true strength.

Norton, preparing to move out, had the Patriots quickly disband. Scott Brooks, unbeaten, picked up his jacket from the ground, waved his men to follow, and prepared for the assigned mission.

The outcome of the fight had surprised the Patriots. The balance of power had shifted. There was a new commander in town. Both Norton and Elliott were still bewildered at the newcomer taking the banner from who was revered as the toughest man among them. As a result, the allegiance of the Patriots might be in question. Something had to be done. With the three commanders presently headed for the headquarters, Norton shot a glance at Brooks. "What are you?"

Brooks had promised himself never to reveal the closely kept secret by the agency. There was no need. It would only cause contention among allies and rivals alike. Mistreated, bullied, and tormented as he'd been through his growing up years, being feared by everyone would be just as bad. People would shy away from him as well, knowing his destructive powers. He took his time before giving an answer. "New breed of fighter." It was all that needed to be said. There would be more questioning later, but, for now, it was a good enough explanation. Norton respected the response.

He instructed Elliott, "Take care of him."

Brodie complied with, "Whatcha need?" He was referring to the armament Brooks might need to accomplish his mission.

"Speedboats," Brooks responded. "A whole fleet."

It was something Brodie could accommodate. He explained, "There's a flotilla waiting by the lake." Brooks had been unaware of the fleet of patrol craft held in possession by the terrorists who had been encroaching on the shores of the Great Lakes. The only reason they had not been able to acquire Milwaukee was the concentration of Elliott's infantry forces in and around the city.

"Why Milwaukee?" Brooks was curious why the Patriots hadn't claimed their stake in Chicago.

"Strategic reasons," Brodie willingly responded, then, with a witty hint, he said, "Beer."

Brooks looked confused. "Beer?"

"Look around." Brodie gestured at the body of lakes near and far. "Got enough water," he explained. "It's beer the fighter craves." Though Scott was not a drinker, he understood. Even he enjoyed an occasional cool mug of fine brew.

"Just kiddin'," Brodie finally giving in, said. "We'll convert into refineries."

"Refinery?"

"Processing fuel for gasoline."

"Understood."

Elliott turned factual. "How much of an army do you need?" He needed to know how many of his soldiers he could spare.

"I'll make it easy for you. None for now," Brooks offered. "But once I get the boats I'll need support."

"You've got it." While Brodie was surprised at not having to give up any of his forces, he accepted it at face value. *Time will tell,* he mulled, *how much weight this fellow's worth.* "When you plan on movin' out?"

"First thing when morning comes around." There was no sense in rushing into the next phase of battle. Besides, his team was already too mellow from the ample supplies of beer served after the fight with the Enforcer. They would march off hangovers come morning. "One thing," Brooks wanted to know. "Where can I find Bad Man?"

Brodie thumbed to his right. Brooks followed the gesture. As soon as his eyes caught a brightly lit sign he understood. "Freedom Brewery." It was the direction he was headed. When he walked through the gates, the hall fell dead silent. All eyes were fixed on him, including that of a still battered Bad Man.

Brooks showed no emotions when he walked up to the once feared, but still revered Enforcer. Unsure what to expect, Bad Man haltingly removed his body from the bench to face the victor.

Scott, in his customary relaxed and self-assured manner, took a couple more paces, closing the distance between the two. Facing off his earlier opponent, he reached for the man's closed fist and slowly raised it overhead, then called into a tense hall, "He's still your Man."

Immediately, cheers and shouts broke out loudly, roaring through the Patriot's packed beer hall. "No hard feelings?" Brooks said to Bad Man.

"No hard feelings." It became clear. Bad Man had his honor restored as Enforcer once more, if only for the Patriot forces.

Brooks turned on his heels and left the hall thinking, *Good man for a good cause.* He did not need to have Bad Man's respected self-esteem challenged. Though an ex-con, the Patriots gave him all the respect he needed and deserved. Balance had been restored between two interdependent forces, one strategic, the other tactical.

With Brooks watching his back, the time had come for Norton to assign the forces under his command. "Elliott," Rusty Norton ordered. "Your command is with Fort Knox. Permanent HQ. Leave immediately." With the ex-con having taken a beating by Brooks, he had been watching an almost broken man over the last few days. He had something in mind that would lift his spirits. "Bad Man," he could not suppress a compassionate grin. "You're in charge of beer. Take your men back to Milwaukee and manage the brewery."

The announcement caused unified cheering among his team. "He'll do well," Norton mused.

Next, he turned at Brooks and ordered, "Mississippi border. Hold under any circumstances." He then provided him with a running account of the present state of resources at hand.

"Big Red and Red Brigade are coming back as soon as HAARP is back in our hands. Your ranks will be filled with their resources."

"Big Red?"

"New division I'm creating."

"Okay by me."

He did not approve of renegade vigilantes but made an exception for Tracy and stated, "Stinger's doing her own thing. She's subject to the same constitutional ruling. No exception. Foster's got control over Pacific assets. So far," he explained, "there are no threats from Asia. Government," he stated. "Can't depend on it. Doing their own thing. Don't want anything to do with Wilmot and his minions. National laboratories," he continued. "Spencer's in charge. Secretive clan, don't know what's brewing there. ISS," he reported. "No word from the crew. Vandenberg and Baikonur are working on a rescue solution. NORAD," he stated. "Hear nothing from there. Supported by Bauer, don't mess with him. He's off limits. Gave him my personal guarantee. Besides," he said, "he's holding down the Central Sector. That's all." He'd said his piece. Now it was up to his commanders to enforce the constitution. Norton, at this time, was still clueless on how to monitor progress. *Time will tell,* he calculated.

TRACY BAUER

Returning from her last stop along the shores, Tracy tossed the coat and weapon in back and dropped her body behind the wheel. She could see the question on Buck's face and said, "Don't ask. Won't get an answer." It was enough to shut him up. With a grin on her face she tossed the copy of the Koran at him and said, "Here. Your new bible." All she got in return from the two was a quizzical stare. Buck apparently had never heard of the Islamic Bible. After several attempts to spell out Qur'an, Emma chastised him once again, "You're such an idiot."

"Let's not fight," Tracy interfered. "We're off to the falls."

"Niagara Falls," both chimed in unison. "Here we come."

Buck had handed Emma the Koran, who, in turn, read some of the verses out loud. Shaking his head, he kept interrupting. "Don't make any sense."

Tracy had been deeply immersed in her personal thoughts for some time when Emma interrupted her from the backseat. She proclaimed, "I wanna be like you. Can you teach me?" Apparently, reading some of the verses must have affected her sense of complacency. Tracy glanced at the rearview mirror. There was serious concern in the girl's eyes. It was enough for Tracy to slam on the brakes. The sudden reaction jolted both into reality.

"Switch positions," she shot at Buck, who again had serious difficulty understanding. "Emma," she ordered. "Up front." That made it clear. Both switched seats in barely enough time before the Humvee careened off once more.

"Let me tell you a story," Tracy began. "There once was an innocent girl much like you…" She then proceeded to tell her about her own life changes not that long ago. She talked for hours, unloading the immense struggle she had endured during the initial attack on the nation. Being taken hostage several times, the misery she had endured fighting off personal confrontations, her frustration at not being able to retaliate, relationships torn apart, loss of friends and family, hardship on the nation, and, most dramatic of all, an entire city, San Francisco, annihilated.

"All happened to you?" It sounded too incredible.

"Me and my dad."

"No wonder you're so merciless." Emma kept shaking her head.

"Now you understand?"

"I do."

"Still wanna be like me?"

"Not sure if I could."

"Believe me," Tracy discouraged her somewhat naive passenger, "there's no going back."

As usual, Buck butted in, "You got me. I'll protect you."

The face she pulled said enough. "Sure, you will." She remained silent for the rest of the trip.

It took close to eight hours to reach their destination. Tracy decided to stay the next day since she had never been here. Niagara Falls was breathtaking. Pictures and documentaries may be nice to watch but gave the real extent of the falls little justification. Tracy had no idea of the volume of water flow dropping over the Horseshoe edge 175 feet deep. Fed from Lake Erie, the water flowed on into Lake Ontario to empty out into the Atlantic via the Saint Lawrence River.

It was the day Tracy parted from Emma and Buck. She had achieved her objective, giving a young couple a chance to see the falls where it may have otherwise only been a dream. Feeling slightly regretful, in spite of their frequent bickering she'd grown fond of the young couple. Much like family life from a distant epoch she'd felt a sense of belonging. "Be good now," where her parting words. Emma was sobbing. Tracy even detected moisture in Buck's eyes. Watching through the rearview mirror, she could see both standing there forlorn until the tail lights of the Humvee disappeared in the distance. Saddened, Tracy headed east, destination New York City. Under normal conditions it would be a leisurely drive within one day. These days, however, with the country under siege, her guess was as good as anyone's as to what might lie ahead.

The ether had been silent since she had left Chicago a couple days ago. It was time to check in with home base. "Stinger," she broke the silence. "Status check."

Alex must have been anxious to hear from her. He responded immediately. "Specter…Go."

"Destination New York…What's ahead?"

It took a few minutes for Specter to respond, "All clear…State your intentions."

"Investigating the city…May stay awhile."

"Any word on Brian?"

"Nothing here. Any word from ISS. Liz?"

"Still working on a rescue mission."

"Any timeframe?"

"Making progress. Few more weeks."

"Good luck. I'll miss you."

"Keep me posted…Daily," he insisted.

"Will do." With advanced technology in the hands of the enemy, locating transmission sources through triangulation was swift. Unlike the old days where time was the determinant factor, today, with GPS and satellite monitoring, source identity was instant. Tracy would have liked so much to keep her dad informed about her ploys. Perhaps later, after things had settled down, she'd be able to pay him a visit. For now, her focus was on the destination ahead. Anxious to see what'd developed since the EMP attack years back decimating the mega city, her anticipation was heightened to the utmost.

Closing in on the New Jersey shores, she could barely make out the city skyline in the fading daylight. Nighttime was closing in fast with miles still ahead. She decided to spend the night in the relative safety of the Jersey side on the Hudson River. Prior to the 9/11 attack, where once the twin towers stood, now, the spire from the newly-erected One World Trade Center was clearly visible. Her sense of grandeur would have been heightened by the sheer magnitude of the structure if it had not been for the recent destruction. All that was left was a skeleton. It'd be the first spot to visit come daylight. "Specter," she called in. "Checking in for the night. Also, need blueprints on the new tower."

"Roger."

He would have the information available for her in the morning. Tracy checked into a local inn close to Fort Monmouth, once a desirable vacation resort. With the state the nation was in, not many vacationers could be found. Many inns and motels had been converted into residential dwellings, as was this one. As always, the ones closest to the body of water came with a high price tag. With Tracy checking in with a few gold and silver coins for barter, there was always a room available.

Once settled in she inquired from the host, "What's it like in the city?" He was only too willing to give out information to the peculiar and atypical appearing, but stunning, visitor. His private thoughts and that of his family were clearly painted across their faces. Provided by most inns in the present economy, she was invited to a communal dinner. For that, everybody had to pool their resources to manage the meager, but healthy, meal dished out twice daily. In order to survive an undermined economy, family living and pooling had become a necessity.

Dinner was pleasant in the company of family and occupants. Conversation was lively over tea and homemade cookies for desert, with current news being exchanged by all parties: hers from the west, theirs the Eastern Seaboard, with much speculations in-between.

"Muslims are taking over businesses," she was told. "Want us to wear Arabian garb." It was further explained, "If you wanna live in the city." Hearing that bit of news did not go over well with Tracy. Concealed anger surfaced from the pit of her stomach once again. It fueled her suppressed rage even more. It was an added incentive to settle here, for the immediate future anyway. Manhattan, she anticipated, would be her most likely battle ground. Harbored by troubled thoughts such as these, after a fitful rest she could hardly wait for dawn to emerge.

NEW YORK CITY

It was early yet. During the night Tracy had thought up the best way into the city. Her concern was for maintaining her cover as much as possible, to stay undetected by the adversary, who, she suspected, was searching for her. Driving the customized Humvee would be too blatant. It'd attract everybody's attentions. "Just take the ferry," the inn's host suggested. "Only a twenty-minute ride. You can put up your vehicle in the garage. Plenty of space there." The night chill was still in the air, especially so close to the water. The first ferry had not arrived yet. She was not alone huddled by Paulus Hook pier, as the sign proclaimed. There were other passengers anxious to get across the Hudson River. The ferry would drop her off just a couple of blocks from the plaza. From the Jersey side, she had a clear view across the Hudson. Her eyes immediately sought out the tower. It was easy to spot. What she saw made her blood boil. Suppressed emotions, disgust, loathing, revulsion, the whole spectrum of hatred surfaced from the depths of her very being. What was left of the recently erected new Tower One was nothing but an empty skeleton. The basic structure still stood. What was missing was the majestic design of the ill-fated, glass-embraced, iconic mark, the symbol of freedom. "Didn't even have a chance to visit," regretting the missed chance, she muttered into the brisk river breeze. With determined strides, she stepped on the ferry. It would be a new segment in her arduous journey.

While she did not anticipate any hostile confrontations today, her senses were on guard nevertheless. Today would be a day for pleasure. She planned to enjoy the bustling atmosphere of a city alive once more. And that she did.

Time had passed quickly over thoughts about the past, the present, and the future. Striding along Lower Manhattan, two hours had gone by when hunger pangs made their appearance. She headed for the cafeteria close by. After getting seated, she was served breakfast. Watching visitors come and go, Tracy studied their faces. Regardless of the current political and economic situation in her country, she concluded, "The rest of the world must be thriving." One thing she did notice: almost everybody was speaking a foreign language. It made sense if one considered the world at its present.

Exposed to many foreign languages when she worked for the NSA, she could detect a number of tongues. There was Russian, Chinese, Indian, German, French, and more. Predominantly spoken, however, and not surprisingly, was Arabic, with matching facial features and attire.

She then noticed something else, American women wearing the veil. This revelation came as a total surprise. Gazing around the spacious café, her eyes caught that of such a veiled woman seated alone nearby. She could not contain her curiosity any longer. She had to find out. Determined, not wearing the concealed weapon she left in back of the Humvee today, she picked up her leather coat, slid from the bench, and casually approached the woman. Politely, carrying a friendly smile, Tracy said, "'Scuse me. You speak English?"

The woman, pleasant in appearance from the little her veiled face revealed, replied with equal friendliness, "I should. I'm a New Yorker."

"May I join you?"

With a fleeting gesture, she welcomed an invitation, "Please do." It was a pleasant voice. After seating herself across, Tracy ambiguously sized up the woman. *No threat here,* she presumed.

"So," the woman remarked curiously. "You visiting?"

"I am. Been many years since my last visit. Freedom Towers back then."

Her comment was accompanied by a saddened sigh. "Ah yes. Good old days. What's your name?"

"Tracy…Tracy Bauer."

Her hand stretched across the table when she said, "Hannah Thompson. What brings you here?"

"Business."

"Business?" Her question was underlined by a quizzical stare. "Rather exposed, aren't you?"

"The clothing?"

"I should say so. Taking chances for harassment," she indicated.

"Actually," Tracy replied, "it's the reason I wanted to talk with you." Since setting foot on Manhattan this morning, she became exceedingly aware of her somewhat daring attire in the present environment. "Why the kurta, the veil?"

"Actually," she was corrected, "it's a Jilbob and Hijab."

"Why you wearing it?"

"Have to," she explained. "Otherwise no job."

"Really? What do you do?"

"Language interpreter—U.N. Secretary General."

"You Islam?"

"Of course not," Hannah insisted. "Been there with the previous administration, what's left of it now."

"Building shut down?" Tracy made reference of the recent assault on the U.N. complex.

"Main building, Yes," was the reply. "Presently occupying auxiliary buildings. Don't know future plans. Probably no United Nations, with Jihad taking over the world."

"Who's head of U.N. now?"

"Kazim Rashid, former tribal elder," she explained. "Pakistani Mountain Region."

"Ah yes," Tracy recalled. "I remember now." The connection began to make sense.

"Know him?"

"Not personally."

"You connected?"

"Used to work with NSA."

"Really!"

"Jobless now," Tracy added. "You know."

"I understand."

"Wanna go someplace?" Hannah offered. "Want company? Like to do some sightseeing."

Tracy did not have to think twice and said, "Lead on." It was a rare occasion for her to accept a stranger's company. But she felt comfortable with Hannah. She might be a perfect connection in the city and its changing society. Besides, the woman was willing to be her tour guide. From what Tracy gathered, the feeling might be mutual in due time.

For now, today, all she wanted was to savor the mega city to the max with its hustle and bustle of millions of people. Preparing to leave, Hannah called her office, taking the rest of the day off. "I'm all yours," she beamed.

They trekked the whole day in and around lower Manhattan, taking in the contrast between modern office complexes, fashionable showcases, restaurants currently in vogue, and the constant presence of underlying poverty. Most impressive that the city had to offer was the Bowery with its diversified ethnicity, a cultural melting pot, exactly as she remembered it from college. With modern day transportation limited, this section of town had even reverted back to the horse and buggy days and, with them, the muck and smell. "Some things never change." Tracy gestured at the many homeless homesteading on and along sidewalks.

"Understandable," Hannah agreed. "With all the poverty in the country."

Hannah seemed to enjoy Tracy's company as much as Tracy did hers. If it had not been for her passionate conviction, driving the enemy from American soil, life in New York could have been a pleasant experience. At times, Tracy couldn't help but express her dislike of the imposing Islamic culture on her once free nation. "Someday soon," she'd mutter. "I'll take my city and my country back."

"What?"

"Oh, nothing. Just thinking out loud."

At the day's end, Tracy bade her newly-acquired friend goodbye and hurried back to the docks where the last ferry crossing for the day would be waiting.

Over the next few days they spent many more hours together, exploring the city in each other's company above and below. It appeared the subway system was working once again, if only partially. Where Tracy asked many questions about Muslims and Islam, indiscreetly at times, her companion was only too willing to provide the answers. Over the following days and weeks, she was able to map out the city above and below ground with unprecedented precision.

WAR DOGS

Settled by the Mississippi River, it was their first assembly of its kind. His scouts had gathered around expecting to receive their orders. "First task on the agenda," Brooks reminded his lieutenants, "is to stop the damned invasion." He and his scouts had proceeded south to the designated target, St. Louis, once Gateway to the West. It would be a gateway once more. "But this time," he underscored the promise, "we are the gatekeepers. Nobody gets in and nobody gets out without our permission."

"What about our own people?"

"Nobody. There's no need for Patriots to seek refuge elsewhere. Their place is here, the plains."

"What about people that wanna join?"

"We'll deal with it later. For now," he emphasized once more, "nobody gets in. Nobody gets out. Understood? Nobody. It's the only way to enforce our ruling. There are spies everywhere. It is those we must filter out and eliminate."

"What's our immediate task?"

"Okay." Collecting his thoughts, he then stated, "We need an identity. From here on, we'll be known as…" He halted the sentence to let the next words sink in. He needed everybody onboard. "War Dogs."

"What?" There were a number of outcalls. It was new. It had to be digested.

"It's ours. It's up to you to make the name, to gain the fame."

Now fame was something everybody understood, something everybody desired. "War Dogs it is." His closest followers accepted it without further objections. The next question was, "What're the assignments?"

"You'll all get commands," Brooks promised. "Our ranks will be filled from the 1st Armored as soon as they return from Alaska. Let's get hopping," he urged. "We have much work to do."

First on Brooks' agenda was dispatching his scouts up and down the river. As long as the borders were still open, he would send his men east and south as well. He needed resources, lots of them. Without power and access to mineral mining he had to do with what has already been manufactured and produced. He needed parts. There were plenty. Everywhere he looked, there were parts waiting to be taken. Aside from an abundance of wrecked automobiles stacked up, crashed aircraft heaped in piles, idle ships, spare parts in uncountable numbers were stowed away on shelves, storage bins, and lockers. It was a goldmine for whoever could get his hands on it.

On his travels, Brooks had realized the wealth of materials abandoned, discarded, and dumped wherever vehicles and craft had quit with the EMP strike. There was some salvage taking place from people claiming their possessions, mostly automobiles. But without fuel, these possessions were rendered useless. People were hoping that one-day fuel would flow again. It was no exception for Brooks. He needed fuel as well. He had one edge up. He had the forces for taking over mines and oil rigs to get them going again for feeding his fleet. Problem was refineries. There were none left in the nation. For that, he sent out his scouts.

"Can't be that difficult," he surmised when discussing the dilemma with Norton and Elliott earlier. They had ample experience with alcohol from brewing beer. Extracting refined fuel from crude oil should not be much different. "How about Anheuser?" he'd suggested. "St. Louis?" He was referring to the famous Anheuser Busch brewery down south. "Recruit the scientists. Use the facility. Modify if you need to. We'll have plenty materials for that."

"Settled then," Norton and Elliott agreed.

For Brooks, building an army of tactical squads and seaworthy crews, he needed everything he could get his hands on. Not only that, he also needed to recruit helpers, technicians, and engineers for tearing pieces apart, getting them fitted, and putting them back together in working order. He needed a fleet of land vehicles. He needed a fleet of seaworthy vehicles, and perhaps later on, to get an air fleet going as well, but that had to wait. There was too much work on the ground to even think that far ahead.

Dispatching his men into the field to acquire transportation was the immediate task. Hauling in wrecks and abandoned scrap was next, followed by creating workshops for every conceivable restoration process. Machine, body, and paint shops were sprouting up like a field of mushrooms. Spaces abandoned in the city and its outskirts were taken up by groups of entrepreneurs. The city of St. Louis began to flourish once again. It did not happen overnight. It had taken close to a year for Brooks and his fleet of vehicles. Aside from a flock of automobiles, mostly customized and designed for personal tastes, he also had a sizable fleet of attack boats under his command. Mostly souped-up speedboats, they were dispatched as fast as they could be rebuilt, assigned, and put into commission.

Manpower seemed to be of no issue. Folks that used to be idle and unproductive, with food for work as compensation, now, helped the economy in the plains begin to thrive once more. Tailors, shoe stores, gun shops, and more went up. Footwear, belts, ammunition, knives, canisters, and other personal items had to be manufactured. Shop owners had their hands full satisfying daily orders for producing clothes, shoes, boots, and uniforms. And so, did other craftsmen.

Brooks had added specialists wherever needed. Most desirable were clothes and gun designers. He had a uniform fabricated that was especially designed for the War Dogs. He took possession of the first unit delivered. It was a great piece of work. The cut, the style, the artwork would be worthy of his nation.

Dressed in the tailor cut uniform, looking sharp and tall, facing a full-length mirror, "It'll definitely set new trends," was his comment to his scouts. "It'll leave a benchmark on the nation."

"And the world," someone chimed in.

Scott Brooks was set to wage war. And wage he did.

Once the War Dogs were mobilized, it did not take long for word to spread across and up and down the Mississippi that a new order was in force.

MANHATTAN MASSACRE

New York City, the mega city it was, had grown to almost twice its size in only a decade. Many of the original inhabitants had taken to the woods years ago after the initial collapse. The new city, as it were, was made up mostly of new immigrants and foreign subjects. "Where are all the people from?" was a popular topic among public media, news broadcasts, and talk radio hosts. Money was spent freely among the arriving entrepreneurs. Old buildings were torn down, replaced with new structures. It seemed that the Globalists had arrived. With world economy thriving, the U.N. managing and controlling foreign influx, oil being traded more prolifically than ever, the city was rapidly growing into an international commerce and trade hub with virtually every technology and currency in the hands of foreigners.

"Hannah." The U.N. department secretary seated at the front desk of the temporary auxiliary building shouted across the spacious office complex. "Turn on your monitor…Al Jazeera's got a newsflash." It was the prominent news station in the world. The once fledgling agency out of Qatar, reporting mostly Middle-Eastern terrorist activities, had grown into a major broadcasting complex.

She was busy preparing a weekly report for the department heads. Sensitive as it was, she closed the lid on the laptop computer with a snap, paying full attention to the newsflash.

"*…just received word that a local mosque has been attacked early this morning…Detailed information is still sketchy, but it was confirmed that several functionaries have been killed. Mostly male…*" The report went on broadcasting the limited information it had available on the massacre with a promise to deliver more as soon as additional details became available.

Hannah, interested but not surprised at the news, since it recently happened at other places such as Chicago, gave it some concern. After all, it involved her directorate, the U.N., directly. *Resistance group,* she gathered, *tired of being oppressed. Who can blame 'em?*

She then took a few minutes to rationalize the new phenomenon. Although highly unusual for a people used only to democratic ruling, it was bound to happen. By birthright, American people were not prone to mass violence and forced takeovers. Demonstrations yes, but overthrowing governments, no. But times have changed with foreign powers in charge. History had demonstrated over and over that an oppressed people would only put up with things for so long before a rebellious group would surface. Comprised of young adults, mostly college age, any resistance began with someone's thought germinating for some time to eventually grow into a movement. A minority at first, testing its waters, as word spread, quickly avalanched into a full-sized, unstoppable force. By that time, it had either been squelched by the government or dictatorship or, if fortunate for the citizens, toppled whatever ruling power had hold over the nation. From there, a new cycle would begin all over again.

Locally, the present cycle was in the state of revolt with the local population severely suppressed by foreign ruling guaranteed to grow on a national scale. Knowing the American spirited heritage, as demonstrated during the civil war, it would not stop here. Making sure there was not anybody else within earshot, Hannah silently reflected, "There's hope." She was not the only one harboring similar private thoughts. As far as she knew, there were many discontented people. But private thoughts like these had to be contained for personal safety reasons. To her knowledge, others had disappeared without a trace. It was held open only to conjecture and speculation what might have happened to those individuals. Rumors of beheadings had surfaced more and more in recent months. If things were not already scary enough, this one topped every conceivable punishment on mankind. It must be stopped.

Must tell Tracy, she urged herself, *next time I see her. By the way,* she wondered, *where is the woman? Come to think of it, she hasn't been around the past few days.* She reminded herself to get a contact address from her so she could share more time with who she considered her Mystery Person. She had grown fond of this woman who so suddenly had appeared in her life out of nowhere. Smiling at the heartwarming thoughts of her newly found friend, she was hoping to hear from her soon. "Wish she'd call," she muttered.

She was slightly startled when a coworker appeared by the desk, dropping off a document file, asking, "Who?" She had obviously overheard the personal comment.

"Oh, nothing," Hannah responded, squelching any further chat. She was not in the least interested in sharing her personal life with any office worker, especially not with other veil-clad women predominantly running the place. Though Hannah was dressed in the mandatory Islamic garb, her heart felt otherwise. She had made a promise to herself years ago that the once free nation would always be her home at heart.

Earlier that morning, on the way to their shops, dozens of worshippers had hastened to the city's most popular mosque in town, a prayer place near Ground Zero. Once a controversial issue with New Yorkers, especially right after the 9/11 attack on the World Trade Center, over time the place eventually was accepted by the citizens. It had proven the fact that time healed all wounds. New generations were born and with them came new ideas, new dreams, and new challenges. The old was quickly forgotten. The only memories remaining were with friends and loved ones who were directly affected, and the older folks, the ones trying to preserve local customs and cultures from rapidly fading memories.

As usual, it was a sizable congregation early this morning, the first homage of the day paid to Allah. This morning's prayer was led by the designated Mullah who, with copy of the Qur'an in hand, was bowing in chorus, guiding the congregation through the session. In his native tongue, he chanted one of his favorite verses from the Holy Scripture:

Qur'an (3:56) – *"As to those who reject faith, I will punish them with terrible agony in this world and in the Hereafter, nor will they have anyone to help."*

Before he could continue on to the next verse, a voice suddenly sounded off amid the worshippers. "I'd like to challenge that." Where normally only the rustle of silken cloth or an occasional nervous cough was heard, the silence had been broken by a voice unheard of, that of a woman. The female voice still echoed through the hall when a woman dressed in dark jilbob and hijab deliberately strode towards the Mullah. The prayer hall had turned eerily silent.

He was taken aback as much as everyone else in the halls. With heads turned in her direction the suspense became overwhelming. The turban clad male congregation was fervently staring at the unexpected interruption. One had to assume that the women worshippers beneath their veiled headdresses were stunned as well.

With faces frozen in time, each pair of eyes followed the woman's every move. What came next, after it was all over, each member was able to account for every detail taking place. First, her left hand reached inside one sleeve and reappeared with her own copy of the Qur'an. Next, her fingers nimbly leafed through a number of pages, then halted at a specific verse. Her voice again echoed through the now deadly silent hall as she read:

"Qur'an (8:12) – *"I will cast terror into the hearts of those who disbelieve. Therefore, strike off their heads and strike off every fingertip of them."*

All the faces lingered expectantly at the stranger. There was a brief pause before she spoke again. "My God, the Lord and Creator of this land," she proclaimed, "is the same God as your Allah." Probably for the first time since the Islamic invasion by the Moors in eighth century Europe had these words been uttered. They were calculating words spoken with intentional deliberation directed at the Muslim congregation.

After a halting pause to let the immensity sink in, her voice broke the silence once more. "And the Old Testament says: An eye for an eye...a tooth for a tooth." If there was any sound before, the hall fell in complete silent then, she said, "Here is my testament—a life for a life."

It was at this point that clusters from the male congregation jumped to their bare feet, rushing to the front of the hall. Extremely alarmed following the words of the challenge assaulting their faith, they rushed to avenge themselves. But their efforts in the midst of the forthcoming turmoil were in vain. In one swift motion, the woman's robe dropped to the floor, fully revealing her warrior-like outfit. Clad in her custom-cut leather jacket, boots and ammo belts slung across her chest, the first burst of deadly-aimed projectiles sought out their targets. Any male daring getting on his feet was mercilessly cut down.

Accompanied by heroic shouts was a vengeful act unlike witnessed in recent times. "This is my land...I'm taking it back." To Stinger, they were words meant not only for her but for her country as well. She was fighting in the name of justice. It was to free a once proud nation, her nation. Her warlike shouts echoed through the halls, reverberating off the walls. Tracy swept Serpent Slayer at hip level at any man that moved. It was a bloodbath.

The next second the terrified worshippers took stock; the woman warrior had slipped away as ghostlike as she had appeared. There was much wailing among the horrified brethren, mostly from the women. The male population had been reduced by the numbers. Numbers increasing with each attack.

From here on out Tracy realized that her future attacks would not be as easy. Word spread rapidly especially when innocent lives were at stake. With American news media owned, operated, and managed by the Islamic order, the killing would most likely be portrayed as a massacre of innocent worshippers, likely labeled a hate crime. In the future, Mosque worshippers would be guarded by armed Jihad warriors. She would have to change her assault tactics. Her strikes would have to be well planned and swift.

Hurrying back across the Hudson, she contemplated, *Perhaps I'll need some help.* The thought of Hannah crossed her mind. To be more flexible and effective in future missions, she might have to strike during nighttime. For that, she needed a hiding place in the city.

THE SERPENT

Hammad was surrounded by his field commanders. After the distressing news just received from New York, he had called an emergency meeting. It was confirmed; Stinger had struck again. Though illustrated as a ferocious killer, Hammad was not greatly concerned. After all, it was only one person to deal with. Probably the usual reaction when death and trauma was involved. It generally got blown out of proportion. Most likely that was the case here but, in any case, he could not afford to let rumors get out of hand. "Need people for New York," he ordered. "Volunteers?"

From the cluster of commanders, one bolted to his feet first and said, "I'll go." It was the familiar face everyone recognized, that of Yusuf.

Hammad shook his head at him. "Need you here."

"But," he openly protested, "you promised. Remember?"

"I did," was the stern comeback. "I still need you here."

"Who's better than me at protecting the cells? It's my hometown...I know the place." He was determined to be the one sent off.

"True." Hammad realized he was trapped. If he did not live up to a promise in front of his lieutenants, made years earlier, he might lose credibility. He could not afford that. *Perhaps,* he thought, *it's not such a bad idea.* "Take a squad of the best with you."

"I'll make you proud."

"Just promise to take care of her," he ordered. "Whoever this Stinger is."

"I'll bring back her head," Yusuf vowed, "mounted on a stake. It will be my trophy gift to you." It was settled. Yusuf was beaming with anticipation. He could see himself already striding the streets of his beloved city. It did not take him long to gather up his belongings. Early the next morning, he was off on the shortest route possible east, leading a small detachment of Jihad fighters. Whether someone was there to greet him or not, it would be a homecoming for him.

"Tracy!" Hannah called out when she spotted the familiar shape by the entrance, leaning against the door post with a smile on the face. Dressed in her usual body-tailored apparel, Tracy appeared as casual and self-confident as ever. Closing the distance, Hannah planted a kiss on Tracy's cheek, asking, "Where have you been? I've missed you." Leading the way up to her apartment, she offered, "Come in, dear."

"Oh..." Tracy avoided being committed. "Just keeping busy."

"Sightseeing?"

"Something like that."

Hannah challenged her friend while extending a glass of freshly-poured cabernet at her guest, warning, "Don't you dare going shopping without me. Come," she then invited Tracy to the guest chair, "sit with me. Tell me all about it," she bubbled on. "What's new with you?"

Averting any embarrassing topic, she could not or would not explain, Tracy lied, "Nothing new with me. What's new in the city?" Unsure about how to handle personal matters, she'd learned to answer a question with another question. It was a tactic she had acquired ever since turning vigilante. It was the safest means to avoid personal commitments.

Hannah was only too eager to comply. "Haven't you heard?"

"Heard what?"

"Massacre," she blurted out. "Mosque by Ground Zero. Been all over the news...Even today," she affirmed. "Panelists are still talking up a storm. Speculation only. Nobody seems to know much about it. Jihad dispatched a strike force to the city. Ever hear of the Prophet?" She took a break to catch her breath, then asked, "Where have you been anyway?"

"Mountains. Catskills," Tracy lied again. "Needed some time alone."

"Have I offended you in any way?" Hannah posed the question. Her exuberant display seconds earlier changed to personal concern. She seemed sincere when she added, "Please tell me." Then, with a hint of disobedience, she chastised her friend, "Don't you dare disappear on me." It was meant as a friendly gesture.

Genuinely sincere, Tracy explained, "You did nothing wrong. I've got some personal issues to work out."

"Talk to me."

"In due time," Tracy stalled. "Now, tell me about the latest news."

Hannah did. They sat up into the early morning hours. She did most of the talking while Tracy patiently listened. Their talks touched on topics of art, politics local and foreign, cultural and current events. Tracy asked many questions. They were about the new law of the land encroaching on the Atlantic seaboard, that of Islam, the Sharia Law.[49] While Hannah had ample amounts of information, Tracy made uncommitted remarks and comments. She still had reservations about her friend's political views and personal standing with regards to the Patriots, the New Republic, and the Muslim influx on the continent, along with its cultural changes. This evening's talks were informative, nevertheless. She got to know her friend better a little bit at a time.

In spite of having developed a renegade position carried out alone for most part, Tracy silently admitted, *it's good to have a friend.* She even accepted Hannah's offer to stay the rest of the night. Since there was no ferry service during nighttime, she readily accepted.

"Why? Why?" a weeping Ground Zero Mullah wailed at the surviving congregation attending the funeral wake.

"I'll tell you why," a stranger stepped up and proclaimed. He had pushed his way through the attendees to the front. The sound of the voice seemed to appear very familiar to the Mullah. He turned in the direction of the speaker. It took him a few seconds to recognize the face. Overcome with joy between cries and laughs, he exclaimed, "Yusuf!" then rushed up to his former student. Both embraced with compassionate zeal.

"Come...please come," the Mullah ushered the unexpected visitor to his private quarters, still intact next door. Waving at his squadron of warriors nearby, Yusuf gestured, "These are my comrades."

---

[49] Sharia deals with many topics addressed by secular law, including crime, politics and economics, as well as personal matters such as sexuality, hygiene, diet, prayer, and fasting. Where it enjoys official status, Sharia is applied by Islamic judges, or qadis. In contrast, the Imam has varying responsibilities depending on the interpretation of Sharia. While the term is commonly used to refer to the leader of communal prayers, the Imam may also be a scholar, religious leader, or political leader.

"Please…please come," he invited them in as well. Whereas the outside of the mosque projected a modest storefront appearance alongside the megastructures of downtown, once inside, the place was spacious. The Mullah's primary residence was configured for housing numerous guests. When Yusuf commented on it, saddened, he wailed, "All empty now. You're welcome to stay," he offered, "all of you."

After seating the guests, they were offered tea and French pastries by his servants. The Mullah joined the party, then explained in distain, "Don't have to tell you about the dead. You probably recognized many." Yusuf nodded his head in agreement. "Best fighters in the nation," he emphasized once more, "entire cell dead, massacred."

"How did it happen?"

"Woman," he sobbed. "Appeared out of nowhere. Recited verses from the Qur'an then opened fire on us." His servants rushed up, comforting him.

Yusuf gave him time to compose himself, then pressed on. He wanted as many details he could get out of his once mentor, urging, "I need to know all you can remember about this woman. Please continue."

Somewhat composed, he proceeded to illustrate the events in their gruesome details. First, there was the woman. He described her attitude, her demeanor, and her appearance in detail. Next were her actions. Again, he described the woman's swift and merciless deed by striking down each and every male member in the New York City-based Jihad cell. "Entire cell," he was sobbing once more. "Wiped out. They had no chance. My brothers," he wailed. "All gone. May Allah bless them."

Quietly embracing his mentor, Yusuf consoled the Mullah, "Fear not. Justice is near." He then gestured for his squad to go outside to identify their fellow warriors. He needed to know precisely who, and how many, had fallen to report back to Hammad. He could already envision the rage the massacre would cause in the leader and his dedicated commanders. With an entire squadron getting wiped out, fellow warriors would call for immediate justice and revenge. It would mean retaliation. Every conceivable means would be used to subjugate the perpetrators. In this case, however, as implausible as it might have sounded with one lone woman causing all the damages, Yusuf's force might be overkill, but he did not dare deny any of his warriors the pleasure of vengeance.

If all he had heard was factual and true, it would take some planning. Considering various alternatives for catching the elusive prey, he contemplated. *I must devise a special trap*. This was no ordinary person. An adversary so daring as to strike at several places entailing multiple rivals at once would take no ordinary means. Next was his solemn promise to the Mullah. "I will take extraordinary measures to make her suffer."

BATTLE FOR HAARP

At the extreme opposite stretch of the nation, Alaska, facing the imminent reality of a first battle, Big Red ordered the all-female Red Brigade into formation. "Move…move up." Where most commanders were educated and trained through war colleges before leading men to battle, in her case, since there had only been time allocated for basic training before being ordered into the field, she had to develop her plan right now and on-the-fly. There was only one attack mode that stood out in her memory, that of the Amazon warriors. Whether legend or myth, it would have to do. "That's it," she'd decided, then called her squadron lieutenants together for one last briefing. "You…you…" she commanded her most capable to cover left and right flanks. "I'll take the front," she decided. Staged and in position, she yelled her forces into action, "Attack!"

Close to five hundred strong, the battle cry shouted in unison, "Down with Jihad," was heard across this isolated stretch of the Alaskan wilderness. Big Red realized that a battalion of soldiers might be somewhat excessive for one enemy stronghold, but being newly trained soldiers without prior battle experience, it would be appropriate. The all out, all woman army presently in attack mode readily jumped into battle.

Muhab Sadek, commander HAARP defense forces, was unprepared for what came next. Undermanned and shorthanded on Jihad warriors, facing an entire battalion of what he could only describe as Amazons, he felt completely overwhelmed. With only one platoon of twenty-four Jihad comrades by his side, his chances for coming out alive were questionable. Taking fire from all fronts, he quickly retreated into the safety of the command building. Confronted by a continuous hail of M-16 slugs, he and his men kept retreating ever further into the halls of the semi-darkened structure.

Cheering his men on, encouraging them to fight and hold position, he kept shouting, "Stand your ground, men." It was of no use. One by one, his platoon was cut down to a dwindling force. Unless he wanted to face total annihilation, he was forced into retreat attack after attack. He could not fathom being slaughtered by the crazed army of woman soldiers pushing him and his remaining forces into retreat after retreat. He had been pushed too far. Already backed against the far walls of the underground structure, he gave the command for a last stand, "Annihilate the bitches."

It spurred his men into one last fighting craze. It was to no avail. Too crammed for effective firepower, the battle groups formed into hand to hand combat clusters. Overpowering in numbers, in fairness to the Red Brigade shortcomings in fighting skills, but great on spirits, Big Red's band fought well even in close-up combat. Threshing, cutting, and stabbing with individual favorites, wielding swords, sabers, and knives, the battle went on until the last man had fallen.

Crushed by the sheer force, the end of his life could be counted in minutes and Muhab Sadek knew it when he felt an extreme burning sensation bursting from his abdomen. He knew it was not heartburn especially with pain traversing through the chest cavity on out through his back. His body had been penetrated by a swift stroke of a blade. It was the blade of Big Red thrusting the killing stroke. With the Jihad commander fallen, the battle was over.

From here on, the scientists and support staff would regain their freedom to man and manage the site once more. Under the protection of the Red Brigade, supported by her army amid prolific cheering, the protection was welcomed with open arms.

Without an immediate assignment to the next battle front, Big Red and her army of Amazons decided to remain at the outreaches of the Alaskan wilderness. She had a calculated reason for it. Driven by zeal and enthusiasm, though the outcome of the battle was in complete favor of her army, it was the sheer numbers that had won. Next time might not be so favorable. To assure future success, much needed individual training was necessary. The surrounding wilderness would provide the appropriate setting for essential field training. This time, training would involve tactical planning, offensive and defensive strategies, with prepping for survival in the open elements. It would present the chance for turning a novice warrior force into a seasoned and respected fighting unit equal or better than a likewise trained, male counterpart.

Next time Big Red's forces would emerge from the forests, her soldiers would be prepared.

THE NEW REPUBLIC

Tension was felt by everyone. People were anxious for the first national session to hear the new constitution, which had been anticipated for weeks. It had taken years to create it. What had been considered the plains would become a permanent part of the Patriots' new territory. What remained was defining jurisdiction, borders, and laws. As was the case with the original Declaration of Independence, the new declaration would be read here today. It would be a historic moment. The grounds were packed with citizens and so were streets and parks nearby. Shops were closed. Fabrication had stopped. Today, hopefully for hundreds of years in the future, would be a day marked for celebration.

A historic place had been selected for this great day. Several floors up at the Freedom Brewery, the nation's leadership, solidly planted by the edge of the balcony, were clearly visible to all. "People," Norton opened the historic speech. "Today will be a day recorded into the pages of history." He then pulled the veil draped over the balcony off, revealing the nation's new flag. The surroundings immediately turned silent, but only a few seconds. It was quickly accompanied by a roar of outbursts followed by thunderous applause.

"Told you," Norton commented to Elliott poised by his side.

"Right as always," was the commander's reply.

He let the people have their day. There was no rush to terminate the ovation and cheering directed at not only him, but the flag as well. Norton was pleased and so was his staff, who had worked diligently to make the event happen. He went on to delineate the specifics of the design of the flag. He detailed each article in the constitution. He promised to uphold and serve the rights of the people as long as they approved of his leadership and presented a cursory plan exercised for immediate action. Much like any new administration, political or otherwise, his people were cheering him on with every article he addressed. It was truly a day of reckoning.

Amid the cheering, many comments were sounded off like, "God bless our leader…Hail the new nation…Hail to the flag…"

The party leaders quickly left to retreat to Norton's private quarters. Details and specifics needed to be hammered out for sound resolutions acceptable to all citizens. With an established headquarters in St. Louis, with Elliott and his armored division providing infantry support to Brooks patrolling the borders, with Norton in command of the Patriots—the forces were in place. All that was left was to put the plan into action. For that, Brooks would lead the first assault party on the Mississippi River. There was one last issue for the commanders to solidify. Brooks needed to know how far he could push south. Facing Norton, he asked, "What's the status with the bridges?"

"Taken care of," he was assured. "Demolition crew just returned. Last bridges around New Orleans were successfully destroyed. River's yours."

"What a shame," someone commented. "Bridges gone."

"Don't worry," Elliott assured his men. "We'll build new ones once this mess is over." Putting concerns aside, he said next, "Bridges, like the rest of the infrastructure, have been crumbling for years. About time somebody's doing something about it."

"I hear you," was an optimistic comeback.

While he'd been getting bits and pieces from Norton and Elliott, Brooks did not have a clear picture of the overall planning the Patriots' leader had in mind for the new republic. "What's the plan?" he wanted to know. "What's the overall strategy?"

An hour later, the leaders of the new nation reemerged from their private quarters to gather in the Assembly Hall.

Norton took the stand at the newly fashioned pedestal. On the front, it proudly displayed the banner for the New Republic. Simplistic, but effective, it was a clever design. The world would take note. Draped over the podium, in all its colorful glory, was the new flag for the republic. It was a beautiful design. Not only did it project the makeup of the nation and its people, it portrayed the Patriots with their simplistically devised constitution to the world. The nation was set. Its foundation defined, all it needed now was a title for its leadership. It would have to be a benchmark, something novel. Some things still needed to be determined, but for now, today, what mattered most was the protection of the nation from an ever-encroaching enemy.

"Okay," Norton opened the private session. He gestured at his military commander. "Elliott. Status."

Brodie Elliott, Command Sergeant Major, 1st Armored Division to what used to be considered Badlands territory, took the stand. He delivered a first report on his military assets as to where, how strong, their positions, and how they were to be deployed. Since the army was the nation's largest employer, shortage of new recruits was not an issue. The problem was transportation. To mount the ever-growing army, the skills necessary for building out and maintaining the required vehicles was utilized from within its ranks. Though a slow process, with Brooks' skills and added manpower, acquisition efforts for acquiring assets had been drastically improved in recent months.

"Brooks. Status."

Whereas the infantry still had ways to go in logistics, Brooks was ready with his fleet of speedboats. He was ready for the river. He was ready to defend the new nation's borders. His engineers and technicians had been busy at work producing the fleet Brooks had conceived. Anchored by the riverside was proof of their accomplishments in the form of a freshwater navy built by hundreds of skilled workers. Where the fleet represented only a minor waterborne force, by any means it was a respectable force for an inland based navy. Scaled in size for speed and agility, it would perfectly serve Brooks and his men, the freshwater-based War Dogs.

"In summary," Norton concluded. "People have a new nation. A new constitution is in place. All it needs now is enforcing and protecting the nation and its inherited treasures."

For that, Brooks, in his casual way and proven capabilities, gave Norton his personal guarantees. "I'll make sure." The next day, he and his navy fleet were off on their first assignment, to stop unwanted infiltration, illicit trafficking, and prohibited trade in the country. Problem was, Patriots or not, the new constitution called for controlled and calculated growth. But trouble, big trouble awaited him only a short distance downriver.

Scott Brooks, flanked by his fleet of customized speedboats, was testing the nearby waters. He had to find out the seaworthiness of the craft. Where each craft had been individually tested after being built, the fleet, as a whole, was something entirely different. Where he had developed numerous battle strategies, they had to be assigned, tested, and refined. Each boat was equipped with HF radio, sonar, and radar. In addition, turret mounted .50 cal. machine guns had been installed up front and in the rear. Some were even equipped with torpedo launchers. He was proud of his engineers that'd pulled it off.

With headset clamped against his head, mic pressed by his lips, Brooks was shouting out orders to an unrestrained navy. While the label 'Navy' might have been a laughing matter at the present, in due time, he knew, he'd beat it into a formidable flotilla. For now, shaking his head with a tolerant grin set on his face, he watched a force acting more like a wild bunch. "Bunch 'a cowboys," he muttered into the roar of the turbine-powered craft. For now, he let them have their day. What was lacking on discipline, his navy sure made up in spirits. He was pleased.

Each day, the fleet expanded its perimeter. Where one fleet would head up north, another would push further south. A third was on standby. They'd mostly patrol the local shores, keeping intruders from crossing the river alongside the only bridge still intact. Brooks took command of the local fleet. He couldn't help but take pleasure in his newly acquired lifestyle, that of waging war. Completely at home in the sizable flagship under his body with top speeds to boost, he felt like Blackbeard himself heading off a bunch of competing pirates. At present, piloting a fleet of souped-up attack boats limited to a narrow body of water, the inland waterway suited him fine. In time, he'd own the whole river, and everyone would know him and his War Dogs.

STINGER

Headlines were all over the news channels. Most read: *Stinger strikes again.* What made it worse was that similar reports had started to come in from other places. Cities like Boston, Philadelphia, and Washington, DC carried similar news: *Islamic worshippers massacred.* Rumors, as impossible as they may have sounded—Stinger seemed to be connected with all of them. Due to the lack of organized law enforcement throughout the region, whoever executed the heinous deeds got away unscathed each time. The impact of Stinger's acts began to take hold. Word not only spread through the local region, but was carried beyond the seaboard. It did not take long for international media to pick up on it.

Immigrants, visitors, and traders thought twice before making arrangements to travel into America's eastern shores. Though the general sentiment for the victims was empathic, voices began to emerge among the local population about oppression, freedom, liberation. Demonstrations were held in city neighborhoods, quickly spreading out, gaining momentum, but it would be a lengthy struggle without effective weapons. Jihad, as well as city dwellers, realized the fighting could not be won with only bare hands.

Weapons of all kinds—handguns, semis, automatics, swords, sabers, knives, and even gardening tools—had been confiscated years before by Jihad. The government saw to it. Citizens, no matter how loud their just demonstration cries, found themselves facing boundless Jihad warriors armed with AK-47s and RPGs, which beat the mobs into retreat each and every time.

At the Chicago headquarters, Hammad also took notice. Agitated and highly concerned, not for his personal safety, but for the sake of his newly acquired nation, he called an emergency session. He demanded, "Anything new on Stinger?"

"Nothing concrete," he was told by one lieutenant. "Only traces of reports."

"Our Eastern cells are slowly losing ground," another reported.

"We are recruiting," he was assured, "but this will take time."

Hearing only negative reports, there was a sudden change in Hammad's attitude. His normally commanding face filled with rage. Where, in the past, he had been relatively satisfied about the way things were progressing in the new world, he now scoffed at his lieutenants. "No more excuses." Striding up and down the hall, he had a difficult time containing his anger. "You… You…. You…" he spat at his weary lieutenants. "Take your men to the cities."

He then further instructed, "I want this woman stopped. I want her eliminated. I want her head." He could not fathom one person inflicting all the damages. "Don't come back with excuses," he raged on. "Don't come back without her."

Not only was he enraged at the lack of results by his cell's ineffectiveness, he was extremely dissatisfied with Yusuf's performance in New York. He had not heard back from him. If things continued without results, he would have to go there himself to fight. *That,* he surmised with finality, *is unacceptable.*

Chicago was where he planned to stay. It was the command center he had selected to be the most effective. Leaving here would open up a gap. It would expose the Great Lakes. It would make the water bodies vulnerable to attacks and possible loss. He could not have that under any circumstances. His place was here. Thoughts like these made his blood boil. Completely enraged by now, he could not maintain his controlled posture any longer.

"Incompetence…Stupidity…Idiots," he shouted at the assembly, then quickly left for his private chambers. He could not face his incompetent lieutenants any more without completely losing his composure.

Eight hundred miles to the east, across the shores from Manhattan, Tracy had just returned from another outing. That's what she called her missions. She was fatigued. She needed some time off. Her stealthy attacks were getting more demanding with each strike. At times, she wished she had company. Though she had created her own environment years before, she knew it would be a challenge combating alone. She was facing an ever growing enemy. There seemed to be an unlimited supply of terrorists just waiting to fill the ranks. After annihilating one cell, several more sprang up in surrounding neighborhoods. The thought of it was alarming. Tracy realized she needed help. Where she was supported by satellite surveillance, the information she received from Specter was beginning to become overwhelming. She could not operate at several locations at the same time. Reality came in the form of exhaustion. Realizing that, in the privacy of her den, the inn where she kept her few belongings, just before slipping into the world of dreams, "Brian," she muttered. "Where are you?"

Next evening, after a day of rest by the Jersey shores, Tracy decided to head for the city. She wanted to reconnect with her friend, Hannah. *Besides,* she thought, *I need to know the enemy.* Determined to draw the enemy out in the open, wherever they were located in the city, she hopped behind the wheel of the Humvee. Taking stock of the inventory, weapons, and crew bag, after adjusting the mirrors with one hand with the steering wheel gripped in the other, Tracy was off to the city.

It did not take long for the enemy to spot her. Trouble began as soon as she emerged from the tunnel. It became apparent that her vehicle had been identified. It was no surprise to her with all her recent travels, as covert as they had been between the cities. No matter how careful, it was only a matter of time before someone would make the connection. As high profile the vehicle was, it could easily be spotted, surveillance or not. Right now, she was being pursued. Clearly visible through the rearview mirror, several vehicles were lined up. It could only mean one thing. *The Prophet set the trap.* "Let's see what you can do," she muttered at the Humvee.

Being chased was a first for her, but she was not without help. It was for situations like these that she had customized her vehicle. After a quick glance, back at the approaching fleet, she flipped a switch on the dashboard labeled "Execute" and stepped on it. Immediately, the twin turbo units kicked in with a tremendous surge. Turning at greater than 100k revs, their power was instantly transferred to the driveshaft. The Humvee momentarily leaped off the ground and shot ahead much like an animal avoiding pursuit. Streaming south on West Street, her current path, she had the entirety of lower Manhattan ahead. It would be her playground. Weaving in and out of traffic she was set to stay ahead. Her problem was the traffic. It would take her underground. There, signal relay from satellites would be ineffective. Specter would have to direct her through traffic. She could only communicate via HF radio transmissions. She needed help. She needed a map.

"Specter," she yelled into the mic, "need directions." Providing him with a running account on her current location, seconds later, Alex's assuring voice came across the earpiece. "Standby." Moments later, he directed her, "Liberty Street Exit. Now."

Cutting to the right Tracy swerved across traffic.

"South End Avenue…Albany left…Now."

It would take her underneath 9A into Lower Manhattan. The averting maneuver did not work. The fleet was still in pursuit, and closing in. The pursuers had one thing to their advantage. They knew the territory.

Specter did his best to keep her ahead. "Greenwich South…Stay left."

"Repeat," she yelled over the sound of squealing tires and scraping metal. His last direction was broken because she had sped underneath another highway structure.

"Stay left."

"Too late," she yelled into the oncoming headlights. Almost blinded, she had already entered oncoming traffic lanes from the emerging Battery Park underpass. Going against it could be fatal. With the wall of moving metal closing in she tried to avert the facing traffic. Turning back was no option. An entire fleet of maddened terrorists kept pressing on her. They were out to annihilate her. The lead pursuing vehicle gradually inched his way up alongside her, running against traffic as well. A fleeting thought crossed her mind, *must be the devil himself.* She shot a quick glance at the driver but could not make the ID. Road traffic ahead demanded her full attention.

"Left…Right…Slowdown…Speedup…Watch   out,"   were   Specter's   running instructions. Chaotic, but in rhythm with traffic, his voice almost sounded like the beat of a tune. The thought of long forgotten times brought a grin to her face. "What was it again?" Her mind recollected, "Riders in the Storm."

She could not shake the vehicle closing in on her right and left. Sparks were flying from scraping metal against metal. She had to know who gave chase. Again, she shot one quick glance to the right. This time she caught his face. He stared back at her. There was instant recognition by both. She had been identified. Her mind screamed out, *I don't believe it!* The face across the lane was none other than… "Watch out!" Specter shot the warning at her.

Tracy responded with, "Guess who I just ran into?"

"What?"

"Old enemy of yours…Hashim…Yusuf Hashim."

Specter's response was immediate. "Take him out. He'll blow our cover."

Despite already being minutes into the chase, on top of oncoming traffic, the new threat was immediate. Her entire mission was in jeopardy. Her mind raced for a solution. "Eliminate."

With both of her hands tightly clutched to the steering wheel, she prepared for the next move. In one quick motion, she swerved to the right, then slammed the Humvee sideways into her opponent. Yusuf reacted, but there was no space for him to avoid the collision. On impact, his vehicle spun out headlong into the oncoming traffic. One quick glance at his enraged face, and Tracy knew he had been beaten. The crashing and tearing of metal on his car, with the ensuing fleet of Jihadists piling onto him, caused the chase to an abrupt end. Vehicles were piling on top of other vehicles. Some burst into flames, others tumbled through the air, blocking the tunnel. Amid the chaos, Stinger spotted an opening. She headed for it. Emerging from the tunnel exit, she recognized the surroundings. She got her bearings back. Cautiously, she proceeded towards her original goal, Hannah's high-rise.

Earlier in the evening, Hannah was speculating on her friend's whereabouts. Somewhat perturbed and disappointed, she wondered whatever could have happened to Tracy. Seated on the balcony, her favorite place, in the quiet of night she became aware of city traffic below. It normally did not bother her, but tonight something was different. Curious, she stepped to the rail to check on the cause. Twenty levels below, was a car chase in progress. What she witnessed was one vehicle being chased by a dozen others in close pursuit.

"Not gonna make it," she shouted into the night when the lead car jumped lanes. The problem became immediately obvious. The lead driver went against the traffic emerging from the tunnel. The fleet quickly disappeared into the dark, but not without audible tearing of metal accompanied by crashing sounds. "Told you," she muttered from the lofty heights of the high-rise apartment.

It was not much later when the doorbell rang. It startled her from the quiet of night. She headed for the door, curious who it could be this late in the evening. One peek though the peephole and her heart jumped with delight. "Tracy," she cheered. "Where have you been? I've been so worried. Come on in."

Returning the warmth of Hannah's smile, Tracy admitted, "Busy." Hannah rushed up to embrace her late guest. It was a warm and comforting hug that Tracy also returned. She could feel no strangeness in the embrace. It was pure friendship and she liked the security in it. Being a lifelong student studying human behavior, personal touch and mannerism could reveal much. Because of it she was always on guard. *Have to be,* she silently deliberated. *Whole damned world is at my back.* For now, she felt safe.

Tracy took note of the environment. It was another one of her safeguards. She did not like surprises. Anybody could be waiting behind curtains, closets, doors. Not that she considered herself paranoid. It was purely for self-preservation. Only thing out of order was an open balcony door, but the platform was vacant. *Good, nobody else here.* "Whatcha doin'?"

Releasing her friend from the embrace, Hannah stated, "Been watching a car chase. Should have seen it. Too bad you missed it."

"Didn't."

"What?"

"Was in it."

Tracy watched Hannah's features change from joy to disbelief, then to surprise. There was doubt in her eyes when she said, "I don't understand."

"I was the lead car."

She seemed dumbfounded. "Didn't see police. Who's after you?"

Tracy took a split second, deliberating, *Should I...could I...do I dare telling her?* It meant putting a friend in dire jeopardy. Then it occurred to her, *I'll protect her. Perhaps I could bunk with her for a while.* Being in the city on the enemy's doorsteps it might make it safer for her to move about day and night.

Hannah, still waiting for an explanation, offered, "Drink?"

"Sure." Tracy waited until she returned with two glasses filled with wine. "Take a seat. Think we need to talk." She enjoyed a few sips of wine with her friend's face locked on her eyes, waiting in anticipation. "Can you keep a secret?"

"For you, yes."

"You swear?"

Hannah's reply was as pure as her face when she promised, "Of course. I promise. You can tell me anything."

"Ever hear of a Stinger?"

Hannah's eyes took on a puzzled look. She sat up straight to directly face her friend. It took several seconds for her to assimilate her thought processes. Then, with an incredulous transformation in her face burst out loud, "You?"

"In the flesh." Hannah's face had changed from utter shock to bewilderment, finally settling into great pride. Tracy knew it was an innocent reaction. She could trust her.

"Will you stay tonight?"

"Of course," Tracy answered.

"You've got some explaining to do." She encouraged her guest, "More wine?"

"Thanks."

While Hannah got busy at the counter, Tracy considered how much she could reveal to her friend and how much would be safe. *I'll have to feel her out.*

Hannah returned with the wine. "Care for some snacks?"

"Love to."

"Be a minute."

She returned with a tray and took a seat next to Tracy. "Talk," she stated. It was the understatement of the year. "You first."

Tracy opened with a monologue, putting her friend at ease. She told her about growing up at the Castle, her years with the agency. She told her about the personal hardship she'd endured, imposed by Jihad terrorists. She explained the years following filled with exploits, conditioning, and preparation with one thing, and only one thing in mind, retribution. Surprisingly, Hannah seemed to understand. When it was her turn to tell a story, Tracy realized how much they had in common.

There was grief, regrets, and dissidence on Hannah's part. Life to her had not been exactly fair either. Growing up in a once thriving metropolis turned hostile caused much resentment on her part. Unable to see an alternative other than trying to carve out a meager living in the city, she eventually landed a job as language interpreter with the United Nations. That was her story. While it was filled with hardship, it was nothing close to what Tracy had experienced.

"What about your language skills. Interpreter and all?"

"My mom," she explained, "came from Iran. Dad used to work the oil fields. They got married. And here I am."

Dawn was already breaking in the east when both realized they have talked the night away. As before, Hannah extended an invitation for Tracy to stay on. This time, Tracy not only accepted but agreed to move in with her when the offer was made. "When can you move?"

"As soon as I get back to Jersey," Tracy proposed. "But first, I need some sleep."

"It's settled then."

Next morning, Tracy, accompanied by Hannah, went to fetch her belongings at the Jersey inn. Hannah was delighted to have a friend living in, but it was not without surprise piled on top of surprise when she spotted Tracy's attack vehicle, weapons cache and accompanied supplies. Hannah was completely onboard with Tracy's future plans. They sat up many nights contemplating the next move. "You know," she proclaimed on more than one occasion, "knowing you, there's hope for our country."

It was a mutual feeling. There were, however, many more roads to travel. Tracy had an idea for their next destination. It'd take them into adventures of which only destiny had an inkling.

SCOTT BROOKS

Under the bridge above, appropriately renamed "Badland Gateway," sea traffic was heavily patrolled by Brooks' fleet of attack boats. It did not take long for the ever-watchful fleet to get noticed, then respected, then feared. Within weeks, rumors were spreading about their ferociousness from riverboat attacks. Right away, the once thriving waterway, engaged with smugglers and unlawful crossings, became unsafe unless one had a legitimate reason for doing business on the water. Floating barges were allowed passage but not without search and paying a fee. Cargo, transport, ferries were taxed. Goods were bartered as tariff, allowing passage up and down the Mississippi. It was this revenue providing a means to keep Brooks' flotilla afloat, his forces fed, and the bridge maintained.

Hovering alongside another black-market trader, Brooks was about to hand over his usual ultimatum. "What's it gonna be?" he demanded. "Life or death?" He did not have to explain. Word had already alerted the traders months ago about what to expect if caught with contraband. The choice was theirs. Give up the cargo in exchange for life, or get sunk into the depths of the river. Terms were clear and simple. Contrary to common belief, many sea captains and crews might be effectively trained in navigating waters efficiently, but when it came to floating, most did not know how to swim. It was most likely the reason why many went under with their ships.

Brooks was watching the boat pilot. It was obvious his mind was weighing greed against reason. Reason generally won out. His choice became obvious when he turned to the edge of his barge and jumped overboard. It was one of two options allowed by the War Dogs. In his case, he knew how to swim. He would make it to the other shore. The laws instituted by the constitution might have been harsh, but they were necessary for assuring the New Republic did not repeat prior mistakes.

The booty cargo just acquired was towed to the nearby docks, unloaded, and distributed among the local shop owners. The organizers for the New Republic might have been ruthless at times, but the result was fairness to all. Everyone in the nation took benefit. For the republic to have a chance for continued existence, laws had to be abided by without exception.

"Floaters," a watchful voice came across the radio. A group of swimmers had just been spotted trying to make it across the river. Binoculars went up, skimming the surface. "I see 'em," Brooks' pilot announced then gunned the craft in that direction. It was too late for the swimmers to hide. They had been spotted. Being detected was a swimmer's worst nightmare. It meant certain death. There was no option extended by the War Dogs. Every outsider trying to make it across the riverbanks illegally was mercilessly cut down. Everyone knew the penalty: death.

No amount of pleading would help the unfortunate. Their pleas quickly turned into cries for mercy before being cut to pieces by the sword. At times, a trader would challenge Brooks to a fight. To be fair, he would submit himself to the challenge to keep his fighting skills honed. The outcome was always the same, certain death for the challenger.

Much like an animal with prey, after playing with his victim, Brooks would lunge out with lightning speed for one final blow to the ribcage. The victim would gasp for air, sputtering blood, only to collapse seconds later with a final sigh, staring bewildered into their executioner's eyes.

Rumors-turned-folklore preceded Brooks' fame wherever he was spotted. Rumors had it he never lost a fight. It went even further. It was said that, "If you see a twitch in the eye, his left, it's already too late. You're a dead man."

Although there was doubt about the proclaimed fame, in Brooks' case it was fact. The twitching of the eye was a direct result from scarred tissue along the facial muscles from an earlier time he remembered well. With nerves traversing beneath the skin, the muscle contraction initiated caused a reaction much like the recoil of a whip, ending in a retraction to the damaged tissue. It affected the sensory receptors to the left eye. The effects were clearly visible to an opponent, but only for an instant. It was barely enough time for an assailant to realize that folklore and myth had turned into reality. By then, it was too late. Death was certain.

Born invalid, turned super fighter, when news spread of his fame, there was envy voiced by his soldiers with a deep desire to acquire his fighting skills. When confronted about his strength and boundless energy, Brooks' comments would be simple. "Keep eating and exercise." He then would explain the balance between caloric intakes versus expended energy followed by muscle growth. It was usually too much information for the curious to digest who'd readily seek another's company.

What Brooks never revealed was the secret of the head implant. That was to be only between Specter, Stinger, the Condors who performed the implant, and him. The clandestine technologies Allen Spencer possessed and controlled was guarded knowledge. Their technology was used only for the good of mankind. To preserve the cause, the national laboratories were off limits to the public. Only trusted scientists and engineers were allowed access to the facilities. It was a close-knit society with Stinger and Brooks being products thereof, and Alex gatekeeper of the stated technology.

Where on the outside world battles were fought by the masses, within the defined boundaries of the New Republic, they were won through knowledge, skills, and technology. The balance of power was in the hands of the Patriots.

THE SERPENT

Weeks before, with Yusuf having departed for New York City, Hammad had delegated primary mission responsibilities to Antarah Radi, Mission Commander, Jihad, Central Sector Chicago region. It was a necessary choice, but the place, he felt, was not the same without his trusted commander and friend. He had no one to bounce ideas off of or to confide personal issues in. Though he did not need anyone for that, it was good talking things through, especially mission related tasks ahead. From a personal perspective, neither Yusuf nor Hammad had a personal life, especially not here in enemy territory. The mission ahead was too critical to let personal matters such as relationships interfere. That had to wait until the world was his. He had made a pact with Yusuf to that fact. "Soon," he had promised. "We shall rule."

Word had just been received via HF. "Comrade Commander," Hakim Massoud, First Lieutenant, Local Cell, came rushing into the command headquarters. The man seemed out of breath when he blurted out, "There was an accident." Present were Hammad and Radi, along with several other lieutenants.

"What?"

Massoud tried to avoid direct eye contact for good reason. He knew Hammad would not be happy at the news. In fact, he would be furious, affecting everybody nearby. "New York City," he explained. "Yusuf."

"Speak up, man."

"Reports indicate vehicle pursuit in Manhattan. Several deaths…One survivor…Yusuf hospitalized…" As soon as the name Yusuf was mentioned, Hammad flew into rage. It was not a pretty scene. Demanding details, he found that there were none. It enraged him even more. Objects were flying. Furniture was broken. Even a door was smashed. It took minutes for the leader to calm down. When he finally did, he called his commanders to order. "New York," he commanded. "Immediately." He did not even wait for next morning. "Two hours."

Even less time had passed before the convoy took to the road. Short on military equipment, Hammad had to rely on the motor pool for transportation, most of which had been confiscated or acquired by force. Traveling via road would be quicker than taking along his fleet of boats, he decided, and they would have to push for time to make the city by evening.

It was late in the day when the Jihad convoy arrived. First stop was the Ground Zero Mosque. He figured it would be the best place to get information. He was correct. Right away, the Mullah led him to the infirmary where Yusuf could be found. The scene in the room was not very pleasant. Yusuf did not resemble the friend he knew. Stretched out in contraptions connected to multiple tubes and devices unrecognizable, his friend lay in a coma. Hammad demanded to speak with the physician.

"Brain damage," he was told. "Among many other injuries." According to the x-rays, chances were that he would not recover and if he did, he might have permanent neurological impairment.

Hammad pulled the shaken doctor close by the lapels. "You," he ordered. "Make sure he will be well."

"Sir," the doctor pleaded. "We are doing our best."

"Not good enough," was the response. "Put your best neurosurgeon to work. I'll hold you personally responsible."

There was more pleading, but, in the end, Hammad, flanked by his lieutenants, abruptly departed. There was not much more he could do at this place. Next stop, the police station, then back to the mosque. After assessing the state Yusuf was in, Hammad realized he would have to establish temporary headquarters in the city, no matter how long it'd take. He had to stand by his friend and most trusted fighter.

Reports at the local police department about the vehicle accident were sketchy at best. Witnesses described a customized Humvee leaving the scene. It was enough to send Hammad into a series of furies. There was this woman again, Stinger. He had suspected it. Elusive as she was, now he knew that it would call for extraordinary measures. He would have to devise a special plan to track her to justice. He would set a trap. She'd have to come to him.

"Get information on this woman," he ordered his men. "Anything and everything, her habits, education, family, friends, hobbies. Don't come back unless you have the information. I want every bit of detail on her, where she sleeps, eats, does her hair." That just about covered every aspect of a woman's daily life, so he thought. But Stinger was not an everyday woman.

At the lofty high-rise nearby, Hannah and Tracy were talking. "Best," Hannah suggested, "that you get away from the city, for a while."

"You coming with me?" she offered her friend. It gave Hannah something to think about. "I'll be on deck," she informed Hannah about her immediate plan. "Back in a while."

Tracy had thought about taking some time off from her mission. The city was getting too hot. She needed to change her attack strategy. Besides, she had not gotten any leads on Brian's whereabouts. Unlike her leaving a trail of destruction, whatever direction he'd taken had left no clues. It was as if he'd disappeared from the face of the Earth. It was time to call Specter. To have privacy, she took the elevator to the top floor of Hannah's building. Stepping off, she sought out a shaded area. The platform also gave her the best reception.

It was a bright and sunny day, like most days in the city. With the jet stream flowing in from the Atlantic, the morning breeze quickly removed smog and city pollutants. Presently in the relative safety of her friend's apartment, Tracy felt at ease. She did savor the time when her voice went out in the ether. "Specter…Specter, come in…urgent."

As always, Alex was right there for her. "Go."

"Any word from Brian?"

"Negative."

"Status on the Prophet?"

"Watch your back." It was a warning. "Prophet's on your trail." It meant the Prophet was closing in. It also meant Jihad cells were monitoring the airwaves. Their conversation had to be brief. "End trans." Because of the nice weather she decided to remain aloft. It would give her time alone to concentrate on her next plan.

Relaxing for the first time in weeks, Tracy was enjoying the view. From this altitude, she could see a hundred miles out. Detached from city life below, it seemed like another world. Without the roar of jet engines overhead, the serenity gave her a tranquil sensation. Aside from nearby tourists gawking at the wondrous views of skyscrapers, the only perceptible motions were puffs of clouds silently streaming overhead. There was only one sore mark jutting above the rest of the high-rise, the burned-up skeleton remains from One World Trade Center, Tower One recently destroyed by the enemy. What used to be thousands of glass panes adorning the new center, now, only a charred framework remained. Bearing vivid in her mind, that day in 2001, when the twin towers fell, followed with the recent attack, the memory renewed anger that surfaced from within. She had to distance herself from thought like these. Regardless of the past, she marveled at the magnificent sight. *Leave it to man,* she thought, *to do the impossible, to destroy as well as create. Are we becoming gods?*

"Time for lunch." Her stomach reminded her of the present. "Hannah's probably waiting." She would have the usual sandwich, soup, or salad prepared. The minute Tracy walked into the apartment she knew something was wrong. At first, as improbable as it may have seemed, she thought Hannah might have thrown a fit. Furniture was toppled over, curtains torn from their runners, the glass door leading to the balcony shattered with droplets of blood splattered across the kitchen floor. Flabbergasted at the disarray, Tracy yelled, "Hannah!" into each room. There was no answer. She was nowhere to be found. Then it hit her. "Abducted."

"No...no." Her fears were confirmed the second she spotted the black bandana tossed in one corner. Hannah must have torn it from her attacker's head. Picking up the cloth gave Tracy the information. It was headgear worn by the feared Jihad, inscribed with bold audacious lettering, "Insha' Allah." In the name of God.

Searching for more evidence, she spotted lettering sprawled across the dresser mirror. It read, "Her Life for Yours." Tracy would have been devastated if it had not been for the killer she'd become. Callused from waging war, all that crossed her mind was vengeance.

Tracy was puzzled about the abduction of her friend. "How did they make the connection between Hannah and her," she pondered. "Well," she decided. "It didn't matter now." Somehow the enemy had a trace on her. There were two choices she had. Wait for the adversary to contact her further or track him down. The aggressor that Tracy was, she chose the latter. It was time to visit the mosque again. It'd be the logical place to establish contact. It was obvious they wanted her. Her fear was about getting to Hannah in time. Being associated with Stinger, death would be her penalty. Images of Jihad beheadings made Tracy's blood boil. She had seen enough propaganda clips to know how gruesome it was. In the free world society, it was the worst death sentence by far. She could never let that happen to her dear friend.

Hurrying from the apartment, she muttered, "Hannah, stay brave." First stop was the underground. When she moved in with Hannah, she had stowed the Humvee in the carport. To keep the vehicle safe from prying eyes she had it covered with tarpaulin. Tearing away the cover, a quick check revealed that nothing was missing from the vehicle. Nobody had touched any of her weapons. Donning her signature jacket, she placed Serpent Slayer by her side and careened off. Tracy was ready to wage war. This time, it was to free her precious friend.

The second she drove up to the Ground Zero Mosque she knew they were waiting. A group of heavily-armed fighters were clustered by the entrance. There was no purpose in using her weapon. She could not shoot it out without possibly getting injured herself. She needed to find out where Hannah was being kept.

Weaponless, Tracy calculatingly approached the fighters, then planted her body solidly in front of them. With both hands thrown up, indicating she was unarmed, she was immediately swarmed by a group of terrorists throwing threatening gestures and feigning bodily attacks at her, shouting, "We will kill you…you bitch." Their attacks did not go further than verbal threats.

Tracy, confident that she was safe for the moment, cast a challenging smirk at the squad. It enraged them even more. Additional threats were spat at her. "We will have your head." Dragged and shoved into the main hall of the mosque, Tracy was approached by the Mullah. Slowly circling her, he seemed to make an assessment when he said, "So…you are Stinger?"

"That I am," she replied. "Where's my friend?" The Mullah's face held an odd, somewhat surprised expression. It was a rather astonishing gaze. From the expression, Tracy deduced that he'd expected a humble creature begging for mercy. Accompanied by a slight nod, his face gradually changed from daunting to reverence. Where the others raged for vengeance, he recognized and respected the personal strength in the captured. He was admiring her muscle tone and body conditioning. His eyes revealed an admiration never before endowed on a woman. Inviting her into his private chambers, he muttered, "True warrior."

"Where's my friend?" Tracy repeated her earlier demand.

She was invited to take a seat when he said, "In due time. But first," the Mullah stated, "what is it you want? What are you fighting for? What is your cause?"

It was obvious that there had not been a consensus among his brethren and fellow Jihadists about her cause. *Why should there?* he'd reasoned. *A single woman against the whole of Islam? Preposterous!* Thoughts like these were clearly painted across his face.

"Freedom…I want my land back."

"That," he responded, "is not possible. You see," he emphasized, "it is our turn."

"Turn what?"

"To own the world."

There was nothing further that could be said. There was nothing that would change the minds on either side. She had read the Koran. She knew enough about their cause. The book spelled it right out. In the minds of the Muslim world, it was their turn to rule the world. Indications to the fact had been emerging for years. Free world leaders had closed their eyes against the threat. Nobody wanted to face the facts. "Not likely…Impossible…You're imagining things." Unlike the Patriots, the visionaries, farsighted as they were, the whole nation had been blindsided. Timing might have been off with Bin Laden, but with the Prophet, the balance of power had shifted. Much like Tracy, he was a warrior fighting for a cause. Where he was fighting his, she was fighting hers.

The handwriting was on the wall. They'd been warned. But nobody paid attention. Only one question remained. "Where is Hannah?"

With a shrug of the shoulders, he lifted both hands palm up, pleading ignorance, and offered, "With the Prophet. Of course."

"Where?" Tracy demanded.

There was a mystical grin on his face when he stated, "That my dear, is for you to figure out." He then added, "You have until nightfall. After that," in an instant his face turned brutal, "it'll be too late."

"Let her pass," he ordered his fellow comrades, who were ready to cut this outlandish woman to pieces. Amidst a cussing and spitting Jihad lineup, Tracy abruptly turned and, with steadfast strides, walked through the chauvinistically behaving gauntlet of vengeful, gesturing Jihad fighters. She could practically smell the cultural loathing oozing from their pores.

CASTLE ROCK

"Place's falling apart," Alex muttered. He had been trying to get a hold of Tracy but could not raise her. *Implant's turned off,* he grumbled. He didn't like not having a direct connection with his daughter, especially not now, when she was in the midst of enemy territory. Last thing he had received was Hannah being taken hostage. After that, the transmission had gone dead. He'd never forgive himself for putting Tracy in harm's way. But, he also knew, it was solely her decision. She chose her environment. She created her own future. Where he had done his best to raise the girls, laying out a career, providing the right connections, recent events had showed otherwise. There was no one individual to blame. It was one world against another. It was the world of capitalism against creed. It was two determined factions pitted against each other by the world powerbrokers, neither ever seeing eye to eye. In addition, with the new threat imposed on his nation, from the knowledge he had on Islamic based secular factions, a common ground would never be achieved, ever.

"Stinger," he tried again. "Report." He'd just have to keep on trying. Satellite monitors did not give him a position. Where he normally could spot her whereabouts, the images were currently static with her last position at her friend's dwelling. The only clue he had was that she was someplace in lower Manhattan.

Concerned but not alarmed yet, his mind wandered to his other liability, to Liz. He needed an update on the rescue status. Currently seated by the command center, his hand reached for the HAM radio dials. Though the scanner was continuously monitoring the airwaves, there had not been a call sign for the Castle in some time. Under normal conditions it would indicate a world at peace, but he knew better. The nation torn to pieces with all that was going on within its own borders. The ether should have been buzzing with chatter.

He selected the frequency for the Presidio, hoping Foster had some update on the next space launch. As if it wasn't bad enough to be a nation without a manned spacecraft, everything going in orbit was dependent on the Russians. Though other nations like India, France and China, had been test firing their systems, so far, the only objects launched were satellites, primarily for the free world. For that, since the Western Sector had no currency to trade with, the former United States had lowest priority.

"Presidio," the voice suddenly broke the silence, "Foster."

Alex did not have to identify himself. After a lifetime of working together, people close to him could identify his slightly-accented voice. "Listen, Hank," Alex queried his friend, "any word from the ISS?"

"Negative," he responded. "But I got good news. New launch date, thirty days ahead of schedule. Baikonur is gearing up its crew."

"What about conditions out west?" He was referring to the Asian nations. Everybody was on alert about the Chinese running full speed for the race into space. Other nations were in contention as well. Everybody that could afford a space program was betting on who'd be first to land on the moon or mars. Whoever set foot on alien dust first was bound for untold wealth.

"China's still leading the pack, but India, France, Japan, and the E.U. consortium are close behind."

What the standing inferred was a hastened race for mineral resources. Mostly kept in the dark as uncommon knowledge, the general public was unaware of its economic implications. What the scientists had determined was that there was untold wealth waiting for the taking on other worlds. Whoever arrived first was guaranteed a stake on the resources. It wasn't Americans anymore. With his mind wandering freely, Alex's ears were listening patiently. "We've lost the pioneering initiative," Foster reported. "Perhaps forever."

Alex could clearly see foreign nations staking out their claims. What made it almost unbearable was that America would not be a contender. Once a world superpower, the United States of America, now reduced to a third-world nation without wealth or stature would be completely left out. As for the race, whoever gained possession of Helium-3 and other precious minerals, the moon's abundant energy resources, would control the world's energy prosperity.

"How could anybody be that stupid?" It was a question posed most frequently with American entrepreneurs when social topics touched on space exploration, mineral resources, and wealth. Opportunities were lost when the government stopped funding NASA. It was that simple.

"Are you with me?" Foster's voice shook him back to reality. "By the way," he wanted to know, "how's Tracy?"

"Out east," Alex replied. "Leaving her mark."

"She the one causing all the grief to Jihad?"

"The one."

"Give her my best. I'll keep you posted on the ISS."

"You do that. Bye."

At least, Alex reflected, *somebody's making progress.* "Good news for a change," he muttered. His next task was informing Liz of the updated schedule. *There may just be enough food supplies left 'til the rescue mission reaches the space station,* he thought. Using Morse code, the only mode of communication with her, he felt a bit relieved. *Now back to Stinger. Still need a link with her.* Surrounded by Jihad cells, without his support, she'd be too vulnerable.

FACE OFF

Tracy walked the gauntlet of swears, insults, and threats amid an irate group of Jihadists ready to kill her. The only thing stopping them from tearing her to pieces was the Mullah intervening with, "She is taboo. Her life belongs to The Prophet." Regardless of the imminent danger, she made it to her vehicle on solid strides. Without so much as a clue about Hannah's whereabouts, she headed north on Westside Expressway. She needed to clear her head. A thought had just occurred. *Where was it again?* "I know. Hillview Reservoir." It was the place she had almost died during the biological incident. It seemed so distant, the time the terrorists had held her hostage. She was dying to see the place in daylight. It may be a slight chance, it was a starting point, nevertheless. Traffic on 9A did not present any problems. She was cruising along at a steady pace. Passing the Bronx to the right, the approaching sign indicated the Yonkers turnoff. "Specter." she called. "Need directions. Hillview."

"Finally," he huffed. He was greatly relieved hearing her voice. "Why there?"

"Possible contact."

"East on Riverdale. Take Central Park Avenue north. You'll see the reservoir ahead."

"Thanks," she said driving off in the direction he had indicated. "Hillview Pump Station," the next sign proclaimed. "Keep Out."

So that's it? Tracy killed the engine, stepped off, and headed for the seemingly deserted place. There was no one here and no vehicles indicating any activities. Regardless of the urgency of finding her friend she decided to stay a few moments. She needed time to think. It was quiet. It was serene, striding by the water's edge reliving the incident from the distant past. Looking for possible clues, she saw the pump house. She pulled on the gate, but it was locked. It did not matter; there was nobody here. She sat by the reservoir reflecting. How long had it been? *Years.* She did not remember getting here. Blindfolded back then and unconscious most of the time, *how could I?* It was not until Brian and Scott showed up to rescue her. "Brian," the thought brought her back to reality. "Hannah…Dammit. Where are you?" It brought on renewed hatred for the enemy and more urgency for the present. Her eyes struck the reflection of the sunset against the ripple-free water surface. She had no answer. For that, she had to get back to the city.

Renewed fear welled up within. Tracy realized she was running out of time. With the sun setting in the west, darkness would set in soon. The Mullah had given her no indication. She had no directions. Hannah could be held anywhere. Even with an army of law enforcement and investigators, if there were such organizations in place, there might not be enough time to locate her. It was up to her to figure out. It was the Prophet's game of life and death. It would be his turn now to play the deck of cards. She had lost her hand. She needed help. "Specter," her alert went out into the ether. "Need help."

"Go." His voice projected anxiety. He had been waiting for her to check in. He was fearful for his daughter's life. With an entire army of terrorists after her, outnumbered by a thousand to one, he knew the odds of coming out unscathed were extremely stacked against her.

"Need a fix on Hannah," she pleaded. "Extremely urgent."

"Standby."

Specter's response could mean a number of things. It could take a short few minutes, perhaps hours for him to get back to her, most likely not in time. It was up to her. With that thought, she hopped back into her vehicle and headed back towards Manhattan. Her concerns proved her wrong. He responded within ten minutes. "Got you on monitors. What do you see?"

Odd question, she reflected. Panning her head across the Manhattan skyline, she gave him running accounts nevertheless. On the backend, Alex could see the panoramic view she provided through the implant. Presently headed south on Westside Expressway, lower Manhattan gradually grew out of the horizon.

"Look around you," his voice prodded. "What do you see?"

"Streets, parks, people, places."

"Higher up," he insisted.

Passing the skyline to the left she suddenly spotted it. "This is it…got to be." The tower skeleton would be the only deserving place for a showdown with the Prophet. It provided a symbol for the end of the free world.

"Keep going," he insisted.

What panned into her view was nearby Towers Two, Three, Four, and Five with some presently still under construction. It would have been a marvelous sight if it wasn't for the recent destruction. She regretted not being able to see the 1776 feet tall, in its full glory, the glass panel encased structure reached into the heavens like an obelisk. Once multi-faceted, much like a cut diamond, the tower presented all of man's technological capabilities merged into one gigantic structure. To Tracy, it was déjà-vu. She had experienced the same sensation many years ago on her first visit to the twin towers. *When was it? Polytech, college days.* It had been an overwhelming feeling, taking the elevators up top. Seated at the observation deck one could see forever. *What a view it was.*

"What do you see?" Alex was persisting.

Tracy was still ways from the towers. Speeding along lower Manhattan Westside, she took the next exit and seconds later slammed the vehicle to a stop right in front of Tower One. Oddly enough, there was no construction crew visible here. Crews appeared to be working nearby, cleaning up debris. Visitors, if there had been any, seemed to have departed for the day as well. Only the local shop owners on the ground remained open. The mega city was getting ready for another night filled with thrill, frills, and delight binging on food, drink, with entertainment and hot bodies for sale, the usual amenities of city nights.

Tracy was troubled. It seemed later than she thought. Embraced within the tall shadows of the towers, dusk was settling sooner than at the surrounding midtown, uptown, and cross-town areas. Eyes straining upwards, she tried to make out details, but from her vantage position, the skyline became ambiguous.

Clad in a smartly-cut black leather jacket with Serpent Slayer flung over her shoulder, determined to challenge anything and anybody blocking her path, shooting one last gaze up hoping, if Hannah was in the building, it wasn't too late, Tracy rushed for the entrance. Her passage was stopped by a couple of security guards. Barring her entrance, one yelled at her, "Lady, what's the rush? We're closed for the day."

"Step aside." Tracy felt extreme defiance. It showed in her demeanor. "Not you," she gestured at him. "Not him," shaking her head, "not anybody will keep me out."

Both fumbled with their sidearms to free them from their holsters. They challenged her, "We'll see about that." With both revolvers aimed at her, to Tracy, it was comical. It became obvious neither had ever been seriously confronted. *Approached perhaps, but challenged? Probably never.*

There was no time for further delay. Two swift sidekicks thrust at both hands ripped the steel from their palms. They flinched at the metallic sounds when the weapons hit the concrete nearby. As she anticipated from novice sentries, their gaze followed the path of the weapons rather than keeping a keen eye on her. One mistake followed another. Before either could comprehend what had just transpired, their ghostly visitor had disappeared. "You see that?" one of them gasped.

After some deliberation, considering the security of their jobs, the other muttered, "Ghost." It would be better not to report the incident than have to face their supervisor with an implausible explanation. Therefore, while one was still trying to figure out how his revolver wound up on the ground twenty some feet distant, the other had already collected his. "Better not report it." Both agreed.

Once inside, Tracy found only the main elevator still in operation. It would take her at least up to the base of the spire. From there she'd find a way to reach the top. It was there where she suspected Hannah was being held hostage. With Specter reporting activity on top and guards below indicating public services over for the day, it was the clue Tracy had hoped for. There was no other place worthy enough for the Prophet to lure her. It'd be the ultimate confrontation between the two adversaries. In spite of years of heated exploits between the two, free world versus Jihad, and though neither opponent had ever faced the other in combat, it'd be a showdown worthy of any fighter. Tracy's only concern was that she'd be too late. There had been no confirmation on Hannah's whereabouts. It was only conjecture, logical deduction on her part. "I hope to God," she prayed, "that I'm right."

The second the elevator doors opened she knew it was the right place. In an instant, staring at multiple faces clutching ready-to-fire submachine guns aimed at her, she realized her reasoning was correct. At once, elation and worry flashed through her mind, elation for a final clash and worry for the safety of her friend. She reacted first. Serpent Slayer went into action before any of the terrorists could pull their triggers. The result was a bloody massacre. One by one, the assailants, in rapid succession collapsed with *Allah* on their last breath. Her eyes, remorseful at such a useless deed, swept across the young faces of lives cut short. "What a waste," she muttered into the silent elevator platform. "Hope Allah appreciates your efforts."

What else was there to console these poor souls? They were trained to become killers before any ever had a chance of growing up to enjoy childhood and maturity.

Enough sentiments, she thought, rushing on, hopeful that Hannah was still alive. Darkness had already set in. The platform was illuminated by emergency lighting, but there was still no sign of her friend, or her captor. With a secure grip on the solid composite framework at the base of the spire, leaning over the edge with strained eyes piercing into the night, Tracy probed the darkness. The platform seemed vacant.

The silence of night was only broken by the distant traffic below. Then, suddenly, there was a slight sound penetrating Stinger's ears. She wasn't sure if it was her imagination or the sounds of the night carried to her ears. She trained her ears towards the sound. Now she could hear it. It was an ever so slight pleading coming from above. It was a muffled cry for help. Spurred by renewed hope, she called into the night, "Hannah!" There was more pleading. It became louder, but there was still no sight of her. Cloaked within the protection of darkness, Tracy cautiously advanced in the direction of the sound. One silent step, then another, extremely aware of her hazardous environment, the darkness, the lofty height, the unpredictable, she gradually inched her way ahead. Then, suddenly, overhead floodlights turned on. An intense circle of spotlight illuminated the prey, "Hannah."

Startled and stunned, as Stinger's eyes gradually adjusted to the brightness, she spotted the shadowy outlines of her friend's shape gagged, bound, and tied to the upper trusses of the spire. It was a pitiful sight to see her friend bound by her wrists and ankles, fixed against the steel girders. She had found his bait. All she needed to do was step forward to free her friend, but she knew it wouldn't be that easy. With senses stretched to the breaking point, eyes piercing the dark, Serpent Slayer at a ready to fire, what came next happened in an instant.

Since her eyes were focused on Hannah, she failed to see the silent motion from the darkness. She was hit by a blow to the right shoulder. It hit her like a sledgehammer. It knocked the weapon from her hands. It landed on concrete with a metallic clatter. Her body instantly retracted into a trained protective posture, but not quick enough. The next blow thrust from the darkness struck her ribcage. Stunned by the sudden attack of a faceless opponent, now weaponless, Tracy suddenly felt exposed, but not entirely defenseless. Blinded by the overhead floodlights, she quickly retreated into the shadows. Whatever was lurking in the darkness would be a worthy opponent.

Taking a few deep breaths, her nerves calmed enough for her to think. Her mind took in her surroundings. She listened into the darkness. Fully composed and prepared, she was ready for battle. With every fiber of her body tensed, poised like a hunter, she waited. From here on, her instincts took over rational thinking. She could feel the presence. Her ears were tuned in to the slightest sound. There was elevated breathing from the dark. The smell of danger was nearby. There was no fear, only two animals stalking each other. She was calculating the odds. Whoever was stalking her wanted her alive. Otherwise, she'd be dead already, struck down by a hail of bullets out of the dark. He wanted to gauge his strength against hers. With all the damages, she'd inflicted on the enemy, it would be a fight for death. She knew she had to be stopped. Only one side could emerge. Halting, waiting, seconds passed, then a minute. Stinger's focus was tuned in on two things: the circle of spotlight in front of her and the spire framework above with Hannah wailing from the distance.

Hannah. The thought spurred her into action. A shadow gradually emerged from the darkness, one inch at a time, followed by one solid step. Stinger matched the advances equally, moving out of the darkness. Contours first, then both faces slowly emerged. There was enough light for plotting shadows on their faces. An instant later, her face filled with utter surprise. Her opponent's face contorted with anticipation. There was recognition. In a split second, both faces changed to hatred and revenge, immediately followed by shouts. "It's you!?"

After years of battling a mystery enemy, the face-off was too much of a shock. It had stunned both. With bodies frozen, muscles unable to react, minds too surprised to rationalize, the two adversaries came face to face. There was no rush now. With eyes staring each other off, mind assessing each other, Stinger deliberately reached into her sleeve, retrieving a knife. *It's what he wants,* she thought.

Slightly surprised at its size, with a slight nod of his head, the once Serpent-turned Prophet approved of the weapon. It was not an ordinary knife he was staring at. Like Serpent Slayer, the knife was just as remarkable. It had been custom made to suit her fingers, palm, arm, and shoulder with a length exceeding most hand-fashioned weapons.

There was a smirk on the Prophet's face when his eyes fell on the blade. Stinger could easily read the expression. *Woman, inferior, second class citizen.* She did not blame him for the culturally diverse thoughts. It was his world. It was a world suppressed for a thousand years. It was a world created for man, controlled by men, and manipulated by them. It'd be the same for her nation if she failed. Today, now, this instant was not a fight over two people's lives and deaths; it was more, much more. It was a battle over two worlds. It would decide and shape the future of mankind. One culture would dominate over the other. It would be a silent battle. Words could never describe the personal suffering, the pain, the anguish both had endured for so many years.

Stinger was sure her opponent had likeminded thoughts. His hesitation to act proved the case. The trigger for the new world was hinged on only the slightest motion. *What will it be? A step forward. A thrust of the knife. Most likely the flinch of an eye.* Battle trained, combat experienced, both were matched in one fashion but totally opposite in another. With two blades extending from his wrists, the Prophet was poised to lunge out first for a combat power strike. Stinger, with youth on her side, upright, exerted speed and agility. Both circled each other, stealthy, feeling out the other's strengths.

There it is. Flinch. Stinger let him have the first thrust. She saw it come a fraction later. His knife shot up in one swift thrust toward her throat.

His attack strategy was close combat swings for cutting, followed by a slicing motion through flesh. The thrust would open the wound to expose the inside tissue. The tactic was to cut a major artery close to the surface. The individual would rapidly weaken, then collapse. Fighting in this fashion was executed swift and fatal. It usually lasted only seconds, minutes at the most. It was a conservation of energy on the combatant's part.

Her attack strategy was different. It was thrust for blade penetration and twist for further damage. It was designed to slow the opponent and cause internal injury. The wound would cause much more suffering. Fatality would be slow and deliberate. But the end result was the same; death would come with one quick and fast and the other slow and painful in her intentions.

The battle was swift when it was the Prophet's turn. It was precise when Stinger struck. Right from the onset it became apparent that the fight would not end quickly. Both were skilled fighters. Both knew how to react and counter in an instant. The only sounds apparent were shuffling of feet, ringing of blades, sharp hisses of breath accompanied by mutterings of insults, followed by another thrust of the blade thrown by one side or the other.

As the battle waged, the scenes kept changing. Starting at the platform below, the opponents sought out one advantage over the next. Initially, aside from the hissing between clenched teeth, each thrust was thrown in silence. Two warrior shadows fighting in silence over life and death, not only between two individuals, but representing entire nations, was an eerie sight. Silence did not last much longer. Wherever there was breathing space, one would enter it with the other in pursuit, chased by screams and shout like, "Take this, bitch," or "Take that, you bastard." Both their strengths were measured back and forth, over and over, again and again. The next stage for battle was one level up, then another, and another, followed with cries of, "For my people," or "It's payback time." Aside from terminating each other, her immediate goal was to save Hannah.

In the Prophet's mind, the sacrifice of her friend meant deepening the wounds. In her mind, saving her friend meant victory that he could not allow. Clinging to trusses with one hand, in between thrusts and slashes, grappling for support with the other, both were worthy opponents. Stinger, although superior over many fighters in past battles, here in the darkness of Tower One, suddenly realized she had found her match.

The Prophet, expecting to manhandle just another woman, so he thought, had also found his equal. No matter how quick and hard he lashed out, she dodged his thrusts and lashed out just as swift. For him, the fighting turned more exasperating by the minute. He realized it would not be the quick victory as it had been in past battles. He had to work for this one. His manhood as well as his energy was being tested. In between thrusts and retreats the thought of perhaps losing this fight crossed his mind. In no way could he let that happen.

Stinger's endurance and stamina was tested as well. Despite the brutal onslaught by both sides, defending and counteracting each other's moves, her strength was an even match to his. "Give up," the Prophet kept taxing. She did not relinquish.

"Never," she responded, leaping yet another level up. Fiercely, but gradually, they battled their way up on the sloping tiers of the Spire, level after level. Stinger's goal was to reach the top first. She had to get to Hannah.

The Prophet's aim became obvious the higher the fight reached. It was to prevent Stinger from saving his hostage. He could not let her live or, worse yet, get freed. He would lose his edge for dominance. He could never admit defeat. Not against a woman. Hissing from between tightly clenched lips, he yelled, "Fucking bitch," into the dark amid another thrust of the blade. "Take this."

"Give up?" Stinger kept prodding her enemy. She didn't have to say much. The situation alone, having to deal with a woman one on one, was enough to provoke him. It was the most degrading position to a Jihad. She kept agitating him. Her self-assured composure and coolness increasingly infuriated him.

Between jumps to further heights, grappling for balance, steadying the fighting body, slashing the knife, degrading her with shouts, cursing, and cussing, he was losing energy fast. Realizing his weakening, he sidestepped Stinger, swung his body up, and, with one final jump, reached the top then grappled hand over hand, hurrying up the final slippery incline. His aim was the hostage. If he could get to her first, he could end the fight. Stinger immediately recognized his change in strategy. Panting and straining upward agonizing level after agonizing level she pursued the chase, closing up inch after inch to save Hannah.

Another few feet and both entered the fully-lit uppermost trusses of the spire. Brightly illuminated within a full circle was Hannah, body securely bound to the steel structure. The only parts moving were her fearful eyes. Petrified to death, eyes frightfully shifting from fighter to fighter, she followed every motion. She knew her time was running short. Seconds, perhaps minutes, away, her destiny was imminent. "Tracy," her muffled voice reached out. "Help me. Don't let me die."

The Serpent was one lunge away from his prey. Short by only yards, Stinger instantly realized she was too late. She could not reach Hannah in time. His knife ready for a final thrust, he was already by her side. In one desperate act, her hand reached out, begging him, "Don't." But her cry echoed in vain. The next second Hannah was gone, sliced to death by the Prophet. Blood squirted profusely from the gash his knife left on her throat. Her once beautiful, always pleasant, life-filled head was decapitated. It was a gruesome sight. It brought back horrific memories of almost forgotten visions, the execution style beheadings, the Jihad deeds for justification.

Hands reaching for her beloved friend's head, now agonized in its final death throes, Tracy's face turned toward the killer. Her stare was filled with vengeance, penetrating his soul forever. With the next blink of her eyes he was gone, disappeared into the shadows of the night. He had escaped once more, but not without Stinger's beastlike scream leaving an everlasting, irreversible damaged wound on his soul. "I'll see you in hell!"

For the first time in years, Tracy broke down and wept. Streams of tears flowed like torrents of rain over the head of a once beautiful person, washing clean the face of her precious friend. Kissing the forehead of her beloved friend, with a slight touch of her fingers she closed both eyes set within a beautiful, now lifeless face, sobbing, "Rest in peace, Hannah. I'll see you in Heaven." She gently placed the head wrapped in her signature jacket to be buried with the remains when the construction crew collected the violated body.

"Time heals all wounds," was a trendy saying. It befitted most suffering. This one, however, would take years to heal, if it ever did. There was no reason for Tracy to remain in the city. Every waking moment here only reminded her of her dear, departed friend, filling her heart with deep regret and sorrow. There was one thing left for her to do. The New York Times headlines reported the following morning: *Late last night, the Muslim mosque, better known as Ground Zero to New Yorkers and its worshippers, experienced an explosion, rattling nearby buildings. All occupants residing and sleeping in the building at the time perished in the ensuing fire. New York fire departments responded to the all-out alarm..."*

ISS

The Russian service module Zvezda, much like Harmony, was floating in close proximity amid the general debris blown apart by HAARP. Its two remaining occupants, Mikhail Toporov and Sergei Budenko, between beating each other to a pulp, bloodied and exhausted much of the time from their forced starvation diet, were calling a truce one more time. Sergei, gazing out the porthole, had noticed something unusual. Amazed at what he saw, he called Mikhail to his side. "What do you see?"

Pushing his comrade aside to gain full view, Mikhail's eyes searched for something unusual. Seeing the sea of debris floating nearby, he became enraged once more. In a hostility-laden voice he said, "Space junk. You blew us apart, you idiot." He blamed their present misery on Budenko. It would have been an immediate trigger for another brawl but Budenko held his gaze, pointing at an object.

"You are the idiot," he shot back. "Can't you see?"

"See what?"

"Harmony."

"What about it?"

"It has moved."

It finally dawned on Mikhail. He spotted it now. Where the American service module used to be close by, perhaps a hundred yards distant, it had changed location, shifted ahead. The only way this was possible was through either internal or external propulsion. Something must have pushed or pulled the capsule ahead. At this point, it was a puzzle to both. While contemplating the mystery somewhat civilized at first before heating up into a verbal frenzy, Budenko forcibly removed Mikhail from the porthole. Sailing across the capsule, Mikhail bounced against the far bulkhead preparing for yet another fight.

Budenko now occupied the porthole. He tried to analyze the mystery. He was taking a closer look, then suddenly shouted, "Look!" He gestured wildly for Toporov to move up close and said, "Wire." Staring through the glass, both spotted the green wire connection leading from Harmony. It then dawned on him. "Harmony is connected to the solar panels. We must do the same." What came after, he was not sure at this time. From their present vantage point, he could only see one edge of the trusses. He needed confirmation. For that, somebody had to get outside and walk in space. But who?

To decide, Budenko was trying to think of a challenge. Where it was easy on Earth, the game of flipping a coin, drawing match sticks, or arm wrestling, in weightless space it presented a challenge. Because of the present conditions, neither one wanted to volunteer. But, in order to have a chance to survive, somebody had to. Oxygen, aside from getting polluted by carbon dioxide, was running low, and so were food rations. Since there was no option, Mikhail volunteered his comrade. "You go." he directed. "You spotted it."

It was decided. Budenko, aided by Toporov, squeezed his body into the only space suit left intact in Zvezda. Because of the shortness of oxygen all around, it would be a short walk. It would be primarily to see where the American service module connected. "If they could do it," he rationalized, "so can we." Next step was the interlock. To their surprise it was functioning. Budenko popped the porthole and gradually inched his way out. He checked the wrist gauge for time. Two hours of oxygen left. Without the safety of a tether, he only dared to partially exit the outer latch. Assessing the connection, satisfied, he pulled his body back into the safety of Zvezda, shut the latch, and excitedly reported, "Green wire ground. We must use green wire."

Mikhail understood. Without delay, similar to what Liz and Walsh had accomplished, they went to work. It was a difficult procedure, pulling the green wire from the back of the bulkhead. Padding had to be removed all around. That alone presented a hazard. The heating and cooling effects from the sun and deep space left the module vulnerable to extreme temperature changes. Regardless, it had to be done. Work diligently continued with cutting connections, pulling wires, and splicing them end to end, fabricating a rig for the required distance. "Hundred fifty yards," Mikhail reported after taking another measurement. He had been spacing out the wires against the cross-section of the module, gauging its final length.

Budenko estimated, "It's enough." With each sunrise, the rays would penetrate pearls of sweat, released from their foreheads, floating inside the module, turning the droplets into brilliantly shining objects. With both exerted measured energy during the work, sweat was mostly from the anticipated spacewalk Budenko was facing again. This time, he knew it would be for life and death. There would be no tether line secured between Zvezda and Harmony, his target. The only lifeline in his hands would be the green wire tied to Zvezda at one end. Once connected, he would figure out the next step. Like Liz and Walsh, it was his turn to cling to life, as little there was left.

Crammed inside the spacesuit once more, Budenko got ready to exit the interlock. Once he stepped outside, the rest would be up to him. Other than closing the hatch, Toporov would be unable to aid in the tasks ahead.

He took a series of deep inhalations then cautiously took the step into space. Clinging to the port hold, he watched the hatch shut tight. He was alone. He suddenly felt the impact of empty space. If it was not for the space station and other debris floating some distance out, he probably would have panicked. The sun-filled horizon in the distance was gradually disappearing. Night was setting in once more. Though he was aware of the immensity of starlight in every direction, it was not enough to illuminate his immediate space. He was faced with an extreme dilemma. Should he wait for the sun to reappear, taking a chance on running out of oxygen, or push off and hope he would connect with Harmony? With limited oxygen remaining, he decided on the latter.

Carefully, so as not to lose the wire uncoiling from one shoulder, he tied one end to the latch hold. He tried to remember the precise position of his target, but without a visible horizon, he felt helpless. There was no turning back. One last deep breath, then he gently pushed his body away from the safety of the module. He was freely floating in space. The only tie to the present world was the thin piece of wire. His helpless body floated toward the darkening body of Harmony inch by inch.

He hated it. From here on out, he would be working by feel alone, using extreme caution not to lose hold of the wire, he pushed off. The sun had completely disappeared beyond the horizon. Space had turned pitch black. Without any references to gauge speed and distance against, he was subjected to the elements. Whatever the outcome, he had to deal with it. His action was completely beyond any control. He had no feel for motion, gravity, or position. All he could do was wait for the inevitable. It would either be having the wire ripped from his hand or slamming into an object in his path. Since prayer was never part of his life, he took to cussing. "Damned HAARP. Damned Baikonur. Damned

ISS." Hearing his own voice on the headset gave him renewed confidence and hope. He then realized he was not cut out for space and continued his swearing. "Damned Cosmodrome. Damned space mission. Damned…" It was then when his head slammed into Harmony. He frantically grappled for a hold. His heavily gloved hand got hold of an object. It was made of solid steel. He clung to it for life.

At this instant, he did not know whether to continue his obscenities or euphorically shout into space. He did the latter but the sound waves traveled through space unheard. He did not care. He was safe. He waited for the life-giving sunrays to reappear. Unable to check the oxygen gauge, he hoped there was enough left. With the first glimmer of light on the horizon, he located the entry hatch and headed for it, then hastily tied the second end of the wire to the dark mass. Gradually, so as not to disconnect the wire ends, he pulled his body towards the hatch. He was inside the interlock. He took a minute, assessing the next move. There was one more obstacle to conquer: the American space crew, if they had survived. Another thought just occurred to him, *Toporov*. He was briefly debating what to do about his fellow cosmonaut he'd left behind. Where he could use his help facing the next step, uncertain as it was confronting the astronauts, he did not have the patience to worry or help his Russian buddy. *Let him fend for himself.*

Careful not to cause any noises that would give away his presence, he undid the inside latch. The hatch opened without much resistance. He was inside. He halted to check for activity. There was none. He then closed the hatch. There was no sound coming from the module. Only the dim glimmer from emergency lighting illuminated the space. He was safe.

Liz was asleep. To preserve energy, both bodily as well as environmentally, Walsh and she had come to an agreement to only work a bare minimum. It would preserve the little food and limited water resources that were left. While there was a glimmer of hope with the scheduled launch out of Baikonur, it might be too late for the two. Muscle tissue, along with their strength, had withered away by now. From now on it was sheer survival. Neither had a clear idea how long until rescue arrived. Though Foster had notified them on rescue progress, from experience, there was no guarantee the thirty-day launch schedule could be upheld.

Since there was much idle time on their hands between sleeping and waking hours, they had renewed their relationship. It created a strong bond for supporting of each other to a possible end. At least they did not have to face it in solitude. The thought having each other made the remaining days of their lives bearable. Despite the old adage, "Misery loves company," it was a comforting thing, being together.

Unrestrained and uninterrupted most of the time, Liz and Kenny became a couple once more. Confined within a cramped space, they tried their best to keep up the romance, passion, and love. They were deeply in love. In their makeshift setting they explored dining out and other romantic antics by creating different scenes from bits and pieces found in storage. One day a scene played out would be setting up at one end of the capsule, the next at the other. There was plenty of discarded material in storage to even change the interior decor. Curtains draped to the ceiling would provide a setting one day; it would be something else the next. As long as it kept them busy, there were no restraints in the relationship. In between lengthy rests, they kept busy with solving issues, creating mental challenges, and using Morse code to maintain contact with the Castle and

Baikonur. Each day, was one day closer to rescue. Their hopes had reached renewed heights. For now, everything was in harmony at Harmony.

Currently strapped to the bulkhead, prevented from floating free, Liz was rudely awakened by the piercing beam of a flashlight. Thinking it was Kenny, with a wave of the hand, she said, "Put that thing away," but the beam persisted in blinding her eyes.

"Don't move," a voice ordered out of the dark. It was more of a restrained hissing sound than a human voice. She did not recognize the voice nor did she understand the reason Walsh would restrain her so rudely.

"What," she started to say when a hand clamped down on her mouth. She was fully awake now, realizing something was drastically wrong. It was then she felt the cold blade of steel pushed against her neck. Harmony was just emerging from another ninety minutes of night. Shadows within the module were beginning to take shape. There was enough light for her to recognize the unexpected intruder. Unable to suppress a sudden shock after recognizing Sergei Budenko, a cry for help escaped her lips. She tried to alert Walsh but the hand pressing down on her mouth prevented her from screaming out. She could only struggle, but that was a losing battle strapped to the bulkhead. She could not free her body from the tight hold of her attacker.

"Shut up," he shot out a warning, tightening his grip on her.

In the middle of struggling, she noticed the weapon stuck beneath his belt. Her hope for rescue immediately sank. It gave him all the advantages. Walsh, awakened by the scuffle nearby, was stirring. Unable to alert him, Liz watched his expression change from a puzzled look to stare of disbelief. He, as well as Liz, could not fathom the sudden appearance of the killer Jihad they had thought killed with the explosion. It became apparent that there was something they had that he wanted. Looking at the emaciated intruder, she didn't need to guess. Food was what he wanted, what they all so desperately needed. With Walsh closing in from nearby, Budenko released the stranglehold he had on Liz. He pocketed the knife to exchange it with the semi-automatic. The Glock trained on Walsh, he slowly retreated a distance.

"Food," he demanded. "Where is food?"

It was the only thing the astronauts were unwilling to give up. It would have to be a fight for death. With palms turned up, both shook their heads, indicating there was nothing left. "No food." Walsh had taken the lead in interacting with the intruder. He was firm about it. Preserving the little that was left and protecting Liz from harm were his foremost concerns. He was gradually advancing on Budenko, but was stopped by the weapon pointed at his face. Buying time, he backed down. *There'll be better opportunities,* he reasoned.

Liz, taking the next initiative, nodded at Walsh, indicating she was in agreement. Where presently the advantage was with Budenko, the overall advantage was with the astronauts. Two against one was a better chance even when there was a weapon. "What is it you want?" Liz reasoned with him.

"Food," he insisted once more.

"Forget the food," she persisted. "What else?"

He kept silent for a time. It was obvious he was trying to sort things out. Liz let him have the time. There was not much else they could do as long as he was in possession of the only weapon on board. They let him have his space as long as he kept his sanity. Both knew he was apt to irrational behavior. The whole incidence with HAARP and the waveguide proved that point.

Walsh moved closer to her. He seemed to have things on his mind. At present, it was not so much about taking on the terrorist. Using reasoning, he was trying to negotiate for time. He wanted to find out what was on Budenko's mind. He did not have to wait long.

"Waveguide," he finally stated. "Need to fix."

There it was. He planned another assault on the nation. Trained solely as warrior against the free world, it seemed the only thing on his mind was destruction. Liz realized it would never stop there. As long as religion was the cause, he and his people's battle for control would go on forever. A thought just stuck her. She gestured Walsh to back off from confrontation at this time. He readily understood. They'd talk after Budenko went to sleep. Sleep would be guaranteed. As tattered as Budenko's appearance was, it would not be long for that. He was nodding off occasionally as it was. The problem he faced was two opponents. He had to eradicate them. He at least had to suspend them from causing harm while he was asleep. Careful not to lose aim, he propelled his way to the storage facility sealed off by curtains. He must have reached a conclusion. They kept watching.

With tie wraps clutched in one fist, weapon trained on them with the other, he instructed Liz to tie up Walsh. She resisted but was subdued quickly by the threat of the weapon. Following a warning to shoot her, she tied both Kenny's wrists and ankles. It was her turn next. Again, she struggled. With both being disabled, there was no chance to defend themselves. He cut off any further resistance with a slap from the weapon into her face. It stunned her enough for him to grasp her hands and securely tie her wrists. Much like Walsh, Liz was helpless. Budenko then towed both to one corner and, using more tie wraps, securely tied them to the framework. It only took a few minutes for him to promptly pass out from sheer exhaustion.

Liz gestured at Walsh. Not to awake the Jihad, he whispered, "What?" Budenko's snoring assured them he was sound asleep.

"He doesn't know HAARP is back in our hands."

"You sure?"

"How could he?"

"You're right," Kenny admitted. "No transmitters on Zvezda. What should we do?"

She wanted to share an idea. "Let him keep busy with repairs. We could even work with him. You know," she hinted, "lend him a hand. By the time the waveguide's in place, rescue will be near." Walsh agreed with a nod. It might just work to stay alive. He'd do anything to keep Liz from harm. He was in full support. Aside from keeping busy there was the other, more pressing concern. "What about the food?"

"You willing to share some?"

There was no contest. "Saving our lives?" he assured her. "Sure."

"It's settled then. For now," she said. "No fighting?"

"No fights."

Both agreed. "Let's wake him."

Budenko was surprised and relieved by the astronauts' gesture to share the food, whatever little there was left. Short on showing gratitude, he kept his distance, but always with a wary eye on them. The weapon was never far from a ready hand. To restore the fragmented space station to a somewhat functional unit again, there was much work to do.

First, Zvezda had to be dragged back to the main structure, the ISS, then secured with whatever materials were at hand. It was no easy task, using only the green wire connection to gently pull the unit into place. It took much time and patience to accomplish it. But time, for whatever resources were left, was on their side. Combining Harmony and Zvezda into one unit allowed for added oxygen, electricity, and ambient resources support. Connected to the main trusses once more, power, electricity, and environmental systems were back in service, if only partially.

With half the solar panels, photovoltaic system, and heat rejection radiators torn off during the accident, only minimal services were back. Computers were functional. Heating and cooling systems were back in service. Communication with Baikonur, ground-based radar stations, and the Castle was back in service. The only shortage was food. It remained as critical as ever. There was one added danger. Beyond joy at being rescued, linking Zvezda to the ISS permitted Mikhail Toporov to join his Jihad compatriot. It was two against two again. It had to be dealt with on a later day. For now, as long as there was renewed hope, promises from ground control, and with the crew busy, differences were under control.

With communication restored, launch command was able to provide not only renewed moral support to the crew, but also to suggest various alternatives to prolong life. One of the suggestions was the recycling of waste product. What that meant was rummaging through the waste lockers for edible items. While on the verge of complete spoilage from time and recent environmental neglect, a wealth of garbage had accumulated over the past year. Baikonur, with assistance from Vandenberg, came up with a bypass fix to chemically recycle, reprocess, and reuse much of the wasted refuse.

Water presented no problem. It'd been recycled and reused over and over from the beginning of spaceflight. Rescue was only weeks away. Hope was on the horizon.

Though the waveguide, with their combined efforts, had been restored to full capacity, unbeknownst to the cosmonauts, the use of it had become academic. Unfortunately for Liz and Walsh, to their great dismay, during communication exchanges with Baikonur Budenko and Toporov were informed of HAARP being back in American control. It was disturbing news. Both had lost their entire incentive for being in space. Their only effort from here on was to stay alive until rescue arrived. Depending on the rescue team, their arrival would determine the ultimate outcome over the lives of the individuals trapped in space. It could swing either way, but most likely only one crew would survive to set foot back on Earth again.

CLASH OF TITANS

Tracy's mind was on her destination ahead, Castle Rock, the Castle, Dad, and a deserving break. It was a total distance of 1776 miles on the map. *Ironic,* she reflected on the number, *the year the nation was born.* It would take close to thirty hours of travel. Unless something unforeseen came up, she could make it in a couple of days. Specter would have her on monitors. Besides, she could always switch the implant to active. She was not in a hurry to push it. *Two, three days,* at this point in time, *it won't matter much.* It would give her some time to reflect on Hannah and the direction her future must take. Deepened with sadness each time she thought of her, the pain of her lost friend grew. "Why do I feel such misery?" she'd asked a thousand times. She had never lost a friend or close relative before. Visions of an immediate past crept into her mind over and over, with victims' dead and dying from the people she had slain, and people killed by the adversary. There were many. Guilt sat in with questions like: *What about their relatives, their friends? Do they feel the depths of pain, losing someone dear?* She was not sure. But, at the end, Tracy justified her deeds with *they're the enemy. And enemies must be eliminated. Or must they? What's the matter with me? Am I going soft?* In her world, there was no room for sentiments. Her world was that of warfare. *My world's a cruel world,* she had to remind herself.

She made good headway on the interstate west. Already in her wake were Allentown, Harrisburg, Pittsburg, and Columbus. The drive was boring at times, with terrain being mostly flat ever since leaving Pennsylvania behind, and the thought of Hannah was mostly on her mind. It would have been so much fun to have her dear friend alongside her for the quest ahead, perhaps for a lifetime. But destiny had other plans. Driven by thoughts like these, she kept pushing on. With the Badlands just ahead, she needed a clear mindset. She had to hone her senses. Danger could pop up at any point. She was prepared.

The outskirts of the next city grew from the distance. "Indianapolis," the city sign proclaimed. *Should I bunk here or go on?* The sun was already setting. She wanted to make it to St. Louis, her first travel milestone, but that would mean finding a place for the night. Shops would be closed and so would hostels and restaurants. There was no rush to go further. She decided to find a place here. "Specter." she called for one last check.

Alex was thrilled his daughter was on her way home. With Rhonda, spending much of her time on the West Coast supporting the upcoming launch at Vandenberg, he'd been the only occupant for weeks. "Go."

"Am spending the night."

"Roger. Next contact…Morning."

"Will do. Out."

Tracy was too spent to even consider dinner. She decided to have breakfast before getting on the way and went to sleep at the next inn. Hostels had sprung up everywhere in the nation. When food distribution had stopped to established places such as supermarkets, hotels, restaurants, and the once popular 7-11s, entertainment, lodging, and dining out had collapsed overnight. The economy reverted back to family orientation, much like in the olden days, the pioneering days. Today, there were no credit cards to call ahead for securing a bed or table. The only barter value traded were personal items such as food rations, ammunition, and other commodities used for survival. Without it, chances were that you spent the night hungry under the stars. More often than not, travelers were turned away. Not in her case. She had plenty of coins which she carried within a money belt. Aside from that, when people recognized her along the route, Stinger was treated as a heroine and forced to sit up for hours telling stories of her personal encounters.

People liked to listen to tales, especially when told by a noteworthy person. Though Tracy was not prone to bragging or boasting, she appreciated the opportunity to exchange news. Where she provided a broad spectrum of information, the local folks informed her on regional events. Most times, for that alone she was offered free lodging and dinner. "We're relatively safe here." Asking for the reason, she was told, "Fort Knox's nearby." It reminded her of the encounter at the Great Lakes she'd had with Norton, Elliott, and the armored infantry not long ago. There were many reminders like it. But it saddened her, because it always led to her lost friend. Tracy was in mourning. She realized it would take time to get over her. Lying awake for hours, she eventually consoled her way into another night of troubled sleep.

Up by sunrise the next morning, after eating a hearty breakfast and bidding her host goodbye, Tracy was back on the road once more. Next stop would be the Castle, unless something unexpected prevented her from completing the journey. She planned to make it all the way back home today no matter how long it'd take. Other than St. Louis and Kansas City, there were no major obstacles ahead. Specter would forewarn her in time. It reminded her. "Specter," she called in. "What's ahead?"

Seconds later, he responded. "Open road. Be careful passing through the Badlands."

"Will do."

Although the region considered the Badlands used to have a terrible reputation for massacres and bloodbaths, with the Patriots gaining ground over the plains, some sort of legal control was slowly reestablished. In contrast, there were many clashes up and down the Mississippi with people trying to cross over. Tracy was about to find out firsthand what the local conditions had in store for her. It was already past noon into her journey when the first warning signs appeared.

"STOP…BADLANDS…ENTER AT OWN RISK," the postings announced. There were many more. Tracy, the free-spirited individual and independent warrior she was, ignored the signs. Somewhat surprised, she reasoned, "Probably for keeping out foreigners." She kept on driving, thinking, "Not bad an idea." Speeding along at 75 mph, her eyes caught a sign just passing overhead. It read, "I-255," and, "8 miles to Checkpoint." Her stomach was making growling sounds. It reminded her to take a lunch break. Where she hasn't had much appetite since Hannah's death, most times she forced some small portions of food into her body, mostly snacks. Still physically worn out and mentally exhausted from weeks of battle, she was looking forward to the break at home. She'd be there by nightfall.

Five more minutes and the roadblock, she remembered only too well, would come into view. To her right, the city's landmark, the Arch, Gateway to the West, was clearly visible. It was here, weeks ago, where she met the honeymooners. Anger welled up again at being reminded of the state of the country, her country. Back then she was angry about being blocked from her journey. So close to home, there wasn't anything or anybody good enough preventing her from driving on. One final bend on the interstate and her thoughts were interrupted by the barrier set up across the road. She had to slam on the brakes to prevent from skidding into the lowered boom. To her surprise, it was not the dreaded Jihad she faced. This time, it was a squad of well-disciplined fighters dressed alike in camouflaged battle fatigues waving her to a stop. Aside from the nametag framing the right lapel, an insignia she was unfamiliar was planted on the left lapel that read, "War Dogs."

What seemed to be the sergeant in command, clutching an M-16 between his hands, strode up to her window and demanded, "What's the rush? State your business."

"Wanna get home."

"Papers."

"What papers?"

"Nobody crosses without orders." He was adamant. "Nobody."

Tracy was taken aback. "Ever?"

"Ever!" It was that final.

There were two words Tracy abhorred with a passion, and those were *never* and *ever*. It instantly made her blood boil. She could feel her muscles tighten. Her chest, waist, and shoulders were beginning to twitch. Her face justly reflected her inner state and so did her eyes. She blew up. "What gives you the right? There's nobody in the world telling me what to do."

Pointing at the lapel on his jacket, the sergeant said, "See this sign?"

"So what?"

"War Dogs," he stated. "That's what."

Tracy was getting more frustrated by the second. She demanded, "I wanna talk to the head dog."

"Nobody talks to him," was the reply.

"Who's making the decision?" She could feel it. The situation was getting heated. It was getting out of hand.

"You saw the signs," he gestured back to the road she came from.

"Now you listen," she spat at him. "Listen carefully. Nobody, not you, not them," she gestured at the squad nearby, "not the other side's going to keep me from going home." A fraction of a second later she punched down on the gas pedal. What happened next was another reminder from the past. Her eyes caught the fleeting movement of one guardsmen cranking up the battery charger to radio an alert to the other side. The remaining forces emerged from the shack, reached for their weapons just as she crashed through the barrier. In the rearview mirror, amid the sound of deadly pings from .223 caliber slugs striking the back of the vehicle, she could see wooden pieces flying through space. She could feel the dual mounted supercharger kick in, Humvee leaping into the air, tires leaving black rubber marks on the pavement, with speedometer reaching top speed. Eyes set ahead, Tracy sped across the Mississippi River.

Approaching the far end of the crossing, it was only seconds later when she slammed on the brakes once more. This time the reason was more sinister. Both legs spread wide, hands up in the air indicating the end of the road, planted across the roadway was one lonely soldier tall in stature, with closely cropped hair, grim faced and unyielding, dressed in a similar uniform to the guardsmen. Unmoving, unwavering despite the speedy mass approaching his way, there he stood like a monument, with sun in the west, his body casting long shadows in her direction, barring her way.

Her vehicle skittered to a halt only inches from his knees. To her surprise, he did not flinch once, nor did his body budge. It became obvious that he wanted her to approach him. Outraged, Tracy jumped from the vehicle. A few paces later she was face to face, boldly staring him down. With the sun in her eyes, him wearing tinted shades, she could not make out his facial features. Her words were deliberate, pronouncing each word. "You are either mad," she said, "or a lunatic."

"Neither," his response was short and smug.

"I could have run you over."

"Would be a first."

Dazed at his calm and unruffled demeanor, she said, "You mean to say nobody's ever tried to kill you?"

"Try it all the time."

Tracy was getting irritated at the unnecessary delay, but also intrigued as well. Unshaken, composed beyond approach, he seemed in complete control over his body and mind. The woman's intuition, or was it instinct, took hold over her. What she perceived were both caution and warning signs, but there was also something slightly familiar. It puzzled her. Finally, curiosity got the better of her. "Who are you?"

"Gatekeeper of the Badlands."

"What gives you the right?"

The smug and arrogant man he was, he mused, "Self elected."

"You know," she replied. "You can also be demoted."

"Haven't met one worthy yet."

"You could be looking at her."

"You...a woman?" He laughed. "Get serious." She sensed he was only toying with her.

They were the wrong words to say, to her anyway. Male, chauvinistic, self-centered, arrogant, patronizing on top of a challenging stance, was too much for her. It immediately brought on a much-suppressed temper. There was no way anybody would get away with such insults. Not at her. Much like he projected, she was fearless. Angered, her face abruptly changed from challenge to fury. She abruptly turned and, in lengthy strides, headed for the vehicle, reaching for the backseat. From there, in one swift motion she retrieved Serpent Slayer and, with determined steps, approached the chauvinist once more. But this time, her face was resolute and she was determined to fight.

Still planted solidly barring her way, he had not moved one inch, as smug as ever. His eyes moved to her weapon and he said, unwavering, "What's this?"

"This," she stated, letting go a warning salvo at the ground, "opens every gate." Bullets hitting the pavement around his feet were kicking up pebbles and concrete dust. He never flinched or moved. With both of his palms turned up, still smirking, he indicated, "See. No weapons."

She warned him again. "I could have killed you."

"We've established that already."

His calm response infuriated her even more. The sound of bullets had attracted a small army.

Watching what must be his personal body of renegades moving in on her, all sporting the same War Dogs patch, she demanded again, "Who are you? What do you want?"

"Told you," he insisted. "Gatekeeper."

"Let me get through," she insisted. There was something familiar about his voice she could not place. With the sun blinding her, she could make out the shape of her challenger but was unable to clearly see his face. Besides, he was sporting several five o'clock shadows. *Must be on mission for days* crossed her mind.

"Not possible."

"Why?"

"It's the law."

"Whose law?"

"Law of the land…Patriots."

She could see by now that no matter what, nothing would sway him to move. "Listen," she insisted one final time. "I'm a patriot much like you. Now let me pass." Among the gathering faces she could only read defiance, fortitude, and determination. There was not one flinch, budge, or motion. Everybody stood solid, including her. It was a standoff in the first degree she'd not faced before.

Her demands only provoked a slight shaking of the head. He insisted, with the same smug grin on his face, "Only through me."

"Lady," one of his warriors approached and cautioned her, "turn back if you wanna live."

"If its fight you want," she called out in anger, lashing out at him, "you've got it." Dropping her weapon, she tried to strike him with a punch but missed his face. To her surprise, he had only moved his head lightly. The rest of his body was still planted to the ground. Another punch thrown by her, then another and more, but she had no striking effect. As trained and experienced a fighter as she was, she could not land one punch. It infuriated her even further. Changing her attack tactic, she switched to kicks. Again, it gave her no advantage. In the fury of things, all she could hear was cheers of applause from the midst of his army who had formed a complete circle around the contestants.

He not once countered her advances. The only motion her eyes perceived in between kicks and punches was his upper body shifting and swaying in between cheering and mocking. Minutes into her advances, it may have been from being mentally and physically exhausted, she realized she'd met her match.

Extremely angered, Tracy lashed out one last time. Straight out, she kicked him in the groin. She realized it was a sensitive area to any man. He proved no exception. Before her foot could even make contact, he'd reached down, grabbed her leg and pulled it straight up into the air. Her body followed. In one continuous motion, her other leg kicked out at his face but missed. Her body somersaulted through the air only to land solidly back on her feet. What she had executed was a complete 360-degree turn, twirling through space in-between a double kick to his body. It was a desperate move executed by only the most skilled martial artists, an all-out throw against an opponent to subdue him once and for all. It had worked in the past, it should have worked now. She had put all of her energy and speed into it, but it failed. Landing on her feet on the other side of him, the sun fully illuminated his face. She reluctantly gave in and said, "You're toying with me." It was then that she recognized his face, "Brooks. Scott Brooks?" Immediately, her anger faded changing into astonishment and admiration. "What..." she asked but was interrupted.

What followed were challenges from his squad. Everybody wanted to get his licks in on her "Let me fight her...I'll take her out." She finally realized her plight. It had become obvious she was a worthy fighter. They all wanted to prove and gauge their personal strength against her. Due to her speed and skills, they wanted to impress their leader.

"Sure you wanna do this?"

"You started it," she faced up. "I'll finish it."

With a slight nod at his protectors, he released all restraints. There was free for all now. Tracy had her fight. It'd be a worthy fight.

Circling like the prey she was, in one quick motion her hand swept over her shoulder, reaching for her back. Tracy drew out the sword strapped to a shoulder sheath. The sight of the formidable weapon made her opponents momentarily freeze. Almost the length of a samurai sword, fitted specially for her strength and body, it was a personalized weapon unlike any other. Hewn into the bloodied solid steel in black lettering, engraved on the blade clearly visible was "Serpent Slayer." She had not wiped clean the remnants from the fight with Jihad.

There was a hush followed by low grumblings among the fighters, when out flew a couple dozen knifes in accord.

Although she was no match for him, the others stalking her in an ever-tightening circle, she assumed, would not be able to match her in fighting skills. Unless they were all clones of him, which would be highly unlikely, she would be able to fend off the lot. She recalled something her dad had instructed her during their many years of martial arts sessions. "When confronted by multiple adversaries," she remembered, "the more the merrier." What that meant in the ancient Chinese martial arts was that one opponent was a fair fight. Two opponents were a challenge. Three opponents might be a threat. More than that, and the odds were with the lone fighter. Reason was, all others would get in the way or have no space to move about. It was through this psychology that she regained her confidence once more.

With odds calculating in her favor, she lashed out her blade in a wide swing. A sharp yell followed. *Now we're cooking,* the fleeting thought passed through her mind. From the trail of blood, the injured left on the pavement, it became obvious her blade had struck home. The others immediately backed away some distance. *Now,* she thought, *the real fight begins.* It would be a fight to which she could relate.

With heightened anticipation and in complete control again, her weapon slicing through the air, she challenged her aggressors, "Come on." She egged them on. "Whatcha waiting for?" From here on it would be one on one, more or less. And so, the fighting began. It was not as much as a fight over life and death. It was a fight over skills, dexterity, and dominance. Moving in one by one, every one of the fighters gave it a try, respecting her skillfulness in handling the sword. They soon realized she was beyond their capabilities. There were many injuries from getting bruised, nicked, scraped, and sliced. So far, not one had been able to take a piece from her flesh, but they kept on trying until their leader stepped in. "Enough."

His squad backed off, inspecting the damages on arms, bodies, and torsos. Some wounds were superficial, others were more severe. Tracy, with energy wearing on her, backed off a few paces. The smugness had left his face. She was glad. There was a new presence, that of admiration. "Could have killed you," he mimicked her earlier challenge.

Not without showing a slight smugness on her part, she shot back at him, "Could have killed you—twice."

He replied, with a broad grin on his face, "We've established that already."

Extending his hand, he readily offered, "Brooks, Commander, War Dogs."

Returning his firm handshake, she said, "I'm impressed."

"Heard about you," he further emphasized, "causing all the damages. Your name's all over the country."

One of the injured stepped forward and proclaimed, "You're one lucky bitch that he likes you or you'd be dead."

Tracy was curious about all the fighting for one crossing. "What's with all the killings over a bridge?"

"Enforcing the law," he replied then went on to explain about the severity. Apparently, the Patriot's leader-elect, along with his advisory panel, had created a new constitution. In order to preserve the values, strict conditions existed within the region. But, both knew that no matter what rules and regulations may be instituted, it was only a matter of time before discontent among the citizens would emerge once more. It was the way of man. Mankind, as diverse as it was, could never be content for very long. There were just too many in number. Breaking up the masses into regional clusters might well work, but some emerging leader will always come along and demand more land. The result was that, regions merged, people expanded with growth, and, eventually, one world government was inevitable. "And so," he explained, "the cycle with greed, corruption, revolution, overthrow of government, turmoil, fight for survival, begins all over. At the end of the tunnel, only one thing remains. Hope."

He gestured his people to move on, then turned to her. "Why don't you come with me? I'd like to talk more. Besides, I wanna hear about the east."

A quick glance at the sun made Tracy realize she could not make it home today. Too much time had been wasted with the fighting. She reluctantly capitulated. Where she had lost the fight with him, she had regained immense respect with his crew. With individual strength and honor sorted out, she considered his offer. Only thing was, she'd already promised Dad that she would be there by evening. She'd call him later.

"You knew all along," she challenged him.

"Stinger?" he said. "Had you on monitors for weeks. Implants, you know."

"Why'd you keep silence?"

"Spent time up north. Canada. No satellite feeds. Now you understand?"

Motioning at the Humvee, she invited him for a ride. "Hop on in." He readily accepted asking, "Your work?" He seemed intrigued about the customized vehicle and said, "Will have to get me one of these."

Punching down on the accelerator, he seemed impressed when Tracy demonstrated some of the functions and features of the Humvee. Several turns later they arrived at what appeared to be a base camp housing a small militia. The camp seemed well organized. It contained the customary support facilities expected at a semi-tactical military camp. Mostly temporary, it served several purposes. One, it was mobile enough to break down and move quickly. Two, there was the waterway for mobility. Three, there was a sense of security all around. Four...

Tossing her a bottle, Brooks interrupted Tracy's assessment of the place. "Here," he offered. "Have a beer."

It'd been ages since she'd had a drink. After expending a sizable amount of energy and losing a lot of body fluid from the fighting she gladly accepted. Beer suited her just fine. It'd quench her thirst.

"Tell me," he encouraged her to speak, "what're you doing here. Where've you been all by yourself causing trouble?"

"Trouble's my middle name."

"Got that right," he said. "Whole damned nation knows."

"East Coast. New York City, Manhattan, to be specific. Ran into our adversary."

"Serpent?"

"The one and only. Calls himself the Prophet."

"Really? Changed his title. Take care of him?"

"Got away again."

He noticed that her face took on a mournful gaze. "Why the gloomy face? We'll get him," he promised.

"It's not that. I lost a friend."

"Sorry about that."

Tracy composed herself. She would deal with her loss later. Right now, she faced another personal challenge.

"Why St. Louis?" Her question brought a change to his face. She could detect some hesitation. *Not quite sure yet if he can trust me with military secrets,* she reasoned. He eyed her with certain reluctance. "You mean," he said, "the headquarters?"

"Right."

"Strategic advantages," he offered. "Arch's perfect place for lookout. Busch Stadium, nearby, we use as training grounds. Old Cathedral Museum over there," he gestured in that direction, "assembly hall. Riverfront, gives us quick and easy access for patrolling the waters. Remaining parks and city squares we converted to junkyards."

"Junkyards?"

"It's where I get spare parts for boats and land wheels. Roadways in every direction for quick distribution of troops and supplies. I-64 direct link to Fort Knox and 1st Armored HQ. I-70 for direct access to the Rockies and the West. Mississippi South, easy access to the Gulf. Mississippi North, access to the Lakes. Great Lakes," he explained, "enormous water sources. Fort Knox, untold wealth of gold resources. 1st Armored Infantry Division, mobility in fighting resources. Red Brigade, additional fighting support."

Tracy could not suppress her surprise. "Red Brigade?"

"Yeah. Infantry division made up of nothing but women. My men can't wait to meet 'em."

"Figures," she sniggered. "Hey," justifying their needs he said. "We're only men." She understood too well. Aside from the many confrontations she had in the distant past with Brooks, it turned out to be a relaxing evening. Feeling equal to him, she was able to talk things out without prejudice. Seated on the docks by the river, at times they reclined, watching the stars. Their talks touched mostly on current events such as border clashes, foreign infiltration, international events, and space. Guarded, neither revealed too much information. It kept their social connection alive. When the topic touched on the ISS, Brooks seemed completely taken by surprise. "Your sister?" he called out.

"My sis," she boasted then illustrated the troubles, the battles, and survival accounts Alex had relayed. She saw him suppress a deep yawn. "I'm about ready to crash," he muttered into the quiet of the night. "How about you?"

Near sleep and exhausted, she consented, "Me too. Got an early start."

Reaching out, helping her off the ground, he made the suggestion, "Listen," he said. "Stay awhile."

"Really should get home."

"I'll show you the river."

She considered the thought. Aside from brief ferry crossings over the Hudson River out east, it had been ages since she'd been on a shore, lake, or any body of water, for that matter. "I'll let you know in the morning." For her to consider seemed good enough to him when he bade her a, "'Night."

"'Night," she replied, then promptly fell asleep on the army cot he had provided.

Getting up at sunup next morning, Tracy collected her few belongings. Recollecting last night's talks, she was still undecided about his offer of staying on. She tried to keep quiet so as not to disturb Brooks nearby, but he was stirring anyway. In the morning twilight, she caught his eyes touching hers, then going on, probing the rest of her body. For some reason, she didn't mind. As a matter of fact, she liked the attention. *What the hell?* she decided. *A few more days in the country won't matter. Besides,* she settled, *a trip on the river will take my mind off of Hannah.*

Speeding north on the Mississippi, with winds whipping into her face and tearing wildly at her hair with the speed the craft was flying along, Tracy felt a renewed surge for adventure. But she deserved a long-needed break from combating Jihad, and an extended rest at the Castle would be welcomed. Spending the day with Dad, catching up on things, would be the break she needed. It'd give her the time to think through the next steps she must take. It'd also present an opportunity to work out with her dad. She realized her vulnerability after being beat by Brooks without ever landing a punch or kick at his body. "Must ask him about his fighting secrets," she reminded herself.

The day, however, turned out differently. Stopping here and there, warding off trespassers trying to cross the river, she had a chance to observe Brooks in operation. Stunned initially at the brutality with which he went about fending off intruders, the potential enemy, she was again taken in by his fighting skills. She made several attempts to lend him a helping hand by warding off challengers, but since he successfully managed the combatants on his own there was no need.

Previous to meeting up with him, Tracy thought she was the only one capable of such speed, agility, and power in punches and kicks. Watching Brooks in action gave her new admiration for his capability in personal combat. He was quick. He was powerful. And he was lethal. All focused within one jab or one kick. She'd never seen anyone fight the way he did without taking the slightest hit himself. While she watched, she noticed something strange. Just before making contact with a body, his left eye would twitch and, in one motion from a punch or kick to the body, he would take out the opponent. Death always followed. He showed no mercy if a contender persisted in agitating or further challenging him in a fight.

"What school did you graduate?" she asked him after witnessing several lethal bouts. In his super cool way, he nonchalantly responded, "Self-taught."

"No teacher…No instructions?"

"Nada."

"I'm impressed," she admitted. "Wanna teach me your secrets?"

"One killer on the loose is enough," he offered. "Don't you think?"

"Correction," she countered. "Two."

"Aah yes," he responded. "Stinger." It was a smug response, but touched with a hint of admiration, nevertheless.

Their verbal sparring went back and forth, filled with respect for each other, in between fending off potential intrusions along the riverbanks. The day turned out to be pure joy. It satisfied both of her immediate needs, the thrill of skimming across the water and getting to know the most controversial individual she'd ever come across. During the course of the day, Tracy gained tremendous respect for this lone warrior heralded up and down the Mississippi. *Together,* she figured, *we'd make a dynamite team.*

Watching a wide grin cut across his face confirmed her conjecture even further when he asked, "Stay another day?"

She readily agreed. Whether it was a right or wrong decision, it would be the beginning of a violent relationship.

GAKONA ALASKA

With HAARP back in the hands of the republic, there might just be a chance for the recovery of the nation. Presently in possession of Big Red and her Red Brigade, Foster was trying to talk some sense into her. "Listen," he said for the third time already, "It's not your weapon. It belongs to me."

"Then," she insisted once again, "why don't you come up here and take it?"

The general and negotiator that he was, he had already tried several times to instill some common sense into her. It did not get him anywhere. He was getting angrier by the moment. "Stubborn dyke," he panted into the receiver.

"What?" There was a flurry of cusswords thrown at him, then, "What did you say?"

He quickly realized no matter what his rank he had overstepped his boundaries. "Nothing," he appeased her. "Just thinking out loud."

"Just watch your thoughts," she warned. "I'll cut your balls off." Big Red knew with the weapon in her hands she had him by the genitals.

He knew he had to apologize in order to get anywhere. "Sorry," he offered. "Won't happen again."

"Damned right it won't."

"Now tell me," he demanded. "Why won't you turn over command?"

"Told you," she insisted for the fourth time. "I want this weapon." She then proceeded to tell him her motivation, rationale, and justification. In Big Red's mind, this was the only way things would be made right. It would make up for all the hardship, the unjust, the unfair treatment women had to endure living in a man's world for God knows how long. Here and now was the chance to get equal rights. All she had to do was stand her ground and be firm. For once, it was not only the verbal shit she was used to getting. She wanted something concrete in her hands like a document, a legal draft, a guarantee in the constitution. If there was ever a right time, with the new constitution being written, this was it.

"Tell you what," she summed up the talks. "You send one of your flunkies up here," she couldn't help grinning at her lieutenants listening in, "maybe we talk." Profuse cheering followed among the ranks of the Red Brigade. They were sure they had left their mark on the nation's defense posture. All they wanted was to be treated with respect and equality. "That," the remarkable leader promised her troops, "we shall get. I promise you."

Two days later, with Foster in the lead, the emissary arrived. Stepping foot on Alaskan ground, he could already smell hostility. He was about to voice off his authority once more, *it'll take some doing, keeping the bitches in check,* but held his tongue. He could not afford another war. There was too much fighting in the country already. *How long's it been?* he reflected when led to the camp. *Years?*

Expecting a bunch of wild, misbehaving broads running wildly amid the woods, he was surprised to find that the camp was fairly well organized. His earlier concerns about, "How secure is HAARP?" melted into obscurity. Much like an infantry base, there were campsites, command tents, and auxiliaries, surrounded by sentries securing the facility. Nodding his head in approval, he readily admitted to the blustering host, Big Red, "I'm impressed." With his immediate staff in tow, striding smartly amid catcalls calling for a change, it quickly became obvious how well organized the all-female battalion was.

Festivities awaited him and his staff. He quickly realized he was being hosted and entertained for one reason only, to mellow him down for maximum concessions. For now, he let them have their fun. Makeshift tables had been setup, tree stumps cut for seating, campfires lit, with a smell of roasted deer drifting through the air. *No wonder,* the fleeting thought crossed his mind, *they refuse to leave.* Everything a person needed was right here: *food, drink, entertainment, everything but men, of course.* Realizing that, the shortage of men gave him a negotiating edge. It was men to balance out physical demands. It was the male company he could supply. Though he knew it would be a sensitive topic with an all women brigade, if that's what they ultimately demanded, he would promise them anything as long as he gained control over the weapon.

Regardless of the outcome, he and his staff were being entertained, and for once he totally enjoyed the attention he and his men received. With the nation in shambles, it had been ages since any one of them had attended any festivities. While getting up on age, in his late fifties, he was being wooed and he liked it. It was here he realized how long it had been since he'd been in the company of a woman. Big Red, as belligerent she appeared on the call, turned out to be quite a formidable host. The initial reluctance he felt earlier slowly melted into acceptance and admiration. It might have been the beer, the whiskey being served, or the personal attention, but he actually felt comfortable amid the Amazon and her warriors.

Festivities lasted through the night. Big Red did the right thing. She broke down the male/female barrier presently so prevalent among the ranks. *Integrating might not be a bad thing,* she contemplated while watching her guest pass out from taking in too much alcohol.

Though slightly groggy from last night's celebration, with his body stiff from sleeping on the ground, Foster felt relatively revitalized, invigorated even. Today, he realized, would be all business. It was not long before he spotted his host approaching with her lieutenants by her side. He alerted his staff, "Here they come." Some in the ranks were still absent. "Go," he ordered his aide. "Round 'em up." He knew quite well where they had spent the night, though he did not complain. While keeping his distance, he himself had enjoyed romantic notions surfacing amid the scores of female presences.

Big Red called the summit to order. It was a first since the forsaken freedom of the nation. It would be a monumental landmark to carve out responsibilities for historians to record. Watching the pride and dedication these soldiers displayed to their leader, the general implored, *I may just have a fighting chance.*

"Silence," Big Red called to order. "You all met General Foster," she began. "He's the one that's gonna put you in the history books. A first as such," she went on, "with your support he will command this nation back to the power it once was." She then continued to illustrate the current state and preparedness of her fighting force. "Let's hear it for the general." Prolific cheering followed.

He was genuinely pleased with the way things were going. It was up to him now to demonstrate his willingness as a leader to forge a plan. His gaze swept across the many expectant faces clinging to his every word. "Thanks to all for your support and dedication," he began. "You are an exemplary force any enemy will come to respect and I thank you for it. Now," he explained, "let me give you the state of the nation first." With pointer in one hand, taking a few strides forward, he motioned at a well-worn, marked up field map tacked on a tree.

"Currently," he began, "my temporary command seat is the Presidio, where I have been and will continue to manage the Western sector."

"Wait a minute," Red cut him short. "What about my command center?"

The question immediately put Foster back on alert status. It reminded him to precede negotiations with caution. *This' no ordinary woman,* he reminded himself. *This' a formidable opponent.*

"I'll come to that," he promised. "But hear me out. To get the big picture," he forced himself to take a relaxing breath. "I need to fill you in on the present state of affairs."

"As I said," Foster resumed his position in front of the map. "You and your forces will join up with Elliott's and Brooks' forces currently protecting the Badlands. Beyond these borders is enemy territory. It is my intent," he emphatically stated, "with support from you and other units, to push the confined borders back to the original frontiers as delineated in the New Constitution. That is our goal." Cheering, although slightly reserved, followed his words. The crowd still displayed skepticism about the sincerity of his promises.

"I will take command of all forces," he continued. "My responsibilities, aside from lending you full support, will include commanding the Armed Forces, managing cyberspace defenses, coordinating the ISS rescue mission, and, finally," with pointer encircling the indicated regions, "assurance that we will achieve this goal."

"What about my command?" Big Red seemed to be getting impatient. Her demeanor turned somewhat hostile. She was forcing her hand. Foster was rebuffed with angry catcall from her army.

"Ladies, Please." The second the words left his lips he knew it was a mistake. There were more outcries for ratifications. "We are soldiers…we are fighters…we are the elite." Deliberately approaching his guest, Red defiantly confronted Foster for specific negotiations, the reasons he was here. "This is no cakewalk. Today," she reminded him. "These are no ladies. These are soldiers. This is a formidable army. My army," she claimed. "It can be yours, if you play my cards." It somewhat defused the situation.

Taken aback once more, he hesitantly continued the deliberation. He sidestepped, "Let's look at the other units, our combined total assets."

"1st Armored Infantry Division – Home base Fort Knox, commanded by Brodie Elliott, Command Sergeant Major, Badlands. Elliott will spearhead his forces north and east to push the enemy out into the Atlantic. You," his gaze shifted at Big Red, "will join your forces with him." Approving cheers from the all-female battalion went up in unison. He was sure each one of them had her own reason.

"Eventually," Foster went on. "There will be a unified nation, once more, led and commanded by Rusty Norton, commander-in-chief." You all know the fine job he did forging out the constitution. Once we decide to advance on the enemy, no matter how much of a force we will face, there is no turning back. At this time, the enemy is Jihad with its combined Islamic extremist terrorist forces, centered mostly along the Atlantic coast. There is one additional area," Foster explained, "that of the Great Lakes. It is this area they're most interested in."

"Why?" several of the soldiers wanted to know.

"Water," the general stated. "It's water they want. It's the water they need. It's the water that's gonna be the most precious commodity of the future. We've lost already three of the lakes to the enemy. We must get them back under any circumstance. Furthermore," he affirmed, "there are several strategic areas just as important. Namely, oil fields, national laboratories, and what's left in working order of former military assets. Much of it has already been cannibalized and lost. The rest will have to wait for repair and rebuilding once the nation's back on its feet. Without currency, and with practically no support from other nations, there is not much we can do at the moment. For all practical purposes," he further stated, "we have to rebuild the new nation from scratch to get a currency back. It's gonna be a monumental effort, but it can be," enforcing his statement, "and it will, be done."

There was more cheering and much speculation among the soldiers. Foster gave them a few minutes to digest the information and calm down.

He was ready to play his trump card. It may just sway Red's army to combine forces. "We have a newcomer among the ranks," he continued his delivery. "The name's Scott Brooks. He is a vital link among our emerging forces. Aside from building out an entire fleet of water-based attack craft, he's made it his mission to reacquire much of our transportation assets. Possessions amount to mostly abandoned assets, such as cars, vehicles of every make and model, fleets of aircraft wrecked or unflightworthy at the moment, machinery, specialty shops, artisans, craftsmen, and much more. All in all, between him and Elliott, they have managed to protect much of our industrial resources within the Badlands. But resources," he continued, "are meaningless for the state the rest of the nation is currently in. Without electricity in many parts of the country, everything powered by electronics is worthless. As for communication, a few major satellite feeds have been reestablished, but at this time only for official use. Satellites above American airspace, incapacitated with the EMP strike, still need to be replaced. Without trade currency, it could take more years. Therefore," he concluded his delivery, "it is of urgent importance to drive the enemy from our land."

"Who's this Brooks… Where'd he come from… What's he like?" where some of the questions shot at the general, who was unwilling to comply at the moment.

"Let me just say this," he offered in a mysterious gesture. "There are two kinds of people who have met up with him: very few alive and the rest dead. Supposed to be a super warrior unlike anything that's ever lived."

"Wanna meet him…He's mine…Can't wait to get my hands on him," were some of the calls yelled out by the Red Brigade.

"You'll meet him and Elliott's men as soon as you get on the road. Presently," Foster enlightened the listeners, "he's patrolling the Mississippi, keeping the enemy at bay. Latest rumors," Foster shared with Red's contingent, "say he's been joined by Stinger."

Another onslaught of questioning was thrown at the general. "Where's she from… What's she like?"

"In due time," he responded. "Now let's get on to the rest of the forces. Allen Spencer, in charge of the Condors, self-elect to our national laboratories. He's head of the secret organization."

"Here we go again," someone shouted from the floor. "Secrecy, classified, concealment all over again. It's what brought us down in the first place."

"Now hold on," Foster objected. "There's a place for it. Granted, we," he checked himself to be politically correct. "The government went overboard with spending, growth, and waste. But no matter what you might call it, there is a need for it. It provides for check and balance."

He let them have the moment. After all, he was part of the former government. Where many had retired, been retired or passed on, he was one of few still in business. "This time," he vowed a promise, "we'll do it right. Then there's Ben Jackson at NORAD supported by Alex Bauer at Castle Rock nearby…"

Foster was interrupted, "Wasn't he the one who'd launched the missile on North Korea years ago? Thought he'd retired."

"Retired, yes, but not inactive," Foster replied. "He's connected with the outside world. Besides, his daughter's one of the astronauts trapped on the ISS."

"Wow…Amazing…Better get that woman back," were some of the demands.

"Got a rescue mission on the way," he promised. "Let's get back on track.

"There's one other problem we've got to solve. Derek Wallace, head of the Anarchists, is roaming the South. They've been pirating the region from the Oklahoma panhandle to Baja and everything in between. Into drugs and illegal weapons business, they smuggle everything contraband from Mexico. Rusty Norton's had his hands full keeping his troops clean. But there's always someone daring to break the law when the goods are available. Like alcohol, drugs cannot be eradicated. It's one of man's sustenance. Best we can do's control and manage its use."

"You got that right," someone shouted from back. "Gotta have some fun."

Foster ignored the remark. He knew man's fallacies and weaknesses. Even he, at times, enjoyed a fine glass of wine or a shot of cognac at the dinner table. Alcohol, pot, drugs: *what's the difference? All the same.* Where the results are instant gratification, the consequences are clearly visible in complacency, indifference, but worse yet, lack of individual motivation. He'd seen it many times. But, he was also a realist. Life without some pleasures, as long as it contained some direction, would be intolerable.

"And last, the Naval Fleet," he noted in closing. "All of our former naval fleet's been placed under NATO's administration, based in Belgium for the Atlantic fleet and Hawaii for the Pacific theater namely, Emmett W. Fletcher, Flag officer, U.S. European command, NATO…Any questions?"

There were many. "Who's leading Jihad?"

"A genius," the general replied. "Known only as the Prophet. After Bin Laden's death, a Pakistani mercenary worked himself up the ranks. Tribal-elect, current supreme leader Al Qaeda, Taliban, Jihad, and all other combined terrorist forces. He's taken on the Muslim cause for conquering the world. It's he," Foster stated, "the Prophet," he strongly emphasized, "the snake's head, we must eliminate."

The question and answer session lasted hours. The following day it was decided to break up camp, leaving behind a fighting contingent for the protection of the HAARP compound. With the chance of battle, and men in sight, there were not many volunteers left for Alaska. The unfortunate ones selected were based on the draw of the straw.

"One last item," Foster specified before taking to the road. "I want you at Fort Knox. Five days. Your missions will be assigned there. Now go with God." He had won the negotiations.

ISS

Several more weeks had gone by since the space crews had reunited, though reluctantly and not without friction between astronauts and cosmonauts. Word was received daily about the progress of the impending launch. Back on the ground, preparations were underway. "Korolev Mission Control," the Cosmodrome chief flight controller demanding the final check via the intercom. "Report status." Within seconds, the various command stations reported in: "Power – Go… Telemetry – Go…Attitude control systems – Go…Propulsion – Go…Thermal – Go…Orbital systems – Go…Reentry systems – Go…" It appeared that all control sections were on standby and ready for launch. Gazing around the mission control center, the launch chief, though in a state of heightened anticipation minutes prior to launch, gave the station a once over. Today, much like the former Johnson Space Center in America, the mission center had a quiet, almost casual look in appearance compared to years ago when the Russian Federal Space Agency was supervised and controlled by the USSR and the KGB. Satisfied and relieved at no last-minute system alarms, *Times sure have changed,* the chief reflected during the final minutes of countdown.

Other than the showcase setting visible to mission crews, news media, and spectators, invisible to the outside world was an army of support personnel busy in the background, conducting last minute checks that made the space launches possible. Unsung heroes, if things went well, the thousands of scientists, engineers, technicians, and ops personal busy between contractors, subcontractors, and support staff were in a state of heightened elation. Today was no difference. On the frontlines was a team of flight controllers responsible for manning the individual section stations. Second level ranks were the support teams contained within the Korolev Mission Complex, conveniently situated in the city of Korolyov near Moscow, formerly known as Kaliningrad. Third level was ground control overseeing the physical launch at Baikonur in the midst of the Kazakhstan deserts many miles to the south. It was here, the Gagarin Launch Port 1/5, where today's action took place. The capsule, protruding majestically into the air, sat on top of a Soyuz-TMA[50] anthropometric version, an American technology, permitting interfacing with NASA and Orlan fashioned spacesuit-clad crew members.

Whereas the last U.S. space launches in recent decades had been geared toward the space shuttle orbiter, an airborne spacecraft specifically designed for the International Space Station, the Russian capsule design, aside from its ISS docking capability, in contrast was geared for manned orbital, space exploration, and moon landings. Where the ISS had been the center of attraction for many years, today it was an aging space platform. Most of today's space launches were for placing satellites in orbit and deep

---

[50] Soyuz Spacecraft – Major Components.
Orbital module: Capsule, Docking mechanism, Kurs antenna, Television transmission antenna, Camera, Hatch.
Descent module: Capsule, Parachute compartment, Periscope, Porthole, Heat shield.
Service module: Module, Attitude control engines, Oxygen tank, Earth sensors, Sun sensor, Solar panel attachment point, Kurs antenna, Thermal sensor, Main propulsion, Fuel tanks, Communication antenna.

space exploration modules with focus shifting toward passenger carrying, private space flights. It wouldn't be long before the affluent citizen would be able to spend his vacation in space, at a Moon or Mars colony developed by international resort consortiums.

Back on the launch pad, the Soyuz-TMA spacecraft, the most recent design in Russia's rocketry arsenal, specifically developed for taking cosmonauts into space to link up with the ISS, was hissing and spewing liquid-cooled hydrogen from the bowels of the space monster situated within the desolate landscape in central Asia. Added to previous models were new thruster rockets specifically designed for a softer reentry landing upon the return of a mission. Days ago, the assembled launch vehicle had been moved to the launch pad on a horizontal railcar, after which the space vehicle was erected and a launch rehearsal had been performed that included activation of all electrical and mechanical equipment. On launch day, the vehicle was loaded with propellant and the final countdown sequence began three hours before liftoff time. Presently, all elements were keyed to elapsed time from liftoff. Intensity on the launch pad, as well as back at mission control, was building up in magnitude with the shrinking in time. The well-rehearsed, periodic voice from the launch center was heard over the intercom.

"Liftoff minus 2 hours, 30 minutes."

For the spectators' present, they could see the crew enter the orbital module through its side hatch, used for command crew and operations during the orbital phase of the mission. It would take the remainder of the countdown to check, verify, and validate each and every test component from interfaces, connections, to computers, software, and personnel, in preparation for liftoff. The clock was ticking down rapidly during final preparation phase.

"Liftoff minus 5 minutes." Systems were switched from ground to onboard control.

Securely strapped within the descent module, the three-man space crew was occupied with last minute instrument checks. With checklists in hand, each was comparing the digital readouts with the well-rehearsed instruction sets. Today's launch was for one and one purpose only, to rescue the remaining ISS crew from certain death. The urgency was visible all around. The tower elevator had just retracted to allow the Proton rocket free access to space. Only seconds away, the countdown had been on hold for the final check results. It was "Go" all around.

"...Three...Two...One...Lift off." Soyuz launched. All at once, timed precisely at zero seconds, ignition for the first stage boosters and the second stage central core thrusters occurred simultaneously. A visible trembling surged through the monstrous giant, now only supported by its umbilical cords. It was feeding and receiving automated launch commands. The hesitated delay from the initial gravitational inertia in lift followed. It took precious seconds for the energy transfer from ground to the craft. Gradually at first, then with accelerated speed, the monstrosity lifted off the ground with ever increasing speed and boosted into the atmosphere.

The space crew commissioned for the emergency rescue mission, two cosmonauts accompanied by one astronaut, clad in latest designed pressure suits for functionality and comfort, securely strapped inside the contoured command seats, felt the tremendous tremors surging up from the quad-configured rocket boosters through the three functional payload stages, the service module, reentry module, and orbital module. The most critical stage in the launch, it would take several minutes for the rockets to be depleted of liquid and solid fuels, after which the tremors subsided with weightlessness and silence settling in the capsule. Concurrently, synchronized time pieces and monitoring stations around the globe kept tracking and reporting.

"Liftoff plus 1 minute." All seemed well minutes into liftoff. Computers were tracking trajectory, boosters were supplying kinetic energy, guidance control was updating their inertia systems, telemetry was feeding the array of databanks, and the cosmonauts were settling back, taking pleasure in the spectacular sight ahead. Soyuz-TMA was on its way to rescue the ISS crew. Though only 250 miles up in space, it would be close to 64 hours before docking would take place.

"Liftoff plus 1 minute, 58 seconds." It was 118 seconds after liftoff. The predefined velocity was reached for first stage burnout. First stage booster separation occurred. All four boosters simultaneously separated from the main body, being jettisoned outward to eventually fall to Earth captured through automatically opened parachutes. Second stage rockets kept thrusting the rocket farther and farther through the upper atmosphere. Though accelerating at speeds greater than 4g forces, the overpowering sound and vibration felt during initial ascent diminished with the first stage jettison. The intensity and most critical stage of initial space flight, during which phase the crew was without communication capability, had passed. From here on out, the crew and onboard computers could communicate with mission control once more.

After passing the sound barrier, the interior of the crew capsule turned silent. The crew was able to talk with each other via onboard closed-circuit radio.

"Liftoff plus 9 minutes." Soyuz separated. The third stage engine was ignited. Separation of the two stages occurred from the direct ignition forces of the third stage engine. The third stage engine would be fired for about 240 seconds, then cutoff occurred with the calculated velocity increment reached. After cutoff and separation, the third stage performed an avoidance maneuver by opening an out-gassing valve in the liquid oxygen tank.

From here on, the crew was able to remove their helmets, external oxygen support, and essentially transfer to the orbital module. It was here that the crew would spend in orbit until docking with the ISS. Three days of spaceflight before docking might seem a somewhat excessive duration to the space station only 250 miles up in orbit. The flight itself would take no more than a few hours. The extra time was allocated primarily for safety concerns to the crew. There were many tasks to perform prior to linking up with the ISS. The seemingly excessive time, however, in the near future would shrink with technological advances, modernization in space travel, and commercialization of space flights. For now, the path was set as it had been for fifty years. The programmed orbital schedule was following:

Flight Day 1, Orbit 3.
Engines were fired to begin moving the Soyuz toward the station by changing its velocity slightly with a Delta Velocity Burn #1 or "Phasing Burn."

Flight Day 1, Orbit 4.

Engines were fired again with Delta Velocity Burn #2 for another phasing burn during Loss of Signal (LOS)[51] period.

Flight Day 2, Orbit 17.
Engines were fired one more time to place the Soyuz in the correct position for rendezvous with the International Space Station the next day, during LOS.

Flight Day 3, Orbit 31.
The crew changed into Russian-fashioned Sokol spacesuits, entering the descent module, which contained all controls and displays needed for critical flight activities. The crew closed descent module/habitation module hatch.

Flight Day 3, Orbit 34.
Space crew preparation takes place for final approach and docking procedures. The crew transferred to the habitation module and removed Sokol suits.

Flight Day 3, Orbit 35. Docking orbit.
Station/Soyuz pressure equalization took place. When pressure on both sides of the hatch was equal, the crew opened the transfer hatch to enter the space station.

The rendezvous and docking were both automated, but the Soyuz crew had the capability to manually intervene or execute these operations. Under normal space flight conditions, at least one Russian Soyuz spacecraft was generally docked to the space station at all times. In addition, a Progress supply vehicle and a space shuttle could also be docked at the same time. The station was well supplied with docking ports for all three types of vehicles. Up to three crew members could launch and return to Earth from the station aboard a Soyuz TMA spacecraft. But current space flight conditions were not normal.

Presently, within the confines of the space capsule, finally, after 64 hours of suspenseful waiting, Soyuz, preparing for the docking procedures, was on final approach with Zvezda. With the rocket launched from Baikonur in final orbit, Korolev Mission control was taking over spaceflight and docking controls. Korolev had a clear vision of the space station. Wholly alerted at the sight of utter destruction, modules torn apart with hundreds of pieces of debris floating nearby, the rescue team was instructed, "Make it quick, and…" with the signal fading from mission control, "…be careful." The sun was quickly losing its brightness in the distant horizon. With another nightfall moving in, the rescue mission would be out of touch again for at least fifteen minutes.

Inching its way toward the docking port of the only remaining capsule what used to be a magnificently constructed ISS space platform, lined up perfectly via targeting scopes manipulated through vector jets, the team was ready to manually intervene in case

---

[51] LOS – Loss of Signal occurs with each orbit as the orbital vehicle enters the far side of the globe or backside of the moon, etc.

something went wrong. A final motion toward each closing port, one critical inch at a time, there was the sudden clank of metal against metal as the two capsules met. Seconds later, pressure equalized and the hatch opened, allowing passage of the crew.

Since both capsules and space vehicle and ISS were pressurized with oxygen, there was no need to slip on the bulky space suits. It would be a quick one-way rescue transfer for the crew in peril. Expecting a hearty welcome as was usually the case after a lengthy stay in space, here and now, there was no friendly face to greet the rescue team. Puzzled and somewhat surprised, the crew of three decided to investigate. Leaving the safety of the Soyuz craft, careful not to bump and bang against the sealed capsule's interior, they gradually made their way into the interlock. Grappling their way forward, without gravitational pull their bodies floated weightlessly across the tunnel-like passage ways. Once on the other side of the interlock, there was still no motion from within. The rescue team, in great anticipation at the emptiness, was about to enter the Zvezda service module.

The hatch on the station entry was shut tight. First one, then two of the cosmonauts tried to open the hatch. Twisting and straining against the locking hold did not budge the hatch. It seemed jammed from the inside. "Korolev," the crew chief called in. "We have a problem." Outside of reach of communication at the moment, there was no answer from ground control. He switched to closed circuit. "Zvezda," the commander called locally. "Open the hatch."

After trying and trying again, there was a sudden motion on the inside of the porthole glass plate. A grinning face suddenly popped into view. It was that of Budenko, waving at the rescue team. His face was barely visible behind the glass-covered helmet of the spacesuit. Relieved, but puzzled at the sight since there was no need for the spacesuit, the crew reacted with joyful cheers. In the next second, the cheers went unanswered. They were lost in space forever.

Watching in heightened anticipation, what transpired seconds later was Budenko's face going askew. The cheering grin cast at the rescue team suddenly changed to a face set in harsh determination. It was a determination over life and death, only Budenko knew its purpose. Puzzled with trepidation, it was the last act of which any of the rescue crew was capable. A fraction of time later, the surrounding space exploded into a bloody mess.

On the other side of the interlock, the porthole inside Zvezda, Budenko, aided by Toporov, was engaged with another of his repulsive plans. The confused individual he was, there was only one person he could ever trust. And that was himself. With the rescue mission on its way, he had been feverishly calculating the odds as to his impending future. With his mission, the takeover of ISS, in complete failure, his future would be a failure as well. He faced certain imprisonment, perhaps death, after his true mission had been revealed: A Jihad infiltration into the space mission. He was not about to let that happen.

For days, he had tossed possible thoughts around his head about how to go about saving his skin. It came to him in a flash as soon as the rescue team prepared for the docking. The interlock would be the solution. Relieved from anxiety, he was ready to execute his desperate act. Confiding to Toporov about his plan, they waited for the right moment. The right moment came when the crew of three unprepared, unprotected, and exposed, entered the interlock and hurried to get to the crew in peril as quickly as possible.

With cheering faces on the other side of the porthole waiting to gain entrance, hatch cover purposely jammed by a crowbar, Budenko went into action. It was a desperate action. It was an act only to suit him and his future. In one resolute action, he punched down hard on the button labeled, "Depressurize."

What followed next were three faces turning from welcome smiles into grotesquely distorted grimaces. Within the blink of an eye, he watched their eyeballs pop from their sockets, blood squirting straight out from ears, nose, and mouth as the three bodies exploded. With blood spilled in every direction inside the interlock, his vision was presently impaired by a red-painted porthole. He did not have to speculate on the damages he had just caused. It was instant death. Next, a punch on the second button, "Pressurize," he could hear the stream of oxygen being rapidly pumped back into the interlock. It would allow his and Toporov's passage into the rescue capsule.

During the previous sleep cycle some eight hours before rescue, Budenko, with Toporov's help, had surprised Liz and Walsh while they slept. As part of his plan both were overpowered and tied to Harmony's framework structure, preventing their escape. Though unsuccessfully struggling to get freed, Liz and Kenny were held captive once more. Already a bad omen, both realized Budenko was up to yet another of his deadly schemes. Liz voiced her concerns. "Got a bad feeling."

There was no need to speculate any further. "You're not kidding." Both knew what the Jihad was capable of inflicting. "Gotta get outta here," Walsh agreed. But the immediate events that followed overshadowed further attempts. Cutting tie wraps without a cutting instrument was close to impossible, especially in a badly weakened condition. Chewing free would be a possibility even if wrists could be moved close to the teeth. With both pairs of wrists strapped firmly to the module frame, that proved to be impossible. Both surrendered, hoping for quick rescue. With both unable to follow Budenko's action from their vantage points, they could only listen to the activities taking place by the interlock.

The bad feeling was further exacerbated with Budenko smashing the radio gear just before departing Harmony. He made one more gesture. It would be a lifesaving one. With knife in hand, Budenko turned one final time, bidding his goodbyes. "No hard feelings," was his departing offer as he flipped the knife toward the helpless prisoners. The steel tumbled freely through space, bouncing against the various sections of bulkhead toward an eventual catch by one of the astronauts. It could take only minutes or hours or days, but eventually the odds were in their favor that one of them would get a hold of the cutting tool.

Desperately trying her best to struggle free, Liz yelled, "You'll rot in hell," after the retreating cosmonauts.

"We'll never stop hunting you down," Walsh shouted after them. The next sound penetrating the far end of Harmony was that of depressurization within the interlock, immediately followed by screams seeping in from the outside, re-pressurization, and the metallic thump of the opening of the hatch cover. There was distant scraping, muttering, and shutting tight of the cover. An eerie silence followed.

Ten minutes later, with the next sunrise, a broken-up sound echoed through the radio. "Rescue One. Report in." Strapped securely into the contours within the crew seats, it was time for Budenko to report to Korolev mission control. By now, another dawn had risen.

"Rescue One," the unexpected voice announced over the Korolev intercom. "Budenko here." Then, after another static delay, "ISS and Rescue One crews lost…Two survivors…Budenko and Toporov…Advise."

There was not much advice to offer from ground control other than, "Follow return procedures. Report on reentry…Return flight on automatic controls."

When word got out on international news wires about the two lost astronauts and rescue crew, the world mourned. There was no chance for another rescue mission. Time would be running out. The two beloved and so dearly hailed astronauts, clinging to the desperate chance for rescue, Lisa Bauer and Kenny Walsh, were declared dead by the world. Grief and mourning set in for families, friends, and fellow astronauts alike.

Days later, amid thousands of mourners, their respective governments held official ceremonies, laying the spirits of five brave space travelers to their final resting place at Arlington, VA, and across the Atlantic in Moscow. The same held true for Dieter Fuchs, German, as well as Hiroshi Nagata, Japanese astronauts. As for the rest of the world, space travel and exploration came to a halt for some time to follow. It would be years before much needed newly developed technologies would take hold on the vast expanse of space.

SUMMIT APEX

Five days had passed since the call for summit. Since Fort Knox was built to contain only a certain number of military, it had to expand rapidly to accommodate the additional forces called to action. A tent city was quickly erected in the surrounding countryside. Most newcomers to Foster's army, who had been commissioned, were cramped outside the security barrier. To protect the new republic's wealth, with gold stored at the fort, security was tight. It was strictly enforced by some of Brooks' contingents. Where Rusty Norton was head of state, law enforcement fell directly under Foster's for military and Brooks for civilian jurisdictions. For anyone breaking the law, the end result was just and swift. Where Fort Leavenworth contained criminal soldiers, the few remaining stockades across the nation housed civilian criminals.

Local jails were used to contain temporary lawbreakers within the specific locale, as they had been utilized in the past. With much reduced and revised amendments to the constitution suitable for the present conditions in the nation, legal guidelines were precise and exact. Everybody knew the law. If not, they learned quickly through illicit contacts. Then, there was always the bad apple, the troublemaker, the criminal in every crowd. Nobody wanted to deal with the problem. Special sectors were set aside for it. Those, rather than putting the burden on the region, were sent into the front lines to defend the nation. It was these characters that made up much of Brooks' brigade. The unruly were conditioned through extreme training, where the hardcore were either beaten into submission or terminated by Brooks himself.

He was the one that would shape the individual into some useful instrument. No matter how mean or how bad one behaved, that individual had to go in front of Brooks. No matter what the challenge, he was judge, jury, and executioner. He was fair to judge. He was the jury if someone would not conform. He was the executioner for the extreme cases. It kept him in shape. It kept up his proficiency. It solved the problem. The only outcome to the dissenter, the nonconformist, and the unmanageable was death. Much like in the pioneering days, that was the new law of the land.

Wendell Nelson, former commander for Fort Knox, had been reinstated to be in charge of the fort. To accommodate the rapidly growing forces, he assigned the various regiments to specific sectors. Set up in temporary housing were sleeping facilities, eating places, and restrooms. Also housed in temporary shelters were hospitals, equipment, and supplies. Most prominent was the command headquarters. It was here where the command staff was getting ready for the summit.

Hosting the summit was Foster. Attached to the wall was a map of the nation, representing the original fifty states. Overlaid was a transparent sheet marked up copiously, with colored markings, primarily concentrated in and around the eastern seaboard. It was there where the next battle would be fought. It might not be a final battle. It might only be the first attempt to uproot the enemy. Depending on the strength the enemy would throw at them, it could mean the beginnings of many battles.

"In the past few years," Foster began the presentation. "We were mostly fighting for survival." Pacing in front of the map with pointer in hand, Foster promised, "This is going to change. Combining our forces, with surprise on our side," he further stated, "we'll drive Jihad from the land."

Most of his statements had been complemented by cheering and applause. The further he pressed on, the more energized his forces became. Using the full name for each battalion for the benefit of the newcomers, he summarized today's summit, "There'll be three waves of battle forces initiating our advances."

"Brodie Elliott, Command Sergeant Major, 1st Armored Division, will lead the first wave. His forces will spearhead the armored division directly east as fast and as far as the equipment and supplies will allow. His goal will be the Atlantic coast and everything in between. In the process," Foster pointed at the map, "enemy sectors and cells will be overrun. It does not stop us from advancing east."

"The second wave," he gave full attention to the all-female newcomers, "Big Red and the Red Brigade, will spearhead for Washington, DC." There were cheers of approval mixed in with cat calls from the admirable warriors. From here on, "DC…DC…DC," was the battle slogan for the Reds. Many of the male soldiers around the tables jumped to their feet applauding. It took several minutes for the roaring sound to subside.

"Third wave," Foster gestured at the formidable warrior quietly seated by the table projecting complete self-control, "Scott Brooks." Another round of cheering went up.

The crowd finally subsided enough for Foster to continue. "Like Jihad and its forces have demonstrated their ideology through ruthless actions," Foster went on, "Brooks, likewise, will show no mercy." What followed was more cheering, heightening the already charged atmosphere.

"As already stated," Foster gestured at the legendary warrior, then stated, "Scott Brooks will command the War Dog battalion. He will not only continue patrolling the Mississippi, but will sweep the countryside for pockets of resistance using his newly built, land based assault squadron.

"What about the Great Lakes," Elliott wanted to know. Since he had been stationed in the region, to him, the area was a cause for many of the terrorist problems. As he saw it, it was the reason for the entire Jihad push on the nation.

"We'll deal with it later," Foster stated. "For my success," he insisted, "I need all the forces on the eastern front. The main objective here," he maintained, "is to rid the nation of anybody showing resistance or causing conflict in our patriotic nation once and for all. As our forefathers stated in the original constitution, the separation of Church and State will become even more important. We, the nation," with a gesture thrown at Rusty Norton, presently occupying the head of the table and returning a nod of consent, Foster emphatically insisted, "will respect any denomination of religion and faith, as long as it does not interfere directly with the republic and its citizens." The cheering that followed lasted several minutes. Foster let them have their day. What he and the country's leadership projected was what every citizen had desired from the onset of the constitution.

Unfortunately, he contemplated over the cheers, *with time, population growth, and commerce with foreign nations, the nation's heritage is subjected to mitigation and dilution of law, tradition, and culture.* Based on historical accounts, those were the bare facts experienced over and over in the expansion of mankind.

With the battle plan forged out and responsibilities assigned to Foster's regiments, the day for retaliation had arrived. It was a formidable convoy spreading out from Louisville on east, occupying interstates I-64 and I-71 headed for the hilly Virginia, Maryland,

Delaware, and New Jersey coastal areas. The 1st Armored Infantry Division's main objective was swooping up any resistance along the path and cutting off everything trapped in between. Brodie Elliott would make sure he had paved the way on and along the major transportation links between Louisville and the coast.

The second wave, the Red Brigade commanded by Big Red, would plow straight east through the Appalachian Mountain range. There was no direct route to head straight for DC. About 600 miles distance, it could take as much as a week for the Red convoy to forge forward on routes I-64, I-79, US-33, and I-66 to their final destination. The route through the Appalachian Mountain range was chosen with specifics in mind. Big Red would be able to recruit many more potential bodies to her ranks. It was this region where many escapees had sought refuge after the eastern cities collapsed. It was the region most suitable for the survival of any individual or group that had sought out shelter.

Once the final destination was reached, it would be her responsibility and pride to take repossession of the once politically charged capital city and its nearby naval establishment, Baltimore, MD. Between the two cities, much of the eastern waterways would be in Big Red's control. Once again, it would be the capital city, but under new stewardship, a patriotic nation, the New Republic.

Last in the formation but first to depart was Brooks in command of the War Dogs, free to roam up and down the Mississippi, the Missouri, and Ohio Rivers, the Great Lakes, and every channel and waterway connecting to the seas and the Atlantic. Lending support up north would be Duke Wheeler, aka Bad Man, protecting minerals, grain assets, and refinery.

Once the objectives were reached, borders would be locked tight through strictly-enforced immigration laws. Initially, nobody would be allowed into the nation and nobody would be able to leave until things were sorted out through international laws and travel/trade agreements. With the republic on a barter system, it would be impossible thinking further ahead than the immediate future. There was much work ahead to reestablish trade and commerce relations with other nations. Unlike many third-world nations' struggle for democracy, one advantage the New Republic had was it had been accomplished successfully before. It can be done again. This time, however, the reign would be tight, with policies strictly enforced.

MISSISSIPPI CROSSING

Tracy's past few days had been rather chaotic. Life for her had taken a new turn. She had become physically involved with her once capturer and antagonist. She could remember the agony well being detained by him and his CIA henchmen in the Arizona deserts. But the once loathing feelings she harbored against the brute was broken down in the past few days succumbed to need and desire. For the day, it was enough. For a lasting relationship, it would never happen. Her longing for a meaningful relationship filled with desire and passion she had felt for Brian was too great to forget. For now, it was nothing but violence, brutality, and sadism. Whereas her body loved it, even thrived, her mind hated it, but she could not tear herself away. Where the days were filled with exploits, confronted with adversary encounters in and around the region, the nights were just as fierce, but on a one on one battle. Whereas the intensity of their lovemaking was at a height of toxic throws, the resultant satisfactions for body and soul equaled in intensity.

As always, he'd take the initiative, commanding, "Spread it, bitch."

"Give it to me, baby," she'd encourage a thrust of emotions, then another and another into the depths of pure lust.

Bewildered at first at the sadistic exploits, Tracy would complement his lust with equal intensity. At times, when things got too heated, her outbursts would entail violent verbal abuses like, "Ouch…ouch…You're hurting me…You fuck!" It was more trash talk than comprehensible words to describe the need to turn each other on.

Their lovemaking, if such could be called, went on not only once, but over and over, again and again, beyond the bliss of complete exhaustion. That was how Stinger and Brooks had spent the past nights. The nightly bouts were intoxicating to both. Much like an alcoholic or drug addict, it was like each was addicted to the other. They could not get enough. And so, five days went by in a wild ride of ecstasy and agony. Tracy was torn between lust and insatiable desire for him and loathing for being involved and dependent on such uncontrollable desires. She needed to break away.

The night before Foster's offensive was the best and the worst yet. Both knew that their relationship would end with each headed in a different direction. It would be a night they would remember forever. There was no break. There was no time for sleep. It was a night of final battle between two bodies aching for each other. Spent and sore all around, both got up with first daylight, sweaty and smelly from hours of lovemaking, jumped into their respective wear, and headed into the morning dew, leaving a trail of personal scent in their wake. Brooks went on to lead his horde of sea craft pilots to an awaiting battle up north, and Stinger, totally spent of energy but completely satisfied just the same, headed west for Castle Rock.

Alex was thrilled when he saw his daughter on the monitors headed his way. It had been ages since she'd left. Besides, he was worried since she had not called in for the past five days. As a father, guardian, and protector, his concern was understandable. The last he had heard, she was her crossing the Mississippi. Sure enough, there was the call. "Specter," her voice chimed into his weary ears. "Come in."

"Go."

"Be there by nightfall…Keep channel open."

"Will do…Later…Out."

As promised, Tracy showed up at the gates after dark. Downtrodden in appearance, disheveled and beaten looking, Alex led her into the home. Slightly taken aback at the neglect in her appearance, he followed her long strides as she hopped up the stairs, but playing the host, he offered, "Beer or wine?"

"Make it brandy. Need a shower first," her trailing words fading.

Dressed in casuals, looking refreshed, Tracy reappeared thirty minutes later. Wearing a befitting smile, taking the filled brandy glass, he offered, she said, "Napoleon? Treat of the year."

Alex settled in the recliner opposite her while she made herself comfortable on the couch. There was a halting silence with each appraising each other. Tracy's face had changed. The usual softness of the beauty in her face had turned into a determined, resolute, almost hardened feature he was not familiar with, but he accepted the change, realizing the hardship she must have endured. He could only guess the strain on her body and mind dealing with daily encounter with the enemy on top of losing friends along her warring path.

Alex finally broke the silence with, "Sorry about Hannah." He suspected it would open new wounds, but a condolence had to be paid. He hoped it would bring closure with her. She did not answer, but he could see the pain on her face. "Take some time off," he suggested. "Patriots' taken over your fight."

Her eyes finally sought out his, then lingered for some time before stating, "There's Brian and," after thoughtfully shaking her head, "the Prophet's still on the loose." Where Tracy had never suspected her archenemy, the Serpent, being Hammad and Prophet, her principle adversary, in contrast to Alex, lately had recognized similar traits in strategies between the former Serpent and present Prophet, but had no proof to support his suspicions.

"It can wait." Alex knew how important it was for her to succeed. She had set out on a path of hope and anticipation. It was not meant to be. She had tried her best, but the odds were overwhelmingly stacked against her from the onset. One person against an army of Islamic extremist infiltrators was too much even for the best of warrior.

Gazing at him, shaking her head, her face reflected her state of mind when she said, "I've failed the mission."

Alex demonstrated his absolute support when he stated, "Not true. You, my dear," he insisted, "have paved the way for the Patriots. Now," he turned as factual as ever. "Let's look into the future. What are your priorities?"

Her face took on a deep shade of sorrow once more. In a compassionate gesture, she wavered. "Liz needs payback. I have to settle the score. It's the least I can do."

"It won't bring her back."

Defending her boundless wrath, she insisted, "Yeah, but it's something I've got to do."

"I understand." Alex could easily recall the passion and enthusiasm he bore during his younger years when facing a challenge. But, over time and with age, reasoning and rationale now usually won out.

"Okay," he finally conceded. "What's it *you* wanna do?"

"Track down her killers."

"That'd be Budenko and Toporov…Next?"

"Locate Brian."

"Next?"

"Get the Prophet."

"Now," Alex cautioned, "we've got a list. But you realize the danger. Moscow's not gonna be happy about it and neither is Dubai." He was referring to the respective governments. What she hinted at was infiltrating the nations from a covert perspective. With the fame she had acquired as warrior, there was no way any foreign nation would permit her entrance.

She had an immediate comeback. "Who cares? They're all over the map too with spies, and agents, and killers. Besides," she paused, letting her opinion gain weight, "we've had no help from any of these greedy nations. All they've done was alienate us further."

"That might be true," he agreed. "But it won't help international relations."

"Screw international relations." Her head shaking in protest, she asked, "You've gone soft?"

"Not at all," he objected. "It's called 'diplomacy.'"

"Where were the diplomats when we needed them?"

"Time's changing."

There was certain reluctance for her to accept his rationale. "True," she admitted. "But where's justice?"

"Sometimes," he proposed, "to serve mankind as a whole, we have to forgive."

Her next response said it all. "Bullshit," she spat at her dad. "Everybody's out for themselves." Seeing his saddened reaction, Tracy immediately regretted lashing out at him. Regardless, it was her opinion. "It's my fight."

He finally yielded, "If that's what you want, I respect that. I will support you wholeheartedly."

"That's my decision."

"Okay then. Here's what must be done."

Tracy and Alex spent the next several days developing an attack strategy. Aside from the surveillance he would provide, there were logistics considerations. It would not be easy to just cross borders. Acquiring passports and visas legally was out. American travelers were typically banned and had been for years from international travel. She would need full, but unsanctioned, support from friendly nations.

Once the political obstacles had been identified, next would be mission specifics. It took more days to explore potential passages with local support from friendly factions. Immediate logistics to solve were the Atlantic flight; transportation to border crossings; escape routes and backup plans; safe houses and payoff money; currency cash; and information drops. There would be some help from local sympathizers, but that could not be depended on. For all practical purposes, Tracy would be alone and on her own. It would not be the first time. Years ago, during her days working with the NSA, she had been through similar situations a number of times. There was, however, always agency support either from the local embassy or through some covert CIA agents on mission. This time, she would have to solve every contingency on her own.

The plan slowly fell into place. The mission was defined. The date was set. The only essentials remaining were identifying the precise routes, notifying foreign elements, and tracing the respective targets to their last known whereabouts. Primary marks targeted for termination were two Jihad cosmonauts and the ever-elusive Prophet. Stinger, once more, aided by Specter, was highly confident of a successful mission. If succeeding, at least her sister Liz and her friend Hannah would be vindicated.

BATTLE FOR FREEDOM

Over the past weeks, when word leaked about the pending liberation push, the Patriot army had grown to a formidable size. There was no need for draft. Showing their patriotism, volunteers signed up in droves. Unearthed were many of the formerly abandoned military vehicles left in and around the plains to rot. Without fuel, there had been no reason to keep them serviced and combat ready. But, with the call to war, an army of Brooks' skilled mechanics was already at work de-rusting, fixing, and preparing many of the idle troop carriers for roadworthy condition. Equally reconditioned were assault vehicles, light armored field guns, machineguns, and cannon-mounted artillery, with a whole slew of army corps of engineers recruited for building bridges, camps, and fixing roadways. Signal corps were at hand for keeping up communication, command and control systems as much as current technology would permit. With most computer equipment inoperative, the plan was to get signal support through communications links, components from local and wide area networks, such as voice and data networks employing troposphere scatter, terrestrial microwave, and other line of sight related systems, mobile and tactical enough to assemble and break down as quickly as HQ demanded.

For the first few days progress was unobstructed. The army units advanced at a speed allowable for keeping up with forward scouts and bringing up supply lines. The problem was fuel supply. Since most of the army vehicles depended on diesel fuel, a fuel not readily available anymore, most engines had been converted into alcohol-based operation. For that, breweries had been commissioned for processing pure alcohol. Some was industrial grade to run engines; the rest was processed into beer, whiskey, and other form of liquor suitable for the ever-thirsty Patriots.

With forces on the way, resistance was not experienced until the convoy crossed the Appalachian Mountains. Prior to crossing, based on information returned by forward scouts, the army units fanned out north and south. The aim of the northern division was to advance into Pennsylvania then on toward New England. The southern division headed toward Atlanta into Georgia. The central and main thrust of the body kept plowing straight across the mountain range. The combined goal was to encircle the eastern sea-based cities such as Norfolk, Richmond, DC, Baltimore, and on to New York with Manhattan as the final destination. It would be there where much of the resistance was expected. Concentrated in and around Manhattan, the seat of the Jihad faction, as reported by scouts, was suspected to be entrenched at and around the damaged remains of the U.N. headquarters. Chicago, presently occupied capital seat for the Jihad headquarters had to be dealt with later once the eastern seaboard was cleared. Brooks' henchmen would see to it.

Without a formidable resistance front expected from the enemy until the shores were breached, success for reaching their respective goals was anticipated all around. That, however, did not preclude the fierce fighting units the Islamic extremists had at their disposal. Already years into expanding on American soil and without officially conducted population censuses, it was anyone's guess as to the numbers of immigrants settled from both friendly and hostile nations.

Over the past days, Foster's army had grown with each mile, especially when nearing the Appalachians. Tired and weary from years of suppressed living conditions, people were ready to join the general's forces. Due to the lack of time to fabricate uniforms, many came dressed in tattered clothes from years of wear, clad in jeans, sweats, overcoats, and overalls. Every type of wear and tear was invited as long as a weapon was at hand. Some even showed up with nothing but hunting knives. It did not matter. Everybody was accommodated. Additional weapons were expected to be acquired from the slain enemy.

Enemy resistant pockets at places such as Pittsburgh, Harrisburg, Hagerstown, Allentown, Reading, Wilmington, Charlottesville, and everything in between were quickly eliminated by the army. Smaller towns were simply overrun by the varied units with many of the Jihadists left dead. Wherever possible, women, children, and family members were spared and dealt with at a later date after the fighting was over. According to Rusty Norton, anyone not conforming to American law and tradition would be deported. Others, conforming to the law of the land, would be extended eventual citizenship. But that was months, perhaps years away. For now, forging ahead towards Manhattan's shores, more pressing issues were at hand.

Advanced scouting parties returned with news from the various sectors. Crossing the Hudson River was anticipated to be the most difficult obstacle. It was there where Jihad had entrenched its forces, defending its settled population. New York City, right from the onset of the foreign invasion, had been selected as western hub for trade, commerce, fashion, and entertainment. Eyed for decades by the Middle-Eastern cultures, the mega city had always been targeted to be the foreign visitor's new cultural paradise.

Foster, commanding all forces, had just reached the shores of New Jersey, specifically Fort Lee. Located directly at the base of the I-95 crossing, the George Washington Bridge, across the shores from midtown Manhattan, would give him easy access to the Hudson crossing once resistance from the opposite side had been removed or weakened. From a tactical perspective, it was the best battle position for his command. Gathered for the initial assault, he was currently watching his personal communication aid, a platoon leader. Fiddling with the control knobs on the comm unit, he seemed to have difficulty operating the equipment. Waiting for a response from Elliott and 1st Infantry located to the south, the general approached the frustrated soldier with a comment, "Thank God for old technology."

"Sorry 'bout that," the man apologized. The soldier tried his best to get a response out of the box. Under pressure as he was with the general breathing down his neck, the poor guy was getting more and more frustrated by the minute. Only the static sound of white noise emitted was audible. Foster tried to calm the fellow. "Don't worry," Foster said, reaching out at him. "Let me."

That completely startled the young man. *The general helping me?* His thoughts were clearly reflected on a surprise-filled face. Hesitatingly scratching his head, he stepped aside to let the general have a go at it. Kneeling on the ground on one knee, it did not take Foster long to get a response from the ancient box. Getting up, he wiped his hands clean on his trousers, handing back the box and offering the astonished fellow, "Here we go."

There was one thing that could be said about the general—he was not above getting his hands dirty when needed. What the platoon leader forgot was that Foster also was a young soldier at one time. Long ago, as it was, the box presently seated on the ground back then was hot technology. It was the latest in communications used in battles such as the Korean War, Vietnam, and others. The piece, though dated by decades, had been re-commissioned from the storage arsenals of Fort Monmouth.

Located to the south 50 some miles also along the New Jersey shorelines, Fort Monmouth was the Army's principal storage facility, the Army Material Command. Aside from being the nation's largest storage complex housing battle equipment from every war fought since the civil war, at one time it was also the home of the Army's signal corps training center, now located at Fort Gordon, GA. Slated for closure through the Base Realignment and Closure Commission, as luck had it, the closure had been delayed several times. It was here that Brodie Elliott had supplemented the needed communication equipment for the 1st Armored Division.

Brodie, miles to the south, his hands presently on dated equipment, had a difficult time getting a comm link established with the battle front. "Fort Lee," he yelled at the base unit's mic for the umpteenth time. "Come in." Testing out various equipment, trying this and that, his signal platoon had been switching knobs and dials without much luck. Again, nobody was familiar with the outdated equipment. There was one thing about the base that came to his advantage, and that was its unlimited materials supplies.

Being the Army's major storage facility, housed in a cluster of buildings a quarter mile long, manual operation had taken over years ago from a formerly computerized and automated store and retrieval system. Entire mainframe computer systems alongside comm equipment and radio gear of all sorts, shelved for backup and potential replacement parts, were in storage, waiting to be deployed. Many of his soldiers posed the question, "What for?" There was no rational explanation. Nobody actually knew. It was suspected that the dated armory arsenal was kept airtight in mothballs mostly for sentimental value, since nobody ever anticipated technology running backwards.

But today was such a day when the dated equipment came in handy. Locating specific gear presented no problem. The problem was getting it to work. Plugged into DC-powered vehicle outlets, many units sprang to life, but without a handy instruction booklet, operating the set was a challenge. It was not all challenges. There were lighter sights as well. To attract one man's attention, Elliott yelled, "Hey, Rich." He gestured at another row of neatly shelved gear. "Try this one." Hardened from fighting several battles, Rich was one of his senior combatants. The radioman recognized the gear right away and enthusiastically yelled back, "Prick."

"What?" Elliott was not happy about being called a prick.

Surprised at his commander's reaction, the man quickly corrected, "Not you." He reached for the unit labeled AN/PRC-25. "Gear," he explained. It was something Rich was familiar with. Used in the Vietnam War, it was the infantry's primary mode of comm operation. As was customary with soldiers, everything was given a nickname, usually derived either from its fickle operation or more often from an acronym.

Today they lucked out. The gear, transmitter secured within a backpack with base unit mountable to the vehicle, powered up right away. Elliott was handling the controls. Still unfamiliar with some of the inscriptions, he asked Rich, "What's Squelch?"

"Noise suppression."

"How 'bout Retrans?"

"Oh that. Relay comm to the next hop. We'll need that." The radio was designed for front line communication, but, depending on terrain conditions, had a limited radio range at less than twenty miles. For distance and over horizon communication, HF was required. When Rich explained the specs, Brodie's immediate assessment was, "Not good enough. Gotta find something better." Something better would still have to predate modern day sensitive electronics. Anything more recent containing microchips and internal computer chips were destroyed with the EMP.

They eventually located a model more recent but robust and usable. "SINCGAR,"[52] the label proclaimed. It would be suitable for the present terrain and range. Once popular gear, there seemed to be dozens of them stored away. A line-of-sight instrument and as flat as the terrain was along the Jersey shores, the set carried the distance to Foster's command position. Communication had been the only restraint against moving forward. With the last element in place, Foster's forces could move ahead.

---

[52] Single Channel Ground and Airborne Radio System

STINGER

Where do I begin? It had probably been the most popular question posed by any immigrant. Though Tracy did not fall into this category, it was her first visit to—*what did Dad call it*? "Oddball Nation." *Why Oddball?* she'd asked. He had to reach back into history to give her a sensible explanation. There seemed to be no clear cut historical account about this vast region of land known as Russia and Siberia. Questions still lingered in her mind: Who had carved out this section of land? When was it created? Who were the original settlers? Its history may have been rich and colorful, dictated by noble and cultural measures through stately events hosted by its regal rulers. That imperial epoch, however, was only of recent times of the Czars, the Mongols, and the Huns. Aside from vague descriptions with reference to mystical Viking heritage, what transpired before was anybody's guess. Written accounts on the land were sparse to almost nonexistent in the western world. What did exist were accounts of a nation riddled by famine, hardship, and wars. It was this challenged heritage reflected so much in the people's distrust of today. "In plain words," Dad explained. "They don't trust anybody from the outside world."

That in itself was a powerful statement. It left a lasting imprint on her mind. What about the fear this nation left on the free world? Until today, she could clearly recall the mark it had left on her and the American population. Her entire nation had succumbed to fear instilled by the USSR, especially during the fifty years of Cold War. Pushing the superpowers close to nuclear annihilation on several accounts, having been on the forefront of conflicts with the NSA, she still questioned the political leaders' objectives. With the Cuban missile crisis, several software malfunctions by NORAD, and covert over-flights into enemy territory, driving the nations into the brink of war, were still vividly on her mind. But that was many years ago.

Today, now, on her way to this strange nation, she still mulled over unsolved encounters of distant and near events. With a faked passport in her possession, counterfeit paper currency, and sporty appearance, after a drop off at Miami's shores, Tracy was able to secure passage on a freighter out of Havana, Cuba. Part of the working crew, though there was not much to do outside of laying another fresh coat of paint on the already overburdened framework, her plan was to jump ship once she got close to her destination.

Presently on break, enjoying a salmon sandwich, a popular spread on a freighter, the implant stirred her from the present serenity of ocean swells. "Stinger. Radio check."

"Go."

"Got a lead on the marks," Specter announced. What followed was a string of orders. "Destination Istanbul. Proceed…Rostov…Volgograd…Kazakhstan…Contact—Dimitry Garin."

To keep the connection as brief as possible from being intercepted, terminating the call, Tracy acknowledged, "Over." Not overly surprised at the passage, she had her work cut out for her, nevertheless. The orders meant getting off at Istanbul, taking passage up the Bosporus, crossing the Black Sea to Rostov, and then on to Volgograd near the Kazakhstan border. The early part of the journey would not present much of a problem. It was the border crossing and last 2,000 km to Baikonur she had to worry about.

Istanbul, Turkey, city of cultural diversity, Kasbahs, camels, shopper's paradise, gateway to the unknown, every conceivable scent and sound converged on Tracy's senses as soon as she stepped onto the grounds of this Middle-Eastern mega city. Contrasting between Islamic heritage, Middle-Eastern concepts, Russian influence, and, of late, modern day E.U., the cultural clashing was irresistible to any visitor. To Tracy, the traffic, the incessant noise, the enormity in population, the poverty was nothing new. She had experienced it on numerous occasions when on field assignments to Asia with the agency. To the traveler's senses, bearing an open mind, it was nonstop entertainment. The days were crowded with shoppers and the nights filled with anticipation, expectation in hope of being entertained further. Life was conducted out in the open around the clock. The city was too overwhelming for only a brief stopover. For Tracy, it was a one night stay to make arrangements ahead. "Must come back here," she promised herself.

After a few hours of sleep, she was off to the docks. A ticket purchase in Turkish lira bought her a one-way passage north across the Black Sea. Crowded as every mode of transportation was in this part of the world, Tracy blended in perfectly with the other passengers. She was just one of many tourists making her way to a destination. She even met a Russian friend who was on her way back home to Volgograd. Elena, like many Russians, since the liberation from the communist regime, had learned and spoke English, although not fluently. Talkative and proficient in Tracy's language, she was a treasure trove of information. In her newly acquired company, aside from picking up everyday language terms in Russia, Tracy was able to easily shuttle to the Kazakhstan border. Once they arrived in Volgograd, Elena even invited her to stay with her.

With logistics issues solved for the time being, Tracy was able to enjoy the company of her Russian friend, as well as taking in the beauty of this strange land. The Black Sea region, she was told, had its environmental issues, just like every other water body in the world. Plagued by overpopulation and pollution, it almost followed the extinction trends of the Caspian and Aral Seas not far off from here. Exchanging information, both learned much of each other's country history.

After 2,000 km plus distance, with a three-day journey between sea and land, both travelers arrived at the city by the Volga River relaxed and revitalized. "Come," Elena directed Tracy to her place of residence. "You stay with me." Unlike the majority of urban dwellings in America, most people here were residing in one of endless rows of apartment complexes. Accommodating the rapid growth in the nation, housing structures were plain, humongous in size, dreary in appearance, but kept orderly and organized. Every household had its dedicated responsibility for keeping stairways dirt free, apartments clean, and common grounds groomed. Custodial services were, for most part, shared among the tenants.

Elena's apartment was no exception. Gainfully employed by an architectural firm, she was able to afford a balcony with a spectacular view over the Volga River. Up to here, awaiting further instructions from Specter, Tracy found the journey had been a pleasant experience. What lay ahead would be tomorrow's problem. For now, she enjoyed the pleasant company of her host with offerings of pickled herring for appetizers, followed with a plate of borsht, Chicken Kiev or shashlik (skewered marinated meat), and, based on the occasion, served with a loaf of black bread, black tea, and finished with shots of vodka, lots of them. It provided for sound sleep after a day of political uncertainties. Tomorrow would be a repeat.

Linked to tradition, the Russian did not eat out as was customary in the western world. It was a home cooked meal for most part. Usually a woman's chore, she would visit the local market daily to purchase meats and produce for the day's meals.

Tracy and Elena sat up talking, giggling, and just plain enjoying each other's company. If it were not for the impending mission, life for Tracy, for a change, would be bliss. With each awakening, however, looming ahead was uncertainty. The call came a few days later. "Stinger," the familiar voice drilled into her brain, "Dimitry…Arriving…Central Station…8:00 pm."

There it was. Vacation over. Back to work.

"What is it?" Elena sensed the change in Tracy's behavior after the call. Not privy to the mission, Elena knew something was about to change. Her face took on a hint of concern.

"Have to go."

"Where? Why? Why so soon?"

"Baikonur."

"Nobody goes to that place," was her stunned reaction. "Government…Secret…Off limits," was her truncated response. "You'll get shot." It was a statement of caution.

"Don't worry," Tracy consoled her friend. "I can take care of myself."

After a contemplating pause, "Are you spy?"

Trying to divert the topic, shrugging her shoulders, Tracy laughed out, "No spy. Goodwill tour."

"I come with you. Da?"

"No, Elena," she said. "Too dangerous."

"You are spy."

The statement went unanswered. It was time for Tracy to get going. "You take me to the station?" she asked her friend.

"Of course. You take me with you."

"Elena." There was no more to be said. A quick look of denial shot at her friend was the final answer. Anything beyond would be pestering. A sigh of reluctance by Elena followed.

Elena gave Tracy a lift in her recently acquired economy-sized Yo-Mobile. A small, but stylish, hatchback crossover, even the Russians had sliced up a piece of the environmentally fashioned pie, it seemed. It was only a short ride to the central station. "Please," Elena requested one final time, but was refused again. They had arrived at the station. Elena, a worried look on her face, watched her friend seeking out something and asked, "You meet somebody?" Someone was waiting near the entrance.

Nodding at the person striding toward the car, although reluctant, she answered, "Yes."

"Don't like him," Elena muttered at her friend when the stranger approached. "Russian Mafia." It was apparent from his facial expression that he had been anxiously waiting.

"Tracy?" He seemed anxious to get going.

"Dimitry?" she acknowledged.

He nodded briefly and pulled Tracy by the sleeve of her jacket to a train ready for departure. "You're late," he said, then motioning at Elena, "Who's this?"

"A friend."

"She stays," he commanded.

Tracy shot one last glance at her troubled friend and promised, "I'll be back."

"Bye." There were tears in Elena's lovely eyes when she turned to face loneliness once again.

When Tracy asked about the travel, Dimitry replied, irritated, "Thirty hours." Unlike Elena, this guy did not talk. He seemed to have all the traits of a hired assassin. Secretive, guarded, cautious, hardened features, he must have said no more than a dozen words during the train ride. It suited her fine. Rather than making a new friend, especially one so reclusive, she could concentrate her energy on a plan. From the intelligence Alex had gathered, both Budenko and Toporov were on location. It was the usual procedure for getting acclimated and debriefed after a lengthy stay in space.

It would make it so much easier without having to track them down across this vast, desolate stretch of land. Kazakhstan may have been populated, but it sure did not seem that way from the windows of the train. The terrain did not change much once they entered Kazakhstan. 2,000 some km to the east, near the Aral Sea, would be her destination. Tracy settled down in her private compartment. Aside from the monotonous clacking sound of the wheels going over the periodic spacing between the rails and a slight swaying of the coach, it was relatively quiet in her surrounding area. The first part of the journey would be mostly night time. Without companionship, there was nothing to do but rest. Tracy now wished she had Elena by her side. Time would pass so much quicker. Dimitry would stop by her compartment once in a while to check on her. He invited her into his compartment, but she refused. With Tracy a non-smoker, and Dimitry reeking from tobacco fumes every time he was close by, he seemed an incessant smoker, which was a turnoff for her. Other than snacks offered by some enterprising train vendors, there was not much else available. Magazines sold were all in Russian, she couldn't read.

Tracy woke up refreshed the next morning, form a night of sound sleep. Time passed a little faster with a daytime view of the passing countryside. As expected, this part of the continent was pretty much flat too. Barren, brown-colored wasteland, it reminded her of the American Southwest. The train made a couple more stops along the way. Close to thirty hours into the trip, the conductor announced, "Baikonur. Twenty minutes."

Dimitry showed up shortly after. "Ready?"

It was already late afternoon when the train rolled to their final stop. It was not only the end of her journey, it was also the end of the railroad line. "Come." Dimitry gestured for her to follow. Taking big strides to keep up with his lead, as expected, the city was pretty much built in support of the Cosmodrome. In the distance, her eyes caught the cluster of missile launch pads reaching into the blue skies. There was a reason the site was selected for space launch. At one time a super-secret location, it was built to have no prying eyes around for hundreds of miles. Whatever local tribes had resided around these parts at the time, with industrialization had either been driven off farther into the steppes or migrated to the cities far away.

Today, here, standing beneath the launch towers surrounded by a once desolate region, some evidence of tourism was visible. Straddled alongside the river Syr Darya, not far off, was a light brown colored, star-shaped complex. Striding closer, the sign identified the building as, "Sputnik Hotel."

"It is where officials reside during missile launch," she was told by her mission guide.

Street names such as Gagarin and Korolev in honor of then Soviet space pioneers were indicative of the activity conducted nearby. Aside from being two casual visitors striding along the most famous streets, Tracy and Dimitry planned to keep a low profile during their stay. What had to be accomplished was within walking distance. In and out, as quickly as possible, no trail left behind was the immediate plan. Their goal was a housing complex in view directly ahead. "One minute," Tracy was told when Dimitry stepped into the complex. "You wait."

It turned out more than one minute. He reappeared ten minutes later with a package tucked under his arm. Waiting by the entranceway, a wave of the hand indicated his intentions for her to come close. Tracy stepped inside the hallway. Poised beneath the stairway, he quickly unwound the string holding the package together. Weighed between his hands was what appeared a weapon, looking like something between a handgun and assault rifle. Dimitry expertly showed her how to operate it. "Brand new," he explained. "AK-12." Fingering the selector switch, he explained, "Three firing modes. Single round, three rounds, automatic."

Tracy took the weapon from his hands to get the feel of it, then slammed the 95-round magazine into place. Just recently released, still illegal, untraceable, and untested, apparently it was a new design by Kalashnikov. Though much bulkier than Serpent Slayer, her personalized weapon she had to leave behind, it felt comfortable cradled between her palms. Tucked under her jacket, Tracy gave him an approving nod, then stepped outside. Where she was anxious to get it over with, it was still too early to execute the mission. "We wait," Dimitry insisted. It was not until after two more smoke-laden hours had passed, waiting by the river, when he decided it was time. Not familiar with the living habits of the Russian, Tracy could only speculate on the delay.

She took the time to reflect on the reason why she was here. The hunt for Hammad had taken second priority for the moment. Immediately ahead was the act of vengeance for her sister. This close to the mark, almost forgotten images of Liz surfaced her mind. *How long has it been?* Recalling the distant past of childhood, a happy occasion, a sudden sadness swept over her face. *Why did you have to die?* Lost in thoughts from the past, intertwined with the present, her reflection swayed between grief and hatred for a senseless act. An act executed by a deranged mind only out for hated retribution, driven by religious root. Tracy needed the reflection. It helped her justify her cause for vengeance. "Liz, dear sister," she silently promised. "You'll be vindicated."

The sky had darkened. Day had turned to night. There was no reason to wait any longer. She wanted to get the mission over with. It was only a short walk to the dormitory, the temporary residence of the cosmonauts.

In the Russian equivalent, Budenko currently voiced his anger at his roommate, "Bullshit." Like most days, he was involved in yet another argument with Toporov. Their incessant fighting had not stopped with the return from space. It had continued on, and would continue as long as they had to put up with each other. Completely contradictory in character and habit, there was not one day that passed without squabbling. At least here, before an argument would escalate into a fistfight, one or the other could walk away or step outside. It was usually Toporov who had the common sense.

To appease his roommate once again, with vodka glass in one hand, Toporov toasted at him, "Na Zdarovye" (To your health). With drink poised in midair, he was startled by an unexpected knocking by the hallway entrance. In spite of the late hour, Budenko lifted his weary body from the relaxed atmosphere of the apartment and headed for the door in his well-worn flip-flops, but not without taking hold of the handgun conveniently placed nearby the living room table. The 9mm Lugar had been his faithful companion ever since joining Jihad.

"Da?"

"Landlord."

"Too late. Come tomorrow." His words were already slurry from his daily dose of vodka.

Accompanied by a persistent knocking, the voice insisted, "Now."

Budenko had no choice but to open the door. It was not customary in Europe to have a peephole centered in the door. To see who a caller was one had to open the door. Casually, but still guarded, he unlocked and slowly pried the door open just enough to see the person in the hallway. His eyes took on a quizzical stare at the stranger poised a few feet distance. What he did not expect was the tremendous blow from a kick to the door. The full force of the blow landed against the center of the door, tearing it from its hinges. He did not expect or see the shadowy figure stepping from the dark. Amid splintered wooden pieces, the battered door landed against his body and face, temporarily obscuring his vision. The frame of the wood shattered against his body. It knocked the weapon from his hand. Taken off balance, he flew backwards into Toporov who, trying to rush to his buddy's aid, was taken down to the floor as well.

Too stunned to react from a relaxed-suddenly-turned-shattered atmosphere of a settled evening, neither could act fast enough to get to their weapons when in stepped a stunning looking woman, clad in combat boots, jean-fitted legs protruding from beneath a smartly cut leather jacket, clutching what appeared a Kalashnikov, kicking aside the remaining debris. With the weapon shifting from Russian to Russian, the stranger demanded, "Budenko?" It was Toporov pointing at him. Taking lengthy strides, she promptly closed the distance to her target.

Tracy could have fired to end her torment but she needed information.

Budenko, staggering off the floor, clinging to the wall to steady his body, managed to say, "Who are you?" His eyes had taken on a hated stare. Never in his life had he been so humiliated. It was incomprehensible to have been beaten by a woman even before he had a chance to put his hands on her.

Ignoring his demands, stepping into the room, the second intruder responded with, "Never mind that." Dimitry, his own weapon drawn, trained on Toporov, now stepped forward. He gestured for both to take a seat by the table. It would be interrogation time if information was not given willingly. Extracting information was what he was getting paid to do by the American agent.

During her journey here, Tracy had much time to rethink her position and reevaluate her past, present, and future. She also realized that she had broken past promises to the man she once planned a future together. Although it seemed a long time ago, her memory, with time passage and disappointing relationships, had forged a closer bond with Brian. She suddenly realized how much she missed him. It became even more important for her to locate him. Unable to find him anywhere, she had to assume he had been taken hostage by Hammad. "But for what purpose?" It suddenly dawned on her. "Draw me out in the open. Come to him. Deal with me in his territory." It made sense now, especially since he lost his game plan on American soil. It was the only realistic explanation she could come up with.

At this point, Tracy did not know if, what, or how much these two knew about Brian. All she suspected was the two had rejoined Jihad. She had to assume that rumors about a potential hostage may have spread through the ranks. Regardless, she had to find out. She could only hope they knew something. The end result would not matter. Their days were numbered, if only for retribution for her sister, to avenge her death. She pressed on.

"Brian Harris. Name sound familiar?"

"Do not know." The denial was an indication he was not going to cooperate. Why would he? He was a member of a terrorist group. There was no compromising. It was a one-way path from recruitment to certain death. It would only be a matter of when until Allah and his minions would be sanctioned with another sacrifice. It was the only destiny for the Jihad.

"Brian Harris?" This time, the stranger was more demanding.

"Do not know." It was the same reply. The denial would go on all night unless Tracy demonstrated some example. It came in the next second. The shot landed in one of his knees. Reaching for his splintered leg, Budenko yelled out in pain, spitting a series of cusswords at her, then, "Told you…don't know." The reaction, a mix of hate and pain, caused excess saliva to ooze down both cheeks. He was already a mess before the torture had even started.

It did not matter to her how long he'd hold out. There was still Toporov.

Pulling the trigger again, the second bullet landed in his other knee. Aside from letting go another wild scream, cradling both legs pulled up against his chest, Budenko's face showed more hatred. This time, however, there was a hint of fear.

Toporov, fearing he would be next, held up one hand and spat at her, "Desert base. Sudan."

"Idiot," his buddy lashed out at him. "You just killed us." He was the only one realizing that, with information in the enemy's hands, there would be no reason to spare anyone. He let loose a series of cusswords only the Russians could understand.

Toporov understood the mistake he had just made. In trying to salvage what little there was left of their lives, he begged the intruders, "Please. Not death."

To Stinger, his pleading appeared sincere. Supporting space missions at one time, the cosmonaut-tuned-Jihad might have been a just person. He might have been forced to join through intimidation and coercion. She was not far off with that assumption. Unknown to her, to make Toporov comply with Jihad demands, his family had been detained and held hostage at the desert camp. He was forced into joining the last space flight against his will to save his family from getting executed. He was playing along to achieve the terrorist's goals for getting their hands on HAARP.

With the mission ending in failure, Toporov, now facing imminent death, did his best to prolong his life. "Will tell," he pleaded again. "Everything."

"Traitor!" Budenko shouted at him. He would have strangled his companion if it were not for the shot-out knees.

Stinger posed the next question. "Prophet."

"Dubai…Somewhere…Do not know."

The voice of a pain-stricken Budenko cut in once more. "Traitor." He was grappling to reach for his weapon, resting on the floor nearby, but Stinger stepping forward kicked it off before he could get a grip on it.

"Other base camps," she demanded next.

Toporov rattled off some names foreign to her, which would be recalled later when Specter retrieved the data from her implant database. There was no use trying to get more information on the Jihad cells located around the world. There were too many. Besides, most had been dormant and isolated, known only to local organizers.

Stinger had enough information. "You'll live," she appeased Toporov and, the same instant, pointed the weapon at Budenko. She fleetingly considered giving him a fair chance to die through hand to hand combat, but too much time had already been wasted. With one single shot to the forehead, she terminated what had been a troubled life for most of the man's existence. Toporov did not need more persuasion. He promptly promised to lead her to the camp. Stinger and Dimitry, with Toporov as involuntary host, occupied the apartment until morning. They caught the first train, leaving Budenko to the local authorities.

The party of three backtracked through Volgograd and Rostov, with a final destination of Istanbul. It would take several days for the team to get new passports, cash, and to make travel arrangements to their next destination, the Sudan.

FORT LEE

Foster's army[53], though largely reduced from a standard army configuration was positioned on all Manhattan entrances on the New Jersey side. Holland Tunnel, Lincoln Tunnel, Washington Bridge, Verrazano-Narrows Bridge to the south into Brooklyn, Tappan Zee Bridge to the north, and ferry landings crossing the Hudson River were all spearheaded by Foster's mobile forces with support from Brodie's 1st Armored Division. The outlying crossings were still moving into position when Foster gave the signal over the radio. "Set your watches. Thirty minutes."

The command was broadcast via HF up and down the ranks. Because of the open structure and vulnerability for a potential loss of the George Washington Bridge, the brunt of the assault was concentrated near the western end of the bridge. The tunnels were a straight forward push. Battalions, platoon, patrols, squads, and fire teams were in position, ready to move. Thirty minutes later, Foster's signal, "Advance," triggered the assault. All at once, an army close to ten thousand strong mobilized across the breadth of the passageways, but the assault did not go as he had envisioned.

It might have been the lack of preparation time, inexperienced commanding staff, hurried preparations to get across the Hudson, insufficient explosives experts, shortage of affective communication gear, but none of the assault teams made it across. Only minutes into the advance, the first indication of resistance became evident with a huge explosion. A fireball equal to a small nuclear charge went off at the far end of G.W. Bridge. It tore one end of the steel-bearing infrastructure to pieces. Between the upper and lower decks fourteen lanes tumbled through the air and with them, half of the forward moving battalion. 212 feet up in the air, falling to their death were five hundred some soldiers, lost in the first minutes of battle. None survived the fall.

Simultaneously, but out of sight, beneath ground level, two more charges went off. Placed almost midlevel inside both tunnels, Holland and Lincoln, the explosions went unnoticed until minutes after they had occurred. Due to the communication blackout within the tunnels, a first indication of trouble to outside observers were armored vehicles

---

[53] Typical Army Command List (other than general Foster's current forces)

Name	Strength	Constituent units	Commander or Leader
Region, theater	1,000,000–10,000,000	4+ army groups	general, army general, five-star *****
Army group, front	400,000–1,000,000	2+ armies	general, army general, five-star *****
Army	80,000–200,000	2–4 corps	general, army general, four-star ****
Corps	20,000–45,000	2+ divisions	lieutenant general, corps general ***
Division	10,000–15,000	2–4 brigades	major general, divisional general **
Brigade	3,000–5,000	2+ regiments	brigadier general, brigade general *
Regiment or group	1,500–3,000	2+ battalions	colonel
Infantry battalion	300–1,300	2–6 companies	lieutenant colonel
Infantry company	80–225	2–8 platoons	chief warrant officer, captain or major
Platoon	26–55	2+ squads	warrant officer, first or 2nd lieutenant
Section or patrol	8–13	2+ fireteams	corporal to sergeant
Squad or crew	8–13	2+ fireteams	corporal to staff sergeant
Fire team	4	n/a	lance corporal to sergeant
Maneuver team	2	n/a	any/private first class

amidst scores of bodies whirling through the air from four tunnel exits on both sides of the Hudson. Immediately following were fiery pressure waves filled with smoke and debris, shooting hundreds of feet in the air, only to spread across the Jersey shores. The sound of the immense explosions followed right in their wakes. Because of the size and severity of the explosions, the charges were assessed in the equivalent of megatons of TNT. For that to occur, experts must have been at work weeks and months in advance placing the charges.

Foster, the battle seasoned warrior he was, was too stunned to act. He immediately realized the error in judgment call by his brigade commanders. He also knew what would come next. In terrified anticipation, he and the fortunate survivors witnessed the horrific events that followed. Seconds after the explosion, an immense flood wave appeared from the collapsed Holland and Lincoln tunnel exits. Much like illustrated through biblical accounts, the ensuing flood waves expelling from each tunnel came sweeping across the countryside, taking with them everything mobile. Armored carriers, troop transporters, howitzers, artillery, tanks, assault vehicles, halftracks, trucks, personal armament, and everything mechanized and human churned violently through water and waves.

What saved Foster and his command was the elevated position he held at the far end of the bridge, two hundred plus feet up at a safe level. Each burst was so violent that nothing could stop the watery onslaught. From his elevated position, he could clearly watch the vortex surging inward. Where air filled the infrastructure used to support the tunnel from within, now fractured and collapsed, an endless stream of water was being sucked into the abyss, creating a tumultuous funnel in mid river. Boats, ferries, barges, and sea craft floating nearby were all pulled into the whirlpool of mayhem, only to emerge on both sides of the Hudson, in Midtown Manhattan on the one side and the Jersey Shores on the other. It would be a vicious cycle until the tunnel break could be plugged up or shored off. But that would most likely not happen for months, perhaps years. For now, lower Manhattan was flooded, uninhabitable, and would remain so for some time. Casualties among the city dwellers would not be accounted for until the flood waters had receded and salvage operations could take over drying up the submerged city.

Body count estimation was in the hundreds of thousands on both sides of the river, Manhattan and New Jersey. Most of Foster's army had been wiped out, and so was Elliott's armored division. Spared was the Red Brigade located to the south, and Brooks' battalion advancing from the north.

It took three days for Brooks and his souped-up river fleet of War Dogs to reach the Hudson River via canals and waterways. When word got to him that Foster's advance on the city had been splintered to pieces, the power of burden had suddenly shifted in his direction. It would be up to him to continue the mission. Where Foster was still in charge, his command was directed from a rear based position until such time as the remnants of his land-based forces could remobilize.

Due to a superior design and power of his command craft, with Brooks in the lead and closely followed by a fleet of customized sea craft, a highly maneuverable regiment of waterborne force, the fleet had just arrived at the base of the wrecked G.W. Bridge. Seated two hundred feet up at the intact end of the bridge, Brooks established direct communication with Foster. From his lofty command, the general had cautioned Brooks on the two water funnels drawing in all floating objects nearby. When the caution call went out, "Stay clear of any spout," some of the heated warriors in the pursuing fleet, as usual, disregarded the warning.

It was too late for them. Whoever came near the watery event edge was inadvertently drawn into the centrifugal vacuum, pulled through the tunnel, only to emerge on one end as projectile shot from a mega-sized, now severely damaged, concrete encased cannon. It took several more warnings from above to avoid further deadly incidents. The remainder of the fleet was regrouped into a more organized unit.

It was decided that Brooks' base of operation would be the partially submerged grounds of the former World Trade Center in the lower part of Manhattan. His attack forces were in position for a first assault on a presently invisible enemy. Any sizeable structure within the city could be a defensive/offensive barrier. At the present, it was anybody's guesses about the force or numbers of resistance. It would be up to Brooks' fleet to flush them out, and he did this with the first assault wave.

Currently under Brooks' freshwater command was nothing like the usual count of cruisers, destroyers, and frigates in a naval attack fleet. At his disposal were much lighter, less armored, but much speedier craft, capable of outrunning everything currently floating on the water. His Navy was a task force sectioned into three groups of five units, each with customized speedboats ranging from light to medium armored craft each manned by a minimum of five-armed seaman and chiefs. Armament was comprised of turret mount .50 cal machineguns and forward mounted .30 mm cannons.

Presently cruising cautiously along the flooded avenues within lower Manhattan, partially submerged street signs with names such as Liberty St., Fulton St., and Broadway slowly crept into view. A sharp turn north off of Fulton brought the task force onto New York's major traffic artery, the famous Broadway, now submerged under water. City blocks were gradually passing on both sides of the slowly advancing armada. Aside from the rustle of water rushing past, the subdued hum of a few dozen inboard engines, fashioned from automobile vehicles, slowly pushed ahead at idle speeds through a city normally occupied with bustling traffic sounds-turned silent. All business had stopped when the water rushed into basements, street level floors, and utility rooms, shorting out much of what little backup power remained in the once thriving metropolis.

Brooks and his vessel pilots were on the lookout. Their eyes were keenly tuned in on any activities in the flooded part of the city. It would be here, extending from lower Manhattan to Midtown, where the enemy was entrenched. His immediate plan was to uproot any pockets of terrorist resistance. Though city based, past reports indicated Jihad forces had sizable water borne forces themselves. Modern day attack cruisers had been seen skimming along eastern waterways for years. Witness accounts, carried reports of hijacked freighters, patriotic resistance clashes, and, more essential to survival, the ransacking of locally-owned fishing boats.

It was these atrocities Brooks planned to put an end to. Enemy strongholds were reported, concentrated mostly along the waterfronts from this part of town. Where a number of enemy craft were seen at anchor along loading docks on the south end of Manhattan, their crews would most likely reside in quarters nearby. It was these quarters Brooks and his fleet was presently seeking out. For the first time, he wanted to make use of his implant. It still needed to be tested for battle effectiveness. He switched it on and made the call, "Specter. Come in. Black Knight."

It took some time before there was a response. Up to now, he'd had no urgent need to use the gadget, even with Tracy. But with the tragedy of Foster's losses, and the present danger tracking the enemy, he needed their support.

"Black Knight. Go." Alex's voice came through the earpiece. "State your mission."

"Recon. Lower Manhattan. Need Stinger support. Urgent."

"Impossible," Specter responded."

"Clarify."

"Stinger on assignment. Foreign land. Out of reach." It took Brooks by surprise. When they parted she was headed for home. In spite of the present predicament, his face turned into a wide grin carried by recent memories of wild and untamed lovemaking. "Miss you, Woman," he muttered into the slight breeze carried through town. He expected her to be at the Castle. "What has changed," he questioned himself. "Must be after Brian or the Prophet. Or both," he reasoned but couldn't asked Alex for fear of compromising her mission. He remained quiet because from the distorted picture he received through visuals, satellite coverage must still be impaired in this region. "Get me coverage," he advised Specter. "As soon as you can. Out." For the present, he suspected, he was on his own.

The prowling fleet was presently carried along by swiftly flowing currents rushing in from the west, moving in an easterly direction from waters gushing into the city through the Holland and Lincoln tunnels. Floating alongside the craft, the ungodly sight was clearly visible from remnants of the explosions. Scores of dead bodies, bloated to bursting from drowning effects, were slowly bobbing on and under the surface.

Brooks, in the lead vessel, gave another signal to tighten up formation. "Gettin' close to Union Station," were some of the running accounts made by the crews. They knew the mission but had not been briefed for details. Details would unfold as the fleet floated along the city streets. Up to this point, there had not been any direct clashes.

Slowly passing in the fleet's wake were the remnants of One World Trade Center and former financial district Wall Street. They had just past Canal Street with the next focal point coming up ahead. One of the city's busiest transit stations, the fleet was advancing on Union Square. It was here that the fleet encountered its first resistance. It came in the form of a cluster of torpedoes launched in their direction, followed immediately by a fleet of attack boats occupied by weapon wielding terrorists.

"Fan out," Brooks yelled out, followed with, "Attack!"

It was the signal many had been waiting for. After weeks and months of patrolling the Mississippi, shooting mostly at defenseless swimmers trying to breach the Badlands, this was real action. "Down with Jihad," and, "Long live the Republic," were the battle cheers sounded off in every direction.

The rapidly advancing enemy fleet, lightened by the just released load of torpedoes, came rushing in much like the tidal waves gushing from the tunnels. Closing distance with increasing speed were dozens of streamlined metallic fish, tipped with lethal explosive charges leaving a stream of bubbles in their wake.

The battle for liberating the nation had begun. Whatever craft was not hit by the incoming fish, the first wave of enemy was dealt with much like pirating ships from an epoch past. Each side was out for revenge. Each side was out to inflict the most damaging harm to the other side. Individual craft were seeking each other out for hand to hand combat. Long pent-up frustrations would finally be released through a one on one battle. Each individual, no matter what side, would give his utmost to pay back the insurmountable hardship endured, a thousand years for Islam and, more recently, years of misery in a patriotic cause for a new republic.

The advancing craft took severe damages from plowing into each other during the initial attack wave. Some sank right away where others took on water, floating on for some time before sinking, taking down with-it crew and weapons. Brooks' crafts and crews, for most part, survived the initial onslaught from torpedoes. After making contact alongside each other with weapons of choice in hand, mostly combating knives for individual effectiveness and powers of strength, combatants swung onto each other's craft to battle out cultural detestation and hereditary hatred.

As the fighting raged on, more and more craft joined the waging battle. When word of the battle reached the outlying areas over the ether, mostly HAM and SINCGAR, every friendly fisherman, recreational vessel, and diving boat in the vicinity took to the water. Some, coming across from the Jersey shores, unaware of the vortexes in the middle of the Hudson, were pulled underground by the tremendous water surges. A few, mostly divers with trained and extended lung volumes, landed in Midtown still alive. For the lucky ones would have a tale to spin for many generations to come.

On the battle front, Brooks was in his true element. The one-time-born invalid turned super hero wreaked death and destruction. He showed no mercy. He spared no life. There was only one question he'd pose before striking. "Friend or foe?"

The answer either way wouldn't matter. Most foreigners were unfamiliar with the phrase. Returned was either a blank stare, gaze of confusion, or grimace of hatred. It would only last a second before death struck home. Brooks himself was indestructible. He seemed to have an inexhaustible source of endurance and power. He seldom had to strike twice. It was one kick, one punch, or one slice. Any one would reach its target with lethal effects. The enemy recognized his destructive powers right from the onset. He was pressured in by more and more advancing boats headed his way. Surrounded on all sides, he leaped from boat to boat, inflicting his personal and deadly wrath.

After eliminating one cluster after another, he would chase after a fleeing craft to demobilize the escape. The battle would rage on until every enemy craft and fighter was eliminated, then they moved on to the next potential front. Consequently, Union Square, Grand Central, Penn Station, Times Square, and the other midtown centers of resistances were eliminated one by one. Only one pocket of resistance remained: that of the terrorist headquarters, the United Nations complex. That, however, would require a special strategy. What he had in mind for it would make history. It'd leave an everlasting impression in the annals of mankind.

RED ARMY

On the other battle front, as had been anticipated prior to departing the summit, travel on the comparatively narrow roads headed through the Appalachians took its time. The first segment was relatively effortless travel. It was after crossing into the mountain range that the convoy slowed down, at times, to a crawl. The slowing served two purposes. First, it allowed safe passage on the narrow hilly roads. Second, it took time for word to reach the many outlying towns and settlements spread across the mountain to enlist new recruits to join Big Red's army. There seemed to be no shortage of volunteers. People came in droves. Once word spread, both sexes were hyped up at the opportunity to get the nation back under control. Trucks and pickups all sizes showed up to carry the additional loads. Weapons were no problems. Everybody in this part of the nation owned not only one but several guns. People showed up with automatics, subs, pistols, revolvers, knives and other hand-wielded weapons long and short. Heck, some even carried machineguns on their shoulders, draped and loaded down with belts of .50 cal ammo, enough to kill a platoon.

"Sign up," was the slogan of the day. "Join the Army." Volunteers lined up, young and old, in multiple files, waiting to sign up. At times, despite being surprised at the inexhaustible enthusiasm displayed by townsfolk, there were many rejections, with gestures aimed at recruit's heads. "You…You…You."

"Yep, me," would be the drawled-out response.

It would be immediately countered by recruiters with, "You're a man. You've got your own army. Go and sign up with 1st Armored." Big Red's standing order was, "No male recruits." It was an all-female force and would remain this way. It was her army and no male would ever dominate it. Besides, she had secret notions of dominating the Pentagon, if and once she took possession. A broad smile swept across her face at the mere thought of the possibility only days ahead. Along the route, word had reached the south about Brooks' successes up north. It'd spurred the Reds on to new heights.

The day everybody was waiting for had finally arrived. Striding up and down the ranks to assure conformity and maintain order, "Let's head 'em out," Big Red urged the morning of their final departure from the Appalachian hills.

It had taken three days to process in the volunteers. The rest of the journey would be a breeze, reaching the Potomac. Reports carried back from scouts were that what used to be isolated cells of Islamic extremists had formed into a united front of a Jihad resistance force. DC would be an aligned battle front. Crossing the river would be a challenge, taking the Capital even greater. It would be a "make or break" for the Red army. For Big Red, there was no option. There was no room for failure. "Make" would be the only path ahead. She had worked hard to get this far. There would be nobody spared to achieve what the women had fought for so many years, equality. Equality not only for the general ranks for citizens, but reaching all the way up into the upper echelons of government.

She could already envision the cheering, the prestige, the standing of women among the greats. Visions with leadership in politics, in government, and stratum positions held by Washington, Lincoln, Adams, Eisenhower, and Kennedy passed across her mind.

As predicted, Big Red's 2ⁿᵈ division ran into resistance as soon as it came against barricades set up on the western side of the Potomac River. Every river crossing, between 14ˢᵗ Street to the south, Arlington Memorial, Roosevelt Memorial, Key, and Chain Bridge to the north, was barricaded. If it had not been because the army had tripled its size in its Appalachian crossing, Big Red would be in serious trouble.

Currently behind the wheel of the Humvee command vehicle, as usual flanked by her brigade lieutenants Kelly, Kim, and Mac, Big Red was leading the convoy. After taking the vehicles up and down the frontline, then skirting the western end of the Beltway, assessing the enemy forces, she had just returned to the main crossing near Fort Myer, their temporary headquarters. She was stunned at the fortified bridge crossings. They all were stunned.

"How can that be?" Kelly voiced everybody's concerns. "All crossings are blockaded."

Big Red, angered every time by the sheer thought of allowing the nation to go to pieces, answered, "I'll tell you," she readily volunteered. "Greed… slacking…recklessness. That's how."

When expressing her fury, a shaded wrath was distorting the leader's otherwise amicable face. Stony faced and seasoned from years of career challenges, it was a face, however, that still carried the softness and beauty of a once innocent child. With shoulder length, auburn colored hair gently flowing with the breeze carried through the open window, almond-shaped gray eyes thoroughly searching the terrain ahead, over six feet tall, trained in combat and well-conditioned, Big Red was a formidable woman. Her strength became obvious once she stood erect on her well-shaped, muscular legs. Seated in the command vehicle at present, she looked her part, a leader equal to any battle commander.

Arriving at the temporary command position set up at Fort Myer, located adjacent to Arlington and opposite the Roosevelt Memorial Bridge, the Humvee slid to a hard stop back at the western crossing into the city. Surprisingly, the fort had not been occupied. It could have been because of its limited size and vulnerability against a possible invasion. It proved to be the perfect command position for Big Red. The fort was central to all of the targets the Red Army had set out to conquer. Located directly east from their HQ was the Pentagon. Slightly to the south was Washington National, the city's former, now dormant, air travel hub, all in the hands of Islamic extremists.

Once the two key positions were secure in the Patriots' hands, the army could proceed to cross the river into the capital city, securing its historic landmarks and political seats. To achieve it, nobody at this time had an idea about the effort and time needed. The battle could be brief or it could be lengthy. It could be over in days with a minimum of casualties or could take weeks and months on end, leaving many casualties. At this point, all the command could hope for was a swift and successful campaign.

Back at headquarters, the Brigade leaders had gathered around Big Red to work out the immediate attack strategy.

"Kelly," she commanded. "You take the northern sector." Addressing Kim, she said, "You've got the south. And Mac," she gestured at her favorite lieutenant, "you get the central push. You've got your work cut out." She then addressed the assembly one final time before moving out.

"All of you," were her final orders, "don't give in. Don't give the enemy an inch. Success rests on each and every one of your shoulders. It'll be you that will run the New Republic. Make your nation proud. Now go with God."

Amid cheers of approval, she abruptly turned, collected her automatic, an M-16, and stormed from the hall, leading the three battalions into battle.

BATTLE FOR MANHATTAN

"Fan out," Brooks ordered on the closed-circuit radio. At this point, whatever enemy force was left in the city had retreated to another water-based stronghold. Much like Brooks and his War Dogs were fighting from worthy sea craft, the Jihad forces did too. Streamlined, sizable, Italian-made speedboats converted into attack craft, the enemy had speed and torpedoes on its side. Brooks and his fleet were limited to salvaged, homogenous, with spare parts, built craft. His advantage was years of attack, assault, and retreat along America's largest riverbeds. His advantage was tactical skills and experience.

Presently leading the fleet in stealth mode, he shot another glance at the geological map tacked to the bulkhead. It was a map of the city. He was mostly interested in the ground terrain of lower Manhattan. Based on submerged ground elevation, his fleet would be running out of water depth shortly. The only possible defense block for the enemy craft left would be the U.N. complex. After that, 48th Street and north of it would be above water level. Skirting along the East River, that was the direction he was currently headed. The body of water embracing Manhattan to the east was relatively quiet. When the shooting had begun in lower Manhattan days ago, whatever sea traffic remained on this part were barges delivering their cargo laden with mostly foodstuff and provisions to the city dwellers and businesses, mostly foreign occupation.

Brooks' strategy was to draw the enemy from its stronghold. It was the open water where he had the advantage. If not, he would have to attack the buildings. It would be a last resort. A fight drawn into the depths of the United Nations complex would cause excessive casualties. It'd meant fighting his way floor to floor and room to room. There were always heavy casualties in such a strategy. It was still early in the day. The craft had been refueled. The War Dogs were prepared for yet another battle, perhaps the final one. He could read it in his people's faces. One more hurdle, one more battle, one more fight would bring them closer to freedom, a forsaken freedom close to being redeemed. It would be only a matter of minutes now for a long overdue fury to be unleashed on the enemy.

"Hold formation," his voice echoed above the throttled drone of the engines once more. Due to the limited numbers of Brooks' task forces, the battle strategy was for three task units to attack from three different fronts. Task Group South would swoop in on 42nd Street. Task Group North would approach from 48th Street. Task Group Central, with Brooks in command, would take the central route straight in from the East River front. The battle front was anticipated to embrace 1st Avenue on the far opposite end of the U.N. complex.

Brooks was currently scanning the U.N. waterfront for activities while his task forces fanned into position. He spotted sporadic movement within the building. Shadowy figures were dodging in and out from behind windows. The attack would approach simultaneously from three directions, swooping in on the garage port levels. The first wave would take out communication to the complex, the large microwave dish prominently located on the southern edge of the grounds. His tactical team South would take care of it. He took one last glance at the sky—the sun was directly overhead; it was time.

"Advance," Brooks gave the command. "All units."

A sudden roar surged through the noon hour. The sound reverberated up and down Manhattan's midtown streets and avenues alike. On the approach was a combination of hundreds of hyped-up advancing seamen amid the pitch of dozens of souped-up sea craft engines. The surge from revving propellers cutting through water threw up swells of waves rushing out south, north, and onward, gradually being absorbed by the East River. What approached the enemy was a wall of water-spewing attack craft manned by battle-seasoned, gun-wielding War Dogs ready to tear the complex apart.

As soon as the first wave of the armada rushed in, fire opened up from above across all lower levels first, second, and third windows and balconies. The fleet was drawn into battle, swerving around a hail of bullets coming their way. It was a gauntlet run from the East River's edge to the base of the building complex Brooks and his fleet had never before experienced. Rushing into the carport levels at full throttle, most attack craft made it without losses other than splintered and chipped body damages from direct bullet impacts to the hulls.

Once in the safety of the complex, past the first level defense, the fleet slowed to stealth mode. To his surprise, there seemed to be no onrush or immediate counterattack from the enemy's fleet. It spurred Brooks' inborn warning signals to action. He sensed something was not right. It could be a trap. He recognized the signals from past encounters. It was the terrorist's strategy to draw the enemy into battle. Regardless, he had to take a chance. There was no other way to converge on the buildings. His fleet would have to cover the space ahead at full speed. It wasn't Brooks' first choice, but he would have to do it to engage the enemy head on.

The flooded car port level was his target approach. Sure enough, the enemy forces were waiting. A combined front of fiery hail, mostly from AK-47 automatics, opened up from above as soon as Brooks' fleet approached the complex. Brooks' task force[54] ran straight into the wall of fire. Anticipating such an attack, Brooks had the foresight to install bulletproof windshields. All of his crews made it through the first fiery onslaught. Once inside, the shooting stopped. Aside from the hum of engines it had turned quiet.

The fleet of War Dogs, cruising by guard rails, staircases, and submerged vehicles, prepared for the next onslaught. Only seconds passed before the shooting started up again, this time from the core of the building, from behind staircases. Dodging streams of bullets headed their way the advancing fleet was forced into seeking protection while returning fire. Salvo after salvo swept toward Brooks and the approaching fleet. To gain entrance to the complex, staircases had to be secured. Under the combined fighting skills, speed, and effort from every member of the crew, ten minutes into the fighting, the objective of taking the carports was finally achieved. The enemy had retreated into the stairwells.

---

[54] Brooks' Fleet of salvaged speedboats spread out over three theaters:
Theaters: Great Lakes, Mississippi River, East River, Potomac River
Task Forces: Three task forces containing five task groups each
Task Groups: Five task groups containing ten Patrol units each
Patrol Units: Ten Patrol units containing five seamen per unit
Total force: 750 craft-based warriors with equivalent combat and underwater training of the Navy Seals.

From here on the fight would be man to man. Jumping from still moving craft the energy-charged War Dogs, between floating, wading, and jump skipping forward, sought cover behind submerged vehicles, staircases, and stairwells, and wherever there was a concrete wall for protection.

Immediately after leading his fleet into the U.N. complex, he spotted it. "Trap…It's a trap," he shouted over his shoulder, warning the crews. It was a call of desperation, but the warning shout was lost amid the confusion and chaos of speeding boats, firing weapons, shouting seamen, and screaming engine sounds. Brooks and his fleet had been drawn into the building by design. He realized it too late. What gave it away was the absence of enemy craft. There were no craft.

Directly ahead, cowered within stairwells, were squadrons of enemy fighters. Above, positioned on the next level floors, was a swarm of terrorists' ready to massacre anything that approached. All that was left to close the trap was an enemy assault from the outside.

Sure enough, seconds later, there it came. He could already feel the roar of approaching engines from attack crafts that had been lurking, waiting within the U.N. assembly building by the waterfront, ready to encircle the fleet of War Dogs. Brooks' home-built fleet of sea craft was about to face off against a Jihad-based, technologically superior fleet stacked with torpedoes, deck-mounted cannons, and machinegun manned attack crafts. After years of pursuing each other, playing hide and seek on the Mississippi and in the Great Lakes, both fleets finally came to a head-on. It would be the ultimate battle for dominance within a once thriving metropolis, now partially submerged by flooding.

Ever since Yusuf Hashim had been taken out of commission in the tunnel incident, presently incapacitated in the intensive care unit for burnt victims, Bandar Malik, First Lieutenant, Jihad, was elevated to local commander U.S. Cell Alpha, New York City. Since he had not known the Prophet's exact whereabouts, he had placed himself in charge. Like all lieutenants, ambitious as they came, he had been eyeing for the position for some time. No matter what the conditions, as soon as a commander faded into obscurity, as was the case with Bin Laden, there would always be somebody anxious to take over leadership. Such was the case with Malik.

Taking over command, Bandar Malik recalled a proverb from the old scriptures: "Give a man a fish and he will live another day. Teach him how to fish and he can feed his family for life." He added, "Taking charge of the waters, I will be in power."

It was the later part he had been vying for. Much like other lieutenants, he was no different. He wanted power. He wanted "The Power." Today, with seemingly nobody in charge of the city, the region, the defensive perimeters, his opportunity had come. Here and now, it would be his chance to excel to supremacy. He made it clear with the first command. "Follow me…this is for Allah…take charge."

Unbeknownst to his lieutenants, the Prophet had bigger problems to solve than New York City. With North America on the brink of perhaps being lost to his cause, his focus needed to be redirected, to that of a global sphere. To achieve that would require a different set of strategy and connections, that of political, military, and social orientation. He was forced to seek out help from newly sought functionaries. That of the new world order, the Globalists. It was the world's power brokers he needed support from. For that, he had to retreat to Palm Jumeirah, his home-based headquarters. Having been absent for quite some time from this sanctuary, he could already see the many changes the island had undergone.

Hammad's visibility had to be redirected as well. The notes and statistics he kept at his lofty abode provided the contacts, numbers, and figures he needed. He had to establish connections with Moscow, London, Frankfurt, Lisbon, and other world HQs in Africa and Asia. Then, there were summits to attend for the cause of Islam and the Muslims. "Dammit," he cussed at no one in particular. "Lost the damned HAARP." He was further cussing out the incompetence of his lieutenants. He knew only too well, that without his super weapon, chances of taking America by force was pretty slim.

Presently observing from the quiet of the lofty balcony, his gaze struck the beauty of the gulf with its colors, waves, and crest below and winds, sky, and clouds aloft, gliding silently across the Persian skies. He fetched the contact list and placed several urgent calls. Connections were made to the respective world leaders. He needed their buy-in. He needed the current state of international affairs, their planning, and future goals. The alliance was an important element before executing his next steps.

There would be resistance from some of the leaderships. After an unsuccessful attempt at taking America, the mineral resources and Great Lakes for their waters, he knew there would be repercussions. It was a dilemma he presently was dealing with. In the current scheme of things, he had lost face. On a broader scale, however, they needed him. Although there were many other nations making overtures to take charge over the globe, clandestinely, the leaders had sanctioned Jihad as the forerunner to pave the ways. Slated troublemakers for decades, the Jihad was a front funded by power brokers who would swoop in, taking control once the battle for dominance was won. For once, the Islamic nations would be given equal statue among the nations for playing in the same pool of global trade, commerce, and currency.

As splintered and obscure as the Islam cause was at this time, it would be consolidated into one cohesive nation much like any other entity on the globe. By desire, due to national resources and geological preference, there was still hope that North America would be home to the new order. Currently positioned for the all-out attack to regain lost footing on American ground, for now, success rested on Bandar Malik's shoulders.

While waiting for the calls to connect, Hammad took the time to visit the bathroom. Striding down the hallway, he momentarily stopped to inspect his reflection in the mirror. Absentmindedly and in deep thought, his fingers gently touched along the deepening lines reflected in an otherwise exemplary youthful face. They had deepened considerably in just a short time while executing Phase II in his master plan. To move forward he had to focus. He had to get his thoughts in order.

In recent times, his thinking had been clouded more often than not. It was always the same image. It was the same woman's face. It was the face of Stinger that had appeared from nowhere. Ever since the incident on top of One World Trade Center, he'd had nightly visions of her. On the one hand, he was extremely captivated with her beauty, her extraordinary skills, and her abilities to battle. On the other, a hate-filled rage emerged from the pits of his stomach at every vision.

He still could not come to terms with the outcome of their battle. "Beaten by a woman," he reflected in nausea and vowed, "Never again." He would be more prepared with exotic fighting skills in the martial arts practiced by such as the samurai and Chinese monks. *Who'd have ever expected,* his mental anguish lingered, *great Prophet beaten by a woman.*

SUDAN

How do I takeout a terrorist camp alone, by myself? The question had been on her mind for days. Not that Tracy was fearful or anything like it, but it was a concern, nevertheless. No matter how she twisted and turned the predicament, the results were the same: strange land, open territory, foreign culture, and lack of Intel. There was a complete lack of foreign intelligence on the nation. She had virtually no knowledge about the target she was about to embark. Still laid up in Istanbul, three days had gone by since Baikonur, as they processed new papers and identity for her, but she had no complaints. It was a well-deserved break away from the battle grounds in New York and the Eastern Seaboard cities. It gave her the time to put an attack strategy together. It was to no avail. She had insufficient knowledge about this part of the region, probably because it was located in the southern hemisphere. She needed help. Radio silence had to be broken.

Presently located on the opposite side of the globe from the American continent, and it being night time, it might take hours for Specter to respond. Regardless, she placed the call. "Specter," she called in. "Need help." It'd flag him into alert by morning.

With travel documents in hand, passage booked on a freighter, Tracy was set for the road again but had a number of issues to iron out. Where it'd be only a six-hour flight to the next destination, the Sudan, she could not take a chance with weapons in her possession. She would have to trade the convenience of flight and a short hop with a sea voyage of several days. *Besides,* she contemplated, *getting passage on a freighter will be the safest way.* There would be no search for weapons. And she needed one. It was the vote of confidence she could not be without.

Conveniently stored with Elena on the trip to Baikonur in Volgograd, she collected her personal things. As a matter of fact, amid all the wishes and denials, after much begging and pleading, Tracy finally gave in to letting her Russian friend join the team for the next mission, that of locating Brian. It would increase her personal taskforce to four in number. At this point, she had no information on Brian's whereabouts other than him being held in captivity in some Sudanese terrorist detention camp. Any additional information would have to come from Specter. Her questions such as *what do I know about the target,* up to now, had always drawn a blank.

Her companions were presently enjoying a Turkish breakfast. In contrast to American breakfasts, always in a rush to get to the office, here, people took their time to eat. Neatly served on a large plate, topped with cold sausage, was feta, a somewhat aged looking cheese, sliced cucumbers and tomatoes, black and green olives, butter, honey, jam, centered with a boiled egg, alongside ample slices of white bread. Just looking at the assortment of servings made her feel full. Her mind was not on the meal. It was on the mission ahead. She was not even part of the table conversation held between Elena, Dimitry, and Toporov. While nibbling away on the plentiful feast, it suddenly came to her. *Local library.*

Jumping to her feet, she announced, "I'll be back," then strode off on the sidewalk which bustled with shoppers, office goers, and local traffic.

The library, when asking a passerby, she was told, was within walking distance. Headed in that direction, she was constantly approached by local hawkers trying to pawn off merchandise to tourists. Not being the average traveler and especially not a tourist, she casually waved them off and marched on. Ten minutes later she arrived at the library. Without a member card, she was not allowed to check out any reading material. It did not matter. There was enough reading on the shelves for a crash course on Sudan, the target place ahead.

Reading through geological, political, and cultural archives on Sudan, she was amazed about the diversity of the place. Despite considering herself fairly informed on global issues, the African continent was never one of interest to Tracy. Born into a western society, then the U.S., Africa was never much of a news item to the free world. Sure, there were media reported incidents on conflicts such as Darfur, regional clashes with neighboring Chad to the west, and internal fighting between northern residing Sunni Muslim with Christians located in the South, but all in all, the American public was not much enthralled with news carried on in nations outside its own borders. The American citizens, especially in recent years, had enough internal issues to deal with.

There was a fair amount of information available geographically and culturally. Reading on, she learned that, though blessed by a rich and ancient history, Sudan had fought its share of wars, battles, and conflicts. Mostly of Islamic heritage, about 97 percent of its population, a once sparsely populated region, in recent times had undergone similar growing pains like many of the surrounding nations on the African content. Bordered by Egypt to the north, Chad to the west, Ethiopia to the east, and South Sudan, a separate nation, it straddled both sides of the Nile, with the river being an extension of two large bodies of water, the confluence of two rivers, the white and blue Niles at Khartoum, the capital of the Republic of Sudan.

Tracy read on. Studying a map on Sudan, from a satellite's perspective, this region in Africa, much like most of its centrally-located nations, seemed to be mostly a desolate body of unpopulated deserts. Zooming in to a closer view, however, primarily due to the discovery of oil on the continent, Khartoum, as well as other cities and towns, and outlying regions had seen tremendous growth in recent decades. What used to be a nation consisting mostly of tribal nomads, today had seen many settlements sprout up amid sand based, seemingly arid, terrains. Among developing settlements, aside from producing and refining fossil fuel, water projects had the highest priority. Canals, dams, and irrigation project were going up in many regions to support the ever-growing population.

From a political perspective, the Sudan was undergoing similar changes. Plagued with growing pains, it would take some time to align with the rest of the free world. Dependent mostly on the U.N. to accomplish that, with the battle currently taking place in New York for world trade dominance, it might take some time to achieve that goal.

Several hours had slipped by when suddenly a voice broke into the serenity of the library making her jolt up. "Report." It was the call from Specter for which she had been waiting.

Tracy switched to transmit, "Go."

"Proceed   Port   Sudan…West   Khartoum…New   contact   three   days…Sahib Mahmud…Over."

The instructions were brief as always. Tracy would have liked additional information, which she hoped the new contact would provide. It would have to do. A bit more reading, she learned that Massawa was a seaport approximately 3,000 miles to the south on the shores by the Red Sea closest to Khartoum.

She had enough data on the target region, but was not thrilled at the target location. One of the hottest cities, desolated, isolated from the rest of the world, it'd be a brutal experience no matter what. From here on out, the past day's leisure life would be all business once more. It'd be Stinger in the lead supported by three more mercenaries, Dimitry, Mikhail, and Elena, a group of seemingly casual tourists on their way to Sudan's capital city.

There was no easy way to get there. With everybody loaded down on weapons and ammo, there was no way getting past airport security checks. Sea voyage it was. "Another delay," Tracy sighed. She'd have to make the best of it. *What's three more days?* The voyage turned out to be a pleasant journey. Hired on as part of the sea crew, the workload on the freighter was easy. Mostly cleaning, scrubbing, and painting, time passed by quickly. Fighters turned swabbies, they had mostly leisure time on their hands. The sea breeze was welcomed. The nights, with countless stars slowly moving across the sky, meteors shooting in and out of the atmosphere, ship horns blowing to give way, were especially enjoyable. Initially fairly cool, the farther south they traveled, the hotter it got, especially after passing into the Suez Canal. The sights, the scenery, the open waters, the conversations, were worth the extra few days. The team was getting to know each other. The synergy between the four seemed to be in relative harmony.

Mikhail Toporov, cosmonaut turned Jihad, the Russian Tracy thought she would have a problem with, turned out to be an honorable character. They listened to his story. Scheduled and on standby for the space flight, he had a visit one day from what turned out to be Jihad operatives. To assure collaboration and compliance with taking control over the ISS, his entire family had been taken hostage. He had been devastated but had no other option but to cooperate. That was the reason he was so willing to join Tracy's team. Like Brian Harris, his family was still held prisoner in some terrorist camp. Tracy promised to get his family back.

Elena, a novice to fights and battles, received Tracy's personal training in weapon handling and hand-to-hand combat. She was a willing student. "Tracy," she kept insisting over and over, "you are my idol." Having a fan suited Tracy fine. On the first night, with starlight illuminating the deck, they had a surprise visit from the ship's captain. He had been alerted by one of his mates about the shooting practice on deck. He came prepared, flanked by two of his crew armed with handguns to investigate. The standoff was short after Tracy explained they were a Russian commando team on a classified rescue mission. The captain eventually released them from their swabbies duties, but kept a wary eye on the team for the following days. It suited everybody fine. There were no further complaints.

For the rest of the sea journey, Tracy watched with delight as Elena took a liking to Dimitry. In time, perhaps after the pending mission was over, they would make a nice couple. *He sure could use someone to cheer him up,* she thought. The next morning, Port Sudan was approaching in the distance. It was time to prepare for exit. They thanked the captain for his discretion on not reporting the unwelcome intrusion and departed for the next stretch, Khartoum. The last leg, a twelve-hour ride by bus, would be a boring journey. It turned out to be exactly that. Seated amid provincial merchants, local tribesmen, and returning travelers, with the daytime sun beating on the roof within a sweltering bus, was brutal. Then there was the endless chatter of family and friends amid squawking and tied up chickens on the way to market. The bus seemed to make stops in the middle of nowhere, dropping off passengers and small livestock. In the hot desert breeze, with windows open all around, the animal stench was ever present, but bearable.

Amid the seemingly endless wasteland spreading out in every direction, soaking wet with sweat, there was not much other than sand to inspire the mind. Tracy was making conversation. "Must be hours of walking," she remarked.

"In my country," Elena explained. "People are used to walking."

"In my country," Tracy replied. "People have been spoiled. But that was before the war. Now," she clarified. "Nobody travels. Too dangerous."

There was light conversation like it throughout the bus trip. Concentration was impossible with all the sound of chatter. A long twelve sweltering hours finally came to an end close to nightfall. The team had arrived in Khartoum. They found refuge for the night at a small, but clean, motel situated at an alley off the main street. Contact with Mahmud would not be made until morning.

Tracy tried to get some sleep but was troubled by the sounds of night prevalent in this part of the world. It seemed that trade never stopped. It might slow during the early morning hours, but street hawkers selling their gods went on around the clock. She tossed and turned for the greater part of the night. Her mind kept drifting from the present to the past. She'd prefer to stay with the present because the past held nothing but tragedy.

It began many years ago with Dad's marriage falling apart, and moved onto the recent past with her sister perishing in space, her mom sick with cancer from the nuclear attack on California, and her nation in turmoil. Then there was her recent love affair with Brooks, if you could call it as such. Though the sex part was beyond belief, it was all there was, two animal-like bodies tearing into each other.

Tracy then realized she needed something more. She needed passion. She needed romance, and, foremost, she needed belonging. Her mind honed in on Brian. He was so close. She could almost reach out and touch him. The concern she had was for his safety. The thought brought on new rage.

"Oh well." She eventually succumbed to a fitful rest knowing that tomorrow would be filled with challenges. "Perhaps," were her fading thoughts, "I need the thrill of fight to get a good night's rest." She was actually looking forward to tomorrow.

BATTLE FOR DC

Today was the day. No matter what the outcome, this day would make history. Since the New York advance across the Hudson by Foster's army had faltered with the tunnel breaks, it would be up to Big Red to pull this off. If she failed, the nation would be lost to the enemy. With the District of Columbia, the federal seat, being the most strategic position in the nation from a government and political perspective, Big Red intended to live up to her promise to retake the city. With the very limited resources at her disposal, it was a big gamble, trying to achieve her goal. Without an accurate account of enemy forces due to the lack of forward scouts, with data on hand only based on rumors, Big Red was at a major disadvantage right from the start. What every battle commander relied on mostly were reports on the status, position, and numbers of the opposition forces. Every battle strategy was based on this information. For all practical purposes, her strategy would be mostly based on her personal intuition.

"What're you thinking?"

Big Red was torn from her concerning thoughts by Mackenzie, who was getting ready to head out for the central push across the Potomac River. It would be her task to spearhead the major brunt of the forces into battle head on across Roosevelt Memorial Bridge, pushing east to Constitution Avenue. "I'm worried," Big Red said.

It was her responsibility to look out for each and every one of her fighters. With only one battle win under her belt up in Alaska and a fighting force filled with mostly unproven novice recruits from the Appalachians, she had a right to be worried. On top of it, the combined tally of her force was less than 5000 in numbers. That was the negative aspect of the pending battle.

On the positive side, the Jihad forces, as much fighting practice as they might have, were based on tactical cell structures without established battle cohesiveness. From all accounts she had gathered, this would be the first battle front by the terrorist forces.

"Look at it this way," Kimberly added. "We have the shock effect advantage on our side."

"You got that right," Kelly chimed in. "We'll scare the robes right off of their scrawny bodies."

"I may have me a Jihad for breakfast," Mac fired back. It was pep talk like this that inspired the battalion commanders into action. It was their responsibilities and mind-sets that essentially spurred on the rest of the forces. The day was still early. The commanders had just finished a morning meal prepared at the fort's main mess hall. At this point, none of the commanders knew when the next solid meal would be served. It could be hours, days, or weeks. It was all hinged on the success of the army. As it stood overall, Red made a last calculation on her battle readiness:

Artillery – Normally comprised of a cavalry of armored Halftracks with spindle mounts of .30 and .50 mm machineguns including large caliber size Howitzer combat units. Her brigade consisted of pickups with bed-mounted machine guns flanked by automatic wielding Patriots clinging to motorcycles.

Infantry – Normally a mechanized force of armored personnel carriers (APCs) fighting vehicles for transport and combat with fire support weapons such as machine guns, cannons, small-bore direct-fire howitzers, and even anti-tank guided missiles. Her mobile forces consisted of trucks and SUVs mounted by Patriot recruits wielding personal weapons of all sorts, like pistols, revolvers, shotguns, and semi-automatics. What they lacked in automatic weapons support was made up by enthusiasm.

Signal Corps – In modern times, was comprised of a highly mobile attack force from military intelligence, weather forecasting, and aviation using communications and information management systems support for the command and control of combined armed forces with the aid of information dissemination management, network management, voice and data communications networks that employ single and multi-channel satellite, troposphere scatter, terrestrial microwave, messaging, video-teleconferencing, visual information, and other related systems. In Big Red's army, it was a mere cluster of SINCGAR radio gear equipped with hand-cranked chargers, and antenna-mounted battery backpacks.

Where her mobile division was limited to mostly commercial vehicles, the battle strength came from the numbers of an enthusiastically charged fighting pack. Big Red was ready to lead her brigade[55] into battle. "Mackenzie, Kimberly, Kelly," were her final orders, "move on out. You know your positions. You know the mission. We'll join forces on the other side of the Potomac. The goal is the Capitol and White House. Let's move it…move it…move it." Initiating the command, she stepped on the pedal of the lead vehicle, a Humvee, spun up wheels, gravel, and dirt, and headed out east onto Arlington Boulevard and onto the bridge crossing. Taking out the Pentagon and National had been deferred to Brooks, by Foster, who was staged to take care of the remaining strongholds.

Following in tight formation leaving Fort Myer, the battalions were fanning out to their assigned destinations. Kelly was making up the northern flank headed for the Key Bridge; Kim, making up the southern flank, headed for the 14th Street Bridge; and Mac, taking the central approach, headed for the Roosevelt Memorial Bridge. Aside from assigned crews and soldiers manning each vehicle, signal corps members were staffing mobile units, creating a closed-circuit net of instant communication between battalions, companies, platoons, and squad leaders.

Being the first major battle for the Red Army, chatter was making up most of the airwaves with the pure energy of enthusiasm. Red's voice broke in every so often to remind them of the mission ahead. It did not take long for the respective convoys to reach their target crossings. One by one, status reports returned from each unit on the local conditions of resistance.

---

[55] Big Red's Army Battle Formation

Big Red BRIGADE	3,000 to 5,000	Brigadier General	BG	1 Star
Mac BATTALION	300 to 1,000	Lieutenant Colonel	LTC	Silver Oak Leaf
Kelly BATTALION	300 to 1,000	Lieutenant Colonel	LTC	Silver Oak Leaf
Kim BATTALION	300 to 1,000	Lieutenant Colonel	LTC	Silver Oak Leaf

Closing in on her target, the Arlington Memorial Bridge, Big Red's brigade immediately stalled. "Incoming…Incoming…Incoming," was a warning alert echoed through the radios.

They had come under heavy artillery from across the river. Shocked at the fiery blockade, Mackenzie frowned. "Don't like this. Jihad's not supposed to carry heavy munitions." She, like most of her crew, at the most had been expecting only automatic rifle fire.

Big Red immediately recognized the charges sent across the river by the smoky trail left in their wake. "Not munitions," she yelled into the mic. "RPGs…take defensive positions."

"Remotely-propelled grenades?" Normally used as shoulder-launched anti-tank weapon, today it was used very effectively against the light armored vehicles under Red's command. Several of the forward positioned trucks were already burning up in smoke, spilling out the passengers that survived the initial onslaught. All three battalions had come under similar attacks. Only minutes into the battle, Red's army had already taken a sizable casualty count.

Big Red was shocked by the unforeseen resistance that forced her advance to a halt. "It's sure going to affect my fighters' morale," she rationalized. *I'll have to take a different strategy.* With that thought in mind she called an ad hoc battle meeting. Twenty minutes later the commanders met at the major crossroads, the Arlington and Roosevelt interchange. Although there was an expression of concern in their faces, it was far from defeat. "Need your assessments," Red instructed her three commanders.

"Lost a squad of my best already," Kimberly reported.

"Same here," Kelly indicated.

"I took the biggest hit," Mackenzie said. She among the three was most devastated over the loss of their former buddies, friends, and associates. It was one thing to lose a friend in hand to hand combat. But watching them fall by the dozen without ever having a chance to defend themselves was shocking.

"Told you," Big Red scolded them, "not to be friends with your soldiers." She knew the consequences very well. She too had made the mistake years ago before losing friends in similar ways. Since then she'd learned the hard way from her superiors. "Follow the chain of command…Observe the ranking system."

What none of them were aware of was the military policy taught in war college. "Enforced ranking discipline." It was why officers were strictly kept separated from non-commissioned officers. It's why higher ranks were kept separated from lower ranks. Disregarding the rules would not only cause personal pain, but, more importantly, it damaged discipline and broke down authority. Without authority, there was no discipline. Without discipline, there was no cohesiveness. Without cohesiveness, there was no army. The force would be reduced to a militia, individual clusters of renegades.

Today, however, there was no reprimand. Big Red knew it wasn't their fault. The blame was on her. She had failed to instill enough discipline into her ranks aside from the lack of recon.

For now, all had to deal with their own losses of buddies and friends. In the cause of an instant, many had learned what war was all about. Aside from the personal combat experience fought in Alaska, today, as a fighting force, they had elevated from being a component of greenhorns to the beginnings of a combined element of power, but not yet a group of seasoned warriors. To achieve that would take many more battles.

For now, the Red Army was on hold for whatever time it took to come up with a new battle strategy. To obtain just that, Big Red kept calling the man who'd have the answer.

"Foster," her signal core kept yelling into the airwaves. "Urgent situation…come in…come in."

But with all the shouting, there was no response. Foster's army had run against its own demise but for different reasons. Because of the limited reach of the legacy communication, he was out of reach of the 2nd division fighting for DC. For getting word to him, Big Red would have to dispatch a detachment of combat resources she didn't have. *Besides,* she reasoned, *it's my battle, it's my soldiers, it's my responsibility.*

SUDAN DESERT

Tracy was awakened by knocking at the door. She must have pulled the curtains sometime during the night to darken the room. She did not remember. Bright sunlight doused the room as soon as she opened the door. It was Elena, looking concerned. "You okay?" She was okay but had overslept.

Inviting her friend in, she said, "Give me a minute." There was no reason to cleanup with what lay ahead. More heat, more sand, and more dust. It took two minutes to finish her morning business between splashing water on her face, brushing teeth, and collecting her travel bag. Loaded down mostly with weapons and ammo, as was usually the case on her missions, she slung the bag over her shoulder, shut the door, and marched to the waiting team. As promised by Specter, a British-made Land Rover was idling nearby, waiting for her to take to the road. Next stop, Mogran Botanical Gardens. It was the rendezvous point with the local contact.

Anxious to get going, he was waiting when they pulled up. "Stinger," he muttered.

Viewing him cautiously, she gestured for him to hop in, "Desert Sands." It was their codeword. Taking a seat in back, he replied with a nod, squeezing his body between the occupied seats. "Sahib Mahmud."

Staring at the three faces in the vehicle, he immediately complained, "Too many people."

"You fight?"

Offended and angered at the mere suggestion, he readily proclaimed, "No fight. Contact only."

"Then shut up," Tracy insisted.

With him onboard the vehicle was packed. At this point, except the contact, none of the crew knew the destination. Impatient to get going, Tracy sat behind the wheel waiting for directions. "Well?"

It took a few seconds for Sahib to respond. Indicating the far reaches of the desert, he muttered, "Okay, take west." It was in the direction Tracy headed.

"How far?"

"Don't know…maybe four, five hours."

Tracy realized it would be a one-way trip and she voiced so. There was not enough fuel in the tank to get back unless there was a fueling station along the route, which she doubted. Hour after hour went by spent mostly in silence. Each was occupied with their own thoughts. Only an occasional grunt or cussword would slip from lips when the vehicle hit a bump. There was a road cut through the desert but it was seemingly not heavy traveled. It was mostly gravel leading the way straight into the desert.

Though the wasteland seemed endless, there was an occasional bend or crossroad with signs proclaiming the next speck of settlement. Sahib guided them through each turn, indicating he knew the route. As suggested, it took close to five hours when another sign appeared from the distance. Unfamiliar with the Arabic language Tracy asked, "What's it say?"

"HALT," Sahib read on. "Get shot—Own risk."

Tracy wanted to make sure it was the target. "Base Camp?"

"Base Camp Three," the contact confirmed.

"What now?" Elena said.

The Land Rover rolled to a stop. "Now we walk." Tracy gestured ahead. They had arrived at the bottom of an incline. Straight ahead was nothing but rolling sand dunes giving off waves of heat, distorting the landscape, and the same was in every direction one turned. Planting a foot on soil caused a burning sensation as soon as the grains touched skin.

"Don't wanna stumble here," Tracy warned at the heat the ground was giving off.

"That's for sure," Dimitry chimed in with a wide grin. "Burn butt."

It was the first time he had spoken in days. *There is some humor,* she mused, *in all of mankind.* It immediately lifted everyone's spirits in otherwise depressing surroundings.

A couple hundred yards later they arrived at the top of the sand dune. Gazing ahead, their eyes caught the shimmer in the distance below. Sprawled across the valley basin was a camp of considerable size, completely fenced in from all sides. Tracy dropped her bag to the ground to free her hands. "Go fetch the tarp," she said to Elena, who backtracked to the Land Rover for the tarpaulin and mats. The ground was just too hot for comfort. Because of the considerable distance, it'd be easier propping their elbows on the ground to steady field glasses. Three pairs were shared among the team.

With binoculars trained on the distance below, Sahib warned, "Motion sensors, cameras, minefield, all around camp."

"That's," Tracy remarked, "gonna be a problem."

Sahib gestured ahead. "Only approach free of mines. Road."

"How're we going to cross the mines?" Elena voiced. Dimitry had likewise concerns. "I'm out," he insisted. "Don't like mines. Never did, never will. I'm out," he repeated.

Scanning the camp perimeter amid prolific training activities held by dozens of camp operatives, Tracy, using the implant, could make out the cameras and motion sensors but was unable to spot any of the buried mines. It was impossible to take an accurate count of trainees and militants with occupants disappearing each time a surveillance satellite passed overhead. From a Birdseye perspective, several hundreds of miles in space, the camp appeared deserted. No matter where a camp was located, Jihad forces were very familiar with orbital spy satellite schedules. Entire daily activities were centered abound spy and surveillance satellites.

With the new information at hand she could at least formulate an approach tactic.

"We wait 'til nightfall," she decided. Gauging from the sun's position, it wouldn't be that much longer. They'd spent most of the day trekking here. Taking the hidden mines under consideration, it would be their only chance for an approach. She silently thanked herself for the foresight to acquire several pairs of night vision goggles and thermal scopes for the weapons; they'd be a savior. Without them, she'd have to abandon the mission. Her major concern at the moment was the minefields. She then had a thought: *Specter.* The airwaves had been quiet all day. Calculating the time difference between Africa and America, she thought, *Good. He's gonna be awake.*

To make contact she needed privacy. Turned to head back to the vehicle, she ordered the team, "Stay here." Squinting into the sun on the western horizon, she noticed that the air had cooled quite a bit since they arrived. "Specter," she muttered in the quiet of the vehicle. "Come in."

Within seconds his voice was on the implant. "Go."

"Base Camp Three," she identified her present location. "Need your best surveillance gear."

"Shoot," the order flashed back.

"Come night time," she informed him, "I must cross minefields."

The ether suddenly turned silent. She knew he was calculating the odds. She knew how his mind worked. It'd immediately switched into analysis mode. He was not only considering pros and cons of the impending danger of crossing a minefield in the dead of night, but also alternatives for getting spotted and how a person, no matter how seasoned a fighter, would react when suddenly detected within trip-activated explosives. Many would panic on the sheer thought of not knowing what step would be fatal.

Specter had the answer. Breaking the silence, he advised, "Keep channel open. Will guide you through…Over."

It then came to her. Years ago, just prior to the EMP strike, NASA had placed highly sophisticated infrared sensing satellites into orbit for USGS. The purpose was to penetrate Earth's crust to identify subsurface minerals and oil deposits. The technology, ineffective though it turned out to be for the North American continent, now, here in the deserts of Sudan, came to the team's rescue.

Tracy returned to the spotter location with the answer. "What? Elena burst out. Cross the minefield? In the middle of night?"

"We'll be safe."

"But how?"

"Trust me. Have I ever been wrong?"

Another hour it'd be night and cold. The desert, as soon as the sun slid beneath the horizon, took a complete turn where temperatures soared to extreme between day and night. When the sun was up, an individual might get fried in contrast to the night, when a body could freeze stiff. People who were not aware of the extremes did not last long in the desert. Almost always they perished unless they came prepared with shade, water, and blankets. Barring the weight factor, the team had at least the foresight to come semi prepared, carrying essential survival gear. Sustainability, however, was yet another issue. They'd have to strike quick. Provisions on hand would not last more than a couple of days. There was no room to get bogged down in a lengthy confrontation. Besides, the base would call on reinforcements from other camps in the nearby regions. From what satellite surveillance indicated, the Sudanese deserts were full of terrorist training camps.

Though Sahib demonstrated a certain measure of collaboration, Tracy did not put her complete trust into the contact. Just observing his personal behavior caused her distrust. He might have had good reasons for helping out a foreign assault on the camp. But, personally, Tracy did not trust anybody but herself. That was Specter's rule. It was her rule as well.

"What do you think?" Mikhail broke the silence.

"We wait," Tracy opted, "'til the camp quiets." Once darkness set in, most operatives would seek out sleep from sheer exhaustion, training under the desert sun. She further suggested her team taking a nap until it was time for the assault.

BATTLE FOR MANHATTAN

Scott Brooks, as soon as he heard the sound of the approaching enemy craft, immediately realized the trap. During his initial approach on the U.N. Headquarters, he had failed to check on the other buildings clustered around the complex. Some had been spared from the HAARP attack. It was the main building that had been targeted for destruction. Considerable in numbers, the most obvious would have been the Assembly building, also partially flooded. It was this building from where the new threat was launched. He was trapped between two fronts, one directly in front, squadrons of heavily-armed terrorists fighting from the building, and that of a naval fleet of heavily-armored speedboats on the imminent approach from the rear. It would require all of his cunning and years of fighting strategy, supported by a seasoned crew, to get out of the trap. The U.N. halls, once occupied by hundreds of humanitarian-seeking emissaries from every corner of the globe, today was besieged by a fleet of Patriots defending their once-venerated superpower taken hostage by a rogue force. It was this hostile and antagonistic threat of terrorists that Brooks and his fleet of dedicated was in the process of eliminating. To accomplish that, he first had to remove their leader. It was Malik and his renegade fleet[56] he was currently seeking out.

The crew's first reaction was to follow the retreating threat, but Brooks' warning, "Explosives," immediately stopped them from charging ahead. Not all of the crew heeded the warning call. Some perished when the first charges went off. It stopped others from proceeding. There was no escape. The rapidly closing-in threat had to be dealt with on a leveled front, a one-on-one battle within the flooded carport arena. Brooks' blood began to boil when he recognized the head of the advancing Jihad force, Bandar Malik. He'd battled him on several occasions on the Hudson River, as well as in the Great Lakes.

Brooks' fleet was shaken into reality with the first hail of enemy onslaught amid torpedoes trailing streams of bubbles tracing their way in addition to taking heavy fire from onboard cannons and machinegun fire. The last battle for Manhattan had begun. There was no escape other than fighting his way out of the trap.

---

[56] Bandar Malik's Naval Fleet—General characteristics.
Brand: Colombo Class Series III
Builders: Sri Lanka, Colombo Dockyard Ltd.
Commissioned: 1996
Type: Ultra-Fast Attack Craft
Displacement: 56 tons
Length: 24 meters
Beam: 5.70 meters
Draught: 1.1 meters
Propulsion: 2x Deutz Tbd 620 V16 main engines (4570 hp each) and two Arneson ASD-16 articulating surface drives
Speed: 53 knots
Range: 500 - 600nm
Complement: 10-12 crews
Armament: Typhoon stabilized system with M242 Bushmaster machineguns, 20 mm Swiss made Oerlikon cannons, and sonar tipped torpedoes.

With the satellite dish disabled, so was Brooks' comm link with Foster. There was no possible means to call for support. It'd be solely up to the War Dogs to win the ensuing battle. Water in this part of Manhattan was still rising from the tunnel breaks. Carports and ground level floors, partially flooded initially, were rapidly filling with seawater. Brooks' fleet of speedboats, trapped within the carport, was sandwiched in between rising water levels and closing in ceilings. Pilots were testing routes to gain escape to higher ground. What used to be dry concrete connecting floors had turned to watery channels. It was these channels Brooks' fleet used to speed upward to the next level carports.

Aside from being the only way out of the present trap for Brooks, it prevented Malik's fleet from pursuing the entrapped. They were stranded outside by the edge of the lower building levels. It would be the last fighting front Brooks would have to face after leaving the complex. But for now, he faced a more pressing threat, that of an army of terrorists hovering immediately above his present position.

The flooded ground had reached enough depth for Brooks' fleet to charge the first level headquarters floors. What used to be the spacious halls of the complex had turned into waterways. It was these waterways the enemy was defending. With the water still on the rise, Brooks' fleet forged ahead, but not without taking heavy fire. As they charged in and out the assembly hall, speeding up and down the spacious hallways, enemy fire erupted from every corner of the building, killing his crews and sinking crafts.

In spite of the entrapment, Brooks' fleet fought on merciless. His fleet of speedboats sought out, detected, and eliminated the enemy wherever it was confronted. In spite of the fearless instinct Brooks instilled on his fighters, trained and conditioned to kill, there was a limit to every fighter's energy and stamina. Eventually, every battle and fight slows down. Though his being a superior being, he could feel the physical drain on his own body. He was taking stock. He was seeking a way out of the present entrapment when he spotted it. The opportunity lay just above. The escape route was the picturesque windows partially submerged by the flood.

"Assemble," he ordered on the radio. "All craft."

The call brought the speedboats to a crawl within the halls of the assembly building. Steering his direction, all came idling closer to receive new orders. Apparently, the enemy was regrouping as well. Other than the idling engines, with the enemy force eliminated within the building and the shooting at an end, the halls had turned quiet when Brooks spoke.

"We have one more obstacle to eliminate," he commanded. "One that's waiting outside."

"But," one pilot voiced the concern they all realized, "we're trapped."

"Not so," he readily informed his fighting force. "There's one way out." He mused at the expectant faces staring at him in heightened anticipation.

He gestured with a nod shot at the windows. "Our way out."

They understood. It'd be their break from this building. It'd come as unexpected surprise to the enemy waiting outside in and around the carports.

Bandar Malik, at first in hot pursuit of the water-based War Dogs, had run against an unexpected resistance. It was the onslaught of fire returned followed by an escaped enemy up to the next level. With the Patriots' fleet disappearing ahead, his pursuit had stalled. He was unable to follow. Each time a group of his pilots made an attempt to pursue the enemy; they were shot out of the water. His charge of torpedoes proved ineffective, leaving only the deck-mounted cannons for distant firing.

With his craft being larger in size as the Patriots', drawing a deeper draft, for the time being he was immobilized, unable to move ahead and unable to eliminate the detested enemy.

Malik was still contemplating his immediate choices when all of a sudden, the world around him exploded. He and his crew of Jihad warriors could not comprehend fast enough to react. Stunned by the unexpected turn of events, he called on his team to regroup, "Take defensive action."

It was an act for which he was not prepared. For a terrorist, it was always attack and forge ahead. There was no room for retreat. In the name of Allah, it was either win and live or perish in the process. Retreat was never an option. To be a Jihad was a one-way course: ahead. That, however, became unattainable as they were charged by Brooks' fleet from every direction. The tide had turned, putting him at a disadvantage. He was placed on a defensive course. He had no training for that and neither did his devout warriors. It would be one on one, boat against boat and man against man. It was a fight with the balance of power shifted to the enemy.

With the shift also came the immediate realization of a promise he had made his leader, the Prophet. He had drastically let him and the cause of Islam down. Unless a miracle happened, he was about to lose the last stand on the newly gained territory, that of North America.

Minutes earlier, Brooks was surrounded by a fleet of trusted warriors. After instructing his pilots and crews about the immediate plan, he prepared to lead the charge. As the day's sun was setting in the distance, the last streamers of sunrays broke through the stained glass encased windows. It was as though destiny was showing the way out. The waning rays provided a perfect path out from their entrapment. With one fisted arm thrust overhead, he gave the order. "Charge!"

In one combined assault, with engines roaring at maximum speed, wave after wave of screaming speedboats spilled from the building complex, splashing wildly onto the waters below. In one sweeping blow, Malik and his fleet were encircled from all sides. It was he now trying to fight his way from entrapment. The wall of flying boats from above had caught him in complete surprise. His entire fleet was encircled by the inferior, but highly capable, homegrown craft. He found himself unable to push his way through the speedy barrier of seaborne, bullet spitting craft.

Bandar Malik was hopelessly trapped. When he realized his demise, it was too late to save his fleet of superior design. It was cut down one by one within a few minutes. Brooks was merciless. He did not want any survivors. It'd only mean delay, recourse, and eventual judicial justification for an act of extermination. He did not have the patience to face the courts for lengthy and prolonged humanitarian processes in the name of international legalities. As far as he was concerned, he had attained his objective in removing an ineffective arm of the world's power brokers, the United Nations.

BASE CAMP THREE

It was so quiet she could not only hear herself breathing, but the others resting nearby as well. Tracy lay flat on her back staring at the brilliance of a star-covered sky overhead. It was a sight not many people had the pleasure of experiencing. One had to travel far away from cities and dwellings. This was such a place. Only thing alive were the stars. The team had retreated to the safety of the mount to seek protection from being spotted. They would remain there until it was time for the assault. Tracy was presently recapping her attack plan. Though activated, the implant had remained silent since Specter's latest instructions. It would remain silent until the attack. She'd decided to wait until well past midnight.

Ever since the clocks had stopped working after the EMP strike, she had to rely on the sun, moon, and stars to approximate time. She had the knowledge of it all since she majored in astronomy. The knowledge had come in handy over and over in recent years. She never gave the watch a second thought. Mankind, she reflected, can learn to live without electronics. Whether it was a good thing or not, technology kept closing doors to the past as readily as new inventions came about. *Perhaps,* she dwelled, *it takes a setback for man to appreciate the things otherwise taken for granted.*

Another check on the stars, her current timepiece, and she swiftly stood up, strode to the campsite, and whispered into the silence of the night, "It's time."

The sleepers began to stir. As was generally the case on waking, there was body stretching and stepping out for personal business amid coughing to clear a parched throat, especially in this climate. Tracy had to caution each, "Keep quiet."

Each understood and quickly turned silent. She allowed five more minutes for personal preparations then, "Gather up." she said. "Here's the plan."

Mikhail again voiced the personal concern on everybody's mind. "What about the minefield?"

"I'll get to that," Tracy stated. "But first off," she stressed, "Nobody steps. Every movement from here on is stealth until we reach the perimeter. Understood?"

All gave her an assuring nod.

Elena had her concerns. "What about the mines?"

"My responsibility," Tracy readily informed her. "Not yours to worry about."

"You a mine detector?" Dimitry insisted on the major point of their concerns. "How you gonna keep us from blowing up?" He still was not convinced.

A hint of mystique swept across her face when she responded to the mutual concerns. Throwing him an assuring nod, she insisted, "Trust me. I've got a sixth sense."

"You go first," was his smug comeback.

"I go first," she stated. "I'll lead you. Just follow my footsteps, even if we are spotted."

"You mad…?" Tracy did not answer.

It was time to focus on the attack plan. Tracy allowed no more interruptions. "Dimitry, Elena, you two take the right flank once we break through the barriers." She was pleased to see both nodding in agreement.

Facing the cosmonaut and addressing him, she said, "Mikhail, you cover the left flank." He returned an approving nod. Her face sought out Sahib. Tracy was uncertain about the Arabian contact. "You," she gestured at herself, "stay close." She could not allow any unexpected fuckups due to a loss in language translation. Close by her side, she was sure he would not deviate from the gauntlet of mines they had to cross. For one final time, her eyes swept across the small, but willing attack squad. "Ready?" It was time to move out.

Tracy alerted Alex to action with a whispered, "Specter." He had been glued to the ether waiting for Stinger to come online. "Proceed," was the initial order. "With caution." Although the warning was superfluous, she was thankful for the advice. It meant he was watching their every step. "Stay to the right…proceed…don't stray too much to the left…proceed…stay on course…slightly more to the right…"

Instructions through the implant came in with precision to the inch. Testing the loose gravel ahead with her boot, each step was deliberated one by one. The closer Stinger took the squad toward the perimeter, the greater their respect grew for her vanguard skills. With her in the lead, each replicated the careful steps and directions taken.

It took close to fifteen minutes of stealth to cover the quarter mile crossing the explosives-charged field. Step by step they made it to the fence without triggering a motion sensor. The next move would be more difficult. It would mean cutting through the wires without setting off the perimeter alarm. For that, Stinger used her skills in electronics. Using battery bypass clips to close the circuit, she created an electrical field at each layer of sensing wire before snipping it in half. With the last piece of wire cut, "Pull up," she instructed Sahib, who lifted the layers so everybody could pass through the mesh of barbed wires.

One by one the squad stepped into enemy territory with one final order, "Check your weapons."

Over the past fifteen minutes a visible transformation had taken place. Who, during the past few days, had been the travel companion, the casual warrior, Tracy had gradually turned into Stinger, the legendary fighting machine. From here on it would be advance, battle, and kill. The attack would have to be swift. There was no room for error. She'd call each and every move the squad had to execute. "Here we go," she whispered into the still, silent night.

The first sound echoing through the stillness of the camp came from Serpent Slayer when she pulled the trigger on the grenade launcher. With an audible thud, the projectile sought out its target. In quick successions, she launched several more grenades, hurled in the direction of each hut. There were dozens of makeshift desert shelters. Each and every one turned to blistering flames from internal explosions caused by stored munitions.

The camp came alive within seconds, thrown into deadly combat. Combat trainees torn rudely from sleep were not given a chance to fully wake up. They were cut down by the hails of bullets released from multiple assault weapons seeking their targets.

"Right flank," Stinger shouted at the Dimitry team. "Fan out."

"Left flank," she alerted Mikhail. "Give cover."

Pulling the rather reluctant contact along, she yelled, "Sahib, follow me." It became clear to her that he was mostly afraid of getting killed. Covered by the team, her next aim was the detainment cages. She had to get to them before the terrorists had a chance to retaliate on the held captives; otherwise it'd be swift executions. "Where?" she yelled at him.

"Come. Follow" He hurriedly led the way to the far end of the camp. A few strides later, she spotted it. It was a rusted grill topping that seemed to lead to an underground bunker. A clever disguise, it kept the prisoners hidden from overhead satellites. It was one thing to keep surveillance trained on a camp. It was another, an unacceptable one under any convention, to retain prisoners of war, especially where no war was declared by either side.

Stinger was keenly aware of the environment. Dodging amid screaming and rushing bodies seeking cover, her focus was directly ahead on the detainees kept below ground. The grid was secured with padlocks. A burst from her weapon and the cover sprang open. The path was clear. A few strides later and she was below ground with Sahib on her tail. The fighting did not end here. Stinger faced another obstacle, that of a barricade set up by the prison guards.

There was a halting silence. It seemed the guards recognized her companion. "Mahmud," his name echoed through the halls, then the firing began. Sahib Mahmud was recognized as traitor and immediately paid the price. Before she could protect him from the hail of bullets, his life was terminated by a bullet to his head. She never did learn the reasons why he compromised his position with Jihad. Whether career related or personal issues, it didn't matter anymore. It was too late to save him.

In one motion, Stinger selected the mode setting, leveled the weapon at the guardsmen, and released the trigger. In rapid succession, three canisters of RPG grenades made their ways to the targets. The resultant explosions tore up everything in close proximity to bits amid the sound of metal hitting concrete, more screams, and the blistering stench of burning flesh. The resistance was removed. Mikhail Toporov had moved up close to join her. Together, they broke through the debris.

When Stinger entered the bunkers, she spotted dozens of containment cages. Each cage was locked. One burst from a shotgun blast removed each padlock. The prisoners were freed. Her eyes were darting from face to face without recognition. Mikhail, by her side, let out a brief shout then moved ahead as soon as he spotted his wife, daughters, and more family members. Tears of joy were streaming down their happy faces as they clung to each other with compassionate embraces.

Not recognizing any of the faces, Stinger, beset with frustration, called his name, "Brian." There was a stirring at the far edge of one cell. In shackles was a completely emaciated body barely alive and unable to move. She quickly approached the filthy space then recognized his face. "Brian," she whispered. "It's me, Tracy."

As if in a dream his eyes sought out hers. He slightly stirred to face her. There was recognition. He tried to lift his body from the filth and stench but was too weak for an embrace. Collapsed within the reach of her arms, his body gave away one final exhausted sigh before slipping into eternal darkness. It was too late to save her once devout colleague, partner, and lover. Tears that had been suppressed suddenly welled up in Tracy's face, releasing a stream of pent up frustration, hatred, and revenge on a world gone mad.

The feeling of tragedy was too overwhelming. She renewed her vows of vengeance on the cause of all this evilness. Her mind was suddenly distracted from the heaviness of grief. There was some commotion by the hallway. Dimitry and Elena had made their way underground, shoving along a live trophy. It was Shakir Murad, the base camp's commander. It was he in charge of the prisoners. It was he that inflicted this misery on the hostages. It was he that killed Brian. She had lost the last of a companion she'd so treasured. One after another, she kept losing dear friends. "There's nobody left except Dad," she mourned.

With hands tied behind his back, seeing his face set in defiance, loathing, and hatred brought out an immediate revulsion in her. In one swift motion, she trained her weapon on Murad and was about to release a burst of bullets into his body, but changed her mind before pulling the trigger. A thought had just occurred to her. He would serve her better alive.

In an instant, his face had turned an ugly grin. He was still reeling with repugnance from having lost the camp to this woman. He had heard of her. His comrades had spoken many times of her. There had been bets placed on the head of Stinger for whomever in the ranks of Jihad could kill her first.

Most bets were on the Prophet with one exception, that of Shakir Murad himself. Since he had the bait in his hands, he suspected she would come to seek him out directly. Today had been the day but, *look at me now,* he reflected in disgust and self pity, *taken prisoner myself. Prophet's not gonna like it, losing the camp. There'll be consequences.*

Tracy moved in the direction of what appeared to be the interrogation room. It was barren, containing only a table and chair. She gestured Elena at the chair, who forced the Jihad commander to sit. Face still set in a grin, staring his captor down, he deliberately slouched his body into the seat. Stepping close, "Listen carefully," Tracy instructed the terrorist. "I'll let you live under one condition."

The grin immediately broadened on the Jihad's face. He was no recruit. He was a seasoned combatant who appreciated life. Unlike new recruits, he was not willing to give up his life to Allah on the mere promise of everlasting delight. He liked the presence on Earth with its indulgences, gratifications, and pleasures. *The heavenly virgins can wait,* was his motto.

He quickly regained his confidence back at the prospect coming out alive. "Eh?" he challenged her.

"Carry a message."

"Message?"

"Hasan Hammad," she spat at him. "Your leader."

"Eh?"

"My message to your leader is following," Tracy commanded. "If he ever spots my flag, that of the New Republic, riding the ocean waves in his territory," she stressed. "Come looking for me."

"Do not understand," Murad replied.

"He will understand," Tracy responded.

Her path was set. It was focused on the seat of all evilness, Palm Jumeirah, home of the Prophet. Specter had traced him to this island. It would be her next destination.

With the exception of Brian, Stinger and her crew stayed at the camp long enough to bury the dead. His remains would be shipped to the Castle. Since he had no other contact or family alive, she or Dad would tend to his grave. After one last sweep around the camp disabling the enemy's weapons, mostly AK-47 automatics, she assisted the surviving prisoners onto the camp's troop carriers destined for Port Sudan. From there, the survivors would be assisted by the Red Cross back to their respective homelands and waiting families.

For Stinger, the mission was not over yet, but for the rest of her crew it was. For Elena and her newly found mate Dimitry, it was back to Volgograd with a promise to keep their friendship alive. Tracy invited her to the Castle and the New Republic once the global conflicts had settled. For Toporov, in the company of his family, it was back to Russia. He was bound for leadership in some directorate.

For Tracy, it was on to the Gulf of Hormuz. She would not stop her relentless pursuit until the world's fiercest enemy was terminated. She had a plan already laid out for that. The bait was set. All she must do now was lure him from his lair.

BATTLE FOR DC

In spite of the initial loss of combatants, the sun had risen over the capital city as it did with each day. Deliberations about a battle strategy for a new approach were still going on. The strategy would entail breaking the forces into smaller tactical units of individual squads trying to make it across the bridges. The plan was to protect the units with trucks and SUV vehicles spearheading ahead. To achieve that, reinforced metal deflectors would be used, much like a medieval knight carrying a shield against an oncoming blow. But that would take time to construct. No other option was at Big Red's disposal. They had to be constructed.

It took several days of intense labor and bodywork to fabricate the protective shields made up of wood, sheet metal, and grill works gathered from local shops and farms. In the prospect of peace, country folks were only too willing to help. The day finally approached when the Red Army was ready for battle once more.

It was an uncanny sight to see the makeshift might of vehicles lined up on the western edge of the Potomac. It was a monstrous force unlike anything ever seen. Presently striding along the bizarre-looking mobile assault vehicles, Big Red gave it a once over. Proud and confident that it'd work, she made a final declaration at her three commanders, "Think we're ready. Are you?"

Almost in unison, "Ready as can be," were the answers accompanied by smart salutes. In addition to getting the vehicles battle ready, the commanders, setting an example, also adhered to the rank discipline for themselves as well as the soldiers. From here on out, commands would be passed along up and down the ranks. Accompanied with a proud grin, Big Red striding along the ranks nodded at her battalion commanders, *you did it. Be proud.*

The final hour for the assault on the city approached. All fighting units were in place. Trucks and SUV drivers were in place, ready for her command. It came minutes later via radios.

"Moving out…Ahead, all units."

In an instant, the roaring sound of hundreds of mechanized vehicles moving toward the bridges filled the air along the Potomac. The combined forces of vehicle-protected, rapidly followed, foot-based fighters were on the move. Taking the last turn, entering the western edge of the bridges, a barrier of wood, metal, and steel were pushing their way across the river. A formation of Trojan horses was on its way to retake the city.

To the astonishment of the commanders, the initial push went without taking on fire. It came as surprise to all. There were only erratic bursts of gunfire coming from the other end of the bridges. It was as if Jihad had exhausted its supplies of RPGs during the initial assault. Realizing that, it spurred the soldiers on even more.

"Looks like the shield's holding," Mackenzie shouted into the radio. "How're your units doing?"

"Charging ahead," and "taking light fire," were their responses.

"Stay in formation." Big Red's voice was heard with precision intervals. Her concern was to not recklessly charge into the city. Her concern was for the protection of every soldier from getting injured or getting killed. To achieve that, the three mechanized battalions had to be precisely paced across the bridges. To be a most effective force they had to arrive as one combined brigade on the other side. The entire strength of the force had to be felt by the enemy. It was this combined force that could drive the terrorists from the capital city once and for all.

"Keep formation," the orders kept coming through the radio. Pacing the three independent battalions across the bridges was making progress. They had advanced one fourth of the way across without taking serious fire. The sporadic return by mostly AK-47 rifles proved completely ineffective on the advancing forces. It only afflicted light damages on the vehicles but not on the Red Army. A few of the mobile barriers stalled out due to damages to tires, windshields, and radiators from overheated engines. Pushing on, the major force made solid progress.

Now halfway across, there was still no resistance to block or stop her army. As most seasoned commanders would also realize by now, advancing into enemy territory without so much as one casualty, Big Red was getting concerned. An uneasy feeling made its way up her throat. Her woman's intuition crept into play. "Something's wrong."

"Report your progress," her voice came thought the radios.

"This' a breeze," Kelly reported from the Key Bridge.

"No resistance," Kimberly reported from the 14th Bridge.

Watching Mackenzie's progress directly ahead crossing Roosevelt Memorial gave her renewed confidence. *My plan worked.*

"Keep your eyes open," she cautioned. The three battalions had advanced almost all the way across the bridges. They were on the doorstep of the city. Hollers and cheers about the rapid progress were heard throughout the ether. By the time Red realized that something was seriously wrong it was too late. Reality came on so sudden there was nothing any one of the commanders or soldiers in, on, or around the vehicles could do.

The explosions simultaneously set off by the terrorists were timed to precisely the same second. They were timed to a point when the bridges were loaded down for maximum casualty effects. It was a strategy used by Jihad over and over in the past. The knowledge should have been a caution to the commanders.

It was too late to contemplate, rationalize, or even justify the event. In military jargon, it was what it was, a "fuckup of royal proportions."

No matter what the cause and consequence, Big Red had to take the blame. She knew the instant the charges went off. Her career path to a military echelon rank status would most likely be over. Time would tell the true events. For now, her work was cut out for her. It was that of immediate assessment and salvaging survivors. Those who had not been instantly killed by the explosive mega forces pushing up vertically and incinerating most of the bridges were killed by tons of debris falling back. Even more died from being thrown up, only to land on the water surface. Injured and unconscious, what followed was drowning. The force alone would have killed a healthy person. Having lungs collapsed and mangled bodies was enough to kill many of the survivors.

Big Red watched on in horror as the events played out. Like the airwaves, she had turned silent from shock. Her ashen face reflected the inner battle her mind went through. The battle was over before it had even begun.

In hindsight, the only thing that could be said about the disaster was, "Live and learn." To earn the skills and experience needed to prevent disasters came with practice. Practice in war, however, gave grounds for casualties. Casualties were precious resources, and resources were the humans. One second alive and the next second expired. It was not anything a commander would wish. In the end, to justify a cause and its effects, especially taking to war, history would have the true accounts.

What would be most important for now and the immediate future for the surviving armed forces was to take care of the injured and to collect the dead. It would take days to assess and report the damages.

Word had already reached Foster up north. He promised support as soon as it could arrive at the disaster zone. For additional resources, Scott Brooks and his seaborne fleet would be available as well. But, for the present, he was getting ready to stage an all-out battle himself.

What neither force had taken into consideration was the cunning strategies with which the Jihad forces managed their skillful attacks. While the rest of the world was asleep at the wheels, Al Qaeda, Jihad, and the rest of the terrorist alliances had taken the time to educate, train, and teach their soldiers on how to fight an effective battle as a feared and formidable force, a unified army.

The balance of power had shifted to an army the future world would have to contend with. The Prophet and his team, aside from a few localized setbacks, had achieved his goal. It was that of dominating free world nations.

BATTLE FOR THE PENTAGON

What Brooks had achieved for the New Republic was extraordinary. Short of taking back a crumbled nation, he had uprooted the enemy, neutralized its power, and pushed its main contingency out to sea. What was required now would take strong leadership. It was time to dole out responsibilities for exactly that. There was one more issue to solve, that of retaking the Pentagon. From scouts reporting on the status of the once most powerful and influential command complex in the world, he still had some work cut out. Consolidating the combined forces from his fleet, Foster's remaining army, and Big Red's, the effort was achievable. The problem at the moment was cohesive communication. With everybody forced to use dated equipment, none of the units were capable of effectively keeping in contact. Regardless of the outcome, the attempt to take the Pentagon had to be made. There was no alternative in securing the nation. Using the signal core protected by advanced scout detachments, though it took time to dispatch, Foster established a relay link from the Eastern Seaboard along the shorelines all the way into Chesapeake Bay.

"Foster," the call went out on the radio. "Come in. What's the condition?"

The link worked. He had a response within minutes from all units. Brooks gave him a brief status on the East River and his success retaking the U.N. complex. Foster had good reasons for the call. He wanted to establish a New Republic presence at the former United Nations complex. It would serve as eastern command for now until a solid presence could be reestablished at the Pentagon.

Using War Dog vessels, the general was shuttled to the East River within the hour. Still partially submerged from flooding, Foster used the upper floors in the U.N. assembly building for an ad hoc summit. The meeting was sure to make history. "What's your take?" Foster demanded. Since he had lost much of his forces in the Hudson River, he would have to fill his ranks from what was left from the Red Army. Accurate accounts at this time were not yet established. For that, he needed to meet up with Red himself. It would take a couple of days to do that.

Brooks assured him, "My men are ready." In spite of the urgency, he allowed his waterborne attack force one day of rest before calling them back to action. Foster notified Big Red via established relay stations. "ETA: 48 hours."

It took close to the projected time for both forces to arrive in DC. Brooks, skirting the Atlantic coast south, making his way through Chesapeake Bay, then up the Potomac River, landed by the shores of what used to be the nation's busiest airport, DC National, now deserted grounds. His plan was to establish a temporary naval presence to host his fleet of speedboats.

Headed directly south on I-95, Foster's units arrived on the same day. His immediate aim was Fort Myer, currently occupied by the remnants of Big Red's units. With the New Republic leaders assembled at one place, an effective battle strategy now was possible. The first of several strategy meetings kicked off shortly thereafter.

General Foster was once again in an effective command position. "First off," he demanded during the initial briefing session, "I need a status count from each of you." His grayish-colored eyes, set within a seasoned, battle-hardened face, sought out Big Red. It gauged the woman with a piercing stare. It would be a first for him, sharing his established grounds with a female counterpart. Like many his age, Foster grew out of the establishment, an epoch that went by the wayside with the '70s. It seemed long ago when the world was shaped by men, managed by men, and commanded by men. It had been a man's world.

Growing with the changes brought on by equal rights movements, he struggled, like many of the commanders, through a decade of adjusting. Some never adapted. Those were quickly phased out with retirement. The prolific rifts that followed were felt up and down the ranks. Soon after, the result was an integrated army with balanced rights to both genders. As he had predicted, there was much friction in the early years. Both genders had to share not only space and inherited habits, but common facilities as well. It was the latter causing the biggest problems. But, in the end, after much controversy, the system worked itself out.

Today, a hardcore military man, Foster accepted the changes. Presently, his eyes lingered on Big Red for a status input. She was slightly affected by Foster's commanding presence. "As you've heard by now," she reported, "I've lost many of my warriors with the destruction of the bridges."

"Every commander has losses," Foster gave her a somewhat comforting assurance. "Skills and expertise will have to be earned, just like individual reputations."

"A hell of a price to pay," she admitted. It was to be the last remark made on the losses. From here on out, the focus was entirely set on the immediate mission at hand. And that was of routing out the last remaining Jihad forces from the Pentagon. What made the task somewhat questionable was the support the terrorists enjoyed from the anarchist forces currently patrolling the grounds from here to the Mexican borders. It would mean fighting the enemy from abroad while cleaning house within the new nation's own borders.

"I want complete annihilation," Foster ordered. "I don't," he insisted, "want any long, drawn out trials and disputes from international tribunals."

Brooks readily agreed on the subject matter. "Got my vote." From his perspective, this had always been his position for the judgment of the terrorists. It was his policy not to take prisoners. Given the opportunity to the enemy was associated with too many repercussions from the media, the mediators, and the liberals. To create a strong nation, rules and regulations would have to be enforced as spelled out in the new constitution. Some might object to such harsh rulings. "Too bad," would be his comeback. There was always resistance to change. And changes were about to be instituted. All there was left was the retaking of the Pentagon.

As soon as Foster had an accurate count of the combined forces he was able to build a battle strategy. The numbers were in. Brooks reported 675 seamen at a ready. Although hardened in character, he was still cringing at the loss of 75 of his men, with some dead and the majority too injured for battle. The rest of his forces were ready to man whatever seaworthy fleet was available.

The Red Army had dwindled down from close to five thousand women to less than two thousand. Adding Foster's skeleton force, the combined count of battle-ready fighters was close to three thousand men and women. It would most likely match the enemy's count evenly.

"Here's the battle plan. Red Army," his eyes shifted to Big Red's face, filled with anticipation. After her heavy losses, she had lost some of her confidence. She had questioned whether the general would bestow another command on her. The only positive thing that came out of the bridge fiasco, enormously grateful for it, her battle commanders had survived. Though frayed and battered, the wounds proved not serious. The next words eased her visible strain. "You and your forces proceed to Constitution Avenue. Once you reach 17th and 15th Avenues," he emphasized, "you split your forces into two assault groups encircling the Capitol and White House grounds. Your goal is to take possession of both."

Some of her lieutenants voiced some legitimate concerns. "What about the bridges…The enemy forces?"

"I'll come to that," he said. "But first, the plan."

"What about backup?"

"Leave that to me. I will shore up my forces wherever needed. The battle does not stop there. Next up is the treasury, the mint, monuments, Smithsonian, and the rest of the historic places. Once the capital city is secure," he went on, "we push on to Baltimore. I want both cities in my hands, especially the naval academy grounds."

"Annapolis?"

"That's right. That, the harbor, and Chesapeake Bay. We won't stop until the entire East Coast is back in our hands. Understood?"

"Understood."

"Now back to the river crossing. Brooks here," he gestured at the renegade elect to naval commander, "will shuttle all of you across the Potomac. He'll set up a floating bridge much like a conveyor belt. You," he addressed Big Red directly, "will have your troops in formation, ready to board as quickly as a craft comes along shore side." He took a few paces to the regional map tacked on the wall. "Enemy's gonna be waiting here, here, and here." What he indicated were three major crossing points. It was the locations where the former bridges had stood.

"We'll be ready."

"Whatever the outcome," Foster reminded his forces as closing statement, "it's not only a fight over life and death," he stressed the point some more, "but a battle to retake a nation. Our nation. Let's kick ass." It concluded the briefing. Battle commanders headed to the fort, taking command over their respective sectors. Brooks' sea pilots were already anxiously waiting for getting the fight underway.

"Muster up, ladies." Big Red took the lead, flanked by her three battalion commanders Mac, Kelly, and Kim. Troop assembly was by the edge of the river. A junction point for it was dedicated at the intersections of Arlington Blvd., G.W. Memorial Pkwy., and on-ramp columns that used to support Roosevelt Memorial Bridge.

Brooks and his pilots, positioned within the protection of Roosevelt Island, were waiting with engines idling at three loading spots by the shores. The island, situated in the middle of the river, gave him the surprise edge he needed for getting a jump on the enemy. He was keenly aware that the sound from hundreds of engines carried across the waters. The enemy would be alerted but would have no evidence until the assault. By then, his fleet would be less than half a mile within reach to beach the DC shore front. Surprise would be with him.

Boarding was swift. Much to the delight of Foster, who was intensely watching the loading, the crossing went like clockwork. The first files made rapid progress until they reached the open waters. It was there when the first salvo from the enemy struck.

"Fan out," Brook's voice urged on the radio. "North and south." His quick reaction probably saved hundreds of soldiers who would have otherwise perished in the fire. The speedboats were swift to maneuver to any command. Hanging onto rails, stern and bow, the Red Army was thrown from side to side with each direction change to avoid the RPGs launched in their direction. There were many. Some found their targets where others missed. Whoever survived the initial onslaught faced the next line of enemy defense, automatic machineguns. Set up to crossfire, there were more casualties from whoever crossed the hail of .50mm bullets coming their way.

Brooks was expecting it. "Wave jump," his voice echoed through the radio receivers. His pilots and crews acted accordingly. It was a coordinated effort for getting as much of the load across safely. Since the load was a mere remnant of Red's and Foster's former armed forces front, it would be their only chance for winning the battle. Based on his experience speeding up and down the Mississippi, Brooks gauged the waves created by the craft's hulls for how and when to jump the crests. It was an important strategy he'd taught his pilots. They did not have to be told twice. Wave jumps came natural after having been practiced on the river for months. It prevented the enemy fire targeted on the craft from getting a solid fix.

Although the maneuvers forced the assault teams to fan out in different directions, many more made it across the river without getting sunk. The primary beachhead on the DC side was the Lincoln Memorial grounds, from where Foster's forces would reassemble into units once more. All commanders made it across, but not without injuries. Kim had taken a headshot. The caliber had bounced off her skull. She survived to fight on. Kelly had taken two bullets. One lodged into her shoulder while another buried into her thigh. As tough as Big Red's commanders were, they all moved on, leading the battalions across the river and on toward the ultimate target.

But the fight was far from being won.

When Foster called up his forces for the push on DC, enemy scouts reported the progress back to their headquarters. An alert went out immediately to every cell in the vicinity. The fact that Jihad had been building up its forces locally, as well as globally over the years, was unknown to the Patriots and the people living in parts west of the Mississippi. Having been isolated from the world since the collapse of the nation, they were not aware that recruiting by Jihad for their cause had not stopped. It continued in a highly prolific manner throughout much of the Islamic communities.

For the common cause in gaining world dominance, every nation on the globe, politically and economically not entirely stabilized, was subject to infiltration with North America as the primary target. To the concerned citizen the reason was obvious. But politicians and policy makers had completely ignored this. Too much trust had been placed into the hands of the U.N. who, over the course of decades, gained much political weight in favor of resentful nations against the free world.

It was the lack in effective leadership from troubled nations, and there were many, that essentially provided the foundation to gain global Islamic footing. The climate had shifted from a free secular world to the power of Islam. The effects were felt by every westernized nation near and far. The impact in and around the Eastern Seaboard and on both sides of the Atlantic had been obvious, but was mostly ignored by the leaders of the regions. It was only the mindful ones noticing the changes. The most visible was the shift from western fashion to Arabian garb, that of a veiled face, loosely fitted clothes, and worn-in sandals. Where many fit the general Arabian heritage, the profile for recruited members acquired in recent times, now, could match any ethnic group.

Assigned years earlier to take command over Jihad forces, U.S. Cell East, headquartered at the Pentagon, Washington, DC, Tariq Amman, First Lieutenant, had been waiting for a chance to prove himself. Today, after regrouping at the eastern side of the river, taking up a defensive position to repel the advancing Patriots, would be it. The combined forces of Jihad, Al Qaeda, foreign mercenaries, and local sympathizers were waiting on the shores of the Potomac for the enemy to advance.

"Spread the word," he instructed his forces up and down the banks of the darkened body of waters relentlessly feeding the Chesapeake Bay to the south. "Nobody gets across."

His chest swelled with pride from the successful triumph he had attained a few days earlier. Squashing what his scouts had estimated to be a brigade at close to three thousand men, women to be more accurate, his men were still cheering him on whenever he set foot among the ranks. "Women," he earlier confided to his most trusted lieutenants, "will never make it in battle."

His point was proven after he annihilated much of what the infidels called their Red Army. In spite of the detested brigades of nothing but women, he boasted, "Wouldn't mind getting my hands on their leader."

"The Amazon?" one of his lieutenants asked. He wanted to be sure he had heard right.

"The one." Where most harbored private thoughts about the female subject matter, the openly discussed dialogue brought on wide grins among the comrades nearby. Reading from their faces, one could readily guess the personal thoughts each held.

"Never saw so many tall, well-proportioned women in my life," one remarked. "Where do they breed them?"

"It is in the water," another replied. "Think it is why we are fighting for the Great Lakes."

"You are right."

"Don't expect to find any virgins there," another added.

"Why?"

"They are born virginless," he boasted. "I was told."

Amman suddenly held up one finger against the lips. "Shh," he cautioned. "You hear that?"

"The sound?"

His face turned quizzical. "Yeah."

"It has been with us all morning," the lieutenant replied.

"What is that?"

His face had turned uneasy at the sound coming from across the river. He brought up a pair of binoculars to his eyes to search the river. "Nothing."

"Could be construction."

"Nah. Not with the state the economy is in. Sounds like engines?"

Minutes later, the Jihad forces were promptly interrupted from their private gathering by a resounding radio transmit. "Red alert," the harsh words from a forward spotter resonated through the ranks.

Tariq Amman immediately jumped into action. "Attack...Attack...Attack."

The enemy forces came in the form of multiple fronts from across the river. Amman had been expecting it but did not know how the enemy was going to breach the Potomac. When the enemy push from the north took place several days ago, based on the sheer numbers of the attacking army, he had made a safe retreat across the river. Having only one convenient battle front facing directly ahead had provided an immense advantage. This way, he did not have to worry about getting flanked from the sides.

What he did not expect was an enemy recovered from the heavy losses inflicted by his fighters. With the bridges destroyed, without an air force at hand by either side, the options had been minimized to either a vessel crossing or forced march approach from the Baltimore front via I-495 after rounding the DC region. That, however, would take time and resources the enemy did not have, he figured.

Being a battled-seasoned warrior, he had ruled out the latter option because it meant close combat in and through city streets. From combat strategies executed by the enemy, experience showed that the American infidels did not have man to man fighting experience nor did they want any part of it. As history had demonstrated over the span of several wars, the infidels preferred to let technology do the dirty work, that of cutting the enemy onslaught to pieces using metal projectiles such as bullets, grenades, rockets, and bombs.

It only took Amman a few seconds to assess the enemy's strategy. With elbows propped against the historical building's windowsill he had selected as his command post, one visual sweep along the riverfront using a pair of field glasses gave him an initial battle measure. The combined enemy threat came in the form of three fronts. He was taken by surprise by the type of transportation in use. The speed of battle in itself was alarming. He could not let what seemed to be wave after wave of armored sea craft skim across the waters. A quick tally of boats gave him an initial count. It was much like a conveyor belt feeding a manufacturing process. "Brooks," he snarled at the approaching front when he spotted the much-feared enemy commander in the lead. *There'll be no hostage taking,* was a troubled thought after recognizing the fleet commander homing in on his defense bastion.

"Fire at will," Amman ordered. "Show no mercy."

Brooks spotted the incoming fire lines as soon as they left the barrels. From the direction of the fiery streams he was able to assess the major enemy positions dug in across the river. Using the onboard radio, he shouted rapid orders from the lead craft he piloted. Much like other great warriors depicted in historical records, he was always out front leading his forces. He preferred that position over handing out orders from the safety of a rear command position. It gave him first choice for cutting down the enemy. Wherever possible, he sought out the attacking force's leaders. At this point he was uncertain of what enemy commander was in charge.

His eyes were watchfully scanning the horizon, trying to spot the enemy's leader. At the moment, he was unable to detect the command position he was seeking out. It seemed the entire waterfront was lit up by fiery tracer rounds. "Watch out," he shouted into the infernal hail of death. "Crossfire."

It was here when the wave jumping commenced. For anyone unaware of the crossfire tactic, any approaching force would have been completely annihilated right from the start. After the Civil War, with the end of fighting the gentlemen's war, many command changes had been instituted. One major change was the crossfire tactic. It was a strategy implemented and proven effective over and over with a resultant successful outcome. The strategy was simple. At its basics, it only required two machineguns positioned some distance apart at the same firing line, crossing angles aimed some distance ahead. Creating a perfect "V" formation spread out wide at the enemy front, the ensuing hail of fire would cut down every living thing entering the continuous stream of bullets coming their way.

It was this unyielding barrier Brooks and his pilots were trying to avoid by jumping the crests of waves his speeding boats created. Up to now the tactic seemed to be working. What made it possible was the distance. With it came the lag of reaction applied by the shooters pulling triggers. Without being able to anticipate the pilots' changing directions, their aim was always a fraction of a second behind the speeding target. A few minutes more and the first wave of brutally charged, armored War Dogs jumped ashore. The battle for DC had begun.

Crouching below the rails for protection from a continuous stream of incoming machinegun rounds, Big Red's all-female army, flanked by Brooks' squads of battle-seasoned seamen, jumped from the craft as soon as they made contact on the sandy shore. What awaited them were merciless killers ready to slice off heads. That thought alone brought on chills. Earlier in the morning, Big Red, aware of the deadly threat ahead, gave her fighters the necessary pep talk. It'd taken the edge off the chilly horror.

"Ladies," she'd said. "Don't let the upcoming fight break your spirits. It's only men waiting on the other side."

"But," were some of the objections, "what about the infernal hatred, the extremists, and the beheadings?"

The fear she tried to instill on her fighters was greater when she said, "I want you to envision one thing and one thing only. See yourself walking six paces in back of your Arabian husbands clutching the Koran on the way to the Mosque." That did it. She did not have to explain further. The immediate uproar was the greatest battle cry three thousand screaming throats had ever produced. "Down with Jihad."

It was this cry the enemy was facing head on when the boats dislodged loads of irate warriors' ready to demand justice in the name of past, present, and future women. Where the bodies provided the energy, the earlier instilled images on the women's brains did most of the fighting.

Hand to hand combat was not new to the Red Army. At a smaller scale, they had experienced close combat during the Alaskan encounter. But directly facing ahead, today would be the make or break of the proud, single-gendered army. After the fiasco days earlier, losing close to two thousand inexperienced but dedicated soldiers, Big Red needed a win. Leading the first wave up the banks looked promising.

As anticipated, her fighters did well. Though not everybody made it up the shores, with some cut down by the wall of oncoming bullets, the ones that made it did her name proud. Perhaps unevenly matched in strength and fighting skills, what gave the women the killing edge was fearful beheadings and Islamic dress code images instilled into their minds.

Big Red's lieutenants kept up the battle slogan. "Down with oppression. Down with mutilations. Down with Jihad."

The shouts were repeated up and down the ranks just as passionately. Agonizing yard by yard was battled out. Once the army advanced toward the city, it was mostly woman to man combat, retaking building after building. The first ground assault took place by the Lincoln Memorial. From there the army spread to the federal, historical, and other major complexes in and around the capital. The ultimate goal was to retake the White House and Capitol, presently in use by the Jihad command.

Where the general advance forces made initial progress, retaking the city proved not as easy. The stronghold force concentrated within the nation's foremost residences presented fierce resistance. Being Jihad's last stand, they were not about to give up their hold on the newly acquired Promised Land. It was die here defending the capital or die later on the execution block. Losing the battle, either way would be death.

The first day came and went. The battle carried into the second and third days with equal intensity. It was not until the fourth day when the Red Army finally gained ground. It came in the form of new recruits. When the battle started, word spread rapidly into West Virginia, down the Carolinas, and up the Appalachians. Help came from as far away as Alabama, Kentucky, Tennessee, and farther out. Recruits were only too willing to put their lives on the line for the country, especially since rumors of initial successes were carried back. It just took time for their support to get to the capital. Once reinforcement arrived the battle for DC was pretty much in control of the Patriots.

There was one more task: a personal vendetta pitted between Big Red and Tariq Amman, commander, D.C. forces Jihad.

Over the past several days, he had been in constant contact via satellite relays with the Prophet, begging for support. "Do not give up the city," he was ordered. "Reinforcement is on the way."

There was, however, no timeframe for the promise. If help could not be mustered up within the next few days, with Amman's forces rapidly dwindling, the city would be lost. He did not dare voice his concerns to the supreme commander. Instead, he kept on fighting to the last man. He followed the progress from his watchtower, the Washington Monument. Perched atop this lofty icon, he was able to command every phase of the advancing army. When he realized the tower could be a potential trap, it was too late.

During the first day of battle he became alarmed. He could not believe the ferocity with which the women soldiers were fighting. Aside from a secret admiration he had held for these foreign women, he had gained a tremendous amount of respect. In the following days, however, the enemy's forces seemed to grow to a force he could not gain hold of. His fighters were losing ground quickly. Already pushed against the wall he made a last-ditch effort to save the remnants of his diminishing forces. "Fall back," he ordered.

His once feared mercenary killers had shrunk to only a few squads of fighters. His forces had already been pushed back into the National Museum complex. It left him and his contingents of close lieutenants exposed without backing. It was then he realized the battle was lost. Defeat was imminent. He was facing the last stand. He could already hear the hurried footsteps sounding up the staircase. In the lead was the woman of great legend, Big Red. He was waiting for her to turn the last corner when he spotted her superior physique.

The first words from Red's lips were, "Judgment day." She was surprised at facing only a small core of Amman's trusted comrades shielding him. Not that he was incapable of hand to hand combat, but the prosperous life as field commander had taken its toll. Amman was not the tough fighter he once was, and neither were his remaining lieutenants. With Big Red flanked by Mac, Kim, and Kelly, facing an equal strength of opponents, the fighting turned personal.

After Brooks delivered the Red Army to the DC shores, he and the armada headed straight south to meet up with Foster. His immediate aim was a complex he promised Foster to help take back from the enemy's hands. The five-sided Pentagon complex was clearly visible from the river with the general giving directions, "Ahead one mile," and when the marker was reached. "Boundary Channel."

After delivering Red's forces across the Potomac, Brooks' fleet followed in tight formation. They had just passed beneath the old G.W. Bridge into an age-old estuary containing the marina. What used to be a flotilla-based berthing place for the political elite today was a neglected piece of real estate much like the rest of the terrain in and around the Pentagon plaza. Years without tending to the place had taken their toll. Construction cranes that used to be busy expanding housing and commerce projects, like gigantic storks, were projecting their ironic frames up into the sky, frozen in time.

Foster's face was locked on the familiar silhouette growing from the horizon. "Soon," he fumed into the spray whipped up by the bow, "you'll be mine again."

As soon as the first boat beached, Foster jumped onto solid ground. It was like setting foot on his homeland after years of absence. He stopped for a moment to inhale the familiar scent of musty seaweed drifting in from the surrounding marchland growing alongside the Potomac. Jefferson Davis Hwy. and Boundary Channel Drive, directly ahead, were the last obstacles to cross. Throwing a determined nod at the target ahead, he huffed at Brooks, "Let's do it." No sooner had he said it when the first stream of fiery tracers from the eastern front of the complex darted his way. It was obvious where the fire originated. Most of the windows on this side of the building lit up with automatic fire. The battle for the Pentagon had begun.

THE PENTAGON

Derek Wallace, self-elect Group Leader, Anarchists, Sector Three, knew he had it coming. But so, did every gangster boss, dictator, and tyrant before him. What was common to all three undesirable elements operating against mainstream society was the self-centric, arrogance, and egotistical disposition set out to purely satisfy lust for personal gain. Fortunately, with all that was going on in the disintegrated nation over the years, he had been able to keep abreast from other undesirable elements roaming the nation. He'd had some good run lasting years. Aside from the vast land he controlled, the perimeter south of Route 66 from east to west all the way to the Mexican border, he had acquired great wealth. The riches were his. He'd earned it. Since there was no currency in the nation, the riches could not be counted in dollars and bank accounts. It was all bartered goods.

Even before the EMP strike he knew what the people desired. Years earlier he had a notion something was amiss with the nation. There was too much deception and dishonesty among the ranks embracing politicians, industrials—including banking—corporate America, and more. Where stability, honesty, and integrity used to be the norm, dating back to the creation of the nation, in recent decades these values holding the infrastructure together had disintegrated. Even before the last turn of the century, the once honorable values had taken a complete flip. In today's world, the standards were greed and deception. When held accountable for their misdeeds, "Hell," was the justification. "Everybody's doing it. I want my share."

It might have been an understatement, but in the process of everybody having a windfall, the consequences proved to be severe. The past years showed the end results. It was the collapse of a once powerful nation.

It was the disintegration that provided great opportunities to individuals like Derek Wallace. Though he was not a bad person, he considered himself an opportunist, nevertheless. And that was the skill with which he had acquired the enormous wealth. Where everybody was fighting for survival, he took his skills to trade. Wallace knew exactly what the people needed during bad times. It was commodities. People need commodities at least until manufacturing was established again. That could be years. Trading goods was exactly what he banked on. Where everybody was struggling for food, clothing, and shelter, the bare necessities, he supplemented what people desired most: drugs, alcohol, and guns.

As with most bad times with a war, a black market was created. A market solely based on barter. "What do people trade for the commodities they desire most?" he'd asked himself. "Personal possessions." And, if there was nothing left aside the home and property, it was this that was traded.

It was deeds to land and property that Wallace had acquired by the thousands. Keeping a ledger on values traded, he had made deals with everybody, supplying what they needed with his suppliers close by, just across the border.

They had all the goods he needed from alcohol, to guns, to drugs, and it was drugs that were high in demand. Though he preferred deeds and trusts sealed in paper documents, for payment he took everything people had to trade to satisfy their needs.

Today, Derek Wallace was worried. He was worried because the liberators were at the doorstep. Several days ago, when he received word about an army amassing only a couple of miles north, he knew it would be only a matter of time before they showed up here. Years ago, just after he started the business, he was looking for a place he could securely store his acquired treasures. "Where else," he questioned himself, "but the Pentagon?" He was surprised when he found the once so prominent complex almost deserted. Occupied by only a small contingent of Jihad at the time seeking refuge, it was a short exchange driving them from the complex. He took possession thereafter.

The Pentagon served him and the Anarchists well. It was a suitable fortress not only for storing his wealth, but for housing its occupants. Many of the once spacious offices had been turned into a dormitory for his men, the "Traders," as he liked to call them. Where the lower levels were used for storage, the loftier ones' upstairs were used by his people.

Filing cabinets that used to contain mostly classified materials now contained contracts, trusts, and deeds of sales for the enormous property wealth in his possession. Today, so close to a possible surrender of the facility, he had ordered his force to box up everything that needed to be hauled off, just in case. It was this activity he was worried about running out of time. He wanted his treasure mobilized in case his forces were overpowered.

Sure, he had an army. Almost two thousand strong, his men, though everybody carried a weapon, were mostly for personal protection while on the road. They were not trained soldiers one would encounter with a battle-trained army. They were mostly street smart with an attitude. It was good enough to fight off vagrants and vagabonds one encountered along the way, but not nearly conditioned enough for fighting an opposing army. If it came to that, it'd have to be close combat from door to door, and floor to floor. All he could hope for was to prevent the intruders from getting into the complex. For that he had his armed men stationed at every window and entrance door. Short on radio gear for everybody, he had been using the intercom for in-house communication. It'd have to do in case of an attack.

"Alert...Alert." An alarm initiated from the top floor, east wing, sounded through the building. "Enemy approach. River banks."

It was an alert call he had hoped would never come. But wishful thinking had faded into reality. He would have to face whatever was on the approach. As soon as the alarm sounded he bolted for the nearest intercom and ordered, "Fire," and "warning shots only...repeat, warning only."

At this point he still hoped he could negotiate his way out without getting into a long, drawn-out battle. And drawn out it would be. There was no way he'd ever give up his hard-earned treasures. Several seconds passed before he reached for the intercom again. "Advise," he ordered his outlook. He needed feedback on the enemy's intentions.

"On hold," he was told. Tense minutes passed before the next orders came in. "General wants to talk."

There's still hope, he huffed while rushing to the east wing entrance gates.

Rushing for the Pentagon, with Foster in the lead, he was first to take fire. What felt like bullets hitting his face and body in actuality were dust and gravel picked up by the incoming rounds. To his surprise the firing stopped short. He immediately halted the advance when he realized they were warning shots. With one arm stretched overhead, facing his forces, he commanded, "Halt." Unless it was an all-out attack without warning from the enemy, Foster generally tried to negotiate a way out to prevent unnecessary bloodshed.

Brooks, on the contrary, did not see it this way. He wanted blood. He needed blood. He'd conditioned his men, as it turned out in most cases, to "kill first and ask questions later...or never." It was a policy that gained him respect. It was a rule that had earned him his reputation, that of a merciless killer.

JIHAD'S LAST STAND

Taking two, three leaps at a time, with Big Red in the lead, the core contingent of the Red Army, Kelly, Kim, and Mac hastened up the narrow passageway within the Washington Monument. To everyone's surprise there was no fire returned from above. It stayed quiet even after entering the nation's prominent icon. "Must be out of ammo," Red muttered. "We should be so lucky," Mac replied. It would be close combat, one-on-one using swords and knives. "Stay tight," Red huffed as she hurried up the stairwell. No sooner had she said that than she stepped on the observation deck and made first contact. With her team alongside, they halted for a moment. It only took a second to assess the situation. Setting gender roles aside, it would be an even match.

Confronting the enemy face to face for a final showdown, they took the time to feel out each opponent. There was no rush for battle. From the looks of it, wielding combat knives, her earlier assessment was correct. They were out of ammunitions. It quickly became apparent that the enemy gave them the courtesy of a first strike. It gave Big Red a fleeting moment to reflect on a part of a different path, a path that might end here.

Dating back to her growing up years, she always knew she was different from her peers. Taller than most of her age, she stood out. But that was not the only difference. There was the well-endowed bodily proportion, determined features chiseled into her face, richness of full bodied hair set amid the personal attitude that she carried of defiance. It was the combination of her extraordinary features and self-assurance that ultimately determined a future cut out for accomplishments just as extraordinary.

Where she had been conditioned by her parents for great career opportunities, the demise of her parents, her educators, her peers and herself with the fall of the nation had drastically changed that direction. Because of that, all of her dreams and aspirations had been reduced to only one aspect, that of a fighter. As in everything else she set out to accomplish, she was good at this as well. But success did not come overnight. It had to be earned. It had taken years of discipline and training to get this far. Confronting the enemy at close quarters, assessing their physique, their disposition, and their character, she knew she was an even match and so was her squad of trusted lieutenants.

Each fighter took up their respective position to allow the space necessary to move. 555 feet off the ground, within the limited sphere of this marble and granite constructed obelisk, eight seasoned fighters were facing each other for one last battle. At this point, it could be read from their bearded faces, they believed the odds were in favor of the Jihad. Bristling with complete confidence, wielding a chosen weapon—either sword or knife, the women could practically feel the enemy's senses caressing their contours. With minds focused more on the pleasures with a woman, the faces took on a look of shock with the first strike of battle.

Mackenzie moved first. Apparently, she was the least patient. She lashed out but was immediately countered by the Jihad she had sought out. The battle had begun. Red's lieutenants kept their distance from Tariq. They knew he, the leader of the Jihad, DC cell, was a privilege reserved entirely for Big Red. His head would be hers to take.

It was understood by all fighters that nothing but a severed head would sanctify the injustice dealt to both factions. No matter what the outcome of this last fight, the trophy would be the head.

Though Jihad had a reputation for cruelty and brutality, at this stage both sides extended a certain reverence for each other. No matter what was said in the past, damages inflicted through terrorist acts causing endless conflicts and casualties, all was set aside. For now, all that counted was eliminating one individual opponent after the next standing in the way of finally restoring peace and stability once more to whomever would win the battle.

It was here within the walls of this famous icon where the future of the next world power would be determined. Victory would be decided here and now, either in favor of an ever-encroaching Jihad, destined for world dominance, or a newly-formed democratic faction created by the patriotic movement, that of the New Republic.

Containing a lifetime of pent-up frustration in a primal scream, Big Red lunged at Amman. "Take this, you bastard." Her sword was blocked. It glanced off Tariq's steel with a reverberating sound filled with exploding sparks flying in their faces. Still feeling each other out for strength, agility, and experience, it would take minutes for the battle to reach full force.

During the fury of fighting, thoughts of regrets such as *why the fighting, what's the sense,* and *why can't we talk* flashed through Red's mind. *Whatever happened to reasoning?* Each of her thoughts was justified by the passionate gaze set within a determined face from within the enemy's piercing eyes. Her ultimate conclusion was, *It's mankind's destiny. We are meant to struggle. We are born for flight. And we are destined to battle.*

"Infidel bitch," Tariq's immediate response followed. "I will have your head." They were words spoken in broken English. Within the blurry veil of battle, Red could see the immense hatred penned up in her opponent's face. It reflected the very reason for their battle. It was from many generations before, from factions like the Knights Templar, the British monarchy, and Vatican City, when power was in the hands of his antagonists, demanding submission by an ever-expanding world. It was only recently, in a span of a short few decades, when the tides had turned. The power had shifted into the hands of the Islamic cause in the name of Allah.

Now, with the fighting in full swing, the two forces battled each other with the weight shifting back and forth. It was not a quiet fight. It was a fierce battle verbalized in-between shouts and yells filled with profanities of all kinds. Each side had its own repertoire of cusswords. Cussing during fighting was nothing new. It was the way of combat. It inspired the opponents into renewed clashes. There was, however, an endpoint. It came with one losing the vigor of strength first.

It was Kim, making an error in judgment. With her strength gradually faltering, she did not block the last thrust from her opponent's knife. It would be an everlasting mistake. The blade from the enemy found its target. It was her heart pierced by the sword. Stunned by the sudden blow, face contorted in surprise, her body collapsed with a final plead for mercy, "Red. Help me." There was no one to come to her aid. The others were busy fending off their own opponents. Ten minutes into the fight, each warrior, terrorist and patriot alike, was weakening.

Physical battle has a relatively short lifespan. Contrary to battles lasting half an hour as depicted in many movies and films, the human body has a limited supply of energy, running out way before then. Most individual battles over life and death were determined within minutes, with one or the other making a mistake or running low on energy. A thrust or block was missed, inflicting the first damage. From then on, it was generally the wounded losing the fight, or life. Today, it was Kim who made the first mistake. It was Kim losing her life.

Though slowed in intensity, the fighting continued, and so did the onslaught of personal insults. The verbal abuse was necessary to drive adrenaline into renewed height. Unable to rush to her dying friend's aid, Big Red, in wounded desperation, delivered another thrust with the sword, screaming out at Tariq, "You'll pay for this." This time, the sword found its target. Aimed for Amman's chest, the blade glanced off his sternum only to penetrate deep into one lung. It immediately exhausted his air supply. The eyes of the leader, Jihad forces, D.C., took on the gaze of utter surprise. Seconds later, a veil of hushed silence fell over the fatally wounded warrior. One last hateful cuss escaped his quivering lips before his fatally wounded body collapsed. "You infidel bitch. I will fight you in Heaven."

Big Red, her face struck with grief and pain over the loss of Kim, stooping over his lifeless body, lifted his head off the floor and, in one wide swing with her blade, severed his head. The trophy was hers. The battle for America was over seconds later when she went to her companions' aid. In rapid succession, three more lives were terminated by the sword of Big Red.

There was one last task that remained. In one swift move with the tip of her blade, Big Red swooped up the severed head from the floor, strode over to the windows of the lofty landmark and tossed the ashen faced head of Tariq Amman into the wind. After landing unceremoniously on the ground, perched high up at the lofty heights of the monument, the sounds of uninhibited cheering from the remainder of the Red Army reached her ears. To the waiting crowd below it signified a victory over the foreign force that had instilled fear and terror for so many years.

The menace that had caused years of misery to the lives of a once great nation had been vindicated. The name of God over Allah would prevail once more over a nation given another chance to rebuild itself.

Big Red, accompanied by Kelly and Mac, supported by capable Patriots, went on to carry out the new constitution created by Rusty Norton, who became the New Republic's elected president replacing Wilmot and his current seat of government in the Western Sector. The balance of political power had shifted to the eastern seaboard once more, DC, Capital of the old, and the new nation. All war casualties from coast to coast fighting for freedom liberating the nation from the invading army, were honored with ceremonial burials putting to rest the brave and heralded at the Arlington cemetery bestowing deserving rights on the fallen soldiers.

THE END OF ANARCHY

Derek Wallace met up with General Foster at the gates. But as soon as he spotted the familiar face accompanied by a bunch of armed fighters nearby he had mixed feelings. The general, he figured, being a seasoned leader trained at the war college, had a sense of honor code he would abide by. But the young punk, as he called Brooks, was yet another case. It would be a challenge having to deal with him. He recognized the face from years earlier with whom he'd had a run-in. Colorado, it was, Cheyenne Mountain, more specifically NORAD. It was a time when he had just formed his contingent of rebels and was testing the territorial waters that he ran up on the lone scout challenging him. Not being the experienced leader of today, a wise choice in hindsight, he had retreated instead of facing an otherwise certain death. In the years that followed he became aware of the rumors spreading through the country about the killer warrior known as Scott Brooks, head of the War Dogs.

"What do you want?" Wallace decided to grab the situation by the horns, direct on. He did not want to give the general an opportunity for long, drawn-out negotiations. *What is mine will stay mine,* he silently reflected. *I've earned it fair and square.*

Much like Wallace, stern-faced and direct to the point as well, the general did not beat around the bush either when he replied, "You know exactly what I want."

His hand had been forced. It was exactly what he was trying to avoid: negotiations. "Well," he countered in defiance, "you can't have it. It's mine now. You abandoned it years ago. According to the Law," he quickly corrected, "Constitution, I've got squatter rights."

Shaking his head in dissent, Brooks stepped up, fixing a piercing stare at the renegade. "Constitution's changed," he claimed. "No more squatters, drifters, or vagabonds."

Wallace knew it was a direct insult at him, a challenge he tried to sidestep. Avoiding the piercing stare, he ignored the insult and Brooks as well. Facing the general, he made an offer. "How about this," he said. "We share the complex." *There it is,* he contemplated with regret. *The first concession.*

Foster, keenly aware of Wallace's cunning, insisted, "No such thing." He was taking the Pentagon back no matter what the consequences. The complex was built as an icon for national defense and it'd stay that way. It was a landmark for power. It had been a symbol of national strength. And it would emerge as such again. As far as he was concerned, there were only two structures in the world of equal statue worthy of supremacy, that of the Pentagon and that of the Kremlin. And he would be in control of this magnificent tribute to peace once more.

"Then it's settled," Wallace consented. "There's no common grounds." He did not proceed any further. There was no point in dragging the negotiations out. There would never be a mutual settlement. Neither side was willing to give an inch. "So be it," Wallace concluded the face-off, forfeiting any further chance for talks. One quick glance at Brooks assured him what would come next.

The defiant grin in Brooks' face said it all. It'd be nothing less than a massacre. One last nod at the general, one assessing glance at the waiting forces, turning his back on the negotiators, taking solid strides back inside the Pentagon, Wallace had thrown the dice. It would be war.

Foster and Brooks assembled their respective forces by the river's edge. Uncertain about the size of Wallace's forces, Foster had to make certain assumptions. No matter the size, his attack had to be swift. He did not want the complex damaged or destroyed. Minimizing damages and casualties, he would take the time for analyzing alternatives for a most effective approach. There was no haste to rush into battle. Unlike Brooks, Foster was not the ruthless killer the cohort's leader was. Less than fighting a "Gentlemen's War," he still respected the individual's life.

"No cannons…no artillery…no setting fires," he instructed Brooks on the overall strategy. He was adamant on the ruling. There were immediate objections from some of Brooks' troops. "What do you expect?" one sounded off. "Arm wrestling?"

"Only swords, knives. Blade is what I want," Foster insisted. He shot a quick glance at Brooks. "Your team. You tell 'em."

"We have to be swift. General here," Brooks explained, "doesn't want the building to go up in smoke." They took his word. They understood.

Addressing Brooks directly, Foster laid out his plan. "Come first daylight," he said. "Your men will storm the complex from all five fronts. Objective is," he briefly paused, letting his words sink in, "to simultaneously meet up at Ground Zero. There may be traps, there may be barriers, but rest assured," he emphasized this last point by lifting up one arm, "expect an ambush around every corner. Now go with God." It was the signal the impatient War Dogs had been waiting for. Shouts of elation roared through the meadows by the Potomac at the opportunity of battle. It was understood that it would entail mostly hand-to-hand combat. It was something the War Dogs could understand. They had been trained exactly for that. The only difference today was that the battle would take place on land. It would be a slight disadvantage for the sea-conditioned fighters.

"Six hours," the battle slogan spread up and down the ranks. Brooks spread out his forces, equally divided into five sectors spearheaded by ramrod squads. It would take the time to fashion the rams. The ensuing damages smashing through entrance gates could not be avoided. If that was all of the damage inflicted, the taking of the fort-like complex could easily be tolerated.

In the meantime, Wallace hacked out his defense. His forces had gathered within the central courtyard to receive the battle plan. Trapped within the complex, it would be a defensive strategy only. They all understood that there would be no escape. Only one winner would emerge. Every one of the Anarchists would fight for his and her share of the acquired wealth. Whereas the attacker's objective was to regain control of the Pentagon, Derek Wallace's aim was to hold on to his treasure. He could not let it fall into Foster's hands, and especially not Brooks'. It would mean the end of Anarchy and, with it, the end of him. "Should have left weeks ago," he reprimanded his plan for not leaving earlier. He could have easily sought out other bastions to the south for his men and his wealth. "Too late now." He had to fight to stand his grounds.

Facing imprisonment was out of the question. Satisfied for the moment, he made an on-the-spot resolution, "Never give up." With that resolution set, he went to work setting up defensive barriers. Stationed in and around top floors, his scouts kept calling out time, "Two more hours."

Foster's progress was closely watched by Wallace's scouts. There would be no surprise attacks. Wallace had formulated a plan. There would be five levels of lateral defenses. The same would prevail vertically for the upper five and two below-ground levels. Close to two thousand men at his disposal, he would assign between 10 to 12 militia team members per barricade. The rest would be for backup to fill open ranks from anticipated losses. Currently watching the assigned numbers dispatched to the last sectors, Wallace concluded with finality, "It's doable."

With the forces in place, his squadrons were ready for the attack. All he could do now was wait for the inevitable. Short of a miracle, the attack would come within the hour. Being an anarchist by trade, he was also a devout atheist by faith. Making one last round through the corridors and floors taking stock, *I better succeed,* he summed up within the walls of his personal retreat, *or life's all over.* After having acquired the belief and lifestyle between agnostic and fortune hunter, without the security of this fortress and acquired riches, life for him would not be worth living. Consequently, *I better succeed,* he reinforced his personal vows one final time.

Camped out by the perimeter of the river with a direct view to the fortress straight ahead, Foster and Brooks confirmed their plan of attack. Foster was mentally recollecting the specific layout for the complex of his former domain. He was not good with details. He was a commanding officer. He was used to have people do the detailing for him. It suddenly struck him. "Tracy." He used to rely on her for the details. She was good at it. How he wished she was here by his side.

With Brooks and his lieutenants nearby, he drew the outlines of the general layout in the sand. Struggling on, he explained as well as he could remember, "We can expect at least five levels of lateral barriers multiplied by seven levels of floors." With a pentagon configuration and corridors running concentric from the innermost Level "A" through the outermost Level "E," times seven vertical levels, there would be 175 barricades at a minimum.

Recollecting the complex ahead, he relayed the specific sectors awaiting them to his attack forces starting with the north side and moving clockwise: "Mall Terrace Entrance façade, River Terrace Entrance façade, Concourse Entrance (Metro Station) façade, South Parking Entrance façade, and Heliport façade." The current position his forces held was the stepped terrace by the River Entrance, leading up from the lagoon. "E Ring offices are the ones to keep a close watch on. They'll be stacked with snipers and advanced firing lines to slow the attack. The last defenses will be at ground level, basement, and mezzanine."

During normal times, it was possible to traverse a concourse between any two distant points in less than seven minutes. But today, that time could not possibly be accurate with an unforeseen number of barricades in the path. Lifting the heirloom piece from the breast pocket, Foster checked the hour one last time. "Thirty minutes."

"Rams are ready," the lieutenants reported. His troops had cut down trees for lumber from the riverside. The solid tree trunks with ropes attached would do the job to batter down expected obstacles.

Without electricity support for years, Derek Wallace and his contingent had been dependent on candle power for lighting the interior. Now, striding within the darkened bowels of the colossal infrastructure close to zero hour, he took stock of his riches. The space that used to house clusters of mainframes, supercomputers, and paper archives was now occupied by the booty he had acquired over year of pilferage. The space looked like a gigantic treasure trove, much like a pirate cove from the Conquering days. His eyes touched on valuables that used to belong to the affluent and middleclass living in the southern belt of the nation. He was soaking up the glitter from jewelry and precious metals heaped in endless piles of treasures. That did not even account for the rows of steel-encased filing cabinets containing drawers filled with countless trusts, certificates, and property deeds.

Pacing along the glittering wealth—his wealth—he could not bear the thought of losing it to the attacking forces. And lose he would if the outcome from the impending assault was in favor of the attackers. The thought alone made his blood boil. He could never imagine reverting back to a life in poverty. He would rather die. Once he came to that conclusion, the decision laid heavily on his mind. He abruptly turned and stormed out, just in time to hear the distant battle cry from the assailants.

When the time was up Foster gave the order, "Attack." He was charging ahead in the lead when Brooks caught up with him. "Stay back, Old Man," he shouted at the general. "This is my battle."

Taken aback by the rude remark, Foster fired back, "Watch your mouth." With a mind still functioning one hundred percent, he could not quite come to terms with the relentless aging process. Though there was no age limit, under normal conditions he would have been retired years ago. Because of the current state of turmoil, the nation was still facing, he did not see it that way. Always keeping in excellent shape through a prolific, but rewarding career, he felt that there were still many years of fighting in him. But when the bullets started flying in uncontrollable streams of fire right and left of him, *perhaps he's right,* he reasoned while slowing his pace, letting the squads of young soldiers and seamen forge on ahead. Watching determined enthusiasm cut into the many faces with which the young attacked the complex, he could not possibly compete. Sober reasoning took over the general's rationale, although reluctantly. He stayed back, commanding and supporting the overall assault on the Pentagon from the safety of distance.

As soon as the attack order was called into action, Brooks charged ahead. The only weapon by his side was a sword, a formidable blade, fashioned from the steel suspension from one of the salvaged land vehicles, pre-70s model. There was enough firepower, mostly bow and arrow, in the hands of his squads to pave the way. Most of his crew was outfitted with archery equipment rather than semi-automatics and handguns. Spending years in the Canadian wilderness, it was their choice of weapons. Besides, ammunition supply was limited. It would not last long. An arrow could always be retrieved on the fly. Entry to the complex was achieved through sheer numbers. Without trees and shrubs protecting the advances, mostly empty parking lots, facing the exposed terrain ahead Brooks knew there would be casualties inflicted from the defense lines shielded within the protection of the upper level windows. It was the cost of battle. He was banking on success once inside past the gates. It was close combat his soldiers were trained in and excelled at.

Brooks held back yards to let his forward lines clear the path. His focus was on Wallace. It was him, he had to eliminate. It would take dozens of barriers and five sectors deep to get to him. Upon entering the complex, the first line of battle, corridor "E," came heavily under fire.

His men had just cleared the initial barriers, pressing ahead to the second line of defense. With his team at close quarters, Brooks was forging ahead, intercepting every threat coming across his path. Applying his lethal punches and kicks would be sufficient most times to eliminate an opponent. Each punch and kick he underscored with a special personal comment like, "Bad day, eh…shoulda stayed home…oops, what happened…ouch, that hurt."

Where the battle was a last stand for Wallace, for Brooks it was all play. Applying the combination of natural instinct, and acquired fighting skills, he was always seconds ahead in thought, action, and results. Much like slow motion in movies he could sense, feel, and anticipate each and every move coming his way. What gave him the ultimate advantage was incredible speed underscored by the enormous power his body could generate. In spite of his steadfast rule on certain death of any challenger, he allowed an occasional mercy casualty. Depending on the challenger's moral fibers, when he sensed a hint of humanitarian quality, he stopped short of the kill, followed by a smirk and the remark, "Today's your lucky day."

Though marked by injury, the clemency would always be cherished by the survivor. Carried along for life, it fueled the individual's bragging rights. "I fought Scott Brooks."

As soon as the attack call was broadcast over the intercom, Derek Wallace rushed across the corridors to reach the upper level concourse. He did not make it. Halfway there he was met with an impenetrable wall of fighters coming his way. He could not believe his eyes, watching the defense lines he'd built crumble one layer after the other and, with them, his people. He stood there for a moment to witness the collapse of the empire he'd so painstakingly built, then realized the trap he was in.

In a rage, he aimed his automatic, letting go burst after burst of fiery steel while getting pushed back further and further into his domain of treasure. There was no stopping the onslaught. The hails of arrows shot his way kept closing in from ahead, sides, and stairwells within endless passages of corridors. Thinning out rapidly in forces, running short on supplies, even if he wanted to he could not break through the solid barrier of advancing fighters made up by Brooks' forces. Running out of ammo, he quit shooting and retreated.

Pushed back into the final bastion of the basement, he gave the order, "Cease fire." There was no need for all of his trusted Anarchists to lose their lives. He'd made a resolute decision. "I'll fight." It was the honorable thing to do. *At least,* he reasoned into the hushed silence of the halls, *I'll go out a hero.*

Seconds later the bloodied immortal everybody in the nation envied shoved his face through the basement entrance. Where his tattered clothes and face seemed to be awash with sweat and blood, not one drop was his own. It was all splatter from those slain by his sword.

Wallace, in the semidarkness of the vault, surrounded by his riches, stared at what was perhaps the greatest warrior that had ever lived.

"How you wanna do it?" Brooks gave him the choice.

Wallace did the one thing that would assure him a place in history. He gently placed the automatic on the floor and deliberately pulled his knife from its sheath. Even in battle he treasured his personal belongings. A hint of sadness swept over his face as he shot one last glance at his treasures and lunged at Brooks, who easily sidestepped the advance. It appeared the great warrior was only playing with him. It did not matter anymore. He gave it his best. Thrusting over and over at his opponent, his blade missed every attempt he made to inflict injury. It was like he was fighting his own shadow.

Wallace was getting enraged more and more by the second from his inferior fighting skills. He was losing his concentration power as well as his focus. He failed the rules of combat: "Breathe, focus, concentrate." If any one element was amiss or out of sequence, it would signal the turn of events. It was only a matter of time before complete exhaustion set in. Brooks' senses were acutely tuned in on the opponent's weakening. It would be a quick ending.

Wallace did not have to wait long. It came seconds later in the form of a lethal thrust by the great warrior. He did not feel the sword smash through his ribcage, slicing inner organs apart. His gaze was held by the glitter from the treasures nearby that he had fought for so many years. His stare did not last long. His sight was waning rapidly. Due to massive amounts of blood loss to the brain, it was the last vision his mind perceived before his beautiful world turned dark forever.

At the end, his body was buried with honors at the Arlington Cemetery nearby by the remaining Anarchists who, after some time of incarceration, were given the opportunity to join the newly-formed armed services. Foster had decided to extend the offer to the once freely roaming nomads. With the death of their great leader, Derek Wallace, strapped without leadership, following incarceration, the scavenging spirit had left the contingent. They became dedicated soldiers with the redirected cause of the protection of the nation.

CASTLE ROCK

"Stinger…Stinger…Come in." Ever since the Jihad base destruction in the Sudan the ether had been silent. "Dammit," a cussword slipped from Alex's lips. "She's doing it again." With his daughter in enemy territory, he was worried. He shouldn't be, he knew, but could not help it. He was still father, mentor, and protector. He did not always have the close connection with Tracy that he had in recent years. There was a time when he had been too busy with his career to worry much about the family. His daughters had been in good and caring hands with their mom. But since then, he had set his priorities straight. They had become dependent on each other. Heavy hearted, whenever his thoughts touched on her, With the loss of his eldest, Liz, he was not about to lose another daughter. He made sure she was protected at all times. To assure that, he had to stay connected to her. He already had a difficult time adjusting to her drastic changes in personal behavior, manner and attitude. Where they would sit for hours on end into the night, discussing worldly things, now, it was only giving and taking orders. He hated the way things had turned out between them. "Dammit," he cussed again at her not responding and the situation the world was in.

To keep his mind and body occupied during his utter loneliness, he sought out things to do. His thoughts touched on Foster and his retaking of the Pentagon. Waiting, anxiously hoping for success, in the quiet of the Castle he muttered, "Soon, the nation will be back in our hands."

Alex was looking forward to getting involved again, lending his skills and expertise to the general whenever there was need. And needed he would be to help reestablish the nation's defenses. For now, using mostly foreign commercial satellite links passing overhead, he was able to monitor the process of a nation healing itself. He had been crushed when much of Foster's forces met with death in the depths of the Hudson River. He was shocked at the losses of the Red Army. He was devastated at the death of Brian, his longtime buddy. At least his grave was nearby to keep memories alive.

A strong sense of concern about Tracy kept creeping into his mind. He could not shake free from an ominous feeling. He took it as warning. He knew she was up to her killer self whenever there was prolonged silence. She shut the comm link off to have no interference from him whenever she was on a vengeful warpath. He understood but still did not like it. For now, there was nothing he could do but wait. It was the wait, the uncertainty that was eating away at him. It was these times when he just wanted to pick up and join her journey. He dearly wanted to be out there on the front lines again. More often than not, in recent times, reality took over his rational thinking. He had to stay back, lending his support. Without it, she would be stalking in the dark and he could not afford that. It was the over-the-horizon vision he provided that had kept her alive all this time.

His thoughts fell on Rhonda. Since Foster spent all of his time on the East Coast, it was she that held up the command post on the Pacific. With all that'd been happening with Foster and Tracy, his relationship with Rhonda had slightly suffered. He wanted to be with her. She was the only link he had to keep his restless feet planted on earth. "It'll be fine once Foster is back in the seat again," he placated.

Based on initial reports sent by Foster, it would take some time to refurbish and reorganize the Pentagon to its command capabilities, if only partial. Rhonda's efforts would be relocated there as well. He could shuttle back and forth more easily once transportation was back in operation. But for that to happen, the new nation had to settle first. There was much to do. First on the agenda would be creating a trust in American currency again. Without it, the nation would never gain the footing it once held among international commerce.

Where modern technology had taken a thousand years to get to the stage before the collapse, this time around it would only take a short time to recover the nation, providing there was support from all ranks. First, everybody had to be on board with the new constitution. Next, international ties had to be reestablished. Without them, the New Republic would be spinning its wheels much like a third world nation. Once a currency was available, rebuilding the infrastructure could commence. Banking, finance, commerce, trade, transportation, education, health, manufacturing—every aspect of life had to be rebuilt.

For the young, there were many opportunities. The middle aged, after taking the brunt of past hardships, needed a break. For the great majority previously holding and directing careers, many of whom were responsible for the fall of the nation, it would be retirement. For others, the common man, the masses, it would be carving out a mere existence since much of the records had been destroyed, and with it proof of their savings and ownership. Only archived data protected from EMP damages would have survived. And records to that effect had been mostly defense, military, and politically related. With the shift in politics, a new constitution and new national policies and order, new records needed to be created. In reality, lost identities and possessions would draw lengthy legal battles. At the end, not much would be settled. Typical point in case is the aftermath from WWII, with surviving holocaust members trying to proof their heritage.

"First on the priority," Alex supposed, "will be getting a census taken." Rusty Norton, the elected leader, would take care of it. At this point, there were hardly any records left on how many people had perished or how many foreigners had immigrated into the country since the last census. He knew all too well how authorities had ignored the once tightly held immigration quotas for maintaining the vision of our founding fathers. "It's all gonna change," he vowed.

To break the loneliness, he sat by the monitors and waited for the remnants of the ISS to finish another pass overhead, wondering if and when he should hold his daughter's funeral. After much consideration, he decided to wait until her body could be recovered once the station reentered Earth's atmosphere. He hoped there would be some remains left to support a burial. To break the loneliness, he called up Rhonda. He needed to hear her voice—any voice.

PALM JUMEIRAH

Shakir Murad had just returned from the Arabian Desert. He was giving Hammad a first-hand account of the last battle. He vividly illustrated the events that took place a few days back. As executed by Stinger and her Russian crew, he was presently describing to the supreme commander the surprise attack on Base Camp Three in its details.

"Who survived?"

Murad was stalling. He did not want to admit that every one of his squad had been wiped out. Giving it a second consideration, then he thought better. News would leak out eventually of the massacre inflicted by Stinger and her crew.

"How many?" Hammad was getting impatient. He would fly into rage next, Murad knew. He finally admitted, "Nobody."

"You the only survivor?" He sensed intensified scorn from the Prophet. He realized that, for being an only survivor, there had better be a good reason. In actuality, he should be dead. The only reason he was still alive was the mercy act by Stinger to carry her message. Though he had heard stories about her bouts, he had always shrugged them off as myths. It was not until confronted directly by her that he realized the myth has taken on reality in the shape of a ferocious woman warrior. In order to justify his survival, he needed to be convincing.

"Sorry, Commander," he unceremoniously pleaded. "I have let you down." There was not much else he could say. All he could hope for was forgiveness. He would accept any kind of punishment other than death. He loved life too much.

"Why you?"

Hoping to be spared the leader's wrath and a death sentence, he explained, "I will tell you." By now, sweat was profusely pouring down his face. "There is a message the warrior woman directed me to convey."

"Yes?" Hammad's temper shifted from complete anger to curiosity. "Spit it out."

Murad considered making up a lie because the message he carried did not make any sense to him, but thought otherwise when he was impatiently stared down by the leader. "She said," he shifted from one leg to the other, then finally came out with it. "If you ever spot the Patriot flag in the Straits of Hormuz," he stated, "come and get it."

Hammad did not need further explanation. He knew exactly what the message conveyed. Just to be sure, he queried a quivering Murad once more. "Tell me exactly what she said."

Shakir repeated the exact words. He watched the face of the leader relaxing. It had mellowed out. Somewhat elated at a future possibility, Murad silently prayed, *Allah, I shall live.*

Apparently satisfied, Hammad took Murad by the shoulder and walked him onto the lofty deck overlooking the Hormuz Gulf. "See the sunset," he gestured in the distance, "how beautiful it is?"

After spending most of his career in deserts, to see and feel the soothing breeze gently tugging on his skin, it was a sight he would never forget. The sunset drifting below the distant horizon was a sight he would treasure forever. He was grateful to the leader for sharing the beauty with him.

"It'll be your last." In one violent swoop, Hammad picked up Murad's body and tossed him ruthlessly over the rail. Still enraged over the loss of the base camp and its forces, he lingered on while listening to the death-defying scream waning in the distance below from a once trusted lieutenant.

Weeks ago, after the personal encounter with Stinger in New York City, Hammad, losing a personal battle intolerably to a woman, felt a rage he could not remove from his mind. He needed to get a handle on current events. He decided to return to his personal retreat at Palm Island. It was the only place he felt secure. It was also the place that inspired him most. He still could not accept the fact he had been beat by a woman.

Where do they breed them? he wondered sometimes when watching individual feats, especially during the Olympics, partaken by the American women. "Vast land. Enormous resources," he sighed with remorse, thinking about the opportunity lost for getting his hands on its population, minerals, and water. "Water," he muttered in renewed anger. "Fight is not over yet."

Recollecting the past months, he had made almost daily assessments about where he went wrong. Since failure had never been a consideration, the thought kept gnawing away at him. He came to the eventual conclusion that there had been numerous factors involved. What he did not anticipate was the consolidated strengths with which the infidels had recovered from his masterminded Plan. With communication out, and the country in complete disarray, it should have taken much longer for the citizens of America to regroup, if at all. All one had to do is look around African nations collapsing, one after the other succumbed to failed attempts for liberation, only to watch poverty and demise prevail, from after effects of war. "Not so America." He always wondered about that. But giving it considerable thought, he always wound up with the same conclusion, the core of the problem, his most detested adversaries.

In hindsight, there was Bauer, the foreign-born security expert. He still could not fathom the opportunity that had placed him into the world's most sophisticated defense sector, NORAD, and his direct ties with the Pentagon.

Then there was Stinger. Never in his wildest dreams did he expect ever to be beaten by her. He still wondered about her fighting skills and how she was able to anticipate his every move and agenda. There was something mystical about it. He vowed to have her investigated before their next encounter. After Murad's return today, he knew there would be a chance for him to face her again. At this time, he did not know when, where, and under what circumstances. He still pondered about the true meaning of her message for what encounter she might have in mind.

There was one more element he had to guard himself against. Just as lethal as Stinger, perhaps deadlier, was the one they called Brooks. He had not had a personal encounter yet with this ferociously acknowledged killer. Aside from Stinger, whose skills and ability he treated with great respect, the leader of the War Dogs might have power and strength gauged even beyond his capabilities. Ending the disturbing thoughts, hoping to get a chance to find out, he muttered, "Time will tell."

"Perhaps," he thought, "I have to expand my vision." At this point his focus had been concentrated only on one continent. He had chosen one with strategic advantages, offering the most versatile resources. Water had been the most valuable asset. "But it came with a high price tag." Unlike many other places, fresh water there was most abundant, except perhaps for that of Russia. But Russia was a nation he dared not tackle. "Not yet."

There were other opportunities more valuable to his cause. With that comforting thought in mind, he firmly strode over to his personal library and reached for his favorite work. It was the document he treasured most, his design, his creation, the Plan.

For the rest of the day, he idled on the deck and studied it into the night. Reading on he realized it needed changing. Since its inception years ago, the world had undergone changes and he had to adapt to the changes. Using a marker and tabs he made many notations to whatever he had to rework. His vision became clear once more. It would take days to revise the Plan. Between pondering and contemplating, he sat, rewriting his work with an occasional gaze at the distant horizon, the most beautiful view on Earth, that of the Sea of Hormuz. His mind touched on Yusuf, his friend, "must check on him." He made a mental note.

ISS

Both Liz and Kenny were intensely watching the knife tumble through weightlessness within the remnants of the Harmony module, completing one ill-fated orbit after another with much of the ISS remnants in tow. Many sunrise and sunsets took place with the knife bouncing off of walls and framework. On one of the passes, luck was on their side. Liz was able to get a grip on the steel. She caught it between her teeth. Gently manipulating the tool, she gradually slid the edge between her wrist and the plastic restraints. Using a deliberate cutting motion, testing both their patience, she was able to cut through the first strap. The remaining restraints holding her ankles to the framework came off quickly. After days of intense hope and anticipation, they were finally free.

In the wasted shape both were in, moving about was an effort. But there were tasks waiting to be performed. They were lifesaving tasks. The first step was trying to fix the smashed radio gear, but on examining the broken-up pieces, they discovered it would take a miracle to fix. Liz gave it a try but hours later succumbed to the unavoidable. There would be no hope in restoring communication with ground control or elsewhere. Creating sound by banging against the bulkhead crossed their minds, but it proved useless. Sound perceived locally could not be transmitted through the emptiness of space. There was only silence in a space void of oxygen. From here on out it would be only a matter of time before both would perish.

Over the following weeks, in keeping up the spirit of living, Liz and Walsh tried their best to maintain their sanity. They dwelled on personal items that under normal circumstances were either too trivial or too delicate to disclose. But, at a time of certain death, to them it was important, sharing their personal feelings, past and present. Having been friends, mates, and lovers at one time not that long ago, what used to be passionate encounters had turned into a feeling of great compassion and love for each other. Trapped without food, with strength rapidly waning, any physical involvement had become part of the past. The only thing that remained was a great desire for a gentle embrace, and that they did often. The brief periods of night they spent together in an interlocked embrace, exchanging gentle kisses.

It was this sensuality that kept their spirits alive for the weeks to come. Without computers or timepieces to gauge the circadian clock, time became endless. During the last phase of their lives, with the mind unable to comprehend rational thoughts, only the eyes kept up a notion of life. They would follow the daily cycle of the object drifting through space once every ninety minutes. It was the sunlit cycle that would stimulate the brain. During the night time, it would shut down once more. During one of the cycles, Kenny did not respond to her hand seeking his. Her touch went unanswered. His hand had turned cold. Blood had stopped circulating through his body. He had expired. Her weakened whispers went unanswered. "…love you…forever."

After the loss of the last astronaut, her friend and lover Kenny, Liz kept drifting in and out of consciousness. It might have been days. It might have been weeks. She did not know. She did not care. Images of her mom, her former husband, and her children crossed her waning mind. Holding on for dear life, regretting a life cut short, "Kids," she whispered without seeing them flourish into adulthood. "Have to go now. Take good care of each other." Her eye tissues did not have moisture left to produce tears. Her weeping sounds slowly faded into silence.

The few moments of comprehending thoughts left in an almost bloodless brain were barely enough to register her thoughts with her conscience. It was one of these last moments when her eyes caught some slight movement through the porthole that only her subconscious mind registered. The body attached to the movement was gradually assembled by her brain. It had turned into a gigantic bird. Much like a bird of prey, it gradually darted in and out of her vision. It might have been the motion or will to live that awakened her brain into consciousness once more, ever so feebly. It was a beautiful sight, watching the bird projected against space. She was looking forward to reaching the afterlife.

"Heaven," her lips formulated without producing a sound. "Must be heaven."

"Kenny," she began talking to the bird. "Take me there."

She could see its beak moving. It was trying to say something but there was no sound. Then it gestured at the interlock. The motion was repeated over and over before her brain connected with reality. The miniscule surge of energy left in her body was enough to spur her consciousness.

"Interlock," the bird kept pointing and insisting.

Liz blinked a few times to clear the vision. She did not want to miss whatever flight her spirit would take next. It suddenly dawned on her it might be an earthly vision. She pinched herself several times in the arm and face for a reality check. Sensory perception for feeling and pain must be a subconscious act for the brain to decide between dream and waking states. Liz felt the pain from her own pinch. She felt slightly dejected, even disappointed, getting torn back to physical life. Then the survival instinct took over. She began struggling for oxygen. The filtering system had failed days ago. Although heavily intermixed with carbon dioxide, it was the oxygen-filled space within Harmony that kept her alive.

Her eyes touched on Kenny's lifeless body. She did not remember when his earthly spirit had left. His ashen face was enough of an indication of his death. Her sadness was interrupted once more by the vision from the porthole. She recognized a symbol she had not seen for years. It was that of the X-37M Space Sentry markings on the craft's nose section. Though severely weakened, some of her memory capacity was back. She recalled a black project initiated by the Air Force years ago, taking into space for prolonged periods. Now she understood what the bird was trying to say.

Floating by the interlock, she knew what needed to be done. One laborious push of the button permitted the mechanics to allow for docking. Seconds later the hatch opened, allowing a beaming face to push through with extended arms. "Lisa Bauer," he smiled, "I presume?"

He practically tore off his space helmet to offer her some lifesaving oxygen. After several deep breaths of air inhaled from the expelled spacesuit, her face, astonished at first, turned into a broad grin.

"Lee Blackwell," he readily offered. "Extended mission, deep space."

"You guys. Thought the craft was unmanned."

"X-37M," he said. "Modified for manned missions." He then explained that he and the crew had just returned from a mission that was still classified. They had been in space for two years on close-up recon for, "Space matters. It's all I can tell you."

"You know," she enlightened him. "Things have changed on Earth."

"So we've heard," was all he would admit.

"People," she tried to tell him, "won't tolerate secrecy anymore."

"We'll deal with it. Ready?" He was anxious to get going. With his help, they transferred Walsh's and all the other expired ISS bodies from the various shattered space modules into the cargo space and departed shortly after.

When word on Earth was received about the unexpected rescue of the so revered astronaut after she had been declared dead weeks ago, her status as celebrity escalated to new heights. Heralded, Liz was bound for fame and success. But first, her two children, Mom, and Dad were foremost on her mind. There was much to tell about the ill-fated journey and unceremonious end of one of mankind's greatest achievements, the International Space Station.

CASTLE ROCK

After the X-37M, a manned crew of two, added cargo space, modernized version of the prototype space plane set down at Edwards AFB near Death Valley, on her arrival back at Vandenberg, Liz spent two weeks getting debriefed followed by several weeks in convalescence. The strong willed individual that she was, with the help from organically grown food and rigorous exercise, in-between furnishing detailed reports on the mission's success and failures, her body strength gradually returned. This mission had been nothing but a failure. For the authorities putting all of the pieces together, and for future space travel, a detailed account was necessary. It would be used to revise the process and procedures currently in place. "Weapons for personal protection," she was told, "would definitely become part in space travel." Whether she liked it or not, changes were already being implemented for carrying into space man's fallacies and weaknesses, that of a warring being. After everything was said, data evaluated, and officials satisfied with her reports, Liz was finally allowed to depart. Her first stop was Napa Valley, home and residence of her kids where she spent one week adjusting back to a personal life she had so dearly missed while trapped in space.

Next stop was Castle Rock, the bastion, fortress, and home of her dad. A trip there was always filled with joy and pleasure for everybody. Her dad and the kid's granddad was waiting with treats, plans, and hikes into the hills. It turned out a great place to spend summer break for the family.

"…by the way," Liz asked her dad when she noticed her absence, "where's Tracy?"

"Wish I knew. Haven't heard from her in weeks. Only thing I figure," he speculated, "is that she's after the Prophet. She's maintained silence."

"He's still alive?" Liz was surprised to hear that after all that had gone on during her absence.

"Last I've heard," Alex confirmed. "Very much. Here," he readily offered a homegrown apple, "have another piece of fruit." He had opened another bottle of wine. A hangover was assured the next morning, but it would be worth it after all the trauma his daughter had endured, sharing some time together. Listening to all that took place in space might have sounded like action fiction in the first degree, but it was worth every minute he was able to spend with his daughter and grandkids. He had renewed hope that she would just pack up in California and move back here. He made every attempt for that to happen. Aside from a safety factor, having the sounds of laughter and happiness from grandchildren would greatly cheer up his loneliness. In just a short while, he realized how much he had missed family.

"You stayin' for a while?" he proposed when detecting signs of sleepiness. He studied his daughter's face. He could clearly detect a hint of harshness edged into her features. He was not surprised after all that she had been through. He was only too grateful for her still being alive.

"For now," she promised. "Need the break."

"How's your mom?" He realized he hadn't spoken with Annette in years. Having been married and raising two daughters together was still an important phase in his life. Liz was unable to suppress another yawn. "Okay," she said. "Sends you her regards. Gotta get some sleep, Dad."

"Use the guest room. Night."

Alex watched his daughter disappear down the hall. He was alone again with his thoughts lingering on Tracy. His nerves still piqued, he stepped downstairs to his favorite place. The first rays of yet another day made their appearance when his eyes finally turned sleepy. "Stinger," were his last words before falling asleep by the desk, "talk to me."

Alex was rudely awakened by a firm tug on the arm. He opened his still weary eyes only to stare at Liz. "What?"

"Wake up," she beckoned, "you've gotta see this." She then pulled him along to the den. The early morning news broadcast by Al Jazeera had just gotten underway. It was the primary news station he had tapped into years earlier. It provided him with an unbiased perspective for most of an otherwise nationally censored experience.

Early this morning, the internationally-based anchor announced, *the first Islamic-sponsored communication satellite was launched by the European Space Agency, from their Guiana Launch Center. The purpose and destination for the satellite is still unclear since parameters and mission specifications are unknown at this time. Satellite and mission have been deemed classified. Further news will be forthcoming as more details become available.*

"That's just great," Alex sounded off. "As if we don't have enough secrecy already."

"Yeah," Liz readily agreed. "Aside from being hostile."

He would definitely dig deeper into the purpose, but first, "Got coffee?"

"In the kitchen."

The thoughts of his daughter tending to him brought on instant happiness as he watched her preparing breakfast for the family. "Like old times," he happily muttered.

CALL FOR RETRIBUTION

Alex, seated by the monitors, was intensely searching for data. Much like the network tools and software applications used by the former NSA that Brian had installed for him, he had been in search of new materials that would indicate the true mission of the Islam-launched satellite. *And there you are.* He had just struck gold. The data mining software was still feeding its database with intelligence unknown to the free world. Analyzing the data, he realized the critical nature of the Intel. It immediately became apparent that some foreign-based intelligence agency had taken over the abandoned surveillance effort of the formerly dominated American intelligence organization.

"I'll be dammed!" Alex, though flattened by the revelation, had suspected something of this nature. He had expected something like this for some time. There had been too many unexplained incidents about international affairs which gave him the idea.

"What?" Liz, attracted to his unusual outburst, had joined him in the den.

"Jihad's taken over communication in space."

"You mean…"

"Yep," he confirmed. "Entire sphere."

"That means," shaking her head in denial, she stated. "All of our efforts for peace were in vain?"

"Looks that way," he agreed. "Doesn't it?"

"What now?"

Alex did not answer. Evaluating the immediate and long-term implications, his thoughts were miles away. He could already envision another space race. This time it would be with hostile intentions. "Need to stop this madness," he muttered.

"What?" Liz did not hear clearly what he said.

"Oh, nothing…Let's take the kids for a hike."

The rest of the day was enjoyed walking the nearby foothills under a clear sky with plenty of fresh air. To his joy, none of the prevalent radiation from the West Coast had made it across the Rockies. Rain and moisture from the lofty passage of the Jet Stream filtered out most of the damaging beta, gamma, and neutron rays still emanating from the City by the Bay.

Spending several rejuvenating hours hiking the trails, a HAM-initiated call was waiting when the Bauer gang returned. Alex recognized the call sign from his army ally, that of Foster. Somewhat surprised, but also relieved that the general wanted to talk, he could pass his newly acquired revelation about the foreign satellite on to him. Foster answered on the first connection attempt.

"How's life at the Castle?"

"Action never stops…Got news for you."

"Jihad launch?"

"So, you've heard?"

"That's," Foster implied, "what I'm calling about."

"Not another mission?" Alex, though used to disruptions in a life filled with action, for a change, was hoping the globe would settle for a time. He was enjoying the company of his family tremendously and had no intentions to do otherwise.

"Yes." was the reply. "This one," Alex was assured, "you'll enjoy. Bring the whole family."

While somewhat perturbed but heightened with anticipation, he was given instructions for an immediate departure and destination.

"Albuquerque?"

"What's there?"

"You'll see. I'll have transportation waiting."

"See you tomorrow."

PALM JUMEIRAH

Hasan Hammad, as was usually the case in the morning, was seated on the lofty deck making revisions to the Plan. With the passing of time the document had grown considerably in size. Where it had previously been a work of tactical policies and procedures in progress on a local scale, now, it addressed the strategic needs of a much wider sphere, the global scale. Taking success, as well as failure, to heart, he still suffered from a recent setback. But Hammad, by no means, had given up.

"As a matter of fact," he revealed to his trusted lieutenants, "I can focus my energy on the world now." He was freed to expand his horizon. First on the agenda was consolidating all Islam-friendly nations and factions, and there where many. Where most of the world had been preoccupied by one disastrous event after another, the Jihad factions had taken the opportunity to expand into new territories. Recent censuses taken gave alarming results of the spreading of the Islam population.

What was alarming about was not only the subtle takeover of much of free world commerce, but of local industries as well. Even the educational institutions had given way to Muslim indoctrinations. In addition to the influx from Arabian nations, many countries found themselves overwhelmed by the sudden increase in population. Within just a few years, it seemed, the world population had shifted to a majority held by the Muslim culture. Some nations had been sideswiped by the unexpected change in culture, others saw the handwriting on the wall. The shift was inevitable. From a historical perspective, it was Islam's turn to conquer the globe.

The stage was set for the Prophet to reach out. He was ready to deliver a strike that would be felt on a global scale. All he needed was the appropriate weapon. *But what weapon?* He had no answer. To have no immediate solution for a problem was a revelation that puzzled him.

The realization forced him into action. It would be his major agenda to either create something of paramount design or, if possible, unearth something from the hidden vaults of a technologically-advanced nation keeping such an invention secret. At this time, he had no inkling if that was a possibility. He initiated some calls to his scientific contacts in Dubai to come up with a solution.

It had taken some time, but with the help of modern medicine, Yusuf Hashim had made a recovery, ever so gradually. Still struggling with burn issues, he was by the side of his revered leader once more. While still impaired for taking part in physical activities, he made it his mission to relieve Hammad from tedious daily chores. For the time, he was the leader's personal secretary.

"Yusuf," Hammad called to his attention. "What's the status on the summit?"

Hammad had made the necessary political connections to force an international summit, held right here at Palm Jumeirah. His plan was to create an organizational seat for a united, global Jihad headquarters. Issued to all nations, he made it clear to foreign emissaries that there would be no alternatives. It was a direct order. After careful considering the alternatives with his forcedly-acquired powerbase, he allowed no rejections. The summit was mandatory. It was set for ten days from now. It would allow sufficient time for the expected powerbrokers to arrange for accommodation bookings.

"All set."

He was pleased. Based on the responses it meant the world was ready for unified leadership. The scene was set. From here on forward, though it might take some time to promote political uniformity, he was assured supremacy. With the potential threat that used to be economic sanctions from influential power nations exerted on a third world, his threat was one of force. How to enforce nations, especially unwilling ones, was yet to be determined. It was for these that he needed a superior weapon, this time for global application.

Satisfied for the moment with worldly proceedings his immediate focus shifted to local issues. His eyes captured the scenic horizon. As usual, the straits were busy with sea traffic. Gradually plowing their ways in and out of the Persian Gulf, delivering and picking up cargo, international shipping was thriving.

With the recent shift of wealth and investments to Arabian nations such as Bahrain, the Emirates, and the Sudan, with it came leisure and recreation. The results were clearly visible across the expanse of the gulf. Amid the gently rolling waves created by the onshore and offshore winds, water sports had become prolific. Watching the water-based activities jogged Hammad's memories about his own personal desires. His personal pleasures over the past decade had been put off for too long. He decided on the spot to make changes.

"Yusuf," he called on his friend and personal servant. "Get some sales person up here."

"Yes?"

"It is time to do some sailing." It had always been his dream to get a sea captain certificate but had never taken the time. Now, watching the scenes below, seemed to be the perfect timing to satisfy his recreational desires. Where he was an accomplished windsurfer holding down his own among experienced wave riders, owning a sizable seaworthy craft, piloted by professionals, would elevate his personal status.

It would take some time to initiate the sailing craft's purchase. In the meantime, he decided to take flight on the windsurf board. It was a thrill he had missed for too long. Collecting his favorite board, a Mistral, with Yusuf, his surfing partner, out of commission for the time being, he solicited several others from his lieutenants and joyfully jumped into the onshore winds. They readily agreed providing personal protection to the leader while having fun as well. With the winds up for yet another few hours he headed for the distant shores of Iran. He had taken the hundred-mile passage across the straits a number of times before. Coasting along the waterfront of Dubai, if winds were favorable, he could make the crossing in three hours. Checking the time on his waterproof wristwatch, he shot an approving nod at his team, closing up in tight formation. Hammad was ready to test his strength and endurance once more.

With the summit set for next week and no other pressing issues on the agenda, he could give the winds his fullest attention. Hammad was overcome with euphoria. Skimming from wave to wave, protected by his surfing squad, he was in an element only few had the pleasure of experiencing. And the beauty of it was that he had no time constraints. If he ran short on stamina, he could always beach overnight at one of Bandar Abbas' outlying islands, the Iranian beach resorts.

It was pure joy dodging in and out of the busy sea traffic. Daring with intercepts to see how close he could cross the stern; container ships would let lose a string of warning calls on foghorns. Away from battles and conquest, with feet planted steadfast on the 10-ft. racing board, 7m translucent sail jutting up into the cloudless sky with harness hooked into the boom, driven by the westerly wind, he could relax. He felt completely alive.

RETRIBUTION

It was a refreshing break for Alex to have his eldest daughter and the grandkids at the Castle. For the time being, it seemed, the nation had settled somewhat after years of border quarrels and regional clashes from an incessant onslaught of immigrants. Word spread in the lands up and down the borders about the successes of the Patriots. With the terrorist invasion under control, the Anarchists squelched with whatever miniscule forces remained, and a new constitution in place, the once scattered nation was on its way to healing itself. Full recovery would still be far off. For now, whatever stability could be achieved for the once battle beleaguered citizens was enough.

It was early in the morning. The Bauer family was on its way to meet up with Foster. As was usual over the Rockies, the flight was bumpy but otherwise a thrill for the kids. The C-130 Hercules had just touched down at the Albuquerque airport. Ground transportation was waiting for them.

"Where we headed?" Alex asked the chauffer. His curiosity got the better of him.

"Alamogordo."

"What's there?" Though Alex was quite familiar with the once prolific atomic testing grounds, he was slightly surprised and said so. "Thought it'd been abandoned long ago."

"You're right," was the casual reply from the somewhat mysterious driver.

"What..." Alex started to ask, then changed his mind after studying the driver, dressed sharply in uniform he did not recognize. "Who are you?"

"Ever hear of the Condors?"

"As a matter of fact," he responded, somewhat surprised, "I have."

"What's a Condor?" both kids asked from the backseat.

Projecting a mysterious look from the rearview mirror, the driver answered, "Secret society."

He hoped it would satisfy the kids' curiosity but the effects were the opposite. They bore down on him with question after question. "Kids," he finally conceded. He proceeded to tell them as much as he could divulge about the present state of affairs. The limo had turned silent with avid listeners to the intrigue of a story from an underground society that had made it its mission to acquire and gather much of the former nation's technological assets. Between Alamogordo, White Sands, and nearby Los Alamos National Laboratories, the sinister group of scientists had managed to assemble technological achievements from the past and present used for both good and the evil. Their objective was solely dedicated to the benefit of mankind.

With a future open for opportunities hopefully guided by responsible leadership, there was a hint of promise in the air. The next few hours would reveal what Foster had in mind for fulfilling that promise.

They had arrived at their destination. The general was waiting at the scene with a friendly welcome. "Who is this?"

"Grandkids."

Foster then pulled the ex-astronaut close and gave her a heart-filled hug. "Glad you made it back."

"Glad to be back."

"Thought we've lost you."

Liz returned his smile but remained silent. She did not want to be reminded of the hardship she had endured in space. She still had nightmares about the horrific experience. Perhaps in due time she would delve into the recesses of her mind to recall the true events of an ill-fated journey. For now, she was just happy to be alive and was looking forward to what the general had in mind. He was no light-hearted individual. There was a specific reason he'd called the Bauer family together.

"You'll stay a few days," he informed them. "I've made arrangements."

Alex was as curious as the rest of his family. He could not contain his curiosity any longer. "What's up?"

"Patience," was all he got in return. "You'll see. I'll fill you in over dinner." Relaxing in the backseat of the limo, they enjoyed the ride to the seemingly evacuated, desert-based testing grounds of Alamogordo.

"Wished Tracy was here," Liz broke the silence. "Me too," Alex agreed. "Wonder where she is?"

"Unfinished business," Foster hinted. In their individual minds, they could only speculate, but subconsciously each considered only one primary target, "The Prophet." It was anybody's guess. Stinger had not returned any of their ether calls.

Alex was curious about the remotely located government installation. It seemed well organized. Where he'd expected a deserted facility overblown with sand and tumbleweed, the base seemed very much alive. Dinner was served at the base's officers club. The general cuisine on the menu was flavors influenced from across the border.

Alex and Liz had not dined out for months and years, as was the case with the kids. They wholly enjoyed the ample amount of servings. The plates of enchiladas, served on extremely hot dishes accompanied by locally grown wine, were a delightful treat for adults and children alike. The kids, of course, had their fill from buckets filled with chilled cola, also shipped in from the south. It was a treat they had not tasted since early childhood.

In spite of Alex and Liz's pestering the general, it was not until dinner was over when Foster opened up. "The reason I invited you here," he haltingly explained, "is for your benefit." His words were directed at Liz when he spoke. It came as a surprise to her. Where her extended and almost fatal mission in space was disastrous to say the least, she did not expect special treatment or rewards. More so, she'd expected a reprimand from the former head of the Pentagon after losing control of the space station and HAARP capabilities.

But things had not exactly ended in his favor either with the disastrous Hudson crossing. She had been thoroughly briefed by her dad on the tragedy that had befallen the nation's last stand. "You've got my attention," Alex broken in. "Do tell."

"Rather than tell," Foster replied, "why don't I show you?"

Dinner was paid for by Foster, who handed the waiter a voucher. All got up, headed for the limo. It was only a minute's ride to what appeared to be a huge hangar. Foster led the visitors through the entrance gate into the shadows of the superstructure.

"Here we are." Foster gestured in the direction of a covered-up contraption. He signaled two guardsmen to open the skylight roof and activate the massive gear. Starlight was gradually illuminating the interior revealing a mystical shape. Whatever had been hidden from view appeared monstrous. At the same time, a gigantic tube encased by segments of coils, cables, and connections gradually raised from its horizontal rest to an elevated position.

Revealed was a contrivance Alex immediately recognized but had not seen in decades. "I'll be damned," he exclaimed. "Railgun."

"You remember?"

"Should. Worked on the friggin' thing for years."

Liz shot Foster a quizzical stare then shifted her attention to her dad. Alex felt he owed them an explanation. He explained his association with the weapon. "Years ago, before space travel took over, DARPA created this monster. It's a ground-based weapon for managing ill-intentioned exploits in space. More specifically," he explained, "to keep enemy objects under control."

Liz was startled at the revelation and said so. "Never heard of it."

"Nobody did," Foster affirmed, "unless you worked in the community." By community he implied the inner circles of the DOD. "What you see here is a prototype. Only unit ever built. Was scrapped shortly after by runaway space technology."

"ASATs?"

It was much more cost effective to have attack satellites launched in closer proximity to space intrusions. Placed in nearby orbit, it was just a simple matter of programming the software and aiming at the potential target. There was no need for a ground-based space weapon anymore. Consequently, the "Railgun" project had been scrapped and mothballed. It had sat here, dormant, until just recently when Foster unearthed the monstrosity once more. For now, it was the only weapon available for space related threats on the nation.

"That's right." Back then money was no object. The government had unlimited access to funding. Justified as a "black project," this and many other developments had been explained away to an uninformed taxpayer. With an economy thriving, the citizens were busy traveling the world with a newly experienced affluence. It was this unawareness that helped bring the nation to its knees. Spending was limitless on both sides, the public and private sectors. With nobody tending to the treasury, the result was a collapsed economy.

"Today," the general promised, "you'll see vengeance in action." He was directly addressing Liz, who was puzzled at Foster's personal revelation and asked, "Whose vengeance?"

"Yours." The expectancy for what was in store for her grew even bigger. "You'll be the first ever to pull the trigger."

The mood of expectation became almost unbearable. "At what?" she almost yelled at the smirking general. The youngsters were perplexed at their mom's unusual outburst, but they too wanted to know the target for this monstrous gun. Alex had his suspicions but kept his thoughts in check. He wanted Liz to be the first to be told.

They were interrupted by footstep shuffles nearby. A new face joined the crowd. Patting him on the shoulder, Foster offered, "Allen Spencer. Condor society."

Alex and Liz both knew of him but had never met the leader of the secluded society. Also approaching was an engineering crew to prepare the mysterious weapon. When the remaining cover came off, protecting the launch instruments, there was something familiar about the gun.

"Looks like something from a British WWII battleship," Liz remarked.

"You're not far off," Spencer agreed. "Exactly what gave us the idea." He then explained that the Railgun in actuality was built and tested for the Naval Surface Warfare Center. It was only recently that he and his scientists redesigned and modernized its purpose.

"How's it work?"

"Actually," Spencer explained, "it's a pretty simple design. Its main parts here," he gestured at the base, "are EMP armature. Difference's the rails." He pointed at the center piece, sandwiched in by parallel mounted rails several yards in length. "Where conventional bullets propelled through a rifle come from an internally compressed explosive charge within the cartridge, this here," he boasted, "the energy's created externally. The farther the target, the larger the charge."

"Laser like?"

"Almost. Difference is, electromagnetic pulse shoots the projectile. Laser's used only to spot the distant target."

"What's its range?"

"Can't tell you."

"Of course. Classified. Another secret."

He shrugged his shoulders, then went on ignoring her remark. "But," he confided in her. "Be assured at speeds greater than Mach-10. It'll do the job it's designed for." The projectile speed alone was breathtaking. "How's it goin'?" he yelled over his shoulder.

"Ten more minutes," the crew chief yelled back.

"So," Liz turned to face the mysterious host, "what's the target?"

"Can't tell you specifically." He again averted her direct approach. "Let's just say," he shot a devious grin at her, "Jihad will never gain footing in space. You'll have first crack at that promise."

It was an honor neither Alex nor she had expected. "Why me?"

"We've been watching the skies. And believe me when I say," he hinted, "that you deserve it after all you've been through." Liz was humbled by the great honor bestowed on her. "I'm just glad," she replied, "that I'm here to witness righteousness in action for the good of mankind."

"We're ready," the crew chief announced.

Spencer replied with an approving nod and led his honored guest to the world's most powerful weapon at her disposal. He gently took her hand and put it on the trigger guard. "Push the trigger," he instructed, "on count zero."

Her body tensed at the pending action. She was hardly breathing. An assistant stepped up and handed each a pair of ear guards. "Here." Alex watched final preparations handled by the crew. One sat by the guidance system, awaiting instructions. Others were poised nearby watching instruments. Apparently, they were gauging for the precise timing for the shot window to open. It came seconds later when the distant target, although slicing through space at a nominal speed of seventeen thousand miles/hour, slowly crept into the crosshair.

"Ready and counting," the chief yelled out. "Three, two, one, zero!"

Liz pulled the trigger at the count. The reaction that followed was incredible. The monster was bucking much like a gigantic bronco trying to shake off its load. All hell broke loose. The sound was overwhelming. With eyes focused on the sky, Liz perceived several actions taking place simultaneously. First, there was a terrific energy burst through the rails, surging in one end and out the other within the closed-circuit link. The burst was felt rather than heard. It jolted her body off the shooting platform. Next was a concentrated beam of thunder and lightning she had not experienced, ever. Although a seasoned astronaut, used to exploding infernos from rocket thrusters, the nightmarish spectacle she just witnessed was unmatched. Despite her initial shock, from the peripheral vision of her eye she was able to follow the projectile as it left an energy signature in its wake. A fraction later, the immediate space around turned silent again as quickly as it had erupted. Only the gasping sounds from the spectators lingered in the air while trajectory computers calculating time, distance, and target speed waiting for the trigger signal. Then, nothing happened, other than the minute vibrations of ringing ears.

Liz was still enthralled by the spectacle the weapon created. "What now?"

"We wait." Spencer's eyes were fixed on the digital readout display that had been clocking down from a preset 53 seconds. He had been calculating computer telemetry and time of impact based on the 250 some miles distance to the orbiting object. "Watch the sky," she was told as he called out the time. "Fifteen seconds…ten…five, four, three, two, one, strike!"

Although 250 miles distant, what followed was the most brilliant display of glittery sparkles ever created by man. Streamers of light were shooting outward in all directions from the epicenter. Whatever obstacles caught up in the passage of expanding projectiles in space were immediately exploded on contact, creating secondary bursts almost as brilliant. It was a firework none of them would soon forget.

On the ground, a chorus of outbursts from scientists and support personnel alike echoed through the hanger. "It's a hit!"

With the demonstration a success, someone shouted, "Champagne." Within minutes the sparkling contents of a dozen bottles were freely emptied over the successful participants.

"The demo," Spencer told them after being served a drink. "Only the first of many."

He would be proven correct in the weeks and months to come from media reports of unexplained starburst phenomena occurring throughout the northern skies. Alex, Liz, and the kids stayed the few days. Spencer had additional treats in store for them. Being granted temporary top-secret access, the remainder of the visit turned out much like a visit to the once glorious Smithsonian Institute.

Before departing, Foster made a promise to all. "After getting the Pentagon in order," he promised, "next on the agenda is reopening national museums. You'll be the first visitors."

"You got that right," Spencer acknowledged. He seemed in full support of keeping the citizens of the New Republic informed on technologies developed for, and funded by, the people, fully honoring the taxpayer's support.

WORLD SUMMIT

Hasan Hammad was furious when he first heard of the satellite incidence. The broadcast was all over the Middle East. "Dammit," he cussed. "Get in here," he called his lieutenants. "Who," he spat at them. "Leaked it to the press? I'll have your heads." Since no one came forward, his anger was driven to new heights. He was assured by his scientists that the secret he had conceived would be safe. "But no," he fumed at Yusuf. "There is always one shooting his mouth off. Bragging." He thought he had a tight handle on people supporting him. Once again, he had been sideswiped. Where his closest followers were proven warriors and knew his wrath when a mission was compromised, there were many more supporting his cause that he had no direct control over. With the news spread over the globe that Jihad had taken to spying, the incidence had removed a vital battle advantage in his disfavor. For once, he had direct access to surveillance that used to be the sole privilege to the most detested organization in his mind, NSA. His advantage in keeping the lead on international politics had been removed with one shot. He only knew too well who was behind the treachery. He'd have to deal with him, later. "You'll pay for this," he vowed while furiously striding off. For now, he was silently preparing his speech for the immediate issue at hand, getting ready to address the world summit.

He had been waiting for this day forever, it seemed. Impeccably dressed in a white tuxedo with matching shirt, shoes, and bowtie, Yusuf gave him a once over, impatiently urging him on. "It is time."

"They will wait," Hammad replied. Hosting the glitz, the glamour, the location was all part of the plan. He gave them the best. To accomplish it, he did not have to look very far. One look from his lofty den and he knew exactly where to host the summit. He had been watching the development on this beloved island for years. With each past visit to his domain headquartered in Dubai, however brief and short they may have been, he watched progress. *What a contrast,* he'd marvel when comparing this place with the war zone he used to be trapped in. In the past, when supreme commander over his forces assuring the Plan was carried out, he was forced to be on location in the conflict's hot zones. America for the past several years had been the frontlines.

While he longed for the day when he would take possession over the war-torn continent, the place of his abode would always be Palm Jumeirah, his domicile. He had seen it grow from an initial heap of sand piled on by humongous pumps sucked from the depths of the Straits, to a wondrous paradise reserved for the rich and the wealthy. Today, one more element of affluence was added, that of the world's powerbrokers. "Let them wait," he denied Yusuf's concerns again.

He had made sure the setting was perfect. And it was. There was no other place on Earth like it. Grown out of the azure tinted waters from the off shores of Dubai, the island, the first of several, had taken on its present state in just a few years. Created in the shape of a palm tree, it assured every resident access to the water, as well as a view overlooking the Straits of Hormuz. What made it paradise for its predominantly Arabic inhabitants was the contrast between a tropically created island environment surrounded by the blue of the ocean. To many, it was the dream promised by Muhammad. Blessings went out to Allah accordingly.

The sun had set an hour ago. Due to the globe's curvature near the equator, a day's equal sunrise and sunset took place within minutes. Day had turned to night when Hammad stepped out on the balcony. He checked the location he had selected one last time. And there it was, less than a mile distant in its entire splendor, the Atlantis, the dream of dreams. Lit up by millions of candlepower growing from the dark of night, shaped in a pagoda-like structure, the Atlantis Hotel presented a façade of splendor and freedom.

He inhaled one more fill of breath from the ozone laden air, abruptly turned, and headed for the exit. "Let's go." Flanked by his personal security staff on the trip, accompanied by Yusuf and his lieutenants, the assembly quickly made its way toward the station nearby. The rail shuttle was the only access connecting the tropical designer dunes with the outer banks and their immediate destination, the Atlantis.

It only took minutes on the shuttle to reach the threshold of the enormous complex. Builders for this magnificent structure left nothing to chance. Every possible comfort and amenity for the traveler was available. At the appropriate cost, of course. The place was purposely designed for the affluent. Hammad envisioned it as the gathering for the once nomadic desert sheik turned oil executive, today's powerbrokers to the region.

The arriving guests were efficiently ushered in through the lobby and out at the other end of the plaza. Somewhat puzzled, Hammad shot a quizzical glance at his trusted friend. "Yusuf?"

"You'll see," Yusuf replied with a smug grin.

A few paces later Hammad found himself facing a most remarkable setting. It was that of an outdoor-situated combination conference, assembly, and business center surrounded by elegance, glamour, palm trees, and personal waiters tending to the guests' every need. The second he stepped foot into the setting, the prevalent sounds of laughter, chatter, and crystal-like sounds from toasting glasses immediately turned into a hush. Not only had it turned nearly silent, but all their eyes shifted to him. For many it was the first time they laid eyes on him, the charismatic and mystical leader for the cause of Islam. Although he had earned a worthy reputation among the world leaders in recent years, Hammad was received with cautious reservation. The "dictator," as he was unofficially slated by the global media, had not earned the deserving trust for which he had hoped.

Looking over the world leaders behaving as usual within the given setting with drinking, joyfulness, and merriment, it struck a chord in him once again that the world needed strong leadership. From the feared Prophet, there was only contempt for this sort of loose behavior. This evening, however, to fit into the setting he put on the most pleasant face he could muster up. Yusuf, flanked by his security staff, led Hammad for introductions around tables seated with only the most prominent leaders, mostly Arabic. He shook hands with the dignitaries while gently embracing their wives, exchanged greetings and pleasantries with all. He knew he had to make a show for the support they would lend him over the coming years. *As long as there's oil*, he reflected silently, *you people will pay for what I demand.*

A persistent tapping on the crystal by the organizing host indicated the opening for the summit. He gestured the elegantly clad leader up to the podium. With calculated intentions, Hammad stepped up to the speaker platform. "My name," he began his delivery, "is Hasan Hammad. I invited you here today for the most important summit ever to take place." There was no applause, no cheering. Only a halting silence prevailed from dozens of anticipating faces.

His following deliverance took a precisely rehearsed and timed one hour. He demanded the time. He tolerated no interruptions. His security was right on top of any disruption or potential disturbance. He spent the hour laying out the necessity for a world leadership, including its pros and cons. Where the "pros" were many, the "cons" included only one element: "the past."

He reminded the attending members of the struggles and hardship his nation, their nation, had endured for a thousand years. "The time has arrived," he stated one last time before concluding his speech. "It is our time. And the time is now." It was here when the visiting leaders and ladies for the evening granted him applause. It was an overwhelming one.

Keeping up a pleasant face, he silently gloried into the uproar. *You need me. You idiots!*

It signaled the end of the presentation. He did not allow himself to get personal. It would have contradicted the calculated purpose of the summit. As inviting and glamorous as it was, closely guarded by his lieutenants, he abruptly turned and stormed from the place. He felt glorious. He had obtained his objectives. It was only a matter of time before he would achieve the ultimate in leadership, a new world order. But, to secure that, he needed their support. He was not thinking of funding and monetary needs. He had that already. The support he sought was unrelenting, remorseless. It was a power so great it might not exist—he might have to create it.

Deeply in thought, he spent the rest of the evening in the privacy of his lofty domain, contemplating on exactly what was needed. He needed something no other nation had. It would have to be such an awesome power that he could hold the world hostage. It suddenly struck him. "Of course." He knew exactly where to find it. "Fantastic." For that, however, he needed a trained team of scientists. And it would take time to develop his next plan to initiate Phase Three.

His chest swelled up with great pride. Just the thought of joining the ranks of great leaders from the past, holding absolute power in his hands with a battle advantage over the enemy, the free world, he would rank equal only to legendary leaders from the myths and legends of antiquity.

BATTLE FOR FREEDOM

Five miles out, Stinger, with legs firmly planted on her customized windsurfer, was jumping waves. "Yippie," she shouted into the whipping winds executing another somersault leaping off the board, legs reaching for the mast, around the boom, only to land solidly back on the surfer. "Gonna be a great day." For close to an hour she had been headed into the winds, first upwind then downwind, cutting her way closer and closer to the shoreline of the notorious island Palm Jumeirah, exclusively designed and built for the affluent Arab.

Today, riding wind and waves so close to her enemy, she felt elated. Azure tinted waters below her board, blue sky overhead, sea traffic plowing the distant horizon, *what more could one wish for?* she thought. Stinger might have appeared fine to the common observer, and there were many watching the surfing woman from the distant shores as she cut the waves, but not everything was well. "Hannah," she wailed into the winds. "Wish you were by my side." The loss of her dear friend still weighed heavily on her mind, especially now, with the enemy in clear sight. In between watching the shoreline and dodging sea traffic ahead, every so often she shot a quick glance over her shoulder. Something in the weather was changing. Aside from the wind beating against her face, she felt a pressure difference pushing against her temples. Seeking out the cause, she spotted it. It was distant clouds forming ominously on the horizon. Billowing high into the atmosphere, they were pushing in her direction. Bunching up ahead were walls of ocean masses pushed up by the oncoming force. Steering in that direction, she studied the clouds for a moment. It didn't look like an ordinary storm that would occur at times in these waters. What she saw was something illustrated directly from the annals of seafarers. There were many accounts written about sailing ships lost across the world's seas. Depending on the oceans they plowed—Atlantic, Pacific, Indian Ocean—what formed was nothing less than a hurricane or typhoon. In these waters people ran for shelter as soon as signs appeared of the detested, demonized cyclone.

With the sky taking on shapes of gray to black shaded clouds, still in the distance, clusters of waterspouts were sucking up moisture from the violently cresting waves pushing against her bow. For Stinger, even at the onset of the cyclone, it was already a wild ride, dodging funnels and skipping water-laden crests in an approaching nightmare. She knew the ride would be an all-out challenge, but being so close to her goal, she could not quit now.

Clad in a tightly-fitted full-length wetsuit matching the colors of the present sky she was not overly worried yet. She had prepared to fight the current conditions. Ecstatic by the thrilling ride, a tune from a Johnny Cash album cut into her mind: "Ghost Riders in the Sky." Grinning from ear to ear, jumping the ever-growing waves, she shouted the chorus into the winds. "Yippie ya yea!" It was a perfect day for surfing. At this point, she was still playing with the elements. It may be the elements plying with her soon after.

He slept well. Getting out of bed, Hammad headed straight for the bathroom. After a solid six hours of sleep he was in dire need of relieving himself. It was a very rare occurrence for him to allow himself that many hours of rest. But, for a change, he felt it a deserving treat. The evening before he had reached the objective that had been on his

     T. RANDALL

mind for years. He was well on his way achieving it. After a quick shower, followed with the rigor of brushing teeth, he slipped into a casual set of designer clothes. Today would be a day of leisure he had not decided on yet. It could be a game of golf or set of tennis or perhaps a match of racquetball would be in order, but he changed his mind after gazing out the window.

"Storm's brewing out west," he muttered. It was a rare occasion to have the otherwise cloudless sky obscured by clouds. He studied the formation for a moment. "These are no ordinary clouds." These were clouds followed by great disturbances. His vision was interrupted by an approaching servant balancing a set of breakfast trays, suggesting, "Perhaps a cyclone."

From beneath solidly furrowed brows, Hammad responded, "Good time for staying in batting up hatches."

The scent of fresh fruit and dried dates, and the drifting aroma from the freshly brewed Arabian coffee permeated the morning breeze. "Life's great," Hammad grinned at Yusuf, seated leisurely by the table. "Isn't it?"

Yusuf was presently enjoying a light conversation with the ocean in full view. After all the misfortunes that had befallen him in recent months, the failed missions, the imprisonment, the accidents, he considered himself most fortunate being in the company of the great leader. Both were telling their personal encounters from recent battle accounts; the thing men usually do after escaping death on the battlefield. This was a good time to do so. The serenity of the moment, both knew, would not last long. Upcoming schedules would demand their full time and attention.

Hammad suddenly jerked his head up in the direction of the horizon. A frown cut across his face. His squinting eyes tried to pierce through the shimmering layers of heat drifting up from the sun-heated water surface. There it was again. His focus was sidetracked by Yusuf giving his account of the Manhattan fiasco. He needed to concentrate. He cut into the chattering, demanding immediate silence. "Shh." He jumped up to close the distance to the railing, leaning into the morning breeze. "Quick," he gestured at Yusuf, "field glasses."

He was handed a pair of high-powered Nikons. Tightly clutched and pressed against his eyebrows, he feverishly adjusted the focus. His breathing became audible. "Impossible," he shouted. Crazed by the sight, he offered the pair frantically to Yusuf. "Here. What do you see?"

Searching the horizon, Yusuf decided, "Ominous clouds. Could be a cyclone headed here."

"Below the clouds," Hammad insisted. "You idiot."

Yusuf was taken aback. Before now, he had never been insulted by the leader. Mulling over the reason, he took seconds to respond. Puzzled and hurt at Hammad's somewhat erratic behavior, he finally responded with, "Surfer."

Growing more impatiently by the second, Hammad insisted, "The flag. What kind?" He wanted assurance that his eyes were not deceiving him. It then dawned on Yusuf. He had recognized the flag as well. It was a flag only recently commissioned. It was the flag he wished he had never laid eyes on. "Patriots," he shouted, equally astonished. "Atop a surfboard."

"What else?"

"Huh?"

"What else do you see?" Hammad had to restrain his impatience to keep from punching Yusuf in the face. It took gripping seconds before he responded, "Okay. Now I see it." He was equally mesmerized when he identified the surfer. "Stinger! Carrying a weapon?" On closer look, he identified what seemed to be a blade strapped to her waist alongside a crossbow slung around her shoulders. Yusuf could see the fuming vapor, spittle as the Americans would say, escape Hammad's clenched lips with his next outburst. "Damned right," he spat out. "This time," he vowed, enraged and shaking a fist violently at the distant figure, "you won't get away."

"The armory," he ordered a dumbfounded Yusuf. "I want anything and everything that fits on a surfboard." The lieutenant had never seen anything close to a fight on a surfboard, let alone a woman carrying a weapon. Now he wanted an entire arsenal fitted into the board. *Idiotic!* But he held his tongue. He handed back the binoculars with a hint of confusion. "Here," he said, then hastened to a secured armory holding an assortment of arsenals.

After losing the dearest friend weeks ago, on top of having to concede the fight to the Prophet, Tracy had been overwhelmed with grief. She could not forget the deep connection she had developed with Hannah. She'd mourned deeply over her losses, her and Brian. As if it wasn't enough, she had lost the fight of all fights. It was for the survival of her nation. Both losses had drilled deeply into her heart and soul. To force herself over the grieving, she fervently dwelled on making preparations against the enemy. It would have to be a new approach. It would only be a matter of time for the Prophet to surface again. She was taking his global onslaught personally. While his fight was to seek world dominance, hers was to defend the freedom of her country. Both kept pushing with unequalled intensity and commitment for their respective causes.

She could not pull her mind free from the lingering, overwhelming thoughts of a persistent Jihad threat gnawing at her mind. To sooth the intensity, she got busy formulating a plan. "I shall teach them a lesson that will be remembered through history." From that day on, her senses were refocused on the pending tasks ahead. What she had in mind was a mission to an all-out battle for ultimate dominance without any external interference. To resolve their opposing visions once and for all, it would have to be a battle over life and death held between the two ultimate warriors. "This time," she assured herself, "there won't be any help or escape route." She had to draw the Prophet out in the open without any of his forces. After days of pondering, her plan eventually fell into place.

Occupied by such thoughts, Tracy went to work. Her immediate plan was to head for Italy. Since it was the Mecca for sea craft design and construction, she sought out a Milan-based shipbuilder. Working together for several days, they came up with a special design tailored specifically for her needs. The result was awe-inspiring to any seaworthy pilot. It was not an ordinary windsurf board they had created. It was a lightweight, honeycomb composite, shaped with bow and rails protected by an extremely durable metal alloy.

The board was fashioned for extreme speed and agility. Seated on the swivel mount was a mast that could carry an eight-meter sail braced by an aluminum boom for handling speed, direction, jumps, and spins. She had ordered several sails of various sizes to suit wind conditions. Attached to the top was the flag she so treasured.

Beneath the surface protruded a cluster of three tungsten-tempered steel fins dynamically spaced and honed for achieving optimum speed while slicing through oncoming swells.

Tracy made sure her rig was protected against collisions in addition to running never before achieved speeds on a wind-propelled craft. Trial runs in the Mediterranean were clocked at greater than 65 knots. The resultant design was perfect. All she needed now was a challenge and wind to test the board's abilities. There was one spot she had always desired to test her skills. For that, she traveled to the shores of Italy, specifically Pisa. She remembered a place she'd stayed one time during her travels. Built along the sandy beaches nearby Livorno's Riviera stood a single majestic structure planted above the sandy soil, the Intercontinental Hotel.

It was there in the offshore waters where she tested the board. It performed beyond her expectations. Satisfied with the design, days later she departed for her next destination, Dubai. Accompanied by light luggage, the surfing rig, and armament stored in the cargo hold, she arrived completely rejuvenated by the shores of the UAE. Renting an apartment for a couple of weeks, no matter what the outcome, it would be the thrill of a lifetime testing the waters in the Gulf Straits.

Hammad, followed closely by his trusted, headed for the sandy beach fronting his abode. "You stay back," he ordered the squad of surprised faces. Amid their objections, he insisted, "She's mine. All mine." He did not need any help. She was his destiny. She was his bounty. Feet securely fitted into the holding straps with both hands firmly gripping the boom, the Prophet jumped into a perfectly executed beach start, rushing head-on into the oncoming storm shouting, "Here I come. You infidel Bitch." Much like Stinger he was in his natural element on the windsurfer. The sight of his mortal enemy an hour earlier had brought on an infernal rage. The hatred he felt from the relentless provocations by Stinger made him grimace. Feeling the waves beneath the board, provoked by the turbulent seas, in an instant, Hammad turned into the ferocious Serpent-turned-Prophet. Braced against the onrush of salty seawater, he was headed for the battle front. With squinting eyes set within a weathered face scarred from past enemy encounters, he sought out the fast-moving target. Unsure if he could catch up in a direct chase, he estimated her speed and direction for an intercept.

Being an expert surfer, he knew all of the advantages of matching his skills with the current weather and sea conditions. Though expertly prepared for the prevalent winds in these waters, with cyclonic conditions rushing in from the distance, today would prove a challenge. He was gauging the onrushing winds against the wave action. "Gonna be a killer."

To assure maximum performance, beneath his feet and clutched between his hands was the best equipment money could buy. Specifically tailored to his size and weight was a handcrafted Speed-73, 7.8-foot carbon fiberglass, sandwiched Mistral board designed by Chris Lockwood himself. The sail was an Ezzy made, Panther Elite 4-batton downsized to 4.0 meters, ideal for today's violent wave action.

There was one more thing that elevated his confidence. It was the assortment of weapons Yusuf had fitted at the base of the mast. Despite the severity of the elements he had to grin. He'd never thought about how so many weapons could be fitted onto the board. He was familiar with any and all. Yusuf had even managed to mount an RPG launch tube just ahead of the mast. It would be a last resort, using this weapon, since it required two hands to launch. "We'll see," he spat into the winds, "what Stinger can fashion."

He was ready for whatever the elements would throw at him. Seeking out his detested adversary, expertly jumping the rolling waves, he spat into the violent winds, shouting, "This ocean is mine. You Bitch!"

The stage was set for the world's most virulent battle-hungry warriors, preparing to fight each for their own causes of survival, taking place in the wind-pitched Straits of Hormuz. The Prophet for global dominance, Stinger for world freedom. Only one power was allowed to emerge. Throwing a quick glance at his own arsenal strapped to his board, he could not help but laugh out loud, "Stupid woman." It would be an easy win.

FINAL BATTLE

Since two hands were necessary to expertly maneuver the windsurfing rig, the weapons would only be used as last result. Upholding the honor and pride of formidable warriors, the two opponents were expected to carry out their fight based on pure physical skills and endurance. Where the Prophet had brutality with the extreme physique strength of a seasoned male warrior on his side, Stinger, in contrast, had youth and agility on hers. Normally using eight-meter sails for optimum speed, today, to manage the rigs, matching cyclonic wind conditions, each adversary had downsized to four-meter sails. It would be the maximum size anyone could handle without getting the rigs torn off. With excessive speeds reaching 50 to 60 knots, it would be difficult enough just to stay on top of the water surface. It was there where the battle would be fought. Getting airborne, the surfers would be highly vulnerable not only to the elements, but to attack as well.

The Prophet had his feet solidly planted in the foot strap mountings. Leaning into the winds, bronze-colored body loosely hooked into the harness, he was headed straight for Stinger. He could feel the wind pressure building up against the sail more so then ever before. He had never experienced such force exerted against his arms and legs. He knew, today, all previously held speed records on the surfer would be broken. Taking a quick glance at the shoreline to check his position, he could see a few diehard sunbathers craning their heads in his direction, probably wondering what those two surfing fools were doing out in the ocean. In spite of the cyclone headed their way, they kept watching.

The hook was set by Stinger. Taking the personal challenge, he was tacking in on her at maximum speed. With the channel open to talk, clipped to his head was a headset and mic for keeping in constant communication with his team. Positioned on the balcony, allowing clear visibility, several pairs of binoculars were following his every move. A few hundred yards out, closing in fast was Stinger, the sheer sight of her challenging him brought his blood to a boil. He could not contain his fury any longer and shouted into the high-pitched winds, "You're no match. You infernal bitch!" The battle had begun.

Stinger, though her focus was set on the watery turbulence all around, from the edge of her vision followed the Prophet closing in fast. She had been waiting for this moment ever since their last encounter on top of One World Tower. It brought back vivid memories of her deceased friend. The memory of witnessing Hannah cut to pieces by the Prophet spurred on renewed fury. She turned pure killer once more, that of Stinger. When his challenge call reached her ears, she took her board into a tight turn, cutting across his first onrushing pass.

"Come on, punk," she challenged him with equal ferocity, slicing across his bow. It was an expression she knew would enrage his already infuriated temper to new heights. And she was correct. Reading the distorted grimace shot at her, he had taken the bait. She could readily imagine his inner hatred from her direct insult on his esteemed status as supreme Islamic ruler.

Executing another tight slalom-style turn, she watched him rush in, slicing across inches from her bow. Riding the crest of the wave, he was right on top of her, lashing out with one arm. He tried to rip the boom from her hands. His onslaught added to the fury of the cyclone, but she held on. After the failed attempt, his instinctive recourse was to spit into her face before skipping across the next wave.

Her turbulent laughter trailed unscathed after a furious Prophet who had sailed out of reach, preparing for the next assault. With combined approaching speeds of greater than 75 knots, there was only one attempt to lash out at each other. Much like jousting, a missed attempt was over within the whisk of a second. The next round, one or the other was setting up for another thrust. For maximum effect on battle strategy it would take distance and speed. Speed was not an issue today. The winds were increasingly whipping with cyclonic speeds out of the east. It was already getting difficult to hang on to the boom even without battling each other. Not one split second could be distracted from surfing without getting blown into the air. With sails tacked tightly against wind pressure, at the moment, extremely hostile conditions prevailed for even the best of surfer and the battle had just begun.

Both were gauging each other up for strengths and weaknesses. So far, it was the Prophet taking the initiative. Unbeknownst to him, it was part of Stinger's strategy. For the most part, she leaned back into the harness, preserving energy while he was attacking her with ever greater fury. For now, she let him have his day. Her time to strike would come soon enough. She kept egging him into attack after attack. With each profanity she threw at him, he took the bait, only to escalate his fury further. When he was setting up for the next attack, she would lean into the winds, concentrating on his strategy. Time after time she averted his strikes.

"Peckerhead," she yelled into the winds after another of his failed attempts. "Come and get me."

Her personal insults on his manhood seemed to heighten his fury to a level equal to the forces of the turbulent winds. By the time he realized her game plan, he had already lost vital energy. After his next attack Stinger decided to reverse her strategy. It would be her turn to become the aggressor. After gauging his surfing skills and abilities she would be able to anticipate his reaction to her onslaughts. There was more. She needed to identify the arsenal of weapons he had at his disposal. With only light caliber armament mounted against board and mast, they would be lethal projectiles, nevertheless. In addition, tightly strapped to the board was a mobile harpoon launcher ideal for the current conditions. He was armed to the teeth with personalized armament for close combat encounters. But so was she.

Stinger went on the attack. Due to the cyclonic winds, the waves had already picked up, reaching heights in excess of twenty feet. Both bodies were only visible to each other when emerging from the depths, getting ready to ride another foam-crested wave. The seas had turned more violent, creating deep voids of rolling masses of water coming her way. Carried by the winds, angled to intercept his speedy path, her deeply-tanned body shot out from the depths of waves. "Over here," she shouted at him. "Raghead." Her words were swiftly carried ahead in his direction. This one got his attention.

Though not prone to racial slurs, she needed to keep up his fury. It would give her the calculated edge she needed in her advantage. Anger in battle might seem to heighten a fighter's fighting ability, but it achieved the direct opposite. Anger took away concentration off the fight. From his next reaction, it became obvious he had taken her insult.

Stinger waited for him to emerge from the next rise of the wave. There he was. He shot straight for her. It was too late for her to escape. The projectile headed her way had already found its target. She watched in astonishment as the harpoon impacted right in front of her face. The steel was meant for her. What saved her from getting hit was the mast. It had blocked the harpoon's deadly path. It was a stunning wakeup call for her. It was a reminder of how severe their face-off was. Her personal challenges, the cat and mouse play, was over. The fight was getting serious. *Better pay attention,* she chided herself into reality.

The next second she realized his intentions. Due to the speed of the cyclonic winds, with sails filled to the bursting, in a slingshot fashion the Prophet shot directly for her while carrying his fearsome combat weapon, a specially-designed attack sword Arabic fashion. It was a sword so popular with desert dwelling horseback fighters.

Stinger reacted fast. She stopped the assault with a kick to his gut. It knocked the wind from his lungs and momentarily stopped his advance long enough for her to lash out with her own weapon. Her quick reaction saved her from getting pierced. It also inflicted the first wound. Her blade left a visible mark on his arm. She could see blood droplets carried away by the wind. In passing, only inches from her face, staring directly into her eyes, lashing out at her again, was the world's most feared warrior. She was able to block the thrust from the sword thrown at her body just when a gust of wind tore him away into the next go around.

In one fluid motion Stinger cut the rope attached to the harpoon, otherwise her mast would have torn from its mounting. It was just in time to ward off his next attack. He was already on top of her again, poised for the next blow. Amid the tearing winds, with one arm clamped around the boom, she sidestepped and countered yet another blow. Her quick reaction left a second mark on his body. This time the injury was to his upper thigh. Where the action left a broad grin on her face, she could see him wince in pain headed into the next cycle of attack.

During their close combat exchange, the cyclone was bearing down on the two with full force. It took great effort to just hold onto the boom straining against the sail. Though only a four-meter fabric, the sails were already too large for the increasing wind pressure. Between holding on and fighting off the aggressor, it took extreme concentration, strength, and skills to keep in control of the rig. For now, it seemed the Prophet, due to his size and strength, although slightly injured, had gained the upper hand. The conditions were in his favor.

Stinger, due to her lighter weight, had her hands full to keep from getting sucked into the air. It took all of her sailing skills to keep her rig close to the water. Presently, her eyes were seeking out the Prophet's next onslaught. And there he was, emerging from the depths of the waters, firing an AK-47 at her. Her eyes followed the tracer bullets tugging at her board and sail. She quickly reacted with an evasive slalom maneuver to avoid getting more hits. The speed of her board spun right into an oncoming wall of water carried by the cyclone. Her board slammed against the solid wall of hellish destruction. In one swift slingshot motion, she used her momentum to jump off the graying walls of hell directly into the Cyclone's path.

After executing another assault, euphoric at having dealt another blow at his mortal enemy, the Prophet took his board into a tight turn. It gave him just enough time to match her last evasive move. He was confident it would be his last attack. One hand tightly braced around the boom, with the other he kept aiming and squeezing the trigger.

Trapped within the violent wave action, his aim leading the target, it was difficult for him to get accurate aim for a mortal hit. Stinger was just too agile in her maneuvers. "I'll get you yet," he spat into the escalating turbulence. "You bitch."

Having spent much time in her country, he had not only learned to be fluent in the American language, but he also picked up common slurs and slang. In the shambles the nation was in, it had not proved difficult. Everybody had something to bitch about. While asymmetrical in meaning, "bitch," he knew, would bring on instant anger among the citizens of the land, especially to the female kind. Today, here within the inferno of a cyclone, he used the verbal insult to his best advantage. He could see the reaction in Stinger's face after each of his assaults. He had found her weakness.

Somewhat puzzled at not getting a kill from the weapon firmly clutched in his hand, after the misses he shot past his enemy into another assault-bearing turn. To execute the turn, his eyes were averted from the target for a second. It was enough to lose sight of her within the spray-laden air. Directly ahead he spotted something new.

Where the cyclonic forces of the wind where billowing up seven miles into the stratosphere, the lower end was tugging at the watery surface, creating rapidly moving water funnels. It was these darting funnels both Stinger and he were dodging. Unpredictable as they were, they would sprout out of nowhere only to drill another core through the atmosphere. The Prophet did his best to not get caught up within the deadly spouts. It would mean certain death.

Fearful of what he saw, he frantically wiped his eyes, trying to clear his vision. He could not believe what he had just seen. He was awestruck by the gutsy move Stinger was presently executing. Pasted brightly against the gloomy gray of the darting spout he spotted her. Unable to resist the hellish winds, she had been drawn toward the funnel with terrific speed. She had taken the momentum to her advantage, setting up for the next assault. What he witnessed was her jumping the next wave and, in one wide arch, heading straight for the solid wall of watery vortex. The momentum carried her vertically up into the atmosphere with her board sucked against the outer surface of the spout.

He could hear her board slap against the hollow wall of water dozens of feet up in the air. Using the centrifugal forces in a slingshot style, the next second Stinger was headed straight for him. Taken by utter surprise at the sheer survival skills he was unable to react fast enough. He tried to avert her onslaught by jumping the rising crest. Next, he took his rig sailing into a horizontal roll, but not quick enough.

The next sensation he felt was that of intense burning across his back. He could not see, but in an instant, became extremely aware of the damages she left on his body. In one swift motion, Stinger had sliced the tungsten-studded, finned board across his back, leaving three deep welts burning intensely in the exceedingly salty waters of the Sea of Hormuz.

Speeding away, Stinger clearly heard him wince in pain at her last maneuver. Seconds earlier, taking the incoming waterspout head-on was her only option to escape the hail of bullets fired at her. The event took place without any conscious action. Her reaction was purely based on survival instinct. It happened with such immense speed that there was no time to prepare. As in any instinctive reaction the outcome was unpredictable. The maneuver was over just as quick. One second she was drawn into the vortex, the next she had landed on the Prophet's back. She had survived the impossible, an escape from the turbulence of the cyclone.

Touching the water's surface once more, her eyes immediate sought out the enemy. He was gone. His body and rig must have been sucked into another void that had opened up between the growing waves. The wind forces had reached speeds of immense proportion. It was almost impossible to negotiate the surfing rig between the watery turbulence. The thought of flight entered her mind, but there was still the enemy to deal with. *Perhaps,* she considered, *he gave up,* but then her eyes caught hold of him. He had reappeared, but this time he was not alone. He was flanked by a fleet of equally-armed Jet Ski riders. All she could make out in between waves breaking in over her were fiery streams of bullets seeking her out as a target.

The tide had suddenly turned in his favor. This time Stinger was forced into flight. Outnumbered and outgunned, she needed to getaway, and fast. But, in the midst of the ocean, there was no hiding. She desperately needed help. Exposed, she had to battle it out no matter what the consequences. She had been so busy with preparing for the final confrontation with the Prophet that she had completely forgotten. It was time to activate the implant. A touch on back of the skull connected her with Specter. As always, he was right there for her.

"Stinger," the familiar voice reached out at her. "Got you on monitors."

Pushed up against overwhelming odds, she shouted, "Need help."

With deafening winds hauling around her, it was almost impossible to perceive communication through the static-laden ether so close to the cyclone's center. She felt the intense cracking created by the thunder and lightning reaching for her skin. Their communication was washed out by the static interference. In between the chaotic conditions she fretfully waited for his directions. Finally, there was a faint response, "Standby." He was ready to guide her out of the present jam.

With her body fitted securely into the harness with both feet straining against the board, Stinger had both hands free to make use of her weapons. Where it would take extreme skills to handle any of them while in flight, she was ready for the attack. With waves being pitched up to fifty feet in height and multiple funnels touching water randomly, it took all of her surfing strength and skill to hang on. With each oncoming swell the board beneath her feet was violently tossed up and down by the boiling water. Her sail was filled to the bursting. It created speeds she had never achieved before. She was slicing across the waves at close to 90 knots, leaving watery streamers of contrails in her wake. The onrushing targets were only in sight for a fraction of a second. Depending on attack or flight, disappearing and reappearing was an advantage given to both sides. It exposed the targets only for seconds.

With the Prophet in the lead, surrounded by a fleet of armed terrorists on the attack, there was only one logical recourse for her, that of retreat. With waves, cyclone, and militia encircling her, the odds against her were too overwhelming. She had stopped calling out insults at her adversary. Words were fading unheard into the hellish environment. What was next would take all of Stinger's concentration. She had no plan. Depending on the moment, her flight would have to be executed on instinct. Her eyes were gauging her surroundings. Seconds later an opportunity opened up. Another water spout, gigantic in size, touched down from the air nearby. Stinger headed directly for its center. Racing across the water, one last leap and she shot through the solid wall of turbulent water, disappearing within chased by a hail of bullets shot from the onrushing enemy fleet. The vortex had completely swallowed her up, board, sail, and all.

Yards away the Prophet was in pursuit. Through the last battle exchange, he had realized his strength was waning rapidly. The elements had sapped much of his energy. He was still amazed at the stamina and skill Stinger was holding up. There had never been an opponent, let alone a woman, resisting his every attempt at a kill. Although he was cussing her out at every thought, he never ceased to admire her talent. She seemed to excel in everything living under the skies. He only wished she could be on his side. He would consider her the best treasure anyone could ever hope for. But, her being the enemy, and mortal on top of it, he had to get rid of her once and for all.

It was here when he called on his trusted. They had been watching the battle from the sanctity of his mansion. Bewildered at the distant violence growing in intensity, from their lofty vantage point they could make out the two adversaries in the distance. Where their cheering went unheard by the far-off warriors, each outburst elevated their spirits to renewed heights. At the onset of the distant fight, it would have been considered prudent for their leader to call for any assistance. Besides, he had given strict orders for them to stay back. Along with their cheering, with each successful attack by the Prophet, another round of fine spirits made its way to a toast. And so, the celebration went on in anticipation of the leader's victory.

It must be said that the consumption of alcohol was not part of the Muslim lifestyle. Having been isolated for a thousand years from the modern mainstream of society, their customs and culture had grown apart from the general trading world. Whereas alcohol had developed as elixir of pleasure in many of the globe's societies, in the Arabian Peninsula it was mostly hashish that made its way into the desert dweller's lives.

For the Prophet's closest followers, since many had been exposed to the western world in recent years, their taste had changed with it. A glass of fine scotch or vodka was the preference. When the call for immediate action came on the intercom they were not only stunned, but inebriated as well. There was a brief hush of wonder before the Prophet's crew staggered to the Jet Skis berthed by the private docks. But, with winds and water pitching into the faces of the speeding combatants, it did not take long to sober up. With faces still set in wonder about the call for help, the fleet was closing in fast. In minutes, they were on top of the fight, surrounding a shocked Stinger.

The Jihad commanders were positioned for an all-out attack on the one stigma that had caused so much disruption to their cause. Now, for the first time, they had come face to face with Stinger. Appearing self-confident, arrogant with an unmistakable smugness in her posture, skipping from wave to wave, the pure sight of her was enough to enrage the squadron of warriors. A woman daring a man, challenging him to the very core of his manhood, was something none had ever faced before. It was time to eliminate this evil from its very existence. A unison cry of battle went out into the gusted winds, "Insha' Allah. Your time has come."

No sooner had the sound faded then the female warrior had vanished as well, sucked into the spinning void. The last sight the attackers held was Stinger, with one great leap, bounding through the darkened wall of the cyclone, escaping the violent waters below and bullets released at her.

The Prophet was speechless. His squads of fighters were stunned. Close to the touch one second, the next she was gone, into a void none had ever thought to survive. In one fleeting second, the fight was over, the battle was won. It was time to return to the protection of the shores, the world's most beautiful island ever made by man, Palm Jumeirah.

With their backs turned away from the windy carnage, the squad of warriors with Prophet in the lead was preparing to hurry back to shore when, all of a sudden, the eeriness of an animal-like cry washed from the skies. Turning around to check the unexpected sound, in full view with incredible speed, a hundred feet in the air, Stinger suddenly emerged from the walls of hell, wildly wielding her faithful companion through the air. It was her turn for an all-out attack. Clutching the boom with one arm, cradled in the other was the crossbow, firing arrows at the stunned terrorists as quickly as the manual feed could reload the next arrow.

The sudden encounter lasted only seconds. As rapidly as she appeared, Stinger only briefly touched down on the waves to gain additional speed before disappearing into the turbulent void once more. If it were not for several dead comrades floating in the water nearby, the image might have well been an apparition. It was beyond the comprehension of the Jihad still alive.

When Stinger had taken the leap of faith into the watery inferno minutes earlier, in a fleeting notion she made peace with herself. Subconsciously, she knew her chances for survival were impossible. She did not know what lay beyond the wall of watery fury. With overwhelming enemy forces on the approach, she had no other option. The only escape was through the solid wall of turbulence. Riding the crest of a wave, she headed directly for the center of the watery column. The closer she approached to the inferno, the stronger the draft became. With every increasing moment, she was drawn into the heart of the cyclone.

Only yards away from the wall of solid water, her body strapped into the harness, board, sail, and boom was lifted off the waves and sucked high up into the air. Gathering all of her strength, in one final effort she shot straight through the wall. Caught up in the vortex, her body and rig was violated with an intensity she had never experienced. Almost at a point of unconsciousness, lifted upward, drawn inward, and thrown through the inner wall of the cyclone, Stinger suddenly found herself surrounded by an eerie calmness. Gazing upwards in wonder, she spotted the clear blue skies overhead.

Awestruck by the sudden calmness, all she could think of was Heaven. She had entered the spiritual realm of eternity. Sailing through space, Stinger was at piece with herself. She had finally arrived on the other side of life. She was overcome with euphoria.

Euphoria did not last long. There was a sudden shaking. It became more violent by the second. It rattled every fiber of her body back to reality. Thwarted with disillusionment over her present vision, Stinger quickly recalled the reason she was planted here, but did not want to face the carnage and what was expecting her below. She yelled for help. "Specter."

His voice was calming her when he spoke. "On my command," he gave her orders. "Jump." It only took seconds for him to get back. "Now!"

Pulling together all of her remaining strength, she headed straight ahead for the solid gray inner wall rushing at her. An animal-like battle cry left her clenched lips,

"CHARGE." In one violent leap, she popped out of the hellish turbulence dozens of yards above the surface. Where much of the sound vanished within the storm, her reappearance shocked the terrorists into reality. The fight was not over yet. Using the sail to steer, she maneuvered the rig straight for the closest Jet Skis. In one solid swoop, she sliced across one, then another, and another of the stunned combatants, leaving, in each of the warrior's backs, three deeply cut wounds penetrating through rib cages into their lungs, from the alloy-hardened fins. The strikes were executed with such violence that no amount of aid could save the Jihadists.

Carried by the winds, jumping from Jet Ski to Jet Ski, tearing away flesh, Stinger managed to wound, in one wide sweep, one terrorist after another. Immobilizing one killer another took up position. There was so much blood in the water it did not take long for the scent to attract the silent killers, home to these waters. Stinger's eyes caught the silvery striped reflections only inches below the surface homing in on their prey. It would be a field day for the hungry sharks, the tiger shark. With a keen eye on the new threat, Stinger set off in pursuit of the one opponent left fighting, the Prophet. She reserved the ultimate deathblow for him.

A quarter mile out, the Prophet suddenly stopped his rig and turned at the wildest battle cry he had ever heard. It was a sound that would stop any action. As he turned, he could not believe the sight. From the walls of the cyclone, emerging was the seemingly immortal enemy striking out once again. His heart stopped for a moment. His eyesight turned blurry from sheer fury. He was on the brink of exploding with rage.

"Impossible!" was his only reaction after being witness to his warriors getting sliced to pieces. He was stunned. He could not move. Frozen with rage, he became sitting prey. He'd had enough. He was tired of pursuit. He was weary of flight. His energy was drained. There was only one thing to do: stay and face death one last time. He was ready for the ultimate fight. There would be only one survivor—perhaps none. Searching the waters for his enemy, she suddenly appeared out of the gray on top of a wave rushing at him. He was ready. He waited until she was close enough for his aim, then released the trigger.

A quarter mile out, Stinger was setting up for one last assault. It would be the final run. She could feel her energy waning. The battle with the cyclone had taken out most of her stamina. If she wanted to come out alive, it was time to end the combat. It was here, exhausted and spent, where most mistakes were made, ending in death. It would be one last deathblow either way.

Setting up direction and speed, she headed straight for the Prophet. It was too late for her to react when she spotted the weapon aimed at her. She tried to, but in her weakened condition she couldn't move quick enough. The incoming projectile headed directly for her body. He had released an explosive charge even she could not outrun or out sail. Holding on to the rig, with eyes fixated at the fiery streamer the projectile left in its wake, she headed straight for the antagonist. There was only one recourse action for her. She dove into the turbulent water below while her rig exploded above from a direct hit of the RPG. It saved her life. For the moment, she was stunned but still alive, but more death was waiting in the deep. Sharks were aiming directly for her. Warding off the new threat, she was forced to surface. Shooting straight up, her body landed near the disabled surfing rig. A few strokes brought her close enough to pull her body onto the battered board. Watching a shredded sail carried away by the wind, boom torn from its mounting, the Patriotic flag was still affixed to the mast barely attached to the board. The sight gave her one last glimmer of hope.

Though the intensity of the cyclone was moving off on its destructive course, the turbulent swells still remained. Anything floating in these waters today was bounced around much like a cork. Salty spray was blowing into her face, burning into her eyes and sinuses. She could clearly smell the ozone laden air generated by the turbulence. Shaking her face to clear some of the drenching rain, she spotted him through the rainy haze. There was something else she spotted. At first, she thought it was upturned boards with their fins protruding from the water. But, to her surprise, they were moving. They were coming her way. Then, she recognized the dark shadows below the watery surface. Tracy, having survived many battles in recent months, was callused to fear. But this was different. She was not in her usual element on solid ground. She was in enemy territory, elements of the killer shark.

She had to act fast. Taking an immense volume of air into her lungs, she dove, and not too soon. Dark bodies were encircling her brushing across the skin of her shoulders and torso. Stinger reached for the knife secured in its shed tightly strapped to her leg preparing for yet another battle. She did not have to wait long for the aquatic killers to move in. She struck at the first gaping jaw closing in on her. Her thrust was directed at the snout of the shark. It struck home. The silvery shadow slithered off with another taking its place. Another thrust at the head, followed by another. Shark blood seeping into the waters was attracting even more. Stinger followed every move of the killers through a watery vision. Her lungs were rapidly draining of life providing oxygen. She could not hold her breath any longer. Among the turmoil developing around her, she surfaced, headed for her board which had drifted off with the winds. To her surprise, the dark shadows beneath the waves had stopped coming after her. All she could think was them taking to a feeding frenzy provided by the flesh of sharks she'd killed.

The desperate break she needed to collect her thoughts did not last long. There was another enemy waiting for her. Amid the watery spray still whipped up by the storm, her eyes caught two outlines. Hammad was headed her way, and so was one she recognized from previous encounters, Yusuf. Still dozens of yards out, at full speed they were rushing in on her. After a few more desperate strokes, she reached her board. In one frantic move Stinger unlatched the mast from its mountings, and pulled her body onboard the battered rig. Secured within the hold of foot straps, bracing her body against the winds, swaying in rhythm with the oncoming waves, she strained to reach for the mast floating in the water. Pulling all of her remaining strength together, she was just in time to ward off the Prophet's imminent attack.

With hands clutched firmly around the twelve-foot mast, embracing one end between her body and arm, she aimed the tip directly at his onrushing body when an arrow from Yusuf's spear gun glanced off her shoulder. It momentarily distracted her. Checking his position, Yusuf was reloading another razor tipped shaft. Regaining her focus on the Prophet once more, who was closing the distance at great speed, she gripped the ultimate weapon she had fashioned. It was the perfect weapon to deal a deathblow. When it hit, the joust-like mast penetrated his body hard.

Stinger watched the Prophet's face contort with sheer agony as his battered body tumbled through the air with the flag of the Patriots imbedded into his chest. Passing with great speed, she could even hear ribs cracking. She watched him trying to scream out but two collapsed lungs prevented any sound from being produced. His flaccid body landed yards away with a terrific splash and quickly slipped into the depths within a turbulent sea.

Stinger dove after him. Though he was the most ruthless killer anyone could ever encounter, she still respected him as a worthy warrior. If there was a chance to retrieve his body, she would grant him a decent burial as was deserving a warrior. Diving deep, the grip she had on his blood-soaked arm slipped from her fingers. In the depth, her lungs were bursting with pain. Close to drowning herself, she was forced to release his lifeless body. She released the hold and watched the body of this great warrior silently slip into the depths of the ocean.

Watching the last shadows of his remains disappear Stinger wondered about the great warrior. "Is he really dead?" In either case, she had finally achieved what she set out to years ago, avenging her homeland from the Jihad taking over. Perhaps, with their leader gone, nations could rebuild and focus on the future ahead within their own inherited cultures. The struggle for world dominance had been going on for too long. It was high time to extend mankind a long, overdue peace. As for her, the warrior she had become over years' time, perhaps she could settle back toward a more normal life. "What life," she wondered.

Tracy Bauer felt as if the world had come to an end. She had serious doubts about whether she would ever fit into mainstream society again. Much like a returning soldier from battle, she might not be able to find a place among her people. But first, it was high time for Tracy to get out of this infernal cyclone. One last sweep around the deadly whirlpool, she hopped on an abandoned Jet Ski, headed for the nearby shores.

THE PROPHET

Minutes earlier, just prior to colliding with Stinger at full speed, the Prophet was straight on course to deliver his final blow. Headed directly for Stinger, whose body had just surfaced from the watery turbulence, he was getting ready to tear into her body. "A few more seconds," he shouted into the wind, "your head will be mine." All of his energy was focused on the one thing that kept destroying his dreams, Stinger. It was she that kept faulting his every plan. It was her that had taken out half of his forces. It was her that kept him from victory. "You shall be no more."

Rapidly closing in on her, one final cry for vengeance brought him face to face with her. There was nothing but rage in his eye when he sought out hers. To his surprise, there was no fear emanating from her face. What he detected was fortitude. When he spotted the weapon, it was too late for him to react. The tip of the mast hit him square in the sternum. At the same time, being lifted from the craft and tossed through the air, he felt the intense pain from the blow. The last vision he perceived was tumbling through the air, only to land hard on the surface of the water when he blacked out.

Earlier, training a pair of field glasses on the distance, Yusuf was watching the battle from the lofty height of the mansion. At first, when he dispatched his fighters to assist the leader in dealing one final blow to Stinger, he was undecided about whether to join the departing war party or stay behind. He decided to stay on to assist by communicating through the closed-circuit headset receivers strapped to each fighter. From his position, he could direct the final battle but immediately became alarmed when he watched one fighter after the other being cut to pieces by Stinger. It was then that he decided to join. Yusuf hurried to the shores and jumped into the closest available Jet Ski. Revving up to maximum power, the jets jolted him through the air straight toward the cyclone. It would only be minutes before he could join in the fight.

He readied the only weapon he had clutched on the way out, a spear gun. Cocking the spear ready for flight, he poised for Stinger to reappear from the waterspout. "There she is." He aimed and pulled the trigger. The spear sought out its moving target but missed her heart by only inches. It glanced off on her shoulder, flinging wildly into the air. He cocked the second projectile but hesitated to shoot. Hammad had broken into his line of fire and obstructed the target. He wavered on his next shot. By the time the target cleared, it was too late. All he could do was follow Stinger thrusting her jousting weapon into Hammad. The motion that followed was enough for Yusuf to assess the damages. His master was hit. He watched him tumble through the air much like a football, only to land hard on the watery surface. His body went under. The next second he saw Stinger dive into the depths. With spear gun clutched between his hands Yusuf jumped into the watery abyss and quickly followed suit.

By the time he reached Hammad, Stinger was already headed for the surface. He was faced with a choice. Follow her and let the supreme commander slide into the depths of the ocean, or rescue him and lose her. He chose to rescue his commander with a silent promise at her. "Allah will deal with you." It was too late when Yusuf realized he was running short on air. His body was screaming for oxygen. His lungs were straining to the max. He needed air. To his horror, Hammad's body had slipped away from his reach, sinking farther and deeper. He struggled to follow but was losing his strength as well.

There was one last chance. He cocked the spear gun and fired after his commander. The string unreeled with a swishing sound, leaving bubbles of air in its path. It hit Hammad in the shoulder. One tug on the line secured the tip. Spent of energy, Yusuf surged for the surface. Almost at a point of losing consciousness, his head finally broke the water, taking in five liters of oxygen all at once. From the watery surface, reeling up the lifeless body, clutching his unconscious and injured commander to his chest, Yusuf watched Stinger jet away. He vowed revenge after her with a promise to his silent leader, "We will get her next time."

FORSAKEN FREEDOM is about a once proud nation, the United States of America, succumbed to the forces of pure survival inflicted by hostile and foreign elements. The ensuing aftermath caused by the enemy using the nation's own defense weapon, HAARP, should serve the American citizen as warning for things to come. We, as a nation, after centuries of complacent living not severely subjected to internal turmoil caused through unrest, conflict, and war have forgotten what life was like for our forefathers that have fought for freedom and independence, American Revolutionary War (1774-1783) and American Civil War (1861-1865). Assisting other nations in the struggles for freedom, we cannot assimilate the hardship of war as experienced directly by the individuals involved in the conflict. Aside from the soldier in the battle front, we, general public can only observe from the distance through Media, Multi-media, and Television for getting a sense of detached participation.

The author of FORSAKEN FREEDOM is taking the plight of struggling nations to heart by illustrating the interested reader in the trials and tribulations that could easily ignite within any nation not just troubled ones. But as sure as there is a future, there is also hope to the end of any conflict. As history has proven over and over, wars will always remain with mankind and come and go with the passage of time. One can only hope for clashes and conflicts across borders to be resolved through diplomatic means which is not always possible with egocentric, inconsiderate, and at times ruthless power mongers. It should be understood that warring is part of man's inherited predisposition. It will always be with us. It has to be like this. Without it, man's ingenuity, inspiration, and desire striving for a better future, life will become stagnant. It is stagnation that would choke off progress and prevent expanding into the endless horizons of the expanse of space. It is man's destiny to propagate and populate the universe. Without it, life for the human species will come to an eventual end. The galaxy we live in, for numerous reasons whether self-inflicted by man or through cosmic disaster, will perish way before the universe.

NEW REPUBLIC

After the New Republic took over the former White House, Senate, Congress, and other governmental organizations and facilities in the nation's capital, Washington DC, it took many months for reestablishing initial order over the nation. Immediate issues were numerous. Most pressing were selecting suitable representatives for the people of the new nation. Common terms such as "Constituent, President, Electoral, and College" were quickly dropped from the political platform. The once popular terms related to former politics and government had taken on negative connotations for obvious reasons, that of unmanageable entities.

In order to assure a long lasting governing body, drastic changes were implemented based on the new constitution hewn out by the likes of Rusty Norton, Brodie Elliott, Wendell Nelson, Big Red, and Hank Foster. Even Duke Wheeler, also known as Bad Man the Enforcer had his say in court.

Getting the land under law and order again proved a monumental effort. In the years of internal struggles for survival, many regional and local clusters of independent factions had emerged. Where some where fighting for independence from any future federal impositions, others sought personal gains and property acquisitions, more yet were striving for numerous causes from oppression to domination. It all boiled down to one common denominator, that of preference and choice of the individual leadership.

Foremost and first article in the new constitution was an axiom written. It proved to be one of utmost importance for all future endeavors for the citizen and government alike. It read:

"If the citizens are afraid, it's Tyranny asserted by the government."

"If the Government is afraid, it's Democracy for the people at work."

It should be noted that a workable equilibrium can be achieved between a governing body and the citizens of the state. But in order to do so, a "Check and Balance" system must be implemented by either side, the public and the private sectors.

BAUER TEAM LEGACY

ALEX BAUER

Alex, also known as Specter, was offered an advisory position with the New Republic but gracefully turned down the offer. It meant taking a seat in the state capital. He would rather not be directly involved with politics or government. Instead, he chose to remain at the sanctity of the Castle. Once, a team player managing numerous crews on assignments worldwide, in recent years, had gotten used to solving problems and issues from the seclusion of his fortress. Technology was where he felt at home. That, however, did not prevent him from taking frequent trips around the nation whenever called upon for his skills and expertise. And they were many.

TRACY BAUER

Tracy, also known as Stinger, after much deliberation by members from the newly formed government, it was decided that Tracy was too radical a person befitting any of the political organizations. She would have turned the offers down anyway. Where her expertise used to be as field operative and analyst in national defense, due to a multitude in personal dramatizations, her skills had dramatically shifted to successfully warding off personal affronting. She had become a fulltime warrior. Her skills for defending the nation in its final throws had not gone unnoticed. She was heralded as heroine and liberator of the nation for years to come.

There was one position most suitable for her. When offered, she readily accepted. The offer came from the Department of Homeland Security. Although secrecy and clandestine missions were not part of the New Republic but as it had been for eons, they were unavoidable. They were part of man's survival of the fittest. Tracy was chosen for her personal skills heading off the newly formed super-secret branch under the DHS, the Stinger squadron. It was her mission to infiltrate, penetrate, and if necessary, eliminate identified antagonists emerging from adversary and hostile nations.

Once word spread of the newly formed agency, her elite team, though extremely covert in nature, was sought out by many troublesome nations. Without revealing possible future opportunities, it should be said that in only a very short time, Tracy would be called upon by the world council for deploying her special skills once more in warding off the world's most feared adversary.

Brian Harris's body was buried at the Castle grounds. In a personal relationship with Tracy, his legacy would live on through the inscribed dedication memorialized on his tombstones, "Here lies the spirit of an invisible soldier dedicated to the very end." Tracy visited his graves often. Although her remembrance from the extreme hardship of the past waned with the passage of time, the memories of not only Brian, but her dearest friend Hannah as well, always maintained a dedicated spot in her heart.

LISA (LIZ) BAUER

Liz, after enjoying a much deserving break spent with her children, who in the meantime had grown into young adults, was extended a career offer by Hank Foster she could not refuse. She became mission director for the revived space agency. Who else would be more appropriate managing the agency than the sole surviving astronaut from a much-troubled space mission. Among space experts, who knew more about possible space related mission failures and how to cope with them, than Liz.

After much deliberation by the international space agency, it was decided not to rebuild the ISS since it had outlived its purpose. With space exploration shifted from government sponsored missions, commercial enterprise had been awarded future explorations into space. First missions on the agenda were setting up a base station on the Moon supporting colonization scheduled for Mars and other planets in the solar system in the near future.

SCOTT BROOKS

Scott, a once inferior human being had excelled in becoming a super human warrior. His personal power and strength were unmatched. With peace returned to a nation in turmoil for many years, rebuilding again, he found himself at odds with the nation and its people. There seemed to be no place for him and his skills in an orderly society. He longed for excitement and action. It was not long before the opportunity presented itself. It came in the form of global terrorism on the increase. Whereas many trading partners had viewed the collapse of the once mighty United Stated ambitiously vying for their own gain for world dominance, economically and currency wise, others had motives more sinister. Those had taken advantage in pursuit of political disorders for infiltrating weakened nations. As a result, international terrorism was spreading with hostilities becoming prolific.

Opportunist by nature, Brooks recognized his time had come. All he needed was a sanctioned venue by the New Republic's policy makers. It came in the form of a tender offer by the Naval Department, specifically a newly formed team equivalent of the former SEAL 6, surface and subsurface tactical assault unit. It was an ideal match between superhuman required efforts out of their natural habitat, underwater, for the perfect warrior. Brooks was in his element enjoying every mission the world threw at him.

HASAN HAMMAD (AKA) THE SERPENT LEGACY

The Serpent, against all odds had survived from drowning, but not without being deeply wounded. Not only visible from being cut up by the blades from his adversary, Stinger's surf board, but emotionally by her incessant insults and onslaughts as well. He carried deep scars for some time he took to heal at his island paradise. Just when he thought his terror reign had come to an end, newly emerged opportunities presented themselves. For that, reenergized, he headed directly for Paris. It would be a new target base for his quest in world dominance, this time played out on a global scale.

The thought alone was cause for jubilation. Where up to now his take-over efforts were considered only minor quests, what lay ahead would be cause for rattling bones to the entire inhabitants on earth. With the world's most powerful weapon HAARP destroyed, the Serpent had to devise other means for supporting his conquests. It had come to him while embraced in mortal combat with Stinger. When he saw her vanish only to emerge from the infernal Cyclone unscathed, the thought had struck him like lightning. All he needed was getting his hands on the weapon and he would be ruler of not only the world, but for all things to come. Being potential ruler of all things, it would elevate him to supremacy, that of true Prophet.

AL QAEDA/JIHAD

Although the Islamic extremist's attempt in taking over U.S. soil permanently were foiled through the combined resistance from the Bauer team, Brook's mercenaries, and the Patriots, terrorist assaults within this, as well as other nations can never be eradicated. Sometimes dormant for years, sometimes in temporary hiding, hostile cells will surface when their timing is right unless a nation closes its borders tight. Even this option will not prevent ideological aversive citizens from aligning in the fighting for justice, liberation, and freedom to suit their individual needs. Unless the individual brain can be programmed allowing for only peaceful intentions by the government or whatever power is running the nation, terrorism is here to stay.

We can only hope that adverse intentions by extremists will be controlled and managed through tightly held surveillance by elements such as the INS, DHS, CIA, DIA, NSA, and other national minded organizations. Although treading between legal and illegal boundaries by such agency may be necessary at times, moral obligations to the safety and wellbeing for the citizens must be honored and observed at all times.

TEAM LEGACIES

When a nation experiences internal turmoil such as illustrated within this novel, many factions may surface each with their own causes. Anarchy is just one example. But anarchy generally does not last very long unless it is headed off by an extreme ruling power such as a dictatorship in which case it could last decades. Iraq, with Saddam Hussein in power, was a typical example.

Anarchy in this writing lasted several years after which it was eliminated by the leaders of the New Republic with the support from Brodie Elliott's 1ˢᵗ Infantry, Big Red's army, Scott Brook's War Dogs, and the Bauer crew. The nation subjected to Forsaken Freedom was eventually restored with currency reestablished, personal and corporate banking assets evaluated, the nation's infrastructure rebuilt so that all industry sectors could effectively function once more. In order to bring about needed changes to a nation, it is sometimes necessary for tearing down its very fabric of society. It may take extreme hardship for a society driven by affluence and self-gratification in waking up to reshape morals and values as its original founders had projected.

The Condors, the non-political sector in charge of national laboratories, scientific developments, and technological advancements continued their sophisticated presence in the shadows of the New Republic. Comprised of the nation's most capable minds, this group, for most part maintained its anonymity and, in the process, continued watching over the nation's citizen's wellbeing and future prosperity.

The displaced government to the western sector maintained its established powerbase by the Pacific shores. After losing its governing base years before, its internal structure and ruling force shifted to protecting the western shores of the newly created nation. George Wilmot, former U.S. President, along with most of his staff relinquished their positions to retirement. Not doing so would have rekindled new conflicts among political agencies, governmental organizations, and its citizens.

The Patriots came out as heroes. A new national holiday was declared honoring their monumental effort in creating the New Republic. If it were not for the opportunity presented by the Serpent and his extremist followers by throwing the nation into upheaval, the Republic may have never been created. Over decades of demoralization by a social minded public, the nation had been weakened to a point where it was perfectly staged for a takeover. In this case, it did not come from within it came from foreign soil in the form of Islamic extremists. The stage had been set long before. The signs may have been clouded to the common citizen trying to carve out a living in a deteriorating economy but were clearly visible to the informed.

It was these informed groups called Preppers and Survivalists that came out alive. They saw the handwriting on the wall. For them, it was only a matter of time for the collapse to happen. It could have come from within, as many had expected, but in this case, the collapse was triggered by the EMP strike followed with the takeover by a foreign faction. In the end, through the combined effort of the strong willed and dedicated individuals, the Forsaken Freedom was restored once more to a nation that so much valued this Freedom.

The War Dogs, headed off by their exceptional leader Brooks, as a force was disbanded. The extreme force, as it was, was not necessary anymore in an established nation. Its members, confused and discouraged at first for losing their principle aspects, that of fighting and killing, were reorganized by Rusty Norton, elect leader for the New Republic into an alternate, more effective fighting force. For its members, a new tactical branch was created, that of navy SEALs under the auspicious of the Department of the Navy with Scott Brooks in charge.

Although reluctant at first, there was no shortcoming in dispatches for the team to burning points around the globe. Foreign conflicts, whenever help requested from friendly nations, Brook's team enthusiastically carried out mission support.

In hindsight, the traumatic effects on the nation and its people caused by the adversary, the Prophet, could have been avoided if the caution signs had been observed. Since this was not the case, many lives were lost in the process. Losses were heavy throughout all regions. Honors should be extended to those fought in battle and perished as results to the dedicated soldiers and citizens that fought for a common cause, that of freedom and independence. There were many. To mention principal leaders and supporters, following are the nation's honored fallen in battle:

FALLEN HONOR LIST

PRINCIPLE CHARACTER
Brian Harris – Former NSA Analyst, longtime friend of Alex, romantic interlude to Tracy

ISS CREW – CURRENT MISSION
Dieter Fuchs – Astronaut, Crew, ISS, European Union, Munich, Germany
Hiroshi Nagata – Astronaut, Crew, ISS, Asian Team, Nakashima, Japan
Kendrick (Kenny) Walsh – Astronaut, Commander, ISS, Houston, TX, America
Yuri Chenkov – Cosmonaut, Crew, ISS, Soyuz Team, Kazakhstan, Russia

SUPPORT CAST – WESTERN SECTOR
Donald (Donny) Allen – Crew Chief, 477th Fighter Group, Elmendorf AFB, AK
Hector (Heck) Rivera – C-130 Squad Leader, 477th Fighter Group, Elmendorf AFB, AZ
Jack Owens – Captain, U.S. AF, HAARP, Gakona, AK
Raymond (Ray) Campbell – Chief of Operations, HAARP facility, Gakona, AK
Ronald (Ronny) Cook – Commander, Base Command, Elmendorf AFB, AK
Thomas (Tommy) Johnson – Commander, 3rd Wing Command, Elmendorf AFB, AK
William (Wild Bill) – Commander, Eleventh Air Force, Elmendorf AFB, AK

SUPPORT CAST – EASTERN SECTOR
Doug Olsen – Plant Supervisor, Power Station, Three Mile Island, PA
Hannah Thompson – Interpreter to the U.N. Secretary General, New York, NY
Jim Ross – Shift Supervisor, Power Station, Three Mile Island, PA
Kimberly (Kim) – Lieutenant, 3rd Battalion, Southern Command, Red Army, Washington, DC